ILLBORN

Daniel T. Jackson is a fantasy enthusiast, with a love for fantastical worlds and epic adventures. After 25 years of creating stories for friends and family, Daniel finally escaped from his day job to fulfil his lifelong ambition of writing *Illborn*. With *The Illborn Saga*, he hopes to create the next classic fantasy series.

Daniel is married with four children, and lives in the United Kingdom. He also loves hiking, cycling and piano, and volunteers for a number of good causes. *Illborn* is his first published novel.

ILIОТИ

ILLBORN

DANIEL T. JACKSON

Matador
9 Priory Business Park,
Wistow Road, Kibworth Beauchamp,
Leicestershire. LE8 0RX
Tel: 0116 279 2299
Email: books@troubador.co.uk
Web: www.troubador.co.uk/matador
Twitter: @matadorbooks

ISBN 978 1800462 823

British Library Cataloguing in Publication Data.
A catalogue record for this book is available from the British Library.

Printed and bound in the UK by TJ Books Ltd, Padstow, Cornwall
Typeset in 10.5pt Adobe Jenson Pro by Troubador Publishing Ltd, Leicester, UK

Matador is an imprint of Troubador Publishing Ltd

To Elaine, my lovely wife.

THE F

BERGEN

- Karn

NORTH SEA

ANDAR

- Be
- Rednarron

CANASA

Andarron

Septholme

ABASS

THE WESTERN OCEAN

Aiduel's Gate

THE HOLY LAND

- Arron

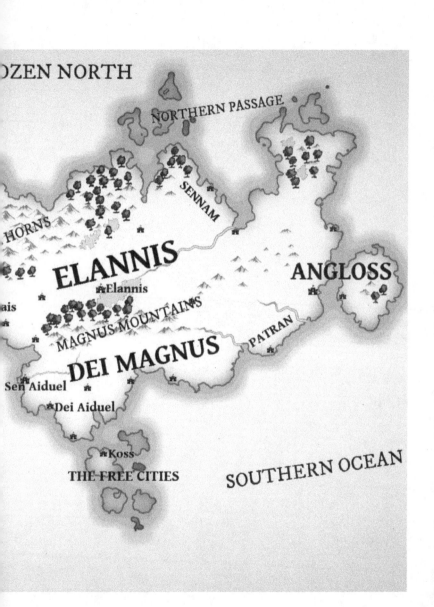

Prologue

Caddin

—

Year of Our Lord,
After Ascension, 761AA

How does the opportunity ever arise for one person to alter the destiny of a world?

Although Caddin Sendromm had a passing interest in matters of philosophy, he had never given any previous consideration to this particular question. Nor was he considering it now, whilst sitting in a dark corner of a grimy tavern in northern Angloss. Instead, he was merely contemplating the direction that his next day's travel might take, at the moment when the stranger approached him.

'Begging your pardon, master,' the unknown man said quietly, while raising a hand to touch a lock of hair on his forehead. 'My name's Sern Maddoc. I'm a sheep farmer out at the Maddoc Farm, seven miles from here. I'm told that you're a healer and a wise man. Is that correct, master?'

Caddin chuckled, the sound a low rumble in his throat. 'A healer

1

and a wise man, eh? A healer certainly, but perhaps not always so wise, friend.'

Maddoc displayed no reaction to the attempt at humour. He had averted his eyes downwards, and his feet shifted restlessly as he stood in place before Caddin's table.

'Please, be at ease, friend,' Caddin added warmly, and gestured to the chair next to him. 'I'm Caddin. Caddin Sendromm. Please, take a seat and tell me what's troubling you.'

The farmer shuffled forwards to accept the invitation, glancing to Caddin's side as he sat down. Caddin knew that Maddoc had for the first time seen the oversized mace which rested against Caddin's chair. The weapon was comprised of three feet of solid oak shaft, topped with a formidable steel head.

Caddin patted the mace reassuringly. 'Please, pay the weapon no mind. It's my travelling companion, and keeps me safe on the road, sometimes. No need for a good fellow like you to be concerned by it.'

Maddoc shifted in his seat, looking around in what appeared to be an assessment of the distance between the two of them and the other occupants of the hostelry. Having apparently satisfied himself on this point, he leaned forwards in his chair, and uttered in a low voice, 'I… a member of my family, that is… have need of a healer.'

'That is indeed my profession, amongst other things,' replied Caddin, also keeping his voice low. 'What's wrong with your family member?'

Maddoc's eyes dropped down to the table, before he turned his head to once again check the proximity of everyone else in the room. 'I can't say, master. Not here. But he needs help. I need to show you.'

Caddin's curiosity was roused. 'You cannot say? Why not?'

Maddoc responded in a voice close to a whisper. 'I've been told that you accept payment for your services, master Caddin. I'd pay you, if you were to come out to my farm with me. But I can't tell you here, master. I have to show you.'

2

Caddin leaned his head in closer to the man, dropping his own voice further. 'I must admit, I'm intrigued by whatever ailment your family member could possibly have to merit your concern for secrecy. However, I'd prefer to hear some details here before I say yes or no. We're past noon already, and a fourteen-mile round trip is a journey I'd rather not take only to find out it's either a matter of no consequence, or some condition for which I can be of no service.'

Maddoc scowled, his expression suggesting that the conversation was not proceeding in the manner which he had planned out in advance. 'Please name a fair price for the journey then, master. I promise you that it's… important. Real important, and I'd be grateful for any help I can get or any learning that you can share. We've no true healers in this valley, see, and people I trust in this town have told me that your wise learning is far above that of any local person. If you can't help my family, well, then I'll pay you for the wasted journey, but I can't tell you more right now. I have to *show* you, master.' By the time that Maddoc had finished, there was a pleading tone in his voice.

Caddin leaned back in his seat, considering the matter. In this case, the decision came easily.

Remember, he thought to himself, reciting one of the mantras which had sustained him on the road over many long years, *Aiduel reminds us that he who does not search shall never find.*

'I shall not take your coin for making a journey, Sern,' Caddin replied, sincerely. 'Let's go to your farm. When we get there, I hope that you'll be more forthcoming and that I'll be able to help. If so, you can then pay me whatever you consider to be fair. Tell me one thing though, before we leave. You said "he" needs help. Who is "he"?'

'My son,' Maddoc replied, his tone softening in apparent relief. 'My son needs help.'

—

Two hours later, Caddin was riding his horse through the northern Angloss countryside. Sern Maddoc was a few metres ahead of him, the shepherd seated upon a rickety horse-drawn wool cart. Caddin gripped his own horse's reins in one fist, and patted the mace which hung from his saddle with the other hand. He then directed his horse to follow as the sheep farmer turned his cart off from the main road, and through a gate onto a much smaller side-track towards the Maddoc farm.

The sky had turned from clear blue to dark grey in the time it had taken them to travel from the town. Ominous clouds had swept in from the east and were now threatening a storm. The gloomy weather acted to emphasise the bleak nature of the countryside in these parts, with open moorland and scrub covering shallow, rolling hills. These features were interspersed only occasionally with jagged outcrops of rock or standalone stunted trees.

Sheep country, Caddin thought ruefully, grimacing in reaction to the miserable surroundings, *full of sheep, shit, and more sheep. Oh, and apparent mystery illnesses.*

'How much further?' he enquired of Maddoc.

'My farm's a quarter of a mile down this track, master, around the hill up there ahead. The gate we passed through marked the edge of my land.'

Caddin grunted in acknowledgement, but did not attempt to engage Maddoc in any deeper conversation. Since leaving the town he had tried to extract more information from the sheep farmer, but most of his questions had been met with a request to wait until they reached the farm. Instead, Caddin shifted the straps of the backpack on his shoulder. He then reached his hand up to touch the medallion which rested against his chest, hidden beneath his robes. Feeling reassured by the welcome contact with the metal object, he stared back towards the main road as it disappeared from view.

After a short time, the Maddoc farm came into sight, its buildings nestling in the shallow valley between a hill to the south

4

and a gently rising slope to the north. The Maddoc property was clearly remote from its nearest neighbour.

The farm consisted of three buildings; a two-storey stone farmhouse, a smaller stone outhouse, and a larger wooden barn. Caddin's eyes focused upon the barn, where two people and a number of dogs were busy shepherding the Maddoc flock through open doors to the shelter within. As they got closer, Caddin could see that the first of the two individuals was a woman of similar age to Maddoc himself, who Caddin assumed was the farmer's wife. The second was a blonde-haired and scrawny boy, who was in his early teens.

'Is that your son?' Caddin asked, while gesturing towards the youth.

'Yes,' replied Maddoc. 'My son Cillian, with my wife Hengra. They're bringing the sheep in before this storm hits us.'

Caddin watched as the son's head turned towards them, after the boy had heard their voices. Whether through a trick of the light or otherwise, the youth's eyes seemed to glow eerily as he focused upon the unusual sight of his father arriving with an outsider.

Then the shepherd boy's stare locked fully onto Caddin. Instantly, Caddin felt the boy's scrutiny and inspection as something akin to a physical impact; assailing him, pushing against him, attempting to *invade* him. Immediately, he felt his breath quicken and his heart beat faster. Associated with that, an emotion lurched into Caddin's mind from which he had long since become detached. Fear.

Lord Aiduel, he recited to himself, *Make my thoughts and actions true, and deliver me from evil.*

The mantra calmed his quickening heart, but his thoughts were still racing, and his mind continued to *prickle* at the sensation of some outside force probing against it. Could he finally have found the thing which he had been searching for, after all of these years?

—

Just minutes later he was sitting opposite the boy, within the small confines of Sern Maddoc's home. A large and sturdy wooden table separated the two of them.

The farmhouse consisted of two rooms downstairs, one for the family and one for livestock, plus a wooden-beamed upper floor reached by way of a smoke-stained ladder. The place reeked of the dilapidation and poverty of the family's meagre farming existence.

Caddin was leaning with apparent nonchalance against the back of his chair, his backpack and mace placed on the floor behind him. The pose on his face was calm and emotionless, his years of training allowing him to maintain this poise despite the twin emotions of excitement and alarm coursing through his thoughts.

Sern Maddoc was seated to Caddin's right, with the farmer's homely wife stood nervously close behind her husband. Neither of those two people held Caddin's attention, though. His entire interest was focused upon the child seated across from him.

The boy looked to be about twelve years old – *the exact right age*, Caddin thought – and was sandy-haired, with a small, wiry build. There was nothing outwardly exceptional about him except perhaps for the dark piercing eyes, which continued to stare shrewdly at Caddin. Staring at him in a manner that did not accord with how a farmer's boy would normally act in the presence of an elder healer.

Caddin also continued to feel a lingering sensation, which he was certain was emanating from the boy, of something *unnatural* probing against his mind. Seeking to find a way in. He had been experiencing this feeling ever since the initial shock of the boy's inspection of him, out in the farmyard. However, he now felt more confident that the internal reciting of calming mantras to The Lord, combined with the security of his medallion, were somehow holding this invading presence at bay. He also sensed that it was *very important* for his own safety that he continue to keep it at bay. He waited, tensely intrigued to see how this encounter would proceed.

Sern Maddoc broke the silence. 'Cillian, why don't you tell

6

healer Caddin here about what's been troubling you?'

The boy frowned, looking perturbed, not taking his eyes from Caddin even as he addressed his father. 'Is he really just a healer, Da? I think he's more than a healer. I think maybe he's a... holy man, Da.'

'What?' replied Maddoc. 'Cillian, don't be rude-'

'That's OK, Sern,' said Caddin, interrupting him, his voice intentionally gentle and friendly. Caddin's eyes narrowed slightly, but otherwise he did not show any outward reaction to the boy's statement. 'Your boy is very astute. I *was* a priest, a holy man as the boy says, many years ago. But for many more years now I've been a travelling healer.' This was not quite true, but was close enough for the purpose of what they needed to know. Caddin's medallion, which might have identified him as something much more than a travelling healer, was tucked away and was out of sight. 'Now, my turn for a question, Cillian. Tell me how you knew that?'

Before the boy could answer, Sern Maddoc interrupted. 'A priest, master? You didn't share that with me when we first spoke? Had I known that, I mightn't have asked you here.' The farmer looked uncomfortable. 'How... strongly... do you feel your beliefs, master?'

Caddin switched his eyes from the boy to the father. 'I'm no longer a priest, shepherd Sern,' he replied. 'I've not been one for over ten years. And if I might save us both time and worry by cutting to what I understand to be at the heart of your question, I have no interest in heresy, or heretics, or the pursuit of heretics, or in helping those who would pursue heretics. No interest. None.'

Maddoc appeared to consider Caddin's response, looking like a man torn between a desire to have never initiated this encounter, and someone who desperately wanted to find out where it could possibly lead. After a pause of a few seconds, a change in his expression indicated that he had made a decision. He looked towards the boy, and his head moved in a small nod, giving his son permission to speak.

'I didn't know it for sure, sir,' said the youth, answering Caddin's earlier question. 'I just... felt it. Felt it coming from you, telling me.'

'Felt it, how?' Caddin's voice was outwardly casual. But the alarming sensation of a probing oily presence continued to circulate around the boundaries of his mind, even as he asked the question. Teasing for a way in.

Lord Aiduel, let me forever walk with you in the light, and keep me from the all-consuming darkness.

'I don't know,' answered the child. 'I just hear things. Feel things. I don't know how, but I find I... just, know things. It scares Ma and Da.'

'What kinds of things?'

Caddin's large hands rested on the surface of the table, fingers splayed out, with palms down. The insistent, probing mental presence made him want to reach up to touch his medallion, to feel its reassuring cold form within his grasp, but he wilfully resisted the urge.

The youth answered, his voice heavily accented but indicative of intelligence. 'Things like... what people are feeling, or thinking. Like that Ma and Da are scared right now. A little scared of you, but more of me. They've been scared of me for a long time now.'

'What else? What other things?'

'Things I shouldn't know. Ma said something to Da a few weeks ago when I was out with the sheep. Something about me. Something I didn't hear. But I knew she said it, and it scared her when I said it back to her. Scared Da too.'

'What did she say?'

Cillian looked across at his mother, who appeared embarrassed and frightened in equal measure, then at his father. The father again made a nodding motion.

'That I may not be right. That I may be a bad one. That there may be an evil spirit in me.'

'And what do you think? Is there an evil spirit in you.'

8

'No,' replied the boy, with conviction. 'I'm a good son. Aren't I, Da? I'm not bad.'

'He's a good boy, yes he is,' said Sern Maddoc, putting out a hand onto his son's shoulder. 'Good boy. Good worker. Ma spoke wrongly when she said that. Tell him about the things you *see*, Cillian.'

'OK Da. Like Da says, I see things, sir. Like, I knew there was a sheep trapped, and where, when I couldn't have known. And I see other things. Things that...' He stopped, suddenly closing his eyes tight, with a look which was somewhat akin to pain contorting his face. He inhaled deeply, appearing to Caddin to forcibly take control of himself, before continuing. 'Things that haven't happened yet.'

'Such as what?' asked Caddin. 'What did you see that hadn't happened?'

'Lots of things. Little things, like knowing that someone will arrive before they come, or what they'll say. And big things, too. Like when I told Ma and Da that Ellie was going to get ill. And she-'

'Let's not talk of that, Cillian,' interrupted Sern Maddoc, before turning to Caddin with a doleful look. 'He told us that our daughter, his sister, was going to die. She died, recently, of fever. But lots of people die. He's still a good boy, master.'

Caddin focused back on the boy, as he asked his next question. 'And did you know that I was going to come here?'

'Yes, I saw you here,' answered Cillian. 'Sitting right there. I told Da I saw you here. That's why he came to get you, isn't it Da?'

Caddin turned to address the father. 'Is that right? You chose not to share that with me?'

Maddoc looked defensive, but responded, 'Yes, master, he told me that he saw me bringing someone here. A healer, like. Said he was big, tall, grey beard, kind of fierce-looking. That's why I came to town. Knew it was you as soon as I saw you.'

'Remarkable,' said Caddin, still resisting the overwhelming urge to grip his medallion, and controlling himself with the repeated recital. *Lord Aiduel, let me forever walk with you in the light, and keep me from the all-consuming darkness.* The next question was asked as casually as he possibly could, although he involuntarily found his right hand twitching as he asked it. 'And did you see how this meeting turns out, Cillian? What happens afterwards?'

'No sir,' the boy replied. 'I only see… little bits. After this meeting…' He frowned, closing his eyes and concentrating. 'After this meeting, I cannot see… cannot see anything. I don't know.' He sounded confused.

So many questions flowed through Caddin's mind, and again he had to force himself to remain calm and to contain his internal excitement and fear. To the family in front of him, his face must remain an impassive mask, and his years of training provided a firm foundation from which he could secure that balance and control.

'What else, Cillian?' he finally asked. 'What else is different about you?'

Again, the farmer was the first one to speak, on behalf of his son. 'Cillian, tell him about the dreams.'

The boy nodded and started to speak again. 'I've been having… dreams. Lots of dreams. Often the same one. Over and over, almost every night.'

'Tell me about the repeated dream,' Caddin responded. His right hand slipped slowly off the table, to rest at his side.

'Ma and Da have heard this lots of times,' the boy started. 'I first remember dreaming it, I don't know, start of shearing season, after my accident, five moons ago. Before the other things started. Before Ellie was ill. It gets… stronger, every time I dream it.

'There's a path, up a mountain. I'm on the path, and there's four others with me. I can see them, they're walking with me, but we don't speak. We walk up the path, and it leads to an opening. Like an arch, a gate. The gate is bright, so very bright. Brighter than a fire, it hurts my eyes. And I get there, and I can see a figure on the other side of the gate. He's… even brighter than the gate. He waits

10

me and makes my heart pound and my head hurt. And then he waves his hand at us, calling us forward. So I try to go to him. So do the others. But then he puts his hand up, shakes it, stops us. And then he raises a single finger. Then I wake up.'

He has no idea what he's describing, thought Caddin, as the boy recounted his dream. *There's no chance that this story could have found its way to him in this backwater. No way that this shepherd boy is repeating something that he's heard before.*

The boy's description of his dream had now resolved Caddin upon his course of action.

'That's an interesting dream,' he said, then casually added, 'But dreams are not something to trouble us unnecessarily. *Four* others, did you say? What do they look like?'

'Yes, four. But I don't know what they look like. Least, if I did, I can't remember that when I wake up.'

'OK, there's a lot to take in here,' stated Caddin, no trace of disappointment in his voice. 'I think though that I'll be able to help you. But is there anything else? Anything else you haven't told me?'

The boy turned to his father. 'Da? Can I show him the, you know?'

Sern Maddoc nodded in response to his son's question and, as if he had been anticipating it, placed an empty wooden bowl onto the table. 'Do it with that, son.'

Caddin watched the boy's eyes switch away from him to focus upon the bowl on the table. Those vivid, dark eyes opened fully, and at that moment Caddin could sense the lingering presence outside of his own mind withdrawing a little. Retreating. Perhaps moving its attention away from him, and onto the bowl? Caddin's arm and hand moved backwards a little, behind his chair. Reaching. If he was going to act, the time would be soon.

The boy's body seemed to tense, his face contorting with pressure, as he continued to stare at the bowl. The more that he appeared to strain, the more Caddin got a sense that the outside presence was receding from him. Then it happened.

11

The bowl began to move. Just inches, a slight wobble, followed by a sideways movement, then a lurch upwards.

In that instant Caddin also moved. His hand clasped on the shaft of his mace at the precise moment that he pushed himself up from his chair, and the weapon whirled above his shoulders in one lightning-quick movement. The motion had been practised thousands of times, across many years and countless environments, and with practise had come the certainty of precision.

The mace crashed down onto the head of the boy, killing him instantly. Not being prepared to take any chances, Caddin spun his body around and a second blow landed on the back of the boy's neck, smashing his small frame face-forward into the table. The separate sound of the bowl, as it fell back down onto the wooden surface, acted as a softer echo of the killing strikes.

The murder of Sern Maddoc and his wife followed swiftly after the killing of their son, neither of them having the speed or skill to escape an experienced killer like Caddin. The husband died first, having barely had the reaction time to climb out of his chair before the murderous mace crushed against him. Then the wife was hunted down as she turned and began to run towards the door.

Having dispatched both of the parents, Caddin turned back towards the inanimate form of the boy. The absence of the probing presence in his mind told him what he needed to know, that the child was dead. However, he saw little gain in being anything less than thorough, and for the next minute his mace crashed down repeatedly onto the small, dead boy.

Bludgeoning him, and breaking him apart.

—

Shortly afterwards, Caddin was outside of the farmhouse, seated on his horse. He could see the tongues of flame at the door of the property, the fire that he had started already doing its work. The smell of burning flesh wafted across the farmyard, turning his stomach, and he was surrounded by the panicked cries of animals.

He reached beneath his tunic and withdrew the medallion resting there. He then gripped this small and precious object, which had been awarded to him over twelve years ago, at the commencement of his mission. After the frantic actions of the last half-hour, the simple act of touching it brought peace upon him, and gave calm to his soul.

Lord Aiduel, make my thoughts and actions true, and deliver me from evil.

He felt satisfied by his afternoon's work, and once he had made good his escape from this place, he would need to write to notify the appropriate people of his actions here. How to summarise what he had achieved today?

One dead. Four more to find.

Part One

—

Allana, Corin, Leanna and Arion

—

Year of Our Lord,
After Ascension, 767AA

1

Allana

—

Year of Our Lord,
After Ascension, 767AA

Allana dei Monis wondered daily about which would be the first to fade away to nothing; her mother's life, or their dwindling remaining money.

At no point in her childhood had she imagined that this was how she would spend her eighteenth birthday, wiping vomit from her mother's chin and changing soiled bedsheets. This drudgery of care for her dying relative had been her life for the past six months, but the deterioration in the patient within the last week made Allana believe that the end was now near.

Her mother had been asleep for the last hour. Allana was sitting in the chair next to the bed, staring at the dying woman. The body in the bed was emaciated and shrivelled, the skin sallow and wrinkled. How different to the looks which Seilana dei Monis had enjoyed a year earlier; a woman then in her mid-thirties with a voluptuous figure, healthy skin and lustrous dark hair.

And with the decline in Seilana's looks as the Wasting Sickness had slowly attacked her, so too had disappeared their source of income. The wealthy male visitors – the merchants, noblemen, even the priest – had stopped coming to their small two-room apartment. And gradually, since that last paid visit, the reserves of cash which Allana's mother had set aside had been consumed.

Allana looked despairingly at the dress set out on the table across the room. It was the last of her mother's expensive gowns, a beautiful green silk garment. During the last three months, all of the other dresses had been sold at the city market, along with a number of their other possessions, to raise cash for food and rent. But Allana had retained this one, which she and Seilana had once made together. This gown had always been her favourite, and had been the focus of childish and romantic dreams of wearing it for a grand city ball. Dreams which she had retained until just six months ago.

You were such a baby, then, Lana, she thought to herself, *always letting Mum protect you from everything and everyone.*

But even after all that's happened, have you really changed? You're still sitting here, pathetically clinging onto keeping this dress as if it matters, as if anything can ever be the same as it was.

It never would be, and at that moment a pain rippled outwards from her empty stomach, reinforcing the point to her. She needed food.

'Lana?' The voice was feeble, barely above a whisper. Her mother had not been lucid for over two days, so it was a surprise to Allana to hear the dying woman speaking now.

'Yes, Mum?'

'Come talk to me.'

'I'm here, Mum.' She reached out a hand to touch her mother's arm.

Seilana turned her head, to face Allana. There was a weak smile. 'Such a good girl. So beautiful. But have you lost weight, my love?'

Allana smiled back, bracing herself for what was to come. Her mother's conversation had become increasingly confused and erratic in the last two weeks. 'A little, Mum. Just a little.'

'Well. You need to make sure you're eating properly. Go buy a nice big ham for us both. From the market. Your favourite.'

'I will, Mum.'

Her mother's voice then abruptly became sterner, chastising her. 'And don't you spend all day playing your silly games with those dolls in that back room, do you hear me? We both need some fresh air. My first appointment's not until this evening, so we can go for a nice walk together. But first, you must practise your reading and writing.'

'OK, Mum, we will. Later.' There was no appointment. The dolls had been sold, months ago. Never again would her mother have the strength to walk outside.

There was silence, then, for a prolonged period. When the older woman spoke again, her voice was suddenly more lucid, more aware.

'Don't be like me, Allana. Don't be a whore.'

Allana was shocked. This was a word that her mother had forbidden in their home. 'Mum. You're not a... that. You're a courtesan, remember?'

'Courtesan. Whore. Whatever. I took rich men's money and let them fuck me. I made you grow up as the daughter of a whore. I'm so sorry.' The coarse language was upsetting to Allana. Her mother had never used such expressions in her presence before, but even more distressing was the bitterness in the older woman's voice.

'Mum, please don't apologise to me.'

'I *am* sorry. You deserve better than... *this*. I was a dei Monis. You're a dei Monis, by blood. You should've been born into a noble house. Should have had servants, money, privilege. Not been forced to live your whole life here, hiding in the spare room of this apartment throughout your childhood, having to listen to me having sex with strangers.'

'Mum, please don't say that. You've always looked after me, made me happy, protected me. Done everything that you could.'

Her mother made a weak noise of protest. 'Listen to me, Allana. Listen! I'll be gone soon. Don't be like me. You can read and write,

19

I gave you that much. You're clever, beautiful. Find another way. Promise me you won't be like me, won't do what I've done.'

'Mum, please don't be upset-'

'Promise me!'

'I promise!' Frustration and pity were mixed together in Allana's voice. At Seilana's insistence she had already made this vow many times before in her life, a pledge not to follow in her mother's profession, but it seemed like the illness had robbed the dying woman of her memory of these earlier promises. Despair welled up within Allana, her voice plaintive as she asked, 'But what other way, Mum? What should I do?'

'Don't go to my family in Monis. They won't help. They cast me out. Cast me out for getting pregnant. Called me a slut. Wouldn't believe me.' The older woman initially sounded angry as she said this, but Allana could hear the voice edging into sorrow, slurred words suggesting that her mother was losing her lucidity again. 'None of them. Wouldn't believe me. Wouldn't help me. Why wouldn't Mummy and Daddy help me?'

'Mum, please don't be upset. We don't ever talk about them, it always makes you upset, remember?' Seilana had refused to discuss her family, throughout the entirety of Allana's upbringing.

The dying woman ignored her, sounding almost childlike now, lost in her recollections. 'They told me I had to say who the father was. Daddy and Mummy were so angry with me. But I couldn't. Couldn't tell them. So they cast me out. I was seventeen! I didn't know what to do!' Her mother's eyes were fluttering, her words slurring further. Then her voice was angry again. 'Don't go to them! They won't help.'

'Then who, Mum? Who will help? What should I do?'

Seilana was losing consciousness, and in later days Allana would often wonder about what submerged and twisted thread of thoughts produced her mother's next words. 'Ronis dei Maranar… he helped me, once. He might…'

Allana let go of her mother's hand as the older woman's eyes slipped shut. She in turn then closed her eyes and sighed, and slumped wearily against the back of the chair.

—

An hour later, she was in the main market of the city of Sen Aiduel, capital of the country of Dei Magnus. She was carrying the green dress, holding it over her raised forearm to keep it away from the dust of the cobbled street. She needed to eat, and therefore she needed to sell it. She had already held discussions with two separate market traders about the sale of the garment, but she was yet to receive an acceptable offer.

This market was a place which Allana and her mother had visited together frequently throughout her childhood, in the safe and contented years before Seilana's illness emerged. The two of them would go there in the morning, once a week, in that quiet time of day before Seilana's clients would require her to return to the apartment. They had often strolled together through the rows of stalls, arm-in-arm, with money available to buy small treats and gifts for each other.

It was always wonderful to come here with you, Mum, Allana thought to herself. *If only we could do that again, just one more time.*

The marketplace was a ramshackle affair, set in a square broadly one hundred metres across, and it was crammed full of vendors selling a variety of wares. Surrounding the square on three sides were buildings typical of the ancient capital, with lines of ageing four storey townhouses jammed together to fully utilise the space within the bustling, crowded city. On the fourth side of the market was another row of townhouses, but two streets back from that was the imposing and majestic sight of the Cathedral of Sen Aiduel.

Allana looked up at the Cathedral, thinking about her mother's earlier words. Somewhere in that building, if she chose to seek him out, she might find Ronis dei Maranar. *High Priest* Ronis, who had been a long-term and regular visitor to Seilana prior to her illness, despite his vows of celibacy. Allana wondered why her mother had suggested

21

him as a possible source of help. She intended to ask Seilana, on the next occasion that the older woman re-emerged into consciousness.

Allana moved further into the market, to speak to a third potential buyer. The market stallholders all knew her by now, and they had begun to recognise that she was desperate. The two insultingly low offers, that she had already received today, had attempted to exploit that recognition.

Try to be strong, Lana. Don't let another one of them see how weak you are. Don't let them bully you.

As she approached the third stallholder, who was a swarthy, unshaven male in his early thirties, his eyes moved lecherously across her body. She had noticed this happening with increasing regularity recently, as she had blossomed fully into adulthood, but never quite so overtly as this.

'Hello there again, pretty girl,' the trader called out, displaying dirty crooked teeth. 'Have you lost weight? Feeling hungry again? Needing to sell another dress?'

'I don't need to do anything,' she replied, trying to sound convincing. She knew that he was both mocking her, and testing for weakness. 'But it *is* a lovely dress, which I may choose to sell. It's silk, beautifully embroidered, in perfect condition. Would you offer me a price for it please?'

He proceeded to make an offer for the garment, at a valuation which they both knew was far below its true worth. She attempted to haggle, but the delicious aromas wafting across from the food stalls in the market made it difficult for her to maintain her resolve. Finally, they settled on a number which she believed was just over half of the gown's true worth. She felt a little wretched as she handed over the dress, in return for a relatively meagre handful of coin.

The market trader gave a leering smile of smug triumph as he took the garment from her, saying, 'It's almost a shame to buy this off of you, a lovely-looking girl like you. I'd like to see you wearing it. Or even better, taking it off...'

She scowled, giving him a look of distaste, then turned her back on him and walked away towards the food stalls. Despite the low value which she had received for the dress, she now had enough money for food for at least two weeks. She would buy some ingredients to make a soup tonight, she would try to feed her mother, and at least she would be able to eat properly herself for the first time in days.

Happy Birthday, Lana, she thought to herself, feeling miserable.

—

In the hour during which Allana had been to the market, her mother had passed away, the illness which had racked the ailing woman's body in the last few months finally claiming her.

Allana did not notice the death immediately upon re-entry to the apartment. There had been too many recent evenings of silence, alone with her own thoughts as Seilana slept, for the lack of immediate noise upon her return to serve as an alarm. However, her first inspection of her mother confirmed that the end had been reached.

Allana chose not to report the death that evening. Instead, she made the soup that she had promised herself, which temporarily sated her hunger. She then sat next to the silent form of her mother, and clasped her hands together in prayer.

'Lord Aiduel, Saint Amena,' she whispered. 'Please forgive me that I've not prayed much in recent times, and please grant my mother's soul a safe journey to heaven.'

Goodbye, Mum. Thank you for protecting me, and for keeping me safe. I'll miss you.

She kissed her mother's forehead, then remained there, seated in prayer, for a long time afterwards.

The first tears did not come until she was lying on her own bed. Tears for the loss of her only family member, and for the end of the life which she had known until now. The tears were still falling as she

23

drifted into sleep, and that was the night when the dream claimed her for the first time.

—

She is standing on a path, on the side of a mountain. She is high up, higher than she has ever been in her life. She looks around, and can see a range of other towering mountains, encircling her.

There are four others by her side. She stares at each in turn, but all that she can see are blazing outlines of light in the shape of people.

No one speaks, and there is silence all around them.

She is walking now, walking with her silent companions, inescapably ascending the winding mountain path. She knows that she cannot stop this climb even if she wants to, and she realises that she does not want to.

In the distance a brighter light appears, a golden, radiant light surrounded by the most beautiful archway that she has ever seen. The light burns her eyes, sears into her mind, and makes her want to weep with joy and terror combined.

But still she and her companions walk on, ever closer, drawn forward like moths to the light. To the Gate.

And then she can see Him. In the Gate. Waiting. Watching. Golden, glowing, terrible, magnificent. Her legs want to collapse, her heart pounds with dread, and she wants to prostrate herself as an unworthy intruder, but still she walks on. Closer, ever closer. So too do her companions.

He moves His hand, a summoning gesture, and once again her body takes her forwards. Seductive whispers of unspoken words assail her.

LUST. POWER. DOMINATION.

But then the gesture of His hand changes, and she is aware that something is wrong.

A single finger is raised. And she knows what she must do.

—

24

The bed sheets were soaked through with perspiration when she awoke. The details of the dream drifted quickly away from her, but the heart-pounding sense of awe and terror which it had inspired lingered inside her for minutes afterwards. Further sleep was impossible after that, and she returned to the seat next to her dead mother's bed, holding silent vigil in prayer until the light of morning arrived to wash away the remaining memories of the dream.

—

Her mother was buried the next day, in an unmarked pauper's grave, and in the week that followed Allana was tormented by indecision and loneliness.

She had enough food to last for a fortnight, and the rent on the apartment was paid for another month. After that, she would need to find a way to support herself. But how? Her mother had always shielded her from many of the harsher aspects of life in the city, and she had comfortably enjoyed that protection. She had never had a job or properly learned a trade. Indeed, she had liked the easy lifestyle that her mother's income had afforded her until six months ago, and she did not know where or how to properly commence looking for work.

She tried to take stock honestly of what skills she did have.

You can read and write, Lana, she told herself, *and how many people in this city can claim that? And you can cook, and clean. And with all of the clothes that you and Mum have made together, you may actually be a good seamstress? Surely there must be a household somewhere which can use all of those things?*

However, even though she knew that she should be getting out into the city and speaking to potential employers, a lethargy had taken hold of her upon her mother's death. She could not work as a seamstress, since she had already sold all of their clothes-making equipment, and she had no money with which to buy any replacements. And although she was aware it was a snobbish thought, in her heart she could not bear the thought of becoming someone else's *servant*. Therefore, for the week after the burial she followed a routine of solitary activity at home, and did not take any further action to search for work.

Allana's mind also kept turning back towards her mother's last ever words. *Ronis dei Maranar.* Her dying parent had appeared to suggest that High Priest Ronis might help, although Seilana had never explained why or how. Could his help be a means for Allana to be able to live without entering into a dull life of servitude? And did she even have the courage to approach him?

After several days of considering this, she finally resolved to seek the High Priest out and to ask him for his assistance.

—

On Seventh-Day, Holy Day, Allana was walking towards the entrance of the spectacular Cathedral of Sen Aiduel. She was amongst the throng of hundreds of people approaching the great building for the Holy Day service.

Allana and her mother had usually attended a smaller and less prestigious church, more local to their home. However, Seilana had once stated that Ronis normally led the main Holy Day service at the Cathedral, so this is where Allana had come to find him.

As she drew closer to the Cathedral, she could hear the foreign accents of pilgrims around her, as they expressed their awe and wonder at the ancient building. She took a moment to look upwards as she mounted the steps to the entrance, and she could share their admiration of the majestic spires and arches, which towered high into the sky above her.

She entered the building within a bustling crowd of bodies, and took her place on a pew as near to the altar at the front as she could. She placed herself at the end of a row, near to the side of the Cathedral, such that she would be able to move forwards quickly once the service ended.

High Priest Ronis appeared shortly before the holy service commenced, and Allana felt relief as she recognised him immediately.

He was in his early fifties, and he entered the public areas of the Cathedral with a slow walk of confident authority, flanked by lesser priests from within the Church. He was dressed in the formal vestments of his office, so different to the anonymous hooded cloak which he had always worn on his arrival to visit Seilana dei Monis. But there was no mistaking the large curved nose and bushy eyebrows, and the heavyset body.

Allana had sometimes secretly watched her mother's encounters, and she had seen Ronis in circumstances vividly different to the one in which she could see him now. Seen him whilst peeking through holes in a door. Seen him above her mother; panting, face red, not in the least bit holy. She wondered to herself, what view would Ronis's church associates have of his secret, forbidden trysts? Would it be deemed scandalous for a senior churchman to have been breaking his vows like that? To have been so full of lust for her mother.

Stop it, Lana! You mustn't think like that, here. Concentrate! Stop these bad thoughts.

High Priest Ronis soon stepped onto the altar and commenced the service, his sonorous voice resonating clearly throughout the grand interior space. 'Welcome, members of the faith! Welcome, pilgrims from all of the lands of the faithful. Welcome! To this sacred place, to this wondrous place, to this heart of the Holy Church.

'We are all blessed to stand here, to be here, in this most holy of places. In this city where, over eight hundred years ago, our Lord Aiduel arrived after His journey from the Holy Land. Think on that! He came from the Holy Land and He landed *here*, in Sen Aiduel. Thus, did His wonder and miracles and teachings first come to us.

'Here, in this miraculous building, is the very spot where He first preached a sermon in this continent of Angall. Think, again, on that! This cathedral, indeed all of us here, all of we faithful here today, stand on the very place where He once stood. Where He once spoke his eternal truths. From where His Word started to spread.'

His voice turned sombre. 'And *here.*' He pointed at the altar, theatrically. 'Here, where this altar now stands. Here is the place where The Tree once stood. Where The Arrows pierced His Body against The Tree. Where He was ready to sacrifice Himself, and where He suffered, to save us all.

'Think on that, believers and pilgrims, as we join together today in our Holy Service devotions to The Lord. Now, in reverence, let us begin.'

Another priest stepped forward, to commence the Holy Recitals. 'Lord Aiduel, make my thoughts and actions true, and…'

'Deliver me from evil,' responded Allana and the other attendees, automatically.

'Let me stand tall and face the darkness…'

'As Aiduel faced the darkness on The Tree.'

The service continued, different priests leading other aspects of the holy rituals. The Holy Day service was comprised of a form of words as familiar to Allana and the congregation as their own names. Words which had been ingrained on each of the followers there from early childhood onwards. The only difference between this, and the hundreds of other holy services that Allana had attended, arose from the splendour of the surroundings, and the eminence of the individuals leading the service and recitals.

She waited tensely for the moment when the religious ceremony would be concluded. She would not get an opportunity for a full conversation with High Priest Ronis, she knew that much. She therefore needed to deliver her message quickly, but had to impart sufficient information such that he would know who she was and where he might meet her. She had already decided how she was going to do that.

Ronis dei Maranar concluded the service himself, with the words, 'Go in the Grace of Aiduel.'

Following this, all of the congregation stood and the faithful, beginning with those on the front row, started to file out slowly through the centre aisle towards the entrance of the Cathedral. At this moment, Allana started to move forwards swiftly along the wall of the building, until she was close to the altar area. This was socially unacceptable behaviour for a commoner and she was taking a risk, she knew that, but if she did not get Ronis's attention now it might be another week before she would have a second opportunity.

The High Priest had turned away from her, and he was still flanked by two other attending priests.

'Your Eminence!' she called. He turned his head to glance at her, but after a cursory look she could see that he had decided that she was beneath his attention in these surroundings. He waved a hand at one of the two priests accompanying him, in a suggestion that they should dismiss her. Before they did so, she added, 'Seilana dei Monis sent me.'

The name caught his attention instantly, and he turned fully, looking more closely at her face. He made a gesture to instruct his accompanying priests to stand in place, then moved a number of paces towards her, his expression inscrutable. 'Yes, child? I have only brief moments. What is it?'

'Seilana humbly requests your attendance, Your Eminence.' Now was not the time to tell him that her mother was dead, not if she wanted an opportunity to speak with him alone.

He frowned, then announced, 'I don't recognise that name.' But she could see his eyes staring again at her face, and she wondered whether he had noted the physical resemblance to her mother. 'Go in the Grace of Aiduel, child.' With that, he turned his back on her, before briskly moving away.

She remained in place for just a few seconds, watching his departure, then she in turn made her way out of the Cathedral, wondering whether her approach would be successful.

—

He came to her apartment late in the evening, on the third night following the holy service.

She had been wondering nervously if and when he would appear, but she nonetheless had prepared for the visit. She had washed prior to his arrival, and had combed through her hair, wanting to be as presentable as possible. The dress that she had selected to wear was that of a commoner, but was the highest quality garment that she still owned.

Earlier that day, as the light outside had started to fade into dusk, she had taken a moment to stare at herself in the mirror. Looking back at her was a petite and beautiful young woman – no longer a girl – with dark hazel eyes, olive skin and long wavy black hair. *How much you resemble Mum now, Lana,* she had thought, with a little sadness.

She had also placed a small object into a drawer next to the bed, an object which she had seen her mother depositing there whenever a male visitor was due to arrive.

Now, with the sky outside black with night, the High Priest's arrival was signalled by the small knock on the outside door.

She opened the door, and he entered the room without waiting for her invitation, pulling the hooded cloak down from his face and revealing his distinctive hooked nose. He pushed the door shut behind him.

'Your Eminence-' she started, but was immediately interrupted.

'Where's Seilana?'

'Your Eminence, she is-'

'Ronis, when I'm here. Cut the "Your Eminence" servility, it bores me. Where's Seilana?'

Allana swallowed. 'I'm sorry, she's dead. She died last week.'

The only emotion suggested by his expression was irritation. 'So, the Wasting Sickness finally took her? I thought it would. And yet according to you she summoned me two days ago, even though she died last week?'

'Not summoned. But she did ask me to speak with you, before she died.'

'And you chose not to mention that she was dead? And brought me here under false pretences. And you are?'

30

'Allana. Her daughter. I'm sorry, I didn't mean to lie. But I didn't know what else to say to get a chance to see you. My mum told me to speak with you, as her last words.'

'Ah... so you're the little brat she always used to keep hidden in the back room?' He moved closer, strolling across the apartment like he owned it, moving behind her such that she had to turn her body to continue facing him. He was tall, much taller than her, and heavily built. 'Yes, I see it now. You *do* look like her. Very much. Still small, like her. But definitely no longer a child.'

She felt uncomfortable with the way that he spoke those words, and she edged away from him, creating space between them. 'Yes, I'm Seilana's daughter.'

'So, Seilana's daughter. What did your mother, or what do you, want from *me*?'

'Mum, sorry, Seilana, I think she wanted me to ask you for help.'

'Did she now? That was very bold of her, assuming that *I* would consider helping *you*. And what form is this help meant to take?' He was still walking in a slow circle around her as he spoke softly, repeatedly forcing her to step backwards and to rotate her body to face him.

'She didn't say, exactly. But I think she wanted me to see if you could help me to find a way to support myself. To work. See, I can read and write and-'

'Help you to find work?' His voice was abruptly icy, his eyes equally cold. 'Help you to find work? Do you know who I am, girl?'

'Of course, Your Eminence, please excuse me if-'

'I'm a High Priest, girl! Do you understand that?' His large body moved towards her, looming over her, and as she retreated the back of her thighs touched the edge of her mother's bed. 'Why would it be worth my time to help *you*?'

'I'm sorry. I don't know.' She was shaking a little, startled by how quickly his manner had turned aggressive. 'Mum – Seilana – told me to contact you. I thought-'

'You didn't think, girl!' He was shouting, the venom in his voice so different to the gentle tones that he had used during the

Cathedral service. 'Didn't think when you almost embarrassed me in front of my priests. Didn't think when you lied to me to waste my time coming here. How did you expect me to react?'

'I'm sorry, Your Eminence. You're right. I didn't think properly, and it was wrong to lie. But I can read and write, and I thought, because you'd known my mum for so long, and because she said-'

'Seilana was a whore! I didn't care to know her, I had sex with her. For money. You're nothing but the daughter of a whore, I don't care if you can read or write. I care about what I came here for.' His look was predatory.

Unwanted tears came to Allana's eyes. 'I'm sorry, Your Eminence. Please excuse me for wasting your time, I shouldn't have lied to bring you here. Please don't waste any more of your time on me.'

She began to move towards the door, but his hand shot out, seizing her upper arm. 'Oh, I'm not going just yet, girl. Not until I've had what I came here for.' The grip on her arm was hard. Painful.

'Please, let go.'

'I came here girl because I thought that your mother was recovered. I had an *urging*, and now I find out that she's not here. But *you* are.'

She tried to prise his hand off from her arm, to no avail. 'Please, I'm sorry. Please, let me go.'

He leaned his face in closer to hers, not releasing his grip, and indeed his free hand took hold of her other arm. 'I came here to pay Seilana money to have sex with her, girl. That's what I'm here for. And what better way for you to start working, to earn some money, than by helping me with my need? By doing what your mother did?'

'What? No, that isn't why I asked you here.' An image shot into her mind, of an easy but meaningless life of sordid decadence here in this room, servicing the likes of Ronis. Submitting herself to him and to others like him, and betraying her promise to her mother. She rejected it, wholeheartedly. 'I'm sorry, I'm not going to do what Seilana did. Please, leave.'

32

'I don't think so.' He moved closer, pressing his body against hers as she was trapped against the edge of the bed. 'The Lord Aiduel wants me to do this.'

'Please. I don't, I'm sorry for wasting your time.'

'Don't act innocent with me, girl. That's what your mother was like when she first became pregnant with you, all virginal and pure and protesting. Did you know that I was the Senior Priest in Monis when that happened? I saw all the scandal, saw her protesting her innocence. Protesting that she hadn't slept with anyone, that she wasn't a *slut*. But her family knew better when they disowned her, on my advice. And I *saved* her. Set her up here, gave her an income, a profession. You both owe me.'

She tried to shake off his hands, unsuccessfully, as she added a last plaintive, 'Please, I don't want to do this.'

'No, but you *will* do it, anyway. Don't worry, though, you'll get paid.'

He lifted her upwards, then pushed her backwards onto the bed, his large body falling on top of her. His mouth was abruptly on hers, breath smelling of olives, and she could feel his sudden arousal pressing against her. She struggled beneath him, but he was too strong, too heavy, too powerful.

He finally released her arms, and she could feel him reaching downwards, shifting his robes, freeing himself. Then she felt him grabbing fistfuls of her dress, lifting the hem, and with horror she was certain that he intended to rape her.

She struggled again, beating her fists against his chest, as he proceeded to push her legs apart. She would not allow this, could not allow him to do this.

This isn't happening, Lana. This cannot happen. This won't happen.

Then, as her flailing arm banged against the drawers next to the bed, three dark words came to her in unbidden whispers, slipping into her mind.

LUST. POWER. DOMINATION.

Time abruptly slowed down for her, and she felt herself

withdrawing from her emotions, her fear, becoming somehow detached from the physical events taking place in the room. And, while High Priest Ronis dei Maranar positioned himself above her, anticipating the rape that he was about to commit, she remembered the object in the drawer.

The knife that she had placed there earlier.

Her hand pushed open the drawer, reaching, reaching... then clasping around the weapon.

As time seemed to move ever more slowly, the choice presented itself to her. Submit, be dominated, become his victim, and accept her mother's life. Or fight back.

No one will dominate you, Lana.

Her arm flashed upwards, burying the short, sharp knife into the High Priest's neck before he could complete his intended act. And then Ronis was rolling off her, gasping.

She pushed herself sideways off the bed, urgently, away from him. He rolled onto his back, and reached up to pull the knife out. Blood gurgled outwards from the wound, and she watched with a continuing sense of cold detachment as he struggled for breath, choking from the ceaseless flow of red fluid.

His eyes locked on hers. Fury, shock, hatred, dismay, was in them. He seemed to being trying to call out, but no words came between his laboured breaths. His face reddened, and then with a last heaving gasp his body shuddered and he moved no more.

You are more than him, Lana. You will be more than him.

Then her feeling of detachment evaporated, the world sped up again, and the screaming sense of her emotions returned to her. Emotions of panic and horror at what had just happened, but also an unexpected and alien sense of triumph. Of power.

But there on her mother's bed was the dead and bloodied body of a High Priest of Sen Aiduel. Whether or not it had been an act of self-defence, she had killed him. She would be tried and burned for this, for murder.

Her life here was over. She had to flee.

34

2

Corin

Year of Our Lord,
After Ascension, 767AA

Corin squatted over the cesspit at the edge of the village, his bowels again betraying his fears over the upcoming raid.

At the end of the next day, his clan would be raiding the land of the neighbouring Anath tribe. Corin had recently come of age, having reached eighteen summers, and his father had told him that he was required to join the raid for the first time.

'Corin, are you OK?' The question came from Agbeth, as she lurked behind the wooden wall which blocked the view of the cesspit from the rest of the village.

'Yes, fine, Agbeth. Please, give me some time.'

He was staring at the Great Forest as he crouched there, looking out towards that vast swathe of trees which marked the edge of their clan territory. And, far beyond the trees themselves, he could see the towering snow-capped northern mountain range, a line of mighty peaks at the very edge of the world.

After he had finally emptied his bowels, he stood and wiped himself with some straw placed near to the pit. He then pulled up his trousers, and wandered round to join Agbeth, who grinned when she saw him.

Corin gestured towards the distant treeline. 'I was just daydreaming about running to the forest, Agbeth. Running there and hiding. Then curling up in a hollow for two days, and coming back after the raid has finished.' He grimaced forlornly. 'Do you think that anyone will notice I'm not here, if I do that?'

She smiled in return, recognising that he was not being serious. 'Sadly, I think that your father, and your brothers, and Borrik, and me, and the chickens, and just about everyone else will notice. So, that'll be a yes.' She then touched his arm. 'It'll be alright, you know'.

'Will it?'

'Yes, we talked about it, remember? Just stay at the back. Stay out of trouble. And if you need to, run away.'

He smiled at her, trying to look brave, and failing. 'I think I can do that much. Run away, at least.'

'You can do so much more than that, Corin. I know that. But if you need to run, then *run*. Good job you won't have me with you for once, slowing you down.'

Agbeth was his only friend in the village. She was five months younger than him, and she had always been there, with him, surviving together. He was short, just four inches over five feet, with close-cropped red hair. But she was even smaller than him. She had suffered some kind of fit when she was young, and the physical effects of that had stayed with her ever since. The left side of her face drooped downwards, with her left eye slack, rendering her features somewhat lopsided. She was also lame in her left leg, walking with a permanent limp.

They walked slowly back into the village, now.

'Try to enjoy the feast, tonight, Corin. Will you sit with me when we're there, and hold my hand?'

36

He smiled at her. 'There's no one else I would rather sit with.'

She beamed happily and blushed, a reaction from her which had been happening more and more often, recently. He sensed again that it was an indication that, for her at least, the nature of their relationship was ready to change. She added, 'I'll hold your hand and speak to the Gods for you. They'll listen to me, and will keep you safe and bring you back to me.'

'Then I will come back running.'

'Running's not important. Just safe.'

The village of Karn always held a feast on the evening prior to a raid. A feast to both praise the warriors who would on the next day be asked to risk their lives, and to make offerings to the Gods. In particular to Mella, God of War, and Banta, God of Death, to seek their favours.

Corin and Agbeth had both finished their chores for the day. For Corin, this had consisted of his usual routine of milking cows, feeding chickens, collecting eggs, chopping wood and cleaning the areas in which the animals lived. Sometimes, after his chores were finished, he would take his bow and head out into the surrounding fields to hunt. But today they both now had a couple of free hours prior to the feast, and they walked in the direction of the lake to the west.

Karn and its surrounding country was the only place that Corin had ever known. He had not seen any other villages. The clan of the Karn was at war with both of its neighbouring clans, the Anath to the south and the Borl to the east. This prevented any travel in either of those directions. To the west of the village lay The Great Lake, and to the north stretched the endless Great Forest.

Agbeth had been Corin's companion throughout his teenage years. Whenever they had free time to allow them to do it, the two of them had escaped together from the boundaries of the village into the surrounding countryside. Despite the impediment of her lame leg, they had even travelled as far as the edges of the Great Forest, but had never dared to explore any further than that.

They arrived at the lake after a few minutes of walking, and they stared out across the glassy, still waters. There were five longboats there, moored against the jetty.

Agbeth pointed at the boats. 'Will they all be full tomorrow, for the raid?'

'Yes,' answered Corin. 'I think up to fifteen men in each. That's…' He tried to work out the number. 'That's a lot of warriors.'

'Yes, lots,' she replied. Her voice was quiet and subdued.

'I've sharpened my axe,' he stated, trying to sound brave. 'It's very sharp.'

'Have you? Do you think that you'll be able to use it?'

'I don't know,' he responded, truthfully. They had known each other for so long, their answers were always completely honest when together. 'I can use it, swing it properly, you know that. But chopping wood is one thing. Chopping a man? I just don't know.'

'Just keep safe,' she said, reaching out to touch his hand.

'But I'm scared, Agbeth. What if my nerve fails me? What if I shame myself?'

She squeezed his hand. 'Just stay alive, Corin. Don't worry about being brave. There's no shame in staying safe. And remember, I'll be praying for you.'

—

They arrived at the feast together, later that afternoon as the sun began to fall. The gathering was held in the Clan Hall, the largest building in the village. The Hall was twenty metres across, constructed from a series of thick logs planted in a circle, enclosed by a thatched roof over which grass and plants had started to grow.

Many of the villagers had arrived there before them. A pig had been slaughtered, and was now roasting on a spit in the centre of the building, with villagers crowding into the spaces around it. The place was already raucous, the noise and atmosphere fuelled by the numerous ale barrels which had been opened.

Corin looked for a place to sit, groaning inside when he noticed that the only available free area was near to a group of his family members. He and Agbeth moved there together, walking at her pace as she limped alongside him.

Corin's eldest brother, Kernon, noticed them as soon as they sat down. He was seated in the midst of Corin's other brothers and their wives. 'Look, it's Runt!'

Corin's size and relative physical weakness had led to only his mother and Agbeth still calling him by his given name. To his father and his brothers, and to the rest of the village, for as long as he could remember he had been called 'Runt'.

Kernon continued. 'Tomorrow's hero has arrived! Father, look at the fierceness in his eyes!' Kernon was over six feet tall, and blonde-haired, a younger replica of his father. He had clearly already been drinking for an extended period.

Corin's father, Akob, was sitting on the other side of Kernon, next to Corin's mother, Orga. Akob looked across at Corin, and there was no kindness in his eyes. 'He'll be no hero. Just mind he doesn't shame us.'

Corin disregarded the comments, accepting Agbeth's hand again as she offered it to him. His father despised him, and he had grown used to that fact a long time ago. The barbed comments which the older man now threw at him no long found a soft target.

Corin was the youngest of five brothers. The other four were all cast from the same mould as their father. Tall, strong, blonde-haired with thick beards, they all looked like warriors. He knew that his father held him in contempt for his size, for his relative weakness, for his lack of facial hair. Corin had always sensed that it was a source of shame and embarrassment for the mighty warrior Akob, that he could have spawned such a weakling.

'Akob, leave him be,' announced Corin's mother, feebly. Corin could dimly remember a time when Orga had defended him with more vigour, but she had become cowed by his father as the years had passed. It was little more than a token protest now.

However, Akob seemed to comply on this occasion. 'Just so long as he doesn't shame me tomorrow.' He returned to drinking the ale in his tankard.

Kernon was not finished yet, though. 'I see that you've come here with the Cripple, tonight, Runt?'

Corin hated hearing people refer to Agbeth with that name, although she had reassured him many times that it did not bother her. She leaned in to him now whilst holding his hand, and whispered, 'Just ignore him.'

Kernon had more to say, however. 'Is she telling you what to do now, Runt?' Then he paused, and smirked, adding, 'Have you fucked the Cripple yet, Runt?'

Corin turned towards him and glared, embarrassed but angry, responding, 'Don't call her that.'

Kernon grinned maliciously. 'What, call the Cripple her name? What's wrong with that, Runt?'

'I said, don't call her that, Kernon!'

'Don't get angry with me, Runt, we both know that you won't do anything about it. So, you haven't fucked her yet?' Corin stayed silent, seething but knowing that a physical encounter with his brother would only end one way. The elder sibling sneered, sensing that he was getting the reaction that he wanted. 'Don't you think you should fuck her tonight? Lose your virginity before it's too late and you get killed tomorrow?'

'Banta curse you, Kernon.'

Corin was blushing, deeply embarrassed by the subject of Kernon's abuse but also furious. Agbeth squeezed his hand again, and Corin knew that she would want him to back away from this confrontation. Knew that she was worried for him.

'Hey, Cripple, don't you think you should fuck him tonight?' The older brother had turned his attention to Agbeth, now. 'I know it won't be like being with a real woman, but at least he'll get a taste of some action before the Anath cut his balls off tomorrow.'

'I said, curse you, Kernon,' Corin repeated.

40

'Or, if he's not man enough, how about you let me take pity on you, give *you* a taste of a real man?'

This was too much for Corin. 'Leave her alone, Kernon, or I swear you'll get an axe in your back tomorrow, from me.'

'Don't threaten me, Runt, or I'll-'

His words were cut off by the entry of the clan chief. The noise levels fell quickly throughout the hall as Borrik Greataxe entered, the chief expecting everyone present to direct their attention towards him. He was so-named after the enormous weapon that he wielded in battle, which he brandished now as he entered the room.

Borrik was a giant of a man, over six inches above six feet tall. His arms were rippled with muscles, and his face carried a purple scar from one eye down to his mouth. That face was contorted into a wild look as he yelled, 'Karn!'

The room erupted with noise around Corin as most people responded with their own shout of the clan and village name.

Borrik appeared unsatisfied with the volume of this response, and again he bellowed, 'Karn!'

This time the response from the assembled villagers was even louder, and Corin joined in, as did Agbeth.

Borrik moved to the centre of the room, the great-axe held in one hand. He was of a similar age to Akob, although he looked stronger and his face held an expression which seemed to constantly threaten violence. He stood near the pig roasting on the spit, then turned his body in a slow, stalking motion, facing each area of the hall in turn.

'People of Karn!' the chief shouted. 'Tomorrow we'll feast on the blood of the Anath! We'll destroy them as Mella destroyed the kraken! But tonight, we make offerings to the Gods, and we feast!'

With that, his short speech was concluded, and the crowd erupted with a loud cheer. Borrik moved away to scoop up a tankard of ale, and the tumult within the room commenced once again.

Corin scrutinised the clan chief. How different was the older man to him; surely weighing twice as much as Corin and no doubt

41

capable of snapping him in two with his bare hands. In a village of strong men like Corin's father and brothers, Borrik towered above all others. He had taken the chiefdom of the village by killing his predecessor in a trial by combat, and he would undoubtedly lead the warriors of Karn into a vicious fight tomorrow, terrifying his enemies. Corin considered how wonderful it would be to go into battle with that strength, that confidence, that ferocity. In contrast to his own weakness and timidity.

Corin glanced towards his own family. Luckily, the chief's entrance had distracted his brother Kernon, who had moved off to talk to an attractive woman in another group. His brother would find a sexual partner tonight, on a night like this, Corin knew that was certain. His brother had been with many of the women of the village, since gaining his manhood. His virginity was long forgotten.

Corin then looked towards Agbeth, who was still holding his hand. She was sitting there with her eyes closed, mouth moving with silent words. Her straight brown hair was hanging forwards, framing her face.

'What are you doing?' he asked her, smiling.

'Shhhh… I'm praying to the Gods for you, silly. Let me finish.' The bottom of her mouth, on the left side, was also slanted downwards, and he could see it twitching as she mouthed her prayers.

He found himself experiencing an enormous surge of affection for her. Without Agbeth here, there would be no one in the village that he could speak to, no one who he could share his thoughts with. The two of them were somehow vastly different to all of Karn's other residents. Different both in how they looked and how they *were*. Perhaps it was as a result of their shared physical frailty, but he knew that they were both so much gentler than the people around them. If he and Agbeth had their way, there would be none of the casual cruelty and nastiness which existed between the members of their clan. And none of the bloodlust which led to murderous raids on neighbouring villages. But in Karn, the two of them were oddities. Freaks.

He waited now, watching her mouth the words, the bustling noise of the crowd in the Clan Hall surrounding them both. Finally, she opened her mouth and smiled, with that lopsided grin which was so familiar to him. 'There! All finished,' she said. 'I spoke with Banta, and Mella, and Cint. And they all promised to keep you safe for me, and to bring you back.'

He smiled in return. 'Oh, so the Gods are making promises to you now, are they?'

'They are,' she said, squeezing his hand again.

He frowned, then. 'I'm sorry for the things that Kernon said to you.'

'I don't mind. Nothing he could say to me would ever upset me. The only person who could ever upset me with *words* would be you.'

He looked at her closely. 'I haven't upset you, have I?'

'No, of course not. Nothing you do upsets me, Corin.' She had a melancholy expression, though, and he knew that the impending raid was scaring her as much as it was him.

'Agbeth… would you like for the two of us to leave here? Just to walk together, outside? I'd like to get away from my family.'

She nodded, and he helped her to her feet, the two of them edging through the crowd to exit the hall. They then moved away from the building. Years of being in her company had taught him to naturally walk at her reduced speed, and they moved together comfortably and slowly back towards the lake.

When they got there, the raucous noise of the feast at the hall was distant to them, and they were alone together. Agbeth looked uncertain for a few moments, but then she appeared to make a decision, and she turned to him and said, 'Corin, you know, the things that your brother said?'

'Yes?'

He could not tell for certain if she was blushing, in the failing light. Both of her hands were now holding his, as she faced him. 'The way that Kernon said those things before was horrible. But you do know, you *must* know, that I think about you that way now?'

He hesitated, before responding. 'I guess I do know that, yes.'

She also waited for a few moments before she spoke again, pausing to see if he was going to add anything more to his response. When he did not speak further, she stated, 'I could not let you go tomorrow, without telling you that.'

'Thank you, Agbeth.'

She waited again, still not looking satisfied with his reply. Finally, she added, 'And what about you? How do you feel? About me?'

There was uncertainty and fear in her voice. He hesitated for longer this time, carefully choosing his words. Then he leaned in towards her and kissed her, softly on her left cheek, the first time he had ever kissed her. 'I'm yours, Agbeth. I've always been yours and always will be. You're in my heart.'

She smiled in response, a smile of delight and relief so broad and radiant that for just a moment her uneven face touched on prettiness. 'And I am yours, Corin.' She placed his hand onto her chest. 'In my heart, too.'

He felt another strong surge of affection towards her. 'And, Agbeth,' he added, 'I *do* think about those things that Kernon said, too. If I return from the raid, I would like to… to talk of this again.'

She hugged him then, her small warm body pressing against his. '*When* you return from the raid, I shall be waiting for you, Corin.'

—

The next day passed in the company of his brothers, preparing for the attack on the Anath. The men had moved down to the shores of the lake, readying their equipment. It was not a time for women to be near, and he saw Agbeth only for brief moments. But he was content that they had said their goodbyes properly the night before, on the shores not far from where he now waited.

As a first-timer on one of these raids, Corin had received the last choice of equipment. The one-handed axe which he had with him was his own, and was of reasonable quality. But everything else that he had scavenged from the residual pile of equipment was of low quality, dented and scuffed. A wooden shield with a six-inch crack angling in from one edge, and a scuffed leather jerkin which covered his body but not his arms and legs. And there was no remaining helmet which fitted him, so he would need to go into battle with his head bare.

The only benefit which he could perceive from his inferior armour was that he was more lightly encumbered than most of the men around him. Therefore, he would be better placed to escape if he did indeed run away.

To his initial discomfort, he spent the day around his father and four brothers. However, the proximity of battle against a shared enemy seemed to have encouraged them to scale down their usual abuse of him. Indeed, his father took him aside at one moment, to offer some words of advice.

'Just remember this,' said Akob, holding up Corin's axe. 'You're weak, we know that. But the sharp blade of an axe swung by you will cut a man's flesh just as well as if swung by me. This is a good axe. Remember, be vicious. Don't hold back. When you see the enemy, attack him. The man who holds back, who cowers, who waits, is the man who dies. If you see the enemy, scream your bloodlust, and kill him.'

'Yes, father,' he replied, feeling scared and finding it difficult to imagine a bloodlust rising within himself.

'And other than all of that, stay near to me and your brothers. You're our blood. Fight with us, don't shame yourself, or shame us, and we'll keep you alive.'

Corin nodded again.

His bowels were no kinder to him during the period of waiting than they had been the day before, and he broke off from the group regularly to make several visits to the cesspit. There were some subdued caustic remarks from others about this, but he noticed that he was not alone in this indication of nervousness.

When the afternoon light started to fade, the men of Karn began to make their way onto the five longboats moored on the shores of the lake. Corin followed onto a boat with the members of his own family and the warriors of two other families, taking a seat on the right-hand side, and grasping an oar.

Whereas in the preceding hours the men had been full of confident boasting chatter, they were silent now. The boats pushed off from the shore, heading south, rowed stealthily and steadily from the lands of the Karn into the lands of the Anath. Corin found the silence on his boat to be oppressive, and he was alone with his grim thoughts although surrounded by the other warriors.

His axe rested on the seat next to him. He still genuinely did not know whether he had it within himself to do the things which his father had said. To swing it into another man. To kill.

They would soon put ashore, close to the main Anath village, and then the work of kill or be killed would start, for him and for each of the other men there.

He was terrified.

3

Leanna

—

Year of Our Lord,
After Ascension, 767AA

Leanna Cooper experienced a holy epiphany exactly one week after her eighteenth birthday, and just two days before her wedding.

It was an ordinary week day, and she was kneeling before the altar in the chapel of the School of Saint Amena.

She had prayed in this very spot, within the religious school, many hundreds of times in the last twelve years. She found great comfort in the small and austere surroundings, alone with her thoughts and safe in the knowledge that Aiduel was with her, as she made her daily devotions to Him. Today would be her last day in the school, and the last time that she would pray in this chapel.

Lord Aiduel, please bless my upcoming marriage to Lohan, and please keep my parents safe and well after I have left their home.

She had known Lohan Marrus for most of her life. He was two years older than her, and for ten of her twelve years at the school he had also been a pupil there. Everyone noted what a perfect match they were; he was four inches taller than her own long, slim frame, and both of them were blonde-haired, blue eyed and comely.

And they were also well-matched in temperament. Lohan was not quite as devout as Leanna herself was, but they both lived by the key teachings of Aiduel's tenets; love, happiness, peace, kindness, respect. Lohan had always been a peacemaker in the school, and from an early age Leanna could remember that he had been attentive to her.

Their families were also close, with both sets of parents owning successful merchant enterprises operating in the city of Arlais. It had therefore not been a complete surprise to Leanna when, twelve months ago, Lohan's father had approached her own parents with the proposal of marriage.

Leanna's family had been delighted. She had not seen Lohan for several months by then, for he had been establishing himself within his family business. However, after her parents' approval, he had visited her. He had told her bashfully of how he had not been able to stop thinking about her, in the months after he had left the School of Saint Amena. He had shared his thoughts on their future, had explained why he would make a good husband for her, and had described the property that he now owned which could become their new home.

It had seemed the most natural thing in the world to accept his proposal. And to enjoy the happiness that her acceptance created in him and in her parents. She was not completely sure that she was *in love* with Lohan, not the kind of romantic love which her friends had sometimes whispered about. However, her mother had told her that a deep and truer love would develop out of the years of working and growing together as a happy couple. And he was a good person. That was enough for Leanna.

They had even kissed, briefly, on a couple of occasions when their parents had left them alone. It excited her a little now to think about those stolen moments, but she admonished herself for having such thoughts whilst in prayer.

This was the last time that she would come here as a pupil of the school. Her happiness at the impending wedding was tempered slightly by a sadness that her life at the School of Saint Amena, here in its tranquil grounds on the outskirts of Arlais, was ending today. The teachers at the school, from Senior Priestess Maris and Priest Hambel downwards, were all warm and kind-hearted individuals. Their teachings had shaped the person whom she had become, and she would miss them all dearly.

Lord Aiduel, please grant me the wisdom and patience to always do unto others, as the kind people here have done unto me.

The carved statue of The Lord Aiduel On The Tree resided on the centre of the altar. The carving was a familiar image displayed in all holy places across the land. The story which it represented was known to all believers, and was one which had been taught to Leanna even before she joined the school.

The Lord's body in the statue was upright, His arms outstretched. Cords bound each of His wrists and ankles, and pulled His arms and legs back tightly against the trunk of The Tree to which He was attached. He wore only a loincloth, and the blood pouring down His chest was clearly visible. As were the two Arrows protruding from under either shoulder, pinning Him to The Tree. And yet despite these twin agonies His face was turned upwards, serene, looking to Heaven and to Salvation.

Lord Aiduel, please bless my home and my family.

Leanna knew that these prayers must end soon, and that she must leave the chapel. Must say her goodbyes, and then depart from this beloved place.

That was when the statue on the altar started to glow.

The light started subtly, a barely noticeable halo around the trunk of The Tree. But Leanna *did* notice, and she was frozen in place with sudden reverential awe as the glow started to spread.

The halo enlarged, and the light on the statue travelled towards the The Lord's Body, illuminating it. Then, with absolute conviction, Leanna knew what she was beholding.

Lord Aiduel, you are here! You are with me!

She instinctively clasped her hands together in devotion, in response to the religious vision which she was certain was being displayed before her.

She also became aware that a warmth, a sensation of bliss, was spreading through her own body in conjunction with the holy light spreading across His Body. And that light continued to build in intensity and brilliance as she watched.

Lord Aiduel, thank you, thank you, thank you, for showing yourself to me...

Ever brighter the Body on the statue glowed, and Leanna felt herself becoming overwhelmed with the blissful glory of His presence. The sensation mounted to a crescendo within her as she witnessed the light exploding from the statue and washing over her. The powerful sensations finally overcame her, and she fell to the floor in front of the altar. Her body was racked with convulsions, as she slipped out of consciousness.

Then, for the first time, the dream took her.

—

She is standing on a path, high up on the side of a mountain.

The world is silent.

There are four others beside her. She looks at them, staring at the four blinding outlines of light in the shape of people. She reaches out a hand to them, beckoning them, but no one takes it. Neither she, nor they, speak.

She is walking now, walking with her faceless and voiceless companions, inexorably climbing the winding mountain path. She senses that this climb has been awaiting her presence for a very long time, and she embraces the moment.

In the distance a beautiful ethereal archway appears, contained within which is a magnificent heavenly golden light.

The light sears her eyes and burns into her consciousness, and fills her with the wonder and awe of divine salvation.

She and her companions walk on, ever closer. To the Gate.

And then she can see Him. In the Gate. Waiting. Watching. Golden, glowing, terrible, magnificent. She is not worthy, not worthy to be here, not worthy to see Him, but still she walks on. Closer, ever closer. So too do her companions.

He moves His hand, a summoning gesture, and once again her body takes her forwards. Angels suddenly sing clarion songs around her, their words reaching into her, inspiring her.

DEVOTION. SACRIFICE. SALVATION.

But then the gesture of His hand changes, and she is aware that something is wrong.

A single finger is raised. And she knows what she must do.

—

Priest Hambel found her prostrate before the altar, her body twitching spasmodically, her limbs jerking whilst her eyes were rolled back in their sockets.

Her first awareness of something other than the vision was the sound of the elderly priest's voice, calling others for help. Her consciousness and her eyesight then returned quickly, and she opened her eyes to find the old male priest cradling her head. Concern was etched into his craggy, aged face.

'Thank The Lord!' he cried out as she focused upon him. 'I thought we were going to lose you, child.'

She realised where she was, lying before the altar in the chapel. 'Aiduel visited me. I had a vision.'

Hambel was a pious man without a trace of cynicism, and he responded by saying, 'Bless you child. What wonderful news!'

The details of the vision on the mountain were already slipping away from her – *Was there a Gate?* – but the image of the light glowing on the statue of The Lord Aiduel On The Tree remained imprinted on her mind.

Lord Aiduel, you have visited me.

She felt certain that The Lord Aiduel *had* visited her. He had blessed her with His holy presence, here in this special place on this particular day. She had been the recipient of a miracle, of sorts.

But two questions followed on from that.

Lord Aiduel, why did you choose to show yourself to me? And why now?

—

Leanna was still pondering those questions as she was seated across from Senior Priestess Maris, later that afternoon. This would be her last meeting, as a school attendee, with the elderly priestess.

Leanna had recounted the little that she could now remember of the vision to the older woman. That remembrance was now limited to the light shining on the statue, prior to Leanna passing out. She had a sense that there was something of much greater importance which was now forgotten. However, try as she might, the memory of that was lost to her.

'I'm so proud of you, Leanna,' said the Senior Priestess, not even spending a moment to doubt her pupil's story. 'The Lord has recognised your virtue and your devotion, and He chose to visit you for that reason, on your last day here. How wonderful!'

'But what does it mean, Mother?' asked Leanna.

'It means that you've been blessed, child. Blessed for your goodness and your piety.'

Leanna nodded, her face not expressing her own concern. The reason for the vision was already causing doubts to seed in her own mind, doubts which she intended to address with her parents later on that day. However, she did not want to share these misgivings with the Senior Priestess.

Lord Aiduel, please give me the wisdom and faith to know your true meaning.

'There is a *small* matter that I want to mention though, Leanna,' added the Priestess, looking a little apprehensive. 'About *news* of this vision.'

'What is it, Mother?'

'Well, how do I say this? As Senior Priestess of this school, I'm meant to report any news of visions or miracles to the High Priest of Arlais. And he in turn should report them to his seniors. And of course, visions and miracles such as the one that you've experienced today are so very rare and special. But… the last time that I heard of a religious school in Elannis making such a report, they were later visited by members of Aiduel's Guards. And there was much investigation and interruption at the school, and very great upset was caused.'

Leanna knew a small amount about Aiduel's Guards. They were the devout military arm of the Holy Church, their mission as she understood it being to eradicate heresy in all of the lands of the faithful. She had only occasionally seen members of their order within Arlais, but they nonetheless had a fearsome reputation, and she shuddered a little as she heard the name.

Senior Priestess Maris saw her reaction. 'Yes, they make me tremble a little, too, child. *If* I report this, they'll be likely to come here and conduct a similar investigation. And even though you'll just recently have been married, there will be lots of questions for you and for your family, too.'

'Will there, Mother?'

'Yes. And sometimes, with Aiduel's Guards, those questions can result in things being found out about, or accusations being made against, good people. Good people who may have strayed a little from the true path but who are not truly heretics. Your vision today has been a wonderful blessing for you, child. But I wouldn't want any investigation, interruption… or upset, here, at the School. Or for you and your family. Do you understand me, child?'

'I think so, Mother.'

'Well, to be direct. I want us both to accept this vision for the blessing that it is. But I will choose not to report it, and I would ask you not to discuss it with anyone other than your parents, and only then on the condition that it goes no further than that.'

'Yes, Mother.'

'Do I have your word on that, child? Your Holy Oath?'

'Yes, Mother. If it would please you, I swear on the Holy Book that I'll tell no one else, other than my parents, about this.'

The elderly woman stared at her in silence for a few seconds, kindness showing in her eyes. She then passed across a rolled-up parchment to Leanna. 'Here then is your Certificate, certifying your accomplishment in this School, child. Go in peace, and may you ever live happily in the Grace of Aiduel. I shall miss you dearly.'

—

Leanna was beset with doubts as she sat at home that evening, with her parents.

She was an only child. Her parents Elisa and Jonas Cooper had married twenty years ago. Her mother was in her early forties, tall and blonde like Leanna, whilst her older father had a short and stocky build. Jonas had inherited his cloth trading business from his own father, and with the support of his wife had successfully expanded it, such that the family now enjoyed a comfortable existence.

Their home reflected that success, being a large two-storey stone building in the wealthier western part of the city of Arlais. It also reflected their devoutness, with a statue of The Lord Aiduel On The Tree in each room of the house. The city of Arlais itself was towards the western end of the country of Elannis, twenty miles from the border with Andar.

'But what does it mean?' Leanna asked her parents, after she had finished describing her recollections of the vision to them, repeating the question she had earlier asked to the Senior Priestess.

'It's a blessing, Leanna,' answered Elisa. 'A blessing from The Lord.'

'Yes. We must pray to The Lord this evening, to thank Him for His blessing,' added Jonas.

That did not satisfy Leanna. 'Yes, but why now? Why did He give me this vision *today?*'

Her mother frowned, considering this, before answering. 'Well, today was a special day, wasn't it? Your last day at Saint Amena's. That must be why He chose it.'

'But that's not all that's special about this week, is it? Could this be connected to my wedding on Sixth-Day?'

'Yes, yes, I suppose it could,' replied Elisa, suddenly excited. 'A blessing from The Lord for your marriage. How wonderful that is, Leanna!'

Leanna did not share that happiness or excitement. In fact, directly contrasting emotions had been tormenting her in the hours since the vision. 'Yes, Mum, that would be wonderful. But what if it didn't mean that?'

'What do you mean?' asked her father, sounding concerned. 'What else could it mean?'

'What if it was a calling? What if He visited me to call me to the Holy Church? To stop me from going ahead with the wedding?'

'Oh Leanna!' exclaimed her mother, sounding exasperated. 'Not this again! Haven't we already talked about this, what, three years ago and then again last year? We love you and we're so proud of your devotion to the Holy Church and to The Lord, but we don't want the life of a Priestess for you. Didn't we talk about this?'

'Yes, we did Mum.'

'And remember what we talked about? If you become a Priestess, you will never marry. Never know what it is to be in a loving relationship with a man. Never have children. Never have a family. And you will live separately from us. That life is for some people, but it's not for you. You have too much love inside you that you could give to a family, Leanna.'

'I know Mum, but-'

'Just hear me out,' Elisa interrupted, her voice a little sharper than her usually calm state. 'You're nervous, I understand that. I was nervous before I married your father. But Lohan is a wonderful man. He'll make a wonderful husband for you and The Lord Aiduel surely also sees that. Today was a blessing for the wedding, not a signal to doubt it or abandon it! Surely you can see that?'

'Yes, Mum, I can,' said Leanna, but in her heart she was not convinced, and her voice betrayed that doubt.

'Your mother is right, Leanna,' added her father. 'This coming Sixth-Day will be a wonderful and happy day. For our family, and for Lohan's family. I could not feel any more joy than to know that your mother and I have secured your future happiness by seeing you married to him. To know that you'll have a chance to have the love and companionship your mum and I have. Please stop these last-minute doubts, they're not worthy of you.'

Jonas was usually a taciturn man, and for him to have made a speech this long indicated to Leanna that the discussion had clearly vexed him. She felt defeated, and did not want to upset her parents any further.

'I'm sorry, Mum, Dad. I'm sorry. You're right, Sixth-Day will be a wonderful and happy day. Lohan will be a wonderful husband. I'm just feeling nervous, having silly last-minute doubts, and of course my vision of The Lord today has truly blessed our wedding.'

They both smiled as she said this, and Elisa patted her hand comfortingly.

Lord Aiduel, please forgive me for my dishonest words of certainty, when I am so suddenly full of doubt and confusion, thought Leanna, as she outwardly smiled back at her parents. *Truly, Lord, please tell me why you sent me this vision, what its meaning is, and what you now want from me. Please.*

—

She lay awake in bed that night considering these questions, her mind alert with recollections of the awe-inspiring vision of light on the statue. Despite the strength of her parents' protestations, she felt sure that the reason for the vision was inextricably linked to her upcoming marriage. Just hours earlier, she had been filled with a serene commitment to her future with Lohan. Now, she was gripped with anxiety and uncertainty.

Lord Aiduel, do you feel that I am rejecting you? If I marry Lohan, am I turning my back on your calling, forever?

She had given serious thought to a life of devotion to the Holy Church, of a religious calling, twice previously in the last few years. The first time had been when she was fifteen years old, the second time just over a year ago, a few weeks before Lohan's proposal. On both occasions, she had initially gone to speak to Senior Priestess Maris about this, and subsequently had spoken with her parents.

The elderly priestess had been supportive and encouraging both times, although she had honestly explained the implications of the choice of a religious vocation. Two years of training would be required at a College of Aiduel for anyone who aspired to become a priest or priestess. For Leanna, that would be the College of Aiduel in Arlais itself.

Any supplicant to a College of Aiduel would have to make the Vows of Submission, giving their lives over to the Holy Church. The accepted individual would then progress through the training ranks of Neophyte and Acolyte, until finally, after two years, becoming an ordained priest or priestess. They would then be assigned their own parish somewhere in the country of Elannis, or a role at a place of learning or healing.

And with the choice of a religious life as a priestess would come the implications. Never to marry. Never to have children. To remain celibate all of her life. To dedicate her life and her existence to the Holy Church, to Aiduel, and to her calling.

These sacrifices had, at the time, seemed bearable to Leanna when compared with the greater spiritual worth of a life of devotion to Aiduel. But both times, when the conversation had extended to encompass her parents, she had been surprised by how strident their opposition to a religious vocation had been. Her mother in particular had been ardently opposed, coming very close to forbidding it.

Following that second conversation, Leanna had acquiesced to their view. And then the proposal from Lohan had followed swiftly afterwards, and the contemplations of a life dedicated to the Holy Church had lapsed into the background of her thoughts. And there they had remained, until today.

Now, as the vision of light played over and over within her, her mind was awhirl with doubts and confusions. Two potential pathways, two potential lives, extended outwards from this point in time, beckoning her. A choice of either would irrevocably destroy the other.

Lord Aiduel, please let me know what the meaning of your vision was. Am I to pledge my future to the loving and lovely man I have promised myself to, or are you calling me to you, Lord?

And she had only two days remaining within which to make her choice.

4

Arion

—

Year of Our Lord,
After Ascension, 767AA

Arion Sepian stood on the battlements of the castle walls, and peered out to sea. He was looking for a first sight of the returning galleon which would be carrying his father and older brother.

Beside him stood his eldest brother, Gerrion, whose eyes were also trained on the entrance to the harbour of the coastal town of Septholme.

'They should be here today,' Arion said. 'They're already four days overdue. When should we start to be concerned?'

'Patience, brother,' responded Gerrion. 'Any number of things could explain the delay. Either the coastal weather has been bad, and the ship has been delayed sailing through the Straits, or the Grand Council has gone on for longer than anyone expected. There's no need for concern, just yet.'

Arion nodded. His brother was expressing what he himself already knew, but he welcomed the reassurance anyway. 'I know.

59

Most likely the latter. I wonder what father has had to deal with there.'

'Lots of scheming and politics, no doubt. Anyway, we'll find out soon enough, once they return.'

Gerrion always managed to talk in a calm and logical manner, and never seemed to lose his composure. Arion recognised that this was just one of a number of contrasts between him and his eldest brother.

Arion had recently turned eighteen years old, and despite being five years younger than Gerrion, he was almost half a head taller and much broader than his sibling. Arion's two older brothers both favoured the looks of their father. They were both black-haired, dark-eyed and of a slim, athletic build. Arion had been told that he had inherited more of the features of his late-mother, and he bore little resemblance to the other members of his family. He was four inches over six feet tall, with brown hair and blue eyes, and a very broad build.

'Yes, we shall,' Arion replied. 'But this waiting is killing me.'

'Is that right, brother?' Gerrion sounded dryly amused. 'And is it the waiting for the outcome of the Grand Council that has put you so on edge, or are you waiting to find out what your fate is?'

'I'm glad that you can find it funny, Gerr. Everything's fine for you, ready to one day inherit our lands and father's title as Duke. It's not you who's being forced to join the damned priesthood!'

'That's just the way it is, Arion, as well you know. First son inherits the land and titles, second son joins the military, third son – *you* – joins the priesthood. As father and Charl have told us many times, that's how we as a family maximise our power and influence in the country.'

'By the Lord! You sound just like a weaker echo of father, Gerrion. Like I said, everything's great for you, and for Delrin. It's just me who drew the short straw.'

Gerrion tutted in response, and shook his head.

Power and influence, Arion repeated to himself, feeling annoyed. *That's great, unless you happen to be the one who has to become a fucking priest!*

He stood in silence then, thinking again about the angry encounter that had taken place between him and his father, many weeks previous. Their furious argument had broken out when he had been summoned to the Great Hall of Septholme Castle, over eight weeks earlier, on the eve of his father's journey by sea to the city of Sen Aiduel.

—

Duke Conran Sepian, leader of the House of Sepian, third greatest noble house in Andar, was a stern and imposing head of his family. His own father had died when he was sixteen years old, and he had now ruled the Sepian House and lands for close to thirty years.

He was black-haired and dark-eyed like his two eldest sons. However, whereas the two of them were both slim, Conran's healthy appetite for meat and exercise had long since shaped his body into a much bulkier and more muscular form.

When Arion had arrived in the Great Hall, that evening in early summer, the Duke had been reclining back in his chair. He had looked up when he had noticed Arion's arrival, his eyes hard.

'So, Charl. Here he is, my youngest son. Fresh from another day of cavorting and not studying.'

Seated beside the Duke had been Charl Koss, the Duke's most trusted retainer and adviser. Koss was fifteen years older than Conran, but he still possessed a tall, wiry body that had lost none of its hardness over the years. More than anyone else, Koss had been responsible for helping the Duke steer through the turbulent times caused by the premature death of Conran's own father.

'I did study, father,' Arion had replied. 'And after that, in my own free time, I chose to focus on the military training which interests me. I wasn't *cavorting*.'

'No, but you have been cavorting recently, boy. That's been reported back to me. Mark my words, I don't want to have to deal with any young women turning up here with your illegitimate bastards. Understand that?'

Arion had blushed, having been completely unaware that his father knew of his private liaisons with some of the lower-class girls in town. 'Understood, father.'

'Anyway, that's beside the point. This military training that you insist on carrying on with. Asking Captain Thatcher to train you in weapons-handling, asking Charl here to school you in military strategy. With what purpose are you doing it?'

'With the purpose of improving myself, father. Making myself ready.'

The Duke had snorted with derision. 'Making yourself ready? I've been telling you for the last five years now that you're to become a priest. You've had more than enough time to make yourself ready for that. But I'm confused. *Why* am I confused, you may ask?' Arion had not answered, and his father had anyway continued. 'I'm confused because a priest has no need to understand how to wield a sword and shield. Or to aim a lance on horseback. Or to understand military manoeuvres. And yet these are the things that you spend your time on, and waste my retainers' time on. So, again I ask, with what purpose?'

'Because these things are of interest to me, father. When I do these things, military things, fighting with a sword or a lance, I feel *alive*. Excited!'

'Alive! Excited! Lord preserve us all! And will these exciting things still be of interest to you, or of use to you, when you begin your priestly studies?'

'No, father, but-'

'No, they will not. They should be and are of interest to Gerrion, who will one day be head of our House. They should be and are of interest to Delrin, who this year will join the Royal Academy of Knights and will one day lead our military. But they should not be of interest to *you*. As I have told you many times, you will join the priesthood-'

'But I have no interest in that, father. As you know, I'm not deeply relig-'

'I don't care if you have an interest or not! We maintain our position and influence by having members of our family in senior positions throughout society. Gerrion and Delrin accept their positions. Your sister Karienne knows that one day, when she comes of age, she will marry to cement our relationship with another house, and she also accepts that. But, as you well know, we now have no one in a senior position in the Holy Church, following my sister Mariett's death last year. We need you to climb the ranks of the church, and using our family influence we need you to ascend to the role of High Priest or even Archprime. Illustrious positions! That is what your role in life will be, that is what you will do. I don't care whether you like it or not!'

Arion had felt frustration and rage building inside himself, growing stronger each time that his father had interrupted him. How could the Duke, a man of action, not understand his resistance to the priesthood? Whenever Arion had been in a classroom reading religious texts, or praying in a chapel, he had always felt bored to tears. He had sometimes lifted his head and looked around during prayer sessions, and had wondered to himself what could possibly make some of his fellow attendees look so interested. So enraptured, so devoted. It just bored him. Effigies, symbols and words which possessed little apparent meaning or relevance, and no interest to him at all.

He had made one last attempt to articulate how he felt, to the Duke. 'But I'm not meant for that father. It means nothing to me! Nothing at all! I ride and I fight better than both Gerrion and-'

'Silence, boy! I'm not having a discussion here. I'm telling you what is and what will be. Cease wasting your time on other pursuits. I've told Charl that no one in the household is to encourage your vanity any further by giving you any more training. Focus on your religious studies. *That* is your place.'

'I will not become a priest, father!' The shouted words had taken an enormous amount of effort for Arion. His father was an extremely dominant figure, and an act of open defiance against his will was incredibly rare.

'Oh yes, you will, boy! In fact, I've decided that you'll set off to the College of Aiduel in Andarron in ten weeks' time, once I've returned from Sen Aiduel. You will make your Vows of Submission as soon as you arrive there.'

Arion had fallen silent. He had been seething inside, appalled to hear that a date had been set to seal his fate. Although he had chosen not to speak, the defiance and anger boiling inside him had been clearly evident upon his face.

His father had noticed and had leaned forwards menacingly. 'I suggest that in the next eight weeks, Arion, you concentrate on your religious studies, and get yourself mentally prepared for your new life in the priesthood. And that includes stopping sleeping with commoners. But know this, and be in no doubt that I mean this. When I return in eight weeks' time, you'll either be ready to accept this role and to travel and make your Vows, or there will be *the most severe* consequences.'

—

Even now, as he stood on the battlements, the recollection of the conversation, and the unfairness of it, made Arion livid inside.

How dare father speak to me like that! Like a common servant, to be barked at and threatened! He never treats Gerrion or Delrin like that!

Arion felt particularly envious of his older brother Delrin, who had travelled with their father to Sen Aiduel. Upon his return, Delrin would also be planning to leave Septholme and to travel to the capital city of Andarron. However, whereas Arion would be forced once he got there to submit himself to the misery of the College of Aiduel, Delrin would become a cadet at the Royal Academy of Knights, and would later be joining the Andar royal military forces.

By the Lord! What a dream it would be, to do that.

Arion had still not decided what he was going to do when his father returned. He had not made any more effort to focus on religious matters in the last eight weeks. No one in the household, under strict instructions from the Duke, had given him any more military training or tuition during that period. However, despite that, Arion had spent more time than ever on honing his martial skills.

But the moment was drawing closer when he would have to confront his father again. He did not feel hopeful for the outcome. The Duke was a man who made a decision, and then expected the people around him to either implement it or comply with it. Arion had seen his father take advice, particularly from Charl Koss, but he had never seen the Duke reverse a decision once he had publicly committed to it.

Lord preserve us! What then do the 'most severe consequences' mean? And do I dare to find out?

'But what do you think I should do, Gerr?' he asked his older brother, now. 'When father returns?'

Gerrion looked across at him, noting the worry in Arion's voice, and he no longer appeared to be amused. 'As troubling as it is for you, Arion, I think that you should do what father wants. He's a difficult man to say "no" to. I think the best thing for you will be to try to embrace the future which he's set out for you.'

'But I hate the thought of it! The fucking priesthood!' Arion took a deep breath as he heard the volume of his voice rising again, trying to force himself not to lose his temper. 'And if I say "no" again, what do you think he'll do to me? What do you think he meant when he threatened me with the "most severe consequences"?'

'Only he knows that, brother. It could be a meaningless threat to bring you into line. But I doubt that. More likely, knowing father, it will have teeth. Forcing you to leave here? Perhaps. Disinheriting you? Possibly. I don't know, truly.'

'You really think that he'd go that far? By the Lord!' Arion's head slumped down. 'You know, Gerr, the thought of being in a College of Aiduel for the next two years, and then spending the whole of my life preaching nonsense while the rest of you are engaged in action, it fills me with despair.'

'It's not that bad brother, surely? Politics and religion are deeply interwoven. There'll be plenty of "action" in that respect. You could rise far.'

Arion's voice rose again. 'Yes, but no fighting! No war! And no sex either! How can I possibly be celibate for the rest of my life? How is that fair?'

Gerrion shook his head and tutted. 'Calm down, brother. No clever thoughts or words were ever born from anger, which is a lesson that you still need to learn. And you should've also learned by now that meeting father's anger with your own is the worst possible way to try to persuade him to change his mind. Specifically, having the argument you did with him, on the eve of his journey to the Grand Council, when he was already stressed and agitated, was *spectacularly* ill-advised.'

Arion felt annoyed by the rebuke and he considered making a sharp retort, but he knew in his heart that his brother's words made sense. Instead, he said, 'I wonder how the Grand Council has gone, and if father will be content with the outcome?'

Gerrion shrugged. 'I suspect that with so many disparate parties and conflicting interests there, it'll be difficult to achieve any outcome which father will be happy with. But all we can do right now is speculate, until they return. Indeed, we still don't even know for what purpose the Archlaw called the meeting.'

Arion nodded. Unlike his older brothers, he had never paid much attention to politics. However, he was aware that the Grand Council was a meeting held only once every several years or decades. It was attended by various heads of state and senior religious figures, from across the continent of Angall. A Grand Council could only be instigated by the Archlaw, the head of the Holy Church.

Arion's father had been summoned to attend as adviser to the King of Andar, King Inneos Pavil. The Duke and King Inneos had been close friends and confidantes for over twenty years, and the King had requested Duke Conran's assistance for what was likely to be a challenging gathering.

As Arion mused on this, Gerrion added dryly, 'If you're lucky, we'll find out that the Archlaw has called for a Third Crusade, and you can beg father to let you head off to find glory in the Holy Land.'

Arion turned towards him. 'Do you think that's a real possibility, Gerr? That the Archlaw may have called for a crusade?'

'It's a possibility, yes. That was certainly Charl's belief before he left for Sen Aiduel. It's been, what, thirty years now since the Second Crusade? It certainly feels possible to me that the Archlaw could have decided that now's the time to once again attempt to reclaim the Holy Land. But, again, we're speculating and we'll find out in due course.'

'Father won't be happy, if they start talking about the Second Crusade.'

'No, he never is when that subject comes up. Grandfather's dishonouring still torments him, to this day.'

Arion was very familiar with the story of the Second Crusade, which had claimed the life of his grandfather. The old Duke had been part of an army of thirty thousand Angallic crusaders, who had responded to a former Archlaw's call for glory in the Holy Land.

Well-armed, and well-provisioned, the tales told of how this massive army of the faith had sailed across the hundreds of miles of the Western Ocean. They had been certain that they would surpass the triumphs of the victorious First Crusade, of sixty years ago. That First Crusade had re-established a foothold in the lost holy lands, after several centuries of that territory being completely controlled by infidels.

The armies of the Second Crusade had been infused with a divine certainty that the holy lands in the west, and the sacred city of Aiduel's Gate contained therein, would fall to them. And with the city's capture, they would secure their places in heaven.

Instead, they had been encircled and trapped between the holy city and a massive host of southern infidels, and had been annihilated. Butchered, without mercy, and without reprieve. The old Duke's body had never been found, and had never been given the proper burial rites. To the best of Arion's knowledge, his grandfather's bones still rested on a distant battlefield somewhere, exposed to desert sands and sun.

Arion was still contemplating this as Gerrion raised his arm and pointed his finger into the distance. 'There!'

Arion lifted his eyes in the direction that his elder brother was pointing, and spotted the ship. It was turning into the harbour mouth, and both its shape and the flag flying from the mainmast marked it out as their father's galleon.

'They're back,' stated Arion. The grim realisation struck him that today was now likely to be the day in which he would either bow to his father's will, or would indeed find out what the 'most severe consequences' meant.

—

Shortly afterwards, Arion and Gerrion were riding down towards the Septholme town docks, to meet the returning galleon. They were accompanied by ten men-at-arms, plus a number of spare horses.

Septholme was a large coastal town on the western side of the Canasar Peninsular, within the country of Andar. The town was built around the best natural harbour on the western Canasar coast. The waterfront stretched in a large circle around the deep harbour, to a relatively narrow mouth out to the sea.

The town was dominated by Septholme Castle, Arion's family home. The castle stood imposingly at the uppermost point of a hill which stretched steeply away from the waterfront. Tightly-clustered properties filled the space between the water and the castle, clinging to the sides of sharply rising streets and cliffs. A large fortified wall stretched around all sides of the town, also climbing the hill in an unbroken line to meet with the walls of the castle.

'Feeling nervous, little brother?' asked Gerrion as they rode beside each other. 'We shall soon find out what sort of a mood father is in, as soon as he gets off the ship.'

'Yes, nervous probably sums it up.' Arion's mouth was dry.

'Well, take my advice and pick your moment for your next conversation with father. Wait until he's rested and recovered.'

Arion nodded in agreement, as they continued to ride along the main thoroughfare of Septholme. Their party passed through various familiar locations within the town, leading Arion to contemplate that he might soon be leaving this place.

Septholme was the only home that he had ever known. The coastal town had stood here long before the independent country of Canasar had been invaded and conquered, by Andar and Elannis, seventy-five years earlier. After the war had concluded, the lands on the west of the peninsular, west of the Canas River, had been granted to Andar and to the House of Sepian, as part of the Treaty of Canasar. All lands to the east of the Canas River had become part of the dominion of Elannis.

House Sepian had forsaken its ancestral lands in the north-west of Andar, in return for the prize of the wealthy Western Canasar peninsular. Three generations of Sepians had now called these lands home since the conquering of this domain, and had ruled Western Canasar from this place. But Arion's time there might soon be ending.

He was still thinking about this, as they arrived at the docks. Their party dismounted and they watched as the galleon dropped anchor in the centre of the harbour. A number of small boats were then lowered from its side. The boats and their determined oarsmen soon closed the distance to the docks, and Arion spotted the distinctive figures of the Duke, Charl Koss, and his brother Delrin.

As the boats moored alongside the dock, Arion was aware that his heart was thumping and his hands were clenched. The Duke's face looked solemn as he climbed the steps up from the water.

Gerrion was the first to speak. 'Welcome back, father. Has your mission been a successful one?'

The Duke grimaced. 'Successful? In a word, no. But here's not the place to discuss it. Let's gather in the Great Hall this evening, and I'll share the disgraceful details of the last few weeks!'

Arion gulped as he heard the rancour in his father's words. Charl Koss and Delrin then emerged from the steps behind the Duke. Koss looked stern and solemn, nodding politely to Arion and Gerrion to acknowledge them. In contrast, Delrin caught Arion's eye and flashed a wink at him.

'Let's get back to the castle then, father,' replied Gerrion. 'I have your horse here, and I've ordered the servants to ensure that your chambers are ready for you.'

'Very well,' said the Duke, mounting quickly and athletically. 'And you can also bring me up to speed later about events here in the last eight weeks.' He glanced at Arion as he said this, nodding to greet his youngest son, his expression grim.

As Arion mounted his own horse and followed his father, he thought to himself, *Lord preserve us! I'm doomed. How can I possibly persuade him to change his mind now?*

No ready answer presented itself.

5

Allana

—

Year of Our Lord,
After Ascension, 767AA

Allana stared at the body on the bed, at the now dead figure of Ronis dei Maranar, High Priest of Sen Aiduel.

She took in a deep breath and held it, trying to stave off the mounting sense of panic building within her.

Murder! You have committed murder, Lana! If they catch you here, you'll burn for this!

The bedsheets around the High Priest's motionless form were soaked in blood, the crime indisputable. No one would care that she had acted in self-defence against an attempted rape. All they would take notice of was that he had been stabbed and killed.

She picked up the knife from the bed, staring at it with grim fascination. A small weapon, maybe four inches of sharp, cold steel. Who would have thought that such a tiny thing could kill a man so quickly, so effortlessly? She wiped the blood from the blade using a cloth, then placed the knife onto the table behind her.

She then walked to the door of the apartment and bolted it, trying to clear her thoughts. She must pack a bag and get out of here, must flee from this place as quickly as possible.

She turned to the mirror and looked at herself, at eyes which looked no different, although she now knew that they were the eyes of a killer. There was no blood on her face or clothing, no visual sign marking her as being involved in violence this evening. But he had died in her apartment, and if he was found here she would be linked to this, and would be punished for it.

Panic crept around the edges of her thoughts, threatening to overwhelm her.

Think, Lana, think!

She had to get away. But it would not be enough to flee mindlessly. If she did that, then they would catch her and kill her. She took another deep breath, trying to force herself to order her thoughts.

How much time do you have to escape, Lana? Work that out, first!

She walked to the window of the room, and quietly opened the shutters. The apartment was on the second floor of a large townhouse which had many such apartments inside, and this window afforded a view of the front entrance of the building.

Sure enough, barely thirty metres away from the spot she now peered from, there at the townhouse entrance stood a burly man. He was carrying what looked like a long, curved sword on his hip, and two horses were tied up close to where he was standing.

She felt certain that this man was the guard of the dead High Priest. Her mother had told her previously that Ronis was not the type to travel alone through the city at this time of night, risking the attention of beggars and thieves. Right now, the guard was just standing there, looking bored, with no inkling that something terrible had happened to his master.

How long before he comes looking for Ronis? Stop panicking, Lana. Think!

Her mother's encounters with the High Priest had typically lasted for two to three hours. That would be the most time which

72

she could hope for before the guard came to seek out his master. She must therefore be well away from this place before that happened.

She closed the shutters, taking more long breaths to try to stem the cries of alarm running through her mind. What did she need? Clothes. Money. Food. She moved back into the apartment and grabbed hold of a canvas bag, then proceeded to stuff it haphazardly with an assortment of clothing and food. All the while, she kept her eyes away from the bed, away from the dead figure which lay as evidence of her deed this night.

She then took hold of her purse, which contained the little money that she still possessed, and pushed that into the bag.

Not enough money, Lana!

There was not enough cash in there to sustain her for any length of time, not if she was fleeing. Again, the feeling of panic began to reassert itself over her.

Ronis! Ronis must have money!

It took a determined effort to turn back towards the bed, to stare at the dead priest. The thought of going near to him, of potentially touching him, repulsed her. But if she wanted to find out if he had money on his person, she would have to search him.

She moved closer towards him, but she could not make herself reach out and start such a search. A horrid fear lurked inside her that if she extended her arms towards him, he would suddenly lurch up, grabbing her and pulling her back into his ghastly dead embrace.

You're wasting time, Lana! Stop being pathetic! If they find you here, you'll die. Do you want to die? No? Then act!

She took another deep breath and forcibly took control of her panicking emotions. Her hand reached out, and she started to search the cloak which Ronis had been wearing, which in his haste to assault her he had not even bothered to remove. There were no exterior pockets, so she spread the cape out to either side of him. Two interior pockets became visible to her. Trying to avert her gaze from the man's face, from the dead shocked eyes staring sightlessly upwards, she slid her hand into both pockets, searching. Nothing.

She stared next at his robes, again trying earnestly to avoid glancing at the area around his groin where he had freed himself for his intended act. Once again, there were no exterior pockets. She grimaced, feeling sick at the thought of opening the garment and pulling the material back. Instead, she slid a hand into the robes where his chest was, desperately searching. Finally, her hands found an internal pocket, and closed around a large object.

She pulled the item out, again breathing slowly to try to avert a panic attack, and then jumped back from the bed with the object in her hand. Relief washed over her when she saw that it was a hefty, fat purse. She walked back to the table, opened the purse and poured its contents onto the wooden surface.

More coins spilled out than she had ever seen. A quick scan of the pile of coins suggested that over two hundred crowns was there. Perhaps an insignificant sum for the High Priest, but this was wealth which she could live on for a year, two years maybe.

This gives you a chance, Lana! You could yet survive this!

She scooped the coins back into the purse, then slipped the item into the pocket of her dress. Again, she paused to collect her thoughts, aware that the time which she had available was slowly ebbing away.

What next, Lana?

She could try to hide the body. Roll it onto the floor on the far side away from the door, cover it in a sheet, then push the bed over it. Doing that might achieve nothing other than wasting a few minutes of her own precious time. But on the other hand, if someone made only a cursory inspection of the apartment from the doorway, it might secure her hours or even days of additional escape time.

She decided to do it. She moved to the side of Ronis. He was now a dead weight so there was no way that she could lift him, but she found that she had enough strength to roll him. All of her energy was put into each rotation of his body, her face reddening, her feet pushing hard against the floor. Desperation gave added impetus to her efforts. Everything that she did now was about staying alive, and as she rolled him close to the edge of the bed, sweat pouring down her forehead, she realised something very important about herself.

You will do what you have to do, to survive this day, Lana. You will not curl up here and cry, will not sit here doing nothing until they capture you and kill you. You will survive this!

This was a side to herself that she had never encountered before, during her cosseted upbringing. The lethargy and laziness which she had lived through in the last week was gone, purged by the terror and necessity of her current situation. And as Ronis's body finally rolled off the bed and onto the floor, landing face down, she felt an odd sense of euphoria, a delight at her newfound determination.

She grabbed hold of a sheet and covered him with it, then moved back towards the bed and started to push it across the room. It was heavy, but again the resources of desperation-fuelled strength took hold within her and she slid it across the floor. The bottom of the bed cleared the dead body, and she pushed the bedframe flush up against the wall. Finally, she pulled the bloodstained sheets off the bed, depositing them in the back room of the apartment, out of sight.

With this done, she went back to the door at the entrance to the room, and looked across at the bed. From this angle, standing up, Ronis was not visible. If someone was to bend down, they would see a sheet covering a large form, but from a standing viewpoint an unobservant visitor might conclude that nothing had happened here. There were certainly no bloodstains visible from this position.

The crime might therefore stay hidden, at least until Ronis started to smell in the heat.

What next, Lana? What next? Get the bag, lock the door behind you, then get away from here. But where to?

She could not stay in the city, she knew that much. There was no one that she could trust to help her, and if she stayed here it would be a matter of time before she was hunted down. No, she had to leave Sen Aiduel, had to leave the only place that she had ever lived in.

75

But how will you leave, Lana? Think! What are your options? Land or sea?

She had only ever left the enclosed walled city a few times in her life, typically when there had been feast day festivals held on the surrounding hills. From this limited experience she knew that, if she chose to leave on foot, she would have to travel out through one of the city gates.

On feast days, large crowds had flooded through those gates to the fields outside. The guards at the gates had stood aside and let people pass for such events. However, she had no idea what would happen if she approached those exit points alone, at night-time. Would the gates be closed? Would they stop her, or question her, or search her? Would it look suspicious that a young woman was travelling out of the city at night, and on her own? Would they remember her, and report it when the High Priest's murder was later discovered?

The thought of even walking through the city at this time filled her with fear, but the idea of leaving the city boundaries and heading out into the night on her own was terrifying. Were there bandits or robbers or worse in the places outside of cities? She would have no idea where to go, and if she chose that option and managed to leave the city itself, it seemed certain that once the murder was discovered she would be tracked down.

They will come after you, Lana. For a High Priest, there will be men on horses, with dogs. You'll be caught within hours or days. And then they will burn you!

The more that she thought about fleeing on foot through one of the city gates, the more appalling that option appeared to be.

Panic continued to linger at the edges of her thoughts, threatening to engulf her as the difficulties of her circumstances became more vivid to her. The image of dying on a flaming pyre, burned as a murderer, kept appearing and re-appearing in her mind. But each time this happened she wilfully forced down the panic, and it reinforced her desire for survival.

The other choice was to try to escape by sea. Sen Aiduel was a coastal city, and had enormous docks on its western end. Allana's sheltered life, however, meant that she knew little more about this alternative than that of a land escape. She had walked down to the docks with her mother a few times in her youth, and on each occasion had been both entranced and a little scared by the activity and noise.

But she did know that there were trade and passenger vessels sailing into and out of the city at all times. And if she could manage to get on a ship leaving Sen Aiduel, particularly if she could do that before any alert was raised, she would be so much harder to trace. Horses and dogs would be of no use in tracking her once the ship had put out to sea.

Escape by sea therefore seemed a much better option. That was what she would try to do.

You can survive this, Lana! You will survive this! You will stay alive.

She pulled a short, hooded cloak over her shoulders, to ready herself for the colder night outside. Then she turned back to the table, and grabbed hold of the full bag, swinging it over her shoulder. She then stared at the knife, which was still sitting in the spot where she had placed it. There was only a moment's hesitation, following which she picked the weapon up and placed it into the pocket of her dress.

She then had one last look around the small apartment, this familiar space where she had spent her entire life, and where she had lived with her only family member.

Goodbye, Mum, she thought. *I love you.*

Then she moved to the door to exit the apartment, locking it behind her, before pocketing the key and then leaving her childhood home forever. She was a fugitive now.

—

She made her way quietly downstairs. At the bottom of the staircase she turned away to the rear exit, leaving by that route to avoid the High Priest's guard, who was standing with the horses at the front.

The quickest and probably also safest way to the docks would be to get to the river, and then to follow the pathways on its banks until it emerged out into the sea. She headed in that direction now, the hood on her cloak pulled up to hide her face as much as possible.

She clutched the bag tightly as she walked. Everything that she now owned was in there, or in her pockets. As she moved through the streets, she found herself repeatedly touching the places on the dress which contained the purse and the knife, reassuring herself that the items were still there. Without the purse, there was no way that she would be able to secure passage away from the city.

Sen Aiduel was an intimidating and frightening place at night, an environment which she had rarely ventured into after dark. She stayed on the main streets as much as possible, which were dimly illuminated by lanterns, and she was careful to cross the street to the other side if she saw groups of people ahead of her.

The hood disguised her precise age and looks, but despite that, she received several catcalls and propositions from passing men as she moved through the shadowy thoroughfares. In each instance, she hurried on by without responding, and no one took things any further.

She moved as quickly as she could, without running. Time was ticking constantly in her head now. How long until the guard investigated his master's absence? How long until he tried and then managed to get into the apartment? How long until he discovered the corpse and alerted the City Guard?

Keep moving, Lana. You will escape. You will survive this!

Finally, she made it to the River Magnus, which wound its way through the city to the docks. Grand paved boulevards lit by frequently placed lanterns flanked the river along its length across the city. She followed these now, heading in the direction of the sea.

On a couple of occasions, she passed members of the City Guard. Each time she was stricken with an irrational fear of discovery.

Don't look at them, Lana. Don't look guilty! They can't possibly know of the murder yet! Keep walking!

The meandering river led unerringly towards the place that she needed to get to, and soon she could see the docks, glittering up ahead of her. The lights alerted her to the place first, but shortly afterwards the dockside sounds were also evident. Noise from boats still loading and unloading throughout the night, and rowdy voices from taverns located alongside the river.

The docks were the scariest part of the city which she had travelled through so far. Again, she found herself patting the purse and, despite everything that had happened earlier in the evening, her hand sought out and took hold of the knife in her other pocket.

This area was also the most sordid. She passed a number of haggard-looking prostitutes who were trying to attract custom, shouting out to passing men. And, despite the hood, she found that she was attracting more attention herself, and that the groups of men which she would prefer to avoid were more frequent and more clustered together. The grip on the knife grew ever tighter.

Just get past them, Lana! Don't be scared. Keep walking!

She had no real idea of where she should head to now, so she carried on walking away from the river and across to the wooden jetties alongside which a number of ships were moored. There was a lot of movement on the quayside, even at this late hour.

She again felt that sense of time ticking away accompanied by the resurgence of panic inside her, and once more she had to forcibly dominate her fear and take control of herself.

Think, Lana! How will you find a ship to take you?

She needed to find someone to talk to. She peered around, searching for anyone who appeared to be even vaguely official. At last, her eyes focused upon a man standing at the other end of the jetty. He was holding what looked like a writing board, and had clothing which, although tattered, appeared to resemble an official's uniform.

She walked towards him, lowering her hood as she did so. He was short and old, with a thin moustache on the top lip of his rat-like face. He turned towards her as she approached, and once again she had the discomfiting moment of a man glancing down across her body.

'Can I help you, miss?' he asked, his nasal voice suitably matching his features.

'Hello, yes. I'm looking for a ship to give me passage from here, sir. Are there any passenger carrying ships leaving here tonight?'

'Where to?' Such a simple question, but her heart sank as she realised that she had not prepared an answer. She paused for a few seconds.

'I, erm… I want to travel. To somewhere overseas.' The answer sounded as weak to her as it undoubtedly did to him, and his eyes narrowed as she spoke.

'To travel, eh? Strange time of night to be travelling, with no particular destination in mind. What've you done?'

She was taken aback by the question, and again took a couple of seconds to answer. 'Done? I haven't done anything.'

His face suggested that he did not believe her. 'Look, girl, I don't really care. It's the wrong time of day for passenger vessels. These are all cargo ships. Come back in the morning.'

Again, anxiety gripped her. 'There's nothing at all? No one who might take a single passenger?'

He studied her for a few moments. 'You really are keen to get on a boat tonight, aren't you?'

She saw little to lose now by being completely open. 'Yes. Tonight. Not tomorrow.'

He clenched his teeth and grimaced with apparent concern, and she realised that he was playing out a little act of inner conflict for her. 'Well. I probably shouldn't say this, but I know of one vessel which might take you.' He paused, and casually raised his arm, the palm on his hand facing up.

'Yes, which is it, please?' But as soon as she had finished speaking she realised the stupidity of asking the further question, as he continued to stand there silently, with palm raised. She placed down her bag and then reached into her pocket, pushing her hand into the purse. She did not want to take the fat purse out in front of him, and for him to know just how much money she was carrying. She took hold of a large coin, which she guessed without seeing was a five crown piece, and slid it into his palm. 'Which ship is it, please?'

He looked down at the coin in his hand and his eyes widened palpably, and with regret she realised that she had paid him far more than he had been expecting. He stared at her again. 'That's a lot of money for a young girl. A thief, perhaps? Or a runaway? But running from what?'

'Nothing. I said I haven't done anything. Now, which boat?' Her hand was clenched around the knife in her other pocket. She could feel a cold sense of anger building inside her, an icy emotion not dissimilar to the one which had possessed her earlier in the evening, before the murder of Ronis.

'Perhaps I need to go and find a member of the City Guard, and ask them to join in this conversation,' he added, a smirk on his face. 'But if you double that, I'll name the boat. Do you understand me, girl?'

No one will dominate you, Lana. You are more than him.

She slipped her hand back into the purse. 'I will double that, sir. But know this, and believe it. If I give you another coin now, and then you choose either not to tell me the boat to which you refer, or you choose to tell me falsely, you'll find out *why* I'm here at these docks tonight. Do you understand *me*, sir?' She was both shocked and impressed with the sudden steel in her voice.

The smirk was gone. His gaze shifted towards the hand in her pocket, the hand clutching a knife which he could not see but suddenly sensed was there, and she witnessed an abrupt fear come over him. 'Just a joke, girl. Please, no need to take offence. I wouldn't go bringing the City Guard into our business down here. Same amount again and I'll name the boat. I won't speak falsely to you, not at all.'

She placed a second coin into his hand.

81

He closed his fingers around it. 'Thank you, girl. It's the *Flower of Andar*, fourth boat on the jetty, just there. It's leaving on the tide in three hours' time, and the captain has been known to be... open-minded... about the cargo he takes. Captain's name is Obnel Rabnar. Going to Andar. Tell him Old Jim sent you.'

'Thank you,' she replied, and after snatching her bag up again she hurried past him. Time was still ticking. Too swiftly.

—

She found the *Flower of Andar* quickly. Gangplanks between the jetty and boat were still in place fore and aft, and a number of sailors were carrying crates and barrels onto the ship. The vessel looked to be approximately twenty five metres long, with three masts.

Still clutching the hidden knife in her right hand, she approached one of the sailors. 'Where is Captain Rabnar, please?'

He took a second to stare at her, leering, then turned towards the boat and with a booming voice shouted, 'Where's Rabnar? Got a female visitor!'

The shout was repeated a few seconds later by another sailor on the deck, with a response then being heard from below deck of, 'Coming!'

Moments later a man appeared, climbing out of what Allana thought must be the cargo hold. He looked around quizzically, then his eyes fastened on her and he walked towards her.

He was tall, maybe a couple of inches over six feet, and was handsome with muscled arms and tanned, darkened skin. His chin was covered with a small goatee beard, his dark hair closely cut. His even darker eyes stared directly at hers, as he said, 'I'm Rabnar. Can I help you, ma'am?'

Be calm, Lana. Be clear.

She needed to get this conversation right, needed to get onto this boat. If she failed, she would in all likelihood be stuck here and being hunted by the City Guard by the time that the sun rose. 'Yes, captain. I was given the name of you and your ship by Old Jim.' The captain frowned upon hearing the name, which she did not take as a good sign. 'I'm seeking passage on a ship to Andar.'

He frowned again. Unlike many of the other men whom she had encountered in the last few days, up to this point he had not displayed any lecherous intent towards her. 'To Andar. Why?'

She had at least now had the benefit of answering this question once before. 'I'm seeking to see a new land, new cities. I've heard many wonderful things about Andar and its people. I have coin to pay for my passage.'

There was a slight creasing around his eyes. 'And do you always decide to travel in the middle of the night?'

'No, but I-'

'We're not a passenger carrying vessel. Look. We transport cargo, not passengers. I'm afraid Old Jim has wasted your time.' He moved to turn away from her but she put out a hand to touch his arm, causing him to pause.

'Please, not passengers. Just *one* passenger. Me. I have coin.' She felt a desperation building up inside her again, images of flames on a pyre revisiting her, filling her with fear. She had to get away from here.

'It's not the coin. We don't carry passengers. We have no spare cabins. And having someone who looks like... well, who looks like you... on the boat could cause problems. Eighteen red-blooded males on this ship, plus me.'

You have to escape, Lana. You have to survive.

'Fifty crowns, captain. I'd be willing to pay that for passage on your ship, to Andar.'

'Fifty crowns? A girl like you is carrying money like that, at this time of night? Just what did you do, girl?'

'Nothing, I didn't do anything. I just want to travel away from here.'

'You don't even know where we're going, yet you come here in the middle of the night, and offer me three or four times what such a passage is worth? You *have* done something, don't insult me by

83

saying otherwise. I've been doing this for long enough that I can smell trouble. I'm sorry, no, find another vessel.'

'Please, seventy-five crowns, then.' This time there was no mistaking the pleading in her voice.

You must escape, Lana. You must survive.

'It's not the money, girl. Look, I wish you well. I hope that you find another person willing to transport you. Just not me, not my boat.' He shook off her hand and again started to move away from her.

Unlike with Old Jim on the jetty earlier, she knew with anxiety that this was not an act on his part to secure more money from her. She tried to think of what she could do, what she must do, to convince him. But the words eluded her. Panic rose up in her, helpless panic. If she could not persuade him to take her, she would be stranded here. Trapped. She would then be hunted, and caught, and tried, and burned...

But then other words drifted back to her, from a dark place.

LUST. POWER. DOMINATION.

On hearing the whispers of those words, mounting desperation again triggered something inside of her. Something akin to what she had experienced earlier in the evening, in the moment when Ronis had pinned her down to the bed. The world seemed to instantly slow down as it had on that earlier occasion, and she abruptly felt an eerie sense of calmness, a detachment from her emotions.

You will not panic, Lana. You will not accept defeat here. You will survive. You must survive.

'Captain, look at me.' The words came from her mouth, but to her they sounded like they were some other person's voice, someone older and more alluring.

His eyes looked at hers again in response to her instruction, and she suddenly felt an unseen connection sprouting outwards from her mind, almost as if invisible tendrils were sighing out from her own thoughts into his. Finding his mind. Entering it. Locking themselves in place. Linking his consciousness to hers.

She could speak directly to him now, she knew, could speak without voice. And the words chose themselves.

You want me. You can have me. But only if you help me. Only if you do what I want. What I need.

Time continued to move slowly for her as she observed him. He appeared confused, the pupils in his eyes dilating, but then he looked at her properly for the first time. *Really* looked at her. His eyes travelled first to her face, then down her neck, across her breasts, then to her hips and legs.

She knew her attractiveness now, in this enhanced state of consciousness, knew it and rejoiced in it. And with the unseen connection that she had somehow created between them, she could feel his gaze as an almost physical thing. Making her feel powerful, in control, dominant. Aroused, full of lust. And then returning that lust to him, magnified tenfold.

His eyes returned upwards to meet hers, and he looked dazed and shaken. She continued to send whispers of words to him through the invisible bond, imprinting them on his subconscious.

You want me. You can have me. But only if you help me. Only if you do what I want. What I need.

Whether or not he wanted to look away now, she knew that he could not. Somehow, she had made him become transfixed on her, mesmerised. Full of an all-consuming and invasive desire with which she was subduing his free will, and overpowering him.

And then, as abruptly as it had started, the connection was seemingly gone, and time restored itself for her back to normal. The captain still looked dazed.

'Captain?' she said, sure that the whole interaction had lasted only seconds for him. 'For seventy-five crowns, will you take me?'

He frowned, blinking and grimacing at the same time. 'Take you? Yes, of course, I… want to help you.' He continued to look confused, thrown by his choice of words, and she smiled with gratitude. 'But, you will have to travel… in my cabin. I will need to keep you away from the men.'

'That's OK, captain,' she said, smiling. 'In fact, it's more than OK, I'm very grateful. Can I come aboard now?' She felt sure that whilst what she had done had planted some powerful impulse deep inside him, the immediate memory of the interactions between her mind and his was lost to him.

'Yes. I'll take you straight to the room. We sail in just under three hours. What is your name, by the way?'

'Allana-' She said the first name before she could stop herself, realising that it would be safer to travel under a pseudonym. 'Allana… Marrone. And where are we travelling to, captain, if I may ask?'

'To Andar,' he replied. 'To the port of Septholme.'

—

He came to her later that night, in the pre-dawn darkness, two hours after the ship had left port.

She had fallen asleep the moment that she had settled into the hard bed in his cabin, slipping effortlessly into slumber following the frenetic exertions of the preceding hours.

She awoke upon hearing him creep into the room. He was carrying a lantern which threw sharp shadows against the enclosed walls. He did not move towards her, and through half-open eyelids she saw the torment playing across his face. He wanted her, she knew that, but he was no abuser like Ronis, not one to try to take what had not been freely given. The urgent need which he felt inside himself, that need which she had somehow planted there, was struggling mightily against this inherent decency.

'Captain…' she whispered, as she lay beneath the bedsheets.

'Allana,' he replied. His voice sounded husky, choked, tortured.

'You helped me, captain,' she said, feeling a heavy echo of the arousal which she had experienced earlier, as time had slowed down with him. 'Gave me what I wanted. What I needed.'

His breathing was heavy, his large muscular body silhouetted by the lantern light. 'Allana. I want… you…'

Her arousal intensified as he spoke these words, sending a previously unknown heat tingling into the core of her body. After the traumatic events of the last few hours, it made no sense for her to be feeling like this. No sense that she was suddenly consumed with this much yearning and lust.

But she was. And he was there, and he desperately wanted her. And despite her inexperience, she wanted this too. 'Then come to me.'

And he did.

6

Corin

—

Year of Our Lord,
After Ascension, 767AA

The longboats put ashore half a mile north of the war party's destination. Flickering flames from lighted torches within the Anath village dimly marked its location in the distance. This murky light contrasted with the now moored longboats, which were bathed in darkness.

Corin followed his father and brothers out of the boat, congregating with the men on the shore. It was dark, but the moonlight above them gave just enough visibility to be able to see the shapes of the other warriors assembling around them.

The giant figure of Borrik was the most easily discernible of anyone there. He gestured for the assembled raiders to come towards him, and then started to speak in a low voice. His quiet tones contrasted with his roars in the Clan Hall on the preceding evening. 'We move to the village in silence,' he instructed the men. 'I'll take the larger group to approach them from the right, from the shore.

Akob will lead the other group to come at them from the left, inland. Akob's group will wait until they see or hear my attack. Once we're in, kill any men we come across, kill their livestock, and kill any women or children who fight back. If you see a lit torch, set fire to anything that you can. Once you hear our horn, get back to the boats as quickly as possible. Don't delay. If you're not back by the time we're ready to cast off, then you'll be running back, with Anath hunters chasing you the whole way. Now, let us make the Anath bleed this evening, so that they never again dare to enter our land or attack our people.'

There was a quiet murmuring of assent, then the war party split into two groups. Corin moved into the group with his father and brothers, which appeared to be comprised of men from two of the longboats. Corin was clutching his axe and shield so tightly in his hands that his knuckles hurt, and he was now wishing that he had obtained a helmet.

Akob's group started to move off inland through the darkness, Akob leading the party with the sure-footed awareness of someone who had been here and had done this before. The group moved cautiously, and as stealthily as possible, without any conversation. Corin slotted in towards the back of the war party, remembering Agbeth's advice.

Stay at the back. Stay out of trouble. If necessary, run away.

His heart was pounding as he walked and his mouth was dry. He still had no idea as to how he was going to react at the moment when he heard Borrik's group attacking, and the men around him charging in response. Even more importantly, he still had no clue as to how he would respond at the instant when he found himself facing one of the Anath. Facing the choice whether to strike and kill.

As they got closer to the Anath village, walking in a crouch alongside a long hedgerow, the details of the place came more clearly into view. There were perhaps ten torches flickering in the night throughout the village, illuminating huts and buildings which looked very similar to those in Karn. Corin noted that the Anath settlement looked somewhat larger than Karn, though it was difficult to tell just

89

how much larger. There was no evident movement anywhere, which was not surprising given the lateness of the hour.

Akob used a hand signal to stop the group approximately one hundred metres from the village, inland from it, and everyone squatted down in a ditch next to the hedgerow. The men were silent, but Corin could hear the constant thudding beat of his own heart as he crouched there.

He peered outwards towards the village, trying to identify any signs of movement, any sighting of Borrik's group in the distance, but there was none.

Then suddenly, there was a blood-curdling sound of a war cry from the other side of the village, followed by a chilling prolonged scream, and immediately the men around him burst into action.

The other warriors in his group were up and out of the ditch in seconds, running fast towards the village. For a moment he was frozen, hesitating with indecision, unsure whether to follow them or to remain and hide. But then he felt a hand on his arm, pulling him upwards, and he turned to see Kernon beside him, his brother using force to encourage him out of the ditch.

The action was enough to press Corin into motion, and in seconds he was out of the hiding place, running alongside his brother across the space between the ditch and the village.

They were in amongst the buildings of the village in no time, the men of the war party spreading out as they moved through the dim light. Corin had no idea what he was meant to be doing, so he focused on his brother's back. Staying near Kernon, and following him.

The first scream which had echoed across the village was followed by several more, as the men of Karn started to unleash their bloody intent on the Anath. The screams were mixed in with frequent war cries, and he could hear Kernon making such a blood-chilling call, directly in front of him.

Kernon then kicked open the door of a hut which they came upon, and moved inside. There was a loud thud and then a cut-off scream, before Corin's older brother re-emerged, blood on the blade of his axe and a maniacal look on his face.

Stay at the back. Stay out of trouble.

Corin clenched his own axe and shield and again followed Kernon, not knowing what else he should do. A building had caught fire to his right, and the flames it threw out served to more vividly illuminate the scenes of violence across the village.

The sounds of battle, of the Anath having recovered from the initial surprise and mustering themselves to fight back, came from all directions. The ringing of clashing weapons was mixed in with agonised screams and terrifying war cries, to create a nightmarish cacophony all around Corin.

Kernon pushed open another door, and charged into a second building. But this time there was no sound from within the hut to indicate that Corin's brother had delivered another quick death. Instead, Corin heard a shouted curse followed by several loud crashing noises. Sounds which suggested that a vicious fight was taking place inside.

Corin hesitated outside the entrance, fear stripping away his ability to think clearly. He should enter, he knew that, but he was too scared. More crashing noises and cursing were audible from inside the hut. Corin quickly scanned the outdoor area around himself, shaking with uncertainty. He could see no other warriors of the Anath or Karn anywhere close. He could run now, he felt sure, run away and no one would know of his cowardice.

If necessary, run away.

He readied himself to flee, but then he heard the shouted word, a bellowed desperate plea, coming from his brother. 'Corin!'

Perhaps it was a reaction to Kernon using his given name for the first time in years, but before he could stop himself, Corin had responded to the call. He bustled into the property, following through the doorway by which Kernon had entered. His eyes then adjusted to take in an alarming scene.

Kernon was wrestling with a man against the far wall, an Anath male at least as large as he was. Both had an axe in their right hand, and were using their own left hand to hold the other man's right wrist, trying to keep the other's blade away from them. Corin's brother was pushed back against the wall, with the Anath man facing towards Kernon and away from Corin.

The two men were engaged in a furious life-or-death struggle, in which the Anath man appeared to be gaining the advantage. Kernon's axe-hand was being pushed slowly downwards. Behind the Anath male was a small woman, who was holding a short knife. She was trying, unsuccessfully, to thrust the blade into Kernon, but was blocked by the Anath man's body in front of her. And there, at the back of the room, crouched as far into the corner as they could get, were two small children. A girl and a boy. Both of them terrified.

In the instant that it took Corin to process all of this, he recognised that he was beholding two parents desperately defending their children and each other, against a violent invasion of their home.

Corin stood there, frozen, seeing the terror and horror on the children's faces, and the anxiety on his brother's face. He again found himself immobilised with uncertainty as to what he should do. Kill? Or run?

Then his frozen shock was shattered by the twin cries of his brother and of the Anath woman.

'Corin, help me!' shouted Kernon.

'Get out!' cried the woman, noticing Corin and then turning towards him, frantically brandishing the knife at him. She was clad in her nightclothes, her hair and eyes wild. 'Get away from us!'

She thrust the knife forwards towards him from her position across the room, in a gesture to warn him to stay back from her. However, she did not make any other effort to move closer to him, or to properly engage him. She was clearly trying to keep him away from both her husband's exposed back, and also from her children.

Corin lifted his shield to protect himself and raised his axe by way of warning, but he did not move forwards either. He stared

92

at her, feeling helpless, seeing the hysterical terror in her eyes. She must know that if he were to attack her with deadly intent, a small knife would represent no defence against his axe and shield. No protection for her or for her children. That it would be easy to brush her aside and plant his axe into the back of her husband's neck, and then with Kernon's assistance to finish off the rest of them.

But still she did not move against him, and he also continued to stand there, unmoving, paralysed by indecision.

The death-struggle between Kernon and the Anath man continued, unabated. The Anath male suddenly pulled his head back and butted Kernon, hard in the face.

'Corin, help, please!' cried Kernon, sounding ever more desperate, his nose bloodied and broken. Kernon's own axe-hand had been pushed down to his side now, his weapon moved out of harm's way, whilst the Anath's man's axe-blade was still in position, edging closer to Kernon's throat.

Suddenly, the woman appeared to recognise Corin's inner conflict, his reluctance to attack. She spoke again, pleading. 'Please, leave, spare us, please spare my children, please, we mean you no harm.'

Corin's eyes cast around the room, panic overwhelming him. Towards his brother, the sibling who had spent his life taunting and humiliating him, who was losing the contest of strength and was likely soon to be losing his fight for life. To the woman, who was weakly waving her knife at Corin and desperately begging for her family to be spared. To the two small children in the corner, who were watching in horror as their parents fought to protect them.

After a few seconds more, Corin came to a decision. He quickly backed out from the hut, cast down his shield, and then turned and ran.

Without shame, he fled. His only thought was to get away from this place, from this village of bloody murder, and to sprint back to the longboat. He could see other figures in the corner of his eye coming towards him, could hear shouting and the ongoing clash of battle, but he neither knew nor cared now whether they were friend or foe. All he could think about was getting away, surviving, and fleeing towards the longboat. Escaping from this evil night, without committing murder.

His axe was still in his hand as he ran, as his legs churned away from the village. He could not hear pursuit, but he did not dare to either stop or to turn around to check. Running without pause, lungs bursting, darting between night-darkened trees. Finally, the longboats came into sight further along the shore.

Then, in the distance far behind him, a horn sounded, long and clear. This distracted him, and he made the mistake of turning to look back while still running. As he did so, his foot caught in a root which was extended across the ground in front of him. He found himself flying through the air at speed, neck still turned sideways. And then he crashed into a trunk of a tree, smashing his uncovered head into the hard wood. Awareness was knocked out of him, instantly.

And then the dream found him.

—

He is standing on a path, on the side of a mountain. The mountain towers over the surrounding lands, within a mountain range like that at the edge of the world.

There are four others beside him. He knows that they are people, although they blaze with the light of the stars.

None of them speaks, none of them chooses to shatter the silence which surrounds them.

He is walking now, walking through the silence, ceaselessly climbing the winding mountain path. His body draws him ever onwards, and he willingly allows it to.

In the distance, a light brighter than the sun appears, a golden radiant light surrounded by an archway which must have been constructed by the Gods themselves. The light sears painlessly into his very being.

But still he and his companions walk on, not wanting to turn away, not daring to turn away. Onwards. To the Gate.

And then he can see Him. In the Gate. Waiting. Watching. Golden, glowing, terrible, magnificent. The need to cry out in shame builds inside him, the need to declare his unworthiness to all around him, but still in silence he walks on. Closer, ever closer. So too do his companions.

The figure in the Gate moves His hand, a summoning gesture, and once again his body takes him forwards. And he can hear the death cries of his enemies, sighing out their final words.

FEAR. CONTROL. ORDER.

But then the gesture of His hand changes, and he is aware that something is wrong.

A single finger is raised. And he knows what he must do.

—

He was roused slowly, to the sound of oars moving through water.

His limp body was lying down along hard wood. Shafts of agony flashed through his head, and he remained there with his eyes closed, not daring to open them lest the pain was magnified further. His hair felt wet.

Conversation was taking place from what seemed to be an echoing distance far above him.

A first voice – *Kernon's?* – sounding angry. 'I should slit his throat and dump him overboard.'

A second voice. 'Not now. He'll get what he deserves, *after* we've got back.'

Then the pain flared up again, and he slipped back into unconsciousness.

—

There was daylight when he next awoke, and opened his eyes. He was caged.

'Corin, can you hear me?' The voice was Agbeth's.

'Agbeth? What's happened?' The pain in his head was still significant, and he reached up gingerly to touch the source of his hurt. His hair felt matted with dried blood.

'Oh, Corin, thanks the Gods! I feared you were never going to wake up.'

He looked towards her, his eyelids opened narrowly. She was on the other side of the wooden bars, her expression trapped somewhere between worry and relief.

'I'm in the cage,' he stated, feeling numb inside. The cage he was locked within was outdoors, in the centre of the village, and the sun in the sky above him suggested that it was close to midday.

'They put you in there when they got back,' she said, sounding close to tears. 'They wouldn't let me help you.'

'Did they say why I've been put here?'

She hesitated before replying. 'They said… you left Kernon. Left him to be killed. Ran away.'

'I did,' he replied. The horrors of the last night, and of his cowardly actions, were coming back to him now. He had shamed himself. 'Is Kernon dead?'

'No. I haven't heard everything, but they said your father saw you running from a hut. He went there, and found Kernon. All of your family have returned, alive.'

Corin closed his eyes and sighed. Despite his actions, the Anath family which he had encountered must anyway now be dead, surely? And Kernon still lived. Corin's craven escape from the village had achieved nothing.

'He was trying to kill a family, Agbeth. A mother, and her children. And to help him would have meant killing the mother. And so I ran. Like a gutless coward, I ran.' Images of the events of the night were flashing into his mind. Of his fear. Of his panic. Of his mindless flight through the darkened woods.

'There's no shame in running, Corin. You survived. You came back to me.'

'But I *have* shamed myself, Agbeth.'

There was silence for a few seconds, before she spoke again. 'What happened to your head? Were you hit in a fight?'

'No, I didn't get into any fights. I didn't attack or kill anyone. When I was running away, when I'd got back to the boats, I think I fell over and knocked myself out. What a hero I am.' He closed his eyes again for a few seconds. The pain in his head was bad, but was becoming manageable, unlike the disgrace that he felt. 'How does my head look?'

'There's a lot of blood. I need to clean it. Come closer, I've a bucket of clean water here.' He did as she said, leaning against the bars of the cage. She reached through, and then gently started to dab his wound using a water-soaked cloth. He winced a few times as she did it. Eventually, she said, 'There, all done. It looked a lot worse than it is. Just a small cut.'

'Have they said what they're going to do to me?'

'Not to me.' Again, there was anxiety in her voice. 'There's a meeting of the war-party in the Clan Hall, right now. I don't know what they're going to do.'

Despondent thoughts were running through his mind. 'I'm sorry. I failed you, Agbeth. All I needed to do was to return without shaming myself.'

She reached through and put her hand onto his cheek, turning him to face her. 'You chose not to kill, there's no shame in that. And remember what we said to each other. I'm yours. Whatever you did, whatever now happens, that doesn't change. It will never change.'

He gulped, before voicing what they were both already fearing. 'And if they banish me?'

They had both seen it happen before, during their lifetimes. The last time had been when one villager had murdered another, during a violent drunken row. The perpetrator had been cast out of the village, told to leave the Karn territories and to never return.

'This wasn't murder, Corin,' she replied. 'They're angry right now, but they won't banish you for this, surely?'

97

'But if they do?'

'Then I will leave with you.'

—

The men came for him half an hour later. Before then, Corin and Agbeth had argued about what Agbeth would do were he to find himself banished. It was one of only a handful of times in their lives that the two of them had forcefully disagreed with each other.

Four men took him out of the cage, none of whom were his family members. With little conversation or ceremony they pushed him in the direction of the Clan Hall, taking up positions surrounding him as he walked there.

He could feel himself recovering from the head wound, and he remained steady on his feet as he moved through the village. News of his cowardice must have spread already, because several villagers yelled out curses and insults as he passed, and one spat towards him.

He looked back behind himself. Agbeth was limping along to the rear of his group, wilfully trying to keep up with them, although she would be denied entry to the Clan Hall for the resolution of this matter.

Then he was at entrance of the Clan Hall, being pushed inside. His eyes took moments to adjust from the bright sunshine outside, to the gloom inside the building. Directly opposite him was seated Borrik, a large bloodied cut on the clan chief's left arm and a menacing look on his face. Flanking Borrik on his right was Akob, and on the other side was Kernon. Various other senior warriors were dispersed around them, in a broad semi-circle.

Corin took his place in the centre of the Hall, standing up. He waited for someone else to speak.

'Runt,' said Borrik, finally. 'You're accused by your brother and father of being a coward and a traitor. That you threw down your arms, abandoned your brother, and ran away. What do you say to this?'

Corin paused, trying to think of something, anything, which he might say to mitigate the shame of what he had done. But the only measured words he could find, that he had decided that saving the life of a mother and her children mattered more than his own brother's life, would mean nothing to them. Eventually, he responded, 'It is true. When my brother needed my help, I cast down my shield, and I ran.'

Kernon was staring at him, his brows narrowed, fire in his eyes. His nose was red and massively swollen. The older brother remained silent, however, turning his head and spitting sideways.

'Why?' asked Borrik. 'Why would you do such a thing?'

'To have stayed would've meant killing a family. I... at the moment when I needed to strike, I couldn't do that.'

Borrik's voice was low, controlled, and grim. 'They are Anath. They're not people, not family. They are less than animals. Kernon is your blood-brother, your shield-kin.'

This time Corin stayed quiet. There was no argument which he could make that would matter.

Borrik continued. 'We lost twelve men on the raid last night. Twelve true warriors. But *you* survived. Not only that, but your kin saved you. Found you and carried you onto a longboat. Knowing what we now know, we should've left you there to die.'

Again, Corin stayed quiet. He looked towards his father. Akob's face bore a look of disdain, full of contempt for his youngest son.

Borrik leaned forwards and stared at Corin. 'Have you anything else to say, in your own defence?'

Corin gulped, his heart pounding. This was his last chance. 'I'm no warrior. That was known to everyone, long before yesterday. Yet my family made me join this raid. I failed, just like they expected me to. I'm no warrior, and never will be. But I could still add a lot to this village, just not as a fighter.'

Borrik grimaced. 'Nothing, then. You're a coward, and a traitor. You've betrayed the trust between blood, between warriors. We

99

cannot let this stand. Karn cannot let this stand. I will not let this stand. Without trust that the man on my left will strengthen my left arm, and the man on my right strengthen my right arm, then we Karn are nothing.

'You betrayed your kin. Kernon would be within his rights to challenge you to combat, to teach you what it means to be losing a fight to the death. And if he'd chosen that, he would've had my support. But Akob has asked for mercy for you, from both of us. Mercy for your life, that's all. And Kernon has allowed that mercy.

'But there can be no place for you in this clan or this village now. You're banished. Before sundown this evening, you will leave the village, and if we see you on any Karn land after sunrise tomorrow you'll be brought to me and killed. Cowards and traitors will not walk amongst us.

'Get your things. We'll allow you to take your gear. But do not ever think to return. For as long as I am clan chief of the Karn this banishment shall stand. This decision is final, sworn before the Gods and the village.'

Corin's chin sagged down to his chest as the judgement and sentence were delivered. From the area outside of the hall, they all heard Agbeth's voice raised in a wailing cry.

—

Corin spent the next two hours pulling his pack of equipment together. Agbeth was seated by him, but she was silent. Brooding.

He would have to carry any equipment that he brought, and he mentally ran through what he needed to take. Clothing, including warmer clothing for when temperatures fell. Axe. Bow and arrows, for hunting. Flint and tinder. Some food provisions for the next few days. Skinning knife. Twine and needle. Bedroll. Sharpening stone. Fishing rod. Two snares. Cooking pot and cooking utensils. He tried to be as meticulous as possible. If he forgot things now, he would have no possibility of return.

The two of them had argued again. Agbeth insisted that she was going to come with him. He was resisting, arguing that he did not want her to leave the relative safety of life in the village, did not want her to exchange that for the unknown future which now faced him.

Neither of them had backed down so far, although in his heart he knew that his argument had the weaker foundation. Because however noble and protective of her he was trying to be, deep down he knew that he desperately needed her to come with him. The thought of leaving the village was an ominous one. The thought of leaving her, of never seeing her again, and of being completely on his own, was a different order of fear.

'I'm not letting you go away and leave me here without you, Corin,' she said again now, her voice defiant.

'I know,' he said, his resistance fading. 'I know you won't. But are you truly certain that you can give up your life here, and can face the life we might now have?'

'I will face it with you.'

'And you know I'm going to go north, Agbeth? To the forest? I can't go south into Anath land, they'll kill me on sight. And I doubt that I would live much longer in Borl land.'

'If you go north, I will go north with you.'

'But you know the tales of the forest as well as I do. Of the spirits, of the felrin. If I go north to the forest, death may find me, may find us both, there.'

'Then we'll face it together. We'll accept it together.'

He exhaled a loud sigh, defeated but relieved at the same time. And once again he spoke truth to her. 'I love you, Agbeth.'

'I know.'

—

The two of them left the village together, an hour before sunset. Agbeth had also prepared her equipment by this time, and together they walked slowly towards the village edge, encumbered by the weight and bulk of the gear that they were carrying.

Agbeth's limp was made worse by the encumbrance, despite Corin having added a significant proportion of her possessions to his own backpack. The weight was already hurting him, and his head still throbbed with each footstep, but he was determined not to allow his physical weakness to shame him again on this walk.

A number of villagers came to see them away, although not in a kind manner. Curses and insults were thrown at them, feral vicious faces yelling unkind words. It reinforced to Corin just how different he and Agbeth were from the people who they were leaving behind.

His own family was in the crowd, some like his mother at least silent and looking sad, while others like Kernon were crying out abuse at him. Neither he nor Agbeth reacted to the vitriol visited upon them, and he reached across to hold her hand in support as she bravely limped alongside him, her head held high.

And then the two of them were outside of the village, and heading north. The never-ending treeline which was the edge of the Great Forest stretched out imposingly ahead of them in the distance. And even further beyond that, the snow-capped mountains marking the end of the world glinted in the late-afternoon light.

They walked forwards and away from the village, maintaining Agbeth's slow, measured pace, one step at a time. Neither of them turned to look back.

7

Leanna

—

Year of Our Lord,
After Ascension, 767AA

On Fifth-Day morning, the day before her wedding, Leanna accompanied Lohan to the place which was to be their new home.

She had slept fitfully the night before, restlessly turning in her bedsheets. And upon wakening, the same questions and choices had re-presented themselves to her as had troubled her on the prior evening.

None of that was apparent to Lohan, though, as he proudly led her by the hand around the small house which he had bought for them. In keeping with her promise to Senior Priestess Maris, she had not told him about the holy vision. The two of them were upstairs now, in the larger of the two first floor rooms, which would serve as their master bedroom.

'Look, Lea, the bed is finished and installed. And take a look at the pillars at the head of the bed.' Lohan smiled as he said this, eager that she see the surprise which he had prepared for her. She leaned in. On both pillars an intricate 'L' had been carved. 'Two "L"s. For Lohan and Leanna. Or Leanna and Lohan. Carnus carved them for me.'

'That's lovely,' she replied, meaning it, and squeezing his hand.

'And look on the wall above the bed.'

She did so. There on the wall was a beautiful carving of The Lord Aiduel On The Tree. It was a foot high, the detail on it exquisitely intricate. 'Oh… Lohan. My goodness. That must have been so expensive. How?'

His face creased into a beaming grin upon seeing her reaction. 'I've been saving for the last few months. I *know* we should be saving our money for furniture, but I also know how important it is to you that our home reflects who we are. That it reflects your piety. So this is my wedding gift to you.'

She squeezed his hand again. 'What a lovely thing to do. It's beautiful.' She stared at the The Lord on the statue for a few moments, this time without there being any trace of a holy light on the figure, then she turned to her husband-to-be. 'You're so thoughtful.'

'That's because you're always in my thoughts, Lea.' He leaned forward to kiss her, and she responded. He pulled her into his embrace, their mouths locked together for a few moments longer, his hand sliding onto her back.

She felt the same sense of physical excitement which she had experienced in her previous embraces with him, and she could also feel his reaction. After more than a few seconds had passed, she broke off the kiss, feeling flushed. 'My goodness, Mr Marrus. And we're not even married yet.'

He looked equally flushed, and pleased with himself. 'No, but tomorrow we will be. And then…' His deep blue eyes shifted mischievously to the bed, and he patted the mattress.

'Stop it now!' she said, laughing.

And for just a few moments it seemed to her that her doubts were lifted, and her misgivings swept away. The two of them seemed so right together, and so at ease together. She was certain that he would make a wonderful husband, and that if she were to choose this life here, with him, that he would make her happy. That they would have a joyful family life.

But as he started to move to the next room, again leading her by the hand, she looked back at The Lord Aiduel On The Tree, hanging on the wall of the bedroom. And once again, she remembered the vision of the statue on the altar and its potential meaning. And the doubts returned.

—

She left Lohan at lunchtime that day, but her secret anxiety remained with her. As a result of her happy demeanour throughout the morning, Lohan had no inkling of her inner turmoil.

This was something which she had to resolve for herself. She could not share her uncertainties with him at a time when he looked so happy, no matter how guilty she felt about concealing her worries from him.

She returned to her home, and by early evening she was sitting in her bedroom at her dressing table, wanting to be alone with her thoughts. A small statue of The Lord stood on the table, facing her. Reminding her.

She placed her elbows onto the dressing table and bowed her head, praying.

Lord Aiduel, please forgive me, but I am tormented with doubt. Please give me the wisdom to know your will.

Tomorrow was to be the day that she would marry Lohan Marrus and start her new life. A wonderful day. A day of new beginnings, of awakenings. She should be feeling excited, giddy and joyful. But she did not hold any of these emotions.

Lord Aiduel, I cannot feel excitement for my wedding, because I fear that I am wronging you, and rejecting you. Please let me know the truth.

Her hands were clasped together tightly, eyes fixed upon the statue on the table. She pushed herself forward from the small chair that she was seated on, to rest on her knees on the floor.

Lord Aiduel, I beseech you, please let me know whether it is your desire that I should marry Lohan?

She closed her eyes then, becoming further immersed in her prayers. And as she did so, the memory of the vision that she had witnessed within the chapel at the School of Saint Amena started to play once more through her mind.

Lord, you were with me. There, in the chapel, I know it was you.

With her eyes closed, she could vividly recall those moments when the miraculous halo of light had extended and poured across the statue. She could clearly remember the physical euphoria which had washed through her own body, enveloping her in His glory.

And as she knelt there, remembering that moment, three words glided softly into her mind, as unbidden notes emanating from a distant heavenly choir.

DEVOTION. SACRIFICE. SALVATION.

The words faded away as quickly as they had emerged, but suddenly the dark clouds of indecision within her were parted, and she was certain that the light of the Lord's answer had shone through to her.

Lord Aiduel, thank you for giving me the wisdom to know your meaning. Lord, I am certain now that the vision was not a blessing. It was a reminder. A reminder that I have a calling to your service. A calling which I have always felt inside of me, although I pushed that feeling aside this last year. But you, Lord, have reminded me of that destiny, and I can no longer ignore it.

And with that, she realised with a mixture of joy and sadness that her decision was made. She could not proceed with the wedding, could not marry Lohan, despite the upset that her withdrawal would cause for so many people whom she cared for.

I must pledge my future to you, Lord, and not to Lohan.

When her prayers were complete, she began to consider the implications of her decision, and what her next actions should be.

She knew that the right thing to do would be to speak to her parents, to inform them. But she hesitated to do this. Once she had told them, they would vigorously challenge her choice, and would undoubtedly become upset and agitated.

She recognised that an eagerness to please other people was a weakness within herself. If her beloved parents became distressed by her decision, her resolve might start to waver in reflection of that weakness. As a result, she could still find herself being encouraged and cajoled into marriage before the next day's end.

Having made her decision to the commit to The Lord and to the Holy Church, she was determined that her actions now had to put that goal foremost above every other consideration. Anything which might weaken her commitment to that objective, whether that be notifying her parents or Lohan, had to be resisted.

Lord Aiduel, I must make my commitment to you irrevocable. And to do that, I must pledge myself to you and to the Holy Church. I must make my Vows to you, Lord, as soon as possible. And I can only be absolutely certain of completing those Vows if I do it without telling them.

Once she had taken her Vows of Submission, she would be committed to the Holy Church forever, and after that nothing anyone could say against her decision would matter. To do such a thing would feel like a horrible deception of the people she loved, but it felt like a necessary action to allow her to commit to her decision. To her calling.

Despite her misgivings, she finally concluded as to what she was going to do. She would make her Vows of Submission at the College of Aiduel in Arlais, in secret, the next day.

She knew, however, that she could not leave her loved ones without offering them some sort of an explanation. As such, she took hold of her quill and ink, and started to compose two letters. The first was to her parents:

> *Dear Mum and Dad,*
>
> *By the time that you read this, I will have already made the Vows to submit myself as a neophyte for training at the College of Aiduel in Arlais.*
>
> *I cannot marry Lohan, and I have chosen to dedicate my life to The Lord Aiduel and to the Holy Church. I believe Aiduel Himself has called me to this life, in the vision He sent to me.*
>
> *Please forgive me for this action and for my leaving earlier today without proper explanation or goodbyes. I know I have to make this choice, Aiduel is calling me to it, and I do not feel strong enough to face you with this news today.*
>
> *Forgive me for the hurt this will cause to the two of you, to Lohan, and to his family. My love for the two of you is as strong as it has ever been, and the hardest part of this choice is knowing how much I will miss you both in the months ahead.*
>
> *Your loving daughter,*
> *Leanna*

And the second was to Lohan:

> *Dear Lohan,*
>
> *By the time that you read this, you will have already been told of my decision to submit myself as a neophyte for training at the College of Aiduel.*
>
> *I cannot go through with our wedding, despite the love that I hold for you. I believe that I have a holy calling, and I have chosen to dedicate my life to The Lord Aiduel and to the Holy Church.*
>
> *Please forgive me for making this decision so close to our wedding, and for any hurt which this causes to you and your family. You are a wonderful person and will make a wonderful*

husband. I hope, with time, that you will find the wife that you truly deserve.

    Yours with love,

    Leanna

Early on Sixth-Day morning, the planned day of the wedding, Leanna awoke in her bedroom. She had been in the midst of a vivid dream, and she came out of sleep with a pounding heart, her ears ringing with ethereal fading sounds. The details of the dream had already vanished, but three words again teased at the edge of her memory, proving elusive.

I must remember this! she told herself, feeling frustrated, and she had a sense that the lost dream had mirrored parts of her forgotten vision.

She started to dress herself in preparation for the day ahead. Putting on ordinary everyday clothing, not the beautiful white dress of a bride-to-be. Next, she filled a small bag with some of her most treasured possessions from within the bedroom, including her newly acquired Certificate from the School of Saint Amena. She then folded the two letters which she had written the evening before, and slipped them into the pocket of her dress, before making her way downstairs.

Leanna's parents were seated at the table in the main room, enjoying a breakfast of eggs and cold meat.

'Here's my lovely daughter, come to enjoy a last breakfast with her parents,' said Elisa, smiling. 'How radiant she looks, Jonas.'

Leanna joined them at the table, smiling at the inconsequential but happy chatter with which they engaged her. They were both outwardly jovial, but she could sense that the joviality masked an inner sadness. Sorrow that their daughter would be leaving them today.

Their sadness made her feel even worse about her chosen course of action, about the deceit that she was now committed to. Lying was a sin, but in this case she justified it to herself as being done for the right reasons, for the greater good.

109

Lord Aiduel, please forgive me for this deception of my parents. I will beg for their forgiveness too, in time, but today I must do this.

As the breakfast finished, she announced, 'I think I'd like to go for a walk for a short time. To clear my head a little before everything gets busy.'

'Really?' asked Elisa. 'Don't take too long. Would you like me to come with you?'

'No, no need,' Leanna replied. 'I just want a last walk on my own, as a single woman.'

Her parents trusted her, and neither of them showed any trace of suspicion.

She moved to the door, then looked back at them both in the room. Her mother was clearing dishes from the table, her father was standing and stretching. She desperately wanted to run to them both, to tell them how much she loved them, and how much she would miss them. But now was not the time for that, not if she wanted to maintain her resolve.

Instead, she said, 'Bye Mum, bye Dad, love you both.'

'Bye, my love,' the two of them responded, in unison.

Leanna was blinking tears from her eyes as she walked out of her home. She moved away from the house, needing to complete one last task.

Some way down the street she found a child playing on the cobbled walkway. Ten year old Mary Tatler, who was her neighbour.

'Hi Mary,' Leanna said, smiling.

The child grinned back, pushing a stray hair away from her forehead. 'Hi Leanna. You get married today, don't you?'

'That's right, and look, the sun is shining for me! Now, would you like to earn two pennies today, Mary? I have a small job that I need you to do for me.' She passed the child the two folded letters and the pennies. 'Please deliver these two letters to my parents at my house in two hours' time, and not a minute before. But keep them secret until then, and you must not read them. Promise me you'll do that, Mary?'

The girl, looking excitedly at her unexpected prize, nodded her

110

agreement. 'I will. I'm good at keeping secrets! But I won't forget to take them.'

Leanna patted the girl's cheek with fondness and then, satisfied that her news would be delivered, she began to make her way on foot across the city of Arlais.

Her objective was the College of Aiduel, on the northern edge of the city.

—

She arrived there an hour later, having travelled through various winding city streets full of businesses and houses.

The College of Aiduel was on the outskirts of the city, and was a large complex of grey stone buildings surrounded by a twelve foot high stone wall. On the far side of the College, the main street which she had latterly followed passed into green countryside, marking the end of the city itself.

She approached the imposing gateway which was the entrance to the College. The wooden gates were open and unguarded.

She passed inside, unchallenged. She looked around and could see the vastness and grandeur of the site. She estimated that there were at least twenty buildings within the walled enclosure, which itself looked to be at least four hundred metres across. In the distance, she could see robed individuals moving between the properties, but none of them approached her.

The most significant structure within the College grounds was the grand domed church in the centre of the site, and she headed towards that now.

As she entered the church, she was at last approached by someone, a middle-aged bald man in a long grey robe who had been inspecting a pile of books near the entrance.

'Hello, can I help you?' he asked her.

'Yes, Father. My name is Leanna Cooper. I've studied under Senior Priestess Maris at the School of Saint Amena for the last twelve years, and this week I've received my Certificate, which I have with me. I'd like to train to become a Priestess, and I'm here today to make my Vows of Submission to the Holy Church.'

He smiled. 'That's wonderful, another of Maris's graduates. I'm Priest Senis. Come with me, I'll find Senior Priest Comrel and we can witness your Vows together.'

Thirty minutes later, after Senis had located the Senior Priest, Leanna found herself in a small chapel with the two priests, kneeling before an altar in surroundings quite similar to the chapel at the School of Saint Amena. Coloured light shone onto her face through a stained glass window high up on the wall.

Senior Priest Comrel, an elderly and shrivelled grey-haired man, asked, 'Would you like me to recite the words of the Vows for you, child?'

'No thank you, Father, I know them all.'

He smiled and then nodded to her, indicating that she should begin.

She took a deep breath. Once she spoke the words, the Vows of Submission, any uncertainty could fade away and her future was defined. She closed her eyes, saying a quiet goodbye to the life that she had known until this moment, then she commenced her vows.

'I, Leanna Cooper of Arlais,' she said, her voice clear and confident, 'coming to this place of my free will, do hereby freely submit myself and my life to The Lord Aiduel and to the Holy Church. I vow to hold my commitment to the Holy Church above all other things, to renounce the sins of the flesh, and to walk in the light along the path which Aiduel has set out for me. I swear before Aiduel and the Holy Church to hold these Vows of Submission true for my whole life, and to never forsake them.'

Senior Priest Comrel nodded as Leanna completed this statement, and said, 'Leanna Cooper of Arlais, we hear your Vows of Submission, and we accept them. You are now bound by your oath, sworn before Aiduel and we two priests of the Holy Church. Now rise, child, into your new life. No longer are you Leanna Cooper

Rise, Neophyte Leanna of Arlais, and be reborn within the Holy Church.'

Leanna smiled, then rose to her feet and into the first day of her new life.

8

Arion

—

Year of Our Lord,
After Ascension, 767AA

Arion was sitting on the edge of his bed, watching the early evening shadows move across the floor of his room within the castle, when his brother Delrin appeared.

'Hey, Arion,' the older sibling said, smiling. 'Why the frown, brother? You look like you're carrying all of the world's troubles on your shoulders.'

'Not the whole world's troubles,' Arion replied. 'Just my own. Welcome back, Del.'

Delrin seated himself on the bed next to his brother, putting his hand onto Arion's shoulder. 'Greetings, little brother.'

This was the first time that the two of them had been alone together since the galleon's return, earlier that day. After the ride to the castle, the Duke and Delrin had retired to their respective rooms, and Arion had returned to his own bedroom to fret about the coming evening.

'Glad to see you back, Del,' he said, meaning it. 'Feeling refreshed?'

'Yes, smell me,' replied Delrin, grinning and raising his arm to present his armpit to his brother. 'Bathed and fresh for the first time in weeks!'

'Please, spare me! Seriously though, good to see you. Things get a bit too serious when it's just me and Gerr, even with Kari around.'

'Maybe not as serious as it's been for me with father and Charl for the past eight weeks, though,' replied Delrin, smiling. 'I take it that you're worried about the follow-up conversation with father?'

'Yes. Has he said anything about me during these last few weeks?'

'Not to me. But we both know father. Once a decision has been taken...'

Arion grimaced. 'I know. He doesn't change his mind.'

Delrin put his hand back onto his younger brother's shoulder. 'Look, don't worry, brother. Things will work out for you, I'm sure.' He paused, suddenly appearing more sombre, looking around Arion's bedroom. 'But one way or another, things are coming to an end for us here, aren't they?'

'Yes, I suppose they are,' replied Arion. 'One or both of us will be leaving in the next few weeks. I'll miss being here, miss you and Kari and even Gerr.'

'Me too, little brother, me too. But I think the one who'll be most upset is Kari. Without you and me here, well... the company won't be the most entertaining for her. As we know, the Duke's not the most affectionate man around.'

Arion nodded, feeling a little melancholy at his brother's words. 'Do you ever wonder, Del, how things would've been different, if Mum hadn't...'

'Course I have. Course I do. I can still remember, even though it was over ten years ago, how different father was before Mum died. But that's done, now, isn't it? Long, long time ago.' He paused, still looking serious. 'Look, Arion, whatever happens tonight or in the next few days, you're still my little brother and I love you. Understand that?'

'Yes Del, understood, and no matter how much it pains me to say it, the feeling's mutual.'

'Good, then let's get to dinner, and hear what father has to say!'

—

They arrived at the Great Hall of the castle at the same time as Arion's fourteen year old sister, Karienne. The three of them were joined shortly afterwards by Gerrion and Charl Koss. Last to arrive was the Duke, who entered looking more refreshed, and significantly less agitated, than he had appeared to be when at the harbour.

The main dining table in the Great Hall seated up to twelve people. The six of them took their places at one end of the table, with the Duke seated at the head and the others around him. The food and drink soon started to arrive, brought in by family servants.

Initially, the conversation at dinner was light-hearted, although Arion was too preoccupied with his own concerns to properly join in the idle chatter. He was still pondering about what he would say if the Duke raised the subject of the priesthood, and he was drinking the wine in his glass more quickly than was sensible.

Lord preserve us, he thought, looking at the almost empty glass. *I have a quick enough temper as it is, without fuelling it further with wine. Remember what Gerrion said.*

Finally, after the third course had been cleared, the Duke ordered the hall emptied of servants, before addressing his family.

'There have been important events taking place in the last few weeks,' he announced. 'Events which could threaten this family, our land and our people. I need to make sure that each of you understands exactly what is happening, which is why I wanted this gathering.' He paused, before turning to Charl Koss. 'Charl, before we get into the detail of the threat which we now face, will you please

116

spare my voice by giving them some of the background to the events at the Grand Council?'

'Of course, my Lord,' replied Koss, solemnly. 'As you're all aware, our King Inneos received a summons from the Archlaw six months ago, to attend a Grand Council in Sen Aiduel, the first such gathering in over ten years. The Duke in turn was requested by the King to attend as his adviser. As some of you may *not* be aware, attendees at a Grand Council start with the Archlaw, along with representatives from his High Council of the Holy Church. Next, there are the heads of state from each of the great nations. Therefore, alongside our own King Inneos, our ally King Kanathar of Angloss attended, and of course Emperor Jarrius of Elannis. Plus various others from the Holy Church and the great religious orders.'

'And all of those parties whom Charl has listed,' interrupted the Duke, 'are sworn to attend under their vows to the Holy Church. Otherwise we might choose not to go, knowing what we're likely to face there! Tell them more about the purpose, Charl.'

Koss did as instructed. 'The purpose of the Council was unknown to us before we set off. I'd speculated with the Duke in advance that the Archlaw was going to call for a Third Crusade, and I wasn't the only one to think this. The Duke, however, was concerned that the Council would unveil plots against Andar. As we'll go on to discuss, your father was more accurate than I was.'

Duke Conran nodded. 'Sadly, yes.'

Koss recommenced. 'A Third Crusade was indeed the first subject raised at the Grand Council, although not in the way I expected it to be. The Archlaw announced that it's *unlikely* there'll be a call by him for a Third Crusade, within the next decade. He stated that he still doesn't think that *now* is the right time for such a crusading call, and that his priority is crushing heresy here on our own continent. Lord Andross, of The Order of Saint Amena, was clearly dismayed by this decision.'

The Duke interjected again, addressing his daughter. 'Kari, The Order of Saint Amena are the main protectors of the Holy Church's territory in the Holy Land. They had clearly been hoping for a new crusade, to provide an influx of warriors to bolster their position.'

Koss continued. 'Lord Andross responded with a strong argument that, if there's to be no crusade for several years, then there's a real risk that our foothold in the Holy Land might be lost altogether, given the increased threat of the infidels. He requested that the Holy Church imposes a one-off tax on all nations, to allow his Order to finance the building of new castles, and the recruitment of five thousand extra men. He argued that this is essential to allow us all to retain our Holy Land territory, until the future day when a Third Crusade finally takes place.'

'That sounds reasonable and sensible,' commented Gerrion.

'Yes,' replied Koss, 'and this request was agreed to by all parties. The Order of Saint Amena was granted an award by the Archlaw to support this holy cause, and all nations are to contribute to this. The Order are to start recruiting immediately.'

Arion sat forward, suddenly alert, as he heard this. He had not given any serious consideration previously to a career in The Order of Saint Amena. However, if the alternative was the priesthood, then a life in a military religious order could hold more appeal. He looked up, considering asking a question, but as he did so he saw Delrin staring back at him. There was a worried expression on his brother's face. The older sibling moved his hand in a gesture which indicated to Arion that he wanted him to keep quiet. After giving a puzzled look back to his brother, Arion decided to comply.

Koss took a gulp of wine, before continuing. 'Unfortunately, after agreeing on that first matter, there was little further agreement during the remainder of the Council. The *second* major matter raised by the Archlaw was the subject of heresy. In summary, the Archlaw wants significantly more powers to be granted to Aiduel's Guards.'

'*Significantly* more powers,' the Duke repeated, before again addressing his youngest child. 'Kari, Aiduel's Guards are a military religious body, controlled from Dei Magnus, answering only to the Archlaw and his High Council. Their *stated* mission is to hunt out heresy against the Holy Church, and to find and punish heretics. And when they have free rein the way they typically do that, more often than not, is to torture their victims until they confess. And then burn them.'

'But not here,' Karienne responded. 'Not in Andar?'

'Correct,' Duke Conran replied. 'Our old King, allied with the leaders at the time of Elannis and Angloss, resisted the previous Archlaw when the Guards were created, forty years ago. Unlike in Dei Magnus, where their soldiers can travel and act with impunity, in our country they're only allowed to gather in groups of no more than five. And they're bound by our law. No torture, no burnings. They can investigate heresy in Andar, can report it, but the consequences of that will be determined by *our* law.'

'And so things have remained for forty years,' added Koss. 'Until this Grand Council. The Archlaw spent a day speaking at length about how heresy is taking root throughout the continent, threatening the Holy Church and all of our immortal souls. Following this, the Archlaw proposed that Aiduel's Guards are now to be allowed to set up military forts in all countries, and to travel within those countries in bodies of up to two hundred men.'

'That can't be acceptable,' stated Gerrion. 'That would be a violation of our sovereign territory, surely?'

'That's not all,' replied Koss. 'The Archlaw also proposed that, in matters pertaining to heresy, Aiduel's Guards be given authority to act in accordance with Holy Law, as determined by the Holy Church, rather than national law. In other words, his proposal is that we allow a force of soldiers, not owing any loyalty to our King, to set up military bases in our country. And then allow them to persecute our people according to laws which are not even set by our rulers, or enforced by our own courts.'

'How did King Inneos react, and what did you advise, father?' asked Gerrion.

'As you'd expect, we both rejected this completely,' responded the Duke. 'Our King referred to the well-established balance between

119

country and church, and in essence he made the same arguments his own father had made a generation earlier. King Kanathar of Angloss also supported this position, and had the same clear resistance to the Archlaw's proposals. And there the discussion might well have ended, but for two things.

'First, the Archlaw then declared that this call for an increase in power of Aiduel's Guards, in the effort to stamp out heresy, had come to him directly in a vision from The Lord Aiduel Himself.' The Duke looked across at Koss, with an expression of cynical exasperation on his face. 'The Archlaw told us of how he'd been praying in his private chapel, *alone* of course, and that Aiduel had apparently come into his presence, and had instructed him to do this.

'But that's not all. The Archlaw and the High Council still wouldn't have had the power to carry a motion like this, if all of the great nations had resisted it, like they'd resisted it forty years ago. But this time, Emperor Jarrius of Elannis spoke up in favour of the Archlaw's proposal. He declared that it's his holy duty to follow Aiduel's instruction as delivered to the Archlaw. Stated that he would allow this in Elannis, and expected all other nations to follow suit.'

'Of course,' added Koss, 'the Archlaw's proposal didn't appear to be a surprise to the Emperor, in the way that it was a surprise to us. It was obvious then that he knew of the agenda of the Council before arriving. The Emperor is clearly not a pious man and therefore we couldn't immediately see what he had to gain by agreeing to this, by agreeing to allow a religious force of persecution into his empire. It was only later that we discovered what his price for giving his agreement had been.'

The Duke continued, sipping from his glass as he did so. 'King Inneos continued to resist the Archlaw's proposal, as did King Kanathar. We argued over this for several days. At one point, the Archlaw hinted at the threat of excommunication for those who wouldn't comply, and King Inneos came close to walking out in fury. In the end, I suggested to everyone that we should discuss and conclude all other business, and then return to the matter of Aiduel's Guards at the end of the Council. I wanted to flush out what the Emperor wanted, or had already received, in return for supporting the Archlaw on this.

'There were then various minor matters addressed, but after a further three days of inconsequential business, the real final issue emerged. The Archlaw, with no prior warning to us, made a proposal to nullify the Treaty of Canasar. He wants to declare it an illegal act and return the dominion of Canasar to the House of Canas, who were of course the rulers until we conquered them seventy-five years ago.'

'That's absurd,' stated Gerrion. 'They've no legal basis upon which to do that. The lands were settled under the Treaty, awarded to our House, to Andar and to Elannis. And the Holy Church ratified that Treaty, in writing.'

'All sensible arguments, son,' responded the Duke. 'But once again, in this *vision* which the Archlaw supposedly had with The Lord Aiduel in his chapel, apparently The Lord made reference to the grave injustice done to his faithful in the land of Canasar, and demanded justice for them.

'This is when we began to recognise just what a long game the Emperor and the Archlaw have been playing. First, the Archlaw and the High Council sponsored this proposal. As we know, the Archlaw himself was once a member of the Elannis imperial family, and for the past ten years the High Council composition has shifted such that it's dominated now by those of Dei Magnus or Elannis origin. Secondly, the Emperor himself supported the proposal. Indeed, he supported the Archlaw's earlier proposals about Aiduel's Guards, because he wants this in return.'

'But why would he do that?' asked Arion, confused. 'Under the Treaty, Elannis received half of the lands of Canasar, everything east of the river. Why would he want a reversal of the Treaty now?'

'Good question. Why? Because we now understand that a sole

surviving member of the House of Canas was captured by Elannis after the war, and was married in secret to the Emperor's cousin. Emperor Jarrius has chosen this moment to disclose that they had one child, a son, who in turn has had children who are all now the Emperor's distant relatives. The Emperor is supporting that the Treaty should be declared illegal, and that all of the lands of the Canasar Peninsular should be returned to the House of Canas. Effectively, to his extended family. To Elannis. To him. They're not satisfied with half of Canasar, east of the river. They want it all.'

'But it was over seventy years ago!' stated Gerrion, losing his usual calm. 'They can't just nullify a legal treaty. We gave up our ancestral lands to take this territory. What did King Inneos say?'

'He told them,' replied the Duke, 'that under no circumstances would Andar ever accept any ruling to reverse the Treaty of Canasar, or to relinquish our lands here. He told them that the House of Canas has no legitimate claim to our lands, irrespective of surviving members. He further told them that any act by the Holy Church, by Elannis or by Dei Magnus to attempt to enforce a ruling of the Grand Council in respect of this, would be deemed to be an act of war.'

Koss joined in the discussion again. 'King Inneos openly accused the High Council of being biased in favour of Elannis and Dei Magnus, and against Andar. At this point the threat of excommunication was raised again by the Archlaw. The King then shocked everyone there by threatening to break Andar away from the Holy Church in Sen Aiduel altogether, if the decisions on Aiduel's Guards and Canasar were supported by the Grand Council. Tensions were at breaking point, with the opposing positions becoming more angry and entrenched.

'King Kanathar of Angloss supported Andar's position. He's as threatened by an expansionist Elannis as we are, and he's already seen how Elannis's empire has conquered and swallowed up his neighbours. However, he's a devout man, and unlike King Inneos, he's clearly terrified by the threat of excommunication. Thankfully,

Kanathar intervened to suggest that all parties should break off from the Grand Council to consider their position, with no decisions being made for six months. After much discussion and further argument, this was finally resolved upon. The Council ended with the finance for The Order of Saint Amena and various smaller matters agreed upon, but no decision made in respect of Aiduel's Guards or the Treaty of Canasar. All parties have agreed to take six months to consider their position.'

The Duke spoke again. 'King Inneos now has six months to decide what to do. His decision obviously has massive implications for this family, and for our lands and people, which is why I wanted to tell all of you this, together, this evening.'

'Surely we're not under threat, father?' asked Gerrion. 'The King would not consider abandoning us to Elannis?'

'No, he'd never abandon us,' responded the Duke. 'However, he's now faced with a very difficult decision. On the one side stands the threat of excommunication, of potential war with Elannis, and of breaking off from the Holy Church. On the other stands agreement to the free movement of Aiduel's Guards and to the relinquishing of our territory. As of today, neither he nor I know what the solution is, but at least we now have months within which to consider our response.'

'Must we get ready for war then, father?' asked Arion, again wondering if this could have an impact on his own fate.

'I don't believe, in my heart, that war will happen,' responded the Duke. 'Nonetheless, we must use the next six months to enhance our border defences, particularly the forts at the river crossing points. And to build our forces, including re-training the militia. Charl and I have already talked about what we need to do. We also need to think further about the political compromises we and the King might have to make to avoid this matter escalating to war.'

'Please involve me in whatever needs to be done, father,' said Gerrion. 'Whether administrating matters here, to allow you and Charl to concentrate on the defences, or working with Charl.' Everyone knew that Gerrion had a natural and brilliant talent for administration, but was not as military-minded as the other males there, and as such his father was much more likely to take up the former option.

Arion felt like there would not be a better moment for him to speak up. 'And the same for me too, father. Anything I can do to support you in any preparations.'

The Duke looked at him, and frowned. 'That won't be necessary. This episode at the Council has reinforced to me what happens when we lose religious influence. My previous decision still stands. You'll travel to Andarron in two weeks' time, and will complete your Vows of Submission to the College of Aiduel there.'

Arion's stomach lurched. For a few moments, he had dared to hope that the events at the Grand Council might have conspired to change his fate. 'But father, everything you've said tonight, this is a time when House Sepian needs able-bodied warriors, leaders-'

'The purpose of this gathering was not to discuss you, Arion,' the Duke said, again looking grim. 'We have many able-bodied warriors. The lesson of the Grand Council for this country and this House is one of what happens when we lose political and religious influence. The matter is settled. You're going. You will travel with Delrin, when he goes to join the Royal Academy of Knights.'

'I won't, father!' Arion's voice was raised, and having been fuelled by too much wine he was quickly losing his temper, despite his earlier warnings to himself. He thought again about The Order of Saint Amena. 'There are other options for me that are better than a pointless life as a celibate priest. I will-'

'Arion, stop!' The shout came from Delrin, who was speaking for the first time since the discussions led by the Duke and Charl Koss had started. 'Don't push this matter any further Arion, until *I* have spoken!'

Arion glared at him, about to make an angry retort, but something he saw in Delrin's face stopped him. A look there of fear, of shame.

Delrin gulped, then turned to face the Duke. 'Forgive me,

father. I don't want to see this clash between you and Arion take place, without having shared my own news first.'

The Duke frowned. 'News? What do you mean?'

'Father, forgive me. I've kept this news from you, these last two weeks, because I wanted to tell the whole family at the same time. But I think it could impact on the decision that you make for Arion.'

'Then tell me, boy,' responded the Duke, his voice neutral.

Delrin leaned forwards. He seemed in control, but Arion could see his brother's hand trembling. 'During the Grand Council, during the long days you spent in the Halls of the Archlaw's Palace, debating, I spent a lot of time in the company of some of the senior men of The Order of Saint Amena. They told me a lot about their mission, about their recruitment drive, about their struggles in the Holy Land. It... inspired me.'

'And?' The Duke's mouth had set into a tight line. 'Get to the point, boy.'

Delrin's hand was still shaking. 'And I took my Vows, father. Before The Lord Aiduel, I vowed to join them.'

'You did what?' The Duke's voice was quiet, controlled, all the more frightening to Arion for being so.

'I've vowed to join them, father. I'm to travel to the Holy Land as part of The Order of Saint Amena, to serve the cause of The Lord Aiduel there.'

'Like fuck you are!' The Duke's outburst exploded across everyone at the table, his face red. He then paused, and visibly took control of his emotion as he clenched and unclenched his fists. When he finally spoke again, his voice had returned to calm. 'Delrin, is this true? You have taken these vows?'

'Yes, father.'

'You understand that by taking them, you've turned your back on this family, and have committed yourself to The Order for your life?'

'I've committed to them, father, yes. To the holy cause of The Lord Aiduel. But I would never turn my back on the family.'

'Nonetheless, you have. I've kept you back here, this last year, so that you could attend the Royal Academy of Knights at exactly the same time as Prince Sendar. I took you with me to Sen Aiduel, so that you could get to know the King and other senior figures in the Royal Household, and get an exposure to politics. And this is how you repay me? How you betray me? By making secret vows behind my back, by abandoning your family at a time like this?'

'No father, not abandoning,' replied Delrin. 'But I'm a second son, father. Gerrion will inherit everything here. I've chosen the cause of The Order in the Holy Land. There's glory and honour to be gained there, even without a Third Crusade. And when the Third Crusade finally comes, maybe I'll already be a leader there, and therefore a leader of the crusade. What glory will there be for the men who finally reconquer Aiduel's Gate, and who bring it back to the Holy Church?' There was fervour in his voice as he spoke, and Arion felt himself becoming inspired by the vision set out in his brother's words, and by the image of glory in battle in a distant foreign land.

The Duke turned to Charl Koss, who looked visibly shocked, and asked, 'If he has taken the vows to The Order, are they irrevocable?'

Koss answered immediately. 'If taken before The Lord, then they cannot be revoked.'

The Duke paused for an extended period, thinking, with a look of distress on his face. Arion realised that he had not seen his father express sadness for many years, not since the time of the death of their mother. But Duke Conran looked stricken with grief now. Finally, the Duke spoke again, addressing Delrin. 'Then, if that's the choice you've made, to follow in my father's foolish footsteps, you're cast out of and disinherited from this House. Take a thousand crowns and whatever provisions and equipment you need. Get Charl to help you. But be gone from this castle within two days, and be gone from Septholme within a week. Go join your new family.'

'Father, forgive me,' responded Delrin. 'I didn't mean to insult you by keeping this from you. I'm doing this to bring glory to-'

'Get out of this hall, or I'll have you thrown out,' responded the older man. 'This is the last time that you and I shall ever speak. Charl, please remove him.'

Arion looked across at his brother. Delrin looked severely anguished. Next to him, Gerrion sat silently, impassive. Charl Koss started to move regretfully towards Delrin, but instead Delrin stood and stalked out of the room, slamming the door behind him.

Arion sat there in silence, stunned by what had happened. He waited to see which of the others would speak first. He was shocked by Delrin's decision, and by his father's reaction, but equally he recognised what it meant for him. In effect, he was no longer a third son. His father now had no other male offspring available to send to the Royal Academy of Knights. An escape from a life in the priesthood beckoned to him. However, he was not going to be the one to voice this, so he waited, his nerves tense.

Be calm now, he told himself. *Be calm and wait.*

After a couple of minutes had passed, the Duke finally spoke again. 'Gerrion, I'll want you to continue to run administrative matters here while Charl and I focus on our military preparations. And I want you to spend some time exercising that giant mind of yours on what potential compromises we might concoct, to avert this crisis.'

Gerrion nodded. 'Of course, father.'

'Arion,' added the Duke, 'Delrin's decision changes things. Prince Sendar Pavil is being groomed to one day lead the King's armies. I need a member of this family at the Royal Academy of Knights with him, strengthening our relationship with the next generation of the royal house. That person was to be have been Delrin. If not him, then it has to be you. That takes priority over your religious duties, as you'll no doubt be pleased to know.'

Arion felt elation inside as he heard these words, although this was tempered by upset about Delrin, so his face did not show any joy. 'I will be honoured to serve, father,' he replied, 'and to train alongside the Prince.'

'I'm sure you will. You will also still be leaving, in two weeks' time. Charl, you may recommence his training, in the meantime.'

—

Delrin left two days later. The goodbye was a sad one for his siblings, but was unattended by the Duke.

Arion, Gerrion and Kari were stood at the castle entrance to bid farewell to their brother. Kari had spent most of the last two days in tears, and such tears were threatening to break loose again now.

Delrin was wearing a burnished steel breastplate over thick leather armour, standing next to a large steed which was laden with his possessions. He was on his way to the harbour to catch a ship to travel to a port in the south, where he would join a large staging post for The Order of Saint Amena.

The second brother embraced each of his siblings in turn, saying words of farewell. Despite the lack of any further contact from their father, Delrin's natural good humour appeared to have returned. When he reached Arion, he said, 'Take care, little brother. I've always thought that you'll be better suited for the destiny which father had set out for me.'

'You take care, too, Del,' Arion replied. 'Really, take care. But I truly hope that you'll find the glory that you seek. I hope one day that we *both* will.' They hugged, then minutes later Delrin headed away from the castle and out of sight. Out of their lives.

Arion felt the loss of his brother, but there was little time for him to dwell upon it. He had less than two weeks now until he himself also left Septholme, and then headed to Andarron for the next stage of his life. And the sharp contrast now was that he was savouring the exciting prospect of his new future, rather than dreading it.

However, given the developments at the Grand Council, would he be leaving his childhood home, and his family, at a time when war was on its way towards them?

Interlude One

—

Year of Our Lord,
Before Ascension, 72BA

—

Interlude 1

A boy

—

Year of Our Lord,
Before Ascension, 72BA

With a final surge of effort from his aching arms, the boy heaved his upper body onto the ledge of the cliff, and then swung his leg around to secure his position. He then wriggled and rolled himself onto the flat and safe surface of the clifftop, and lay on his back, panting.

I made it! I knew we could make it up here.

The late-morning sun was beating down relentlessly upon him, bathing him with heat and causing his thirst to rise. He allowed himself a moment of indulgence to drink from the small leather canteen attached to his belt, then returned to the ledge to check on the progress of the others.

His best friend, Tennus, was only metres away from the top. The boy reached down his hand as Tennus drew closer, and then he used his remaining reserves of strength to drag his friend up and onto the ledge.

Within seconds, the two of them were seated there, together.

'We made it, Tennus. I said we'd make it.'

Tennus, brown-haired and heavily built, was breathing rapidly from the exertion of the climb. Nonetheless, he turned now and smiled, nodding. 'Yes. We did. But we haven't all made it to the top, yet.'

The two of them looked back down along the side of the cliff. Their eyes followed the trail of the very narrow shelf upon which they had ascended; a steeply sloping protuberance of rock which wound its way up from the desert plains two hundred metres below.

Just twenty metres away from them, Pellina was steadily ascending along that rock shelf. She was on her hands and knees, having adopted that position to enable her to overcome her fear of the height of the climb. She was doggedly crawling forwards now, determined to keep moving despite the pain which her bloodied knees had to be inflicting upon her.

The boy had originally not wanted to bring Pellina with them, and he had been annoyed when she had heard about their escape plan and had insisted that she was coming. He had felt sure that she would be too little, too weak, too slow; one more burden for him to have to keep alive. However, despite the fact that she was the youngest amongst them, he could already detect a fierce determination and willpower within the girl. He was glad now that he had relented, and had allowed her to come.

Pellina also now reached the challenging last part of the climb, and this time Tennus reached his hand down to pull her up.

The small dark-haired girl rolled onto her side on the ground next to the two of them. 'Oh my,' she said. 'Just look at that view.'

The desert stretched into the distance in front of them, a dry wilderness of sand, scrub and rock. Seeing it, the boy felt an immense sense of satisfaction. They had survived a journey of fifty miles across that desert, journeying over two nights and one day since fleeing the slave camps. And now they had finally arrived. They had reached these remote cliff-tops which he had spied two months ago, whilst part of a scouting group. Made it to the place to which he had attached an irrational but unwavering belief that he would find his freedom.

'Look, there,' said Tennus, concern in his voice. He pointed to a spot in the middle-distance, perhaps two to three miles away. A dust-cloud rising from the desert surface. 'What is it?'

The boy squinted at the highlighted place. His heart felt suddenly heavy. 'It's an Angall slaver party. They've come after us. They must've found our trail.'

'Oh no,' replied Pellina, sounding scared. 'What now?'

The boy grimaced. 'It doesn't change our plans.' He looked around, satisfied to see that there was much more grass and vegetation at the top of the cliff than on the plains below. And that the cliff extended backwards into the distance, towards the vast mountains behind. 'We need to keep moving. Find water. As soon as Menira and Kellon get here. The Angalls might not even spot the route we used to get up here, but we anyway need to keep moving, keep ourselves ahead of them.'

The three of them looked back over the cliff-edge now, checking on the progress of the last two members of their escape party. The boy felt agitated when he observed that they were still at least fifty metres below.

Kellon would be the one slowing the last pair down, he knew that, and he felt a little guilty now for not hanging back to help the diminutive boy. Kellon was the weakest and smallest of the group, but there had never been any consideration of leaving him behind at the camps. Not after Kellon had masterminded the plan as to how they could escape from the slave enclosures, undetected.

However, the exertions of the last forty hours had clearly taken their toll on the small boy, visible in the exhausted manner in which he was pushing himself slowly forwards upon his hands and knees. Not that Kellon would ever complain. For the smallest boy, escape had been a necessity, because he would not have survived for more than a few additional months if they had remained in the mines.

Fortunately, Menira had chosen to stay back with Kellon, and she was directly behind the tired boy now, encouraging and assisting him along the final part of the challenging ascent.

The boy continued to stare at the last two members of their group as they progressed slowly upwards, but in particular his eyes were drawn towards Menira. He could feel the same strange sensation which he had often felt in recent times, when he looked at her. At her pretty face, at her dirtied blonde hair. A feeling of longing, an uncertain longing which he could not properly comprehend or know how to address.

Minutes then passed, minutes during which his view switched between the ascent of the two slowest members of their group, and the distant dust cloud moving towards them across the desert plains.

Please don't let them find us. Please don't let them find us.

Finally, Kellon and Menira also joined them at the top. Both of them were exhausted but, as she was pulled onto the final ledge, Menira smiled broadly and then laughed.

This unexpected act proved infectious, and the boy and the others also joined in with her laughter.

It made no sense to laugh like this, to laugh like children when they were all still in the greatest jeopardy. The boy knew that. However, they *were* still children, and after the toils and fears of the last two days it felt good to allow themselves this defiant expression of joy, for just a moment.

Eventually, the laughter stopped. Menira smiled again and looked at the others, before her gaze then focused upon him, and she said, 'So, is this how it feels to be free?'

Part Two

—

Dreams and Powers

—

Year of Our Lord,
After Ascension, 767AA – 769AA

9

Corin

—

Year of Our Lord,
After Ascension, 767AA to 768AA

On the evening after they had departed from the village, Corin and Agbeth trekked for an hour until the sun first touched the horizon, and then for a further hour after that within the fading dusk light.

After leaving the village, they had travelled alongside the edge of the Great Lake. At the northern tip of the lake, they had picked up the river which flowed into it from the direction of the Great Forest. They were now following this river northwards.

Their pace that first evening was slow and steady, restricted by the burden of their possessions and by Agbeth's limp. Despite this, Corin was determined to put as much distance as possible between the two of them and the village of Karn, before they made camp.

They would still be on Karn land when the sun rose the next day, and Borrik's threat for them to be killed on sight was prominent in Corin's thoughts. However, it would take them the entirety of the next day to reach the edge of the Great Forest. Corin knew that there was no chance that either of them would be physically capable of walking through the night, to cover that much ground in a single effort.

'I need to stop, Corin,' Agbeth said, eventually, at a time when Corin was also feeling drained by fatigue.

Corin pointed to a tree next to an outcrop of rocks. 'Let's make camp here. But we need to be ready to move off by sunrise.'

He worked quickly to build a small fire and to place their bedrolls to either side of it. Corin was thankful that it was a warm night, and the fire made their camp comfortable despite the cooler night-time breezes blowing over them.

After they had eaten some of the provisions which Corin had packed, Agbeth moved to lie down on her bedroll, and Corin moved over to his.

'Corin?'

'Yes?'

'It's just the two of us, now, isn't it?' Agbeth's voice sounded wistful.

'Yes, I think it is.'

'And this is the first night of our new life together?'

'Yes, I suppose it is.'

'So, could we put our bedrolls next to each other?' Her shyness was evident. 'And lie together?'

'Lie together?' His heart pounded a little faster, uncertain at her meaning, and that uncertainty was clearly echoed in the tone of his reply.

She laughed. 'Sleep together, silly. Lie together and sleep. Tonight, after everything that's happened in the last two days... I'd like to have you here with me, as I sleep.'

He did not answer, but instead moved his bedroll, placing it to the side of Agbeth's, and then he lay down beside her. She turned onto her side, and then snuggled back against him, pushing her back into his chest and stomach, and her legs against his. He could feel her heat, and instinctively his arms wrapped around her and hugged her closer to him. After the traumas of the last day, this intimately peaceful moment of holding her felt wonderful.

'Thank you for coming with me, Agbeth,' he said.

'Thank you for agreeing to let me come, Corin. With you is where I'm meant to be.'

'I promise on all of the Gods that I'll make things right for us. And I'll do everything that I can, to look after you and to keep you safe.'

'I know you will.'

'I love you, Agbeth.'

'And I love you, Corin.'

It was then a simple thing to lean his head forwards, and to softly kiss her on the back of her head.

—

The next morning, they set off again as soon as the first rays of sunlight appeared to the east. They continued to follow the river northwards, making steady progress towards the great line of trees in the distance.

Corin occasionally glanced behind himself to check for any pursuers, but there were none. He knew that it was very unlikely that anyone from Karn would follow them; if Borrik had wanted Corin dead, he would have killed him yesterday. And Borrik himself would have known that it would take Corin and Agbeth at least a day and a half on foot to leave Karn territory.

The sun was soon bright in the sky, the day was warm, and as the two of them trekked through the countryside it was easy to imagine that this was all part of an adventure. A repeat of their earlier journeys together to the edge of the Great Forest, when they had been more carefree teenagers.

Of course, in those days they had never dared to venture more than a few hundred metres inwards from the edge of the mighty woods, and they had never been as heavily encumbered as they were now. The encumbrance of their possessions was tiring for both of them, and throughout the day they needed to stop every couple of hours for a break.

On one such stop, Agbeth asked, 'What will we do when we reach the forest, Corin?'

'We'll have to keep moving north,' he replied. 'Keep following the river. As long as we stay near the river, we'll have fresh water and won't get lost. I'm hoping that at some point the river will lead to another lake. Somewhere we can fish for food. If we find anywhere like that, that's where we should make a permanent shelter.'

'And if we don't find somewhere like that?'

'I don't know. Then we might need to come south again, and think of something else, before winter arrives.'

'And do you believe the tales, Corin? About the spirits? And the felrin?'

'Who knows? You know as well as I do, that the spirits are like the Gods. We all know they're there, but who do we actually know that they've ever shown themselves to? If they *are* in the Great Forest, let's show proper care of and respect for the place, and hopefully they'll leave us alone.'

'And the felrin?'

'I don't know. That's different. We've all heard Crannic's story about how he thought he saw one at the edge of the forest. But that was what, twenty years ago, and everyone knows how much he's always liked to drink. And no one's seen one since. If they are there, though, we've got to be... well, *careful*.' This was an optimistic choice of word. If the stories were true, they both knew that an encounter with even a single felrin could prove fatal.

Given the sombre note to Corin's response, Agbeth's next words were deliberately playful. 'So, hopefully there won't be lots and lots of them, like in the story when Mella leads a horde of felrin to battle against the Outsiders?'

He smiled, also trying to sound cheerful. 'If there is a horde of them, somewhere in the forest, then we'd both better be ready to jump into the river, and had better pray to Banta that they can't swim.'

—

They reached the edge of the Great Forest an hour before sunset, that evening, and made camp a couple of hundred metres outside of the woodland boundary.

By the time that they stopped Corin was exhausted, with an ache in his head from the area around the cut. Agbeth was also suffering pain from her lame leg. However, they were both pleased to have covered so much ground in a single day.

The mighty trees at the edge of the woods were clearly visible now, towering close to a hundred metres into the sky. And that treeline extended as far as the eye could see to both the east and west; an awe-inspiring, unbroken line of foliage.

On this second night, without needing to be prompted, Corin placed the two bedrolls side-by-side, and he and Agbeth lay together. Once again, they shared words of love. But this time, without saying anything further, Agbeth turned her body around to face him. And then the two of them were kissing, hungrily, for a number of minutes. His arms pulled her in close against him.

When she finally broke off the kiss, and turned back around to snuggle herself against him, Corin could feel a new kind of excitement coursing through his body.

—

The next day they entered the Great Forest, still following the river, and moved further into the woodland than they had ever been before.

They were now outside of Karn territory. The vast swathe of trees around them represented the boundary between the mountains at the edge of the world, where the Gods lived, and the lands of man.

The ground was still relatively flat in this area, and as such the river remained easy to follow. Corin had brought enough food to provide for them both for over a week, but he was alert now to opportunities to add to their provisions. He wanted them to cover more distance before making a concerted effort to hunt or to gather further food, but he nonetheless was noticing lots of small animals as they travelled under the forest canopy. Late in the morning, they stopped at a blackberry bush, for several minutes, and greedily filled their stomachs with the small fruits.

Corin kept the river on their left hand side, within a hundred metres, at all times. Sometimes, rocky outcrops blocked their path and necessitated a small detour away from the water, but never to a distance that meant that it was difficult to re-join the waterway again.

It was darker under the blanket of the forest foliage than it had been in the fields outside, but speckles of sunlight broke through the leaves and made it an appealing place to be. Indeed, at mid-afternoon they came across a beautiful and dry grassy glade next to the river, and decided to camp there for the night.

That evening, after they had eaten and had laid out the bedrolls next to the fire, the two of them cuddled together. Once again, this led into a heated and passionate kiss. Only this time, Corin could feel Agbeth's hand sliding down to the drawstrings of his trousers, and he knew that she wanted more. And so did he.

—

Afterwards, as they lay in each other's arms on the bedroll, both naked, Corin was grinning from ear-to-ear.

'Agbeth?'

'Yes?'

'We can't do the ceremony here, of walking under the arches. But will you agree to be my wife?'

'After tonight, in my heart and in every way that matters, I already am. And you are my husband.'

142

He smiled, feeling full of joy, and kissed the top of her head. 'I am. Your husband. And I will always love you and protect you. From spirits. From felrin. From *everything*.'

Talk of spirits and felrin was then forgotten, and they fell asleep all too easily that night, entwined in each other's arms.

The dream came to him later, in the hours of darkness. A dream of a mountain and a Gate. He awoke, feeling angry and confused, but then realised that he was on his side, with Agbeth pressed close against him. He slid back into his slumber, soon forgetting the reason for his anger.

—

During the next three days, they continued to trek northwards through the wilderness of the Great Forest. Corin was more alert now. Both for prey which he could hunt, and also for anything which could potentially be a threat to the two of them. They had not yet encountered any large wildlife which might pose danger, but it was possible that there could be wolves or worse within the deep forest.

The land was gradually sloping upwards, and this was starting to create greater problems for closely tracking the river. It was particularly challenging whenever they reached areas where the waters were rapidly flowing and surrounded by rock walls, or when they arrived at waterfalls. Corin was determined not to divert away from his plan to track the river until they reached a lake. Therefore, they had to make several extended detours to circle around obstacles, and to return back to the side of the water.

'Do you think that anyone else has ever walked where we're walking, right now?' Agbeth asked him, at one point.

'Maybe not,' he answered, recognising the sense of remoteness which had triggered her question. 'This is our land, now.' He did not want to dwell in his mind upon the reasons why no one came to the forest.

On their fourth day within the sprawling woodland, they decided to only walk during the morning, so that Corin could use the afternoon to hunt for food. They would have to split up while he did this, to allow him to tread lightly in a way which Agbeth's leg could never achieve.

Agbeth was to stay behind at their riverside camp. The two of them had by now spent every waking and sleeping moment together for almost a week, and it unsettled Corin to think about leaving her there, close to defenceless, whilst he headed into the forest with his bow.

'I won't be more than a few hundred metres away,' he said, prior to departure. 'If anything comes, you scream for me as loud as you can, OK?'

'Yes, and I've got my knife,' she replied, looking worried herself but trying to make light of it. 'And I'm ready to jump into the river and swim if anything scary comes for me.'

Corin kissed her goodbye then left their camp, heading away from the river and into the deeper canopy of the woods. He and Agbeth would have to become accustomed to splitting up in this territory, he knew that and he was resigned to it, for it was the only way that they would be able to survive. However, he could not resist taking one look back as he came close to moving out of a direct line of sight from her, and checking that she was still fine. She was watching him, and waved.

He clutched his bow in his left hand as he moved onwards, and he had soon settled into a slower, stalking pace of walk. He was concentrating on the sounds and sights around him, grateful now that he had learned to hunt when he was younger. The forest surrounding him was teeming with life; he could feel that, within himself.

And it was life that did not know man, did not know the threat a human hunter could pose. That made it easy for him to secure his first kill, a rabbit which had been sitting within a cluster of its kin outside of a warren in a clearing. Corin's arrow only travelled a short distance, but its flight was true, and it embedded itself into the side of the animal, knocking it over.

The others rabbits scattered instantly, many heading into the burrowed holes leading into the warren.

Corin moved over. The rabbit was twitching, still alive, the arrow through its body. It looked at him, eyes panicked, and for a peculiar moment it seemed to Corin that he could *feel* the animal there. Could feel its beating heart. Feel its life. Feel its terror. And could see himself, through its eyes? Then he clubbed the creature on the head, killing it, and those odd sensations vanished.

After that, he moved back to the same hidden spot, with his recovered arrow and his first kill, and waited for the other rabbits to return. And as he waited there, silent and alert, it was almost as if he could sense the forest around him. Alive and vibrant. Populated with creatures that could be hunted. Could be killed. Could be...

Then another rabbit emerged from the burrow, and it was a simple matter to secure his second kill.

With both kills claimed, he returned to Agbeth, both of them feeling relieved to reunite with the other.

—

They moved north alongside the river for three more days, continuing to enjoy sunshine and warm weather, and then finally they came upon the location which Corin had been hoping to find. Prior to arriving at this place, they had been blocked by yet another waterfall whilst walking in the morning, and had needed once again to take a large detour around some sheer cliffs.

The climb at the point where the cliffs had eventually given way to a steep hill had still been very difficult. Corin had needed to help Agbeth ascend first, without either of them carrying any equipment. He had then undertaken a further four trips up and down the slope, to retrieve their belongings. By the time that he had made the final ascent it was already afternoon, and he was extremely tired.

145

But then, when they had returned to the river and could see their prize, all of their efforts seemed worthwhile. The waterway continued to snake northwards for one hundred metres from the waterfall, but then it joined into a large lake, which was perhaps three hundred metres across. Trees surrounded the lake on the western and northern edges, the great mountains distantly visible behind those trees to the north. To the east, there was a flat area of grass backing onto further cliffs.

'This is perfect,' Corin said to Agbeth, smiling, as they first saw it.

It was a truly beautiful and idyllic place, and Agbeth clearly thought the same as she exclaimed, 'By the Gods! How lovely.'

Corin was excited. 'That lake must be brimming with fish.'

They moved closer to the grassy area on the eastern side of the lake, dropping their equipment onto the grass when they got there, such that they could more comfortably explore. Corin's eyes scanned along the cliffs, looking for any outcrops which could provide cover from the weather, and which therefore would be a suitable position to build a shelter.

He quickly identified the perfect spot. A place where the top of the cliff jutted further outwards than the bottom, and the undulations in the cliff edge formed a small, partially-covered cave area below.

Then he also spotted a wooden lean-to shelter, built against the side of the cliff within this cave. He realised that they were not the first visitors to this place.

'Agbeth, look,' he whispered, while pointing. He reached for his axe, feeling nervous, and shouted, 'Hello! Is anybody here?'

There was no answer, his shout reverberating off the cliff walls. The two of them moved towards the shelter cautiously, but as they got closer Corin's tension eased. Whoever the owner had been, they did not appear to have lived in this place anytime recently.

The shelter was old and dilapidated, and appeared to have been abandoned for quite some time. The wood within the structure was rotten in places, and some leather hides which must once have been attached to the wood were dangling downwards haphazardly. There were also odd assortments of possessions scattered about the floor, as if strewn there by the wind. However, to Corin's satisfaction, the shelter looked like it was capable of being repaired, and it was easily large enough to accommodate them both.

'Where do you think the owner is, Corin?' asked Agbeth. 'They've left lots of their things here.'

'I don't know,' he replied, uncertainly. 'But wherever they are, this place seems perfect.'

'It does.' Agbeth looked upwards, at the cliff jutting outwards above their heads. 'It looks like this area under the cliff will stay dry.'

'Yes, I think you're right. And we have a natural windbreak on three sides, and a ready source of food. It just seems perfect. I think this should be the place we stop at, Agbeth. Do you agree?'

'Yes. I agree. This is where we'll make our home.'

—

In the following weeks, they did just that, and they were the happiest times of Corin's life. The place which they had chosen was beautiful and peaceful, and was rich with wildlife which he could hunt.

The lake was also replete with fish, and Corin taught Agbeth how to use a fishing rod, either alongside him or in the time when he was out hunting. Food caught from the water quickly became a major part of their diet.

The two of them enthusiastically set about the task of restoring and improving the shelter. They were both very aware that, whilst the days and nights were still comfortable, winter was only a few months away. It was therefore vital that they improved the lean-to sufficiently such that it would protect them from the worst of the winter weather. They replaced many of the older wooden branches with newly cut tree limbs, and then Agbeth started to apply a mixture of mud, grass and stones to fill the gaps between branches.

147

After two weeks there, they had their first downpour of rain. They were both happy to see that there was an area of five metres around their lean-to, under the cover of the protruding cliff, which remained protected and dry.

They had encountered no concerning threats yet, from any of the creatures and wildlife of the Great Forest. Occasionally, at night-time, they would hear the howling noise of wolves, far away in the distance, but thankfully never in their proximity. Nor were there any signs of either spirits or felrin, although Agbeth would frequently leave out small offerings to the former, in case they needed placating.

And whenever the urge came upon the two of them, they made love together, unconstrained by any human neighbours. They were both delighting in the newly developed carnal side to their relationship. Corin was aware that they should be more careful, lest Agbeth become pregnant, but that did not restrain him when they each felt a need for the other.

In those early weeks, they both worked incredibly hard in the pursuits of hunting, fishing, building and making. But they each also felt incredible contentment. This was their home. Whatever they built here, whatever they made here, was theirs. And they had each other.

—

After four weeks, their tranquillity was disturbed when Agbeth discovered what appeared to be the remains of their predecessor.

She had wandered away from the shelter to pick berries, and had cut through a particularly dense bramble to reach another crop of fruit, when she came upon the bones.

'Corin!' He had heard the panicked shout from where he was chopping wood, and had immediately sprinted in her direction, axe in hand and full of anxiety.

When he reached her, Agbeth was by the side of the bramble,

looking scared, and was pointing inside. 'There's a lot of bones in there, Corin. And what looks like a person's skull.'

Corin entered the thicket of brambles, and immediately observed what Agbeth was referring to. Bones were scattered all over, only a few still connected together, and some with what appeared to be tatters of either flesh or cloth attached to them. At the back, a human-looking skull rested on its side, detached from all of the other bones.

'Do you think that's what it is, Corin?' Agbeth asked. 'Is it a person?'

'Yes, I think so.' Corin's mind was absorbing the scene. This appeared to have been no peaceful death. 'I think the way that the bones are scattered, it must have been done by an animal.' Having uttered those words, he suddenly felt a flash of fear and looked around himself, checking that nothing was nearby, stalking them.

'An animal killed them?'

'Could be that, or it was a natural death, and an animal subsequently ate them.' However, looking at the way that the bones were strewn in front of him, he felt a grim concern that it was the former. 'Either way, we both need to make sure that we stay careful and alert, now. And maybe stay closer together, when we're both here.'

She nodded. 'It's sad. I think we should bury them.'

———

In the next three months, their idyllic new existence continued, and they both did everything that they could to prepare themselves for winter.

Gradually, however, the nights were becoming longer and colder. Their lean-to shelter was now in significantly better condition than it had been when they had arrived, with Agbeth's work ensuring that there were no wind gaps in the side or at the back. The repaired structure acted in concert with the natural protection of the cliff and cave, to preserve them from the worst of the weather. Each night, they would build a large fire outside, in front of the entrance to the shelter, and would fall asleep in each other's arms as the fire warmed them.

Occasionally, Corin would suffer from a repeat of the dream, and gradually he was remembering disjointed images from it. Particularly the winding mountain path. And the Gate. Sometimes, after he had woken in the morning, he would stare to the mountains in the north and would wonder if the peak of which he dreamed was there, in that range. And if the Gate of his dreams could be the entrance to the home of the Gods themselves?

But then, in their fifth month of living in the shelter by the lake, the weather really started to turn against them. Temperatures dropped significantly, particularly at night, and they endured a number of consecutive days and nights of icy, sleeting rain.

There was little food available to gather, by now, and Corin was having to range further from their shelter to find food. Each time that he did this, he felt an element of fear for Agbeth. Ever since finding the bones, he had suffered doubts about the manner of the person's death, and it therefore worried him to leave her alone. However, he had no choice but to do so, if they were to secure sufficient food to see them through the winter.

He was becoming increasingly concerned about how difficult the winter was going to be for them both. They were higher up here than Karn was, and already it felt like it was going to get much colder than it had ever been in his old village. And although winters had always been challenging in Karn, at least there they entered the winter months with full stores and with livestock which could be slaughtered. Here, although they had stockpiled a lot of dry wood in the shelter of their cave, their reserves of food were slim. For the past month they had been smoking and drying both meat and fish, but what they had hoarded so far did not feel remotely enough to give him comfort.

When the days of icy rain finally stopped, they were presented with a clear, freezing cold day. There was now visible ice on the edges of the lake, forming a glassy crust which was steadily creeping towards the centre of the water. The two of them enjoyed a day of being able to move around again without becoming soaked through with rain, and by late afternoon they were in renewed good spirits. However, by nightfall the sky was again covered by ominous clouds.

The fire was raging outside the lean-to entrance as they lay down that night, huddled together under all of their furs and covers. Corin was feeling a sexual urge inside himself, and he knew that Agbeth was too, as she pressed herself fully and intimately against him. Outside of their cosy shelter, the wolves were again audible in the distance as they howled, a large pack baying out their long, doleful call.

And then another sound abruptly joined their collective canine cries, a shrieking noise which was closer and louder and far more terrifying. Instantly, the wolves fell silent.

The new, and alien, noise was repeated. Corin and Agbeth both sat up, feeling alarm. It sounded like an unnatural mix between a howl, a screech and a scream, each cry lasting for several seconds. It was unlike any sound that they had ever heard before, and came from a location which Corin judged was somewhere between their shelter and the remote wolf pack. And was therefore closer to them than the wolves had ever been.

The cry was repeated and repeated, echoing across the woods and cliffs, and the forest had otherwise fallen deathly quiet around them. Silently listening to the blood-curdling calls.

'What is it, Corin?' whispered Agbeth, sounding frightened. Her hand was on his arm. Corin was scared, too.

'I don't know. A large animal, maybe.' But one word had sprung into his mind. *Felrin.*

The cry continued for minutes afterwards, dominating and intimidating the still silent forest. It was the confident cry of a hunter, of a dominant predator. Marking its territory.

And then the sky outside was interrupted by a blanket of falling whiteness, as it started to snow.

10

Allana

—

Year of Our Lord,
After Ascension, 767AA to 768AA

Allana disembarked from the *Flower of Andar*, onto the Septholme docks.

She had whispered her goodbyes to Captain Rabnar earlier, in the private confines of his cabin, whilst her body had been sensuously entwined with his. He had deliberately chosen not to bid her farewell here, in public, lest his unquenched lust for her betray itself in front of his men.

She shivered now, in remembrance of what the two of them had done together over the last few days. She had boarded the ship as an inexperienced girl, but was undoubtedly leaving it as a woman. In some ways, she could now better understand her mother's choice of profession; she had not remotely anticipated the wild intensity with which she would relish the act of sex.

You were so wicked, Lana, she thought to herself, with a sudden frisson of excitement. *So shameless. Even though you knew he was married.*

152

He had confessed his marital status to her after she had been aboard ship for two days. Had explained that he had a loving wife and family in Andarron. He had seemed confused as he had spoken about them, and had explained to Allana that not only had he never been unfaithful before, but that he had never even *contemplated* being unfaithful. But that with Allana, he could not control himself.

Rabnar had completely forgotten about her actions on the dockside in Sen Aiduel. However, Allana felt certain that their intense yearning for each other had originated from what she had done to him that night. That moment where she had somehow connected her mind to his, and had planted the seeds of desire deep inside of him. Seeds which had also been born within her, and which both of them had enflamed into life throughout the voyage by sea.

She had thought about what had occurred at the Sen Aiduel docks many times during the journey, as she had lain languorously on the bed in his cabin. Remembering the way in which the world had slowed down around her, and how she had felt tendrils of connection curling out of her mind and into his. Whatever she had done, it had not been natural, and an uncomfortable question lingered at the edges of her mind; had she forced him?

Don't feel guilty, Lana. However it started, he wanted it as much as you. Just remember the pleasure.

However, despite the thrill of their encounters, they had both accepted that their relationship must end once they arrived at Septholme. At which point she was to disembark and he would sail onwards. They had agreed that was the right thing to do, for the sake of Rabnar's family, although neither of them could resist the temptation to continue their adulterous liaison for the remainder of the journey.

Allana walked forward across the docks, now. She was again carrying her bundle of possessions, with the knife and her coin purse both inside the pockets of her dress.

Septholme was, on first impressions, very different to the place which had been her home. The harbour was smaller than the equivalent area in Sen Aiduel, although still bustling with noise and activity, and the land sloped steeply upwards away from the sea here. Her eyes now followed that hillside, past the tightly-packed streets of buildings crammed into its slopes, until finally she observed the mighty castle fortress residing at the top of the hill.

This place is so different, Lana. So foreign. But it could be your new home.

The hood of her cloak was raised up as she walked away from the *Flower of Andar*, passing through the harbour area to the narrower thoroughfares beyond. She wanted to be several streets away from the ships before she lowered the hood again, such that no one might notice or remember that a dark-haired olive-skinned girl had disembarked here.

As she walked into the town she thought about that other – *much darker* – event, from her last night in Sen Aiduel, which had also remained prominent in her thoughts throughout the journey. The murder of Ronis dei Maranar, and the subsequent terrifying flight through the city. In the extended periods when Captain Rabnar had been above decks, there had been ample time in the small cabin to reflect upon what she had done. To close her eyes and to recall the image of that moment when she had plunged the knife into the High Priest's neck.

She was a killer. A murderess. And she would always be a killer, no matter what deeds she now undertook in future, whether good or bad. That picture in her mind, of dei Maranar choking and dying on the bed, was seared into her memory. He had been alive, and then she had ended that life.

She had not mentioned anything about the High Priest to Captain Rabnar. Maybe he would hear about the murder during some future visit to Sen Aiduel, and possibly he would then connect it to the mysterious girl who had travelled in his cabin. But if she *had* told him, and if he had asked her whether she was feeling guilt or remorse, she would have answered 'no'. Because that was the truth. She had no regret for what she had done.

Ronis was going to assault you, Lana. Rape you. You asked him to stop, and he wouldn't. You did what you had to do, to survive.

And she knew in her heart that, if the circumstances of the killing were ever to be repeated, she would do the same thing again.

—

On the first night that she was staying in Septholme, she paid for a room in a good quality inn, a few streets away from the harbour area.

Her first conversation with a local resident of the town was with the landlady of the inn, after Allana had cautiously entered the reputable-looking establishment.

The landlady was short, with mousy-coloured hair, and introduced herself by asking, 'Can I help you, miss?'

Allana immediately noticed the sharp difference in the woman's accent, with the landlady's manner of speech being both quicker and at a higher-pitch than her own.

'Yes, I'd like a room for a few days, please.'

The woman peered at her with interest. 'You're not from these parts, are you?'

'No, I'm not.' Allana suddenly felt self-conscious, for both her drawling accent, and her attire. 'Do you have an available room, please?'

The landlady was not about to be so easily diverted, although Allana sensed that the woman merely liked to chat. 'I bet you're from Dei Magnus, aren't you? Had a group of your countrymen through here, once. Sounded just like you.'

Allana smiled in return, but did not reply.

The landlady stared for a second longer, but then appeared to conclude that her efforts to start a conversation were not going to bear fruit. 'You have coin? I'll expect payment in advance.'

After they had concluded agreement for lodgings in a private room for three nights, and Allana had paid, the woman made

155

another attempt to make conversation as she showed Allana to her bedroom.

'There's a handful more of your countrymen in town, you know, if you're looking for company with your own folk? They sound just like you, you know, that funny way you say things.'

This time Allana was more interested. 'Really? Where?'

'Oh, the other side of town. South side. Only been in here a couple of times. Those Aiduel's Guards fellas. You know which ones I mean?'

Allana nodded. Aiduel's Guards were prominent in Sen Aiduel, and she had witnessed some of their burnings of heretics, in the main central square there. 'Aiduel's Guards are here? Where did you say they are?'

'On the south side of town. Got a little mission house there. Handful of them, as I understand. Might want to pop in there to see them, mightn't you?'

Allana smiled, non-committedly, as she considered this information. The news that her countrymen were close caused a small chill of alarm.

That decides it, Lana. Tomorrow, you can start looking for somewhere to work and live. On the north *side of town.*

—

The next day, she started to look for a home to rent, in the northern areas of Septholme.

During her time on the *Flower of Andar*, she had formulated a plan of what she was going to do. Her intention now was to utilise some of the money that she had looted from Ronis, to set herself up in a small home. And from that home she would try to work as a seamstress, utilising the skills that she had once been taught by her mother, when they had made clothes together. The other option which she had considered and dismissed was to seek work as a servant somewhere, but she wanted to try to avoid that if possible.

After their first liaison together in Rabnar's cabin, the captain had insisted that he would only accept the proper fare for the voyage to Septholme. She therefore still had most of Ronis's money to help her to secure her position in this new country.

It took Allana two days to find a suitable available property to rent, which was located on the corner between a quiet alleyway and a busier street. It was a small downstairs apartment at the end of a terrace, with two rooms, and an external door which opened onto the street outside.

Her first night in this new home was very unsettling. She had always shared an apartment with her mother, the two of them comfortably familiar with sleeping near to each other. But now she was in an unfamiliar place, living on her own.

There was also a background bustle of noise from the street outside, which further disturbed her attempts to sleep. She did not find much rest, that first night. Nor did she dream.

Don't worry, Lana. You'll get used to this. Soon this will feel like your home, and you'll sleep properly again. Be brave.

—

The following morning, she awoke with a renewed sense of enthusiasm. She visited a number of shops and stores in the town to acquire the items she needed to operate as a seamstress. She also purchased a small sign with the words 'Seamstress and Clothes Maker' painted upon it, which she hung up outside the front of her home. With everything that she needed acquired, she was ready to start.

And then she set out with a determination to find customers. There was no other way to do this, she realised, than to knock on lots of doors and to speak to lots of people.

Almost everyone she conversed with commented upon her accent, and she was quickly realising that it would be much harder to remain anonymous and ordinary within a foreign country. Whenever

157

she was asked for her name, she answered, 'Lana Marrone'. She could not countenance having to get used to a completely new identity, even though retaining part of her name added some risk.

She noticed a couple of significant changes within herself, as she went out into Septholme that day. Firstly, the traumatic events with Ronis, and her subsequent escape, had completely shaken off the lethargy which had gripped her after her mother's death. No longer did she feel content to just drift apathetically, aimlessly waiting for something to happen to her. She had gained an understanding of how much she valued her freedom and her life, and this was giving her a new sense of purpose.

Secondly, after having witnessed the desire which she had stirred within Rabnar, she now more properly appreciated the physical beauty with which she had been blessed. And that with such attractiveness, there was a new type of power available to her. A power available over men, and perhaps over women of a certain disposition. A power which she now had greater confidence to employ.

And on this day of knocking on doors in Septholme, she did utilise this whenever the person who she addressed was a man. They would answer the door to be met by a young and exotic foreign woman, with long black hair and a petite but curvaceous body. She quickly realised that, for some of the men of the town, the conversation with her was the highlight of their day.

And it was the men who displayed the most outward signs of attraction who were also the most effusive in their promises that, if they had any applicable work, they would remember to give her business a try.

—

Over the subsequent weeks, Allana continued to live on Ronis's stolen money, as her seamstress business began to build up. It started with a couple of small pieces of work, which she completed diligently and to the best of her ability. She passed these back with requests for the customer to use her services again, and to recommend her to others.

Gradually, she was securing more business, although her income was still less than she needed to cover her routine outgoings. However, the work gave her a sense of purpose throughout the week, and she had enough activities to undertake to keep her occupied in the daytime. She would work in her home across First-Day to Sixth-Day. The only break in her daily routine was Seventh-Day, when she attended Holy Service at a small local church.

At night-time, however, she suffered from loneliness. She was in an unfamiliar town, in a foreign country, and she did not have any family or friends. In the evening, she would close and lock her front door from the inside, and then would sometimes sit in silence and boredom, until she felt that it was an acceptable time to lie down to sleep.

And as she stretched out beneath her covers, she often found herself thinking sensual thoughts. Lustful thoughts. Remembering what had happened with Captain Rabnar, and wishing he was there. It was a torment which had not existed within her at all during her time in Sen Aiduel. However, the lingering memories of the events in the cabin, and the sensations they evoked, were taunting her now and making it difficult for her to sleep.

What has happened to you, Lana? Is this how Mum once felt?

She ached for a repeat of what had happened between her and Rabnar, and wished that the captain was there with her. However, she knew that they had agreed to part, and that she was alone. She doubted that she would ever see him again.

Many nights, therefore, under the cover of darkness, she would need to furtively slide her own hands down under her blankets, before she was able to find sufficient relief to allow sleep to take her.

And when she did sleep, she was troubled by an eerie recurring dream. She did not retain the entire memory of this dream, after awakening, but flashes of recollection remained. A mountain. A winding path. A Gate. Something that worried her.

159

Often the dream awoke her in the middle of the night, in the midst of rumpled and dampened sheets. Her heart would be pounding afterwards, her mouth dry, and it would be difficult for her to return to sleep. And then her thoughts would return to the sensual events on the boat, and the cycle of hunger would begin again.

———

After three months had passed of Allana's new life in Septholme, she was working in the middle of the day on Third-Day, when an unexpected female visitor arrived at her home.

Allana often worked with her front door open, to make it more welcoming for potential customers to enter. The newcomer was therefore able to pass through the doorway of the apartment without knocking, and she got Allana's attention by saying, 'Hello?'

Allana recognised immediately that the accent of the woman addressing her was that of Dei Magnus. She looked up, and felt a jolt of fear when she spotted the identifiable red cloak and red sash that the woman was wearing, over otherwise ordinary clothes.

She is of Aiduel's Guards, Lana. Be careful.

'Hello, can I help you?' Allana knew that the woman would in turn recognise her own accent as that of their home country.

'Ah, I'm in the right place!' exclaimed the visitor. She was tall and skinny, appearing to be in her early-twenties in age, with short cropped blonde hair. Allana could see a sword within a scabbard on the woman's belt.

'Can I help you, please?' repeated Allana.

'No, no, please excuse me,' answered the woman. 'I heard just last week that there's another woman from Dei Magnus living in Septholme, and I needed to come find you.' She walked forward and extended her hand towards Allana. 'I'm Nionia, Nionia dei Pallere. From Pallere, of course.'

Allana shook the offered hand. 'Lana Marrone. From Dei Aiduel.' She had never been to Dei Aiduel, but she was not about to tell this stranger where she was actually from.

'How wonderful to see another Dei Magnun woman here! I've been at our mission house here for twelve months now, and you're the first woman from our homeland that I've come across.' Allana smiled but did not otherwise respond. She felt uncertain, and Nionia dei Pallere appeared to pick up on this, adding, 'Oh! Don't worry about my uniform. I'm not here on official Guards' business. This is my first posting after being accepted into the Guards. I've just been so *lonely* in this country. I just came here for a chat, if that's OK?'

Be careful, Lana. She might know everything about Ronis. She might already suspect you. This could all be an act.

Allana gestured to a chair across from the desk at which she was working. 'Please, Nionia, take a seat and let me get you a drink of water.'

The woman seated herself in the chair offered, her long bony legs sticking out as she did so. Allana passed across a cup of water to her, waiting to see what her visitor would do next.

'How long have you been here, Lana?'

'Five months, there or thereabouts.' Allana smiled as she made this lie. Again, she was not about to give the real date, and therefore link herself directly to the time when Ronis had been murdered.

'Oh, so you're still quite new here? Are you alone? And what brings you from Dei Magnus to Andar?'

Allana had rehearsed her cover story in her mind several times, and by now she had also had several opportunities to employ it on other residents of Septholme. 'I am alone, yes. My mother was from Dei Aiduel, but my father, who left her when I was very young, was a sailor from Andar. The last thing my mother knew was that he was here, in Septholme. Mum died earlier this year, so I decided to come to try to find my father.'

'Oh, that's so sad! But did you find him?' The question appeared to be asked innocently.

'No. No one here has heard of him. Maybe he left – or died – a long time ago. But having travelled here, I've decided to stay. At least for a while.'

'You're so brave, Lana. Doing that on your own. I remember being scared when I first left Dei Magnus to come here, and I was travelling with two other Guards. And then to get here, and to find that no one wants us here, was even worse. But you're so brave, to do it on your own. But I'm glad that you did. It's so nice to speak to someone from our country.'

Allana smiled again. For a member of Aiduel's Guards, Nionia appeared to be disarmingly unguarded in her conversation. Allana was quickly coming to a conclusion that either the woman was genuinely lonely and looking for a friend, or that she was an extremely good actress, and therefore could be very dangerous.

Just humour her, Lana. Don't do anything which might annoy her.

'How many of you are here?' Allana asked this question casually.

'Just five of us,' responded Nionia. 'And I'm the only woman, of course! The lowest-ranking skivvy for everyone else! They only allow a maximum of five of us in each mission house within Andar, and even then they don't really welcome us.'

Allana then chatted with the woman for the next thirty minutes, being careful throughout to appear friendly, but remaining guarded about any information she divulged.

After what felt to her like an appropriate length of time, she was going to politely remind the woman that she had work to do. However, before she did that she could not resist from asking one final question. 'Has there been any... news, from home?'

'News? Let me think. Not much. Although you must know of course that the Archlaw is trying to get more of our people here, in Andar? The Guards, that is. I hope he succeeds. It's so quiet here.'

Allana was relieved. Of course, the news that she was alluding to was the murder of a High Priest, in Sen Aiduel, but she took the absence of any mention of that as a positive. The conversation

162

continued, and eventually Allana gestured towards the work that she was undertaking.

Nionia looked at it and blushed. 'Oh, of course. Silly me. But I've so enjoyed today, Lana. I always have free time on a Third-Day. Please may I visit you at this time, every week? It would be so wonderful if we could become friends.'

Allana nodded, and smiled again. But at the same time, she was groaning inside.

—

After the meeting with Nionia dei Pallere, Allana considered packing up her possessions and leaving Septholme, as soon as she possibly could. She thought about walking north from the town, until she got to another settlement, so that she could distance herself from Aiduel's Guards.

However, she decided against this. Firstly, there had been nothing tangible in Nionia's words or actions which suggested that Aiduel's Guards were hunting for the murderer of Ronis dei Maranar. Secondly, if there was a mission house of Aiduel's Guards here in Septholme, it was also likely that there would be one in the next major town that she arrived at. And finally, she was just starting to become settled into her new life in this town, and the thought of uprooting everything again and moving to another place was deeply unappealing. She therefore resolved to stay, and to accept Nionia's weekly visits.

And after the next couple of meetings with Nionia, Allana was becoming more comfortable that the young woman's expressed motivation for visiting her was indeed genuine. The subsequent conversations were equally unguarded on the part of Nionia. Allana could never forget about the burnings which Aiduel's Guards had regularly been responsible for in her homeland, but at the same time her visitor seemed too nice and naive to be sullied by attachment to those deeds.

163

At the end of Nionia's third visit, Allana asked her a question as she was about to leave. 'Nionia, do your colleagues know that you come to see me?'

The other woman gave a lopsided grin, showing embarrassment. 'No, they don't. This is my patrol day. I'm meant to be out on the streets, all day today. Looking for signs of sin, and heresy. I haven't told them about you.'

'So, I'm a secret from them?'

'Yes, you're my guilty secret, Lana! None of them would understand that I just want a friend here. Someone I can talk to.'

On another occasion, Allana tried to understand more about the young woman, particularly why she did not seem to fit with Allana's preconceptions of what an Aiduel's Guard might be.

'Nionia, why did you decide to become part of Aiduel's Guards?'

The lanky woman shrugged, looking embarrassed. 'I don't know, really. My parents met in the Guards. And they both told me to.'

'But doesn't it worry you? Some of the things that the Guards have to do?'

'Not really. I haven't really thought much about it.' This was said casually, and Allana could believe from the relaxed response that the other woman genuinely had not. Nionia did not appear to be a particularly deep thinker. 'Like I said, I'm just the skivvy here. The others do that kind of work.'

More than anything else, these answers comforted Allana that the expressed reason for the visits was genuine. Over time, Allana also began to welcome their encounters, and recognised that their acquaintance was slowly blossoming into friendship.

—

After she had been in Septholme for five months, Allana was visited by an Andarron soldier.

She was at work in her home, with the door open, when

he arrived. His large frame, blocking the light in the doorway, immediately alerted her to his presence.

'Excuse me, ma'am,' he said, to announce himself.

'Hello, can I help you?' She quickly noticed that the man was good-looking. He was over six feet tall, with a squared jaw and completely bald head, and a body which looked thick and muscular. He was wearing a military uniform, which she recognised as being that of a soldier from Septholme Castle.

'I'm Captain Menion Thatcher, ma'am. Am I right that you're a seamstress, ma'am?'

The man appeared to be between ten to fifteen years older than Allana, and it made her smirk to hear an older person addressing her so formally. 'Please, call me Lana. And yes, I am a seamstress. I repair and make clothes.'

'Good. Good. You were actually recommended to me… Lana,' he replied. 'I have a job. I'd like a jacket to be made. A formal jacket. High quality. For my wedding.'

'Well, that sounds perfect, Captain Thatcher. You've come to the right person.'

They proceeded to discuss exactly what it was that he required. Allana questioned him as to what style he wanted, and the material. Following that, they agreed upon a price, and a date for the garment to be ready.

As they spoke, she quickly became attuned to the fact that he had noticed her attractiveness and that, despite his impending marriage, he was openly flirting with her. There was a boldness in the way that he stared at her, which announced his interest. And for the first time since her liaisons with Captain Rabnar, she found that the attraction was mutual, and that months of pent-up desire was leading her to respond to his attentions.

'I shall have to measure you, Captain, before you leave. To ensure a good fit.' She said the words casually, after they had concluded their other discussions. But she could immediately notice the tension within him after she had said it.

165

'Of course.' He raised his arms outwards. 'How?'

She smiled. 'It might be more accurate if you remove some of your upper garments, like your jerkin, so I can measure you properly.'

He stared at her directly, but then without hesitation he stripped off the leather jerkin he was wearing over his shirt, and extended his arms again. She moved behind him, sliding her hands to either side of his ribs to pass the measuring tape in front of him, and then took the measurement of his chest. She then in turn measured his shoulder width, neck, and arm length.

She could hear him breathing, heavily, as she worked. She knew that he was as aware of her physical proximity as she was of his, and this time she needed no unusual slowing down of time to tell her that he wanted her.

She could also feel the lust building inside herself, a craving which had been pent-up now for months. She ached to find an outlet for this. She wanted him. Right there and then.

Without effort, invisible tendrils seemed to coalesce around her, and spiral slowly towards him, teasing at the edges of his mind. She knew that if she wanted this now, she could have him. Despite his intention to marry. Despite any other objections he might make. All it would require her to do was to allow these unseen tendrils to ease in and make their connection. Then to move back behind him again, slide her hands around him onto his chest, and put her mouth to his ear…

But she restrained herself.

Lana, what do you think you're doing? He's a customer and he's already told you that he's going to be married. Stop!

She shivered, and the tendrils dispersed harmlessly. She stepped away from the soldier.

'Do you work up at the castle, Captain?'

The question seemed to take him by surprise, as if he in turn had been expecting the moment when her hands and mouth would touch him, rather than hearing a mundane enquiry. 'Erm, yes, Lana. I'm Captain of the household guard at the Castle. I report to the Duke and Lord Gerrion, themselves.'

166

'That's impressive. Your wife-to-be must be proud. Is she very lovely?'

'Rhuanna? Lovely?' Thatcher frowned, as if remembering for the first time in several minutes that he had a fiancé. 'Oh yes, she is. Very lovely.' He then shook his head, as if trying to dispel something from his thoughts.

'That's wonderful, Captain. Well, I'll make sure that this jacket is the very finest for your wedding. Please come to collect it in two weeks' time.'

Thatcher left shortly afterwards, with nothing else having happened between them. However, that night Allana suffered even more torment as she lay in her own bed, thinking about the opportunity which she had chosen to forsake.

—

Allana was becoming closer to Nionia, with the passing of time. In the week after the encounter with Thatcher, Allana was even looking forward to the young woman's visit. She wanted to gossip with someone about the handsome soldier who had appeared in her home.

However, the other woman had her own news, this time. 'We got an exciting letter two days ago, Lana. If I tell you about it, will you promise to keep it a secret?'

'Of course. I promise.'

'It's an instruction by the head of the Guards in Sen Aiduel. They're looking for a murderess! Who they think fled overseas! They think she may be here, in Andar, and they've asked us to look for her.'

Allana's heart pounded as she heard this. Casually, she stood up and walked to the work counter at the end of the room. Her knife was laying there. 'A murderess?'

'Yes! She murdered a High Priest, apparently. The High Priest of Sen Aiduel! Can you believe it? And then fled. Apparently, they found him with his throat cut, in her apartment.'

Allana picked up the knife from the counter, slipping it into the pocket of her dress. She then moved to the other side of the room, back to the door. Softly, she closed it, shutting out the bustling noise from the street outside.

She told you that she's the only one of them who knows who you are, Lana. The only one who knows that you live here.

Allana walked back over to her visitor, standing by the side of Nionia's chair. Her hand slid into the pocket of her dress, and abruptly her fingers were clenched tightly around the knife handle.

'Who is she?' There was tension in her voice, as she asked the question.

'Some whore, apparently. Let me think... Seilana dei Monis! That was it. She was his lover. His mistress. Can you believe it? A High Priest with a lover! Such a scandal. I think the Church must have been trying to keep it quiet, because it happened months ago and they're only telling us now! But they think she must have escaped by sea. And we've eventually been told to keep an eye out for her, in case she travels to Septholme.'

'What does she look like?' Allana's grip on the knife eased slightly.

'She was in her mid-thirties, the letter said, and has a teenage daughter. The two of them escaped together. We're to catch them both, if we can.'

Allana finally released her grip on the knife, and she removed her hand from the dress pocket. 'I'm not aware of anyone in Septholme who sounds like that. Are you?'

'No. We're the only two women from Dei Magnus here in Septholme. And neither of us could possibly be that old, could we? Unless we look really good for our age! But anyway, it's very exciting, isn't it?'

Allana stared at the other woman.

She's a fool, Lana. Either that or she is wilfully blind to what should be obvious to her.

Finally, Allana replied, 'Yes. It's very exciting.' The knife rested at the bottom of her pocket, feeling heavy with the weight of guilt.

—

Later, after Nionia had left the apartment, Allana was sitting alone with her front door shut, and was reflecting upon what the other woman had said.

Whomever was pursuing Allana thought that her mother was still alive, and had committed the murder. As Allana considered this, she knew that such a conclusion could be possible. The removal of her mother's body from the apartment, and the subsequent burial in a pauper's grave, had been done with a minimum of fuss. Only Allana and a local priest had been at the burial service. And, for people of Seilana's status, no documents were kept to record the death.

Unless any investigators of the murder had spoken with the specific priest and unless that person had remembered the burial, they would have no clear idea that Seilana dei Monis was dead. But they would have been more likely to know that the High Priest had been on his way to visit Seilana, on that evening, because that is what dei Maranar himself had viewed as the purpose of the meeting. They had therefore concluded that dei Maranar had died by Seilana's hand, in her apartment.

Are you free then, Lana? Can you stop running?

With grim resolution, she considered that the answer to both of those questions was 'no'. Nionia, a member of Aiduel's Guards, knew that there was a Dei Magnun woman in Septholme right now, although she appeared blind to who Allana might actually be. And Allana now knew for certain that Ronis's killer was being hunted. And that the Guards had been set upon that hunt, albeit for the wrong target.

The only things keeping Allana safe, right now, were that Nionia

169

had made no connection between Allana and the two fugitives mentioned in the letter, and she was keeping Allana's existence secret from her associates. And in her eagerness to make herself a friend, Nionia's naive questioning of Allana had never been more than cursory.

However, all it would probably take would be for Nionia to casually mention the Dei Magnus woman she knew, a girl who had arrived in Septholme a few months earlier, and suddenly all of the Aiduel's Guards in Septholme would be descending upon Allana's home. Allana doubted that her cover story would stand up to even a few probing questions from a more hardened member of the Guards.

She therefore faced the choices again, of whether to stay or to run. And if she were to choose to run, where would she go? Aiduel's Guards might be in every major town, and therefore she might face the same problem again. She wanted to stay, wanted to continue on with the new life she was slowly building, but from now on each interaction with Nionia would only bring more danger.

And there had been a third choice, of course. Which was still available to her. One which she did not want to dwell upon, but which nonetheless kept infiltrating her thoughts. Of having picked up a knife. Of having gripped it. Of having been ready to use it?

No, Lana, you wouldn't have done that. You wouldn't! You killed Ronis in self-defence. Nionia is trying to be your friend, isn't she? She seems like a good person. You wouldn't have done that!

But as she sat in her home in the fading light of dusk, staring at the knife set out on the table in front of her, she was not entirely convinced about the truth of that. Her hand was shaking, in memory of how tightly she had been clutching the weapon, earlier.

She would need to act soon.

11

Arion

—

Year of Our Lord,
After Ascension, 767AA

Arion looked forward over the prow of the ship as he watched the city walls of Andarron edge closer.

Andarron was both the capital and the largest city within the country of Andar. It was the home of the ruling royal House of Pavil, and the mighty whitewashed stone walls which ran along its entire sea-facing front had long ago earned it the title of The White Fortress. The vessel carrying Arion, named *The Crescent's Wave*, was now sailing towards the gap in that imposing fortified wall, and entering the harbour.

The journey to Andarron by sea had taken six days, on a route which had principally hugged the coastline. *The Crescent's Wave* was primarily a trading vessel, but it also contained a number of cabins for passengers, and he had journeyed in relative comfort. He was travelling alone, and the voyage had allowed him plenty of time for both reflection and anticipation.

Much had happened since the fateful evening in the Great Hall. First, Delrin's departure from Septholme, and then his own parting from the family. Karienne had suffered a repeat of her tears as Arion had said his farewells on his final morning at Septholme Castle. The Duke, Charl Koss, and Gerrion had also come to bid him farewell, although with significantly less visible emotion in each case.

The Duke had used messenger pigeons to ensure that a number of arrangements were made in advance of Arion's arrival in Andarron. The Royal Academy of Knights had already been notified of his intended enrolment in the place of his brother. It was also arranged that retainers with horses were going to meet him at the harbour of Andarron, so that he could proceed with his onward journey to the Academy, without delay.

Tomorrow was scheduled to be the first day in a new year of training at the Academy. The Duke had highlighted that Prince Sendar Pavil, and a number of other high-ranking sons of the nobility, were also due to enrol. Arion was excited to meet all of them, which overcame his slight disappointment that he would not be able to spend any time to explore Andarron itself.

The Crescent's Wave now sailed into the imposing harbour of the city, drawing closer towards the docks. Arion recognised that it would only be a short time until the ship docked, and he returned to his cabin to finalise his equipment before disembarking.

—

The journey to the Academy from the docks, accompanied by a hired guide, took a couple of hours by horse. Arion caught fleeting images of the city of Andarron as he rode through it, although his overall perception was a negative one of bustle, noise and bad odours.

His first impression of the Academy, as he arrived there in the mid-afternoon, was even more underwhelming. It was located in the flat countryside outside of Andarron, its boundaries marked by a low stone wall. From the edge of the site there was a ride of perhaps ten minutes to get to the unremarkable grey stone buildings clustered in the centre, situated around a square, dusty yard.

The most notable sight upon arrival was that of a stocky individual, clothed in a thick leather jerkin, sitting at a table outside of one of the properties. In the absence of any other clear indication as to what he should do, Arion dismounted, and headed towards the seated man.

'Name?' said the individual, speaking in a gruff voice. The man had hard weather-beaten features which matched this voice. He was bald with a thick black beard, appearing short but extremely stout and heavily muscled.

'Arion Sepian, from the House of Sepian.'

'Arion Sepian, *sergeant*,' replied the man, sounding angry. 'I'm Sergeant Kallin. I'll be responsible for your cadet group this year. From the House of Sepian, eh? How very *important* you are. How very *special*. Now, listen carefully, Cadet Sepian. I couldn't give a flying fuck what House you're from. Once you're here you're a cadet, that's all, and the Academy owns you for the next twelve months. You're also the third person who's a member of a famous noble house to arrive in just the last half hour, so it's really not that special anyway, particularly not when we have a royal prince here. But, as I said to the others, including the prince, you'll end your addresses to me with the word sergeant, or you and I will have a problem. Understood?'

By the Lord! What a cheeky bastard, Arion thought, bristling in reaction. *Who does he think he is? Only the Duke has ever spoken to me like that.*

Kallin leaned forwards, his demeanour suggesting that he might actually want Arion to disagree, to give him reason to launch into another tirade. However, Arion had been reflecting on Gerrion's recent advice about controlling his temper, and he recognised that this was a moment for listening and agreeing. He replied with a muted, 'Yes, sergeant.'

'OK, Cadet Sepian. See that building there?' The sergeant pointed without waiting for a response. 'That's the Quartermaster's building, for provisions and equipment. Go there, tell them you're a new cadet and collect your gear. And that building there?' He pointed again, to another larger property. 'That's the mess hall. Dinner at sixth hour this evening. And that building there?' Another finger pointed in a different direction. 'Your lodgings. You're in room three, in the *special* room for the *special* nobility. But that's all the *special* treatment you'll get here, understand?'

'Yes, sergeant.'

'OK, get your gear, put it in your room, room three remember, then get to dinner later. And then muster here at eighth hour tomorrow morning, having already eaten, wearing the uniform you'll be given. Commander Roque will address you all then. Understood?'

'Yes, sergeant.'

'Oh, and one final thing. Get your stuff off of that horse and then tell your retainers to fuck off. We don't have *special* servants for the *special* nobility here. Understood?'

Arion breathed deeply, barely managing to suppress his anger. 'Yes, sergeant.'

———

As he later pushed his way through the door into his lodging room, Arion's arms were full of his possessions from Septholme, bundled together with the items which he had just collected from the quartermaster.

There were already two other men in the bedroom, youths of an equivalent age to Arion. One was handsome, tall, slender and blonde-haired, the other of average height with auburn hair and a thin beard.

The tall individual spoke first. 'Ah, so you must be either Arion Sepian or Jarrett Berun?' He extended his hand.

Arion placed down his various possessions and accepted the handshake. 'Arion. Arion Sepian.'

'Sendar Pavil,' replied the tall man, grinning. 'I would usually say *Prince* Sendar Pavil, but I've already been told several times by

174

our angry friend outside that I'm no longer *special* and *important*, so perhaps I'll drop that title from now on! Well met, Arion.'

Arion grinned back, then turned to shake the hand of the second individual, who looked equally welcoming.

'Lennion Rednar,' the man said, clasping Arion's hand with a strong grip. Arion recognised the name. The House of Rednar owned the lands to the west of the Sepian territory, and the relationship between the houses of Sepian and Rednar had always been friendly.

'Well met, both of you,' Arion stated. There were four beds in the room, two of which had already been claimed by Sendar and Lennion. He moved over to place his possessions on one of the two unclaimed beds. 'Ah, so this will be our home for the next year?'

'Yes,' replied Sendar. 'Quite the gathering of the noble houses in here. I think our friend the sergeant outside is a little upset because my father used his *influence* to insist my room-mates were to come from the leading houses, rather than mixing us in with the minor lordlings. But, you know, if we're to spend a year in the squalor of shared accommodation, better to do that in the company of our peers, don't you think?' Sendar smiled again, and Arion was rapidly forming a view that they were going to get on well together. 'And just in case you're in any doubt, please don't feel any need to address me as "Your Highness" or "Prince" whilst we're here. It will probably be good for my inflated ego to have a bit less grovelling towards me for a few months.'

'Don't worry,' quipped Lennion. 'Not grovelling comes quite easily to me.'

The three of them then exchanged idle chatter as a way of getting to know each other better, with a couple of hours to pass before sixth hour arrived. Arion felt comfortable in their collective company, with Sendar's quick wit putting him at ease and reminding him of Delrin.

They were soon interrupted by their fourth room-mate arriving. The man who came in, bearing an equivalent burden of possessions to that which Arion had carried earlier, was enormous.

175

The newcomer was at least two inches taller than Arion himself, but broader and heavier, and his youthful bearded face displayed a stern expression. Sendar Pavil reacted as he had done with Arion earlier, introducing himself first, and using an almost identical speech about temporarily dropping his titles.

'Jarrett Berun, heir to the House of Berun,' the large individual replied. He returned Pavil's handshake, but otherwise his demeanour did not change and no smile touched his features. Arion and Lennion then introduced themselves, in turn, with Jarrett's eyes narrowing as Arion stated his family name.

Following this, Jarrett looked around the room, noted the three claimed beds, and tutted to himself as he walked across to the final bed. 'Thanks for waiting for me before choosing the beds,' he stated, acerbically, before dropping his gear onto the mattress. 'And if that guy ever speaks to me like that outside of here, in my lands, I'll have him flogged in public.'

Arion glanced towards Sendar and Lennion, who both raised their eyebrows in response. The atmosphere in the room had become considerably cooler.

Arion was aware that the House of Berun controlled lands to the north-east of Andar. This territory included borderlands with Elannis, which were to the immediate north of the Canasar peninsular and the Sepian territory. However, in contrast to House Rednar, the relationship with House Berun was lukewarm at best. Duke Conran had once explained that this was as a result of the decision of Bannon Berun, who was Jarrett's father and the head of House Berun, to marry a member of the Elannis Imperial family. The Duke had made it clear that he did not trust Elannis or its royal family members, and he had shared this view openly and often. As a consequence, there had been little cordial contact between the houses of Sepian and Berun for over twenty years.

The room remained in silence for a few seconds, as Jarrett Berun rooted through one of his packs. He finally found what he was searching for, and extracted a small statue of The Lord Aiduel

On The Tree, placing it on the cabinet next to his bed. He looked at each of them, then, his face still solemn. 'I pray six times a day. Anyone who would like to join me in prayer is welcome to do so.' Without waiting for a reaction, he got down onto his knees at the side of his bed and started to pray, in silence.

In response to this, Arion again looked towards his companions, who remained silent. Their solemn expressions were a precise mirror of how he now felt.

—

The next morning, they were all gathered in the yard outside. There were sixty people in their cadet group in total, all of whom were residing in the same large dormitory building as Arion. They had met a number of the other cadets during the evening before, at dinner. Arion, Sendar and Lennion had naturally sat with each other at the evening meal, and their status had attracted a number of other cadets towards them. However, whether by accident or design, Jarrett had seated himself with another group.

Arion was now clothed in the equipment which he had been provided with the day before, wearing a grey tunic and trousers. All of the other cadets were attired in similar clothing, and in their uniformity they already looked like a military force, albeit a disorganised one. No one had been supplied with weapons.

'Cadets!' shouted Sergeant Kallin, silencing their chatter. 'Stand to attention and get yourselves in line. Commander Roque will now address you.'

The man standing with Kallin appeared to be in his early fifties in age. He was of average height, with grey hair and stubble, but his most distinctive feature was the patch over his left eye. He stepped forwards now, and began to speak.

'Cadets! Welcome to the Royal Academy of Knights. I am Commander Arnas Roque. I'm in charge here, and henceforth you'll address me as Commander, and only as Commander. For the next twelve months, you belong to this Academy, and to us. Irrespective of your background, you will obey our commands here, whether from me or Sergeant Kallin or any other officer or instructor. Fail to do that, and you'll be told to leave. Is that understood?'

'Yes, commander!' Sixty enthusiastic voices responded in unison.

Roque continued. 'You're all here because you want the skills which we can teach you. And if you complete the programme here, you'll be equipped with knowledge and abilities which most of your brethren do not have.

'Why then does this Academy exist? You may already know that we were created over fifty years ago, by royal decree, by King Cenneos. But why? For what purpose did our late King create this place? The answer to that question is that the Academy exists to equip you, as the future leaders of Andar's military, with the best practice techniques as to how to conduct warfare. Andar is a great country, and we've existed as an independent nation now for close to two hundred years. But, compared to Elannis and Dei Magnus, we are also a *small* country. Royal estimates suggest that Dei Magnus has one and a half times our population size, and Elannis is double that again. Think on that for a second. *If* we were to ever find ourselves at war with both of those countries at once, without allies, we might find ourselves facing resources and armies which could be five times the size of ours.

'How then can we best prepare ourselves to combat that? The answer is by being the very best at what we do, in matters of warfare. By pooling the knowledge of our finest generals and leaders, and then by sharing that knowledge with the next generation of leaders. Namely you. Every year, up to sixty new future military leaders of Andar are trained here, and are given the skills to become great commanders. The skills to effectively lead our armies, *if* this country ever needs it.

'You'll be trained here in four disciplines. Physical Training. Military Skills Training. Military Tactics. Military Strategy.

Sergeant Kallin and his team will lead the instruction in Physical Training and Military Skills Training. I will lead the instruction in Military Tactics and Military Strategy, assisted by my colleague Senalis Roque.' He gestured towards a woman standing a few metres behind him and Kallin. She appeared to be in her late-forties, with greying brown hair.

'Before I conclude, let me give you all a warning now. The next year will be hard. Likely the hardest year of your life, to date. I can say with certainty that not all of you will complete this course. Some of you will not have the necessary physical or mental toughness and will drop out. But *most* of you should have the resources and willpower to complete it. And at that time, we will award you with the title of Martial.

'And after completion, as you'll be aware, your time here will be followed by a ten month period of service in a royal military unit, to give you practical experience to follow the theory you'll learn here. Following that period of service, you'll be a free man again, free to return to your homes should you choose. And at that point you'll be entitled to describe yourself as a Knight of the Realm, an honour which less than fifteen hundred people in our country hold.

'I will handover to Sergeant Kallin shortly, but before that I'll make one final point. We have *zero* interest in status here. We don't care what rank or title you hold or held prior to coming here, you will be addressed as cadet and will be expected to address us appropriately. And no cadet will have any greater status than any other cadet.' He looked in the direction of Sendar Pavil as he said this last part. 'Is all of that understood?'

'Yes, commander!'

'Very well, in that case, welcome again, and I wish every one of you success in the trials you will face in the year ahead. And believe me, they *will* be trials.'

—

In the weeks and months that followed, as he was pushed to his physical and mental limits, Arion realised that in his time training at Septholme Castle, he had just been *playing* at being a soldier.

Now, he was being forced to acquire the skills and to develop the mental strength which he might one day need to lead the armies of House Sepian into battle. The overall cadet intake had been split into three sub-groups of twenty cadets each, and Arion's training group included all three of his room-mates. The training that they were undergoing was satisfying and productive, but it could not be described as enjoyable.

The early weeks contained a disproportionate amount of physical training, as Sergeant Kallin and two other hard ex-soldiers enforced a regimen of intensive training and exercise on the cadets.

For anyone who dared to question the worth of this, Kallin would growl in response, 'In a war, the army which marches fastest and furthest, which arrives the freshest, and which fights hardest for longest, will be the army which wins. Leaders must lead by example. They must be the fittest *and* the strongest.'

This physical training manifested itself in wake-up calls at fifth hour, followed by long runs in the early light of dawn. This was succeeded in turn by extensive drilling exercises, marching and manoeuvring as a group to various drum and bugle calls, in the morning heat. This was all mixed in with a number of strength and weight exercises, to physically develop all of the cadets.

Sendar and Lennion both acquitted themselves admirably in any physical challenges, being in the top half of their group in most activities. In what was a boost to Arion's confidence, he typically finished either first or second in most strength or speed challenges. The person who he invariably found himself battling with, for top spot, was Jarrett Berun.

For any distance running challenges, however, Arion was delighted to find that he had significantly better stamina than anyone else. The first time that his group was asked to race on foot from the central square of the site to the external gate and back again, he crossed the finish line a hundred metres ahead of anyone else. In second place, demonstrating impressive speed given his size, was Jarrett Berun.

To Arion's surprise, the giant youth did not acknowledge or congratulate Arion's victory as he finished. Instead, Jarrett appeared to be furious at himself, and he spat into the ground. The phlegm landed close to Arion's foot. Arion tried to ignore the minor insult, and to take satisfaction in another victory in a physical trial. However, Jarrett's rude conduct towards him was becoming increasingly troubling as time went on.

Lord preserve us! he thought, feeling annoyed. *Just what is his problem with me? And how many more times can I suffer his insults and cold behaviour, before needing to do something about it?*

—

In Military Tactics and Military Strategy lessons, it was Sendar Pavil who was the star of the class. By contrast, Arion was struggling to retain all of the information which was being taught to him.

Arnas and Senalis Roque were relentless teachers, both of them clearly expert in their subject matter. In the first lesson, they had detailed the expected syllabus.

Arnas Roque had spoken first. 'In Military Tactics, we will teach you best practice in battlefield formations. How to deploy your troops. How to use ground to best advantage. How to move and manoeuvre your troops. How to place and use reserves. How to communicate on the battlefield. To do this, we will draw on my personal experience as both a commander in the Island Wars, and as a rare survivor of the Second Crusade. We will also teach you the best practice shared with me by great living commanders of Andar, and will study the experiences of the great commanders of history. Senalis?'

Senalis Roque, who Arion had established was the Commander's wife, added, 'I have spent many years studying the texts of the Angallic Republic, and of the great battles since then, distilling those

181

actions and activities which separated the victors on the battlefield from the vanquished. We will study those matters together.'

Arnas Roque continued. 'And finally, in Military Tactics, we'll study siege warfare. How to successfully prosecute a siege, and how to defend against one. Then, alongside Military Tactics – how to win a battle, if you will – we will also study Military Strategy. If tactics teaches us how to win a battle, strategy teaches us how to win a war. Senalis?'

The female teacher spoke again. 'We will study the progress of some of the classical wars based on the ancient texts, including Aiduel's own conquests of the Holy Land and of the Angallic continent, and the later Wars of Secession. We will also study more recent wars, such as the First and Second Crusades, the Canasar War, and what we know about the invasions and conquering, by Elannis, of Sennam and Patran. Within this, we'll aim to teach you about grand strategy, resources, troop placement and movement, and logistics.'

Arion had felt the hairs on the back of his neck prickling up in excitement as he had heard all of this. However, he soon found out that the *idea* of learning about these subjects was more exciting than the dry reality of having to study hard to understand and master them. He also quickly determined that he was not one of the stronger students there.

By contrast, Sendar Pavil found the sessions in Military Tactics and Military Strategy to be easy. Arion was impressed from the first lessons onwards by just how clever the prince was, and how rapidly he picked up on new points. Whenever the Roques had stumped a series of members of the class with a tactical battlefield problem, they would invariably turn to the prince, who would have a workable solution readily to hand. After two weeks, the instructors had already started to refer to him as 'Genius'.

—

By the time that several weeks had passed in the Academy, Arion had become close friends with his room-mates, Sendar and Lennion. The three of them had clicked with each other from the outset, and had fallen into a pattern of relaxed banter and friendly competition. By contrast, Arion found that Jarrett Berun was an increasingly difficult individual to like or to tolerate.

Outside of their shared room, Jarrett appeared to gravitate towards other cadets who were as equally devout as him, spending a lot of time in the Academy chapel. Arion had no particular problem with this, although he viewed Jarrett's piety with the same sense of bemusement with which he had always regarded the religiously devout.

Arion felt less tolerant, however, in relation to the regular nasty comments Jarrett made to other cadets about his comparatively superior social status. Arion had noted that Jarrett was careful to only ever make these statements when out of earshot from the instructors.

When in their shared bedroom, Jarrett was typically either aloof or praying, or would make caustic remarks which would lead to uncomfortable silences for the rest of them. In particular, his rudeness towards Arion was increasing in frequency and vehemence. Arion was not sure whether the targeting of him was connected to the Duke's comments from long ago, or was a result of his success in physical activities, or something else. However, with the passing of time and an accumulation of such insults, Arion was beginning to despise the giant youth. And his temper was building.

This came to a head one day when the cadet group was going through a particularly punishing form of weight training. Sergeant Kallin had left the cadets, in the midday sun, with the challenge of lifting a set of rocks from one side of a field to the other. Kallin was watching them, with an amused expression, from a distance away.

The group embarked on the task with muted enthusiasm. As one of the two largest individuals there, Arion found himself tackling the larger rocks alongside Jarrett as others cleared smaller weights. Having transferred many of the boulders, when they started to reach the heaviest rocks it was clear that even the two of them would need help from others. Lennion came to assist Arion to pick up one large rock, and a minor noble named Roliss Sonder moved to help Jarrett with another.

'Get your hands off this, Sonder,' snarled Jarrett.

'What?' replied Sonder, sounding indignant. 'We need to get this finished.'

'Not you,' answered Jarrett. 'I'm not shifting rocks with some minor peasant. This waste-of-time exercise is already far enough beneath me, without having to labour with the likes of you.'

Arion had employed a lot of willpower to restrain himself from heated responses, in the preceding weeks. However, he could not contain his words this time. 'Don't be ridiculous, Jarrett,' he stated. 'Remember, we're all cadets, there's no status here. And we need to get this finished.'

'Shut up, Sepian!' snarled the Berun youth, causing all of the surrounding cadets to turn towards him. 'I've already had enough of your smart comments by now. Typical House of Sepian. Always got an opinion on everything.'

'What's that supposed to mean?' Arion placed down the rock that he and Lennion had been lifting, and turned to face the giant youth.

'You know what it means! Your father's a loudmouth irreligious arsehole, and it looks like it's all been passed on to you.'

The sensible part of Arion whispered that now was the time to cool the situation, and to follow Gerrion's advice. Instead, the heated side of his nature took control. He stepped forward, fists clenched. 'He may be an arsehole, but at least my father's trusted, because he knows how to marry into families which are loyal to the King and to Andar.'

'What do you mean, loyal? Don't you dare insult my parents!'

Berun's face was red with anger, and he stepped closer to Arion, such that they were now barely a foot away from each other. Arion found himself staring upwards at the bigger man, rage building inside.

Come on, you fucker. Make your move.

'Both of you, cease this, NOW!' The shout was from Sendar Pavil, and it carried an air of royal authority which meant that everyone paid attention. 'Kallin is already starting to take note of this. If it carries on he'll make us shift these rocks for a second time. Back off from each other, and finish this later! I'll help Jarrett with his fucking rock!'

He stepped between the two of them, physically defusing the situation. Neither Arion nor Berun said anything further, but Arion could see the giant youth staring at him, with hatred in his eyes.

—

That was the last exchange between the pair of them before they arrived at their first Military Skills Training lesson, later that day.

Sendar Pavil, exuding the same natural authority that he had displayed earlier, had taken Arion to one side after the incident in the field. 'Look, Arion,' the prince had said, 'I know he's been making comments for the last few weeks, but no good will come out of this if things get worse between you. He's a difficult character, we both know that, but let's try to give him the benefit of the doubt. Remember, he's probably not been around his peers like this before. I'm a second son, you're a third son. We've both grown up around brothers, and we're probably more familiar with having others with us at all hours. Jarrett's an only child, a bit of a rarity coming here as a first son, and he's destined to lead his house one day. This is probably a lot more difficult for him, particularly because of his religious piety. It does none of us any good for you to argue with him. Please, if I speak to him and try to broker it, will you try to make peace with him?'

Arion nodded his agreement, seeing the sense in the prince's words. 'You're right, Sendar. Only bad can come of this. With your help, I'll try to make peace with him when we return to the room, later.'

Sendar had smiled in response and had patted his arm, saying, 'Good man!'

Now, the group of twenty were seated whilst Sergeant Kallin stood in front of them, for the first Military Skills Training session.

185

'So, here we are, cadets!' he announced. 'I hope you all enjoyed shifting those rocks earlier?' He smiled at his own comment. 'Well, in the last eight weeks, we've shifted some of that puppy fat and weakness from you. Now, you're ready for skills and weapons training. In the next ten months, me and the other instructors will teach you how to fight with a variety of weapons, both on foot and from horseback. Sword and shield, mace, lance, axe, we'll teach you all of the nasty little tricks we've picked up from our combined fifty years of service in the military.

'Again, why do you need to learn this? Because, no matter what a great tactician or strategist you are, sometimes a leader has to lead from the front. Sometimes, when the men's courage or resolve or strength is faltering, they need to see their leader amongst them. Standing tall, still fighting. *Inspiring* them. You can only do that if you have the skill and technique to stay alive.

'You will all come here with different levels of weapon skills. We'll quickly evaluate that and will group you according to your level. But before we do any of that, your first session today will be fighting *without* weapons. Wrestling. I want to see how each of you fights one-on-one with an opponent. No weapons. No punching. I want to see you wrestle your opponent and put him to the ground, and pin him until he surrenders. For there'll be moments on a battlefield where you might face that, where you'll be in a true death struggle. Today, you'll fight raw. I want to see aggression, determination. Later, we'll teach you technique. Later, we'll give you weapons. But today is all about showing the willpower to overcome your opponent. OK, let me pair you all off.'

Arion's heart sank as he heard these last words, because he knew how this was going to end. Given their size advantage over the rest of the group, he felt certain that he and Jarrett would be paired together, without having had the opportunity to attempt to make peace. And as Kallin moved around the group, selecting pairs, Arion was soon proven right.

Kallin placed the bouts into order from smallest pairing to

largest, making the opponents for each fight sit at opposite sides of the square created for the contest. Arion was therefore seated opposite Jarrett Berun. His opponent stared at him continuously, with the same look of hatred in his eyes as earlier, and a confident, contemptuous smile on his mouth.

Many of the bouts were evenly matched, and they were all aggressive, the combatants spurred on by Kallin's curses and shouts. 'Aggression! Control! Impose your will on him!' Kallin repeatedly shouted words such as these as the bouts went on, and the spectating cadets in turn added their own cheers and calls.

Lennion Rednar showed a surprising level of aggression to win his contest, both fighters being warned about punching during their violent struggle. By contrast, Sendar Pavil, in the bout immediately before Arion's, was calmness personified. It was apparent to Arion that Sendar already knew a lot of unarmed fighting technique, because he easily tripped his bulkier opponent and then gripped him in a chokehold, holding him there until the other cadet surrendered. Kallin was effusive in his subsequent praise of the prince.

Then it was Arion's turn to fight. He stood up and entered the square, watching Jarrett Berun do the same thing. His opponent continued to smile, with arrogant self-assurance, although the smile did not reach his eyes. Arion was well built, but his adversary had two inches in height and probably a couple of stone in weight advantage over him. Arion would need to win by applying superior technique, but wrestling was not something he had ever learned while growing up.

I've got to win this! Stay controlled and beat him.

'Fight!' Kallin shouted the words.

Then Berun was up close to Arion, grappling him. Arion applied all of his strength to grapple the other man back in return, but felt a hand on his wrist and his arm being twisted. He resisted, pushing back, but then there was another movement of Jarrett's body and a forearm thrust up towards his neck. Arion realised grimly that while he did not have any wrestling experience, his adversary clearly did. He was outmatched.

Their strength seemed equal, but each time Arion managed to counter another of his opponent's moves, he felt Berun's arms and body twisting, making it increasingly difficult to block the next attack. Then Berun had somehow slipped his body behind Arion, and an arm locked around Arion's neck.

A whisper in Arion's ear. 'Don't insult my parents, you Sepian fuck.' The arm was gripping tighter. Arion reached up to try to release the hold, but it was iron tight. A knee pushed into the back of his leg and he found himself losing balance, falling face forwards to the ground, the arm still on his neck. Berun was now lying on the top of his back, legs wrapped around Arion's waist, arm still locked around his neck. Gripping ever tighter.

'Going to choke you, you weak Sepian fuck,' snarled Berun, as he sensed that the strength was leaving Arion's body.

Arion tried to push up and roll, without success, then again tried and failed to remove the grip on his neck. With every second, his energy and ability to resist was fading.

From the crowd, he could hear shouts of, 'Surrender!'

Mixed in with that were cries of, 'Stop!'

But some animal instinct within him told him to keep struggling, keep resisting, even though the humiliation of Berun's dominating victory was growing greater with every second. And the grip on his neck, ever stronger, choking him.

He sensed movement, someone moving towards them with a shout, at the same time that his final breath left him and blackness dawned.

12

Leanna

—

Year of Our Lord,
After Ascension, 767AA to 768AA

Leanna adjusted quickly to her new life as a neophyte within the Holy Church.

She had always been a person who responded well to structure and order, and her life within the College of Aiduel in Arlais was *extremely* structured and ordered.

She would be woken by the great bell of the College church ringing out fifth hour every morning, following which there would be thirty minutes of prayers. There were then two further prayer sessions during the daytime, before the day was concluded with a full holy service. This was conducted in the central church each evening, by the Senior Priest, at eighth hour.

Her religious study and priestly training lessons required six hours in total, each day. Her few remaining spare hours were used for meals and wash times, or for undertaking the various menial tasks assigned to the novices. By the time that she settled into bed each

189

night, at tenth hour, Leanna had ended the day feeling satisfied but tired.

The only break to the daily routine was on Seventh-Day, Holy Day, when there were no lessons. Instead, there was a full Holy Day service in the morning. She would still have to complete her work duties, but typically she would find herself with a few hours free on each Holy Day afternoon, the only time of the week when she had such freedom.

She was sleeping in a large dormitory building with the other neophytes and acolytes. The building was split into twenty cells, each room simple and austere with two beds, a wash basin and a long study desk with two chairs. There were twenty-eight other trainee priests or priestesses at the College when she started, and initially Leanna was placed into a room on her own.

In the first nights at the College, as she ended the day in her cell without anyone to talk to, she felt strong pangs of loneliness. She would not be allowed contact with the outside world for the first three months of her training, and she missed her parents. She took solace during this time in her prayers.

Lord Aiduel, please look after my parents and keep them safe and at peace, until I can see them again. And please ask them to forgive me.

—

After she had been at the College for three weeks, she was in her room following the afternoon fourth hour prayers, when she was interrupted.

Priestess Corenna was standing at the door. Corenna was one of four priests who were responsible at the College for the training of the novices. She was in her early fifties, with thinning grey hair and a plump, pear-shaped body.

'Neophyte Leanna, stand up straight, girl,' the Priestess demanded, sternly. She entered the room, and following behind her was someone who Leanna realised must be a newly-joined trainee.

190

'This is your new room-mate and fellow neophyte. Neophyte Amyss, meet Neophyte Leanna.'

The new girl was very petite, barely reaching above Leanna's shoulders in height, although Leanna knew that to have taken her Vows she would be at least eighteen years old. She was also very pretty, with high cheekbones, dark freckles, and thick red hair falling around her shoulders. Leanna smiled and greeted her warmly, and the girl returned the greeting, accompanied by a broad happy smile which displayed perfectly straight teeth.

'Very well. Leanna, I want you to look after her, and make sure she gets where she needs to get to whilst she's learning the daily routines.' Leanna nodded to confirm her understanding.

After the Priestess had left, she turned to the new girl. 'Hello. I'm Leanna, and I'm so very glad to finally have a room-mate.'

'Hi, I'm Amyss,' replied the girl. 'And I'm glad that I have someone to show me what to do. But I must admit, I'm feeling very nervous. I've never shared a room with anyone before.'

'No, me neither,' replied Leanna, smiling. 'Let's both learn how to do it at the same time, shall we? This bed here is yours.'

Amyss moved over to the bed, placing down her small bundle of possessions. 'Have you been here long, Leanna?'

'Oh, only three weeks. I'm hardly one of the experienced ones here. I was the last to start as a neophyte, before you.'

'Well, I'd still be really grateful if you can help me in my first few weeks.' Amyss laughed then, a high-pitched giggle which Leanna found to be infectious in nature. 'I was *so* nervous taking my Vows today. I forgot half the words, and the Senior Priest had to keep prompting me. I don't think my mum was very impressed.'

'Did you, really?' Leanna laughed in return. 'Did your mum watch you take the Vows?'

'Yes, my whole family travelled down from our estate to watch. Did your parents watch you?'

'No. There were… erm… reasons why I took my Vows on my own. No one watched me.'

191

Leanna was becoming embarrassed, and she was therefore grateful when Amyss did not question her about her response. Instead, the girl replied, 'Well, there were ten of my lot here. I could almost hear the steam escaping from my mum's ears every time I tripped over a word. I almost started giggling too, when my brother sneezed.'

Leanna laughed again, picturing the scene, so different to the quiet formality of her own Vows. 'Did you always want to become a Priestess, Amyss?'

'Oh, Lord, no!' exclaimed Amyss. 'But when you have five older brothers, and your mum is desperately devout, and the other five have all managed to avoid fulfilling her lifelong dream, well, somehow you find yourself being talked into it!'

Leanna frowned with uncertainty, feeling surprised by the girl cursing with The Lord's name. 'Really? You didn't want to come here?'

Amyss laughed once more. 'Don't worry, Leanna, I'm just teasing you. Yes, I've wanted to become a priestess for a number of years. And although my memory isn't that great, my faith is *very* strong. But Mum did a lot of coercing, too!'

Leanna grinned. 'Not fair! I'm way too trusting. Far too easy to tease.' She paused, wondering what else to say about herself and then deciding, for now, not to divulge her own story.

The two of them then chatted further, sharing more information about their backgrounds. Leanna found out that Amyss was the youngest child of a minor country lord, and had grown up on an estate in the countryside, fifty miles north of Arlais. This was her first ever visit to the city of Arlais itself, and everything seemed like an exciting adventure to her so far.

'It's not really meant to be fun, you know,' stated Leanna, eventually, trying to sound more serious. 'There's a lot of study and work to do, too.'

'Oh, shush now, Leanna! If we're room-mates for the next two years, I'm sure it will be a *lot* of fun.'

To some extent, Amyss was proven right in the following weeks. Leanna worked diligently to help the other girl settle into their daily and weekly routine of prayer and study. Amyss was also hard-working and focused during the times that she needed to be. However, at other times, if there was an opportunity to see the funny side in something, the country girl would take it.

In their room at night, as they chatted in the hour before sleep, Amyss could often reduce herself to fits of giggles with observations on the priests and other trainees around them. She had given Priestess Corenna the alternative name of 'Dumpy', and she regularly made jokes about the poor sight of a very old teacher, Priest Parmer. Leanna initially felt that she should be admonishing Amyss for the slight cruelty in her jokes, but then she found herself laughing in turn, and any subsequent reprimand would seem half-hearted.

Leanna had never really had a single best friend in her life, but after a month of sharing the simple cell room with Amyss, she realised that she now had one. The two of them had grown close very quickly, and Leanna was thankful that Amyss was there to share the experience of the College with her.

After several weeks had passed, they were both lying in their respective beds one evening, waiting for tenth hour bells to be rung before extinguishing their candles. Leanna chose that moment to open up to the other girl about what had happened to her prior to her Vows. 'I was very close to getting married, you know, Amyss.'

'Were you?' asked the other girl, excitement in her voice. 'Wow, Lea! You sure know how to keep a secret, don't you?'

'I was just a little embarrassed to tell you. Please don't tell anyone else, here.'

'What happened? I can't imagine you deciding to marry a man. You seem so, well, devout. So committed to this life.'

Leanna was not going to mention the vision. 'I *am* committed

193

to this life. But for a while I thought I was meant to marry, and my parents wanted me to. But instead I finally decided I had a religious calling, so I didn't go through with the wedding, and came here, instead. I caused great upset for my parents and a lot of other people, though, and I'm still a little ashamed about it.'

There was silence for a few seconds.

'Well, I'm glad you did decide to come here,' said Amyss, finally, her voice sounding serious for once. 'And thank you for sharing that with me, Lea. And don't worry, I wouldn't ever tell anyone.'

Lord Aiduel, Leanna thought, feeling happy. *Thank you for blessing me with the gift of my friend, and of her friendship.*

—

In the first three months, their priestly studies were comprised of three main elements. The first was learning the roles and activities of a priest or priestess, and memorising all of the sacraments and rituals which an ordained priest would need to undertake. These activities were familiar to Leanna from the many religious services she had attended in her life, but it was nonetheless very different to have to learn the processes in every ceremony by rote, under the tuition of the stern Priestess Corenna.

The other two parts of the religious study, which for Leanna were more interesting, were the study of theology, and the study of religious history. Theology was something which she found to be intellectually stimulating. In that subject, they considered the nature of The Lord Aiduel and of heaven, and studied the Holy Book and the discourses of The Lord, discussing and deciphering His Meaning from the words He had left behind.

Sometimes, she found herself wanting to speak up about her vision, to get the scholarly Priest Parmer's interpretation about what it had meant. However, she always abided by her vow to Senior Priestess Maris of the School of Saint Amena, and she did not ever disclose her secret.

Most of all, however, she found the study of religious history to be fascinating. And the study of religious history was the story of The Lord Aiduel. She had been taught much about the events of His life before, in the classes of the School of Saint Amena, but never with as much depth and detail as she was learning now.

The first class with Priest Parmer, as he had introduced the subject, had filled her with excitement. The elderly priest had stood at the front of the class, and had squinted as he began to speak in a croaking, crackly voice to the twelve neophytes seated in front of him.

'The story of The Lord Aiduel *is* the history of religion. Before The Lord, we were all ignorant; heathens, pagans, infidels. He came and He shone a light upon us, upon our souls, and He laid open the pathway to heaven and to eternal salvation.

'But He was not born a god amongst men. As we all know, he was born a slave. What, then, is His story? How did Our Lord go from being a slave in the Holy Land, an apparently insignificant and expendable nobody within the cruel Angallic Empire, to ruling and shining a light upon an entire world?

'That is the story which we'll examine in this class. Which we will examine in greater detail than you have ever done before. And by knowing His story, His suffering, we *will* understand the proper history of religion, and we will be able to understand and interpret His teachings that much more clearly.'

Lord Aiduel, Leanna had thought, reverentially, upon hearing this, *please grant me the knowledge and wisdom to fully understand your teachings.*

—

In the early months of the College, however, Leanna was also haunted by troubling dreams.

She would wake in the night, crying out, her bedsheets kicked away from her. Initially, she was left with unconnected flashes of images from her dream, and nothing else.

Ascending a mountain path. Witnessing the Gate. Facing a decision. But what decision?

The meaning remained elusive.

After this had happened a handful of times, she awoke one night to find Amyss sitting on her bed, holding her hand.

'Lea, are you OK?'

Leanna's heart was thumping, hard. 'I… don't know. I think so.'

Amyss's features were barely discernible in the dim light. 'Your body was shaking. Like you were having a fit. It scared me.'

'Just a bad dream.' Memories of how she had been found in a similar condition, following her vision at the School of Saint Amena, returned to Leanna. She felt certain that the dreams were somehow connected to that. She could feel the perspiration collecting on her forehead.

'It's been happening more and more, Lea,' added Amyss. 'You looked so troubled. You were saying things, too.'

'Saying what?'

'I couldn't hear everything. But it sounded like you were protesting, like "Don't! Stop!" Things like that. Except that you sobbed it. You were sobbing. Crying the words.'

As Amyss said this, Leanna felt deeply unsettled, as if someone had grabbed hold of her heart and had squeezed it, hard. 'Please don't tell anyone, Amyss. Please. But… these dreams… they're scaring me, a little.'

Amyss did not respond with words, but instead she lay down on the mattress beside Leanna, resting her head down onto Leanna's chest. She then pulled up the blanket, covering them both.

'Don't be scared, Lea. I'm with you, now.' She hugged Leanna.

Leanna relaxed and fell gently back to sleep, with Amyss sleeping in her arms, and there were no more dreams that night.

—

After three months of her time in the College had passed, Leanna was allowed to receive her first visitors. On the next Seventh-Day, after a Holy Service in the main church at the centre of the College complex, she emerged through the church entrance to find her parents waiting there for her.

Leanna was wearing her formal neophyte gown for the service, and her mother's gaze traced up and down, taking in the new form of dress. The older woman's top lip trembled, and tears were welling in her eyes. 'Oh, Leanna, look at you.'

Leanna stared at them both. Her mother was close to weeping, her father was looking worried and sad, and Leanna was also abruptly on the edge of tears. 'Oh, Mum, Dad, I'm so sorry for what I did.'

Then the three of them were in an embrace, sharing whispered words and tears, as Leanna apologised and her parents forgave her. Within minutes, Leanna's world felt whole again. The shadows which had resided in her mind, caused by her deception and betrayal, were dispelled by the sincerity of her parents' forgiveness.

The three of them spent that afternoon walking around the College complex. Later, they were seated on a bench, when Leanna drew the conversation towards the final component of her guilt.

'And how is Lohan, Mum?' she asked.

'He is… not so good, Leanna,' replied her mother. 'What you did hurt him very deeply, maybe more than you can know. He doesn't understand why you left things so close to the wedding. Why you didn't speak to him. Why you rejected him. Maybe in time it will pass, but sadly I think he still feels very bitter towards you, for what you did.'

Leanna paled. 'I still feel ashamed about what I did, Mum. But you know *why* I did it. I truly believe now that the vision was calling me to this life. And that I've made the right decision, by coming here. But I made an oath that I wouldn't tell anyone other than the two of you about the vision, so I can never really tell Lohan the truth about what happened.'

'That's a shame,' replied Elisa. 'We've never told him, but it might have put his mind at ease, if he'd at least known that.'

In the remainder of the afternoon, Leanna showed her room to her parents and introduced them to Amyss. At the end of the day, they said their goodbyes, and her parents left her with a promise that they would visit every month. After they had departed, Leanna returned to her bedroom and sat on the edge of her bed, reflecting on their reconciliation.

Lord Aiduel, thank you so much for restoring my parents to me, and for shining the light of forgiveness into their hearts. Thank you so much.

She then started to weep, shedding tears which were equal parts the result of both happiness and relief. Amyss came to her and put an arm around her shoulder, while Leanna sobbed with embarrassment. And after that, the world seemed like a better place again.

—

As the weeks went by, Leanna increasingly embraced the peace and goodness at the College. Having had much of the unhappy burden of her secretive flight from the wedding lifted by her parents' visit, she began to more fully appreciate how lucky she was to be there. How blessed she was to be a neophyte, living and praying amongst people who were so committed to serving The Lord, in both their words and their deeds.

Gradually, she could also perceive more clearly how important Senior Priest Comrel was to the successful functioning of the College. Although she had only limited contact with him, and he did not teach any of the neophytes or acolytes directly, he was a clear beacon of calm and kindness.

The evening services he conducted, at eighth hour, were always warm and inspiring. Leanna would listen with admiration as he taught the words from the Holy Book, mixing the sermons in with real life examples of respect, piety, peace and love. She was determined to memorise his approach to services as she went through the year, trying to ensure that she captured his stirring words such that she could utilise them herself in future.

And it was clear from the way that Comrel interacted with the priests and trainees around him, that he lived by the values which he preached. The respect and fondness with which he was regarded by the other priests was very apparent to Leanna. She could see that he maintained strong authority, but never raised his voice in an unkind way to anyone around him.

Lord Aiduel, please let me learn from and become like the good people around me, like Senior Priest Comrel.

Another person who Leanna had limited contact with at first, but whom she began to admire from a distance, was an older lady named Sister Colissa. The Sister was a priestess who had joined the Order of Saint Helena, a religious order dedicated to the arts of healing. Colissa was in charge of the small hospital within the College grounds, and was also its apothecary.

Colissa was in her late-forties, with a kind round face and long black hair. After four months in the College, Leanna had free time one day and decided to enter the hospital, to introduce herself. Sister Colissa looked up as Leanna entered. 'Yes, child, can I help you?'

'Hello, Sister, I'm Neophyte Leanna of Arlais. If it's convenient to you, Sister, I'd be keen to learn more about what you do here.'

'I'm happy to tell you more, child,' replied the Sister. 'And right now is a good time for me. But first, child, tell me, what do you already know about The Order of Saint Helena?'

'Not a great deal, Sister. Only that the Order is dedicated to healing? And runs hospitals and other healing places on behalf of the Holy Church?'

'That's correct, child. But if you'd like to understand what we do here, let me tell you a little more first. Do you know anything about Saint Helena herself?'

'No, Sister.'

'Well, our blessed Helena was born over seven hundred years ago, daughter to a powerful senator within the Republic. And she became obsessed about the appalling quality of healing provisions across Angall. Helena then devoted her life, using her father's power and influence, to encouraging the Holy Church to take on the task of delivering healing to all of the faithful.

'Before she died, the Church had agreed to support some of those from within the priestly order to become healers, and to retain and share that knowledge. She also succeeded in getting the Holy Church to agree to support a hospital and apothecary in all Colleges of Aiduel across the continent, and in all major cities. That is how The Order of St Helena was born, from one woman's persistence and devotion, and now we have hundreds of ordained priests across the continent who can spread Aiduel's word, hand-in-hand with the gift of His healing. Our Saint Helena was a truly marvellous woman.'

'That all sounds wonderful, Sister,' Leanna replied. Leanna could see the attraction of a life such as Sister Colissa's. 'How very wonderful, to be able to devote one's life to the service of The Lord, but also to do such practical as well as spiritual good for people, too.'

'Very true, child. That's why I joined The Order. May I ask, then, might you be interested in learning the healing arts, and in our Order?'

'Yes, I am interested,' replied Leanna.

'If that is the case, once you've been here for six months, you may choose a special area of study, for two afternoons a week. I have a number of novices who devote some of their time to helping in the hospital, child, and I hope I might be able to add you to that number. That will help you to find out more about what we do, and to decide whether the art of healing is for you.'

Leanna smiled. 'Thank you, Sister. I think I would like that.'

—

A couple of weeks later, Lohan came to visit her, late on a Seventh-Day afternoon.

When she first caught sight of him, the two of them were a handful of paces away from each other. She froze in place, and he also made no movement towards her.

'Leanna,' he uttered, a rigid formality in his voice. Indeed, his whole body pose was stiff and ill-at-ease.

'Lohan.' It was difficult to find the right words. 'Hello.'

He paused, staring at her face, and she could see the hurt in his blue eyes. 'Leanna. You're looking well.'

She moved a step closer to him. 'Thank you for coming, Lohan. There's so much I've wanted to say to you-'

'I've come to say goodbye, Leanna,' he interrupted, his voice cold. 'I'm getting married. I've come to say goodbye. I thought I owed you that much, at least.' The rebuke contained within his words was evident.

'Married? Who to?'

'Melissa. As you know, she's always had feelings for me. And I realise now that I... share those feelings.'

Melissa had been a girl in Lohan's year at the School of Saint Amena. Leanna knew very well that Melissa had been smitten with Lohan for a number of years, but he had never returned her interest.

'That is... happy news, Lohan. Congratulations.' There was silence between the two of them then, before she continued. 'Lohan, you must know how sorry I am. For what I did. So sorry for the hurt I must have caused you.'

He shrugged, his expression grim. 'I'm sure you are. But I guess it was for the best. I'm going to end up with someone who actually loves me more than they love The Lord and themselves. Someone who isn't full of lies and deceit.'

The words stung her, as did the bitterness in his voice. She added quietly, 'But I am sorry.'

He did not speak for a few seconds, and the silence was awkward. Finally, with sorrow in his voice, he said, 'I'm going to go now, Lea. And I think this *will* be the last time that we see each other. But please, just answer me this. Even if you have this *calling*, to come here, why leave it so late to dump me? And why humiliate me by leaving on our wedding day, by not telling me?'

The vision, she wanted to answer, but she knew she could not.

'I had a good reason, Lohan. But, please forgive me, I can't tell you. I didn't want to hurt you, and certainly not humiliate you. You're someone I love, someone I'll always love. Please forgive me.'

He stared at her again, and though his mouth was set in a hard line, she could see moisture in his eyes. 'Please know that I've tried not to be angry, not to be bitter, about what you did. But it's impossible. You broke my heart, Lea. Reached in and ripped it out. I'll never forgive you.'

As he said that, Leanna felt a cold heaviness in her own heart, and suddenly three words emerged into her mind, arriving song-like. Three words which had lapsed from her memory.

DEVOTION. SACRIFICE. SALVATION.

And upon hearing those words, Leanna experienced an abnormal sensation within herself. A feeling like a ripple passing over her and through her. Touching and caressing her senses, her mind. A wave of emotion. A wave which seemed to be emanating from Lohan, raw and uncensored by word or thought.

LOVE. HURT. LOVE. HATE. LOVE.

Lord Aiduel, what is that? How can I feel that?

Then Lohan turned his back on her, and he walked away. Part of her wanted to follow him, but she was shaken by the ripples of emotion which were still flowing through her. Instead, she simply stood there, feeling numb, watching him leave.

He disappeared from view, and with his departure the flow of emotion ceased, and she immediately began to doubt her own recollection.

Lord Aiduel, what just happened? Was it even real, Lord, or did I imagine it?

—

In the wake of Lohan's visit, the dreams began to more vividly torment her.

One night, when Leanna awoke from another dream, shaking,

she found that Amyss was already there, in her bed. The smaller girl's arms were around her, with her head resting on Leanna's chest.

'Amyss…' Leanna's heart was pounding.

'Shhhhh… you're safe, Lea. The dreams can't hurt you, while I'm here.' Amyss lifted her head and planted a soft kiss onto Leanna's cheek. 'Go to sleep, now.'

And Leanna did, falling quickly and securely into a dreamless sleep.

But in the half-trance moments before full slumber descended, as she lay there with her eyes closed, somewhere deep within she felt that she could sense Amyss's soul, strangely akin to an almost tangible presence around her. Embracing her. Guarding her. Loving her.

—

In the weeks that followed, religious history lessons with Priest Parmer continued to be her favourite morning of the week.

Today, they had been discussing the early parts of The Lord Aiduel's life, and his epiphany in the desert of the Holy Lands. Parmer was concluding his narrative. 'And therefore, after finishing His twenty days and twenty nights on the plateau, The Lord descended back down to the desert. Only now, we know that He had become more than a man. We know this to be true, because it was all recorded in the Book of Josia. Of *Saint* Josia, who travelled with The Lord from the Holy Land to Angall.'

'And the plateau, Priest Parmer,' asked another neophyte. 'That was the place which He later returned to, where He built the city of Aiduel's Gate?'

'Yes, correct, it was,' replied the priest. 'But that is much later in His story, almost at the end. Not for discussion today, child.'

A question then occurred to Leanna, a question driven by her dreams. 'Father, why is the Holy City called Aiduel's Gate? Is there an actual gate there?'

'Now, we are truly veering off at a tangent, child,' replied the priest, smiling benevolently. 'No, there is no recording in any book which refers to Aiduel having built a gate in His Holy City. It is simply a metaphor, child. The name refers to the epiphany Our Lord had during the twenty days, in the place where the Holy City was later built. The "Gate" refers to the awareness of Heaven which he gained there, the spiritual enlightenment which came upon him there. He passed from ignorance to enlightenment, from mortality to godhood. The "Gate" metaphorically refers to His travelling along and through a spiritual pathway from what He was before, to what He became.'

Leanna nodded. His explanation sounded plausible. But still, in her mind, she could see a memory from her dreams of a shining ethereal Gate, a place of boundless awe-inspiring beauty. However, she did not want to share this thought with the class, and as such she said nothing further.

Lord Aiduel, what is this Gate, which haunts my dreams? And why, Lord, are you showing it to me over and over?

—

The days continued to pass in Leanna's fulfilling life as a neophyte, and it was approaching six months since she had taken her Vows of Submission.

A couple of days before that date, Senior Priest Comrel summoned all of the priests and novices to the central church building, to make an announcement.

'My children,' he stated, as he addressed them outside of the formalities of a church service. 'There is going to be a major development, a change, to our life here at the College. I want to be the first to announce it to you all, lest rumours start to come from other sources. Our venerable High Priest of Arlais, Comenis, only found this out yesterday, and he has shared the news with me today, with permission that I may also share it with you.

'His Eminence the Archlaw has, in his great wisdom, judged that the threat of heresy is growing in our land, and across Angall. As a result of that, he has agreed with our beloved Emperor Jarrius that action must be taken to stop this perceived threat. In their great wisdom, they have agreed that the presence of Aiduel's Guards in our mighty empire is going to increase significantly.'

Leanna looked across at Amyss, who smiled back. Amyss seemed unfazed by Comrel's news, but Leanna felt a shiver of fear, in remembrance of her conversation with Senior Priestess Maris.

Comrel continued. 'It has been further agreed that a garrison of Aiduel's Guards will be stationed here, in Arlais. Their fortress is to be built on the open field to the north of this College. The construction work will be starting very shortly.

'We will therefore soon be seeing a large influx of the holy brethren of Aiduel's Guards, to join us in Arlais. They will no doubt become regular visitors to and fellow faithful at this College. Indeed, I've been informed that a number of their soldiers will be staying in our buildings, whilst their own barracks are being built.

'I would ask you all to welcome them with all of the charity, warmth and hospitality which we would always retain for each other, and for every true believer within the faithful. Thank you all in advance for your support with this. And may you go in the Grace of Aiduel.'

Leanna was unsettled by the announcement. This College had felt like a tranquil haven to her in the last six months, as indeed had the city of Arlais throughout her life growing up there. A haven that might now be disrupted by these new arrivals.

And, despite his seemingly positive words, she sensed that Comrel himself was not enamoured by the announcement he had made.

Lord Aiduel, she thought, as she sat there contemplating the implications of Comrel's announcement. *I am a true believer. I am no heretic. Why then am I scared by this news?*

13

Corin

—

Year of Our Lord,
After Ascension, 768AA

The snowfall marked the beginning of an arduous time for Corin and Agbeth.

That first night, after the snowflakes had started to descend thick and fast, they both struggled to sleep. Corin had felt great disquiet after hearing the chilling calls of the unknown creature, and he had lain there wide awake, staring at the walls of their shelter. Finally, he had roused himself from their covers, had built up the fire again, and then had tried to shake the wooden structure of the lean-to, testing its sturdiness. Eventually, Agbeth had encouraged him to return to bed.

But after he had slid back under the covers, it was still impossible to sleep.

Agbeth broke the silence. 'You think it's a felrin, don't you?'

'Yes. It could be.'

'What would that mean for us?'

'Danger. Great danger. You know the stories, as well as I do, Agbeth.'

'Yes, but I've never known for sure whether they were true? Or if they were just that. Stories.'

'That… noise… sounded like something real.' Corin was suddenly scared that the tales told in their village could actually contain the truth. If the stories were indeed true, he had placed the two of them into terrible peril by coming here. The rational side to him had always imagined that felrin were just a made-up monster, intended to scare children. In making the decision to bring Agbeth to this remote place, he had genuinely not expected to encounter one. But the terrifying call they had listened to had rocked this belief to its core.

The stories recited by the Karn elders had talked about deadly creatures which sometimes fought for and sometimes fought against the Gods. Beasts which were eight feet tall, and which walked upright, like a man. The felrin were reputed to be covered in fur, with long jaws full of razor-sharp teeth, and claws on hands and feet which could effortlessly disembowel a man. A monster which, if such descriptions could possibly be true, would make even a warrior like Borrik look puny in comparison.

'You think it might come here?' Agbeth sounded frightened, too.

'It's possible.'

'What should we do then? Can we protect ourselves? Should we leave?'

Corin paused, collecting his thoughts before answering. 'We can't leave. Not now, not in winter, when the snowfalls have just come in. We'll freeze, or starve, and we've nowhere else to go.'

'So, we protect ourselves, then?'

'Yes, we'll have to work out how to protect ourselves.' But as he lay there, thinking, he was coming to only one conclusion. If it really was a felrin which had been making that noise, and if the legends about the monster were true, then the only protection that he could think of was to avoid it. To stay in this area and to hope it did not come here.

But then the image came into his mind of their predecessor in this place. An image of a scattering of human bones within a bush, close to their shelter. Bones which had been scattered in a manner that suggested an attack by a ferocious wild animal.

And a head which had been ripped off from its body.

—

The next day, they emerged into a world covered in a blanket of white. The small area within their cave had remained free from snow, but otherwise all of their surroundings were coated with a thick layer of whiteness.

The temperature had dropped again, and the ice on their lake had extended even further towards the centre. In the preceding months, Agbeth had used furs to make them both an extra layer of outer garment. However, this only served to make the chilly weather bearable, rather than comfortable. Indeed, it soon became apparent that Agbeth was suffering from the cold worse than Corin was, her teeth chattering uncontrollably whenever she moved away from the fire.

For a number of days after first hearing the blood-curdling calls of the unknown creature, Corin could not find the resolve to leave their camp to go hunting. He was scared for himself, but even more so for Agbeth. Whatever he did now, whatever choices they made, his foremost consideration was going to be about how to keep his wife safe.

He therefore stayed within range of Agbeth, axe and bow always close to hand. But even when he was in camp, he felt constantly on edge, scanning the trees and rocks around them for any ominous movements, any rustle which could signify the stalking approach of a predator.

Whilst staying there, he spent his time fishing on those patches of the lake which were still unfrozen. This was dangerous work, with an ever-present risk of a crack of ice casting him into the icy water.

He also set snares in the treeline on the edge of the lake, although without any success.

They had decided together to reduce the amount of food that they were eating, to preserve their supplies, and within days both of them had aching stomachs and thinner faces and limbs. Corin tried on a number of occasions to slip a slightly larger portion of dried meat towards Agbeth, but she identified his ruse every time and insisted that they both ate the exact same amount.

The cries of the unknown creature were repeated each night, interrupting their attempts to sleep, and then haunting their thoughts thereafter. Corin was cursing himself for not having built some form of palisade wall around their cave entrance, while the ground had still been soft. However, the surface was too hard and frozen to attempt to dig into it, now. The best that he could do was to reinforce the walls of their lean-to, and he also constructed a sturdier frame at the entrance to the shelter. That way, the two of them at least had some reassurance that it would be difficult for a beast to break unexpectedly into their home, once they were inside it.

At night-time, when they were on their bedrolls with all of their clothes still on, huddled together under their furs with the fire blazing outside, they could finally get some relief from the bone-chilling cold.

And each night, despite the rigours of the hard day, he would whisper, 'I love you, Agbeth.'

'And I love you, Corin,' she would reply.

—

After six days in the wintery conditions, Agbeth developed a fever. Her cheeks and forehead were flushed with heat, but she was shivering constantly, and struggling to get warm.

She needed no encouragement to retreat to under the furs in their shelter, and he built up a second fire beside the lean-to, in addition to the usual one close by the entrance.

She called out to him, and he moved inside to lean over her.

'Corin?'

'Yes?'

'You need to go out and hunt. We need food.'

'I can't leave you here. Not with that… creature, somewhere close.'

'You *have* to leave me here. We'll starve, if you don't.' Her eyes were bloodshot, and her mouth looked dry.

He knew she was correct. 'Just one more day. I'll stay with you today, then hunt tomorrow.'

'Corin, we need food today. Do whatever makes you feel better about leaving me. Block the entrance. Raise the fire outside. But we – I – need you to find food for us.'

He was tormented by the choice that he had to make. He was terrified of leaving her, in this state. But she was right. If he did not find some food soon, he might be too weak to hunt at a later time.

'OK. OK then. I'll go and hunt. But I *will* raise the fire. And I'll block the entrance. And you must promise me that you'll stay in here, stay inside, and try to keep warm.'

'I promise. I'm too weak to do anything else, anyway.'

'And if… anything… does come, you scream for me as loud as you can. I'll stay within a few hundred metres, if possible.'

'I promise. And Corin?'

'Yes?'

'You keep safe, too.'

He kissed her on the forehead, then left the shelter, doing what he could to block the entrance, before he departed to go hunting.

—

He had forced himself to move a few hundred metres away from their home, bow in hand, when he saw the fresh tracks in the snow. There had been no new snowfall today, and the crust of whiteness which had carpeted the forest left a crisp imprint of anything which had walked across it.

He did not want to travel any further away from Agbeth, since at his current distance he would be able to hear her calling for him. However, the prints looked like they could belong to a large cloven-hooved animal. Possibly a deer. And they were moving away from the shelter. Moving in the general direction towards where the unknown creature's night-time calls seemed to originate.

He looked at the prints again, then back towards their camp, agonising. If he followed the tracks, he might not be able to hear Agbeth if she called for him. However, they needed food, desperately, and the skins a deer could provide would also be very useful right now. And how many more times would he have such an opportunity as was presented by these tracks in the snow?

He grimaced, his teeth gritted, then before he could change his mind he moved to follow in the direction of the tracks. He walked at a steady pace, crouching with bow in hand, very aware of the crunch of his light footsteps upon the snow. His eyes were flashing in every direction as he walked, searching both for his prey and for sign of anything which could be a predator to him.

This was the furthest that he had been from the shelter since he had first heard the chilling calls of the unknown beast, and he was constantly on edge. More than once, he glanced upwards to the tree branches high over him, feeling concerned that something was lurking above him. Watching him. Ready to pounce.

Finally, he mounted a small rise in the forest floor, and there before him, standing proud and magnificent within a forest clearing, was his prey. He crouched low, keeping most of his body below the ridge line, staying out of view of the animal. Feeling excitement. It was a large stag, and this was a perfect opportunity to kill it. He was downwind of it, and the trees behind him would make him difficult to see as he stood to take aim with his bow.

He took in a deep breath to try to stay calm. A deer like this could support him and Agbeth for weeks. He could not afford to lose this chance.

He nocked an arrow onto his bowstring, then eased himself

upwards. Slowly, very slowly. Concentrating on the deer, looking down the arrow to sight his shot towards its neck. Breathing deeply, focusing. Attention locked onto the animal.

FEAR. CONTROL. ORDER.

The words sighed into his thoughts, and a bizarre sensation gripped him. As he placed all of his focus and concentration onto the deer, it was as if he could suddenly *feel* the animal. Feel it as something alive, akin to how he had sometimes sensed that the whole forest around him was vibrant and teeming with life. He could sense the stag's beating life-force, could hear the blood pounding through its body.

He remembered having had a feeling like this once before, the first time he had killed a rabbit within the Great Forest. But this was different; more powerful, linked to a more majestic and intelligent creature. He stayed his hand for a few moments, and did not release the arrow. It would seem to be such a simple thing, to reach out slowly with his mind, to send out sinuous and invisible tendrils towards the deer, and to-

Then a screech shattered his reverie, and another, much larger form was barrelling across the clearing towards the stag. Before the animal which Corin had been hunting had time to react, this other form was upon it, in a whirlwind of slashing claws and ravaging red maw. The deer was crippled instantly, and Corin could feel its agony immediately within himself, fed outwards to him along this strange new connection with his mind.

He had only a moment to capture the image of gruesome massacre playing out in front of him – *Felrin!* – before his own survival instinct kicked in and he dropped to the floor. He pressed himself to the ground, hidden behind the shallow ridge, and listened to the death cries of the deer as it was eviscerated by this newly arrived attacker.

After that, Corin could not see anything. He was frozen with terror, not contemplating raising his head over the ridge to witness the scene of death before him, nor having the courage to force himself to stand and run. Instead, he pressed himself into the snow, trying not to whimper, as he heard the last squeals of the deer's life mixed in with a snarling, voracious feeding sound.

Corin could somehow sense the very moment when the last vestiges of life ebbed out of the deer, as if there had been a severing of the strange link which had connected him to the slaughtered animal.

And at that moment, he felt that he could sense something else too, something *other*, which was newly connected to his mind. Something different, more intelligent. Something feral, hungry, beastly. The creature. And as if in response to him making this connection, the monster suddenly howled out its long terrifying screech from the floor of the forest clearing.

Celebrating its kill, and screaming out its own dominance of these woods.

Corin buried his head under his hands and lay there for an extended duration of time. He was paralysed with fear, pressed full-length into the snow. In such a condition, he then listened to the creature messily devouring its prey, and was somehow experiencing the feeling of its alien and savage nature inside of himself. In that terrified state he then remained, heedless of the urine flowing down his own leg.

—

At some point thereafter, he realised that the sounds of ravenous feeding had long since gone, as had the feelings of being inside the creature's mind. He had no clear idea as to how long he had been cowering there, but he again felt a brief shadow of the shame he had experienced after the Anath raid, particularly as he felt the now-cooling wetness on his inner thigh.

He raised himself onto his hand and knees, and peered cautiously over the top of the ridge. The death-scene was displayed before him, red blood and gore spattered across the previously pristine snow, central to which was the carcass of the bloodied and disembowelled deer.

There was no sign of the other creature, but Corin anyway spent minutes looking around the edges of the clearing, studying for any sign of the feral beast lying in wait. There was nothing to indicate it was still there; he could see large scuffed marks in the snow across the ground from where the creature had charged, and then crisper prints in another direction, to where the beast appeared to have departed. The latter paw-prints in the snow were much larger than a man's foot.

He could remember the brief moment when the creature had launched itself across the clearing at the deer. He did not have a complete mental image of the beast, but he could recall an instant of seeing long fur-covered arms and legs, and an elongated maw full of razor-sharp teeth. It had been like nothing he had ever seen before. It had to have been a felrin.

And had he somehow shared its thoughts and cravings? And the deer's terror, too? Something strange was happening to him. Perhaps some odd sensation brought on by lack of food. Or the cold. But he was experiencing things at the moment which he had never felt before, and they did not seem natural. Perhaps this was as a result of being closer to the land of the Gods, and of living in an area where men had chosen not to live?

Finally, Corin got up and then moved tentatively closer to the deer, eyes still scanning his surroundings, axe in his hand. Not that he expected the axe to be of any use if the creature was lying in ambush, and launched itself at him.

Half the deer was eviscerated, but there were elements of its hind which were untouched by the felrin attack. It made him queasy to come closer to the scene of death, but his day's hunting had otherwise proven fruitless, and if there was still good meat on the stag he needed to claim it, for Agbeth's sake.

Agbeth!

He suddenly realised just how long he had been gone from their shelter, and what terror she must be enduring, having heard the screams of the felrin so much closer to their home. He had to get back to her.

Quickly, he worked to butcher the unsullied hind part of the deer, his heart beating fast both out of fear for himself and worry for Agbeth. Eventually, he had cut off a large piece of meat for them both. He wrapped this in a cloth, picked up his other possessions, and then started to run back towards their home.

He sprinted the entire way, heedlessly leaving a trail of footprints in the snow, as he ran.

—

He was out of breath when he arrived back at their camp.

Agbeth was sitting up within the shelter, still covered in furs. Her face remained flushed and sweaty with fever, but at the moment when he pushed his head into the entrance of the lean-to, she burst into tears.

He moved in closer to her and she wrapped her arms around his neck, not saying anything, just hugging him tightly as she sobbed. He could feel heat radiating out from her, the illness causing her body to be hot at the same time that she continued to shiver with cold.

'I'm sorry,' he whispered, hugging her back. 'I'm sorry. I got food for us.'

She said nothing for an extended period, sounding like she was struggling to draw breath between sobs. Finally, she said, 'I heard it. Screeching. So close. And when you didn't return, I thought… I thought…'

'It's OK. I'm here. It didn't get me.'

She squeezed him again, still crying, and they stayed like that for minutes afterwards, hugging each other in silence.

Eventually, when her tears had subsided, he said to her, 'It is a felrin, though, Agbeth. And it's hunting. Within a mile of here.'

'I'm scared, Corin. So scared, now.'

'So am I.'

—

215

Agbeth's fever worsened over the next few days, and Corin was becoming increasingly worried for her.

Each night she would suffer from tormented sleep, alternately pressing herself to him when she was shivering, then pushing him away when she became too hot. Her breathing was still laboured, and she was complaining of her whole body aching, of her face and muscles feeling tight.

And each night, the felrin would cry out its ghastly call, broadcasting its terror across the forest, disrupting their attempts to sleep.

Corin's own night-time was also disrupted by recurrences of the dream, which was becoming increasingly frequent. Sometimes, he would awaken full of a lingering sensation of a terrible wrongness. Of something he had done. Or which had been done to him. Or that he was going to do? Whichever way, he was experiencing a sense of unbalance when he awoke each night, wishing that he could forget the dream and have it leave him forever alone.

He was growing certain that the dream was somehow associated with the strange out-of-mind experience that had happened several times now; with the rabbit, the deer, and the felrin. This sense of being aware of and within another creature, of sharing its thoughts. He did not know how he knew this as certainty, but he nonetheless felt sure that the dream and his strange powers were connected. Indeed, sometimes at night, when he heard the felrin's calls, he experienced a peculiar sensation that he was somehow linked to the beast, again. Could feel its alien mind, somewhere out in the cold of the night. Could share in its predatory and murderous instincts. Each time, the feeling made him shudder, leaving him with the same sense of wrongness as did the dreams.

He wanted to talk to Agbeth about these concerns, but she had enough suffering of her own to endure at the moment, without him adding to her worries.

Instead, he focused on looking after her, both of them benefiting from a few days of proper nourishment. He chose to stay at the camp, close to her side, throughout that period. Sometimes he would sit outside the lean-to, and his eyes would scan the surrounding areas, looking for any sign of the felrin.

And sometimes he would hear Agbeth moaning or involuntarily crying out from under her bed covers. And he was becoming ever more worried, for himself but even more so for her.

—

On the fifth day of her fever, Agbeth was beset by a severe seizure. It was something which had happened to her numerous times during her childhood. Something which, at its worst, had led to the permanent physical impairment on the left hand side of her body and face. But it had not happened to her for over six years.

Corin was outside of the shelter, chopping firewood, when he heard an unusual sound from inside of their lean-to. A repeated banging against the wall.

He moved inside, and was aghast at what he saw. Her entire body was stiffened, her arms and legs jerking, one arm thumping against the side of the lean-to. Her eyes were unfocused, rolled upwards slightly, moving back and forth with no sign of recognition. Her breathing sounded even more laboured, and her mouth was clenched shut.

Feeling terrified, he moved to her, turning his wife onto her side and holding her tightly as her body thrashed against his. Corin could well remember her condition from when they had been children, but he had hoped that they would never experience such moments ever again.

He knew that the words would not reach her, but he anyway whispered, 'Shhhhh… my love… I'm here.' Her arms and legs continued to jerk and thrash, but at least now his arms around her were preventing her from injuring herself against the walls.

The seizure continued for several minutes, but eventually it began to diminish in intensity. For a while afterwards, there were minor twitches in her arms and legs, before he finally felt her hand reaching up and pressing onto his. 'It's OK, Corin. I'm back.'

He kissed the back of her head, with tears in his eyes. This was

217

his fault. These conditions, this cold, the fever, the fear of the felrin. And now the seizure. This was all his fault. For being a coward. For bringing her here with him. If he had chosen to stay and fight, in the Anath village, she would not be suffering like this now. Or if his strength of character had been sufficient to tell her that she could not come, could not volunteer to share his banishment. But no, he was a cowardly weakling, and it was Agbeth who was suffering as a result of this weakness.

He had brought all of this misery upon her. He felt certain that the seizure had been caused by all of the other distress and adversity which she was being forced to endure.

'I'm sorry, Agbeth. I'm so sorry.'

She squeezed his hand. He could still feel the heat of her fever, but there was no anger or recrimination in her voice. 'Don't be. Just hold me, please.'

—

After the seizure, she began to recover, albeit slowly. However, Corin's worry continued, and their food supplies were almost gone. He needed to hunt again soon, as a matter of urgency.

Whilst she was in her fevered state, he had been giving Agbeth the greater proportion of their remaining food. He had judged that her recovery was more important than his own nourishment, but now the gradual effects of cold and lack of sustenance were starting to deplete him as well.

Four days after the seizure, he knew that he would have to get back out to find food. Would have to leave her again, alone at the camp. By this time, Agbeth's fever had reduced significantly from the heights it had ascended to, although she was still not fully recovered.

She had moved to sit outside the shelter on this day. She was seated next to the fire, huddled in her furs. It was a sunnier day again, although still cold. He came to sit with her.

'I need to go back out hunting, today.'

She was staring out towards the lake. 'I know. And I know that you haven't been eating your share, Corin.'

He did not say anything in response, for a few moments. 'Will you go back into the shelter whilst I'm away, in case-'

'I'm not sure I can stand another day inside there. I need some fresh air today, to get well again. Need to take in these views. It's so beautiful today.'

'No, Agbeth, I need you to-'

'No, Corin! Today, I'm going to stay out here. I'll be careful. But I want to be useful again. I'll try to make a hole in the ice on the lake, to fish.' The lake was fully frozen over, now.

'But it's dangerous out here, you know that.'

'It'll be no more dangerous for me, here, than it'll be for you, out there, in the woods. And I can't stand the thought of another day sitting inside, doing nothing. Doing nothing, and worrying that *you* might be in danger.'

'Agbeth-'

'I said no, Corin!' There was an edge of steel in her response, one of the few times that she had ever raised her voice against him, and he recognised that further protest would be worthless.

'OK. But I have to go. I have to hunt. But if you're going to be outside, near the lake, please keep your eyes on the treeline. Yes?'

'Yes.'

'And if you see anything even slightly concerning, you get back in the shelter, and you wait for me?'

'Yes.'

'OK. I promise I'll be as careful as I can be, while I'm hunting. Promise you will be, too?'

'I promise.'

He reached out and took her hand. 'OK, then. Let's both keep safe.'

—

The forest seemed vibrantly alive, within his mind, as he headed out that day. It was as if he had gradually, over time, become more alert and attuned to the life around him, more conscious of its presence.

As with his last hunting expedition, he was reluctant to move more than a few hundred metres away from their home, so that he could remain within hearing distance of Agbeth. He again proceeded with caution, continually scanning the area around him for any signs of the felrin.

Once he had walked outwards a few hundred metres, he started to follow a circular route, which maintained what he estimated to be a consistent distance back to the camp.

On this hunt, however, he *felt* his prey before he saw it. He was walking through a cluster of trees when he suddenly got a sense that there was a life near to him. In close range. Waiting. Hiding. Watching him. He got a peculiar sense of being out of balance again, as if he was seeing himself through eyes which were not his own. Feeling himself inside another – animal – mind. A mind that was observing him, and fearing him.

Without thinking, he nocked an arrow, aimed his bow towards some bushes on his left, and then fired. There was a thud accompanied by a high squealing noise, and then again a sense of an immediate disconnection.

He walked over to the bushes, crouched down, and there before him was a white fox. His arrow had gone through the side of its head, and had killed it instantly. He felt satisfied with the ease of the kill, although again confused by this odd sensation, which seemed to be occurring more regularly.

The fox would be sufficient to feed them for at least a couple of days. Therefore, as far as Corin was concerned, he could end today's hunt. He wanted to get back to Agbeth as quickly as possible. He started to move with urgency back through the woods towards their home, still being careful to scan the areas around him for any signs of the felrin.

He quickly re-joined the path he had used on his journey

outwards from the lake, seeing his own footprints in the snow, pointed away from the camp.

But he froze with horror as he saw what was next to them. Prints of a beast's paws in the snow, paw-prints which were larger than a man's. Next to his own tracks, but pointing in the opposite direction. Back towards the lake. Towards Agbeth.

He started to run in the direction of their home, legs pounding in the snow and moving him as fast as he could. Panic was gripping him.

And then, at that very moment, he again felt a connection form, and he was sharing an alien, feral, savage mind. He could feel its urgings; to hunt, to kill, to feed. Could see through its eyes as it moved around a corner of rock, onto a flat area of land next to a frozen lake. And there, before it, was prey. Large prey. By the lake. On two legs.

STOP! STOP! STOP! STOP! STOP!

Corin instinctively shrieked the command through his mind, as he witnessed the creature's eyes focusing upon Agbeth. The order was less an articulated word than an image of ceasing movement, of freezing in place. But then he became aware that the felrin had sensed him, there, in its mind, and suddenly intense rage surged at him and he was ejected from its thoughts. And with that ejection the foreign image he was seeing in his mind, of his wife observed ravenously through the eyes of a beast, was gone.

Corin continued to sprint, the rocks marking the entrance to the lake area being no more than one hundred metres away, now. He was frantic. Terrified. He had never moved so quickly in his life.

And then Agbeth started screaming.

14

Arion

—

Year of Our Lord,
After Ascension, 767AA to 768AA

Within the blackness, the dream took possession of Arion, for the first time.

—

He is standing on a path, on the side of a mountain. Higher than he has ever been in his life, in the midst of a range of majestic peaks.

Four other people stand with him. Four other shining avatars of light.

There is silence all around. Silence in the world, silence in his companions.

He is walking now, inexorably climbing the winding mountain path. He walks with a sense of purpose, a sense that this might always have been his purpose.

Ahead of him, a brilliantly bright light appears, contained within an archway of breathtaking beauty. He gasps as the light shines into him and through him.

But still he and the four silent companions walk on, relentlessly pursuing the end of this path. Onwards. To the Gate.

And then he can see Him. In the Gate. Waiting. Watching. Golden, glowing, terrible, magnificent. He wants to kneel, to bow his head, to murmur his obeisance, but still silently he walks on. Closer, ever closer. So too do his companions.

The figure in the Gate moves His hand, a summoning gesture, and once again his body takes him forwards. And he can hear the clash of distant weapons, glorious ringing sounds given the shape of words.

STRENGTH. VICTORY. GLORY.

But then the gesture of His hand changes, and he is aware that something is wrong.

A single finger is raised. And he knows what he must do.

—

When he awoke, it was with an anguished sense of disorientation. He was lying on his back in the fighting square, throat hurting. But he had been somewhere. Somewhere other, somewhere more important.

Lord preserve us! Think! What was it?

He squeezed his eyes tight, trying to recover the memory, but it was elusive and fleeting. Then it had vanished, leaving him with a sense of frustrated anxiety.

He opened his eyes to find himself facing the close presence of Sergeant Kallin and Sendar Pavil, both of them leaning over him. Other cadets were crowded in behind them.

'He's back,' announced Kallin. 'Sepian! Sepian! Can you hear me?'

Arion groaned and nodded weakly.

'You passed out,' Sendar commented, anger in his voice. 'That… thug… tried to throttle you, despite repeated orders to release.'

'Can you breathe OK, Sepian?' asked Kallin.

He realised that he could. He sat up, feeling his throat, which felt sore but no worse than that. 'I'm… OK. Can breathe fine. Just my… pride hurt.' He looked around, expecting to see Jarrett Berun with a smug triumphant look on his face, but the giant youth was nowhere to be seen.

'I've sent him back to report to the Commander,' stated Kallin, anticipating Arion's question. 'He disobeyed repeated commands from me to release. I had to get him off you.'

'He *kicked* him off you,' clarified Sendar, sounding satisfied. 'I suspect that Berun's feeling worse than you, right now.'

By the Lord! Not sure about that.

'OK, we're done here,' announced Kallin. 'Class dismissed! Everyone clear out.'

As the others began to file slowly away, Kallin and Sendar helped Arion to his feet. Sendar addressed the sergeant. 'Sergeant Kallin. I would like to have a conversation with both you and the Commander. Urgently. Certainly, *before* Berun returns to our rooms.'

Sendar had once again spoken in that voice which effortlessly exerted his rank and authority, and Kallin nodded. 'Very well. Come to see us at fourth hour.'

Arion wondered briefly what that could be about, but he was still recovering his breath and he could not find the energy to ask.

—

He found out later that Jarrett Berun was being switched out of their lodging room, at Sendar's request. Prior to the fight, Sendar had favoured conciliation, but Berun's actions in the wrestling contest had proven to be too much for the prince.

'Is that what you spoke to Roque and Kallin about?' asked Lennion Rednar, when the three of them were back in their lodgings.

'Yes,' replied Sendar. 'In coming here, I'd promised all parties that I wouldn't arbitrarily lean on my royal rank. However, from the outset I insisted that I would select my own room-mates. I've told Roque and Kallin that I no longer want to share a room with Berun, after his actions today. They've accepted that. Particularly given that Roque has now issued Berun with a formal reprimand over his actions, including for the comments he's been making about his superior status. Which I also informed them about.'

'But what about the things you said to me, earlier?' asked Arion. 'About making the peace?'

Sendar shrugged. 'Look, Arion, I know that I asked you to make the peace with him. And that was despite seeing all of the sly little verbal attacks that he's subjected you to in the last two months. But his actions in that fight crossed a line for me. It looked like he wanted to *kill* you. I don't want to be sleeping next to someone who has that much rage inside of him.'

Arion blushed, thinking about his own occasional fits of temper.

'He looked feral,' commented Lennion. 'I know I lost it a bit in my fight, but he looked like he *hated* you.'

'Yeah, I think he does. But he sure gave me a heck of a beating,' said Arion, still red-faced. 'I thought I'd be able to give him a better fight than that.'

Sendar shook his head vigorously as he replied. 'Nonsense! It was obvious to me, and no doubt to Kallin, that you've had no unarmed fighting training previously, whereas Berun has clearly had plenty. It was an extremely unfair contest and Kallin should have ended it earlier, which I told him in no uncertain terms. He should have put Berun up against *me*.'

'So, what happens now?'

'They're going to move him into a room with three of his more devout acquaintances,' answered Sendar. 'It will probably suit him better. They're going to transfer Roliss Sonder out of that room and into here. He seems like a decent sort of fellow, and it might mean things feel a little less tense in here.'

Arion nodded, not feeling at all upset with the outcome.

—

Berun came to the room later, to collect his gear. At first, he packed silently, but after he had collected his possessions he turned towards Arion and Sendar, anger visible on his face.

'So, the two of you have got what you wanted,' he stated. 'Got rid of me.'

Sendar frowned, but replied calmly. 'I didn't want this outcome, Jarrett. But your actions earlier crossed a line, and I think it's better for everyone now if we physically separate you and Arion.'

'This is about my religion and my family, isn't it?' Flickers of hot rage were in the larger youth's eyes.

'Not at all,' replied Sendar, again sounding reasonable. 'I commend your religious devotion, and have nothing but the utmost respect for your noble house and family.'

'No, but *his* family don't,' replied Berun, looking at Arion. 'We've all heard the insults his father has made about my mother, calling my father a traitor for marrying her, which implies *I'm* a traitor. Which he repeated today. And none of you three show the proper level of religious devotion. How is it that I'm the only one who's been regularly praying in this room? How can a prince of the realm care so little for the true faith? No wonder our whole country is under threat of excommunication from the Holy Church, if that's the example our royal family sets!'

'No one thinks for a second that you or your family are traitors, Jarrett, that's nonsense,' replied Sendar, still calm, although Arion sensed that there was more tension in his words now. 'But with your comments about my faith and the Holy Church, you must know that you're crossing another line. One which I will *not* tolerate. I have nothing but respect and devotion for the Holy Church, as does my father, and we're both true followers of the faith. And I would advise you not to say anything further on this matter, lest your comments do stray into territory which *may* indeed be deemed treacherous.'

Jarrett Berun glared back at him, but he did not respond.

Sendar continued, in a more conciliatory tone. 'Can I please suggest that we all move on from this, Jarrett? I don't bear any ill will towards you, and neither does Arion. I think you'll be better suited to your new room-mates, who are as equally and commendably devout as you are. And in time, I hope that all of us will again be friends.' He stood up, holding out his hand.

Berun paused for a second, considering Sendar's comments, then shook the proffered hand. However, he made no movement to extend that gesture towards Arion, and neither did Arion himself make any attempt at reconciliation.

As he moved to the doorway, Berun added one last comment. 'Oh, and Sepian. I hope you enjoyed your beating today.' Then he left the room.

Go fuck yourself, Jarrett.

—

Sendar had also arranged for Jarrett Berun to be moved out of their immediate training group. As a result, Arion began to enjoy his life at the Academy much more.

The next three months passed quickly. The time committed to Military Skills Training increased significantly, and it was another area in which Arion excelled. He had received significant prior weapons training in Septholme, and the only two members of his training group who could match him in weapon skills were Sendar and occasionally Lennion. Sometimes, he found himself wishing for the opportunity to go head-to-head with Jarrett Berun with a weapon in hand, to provide a means to avenge his humiliating defeat. However, the sensible part of him recognised that it was probably for the best that they stayed well away from each other.

Arion continued to struggle with Military Tactics and Military Strategy lessons, but with effort and with the support of his room-mates he was keeping up with the required standard of work.

In his fifth month there, Arion received two letters. The first was from Delrin:

227

Dear Arion,

Hello little brother. I am writing to you directly at the Academy, in case father is intercepting and ripping up my letters!

Hello from the Holy Land! I have been here for two weeks now. And what a place it is! Dust, sand, heat, and beautiful exotic local women!

I am staying in The Order's fort in Arron. In the end, I spent four weeks at The Order's staging post on the island of Abass, followed by a three week journey by sea. What a voyage that was, I can tell you. Even in the late summer months the seas were terrifying!

Arron, as you will know, is the largest city in our territory here. It is a tremendous walled fortification, and so many of the population are warriors such as me, from The Order of Saint Amena or other holy orders.

Like you, I am now embarking on my training, in my case to become a Knight of The Order. It will take me two years. I am shortly to be transferred to a frontier castle on the edge of our territory. I very much hope that there will be a well full of cool water there!

I also hope that your training at the Academy is progressing well? Knowing you, I suspect that the physical challenges will be too easy and the studying too hard. And I hope that the locals haven't had to lock up their daughters yet?

Write to me when you get the chance. Despite being banished by father, I am not ready quite yet to cast off all family links! Send any correspondence addressed to me to The Order in Arron, through the packet service. It will find its way to me, eventually.

Anyway, I haven't had any glory yet, but who knows, perhaps when I am on the frontier I will see my first hostile infidel!

Take care,
Delrin

The second was from Gerrion, and was much more succinct.

> *Dear Arion,*
>
> *I hope you are keeping well and are achieving success in your training.*
>
> *The matters we all discussed in the Great Hall with father and Charl Koss are progressing. I trust you will understand to what I am referring.*
>
> *Father and I will be travelling to Andarron shortly, to meet with the King at the palace on the 8th of Earthsong. Sendar has been invited to attend. Father has indicated that you are also welcome to attend, if you can make yourself free and arrive before twelfth hour midday.*
>
> *Yours,*
>
> *Gerrion*

It was as a result of that second letter that, one week later, Arion was travelling through the gates of the royal palace in Andarron. He and Sendar had journeyed there together, in a carriage accompanied by four men-at-arms. Sendar had once again flexed his royal powers, and his father's authority, to ensure that they were both given permission to leave the Academy for a day.

For a second time, Arion had experienced the fleeting glimpses and unappealing smells of the royal capital as they had journeyed through it, travelling to the royal estates on the northern side of the city.

Arion stared out of the carriage window at the royal palace as their transport drew close alongside it. It was a grand old building, one built for spectacle and beauty rather than defence, and it was surrounded by extensive manicured gardens and lawns.

Twenty minutes later, Sendar was leading him into a great meeting room within the palace. Arion gulped as he entered, feeling nervous about meeting the senior members of the royal family. However, he relaxed when he saw that the only other two people in the room were his father and Gerrion, who were both seated near the end of a long and ornate meeting table.

He moved towards them, shaking their hands and formally introducing Sendar.

The prince smiled. 'Welcome again, Duke Conran,' he said, shaking the Duke's hand vigorously. 'And thank you for developing such a fine room-mate and fellow cadet as Arion here.'

The Duke nodded, smiling in return, and for a moment Arion's father displayed an emotion which could almost have been mistaken for fatherly pride. Arion experienced a surge of gratitude towards the prince.

The Duke then placed a hand onto Arion's arm and steered him away from Sendar and Gerrion. The older man leaned in to speak quietly to Arion. 'Well done for the positive reports I'm getting back about your conduct at the Academy, and for Prince Sendar's favourable opinion of you.' Arion had only a little time to wonder – *What reports?* – before the Duke continued. 'The King has granted you and Gerrion a great honour by allowing you both, at my request, to be here for today's meeting. It will be a good learning experience for you, and will be very valuable for you to meet the King, Queen and Prince Senneos. However, other than greetings and formalities, your role today is to listen and not to speak. And not to repeat anything you hear outside of here. Understood?'

Arion nodded, and then he and his father returned to speak with Sendar and Gerrion. The four of them chatted together for a few minutes, until the doors at the far end of the room were opened by two palace guards. Three individuals entered. At the front was a man who Arion was certain must be King Inneos. The King was in his early forties, and was dark-bearded and balding, with a circlet of a crown upon his brow.

Next to the King, on his right hand side, was a male who looked strikingly similar to Sendar. The man was tall and blonde-haired, and Arion concluded that he was Prince Senneos, the heir to the throne.

However, Arion's gaze was drawn unerringly to the woman

on the King's left, who he knew must be Queen Mariess. Arion had heard the stories whilst growing up of the Queen's legendary beauty, but those tales had not prepared him for the sight now of the most flawless woman he had ever seen. She appeared to be in her mid-thirties, of a similar height to the King, with delicately perfect features framed by long blonde hair, and a slim, regal body.

The Queen was also wearing a royal circlet, similar to the King's. Arion had been told by Sendar that the Queen was a former Princess of Angloss, who had been married to the King at the age of sixteen. Their marriage had been part of a political arrangement which had cemented the close friendship between the countries of Andar and Angloss. Even knowing the age when she married, however, he was finding it hard to fathom that she could have two sons as old as Senneos and Sendar.

By the Lord! She's simply stunning. Stop staring at her, Arion! She's the Queen. And close your mouth.

'Welcome, Conran,' said the King, smiling, and the monarch then surprised Arion as he embraced the Duke like a family member. 'And welcome to your sons, too. How wonderful it is to be amongst friends, in these difficult times.'

'Difficult, indeed, Your Majesty,' replied Arion's father. 'But let's hope that we can agree upon a solution to ease some of those difficulties, here today.'

'Indeed,' replied the King. 'Although it appears that we're still waiting for the Archprime?'

Almost on cue, Archprime Amnar arrived, bustling in through the entrance by which Arion himself had entered. She was a small grey-haired woman, with very sharp features and narrow eyes, and she looked flustered. The Archprime was the head of the Holy Church in Andar, and Arion had been expecting a more imposing figure than the diminutive woman who now scurried into the room.

A few minutes of small talk followed, before they gathered around the table, the King at the head with Queen Mariess on his right and Prince Senneos on his left. The Duke and the Archprime took up the next positions, with Arion, Gerrion and Sendar furthest down the table.

'So, Conran,' said the King, starting the discussion. 'We've corresponded by letter many times in the past four months but, as we agreed, the purpose of today's meeting is to resolve our final position. Summarise your thinking for me, again, please.'

'Yes, Your Highness,' replied the Duke. 'As we all know, we face two problems. First, the stated intention of the Archlaw to introduce larger numbers of Aiduel's Guards into our country. Second, the threat of Elannis against the western part of the Canasar peninsular. And mixed in with that, if we refuse to give any accommodation on both points, is the threat of war with Elannis and possibly Dei Magnus combined. Which could also happen alongside possible excommunication from the Holy Church, with the terrible upheaval that would cause.'

'Yes, unimaginable upheaval,' added the Archprime.

The Duke continued. 'I will speak frankly, now, Your Majesty, in addressing the question we've previously discussed. Namely, whether we can simply rebuff the Archlaw and Emperor Jarrius on these points, in the hope that they're bluffing. I personally think that approach represents an enormous risk, because I believe that Jarrius is looking for an opportunity for war and conquest, now that the conquered territories of Sennam and Patran are both subdued. A continued flat refusal from Andar to any of the requests made would drive Elannis and Dei Magnus closer together. And, as we've corresponded, none of us believe that we can win a war if we're fighting both of those countries at the same time. That's even if Angloss were to ally with us, which is not a certainty given the threat of excommunication.'

'Archlaw Paulius's threats of excommunication don't intimidate me,' growled King Inneos, in response. 'If he chose to do that, we'd instigate our own Holy Church of Andar, with me as head of the church. The Archprime has already said that we could do that without jeopardising our souls, haven't you, Amnar?'

'Yes, Your Majesty,' replied the Archprime. 'I've consulted with my senior and most trusted colleagues within the Church of Andar on this question. We've all adjudicated that, if we were to break off from the Holy Church in Dei Magnus for these reasons, then our immortal souls will not be in peril.

'However, the practical difficulties of such a move are almost inconceivable, and the thought of *actually* breaking off from the Holy Church in Dei Magnus, and from the divine authority of the Archlaw, horrifies me. I've lived my life in service to and have given all of my holy oaths as a loyal follower of that Church.

'Also, I cannot know with certainty what reaction such a move might elicit in the country and within the priesthood. But it's entirely possible, or indeed probable, that such an action could cause the faithful to split in two. Cause them to split between those faithful to the new Church headed in Andarron, and those still professing steadfast loyalty to the Archlaw and to the Holy Church in Dei Magnus. There's no precedent for such an action throughout Angall and throughout history. Even in the Dark Century, after the collapse of the Republic, all of the faithful still made their oaths to the Holy Church in Dei Magnus.

'If the Archlaw were to follow through with his threat of excommunication, and we were indeed to break off from the Holy Church under his authority... well, it could lead to civil war. A civil war within the country between those willing to show allegiance to a new head of the church, and those who would feel unable to do so.'

'That is a real threat, Your Majesty,' added the Duke, 'were you to decide to break off from the Holy Church in Dei Magnus. Which is why I continue to counsel you not to do this. Imagine the worst-case scenario. Elannis and Dei Magnus attack us, invade us, whilst we ourselves are engaged in a civil war where brother turns against brother, and father against son. The realm could collapse under such pressures.'

'Enough!' barked the King, and to Arion's ears he sounded irritated. 'We've covered this ground before, Conran, and I'm *almost* convinced that breaking off from the Holy Church is not a valid option. Mariess, my dear, why don't you share with the Duke and the Archprime the discussion which you had with your father's ambassador? Then I'll finally resolve on the matter.'

The Queen spoke softly, her melodic foreign accent that of distant Angloss. Arion allowed himself a few moments to enjoy being able to stare openly at her beauty, without embarrassment. 'Ambassador Julien of Angloss and I met three days ago,' she said. 'He expressed the views of King Kanathar on behalf of Angloss to me very directly. Firstly, Angloss remains our ally and, in the instance of unwarranted attack upon our territory by Elannis, Angloss will honour our alliance and will provide support. I pushed back as to what that support would entail, specifically would it include a declaration of war by Angloss against Elannis. However, the ambassador wouldn't allow himself to be drawn that far. By which I interpret that we can't be certain of direct military support from Angloss, although I do believe they would provide naval support and other aid.

'Secondly, he made it absolutely clear that King Kanathar will not do anything which brings with it a threat of excommunication to himself. My father will not countenance breaking off from the Holy Church in Dei Magnus, under any circumstances. He's therefore minded to reluctantly accept the increased presence and power of Aiduel's Guards in his realm, but on the condition that they are to be limited to larger military garrisons in *three* locations only.'

'None of which is good news,' stated the King. 'But tell them about his other statement, dear, about what would happen if we were to break off from the Holy Church.'

'The ambassador counselled most strongly against us taking action to do that,' responded the Queen. 'He indicated that any such action would, in King Kanathar's opinion, imperil the alliance between our countries, and would give Elannis and Dei Magnus complete holy authority to attack us.'

'Surely that settles it then, Your Majesty?' asked the Duke. 'We must not lose our alliance with Angloss by doing this?'

'Yes, I know, it's settled!' stated the King, again surprising Arion by sounding angry and a little peevish. The King then slammed his fist down against the table and cursed. 'Lord damn it!'

By the Lord! Arion thought to himself. *I didn't expect to find the King so... petulant.*

The King then took a deep breath, and continued. 'OK. I'm persuaded. Let's abandon the option of breaking off from the Holy Church in Dei Magnus, for now, as much as I'd like to tell Paulius where to shove his holy authority. What are our next options, Conran?'

The Duke responded, 'We need to find a way to divide Elannis and Dei Magnus on these matters. And for me, that means finding a way to concede something in relation to Aiduel's Guards, which the Archlaw wants, whilst making no concessions in relation to giving territory to Elannis through its House of Canas claim. Are we all agreed that we're not prepared to offer any concession in relation to the Canasar territories which we hold?'

'Yes, agreed,' answered the King. 'The Canas River provides a strong natural defence of our borders, and we cannot countenance a situation where Elannis has taken some of our territory. If we give them all or part of Canasar now, we'll be ceding a strong defensive border, and it'll be a certainty that they'll want more. It would be the start of the end for Andar. We must therefore reject their territorial claims. Utterly. And rely on the Treaty of Canasar, and on our legitimate rights to the Western Canasar lands under that treaty. Consider that settled, Conran. What then do you advise in relation to Aiduel's Guards?'

'Well, in relation to that matter, I believe that we have to agree to give *something*,' replied the Duke. 'Kanathar's proposal that they be restricted to three main garrisons throughout the country sounds sensible, so I'd suggest that we also make that a condition in our response. And we should put a limit on their total military strength in any single location, which we suggest should be a maximum of two hundred men. We should also require that there's a substantial distance between each of those garrisons, such that they could not practically muster as a single army.'

'That all sounds sensible,' replied the King. 'Two hundred men is a sizeable force, but if we insist that they're stationed near our existing fortresses, I assume we can ensure we have a numbers advantage in any single location?'

'Exactly, Your Majesty, yes,' answered the Duke, 'and I'd also suggest that we limit the maximum total number of Aiduel's Guards in our country, in all locations, to no more than five hundred. I believe that by imposing these conditions, then Aiduel's Guards' presence in our country will become more prominent and visible, but will not genuinely threaten our security.'

'And do you also believe that the Archlaw will agree to this?'

'I can't be certain,' replied the Duke, 'but this would still feel like a meaningful victory for the Archlaw versus the existing position, so yes, I do believe he could accept this. Particularly if he still believes that our breaking off from the Holy Church is a genuine possibility, which we believe he does.'

'So, your recommendation is that we agree to these numbers, as you've set out here, Conran?'

'Yes, Sire.'

The King looked across at his wife, who nodded, and then at his elder son, who did the same. 'Very well, consider those positions acceptable and agreed, Conran,' stated the King. 'What else?'

'Thank you, Your Majesty,' responded the Duke. 'The next question is then one of what to do about the Archlaw's request that, in matters related to heresy, Aiduel's Guards be allowed to enforce such law directly themselves in accordance with Holy Law. This was a trickier issue, and one for which my son Gerrion has drafted sensible proposals. I also took the liberty of discussing these with Archprime Amnar, who's in agreement with them.'

'That's correct,' confirmed the Archprime. 'Very sensible proposals.'

'Go on,' said the King.

'Well, I'll let Gerrion set this out, Your Majesty,' stated the Duke. 'Gerrion?'

'Thank you, father,' replied Gerrion. 'Your Majesty, if we look at the question of heretical punishment and jurisdiction, there are in effect three elements. First, the investigation. Second, the prosecution, trial and judgement. Third, the punishment. To date, Aiduel's Guards have effectively been toothless within our country, because we've solely allowed them to investigate heresy, and only without torture. However, we haven't allowed them to control the trials, which were undertaken by local lords and magistrates, and we haven't allowed them to enforce their preferred punishment of burning.'

'All understood,' answered the King. 'So, what do you now propose?'

'Your Majesty,' responded Gerrion, speaking confidently and calmly, 'the Archlaw requested that Aiduel's Guards take control of all three elements. That request is clearly not acceptable without putting the lives of all our citizens, including any noble persons, in danger. Taking the three elements, we would propose that the first, the investigation, remains unchanged. We can allow them to continue to investigate heresy in our country, but we cannot allow for the torture of our citizens as a means of extracting false confessions.'

'Agreed,' said the King. 'That is beyond question.'

'Second, I proposed to father that, specifically for accusations of heresy brought by Aiduel's Guards, we could agree each time to convene a special court. There would be three individuals examining the evidence and making judgement at such a court. The first would be the local lord or magistrate who would have had full control of such matters previously. The second would be the High Priest into whose territory the accusation fell. The third would be a representative of Aiduel's Guards. A verdict and judgement would be formed by majority view of those three individuals.'

'I think this is a very clever idea, Your Majesty,' added Amnar. 'We'd be agreeing to give the Church a majority position on each case of heresy, but one of the three individuals will be an Andar

237

Church representative, which would of course control any attempted abuse or overreach of the Archlaw's power. But it does still give the Archlaw and Aiduel's Guards a more visible representation of the Church's authority to stamp out heresy, and therefore I believe it could feel like an acceptable position for the Archlaw. He would not be losing face to accept this.'

'So, you both support this?' asked the King. The Duke and Amnar confirmed their support, then once again the King looked to his wife and eldest son to obtain their assent. 'Very well, that is also agreed. And on the question of punishment?' He looked back at Gerrion.

'That is a more simple point, Your Majesty,' replied Gerrion. 'We either allow burnings as a punishment for heresy in our country, or we refuse this.'

'By the Lord!' exclaimed the King. 'The matters Archlaw Paulius forces me to adjudicate on! Conran? Amnar? Your views?'

The Duke spoke first. 'Sire, I think that giving the Archlaw his burnings will be the point which will clinch his agreement on the whole negotiation. Archlaw Paulius clearly relishes the thought of heretics burning on a pyre, given the visible deterrent that this would provide to others. I wouldn't propose to offer him our agreement to this initially, but it would be a point I'd be prepared to concede to secure a final agreement with him.'

Amnar then spoke up again. 'Sire, we already have hanging as a punishment in our country. To avoid the possible consequences of war and excommunication, conceding this point feels like a small matter by comparison.'

'Another concession!' shouted the King, again sounding somewhat petulant and sulky to Arion. 'It feels like we're the ones giving everything here. What then do we get in return?'

'Two things, Your Majesty,' replied the Duke. 'First, we get an oath from Archlaw Paulius that the status and powers of Aiduel's Guards will not be raised again within the Archlaw's lifetime. That, once we agree to this, it's settled for what will hopefully be decades to come. Second, we demand that he withdraws any support he might have for the claims of the House of Canas to Canasar territory, and that he publicly affirms his unwavering commitment to the Treaty of Canasar.'

The King smiled, grimly. 'So that, in effect, the Archlaw gets much of what he wanted, but that bastard Jarrius gets nothing of what he asked for?'

'That sums it up neatly, Your Majesty,' responded the Duke. 'And for Andar, there would be many positive outcomes. We'd stay united with the Holy Church, we'd not create any religious division in our own country, we'd retain our territory, and we'd hopefully create a meaningful division between Elannis and Dei Magnus. And in return for that we'd be conceding power to Aiduel's Guards, but in a way which we all think is controllable.'

'Very well,' said the King. 'That is all agreed. Don't offer the burnings point initially, but let's be prepared to concede it to secure a final agreed position. Well done, Conran, Amnar, Gerrion. What now?'

'We have to put that position to them, Sire,' replied the Duke. 'And we need to ensure that our response is co-ordinated with that of Angloss. If we both ask for and concede exactly the same things, our position will be that much stronger.'

'I will need you and Amnar to go and present this proposal to the Archlaw and to the High Council in person, Conran,' replied the King. 'Correspondence cannot communicate this properly. You'll need to ensure that this is agreed in person, in Sen Aiduel.'

'Very well, Sire,' responded the Duke. 'With your authority, Amnar and I will travel there as soon as the position with Angloss is confirmed.'

Arion stared at his father, impressed. *Lord! Until today, I had no true idea of just how important father is to the running of this country. Or of just how much the King relies on him.*

'I will call Ambassador Julien back in as soon as possible,' stated the Queen. 'And the four of us can then meet him together. I feel confident that we can get full agreement with Angloss on this, given the awful alternatives.'

'We are resolved then,' said the King. 'Thank you for your time, everyone. As much as it has pained me to concede *anything* to the Archlaw, let's hope that our proposals will be enough to avert war and religious division, and to preserve our country.'

15

Allana

—

Year of Our Lord,
After Ascension, 768AA

Allana was still contemplating her choice as to whether to stay in Septholme or to flee, when Captain Menion Thatcher returned to collect his jacket.

She blushed when he reappeared in her home on the day of collection, remembering the moment when she had been teetering on the edge of seducing him. He was wearing his soldier's uniform again, today, and looked as handsome as he had done on the previous visit.

He tried the jacket on in front of her, and was clearly delighted with the outcome. After he had handed over payment for the garment, she said, 'Thank you for choosing me for this item, Captain Menion. If you or your wife ever have need of my services in future, please don't hesitate to visit me again.'

He nodded, looking at her with a slightly glazed expression. There was still some unspoken sexual connection between them, as if he too knew how close they had come to doing something two weeks before, and had thought about her since. 'I will. Of course.'

'And if there's anyone else that you know who might want to engage my services, I'd be very grateful if you could recommend me to them.'

He nodded again. Then, a few moments later, as he was proceeding to leave her home, he stopped and said, 'Actually, now that you mention it, there is someone who I could introduce you to. Someone who could give you a *lot* of work.'

—

It was as a result of Thatcher's stray thought that, three days later, Allana was for the first time making her way up the main street of Septholme, towards the castle at the top of the hill. She had been invited to go and meet with Ami Randle, whom Captain Thatcher had described as the Head of Household for the House of Sepian. Allana understood that Randle was in charge of all of the servants working in the castle.

Allana had made a new dress for herself since arriving in Septholme, and she was wearing it now, to look as presentable as possible. She was determined that she would have a successful meeting, although she had still not decided what she was going to do following the news that Aiduel's Guards were hunting for Seilana dei Monis. Therefore, if she subsequently chose to flee, this encounter with Randle might mean nothing. However, she would do everything she could to achieve a positive outcome, in case she decided to stay in the town.

As she approached the castle, she could more fully appreciate what an imposing fortress it was. Its walls rose at least eight metres from the ground, the mighty stone sides regularly interrupted by tall rounded towers. She looked behind herself as she drew closer to the castle gates, and was impressed by the view over the harbour out to sea. She had never been this high in the town before, and the outlook was surprisingly pretty and peaceful.

It is lovely here, Lana. Doesn't Septholme feel more like home now?
It will be sad if you have to leave here.

———

Twenty minutes later, Allana had been allowed to pass through the castle gates, and was sitting across from Ami Randle. The other woman was in her fifties, grey-haired with a plump pear-shaped body.

'So, you're a seamstress, are you?' Randle's voice was husky and common-sounding, but was possessed with a lively hint of intelligence.

'Yes, mistress. And I've been working in the northern quarter for a number of months. My mum trained me.'

'Thatcher showed me the jacket. Good work, that.'

'Thank you. It was a good job to take on.'

'Do you know what job is available here?'

'Mostly. Captain Thatcher said that there'd be a lot of work to make and repair clothes. He said there might be other things, too. But he wasn't clear on what.'

'Yes, there are other things. But we'll get onto that. You're a foreigner?'

'Yes.' Allana smiled. 'With my accent, I'm afraid there's no hiding that.'

'Where from?'

'Dei Aiduel in Dei Magnus, mistress.' Allana then proceeded to recount her cover story again. 'My mother was from Dei Aiduel, but my father, who left us when I was very young, was a sailor from Andar. My mother died last year, so I decided to come to try and find my father. Mum had said he might be in Septholme. But I haven't found him.'

'We don't usually employ foreigners, mind. Any offer of a role here would be subject to me checking with Lord Gerrion. Understand?'

'Lord Gerrion?'

'The Duke's son. You'd soon see him. Serious-looking one. He's in charge here, when his father the Duke's away. Like he is at the moment.'

'I understand, mistress.'

'You're certainly a pretty one, aren't you? Nay, pretty's not right. Beautiful, more like. I bet you're always fighting the men off, aren't you?'

Allana blushed. 'I wouldn't say that, mistress.'

'Ah, come on now! You know you are. I'd certainly be popular with the men here if I offered *you* a job.' She suddenly cackled with laughter, before composing herself and becoming serious again. 'You're well-spoken too, girl. Better spoken than most seamstresses I've dealt with. How's that?'

'My mother was educated, mistress. She taught me to speak well, and to read and write, too.'

'Ah? So you have some education? Interesting. I'm the only one on my staff who can read and write, at present. Would certainly be a help to have a second person who could do that.'

'I would enjoy that, mistress. I can read and write, and can do numbers, too.'

'That's useful to know, girl. Shall I tell you about the role, then?' Allana nodded. 'A large part of it is seamstress work. We've a lot of people here, who need clothes mending and repairing. Occasionally, you'd be making new clothes, too, or repairing furnishings in the castle. The woman you're replacing got too old, her fingers had become too slow and clumsy, and I had to let her go. I'm having to farm that work out, right now, and it's costing me too much. Want to bring it back in-house.'

'Yes, mistress. Is it a full-time role then?'

'Yes, certainly. You'd have to stop doing work for others, because there's other things I might ask you to do, too. Not low-level work, mind. No scullery work, or cleaning out bedpans, no nonsense like that. But helping with castle events, serving at feasts, that kind of thing. Could you lower yourself to do that sort of thing, girl?'

'I think I could, mistress.'

'And now that I think about it, there's plenty of ways I could use someone who knows how to read and write, and count, to make my life a bit easier.' Allana nodded again, getting a good sense that the woman liked her and that the interview was going well. 'You've got a place in the northern quarter?'

'Yes, mistress.'

'I could accept you living outside of the castle, but this would be better as a live-in job. And I expect that'd save you a lot of money. Free room here in the castle out-buildings, and two free meals a day come with the job.'

They then proceeded to talk about the terms of the role. During this time, Allana was thinking about the woman's comments. If she was able to get a position here, working and living at the castle, it could possibly allow her to disappear out of the view of Nionia dei Pallere and Aiduel's Guards, for an extended period of time. If she could do that for one or two years, the world might by then have forgotten about the fugitive Seilana dei Monis and her teenage daughter. And she would be free to start her life again.

'So,' stated Ami Randle, as their meeting was concluding. 'Are you interested in taking the role, Lana?'

This is your chance, Lana. This is better than all of the other options available to you.

Allana smiled back at the older woman. 'Yes, mistress, I think I am.'

———

The following Third-Day, Allana shared the news with Nionia that she was returning back to Dei Magnus.

'Really, Lana? Must you really go?' The young woman looked distraught when she heard Allana's news. Allana was sure that she could see the Guard blinking her eyes quickly, to stifle her tears.

'I'm afraid so, yes. I'd hoped to find my father here, but haven't. And I'm homesick, Nionia. I've given notice on the property here, and I'm to leave next week.'

How easily lies come to you now, Lana. But you need to do this.

'But it doesn't seem fair! I will miss you so much. You're my only friend here, Lana.'

'And I'll miss you, too.' In truth, Allana did think that she would miss the guileless woman from her home country, and she wished that they could have met in other circumstances. 'But when I'm home and settled, I'll write to you.' She knew that she would never be writing.

Nionia was still blinking, her eyes red. 'I would like that. And I'll write back. But I will miss you so much.'

Allana put her hand onto the other woman's arm, and patted her comfortingly. However, although she felt sympathy for Nionia's reaction, she was also aware that the young Guard was the sole reason she had needed to make the decision to give up this home.

Harden your heart, Lana. This might be sad for her, but she's the one forcing you to do this. A careless word from her could still lead to your death. Or could have led to hers?

—

A few days later, Allana received word from Ami Randle, confirming that Lord Gerrion had accepted that she could take the job. Shortly after that, she vacated the house in the northern area of Septholme, and moved her possessions into the castle.

Her room in the castle was barely worthy of that name. In fact, it was not even inside the stone castle walls themselves, but was within a wooden outbuilding in the vast castle courtyard. Every live-in female servant resided within this outbuilding, with the exception of Ami Randle. Each of them had a tiny room with a small thin bed, a cupboard, and a basin. Allana discreetly placed her coin purse at the bottom of her cupboard, hidden under a pile of clothes. She kept her knife within her possession, at all times.

She soon settled into the rhythm of life at the castle, and after the lonely times of the last few months, she was appreciating being in the proximity of so many people. At first, she was a peculiarity to the soldiers and servants around her, an exotic foreigner who the men could gawk at and the married women were distrustful of. As a result of this, she was initially reserved around others.

Gradually, however, people grew used to her being there, and she became accustomed to her new routine. There was a lot of work for her to do, catching up on a backlog left by her predecessor's enforced retirement. She was therefore constantly busy, but she was enjoying the activity.

One to two years, Lana, she would tell herself. *Hide here, for one to two years, then you can go back out into the world again. Can start your life again. Free.*

—

During the early weeks in the castle, Allana got to see some of the members of the Sepian noble house, and found out lots more about the family from Ami Randle.

The Head of Household was well-organised and a hard driver of people, but she was also a chatterbox who loved to gossip. Randle had taken a quick liking to Allana, as 'the only other educated one on this serving staff', and she often seated herself beside Allana whilst working. This provided Allana with ample opportunity to hear stories about the Sepians.

Allana established that there were only two members of the family on site. The first, Lord Gerrion, was darkly handsome, but appeared aloof. She had only seen him from a distance, and did not have any direct interaction with him in the early weeks. She understood from Ami that he was the eldest of the Duke's children, and would one day inherit that title. Ami had also told her that

Gerrion would remain in charge for several weeks, until the Duke returned from his travels.

'Is Lord Gerrion married?' she asked Ami one day, as she sewed beside the woman.

'Oh, no!' laughed Ami in response. 'Why, got your eye on him, have you? You just watch it, girl!' She cackled with laughter. 'Oh, he's real choosy, that one. Real choosy. Duke's been trying to arrange him a marriage for a few years now, as I understand. But he's not been having any of it. Mayhap he's looking for a pretty little seamstress, is that what you think, eh?' She cackled again, causing Allana to smile.

Karienne was the youngest of the Duke's children, a teenage girl who Allana perceived as a little plain and shy. Allana had experienced only brief interactions with the girl, in the early weeks.

Ami had also shared an opinion about Karienne. 'Oh, it's sad for that little one. It truly is. Growing up in a household of men the way she's had to. And with the poor little bairn's mother dying so young. So sad.'

'Her mother died?'

'Oh, yes. What, ten or eleven years ago, now? Kari was just a little girl. So sad. Wasting Sickness took the Duchess, it did. Just like it took so many good people that year, may Aiduel watch over their souls.'

'That *is* sad.' Allana was suddenly thinking about her own mother, and without any guile, she added, 'That's how my mum died.'

She was pleasantly surprised when Ami Randle reached across and patted her hand. 'Oh, that's sad too, girl. I'm sorry I'm bringing up bad memories for you. Let's talk about happier things, eh?'

Allana had subsequently asked Ami about the rest of the family. The older woman was only too happy to talk about them. 'Oh, that's interesting, that is. There's a middle brother. Delrin, he was. But he's been cast out of the family, would you believe it? Has gone off to fight in the Holy Land. Real shock it was, I can tell you. Such a funny one, Delrin, too. Always had a kind word and could make me laugh. He really could.' As if to reinforce this, she cackled again at some unshared memory.

'I can imagine,' replied Allana.

'And then there's the youngest son, Arion. Oh, he's proper good-looking, that one. Proper good-looking. Lock up your daughters, I say to all the fathers here, when that one's around. Mind you, if he were here, he'd no doubt be taking a shine to you, too, same as all the other men.'

'Where is he?'

'Oh, he's off at the Royal Academy. Becoming a knight or some such thing. I bet he'll look real handsome in his uniform, when he returns. Real handsome. But that's not for another eighteen months, as I understand, so you'll just have to imagine him until then. Or join me in drooling over our handsome Captain Thatcher.' She cackled once more.

Allana smiled. 'I just might have to do that.'

You will hopefully be gone before this Arion returns, Lana.

Allana had one further question. 'What about the Duke? Has he never remarried?'

'Duke Conran? Oh, no,' said the older woman, shaking her head to reinforce the point. 'He's hard as nails, our Duke. Such a strong one, has ruled us all so well ever since he was a boy, and since I was almost still a strip of a girl like you. If you can believe it. Great man, we'd all give our lives for him, we would. But when he was with the Duchess, he was like a little cuddly puppy. Broke his heart, it did, when she died. Broke his heart. He was never the same again. He was still young, then, mind you. Still young now, in fact. Very eligible man, I'm sure lots of noble women would beat down the castle walls to become the new Duchess. But he won't remarry, that one. She was the love of his life, and he's never even looked at another woman, since. So sad.'

Allana forced herself to look solemn as Ami continued to shake her head in apparent remembrance of how sad the Duchess's death had been. However, Allana could not help but add a further thought.

I bet you could make him look at you, Lana. If you wanted to.

Allana's torments at night-time were not eased by being in the small room within the castle outbuilding. In fact, the thin wooden walls between her room and others' made it even more challenging for her to find the slumber and relief which she sought.

Firstly, as the recurring dream continued to regularly haunt her night-time hours, she became more self-conscious about her restless sleep. Indeed, this was often commented on by the women in the neighbouring rooms, usually in a disapproving manner. All Allana could do in response was to shrug apologetically; if she had known how to stop the dream, she would have done so by now.

The second aspect was that her sexual longing was not abating with time. She was still yearning for a repeat of what had happened with Rabnar, only now it was more difficult for her to achieve her own release at night-time.

Thatcher was indeed the most handsome man in the castle, and on a handful of occasions Allana caught herself staring at him. Contemplating what might have happened between them. And sometimes those stares were returned, for longer than was appropriate. However, Allana had subsequently met Thatcher's fiancé, and she was now glad that she had not acted to seduce him.

Despite this, she was still full of an unsatisfied and growing hunger, and at some point she knew that she would need to act upon it. With Thatcher, or with someone else.

—

After Allana had been in the Sepian household for over a month, Duke Conran Sepian returned from his travels.

There was great upheaval amongst the household staff at the news that the Duke's ship had been sighted in the harbour. Ami Randle instantly cajoled numerous servants into cleaning the Duke's chambers and the main feast hall. She then set about berating the kitchen staff to ensure that they were ready to prepare a feast for their master's homecoming. Allana herself was to be commandeered into helping with serving, on this evening, if the Duke wanted a feast upon his return.

Allana watched Lord Gerrion, Captain Thatcher and a number of men-at-arms ride out of the castle, which she assumed was to meet the returning Duke. She was intrigued to finally see the man who appeared to inspire from his retainers such varied feelings of fear, respect and often devotion.

In the midst of the bustle now enveloping the fortress, she found herself a shaded hidden spot within the courtyard from which to observe matters, in anticipation of Lord Gerrion's greeting party returning soon.

Allana immediately identified the man whom she believed to be the Duke. He was riding alongside his eldest son as they entered the castle grounds. She was a distance away from them both, but she could perceive the features of the older Sepian. He was physically unexceptional; dark-haired, with a ruggedly handsome face, and a solid, muscular frame of average height. However, there was something within the manner with which he carried himself that was striking; this was a man who was accustomed to others obeying him.

Allana watched Duke Conran and his son dismount, with a third older man also joining them, who she guessed was Charl Koss. As the Duke passed through the courtyard towards the main castle keep, Allana could see household staff members bowing or curtseying as he passed by. He appeared to acknowledge such deference with a relaxed authority, and she could hear him engaging in friendly banter with several of his retainers.

This is a man of power, Lana, she told herself. *A man who rules Septholme and all of Western Canasar. This is what power looks like. Be careful.*

—

There was indeed to be a feast in the Great Hall that evening, attended by the Duke and his family, with several of his long-serving retainers also invited. Allana did not fall into this category, and she had been conscripted by Ami Randle into helping with the preparation of the Great Hall, and with the serving of food and drink.

Allana was thrilled to be part of an event at the castle, even if only in the capacity of a servant. To get herself ready, she brushed through her dark flowing hair and left it loose around her shoulders. She had also decided to wear her best dress for the evening, and was satisfied with how snugly it fitted against the curves of her body.

You'll be the most beautiful woman there, Lana. Why be shy about it?

The Sepian family members were seated on the central table with their advisor Charl Koss, alongside four other tables which were principally occupied by household soldiers and their spouses. Allana had been tasked with serving one of the other tables, while Ami Randle was directly attending to the Duke and his party.

Allana could feel eyes upon her as she moved around the room. The eyes of the soldiers she was serving, who were trying not to be too overt in the way they looked at her, whilst they were with their wives. The eyes of their wives, a number of whom were still distrustful of this attractive foreign outsider. And she could also feel herself being watched from the main central table.

Not by Lord Gerrion. No, as usual the eldest son of the Sepian household appeared to be oblivious to the fact that she was there. And not by the aged Charl Koss. But by the Duke himself. A couple of times, she glanced towards his seat and caught him staring at her, directly. The first time, their eyes locked accidentally and then she averted her gaze, blushing. The second time, with slightly more boldness she held his stare for a second, before then dropping her eyes.

He has noticed you, Lana. Did you intend to be noticed?

Towards the end of the evening, after large volumes of alcohol

252

had been consumed throughout the room, Ami Randle sidled across to Allana. 'Lana?'

'Yes, mistress?'

'The Duke would like to meet you. Says he didn't recognise you. Wants to know who you are.'

Allana felt a sense of trepidation, blended with a definite hint of excitement. 'Now?'

'Yes, now. Remember, call him "my Lord" at the end of your sentences. And curtsey when you greet him for the first time. And don't make a fool out of yourself or out of me!'

Allana moved towards the Duke's table. She could see that he had been watching her brief exchange with Ami, and that he was observing her approach now, as he held a goblet of wine in his right hand. She stopped at the head of the table, beside him, and made a small curtsey. 'My Lord.'

Ami Randle had followed her. 'My Lord, this is Lana Marrone. Seamstress and newest member of your household retinue.'

The Duke's eyes remained locked on Allana's face, and he stated, 'I pride myself on knowing all of my staff. But you're clearly not from Septholme. Where *are* you from?'

'Dei Magnus, my Lord-'

Duke Conran immediately turned to both Gerrion and Ami Randle. 'You've hired a Dei Magnun, into *my* household?'

Allana was mildly shocked by the apparent coldness in the Duke's voice. Gerrion in turn seemed to be taken aback, blanching at his father's reaction before replying. 'Yes, father. Ami interviewed her, and she'd been working in Septholme for a significant period of time before we hired her. Ami?'

'And she's a good worker, my Lord,' added the Head of Household, appearing rattled. 'Very good worker. Popular, too.'

The Duke looked at Allana again, his expression stern. She was suddenly worried that his earlier stares might not have been what she thought they were, but had instead been driven by suspicion of her foreign appearance.

'That may be,' said the Duke. 'But she's from Dei Magnus. You must know why that matters, Gerrion? Did you interview her yourself, son? Understand her background? Why she's here?'

Gerrion looked embarrassed. 'No, father.'

'No harm,' replied the Duke, after a pause, and his next words sounded more conciliatory. 'You've had a lot to do, these last few months. Almost too much, and all of that done well. No harm, son.' He then looked up at Allana again. 'Very well, Lana Marrone. I will summon you at some point tomorrow. I'd like to understand more about your background. Make sure that you come, when you're summoned.' His piercing dark eyes locked directly onto hers, and Allana had an alarming sense that he knew exactly who she was, and what crime she had committed.

'Yes, my Lord.'

What does he already know, Lana? And even worse, how quickly will your story unravel if he questions you? And what will he then do to you?

———

At third hour on the following afternoon, a guardsman arrived to inform Allana that Duke Conran had requested that she immediately attend his chambers. The guard then lingered as she hurried to finish what she was doing, and it was apparent to Allana that the man was intending to escort her there directly.

Be calm, Lana. Remember your story. Stick to it. Be brave.

She had toyed with the idea of fleeing the castle at the end of the previous night, but on balance she had concluded that such an act might be a vast overreaction to the Duke's comments at the feast. And would of itself have cast suspicion upon her.

She had therefore been running through the details of her cover story ever since the exchange with Duke Conran, and this had been a distraction to her throughout her day's work. She was trying to make sure that there were no obvious gaps or flaws in the story.

254

Nonetheless, her heart was beating fast when she arrived at the door outside the Duke's chambers, within the castle keep.

The guard knocked on the large oak door, opening it after receiving a shouted instruction from within. Allana entered behind the soldier, walking into an antechamber within which the Duke was seated, at a desk against the far wall. There was an open doorway on the right-hand side of the room, which Allana noted led directly into a larger chamber, which appeared to be the Duke's bedroom.

Duke Conran looked up at Allana. 'Ah, here she is. Hello Lana, take a seat.' He gestured towards the chair which was a couple of metres away from him. 'Thank you for finding her, Callor. You may leave us. But stay outside, in case I call you.'

The guard nodded, then turned and left the room, shutting the door behind him. Allana sat down in the chair, facing the Duke.

He stared at her for a few seconds, in silence. His eyes were locked upon hers, and she felt nervous under the penetrating focus of that stare. He was wearing a grey tunic, his muscular arms and bulky build evident beneath the material. She noted that there was a knife in a sheath attached to his belt. 'So, Lana,' he finally said. 'Are you enjoying your work here?'

'Yes, my Lord,' she answered. 'I enjoy the work, and I enjoy working for Mistress Ami.'

'Good. Very good. Now, don't be nervous, I just want to ask you a few questions. I like to know all of my household staff, personally. Is that OK?' His voice sounded business-like, being neither friendly, nor threatening.

'Yes, my Lord.'

'So, you started at the castle, when?'

'Five weeks ago, my Lord.'

'Yes. And when did you arrive in Septholme, prior to that?'

Allana paused to work this out, and then added two months to separate herself from Ronis's death. 'Nine months, my Lord.'

'And you came from where, precisely?'

'Dei Aiduel, my Lord.' Once again, she had her cover story ready.

'Ah, Dei Aiduel. A lovely city. I've been there, you know. Many years ago, but I can still remember it well. Wonderful cathedral. And those amazing fountains in the town square! Absolutely spectacular, aren't they?'

She did not hesitate. 'Yes, my Lord. Spectacular.'

'So, Lana Marrone, let me ask you this. Why would a young – and if I may so, beautiful – girl such as yourself travel such a long way from the truly magnificent city of Dei Aiduel, to a foreign country and to a rather more *mundane* town like Septholme?'

He thinks you're beautiful, Lana. Remember that.

Once again, Allana repeated her rehearsed story. 'My mother was from Dei Aiduel, my Lord. But she died, last year. From Wasting Sickness.' She said this last part deliberately, pausing to see if there was any reaction from him to the cause of death. However, he showed no outward sign of emotion. 'My father, who left us when I was very young, was a sailor from Andar. After Mum died, I decided to try to find him. Mum had said he might be in Septholme, but I haven't found him yet. I don't think I will, now.'

'That's very sad. Very sad indeed. My condolences for your loss by the way, and may your mother's soul rest with Aiduel in eternal peace.'

'Thank you, my Lord.'

Should you say the same thing about his wife, Lana?

However, he continued before she had an opportunity to resolve this question. 'What was your father's name, Lana? Perhaps I could help to find him for you?'

Again, she had prepared an answer for this. 'Connor Andarsson, my Lord. Any help would be greatly appreciated.' She knew that this was a very common Andar name.

'I'm sure it would. How did you get here, by the way?'

She hesitated. 'To the castle, my Lord?'

'No. To Septholme. From Dei Aiduel. How did you get here?'

'On a ship, my Lord. A passenger carrying ship.'

'Its name?'

She did not have an answer for this. 'I can't remember, my Lord.'

His eyes continued to watch hers. 'Really?' He then paused for a second, before continuing. 'No problem, though, Lana, if you can't remember. You must have been *very* distressed, after your bereavement. And did your ship travel here directly? Or make any stops on the way here?'

'Directly, my Lord.'

Keep calm, Lana. Just keep answering quickly and with confidence. Don't act like a liar.

'OK. And then you set up a house as a seamstress, operating in town? And I understand that you did a piece of work for Captain Thatcher, which led to your interview with Ami?'

'Yes, my Lord.'

'OK. Very good. Very clear answers, Lana. Very consistent and thorough.' He paused, then stood up, leaning back against his desk. 'Apart from the ship name thing, that is. Despite your bereavement, it just feels a bit out of character on your part that you wouldn't remember the name of the ship that you travelled on. Particularly an educated girl like you, a seamstress who I understand from Ami can somehow also read and write.' He leaned forwards, and for the first time she could see menace in his eyes.

'Sorry, my Lord?'

'A few points, Lana, for your story. First, and this may seem like a trivial detail to you. But there are no direct passenger vessel journeys between here and Dei Aiduel. This is a trading port, and I've been running it for thirty years, girl. I know all of the shipping routes to and from Septholme. And the one that apparently brought you here? It doesn't exist.'

She felt the blood drain from her face. 'Sorry, my Lord. I must have spoken in error. Let me think-'

'Second!' he interrupted her, his voice cold. 'There are no fountains in the town square of Dei Aiduel, amazing or otherwise.

I actually have been there. Something which a resident of that city ought to know, don't you think?'

'Lord, I-' she floundered, seeking an explanation. 'I've only just met you, my Lord. I didn't want to contradict you-'

'Stop lying to me, girl. Right now.' There was cold steel in his voice, and she immediately silenced herself. 'You don't come from Dei Aiduel. You've clearly never even been there, which begs the question as to where you're really from and why you're lying about it?' He then reached into his desk drawer, and with dismay Allana saw him produce her stolen coin purse. 'Lastly, what is *this*? My men searched your room this morning. They found this.'

'It's… it's my money, my Lord.'

'Yes. But I've counted it, girl. How does an innocent seamstress come by that much money?'

Allana was frantically searching for answers. 'My inheritance, my Lord. From my mother.'

'Enough!' He slammed his fist down onto his desk, and for the first time his voice was raised in anger. 'Stop lying to me! You lie as easily as you breathe, girl!'

'I'm not, my Lord, I-'

'Silence! You're a liar! You're still trying to lie to me, even now. I don't even believe that your name is Lana Marrone.' He paused, then took a deep breath, and when he spoke again his voice was returned to calm. 'Listen to me carefully, now. And take heed. If you deliberately speak even a *single* further word to me which I think is a lie, I'll have you dragged down to our dungeons, and I'll throw away the key. Understand?'

Her heart was pounding, and she felt dizzy under the sudden verbal assault. She did not know what else to do, other than to nod and to say, 'Yes, my Lord.'

'Very well. Now, what I want to know is *this*. Who are you, really, girl? What are you really doing in my castle? And who do you work for?'

She swallowed, feeling overwhelmed and out of breath. Her

hands fell onto the front of her dress, where she could feel the comforting presence of her knife, hidden in the front pocket. He was staring at her like a hawk, expectantly waiting for an answer.

Think, Lana! What should you say? What should you do?

But as she sat there, with the seconds ticking away, and the Duke's cold eyes boring into her, only one option presented itself.

16

Leanna

—

Year of Our Lord,
After Ascension, 768AA

For a number of weeks after Comrel's announcement about the impending arrival of Aiduel's Guards, there was no apparent change at the College of Aiduel in Arlais. No building work had commenced on the land outside of the College, and there had been no sightings of any of the Guards' soldiers.

Leanna began to wonder whether she had initially overreacted. She started to hope that the impact of the Guards on her time at the College would be much less significant than she had initially feared.

As soon as she had been able to, Leanna had enrolled with the College's hospital, acting as a nursing assistant for Sister Colissa of the Order of Saint Helena. The hospital was in an inconspicuous grey building, near to the entrance of the College complex. Leanna was officially meant to help there two afternoons per week. However, Colissa also welcomed her on Seventh-Day afternoons, and at other times when Leanna had a few free moments.

Four other Sisters and two Brothers of the Order also worked in the hospital under the direction of Colissa, in addition to a number of lay assistants, and a handful of other novices. Leanna was soon eagerly soaking up the knowledge which Colissa and the other priests had to impart, as well as picking up a number of practical points while acting as their assistant.

Until she had started working in the hospital, Leanna had not properly appreciated the large flow of citizens from the city who visited it. Most of these visitors complained of ailments which Colissa would address by means of an herbal remedy. Leanna observed any such treatments keenly. With the aid of a book which Colissa had given her to study, she was soon recognising what each herb in the herb garden looked like, and what maladies they could be used to treat. Colissa commented a number of times on what a fast learner Leanna was proving to be.

Leanna identified from her studies that one particular herb was recommended to aid with a deep sleep. It immediately made her think of her own restless nights. On one occasion, with the permission of Colissa, she cut off a small leaf for use in her own drink, hoping that it might help her to avoid the recurring dream that night.

It did not work, and instead the visions of the mountain path claimed her once again.

—

Indeed, the dream was becoming ever more vivid and frequent.

Whereas in the early months at the College it might have captured her in its restless arms once per week at most, now it had started to draw her into its intrusive clutches almost every other night.

She could remember more about the events within the dream, now. More of the pieces were being etched into her memory after waking, although still not as a fully coherent whole.

She had also told Amyss about those aspects of the dream which she could remember, although the other girl had enjoyed no more success than Leanna in deciphering what it might mean. Leanna had made Amyss promise not to share her awareness of the dream, including its details, with anyone else.

It was an unspoken but agreed act between them now that Amyss would come to her bed and hold her, when the worst visible aspects of the dreaming started. Amyss said that her own close presence tended to subdue the worst of Leanna's restless shaking and thrashing whilst she was within the dream. Leanna herself found that the presence of the other girl, after she had woken, helped her to subsequently fall into a dreamless sleep for the remainder of the night.

One night, Amyss was still holding her after Leanna had come awake, with Amyss's head resting on Leanna's chest. The smaller girl said, 'I tried to wake you, tonight, you know, whilst you were in the dream.'

'Did you? What happened?'

'Your thrashing got worse. And, even though you were sleeping, you got angry.'

'I did? I didn't hurt you, did I?'

'No.' Amyss laughed then. 'But only because I was fast enough to get out of the way of your swinging fist. I won't be trying that again!'

'Oh no. I'm sorry, Amyss. I'd feel so terrible if I ever hurt you. You must really feel like you've had such bad luck, ending up in a room with such a… *disturbed* room-mate.'

'Yes, it's truly terrible,' said the other girl, with a whimsical tone to her voice. 'Absolutely awful. You're obviously completely and utterly mad. Nuts. They should make me a *saint* for what I have to go through at night.'

Leanna laughed. 'Saint Amyss. It has a nice ring to it.'

'Yes. And for my first miracle, as a saint, I would bang you on the head and make these dreams go away.'

'That sounds nice. But only if you promise to bang softly.'

Amyss reached her hand up and tapped Leanna on the forehead, very gently. 'Like that?'

'Yes, that's acceptable.'

'OK. Consider yourself cured then. No more dreams tomorrow!' The girl then lowered her head back onto Leanna's chest and hugged her again. 'But seriously, I feel so lucky to have you as my room-mate, Lea. To have you as my best friend. *Even* with the dreams.'

'And you're my best friend too, Amyss. Thank you for looking after me. I love you.'

Amyss made a noise which sounded like a soft embarrassed giggle, but she did not otherwise respond. Leanna then felt her room-mate shifting position to fall asleep, and she in turn closed her own eyes.

At that moment, sudden waves of emotion passed over and through Leanna. The emotions were coming directly from Amyss. Rippling from her.

The sensation immediately recalled memories of the manner in which the light had passed over The Lord's body on the statue, in the School of Saint Amena. It equally raised forth other more recent memories for Leanna, of the way that Lohan's emotions had also seemed to ripple through her, following his last words to her.

But, right now, Leanna was bathed within a warm radiant waterfall of the smaller girl's innermost feelings.

LOVE. PROTECT. LOVE.

Leanna drifted back to sleep, feeling safe and protected. And much loved.

—

After that, over the following days, Leanna realised that she was beginning to sense strong emotions from a variety of people.

First, it had happened with Lohan. Then with Amyss. Soon, she was feeling the same thing several times a day, across a number of days, with lots of different individuals. Each time, the common factor was that the person concerned was physically quite near to her.

On each occasion, she experienced the sensation of an invisible ripple passing through her, her body and her mind catching wave after wave of some secret emotion. Some private emotion which she knew with certainty was originating from an inner place within another person. Emanating outwards towards her in regular beats, like the steady beat of a heart.

Initially it made her feel like an intruder, an invader, trespassing on the hidden feelings of other people. Sensing things which she was not meant to sense. But she quickly realised that she had no control over when this strange ability was triggered, or when it ceased. As such, she had become a reluctant recipient and observer of these strange emotional waves.

Thankfully, most of the time, given the place where she was, the emotions which transmitted themselves to her were positive. Love. Joy. Happiness. Contentment.

But occasionally, she was startled to receive a negative or a dark emotion, from an unexpected source. One day she saw Priest Parmer looking down at an open book, as she was seated at her desk, working in his classroom. The kind-natured priest was squinting in frustration, trying to read the words within the tome. But failing. Pulses suddenly emitted towards her, screaming his emotions.

FEAR. ANGER. FEAR.

He looked up and saw her sitting near him, gaping at him. He must have realised how sour his expression was, for his face adopted a pleasant look and he tried to smile. Abruptly, the strong emotions lapsed and no longer seemed to emit towards her. She felt somehow dirty, as if she had invaded a moment which should have stayed private just to him.

Thereafter, she repeatedly found that she had to control herself from staring at the person emitting any strong emotions, particularly the negative ones.

And as she experienced this more and more, she began to associate some of the emotions with colour. Positive emotions poured into her mind as bright, golden, white colours. Negative emotions instead slithered into her thoughts, contained within colours which were dark, black, of the night.

Despite her joking with Amyss about being a disturbed person, there were times when she indeed began to wonder herself if she was going mad. Whatever was happening to her, it was not normal.

Lord Aiduel, what is happening to me? How can I feel what others are feeling?

She was certain, however, that this newfound ability – *this power* – was somehow linked to the holy vision, and to the recurring dreams. Everything had started with the vision. With The Lord calling to her, on that day as she had prayed before the altar.

This certainty was the main reason why she could reassure herself now that madness was not setting in. If this ability had started with and was somehow linked to the holy vision, she reasoned, it had to be a gift which had been given to her by Aiduel Himself. And therefore, if The Lord had given it to her as a gift, it was intended to be used, for good, else He would not have gifted it.

Lord Aiduel, why have you given me this power? What am I to do with it, Lord?

She desperately wanted to talk to someone about what was happening to her. However, given her belief in its connection to the vision, and her oath to keep that secret, she kept her own counsel, even from Amyss. And continued to feel like she was stealing into others' hearts, and into their souls, as she shared and experienced their secret emotions.

—

Three months after Senior Priest Comrel's announcement, the peace and tranquillity at the College was finally disturbed by the arrival of the first contingent of Aiduel's Guards.

Leanna became aware via Amyss that the Guards had set up an encampment in the fields immediately to the north. When they both had a free moment, she and Amyss walked to the gate at the entrance of the College complex, and looked out towards the Guards' camp.

There were perhaps twenty tents in total. A number of identical smaller canvas shelters stretched in a semi-circle at the edge of a field. In front of them were two larger tents, next to which was a very large central marquee.

There appeared to be a number of labourers in the cluster of people which Leanna could see in the encampment, but she could also discern those individuals who she assumed were members of Aiduel's Guards. The latter were identified by uniforms which looked like they were more befitting of a soldier than of a religious person, each wearing a sword at their hip. Their most distinctive feature was the red cloak they were wearing, accompanied by a bright red sash across their chest.

'There's certainly a lot of them,' stated Amyss.

'Yes, lots,' replied Leanna. 'And I don't think that's a good thing.'

'You don't like that they're here, do you, Lea?'

Leanna glanced around, checking that they were out of earshot of anyone else. 'I just feel a little sad that it could change how happy things are, here at the College.'

'Do you think so? Why do you think that?'

'I don't know for certain. But someone I trust once told me that... *trouble*... can follow Aiduel's Guards. Trouble that can lead to bad things happening to good people. I'm worried that by them coming here, they might bring that trouble with them. Amyss, will you promise me something, please?'

'What, Lea?'

'Promise me to be careful with what you say, when you're around them. No jokes. Particularly don't say anything about the... you know, my dreams.'

'I'd never tell anyone about those, Lea, without your permission. And I promise to be careful.'

'Good.'

A couple of days later, Comrel again summoned all of the residents of the College to the main central church, for another evening gathering. Leanna took a seat next to Amyss, on one of the pews towards the back of the room.

Comrel was once again standing at the front of the church to address them, but this time he was accompanied by another man, who was clearly a member of Aiduel's Guards. The man next to Comrel appeared to be in his forties in age and was tall, with long black hair and a thick black moustache. His pose was relaxed and confident, with legs parted and a hand resting on the hilt of his sword. The red sash was worn across his chest.

Comrel spoke first. 'My children. As you'll already have noted in the last two days, some of our brethren of Aiduel's Guards have now arrived outside of our College. As I've asked before, please will you show them all of the hospitality and warmth which they deserve, as they carry out their important work for the Archlaw. More of our Aiduel's Guards brethren will be arriving soon, and indeed a number of their officers will be moving into lodgings here within the College. But may I please now introduce High Commander Ernis dei Bornere, commander and leader of the garrison of the Guards which is to be stationed here in Arlais.'

Comrel gestured towards the other man, who now stepped forwards. The High Commander then took a moment to peer around the room, and began to speak.

'Thank you, Senior Priest Comrel,' the man said, with a strongly accented foreign-sounding voice. 'And well met, all of you, my fellow faithful. As the esteemed Senior Priest said, I am High Commander Ernis dei Bornere, and I will be in charge of the garrison of Aiduel's Guards which will be stationed permanently here, in Arlais.

'As you can probably tell from my accent, I wasn't born here in Arlais!' He paused, acting like he expected laughter, but the room

267

was silent, the mood of the audience subdued. 'No, I come from Dei Magnus, which is the country which many of my men also hail from. We are therefore new to Arlais, and will welcome all of your knowledge about the city and the surrounding lands, in conducting our mission.

'And what is our mission, you might ask? Why has His Eminence, the glorious Archlaw Paulius the Fourth, sent us here? And why did His Majesty, Emperor Jarrius also want us to come here? The answer, my fellow members of the faithful, is to find and eradicate heresy.

'Our mission in life, within Aiduel's Guards, is the eradication of heresy and heretics. And please understand that our mission is intimately intertwined with yours. Your duty is to spread and teach the one true faith. Our duty is to destroy those false heretics and non-believers who would undermine your teachings. Your duty is to nourish the souls of the faithful. Our duty is to find and rip out those weeds of heresy which would poison and strangle such nourishment. Your duty is to guide the faithful onto the one true path of belief. Our duty is to keep them there.

'Heresy is a gangrenous wound on the pure skin of faith and belief! It will not be destroyed by words. It will be destroyed by actions. By holy fire! It must be burned out, and only through such burnings will the faith and the faithful be purified. And I swear, by The Lord Himself, that we *will* find purification.'

Leanna looked across at Amyss, and this time the smaller girl did look worried. Indeed, Leanna could feel pulsing emotions of fear and concern from almost all of the people around her, including Amyss. Leanna herself felt anxious. The more the High Commander talked, the louder he became and the more fanatical he appeared to sound. Leanna surreptitiously reached out her hand to find Amyss's own hand, and squeezed it.

The High Commander continued. 'His Eminence, Archlaw Paulius the Fourth, has made it his life's work to eliminate heresy and its advocates! And we, Aiduel's Guards, are his appointed emissaries

268

in that glorious work. We have the Emperor's authority in Elannis, granted to the Archlaw, to find heretics, to judge heretics, and to purify their heretical souls through the cleansing act of burning.

'What then is heresy? What then is a heretic? In the most basic form of answer to that question, heresy is the expression of beliefs and opinions which run counter to the truth set out within the word of Our Lord Aiduel. And it is also the practise of those false beliefs, the promotion of those beliefs. But it is more than that.

'A heretic, also in the most basic form of answer, is a person believing in or practising heresy. A heretic may be a non-believer, a pagan, an infidel. May be an espouser of other false beliefs and religions. But again, a heretic may be more than that. His Eminence Archlaw Paulius has taught us that a heretic can also be disguised from us, can hide their true nature from us. Indeed, the worst form of a heretic may be those hidden amongst us, professing to the true faith, corrupting us from within.

'How then can we identify such a person? There are markers we look for, markers of their evil. The worst form of a heretic may be a person who claims to see the future, who claims the power of false prophecy. It might be one who claims to see false messages and truths, in their dreams and in their visions. Or it might be one who demonstrates evil powers, powers which have not been granted to mortal man or woman by The Lord. Powers to know things they shouldn't know. Powers to do things no mortal man or woman should be able to do.

'All of those things are also heresy, and their perpetrators foul heretics, and each of these abominations are potentially more corrupting, more pernicious and more evil than the spread of false word and belief alone.'

Leanna felt her mouth becoming dry, and her heart thumping with fear, as she heard these statements, particularly the references to dreams, visions and powers. She then felt Amyss's hand squeezing her own in return, and wondered whether Amyss had also picked up on these comments.

Lord Aiduel, please let me know that your vision and the dreams are things of good. Not heresy, not evil. Lord, please guide me.

'It is the duty of Aiduel's Guards,' continued High Commander Ernis dei Bornere, 'and indeed each of you, to identify and eliminate all heretics. We will find them all, and we will burn them all, to cleanse ourselves from their stinking corruption. We therefore demand, under the authority of His Eminence the Archlaw and His Majesty the Emperor, that any suspicions which any of you has about heresy or heretics are to be reported to us immediately. And remember, the knowing concealment of heresy is itself a heretical act.

'Finally, in the coming months, we will be choosing to interview some or all of you. We expect full co-operation from anyone who is so requested to speak with us. And remember, there is no danger to anyone who walks in the light of the true faith and who speaks the truth to us and before The Lord. May you all go in the Grace of Aiduel.'

Following the conclusion of the High Commander's speech, Comrel stepped forwards again. Leanna was too far away from the Senior Priest for her newfound ability to be able to get any sense of his emotions. However, the look of discomfort within his expression told her all that she needed to know about his views on what had just been said.

—

Two weeks later, a very unusual event happened at the College hospital.

Leanna was working there, on a weekday afternoon, when a man was stretchered into the main room amidst a bustle of noise. He was screaming in pain as the stretcher-bearers placed him down onto an operating table, and he was clutching his abdomen.

Ripples of dark emotion washed into and around Leanna, beating outwards from the man at a frantic rate.

270

PAIN. PAIN. PAIN.

Leanna staggered backwards in response to the wave of agony which the man was experiencing. Fortunately, no one else noticed her doing this as Sister Colissa rushed into the room and started to take control of the situation. Leanna placed her hand up to her head, almost feeling the man's hurt as if it were her own.

Lord Aiduel, help me to endure this. Help me to understand it. Help me to save this man.

She was ignored as Colissa and another priestess attempted to diagnose the man, without success, as he was shouting and ranting.

PAIN. PAIN. PAIN.

The ripples of agony were consuming the man's thoughts, arriving at Leanna in the colour of blackness, darkness, oblivion. She stood back from the operating table, trying to ignore his immediate pain. Attempting to concentrate, to focus.

And then somehow the world slowed down around her, and the man's hurt adopted a visible form. She could *see* the spot from whence the waves of the man's emotions of pain were originating. From where they were beating their rhythm of misery. A blackness within the man, residing in his lower right abdomen.

Leanna stared at it, becoming almost trance-like. It would seem like such a simple thing; to reach out towards it, to call to it, to touch it with her mind, and then to use invisible ethereal fingers to *pull* that blackness out of the man. To take away his pain.

Without planning to, she lifted her arm, raised it and pointed it towards him. The waves of blackness continued to pulse towards her mind with each throb of pain that the man endured, but she looked past these now. To the root of the emotion, to the agony.

Within this newly emerged slowness of the world around her, she realised that she possessed the power to heal the man. To cure him, to drag the illness and pain out of his body. She concentrated… focused… staring…

'Leanna! What in the Lord's name do you think you're doing?' shouted Colissa. 'Get my operating tools, now!'

And Leanna's focus was broken, and suddenly the world was returned to normal speed. There was no longer a visible root of the man's pain, no sense of an ability to heal, just the noise and bustle of a hospital with a man screaming, and Sister Colissa shouting at her.

Leanna hurried to do what she was told, and then subsequently watched Colissa and the other priestess operate on the patient.

But it was to no avail, and the man died later that day.

—

That night, as she lay on top of her bed in the minutes before tenth hour, Leanna was finding it increasingly difficult not to share the peculiar details of what was happening to her with someone.

She had prayed for help and guidance that evening.

Lord Aiduel. Please give me the wisdom to know what is happening to me, Lord, and what I should do with it. I truly believe that you have given me these… powers, as gifts, Lord. But if that is so, how can my use of them also be heresy?

No answer was forthcoming, and she had only her own thoughts for guidance. In Leanna's mind, everything that was happening was linked intrinsically to the vision on the altar, and to the subsequent recurring dreams. But for what purpose was she feeling others' emotions? And had she really been certain that she could heal the man in the hospital, earlier in the day?

She wanted to discuss these things with Amyss, but given the speech by High Commander dei Bornere, she felt that she could be putting the smaller girl into danger by confiding. She had therefore been lying there in silent and conflicted contemplation for a number of minutes.

'What's up, Lea?' asked Amyss. 'You're awfully quiet.'

The one matter which she actually could talk about with Amyss were the dreams. 'What do you think it means, Amyss? Why do I keep having this same dream?'

'I don't know, Lea. But it's making me worried about you.'

'I'm sorry. I don't want you to be worried.'

'But I *am* worried. Worried it might hurt you. Is it too late to talk to one of the priests, or even to Sister Colissa? To see if they might help?'

'No, definitely not,' said Leanna, shaking her head. 'They'll probably think I'm going mad. But anyway, we agreed, we can't discuss this with anyone. Particularly not now, not with Aiduel's Guards here, and the High Commander having said what he said.'

'Oh, but he didn't mean you, Leanna!'

'He said that dreams can be heresy, Amyss.'

'Yes, but surely they don't mean the kind of dreams you've been having?'

'Amyss, you promised, remember! You mustn't tell anyone!' Leanna's voice was unintentionally sharp, and in the silence that followed she knew that she had upset her room-mate. 'I'm sorry, Amyss. I didn't mean to raise my voice. I don't know what I'd do if I didn't have you to talk to about this.'

There was silence for a few more seconds, then Amyss finally spoke up again, her voice quieter and more solemn than usual. 'What else, Lea? What else is going on that you're not telling me about? There's something, isn't there?'

Leanna sighed. She looked up towards Amyss, feeling guilty. Lies and deception were becoming so very tiring. 'Yes, there is… something. These dreams, I think they may be linked to… an event which happened to me before I came here. Something I can't talk about. Something which I swore not to talk about, to anyone.'

'Linked to your wedding? To you pulling out of the wedding?'

'Yes.'

'What was it? What is it, Lea? Please tell me.'

'I can't, Amyss. I won't.'

Amyss was quiet again for a few seconds, and when Leanna looked across she could see the hurt in the other girl's face.

'Don't you trust me, Lea?'

A wave of intense emotions, simultaneously both golden and

dark, suddenly passed through Leanna, like a strong and wild caress of her senses. From Amyss.

LOVE. HURT. LOVE. HURT.

The intensity of the feelings shocked Leanna. She sat up and turned towards her room-mate, and reached out to take the other girl's hands. 'I'm sorry, Amyss. I didn't mean to hurt you. If I could tell anyone, I'd tell you. I'd trust you with anything, now, you must know that? But I swore an oath. A holy oath. Not to tell anyone. Please tell me you believe that? Please tell me you understand?'

The red-headed girl looked at her, rolling her thumbs across the back of Leanna's hand. More emotions, more confusing sensations of deeply held feelings flowed out from her towards Leanna.

RELIEF. LOVE. NEED.

'I understand, Lea.' Amyss then squeezed Leanna's hand, and drew in a breath. 'Lea, I-'

The other girl suddenly stopped, and sat there in silence, looking downwards. After a few moments Leanna responded, 'What is it?'

Amyss continued to stare downwards in despondent silence, appearing for a second as if she was going to cry.

LOVE. DESIRE. LOVE. DESIRE.

Then she abruptly shook her head, causing her thick red hair to cascade around her shoulders, and a grin was back on her face. 'Nothing! Hey, what's going on? When did we start to become so serious and miserable? Hey, come on, let's stop depressing each other!'

The flow of emotions had stopped, but it left confusion for Leanna in its wake.

Lord Aiduel, what is happening to me? How is it right that I can be experiencing Amyss's feelings like this?

She felt disturbed by the invasion of her friend's emotions, but she was even more unsettled by the apparent meaning which she could discern from within those secret feelings,

274

The last month of Leanna's first year in the College brought a series of further unsettling events.

The first of these was a burning of a heretic by Aiduel's Guards. The news of the coming burning, of what would be the first execution by fire in living memory in the region of Arlais, spread quickly across the College and throughout the city itself.

A wise woman from a village to the north of the city had been accused of witchcraft and heresy, and had been tried and found guilty by the High Commander and a panel of his fellow Guards.

The burning had been scheduled for a Seventh-Day afternoon, and was to take place next to the encampment of the Guards, outside of the College grounds. Neither Leanna nor Amyss had any intention of watching the event. However, when the day arrived they could not ignore the crowds of people which walked past the College complex, heading to view the pending spectacle of the heretic being burned.

Leanna felt disgusted at the thought that people would regard this murder as entertainment. She was therefore surprised upon seeing her parents arriving at the College complex, this being a Seventh-Day when she had not been expecting them. She greeted them and then they walked together for a short while, Elisa steering her away from any potential listeners.

'What is it, Mum?' asked Leanna.

'We just wanted to come and tell you to be careful, Leanna,' replied her mother. 'These last two months, the city has become a... more dangerous place.'

'And stay away from *that*, today, Leanna,' added her father, pointing his thumb in the direction of the fields to the north. 'No good will come of it.'

Leanna nodded. 'I've no intention of watching, Dad.' She lowered her voice. 'It's horrible.'

Elisa leaned in towards her, and whispered. 'Leanna. You must be careful. The vision, what happened at the School. You haven't told anyone?'

'No, Mum.'

'Good girl. Don't mention it to anyone, under any circumstances. And don't say or do anything out of the ordinary, which could draw attention to you. They haven't interviewed you yet?'

'Who? Aiduel's Guards?'

'Yes,' replied her mother. 'They're interviewing lots of people in the city. *Lots* of people. Everyone is scared, unsettled, it seems like Aiduel's Guards can do what they like now, since the Emperor changed the law. But it's mainly young adults who are being questioned. People your age. A number of your old school-mates have already been interviewed. Well, I say interview. Jess Baker's mother said it was more like an interrogation.'

'Interviewed about what?'

'No one is sure, yet. The interviewees are being ordered at the end of the interview to keep it secret, and no one we know is telling. But be careful. If they haven't spoken to you yet, it's likely they'll be doing so soon. If they do, be good, be devout. But please don't mention the vision!'

'I won't Mum.'

After that, they rejoined Amyss, and the four of them waited tensely inside the College grounds as the execution was conducted on the land outside. The bustling, chattering noise of the crowd was in the background for the early part of the afternoon, and it was the reduction of that noise which indicated to the four of them that the execution was about to commence.

They then heard the distant voice of an individual speaking to the crowd, which Leanna assumed was an officer of Aiduel's Guards, reading the charges.

After this speech ended, the crowd remained quiet, and there was an extended period of silence.

Then the screaming started. A female voice, in agony,

It lasted for minutes, the sounds of tormented suffering joined after a few seconds by the image of smoke rising into the sky from beyond the College walls. Leanna stared at the billowing smoke and felt sick inside her stomach. The screaming seemed endless. She was holding her mother's hand on one side, and Amyss's on the other.

Lord Aiduel, in your mercy please end her misery, please end her misery.

The crowd remained subdued throughout, perhaps the spectacle of the event proving less satisfying than some had imagined. Finally, the agonised calls of the woman ended, and Leanna gave a silent thank you to The Lord.

'Lord preserve us,' said her father, sounding scared.

—

The second unsettling event took place a week after her nineteenth birthday, on the anniversary of the day when Leanna had first had the holy vision in the School of Saint Amena.

The staff and novices of the College were again gathered in the main central church, with Senior Priest Comrel standing at the front and facing them. The Senior Priest looked older and more tired than Leanna could ever remember. This time, he was not accompanied by anyone from Aiduel's Guards.

'My children,' he announced, his voice wavering. 'I have some news for you. Some news which is sad for me, but which in time may also bring happiness. After my thirty wonderful years as Senior Priest of this College, I have decided to retire. I am so proud of all of you, and of what we achieve together in this marvellous establishment. However, sadly I think that, although my spirit is willing, my body is struggling more and more to serve properly. I will be moving to a monastery in the north of the country within the next three or four months, to see out my remaining years.'

There was a shocked silence amongst the people assembled there. Priestess Corenna spoke up first. 'Who is to replace you, Father?'

Comrel's expression remained neutral. 'That is still to be decided. High Priest Comenis will no doubt make the final decision, after having received a recommendation from the Archprime in Elannis.'

Sister Colissa spoke up next. 'A more cynical person might believe that your retirement is linked to the... changes which have taken place in Arlais recently, Father? And to the decision of the Holy Church to ignore your protests about those changes.'

'Indeed,' said Senior Priest Comrel, smiling with sadness. 'A more cynical person might indeed believe that. Luckily, there are no cynical souls in this room, are there, Colissa?'

'No. No cynical souls. Only good souls, Father. And there'll be one less good soul following your departure. Aiduel bless you, Father.'

Leanna looked down at her hands, feeling even more anxiety about the future.

—

The final unsettling event occurred on the day which was exactly one year after Leanna had taken her Vows of Submission.

It happened after fourth hour afternoon prayers had concluded. Leanna was leaving the small prayer chapel, in the midst of a number of members of her novice group, including Amyss, when she was approached by a young soldier of Aiduel's Guards. He stared at her with an impassive expression, his red sash and cloak brilliantly bright in the afternoon sunshine.

'Novice Leanna Cooper, of Arlais?'

'Yes,' she replied, uncertainly. 'How may I help?'

'You are requested to accompany me to our interview tent. We would like to ask you some questions.'

'Now?'

'Yes, now.'

'Very well.'

Leanna turned her head and looked at Amyss, feeling scared.

Amyss's eyes and mouth were wide open in surprise. Emotions pulsed from her, rapidly.

FEAR. FEAR. FEAR.

Leanna tried to smile reassuringly, then turned to follow the Guard, feeling an equal measure of dread within her own heart.

Lord Aiduel, make my thoughts and actions true, and deliver me from evil.

17

Corin

—

Year of Our Lord,
After Ascension, 768AA

Corin sprinted frantically around the rocks which marked the entrance to the lakeside area.

Agbeth's screams from moments earlier were still ringing in his ears, but even worse than that was the abrupt silence which had followed that awful sound. Images of the deer which had been slaughtered by the felrin flashed into his mind as he ran, images which were then transformed into other thoughts, which were too ghastly to contemplate.

As he turned the corner into the flat land by the lake his axe was in his hand. He had no clear plan of action. He knew only that if he was too late, if something had already happened to Agbeth, then he would launch himself at the beast such that he could quickly share in her fate. His cowardice would not unman him this time.

The first thing that came into view was the lake itself; frozen, magnificent, and wholly indifferent to the events being played out upon it.

Then he spotted Agbeth, his wife staggering awkwardly backwards across the icy surface, towards the lake's centre. Terror was etched onto her face. But she was alive, unbloodied, unmutilated. Retreating. Slowly retreating.

She did not notice Corin's arrival. Her attention was focused upon the creature before her, pursuing her. The felrin. She was backing away from it, keeping her eyes locked upon it, her limp restricting her speed of movement.

It was a creature of nightmares. It stood on its thick hind legs, hunched over but somehow still as tall as a man. Its arms hung down almost to ground level, claws close to scraping the ice. Its whole body was covered in fur, and its face was like that of a wolf, except longer and thicker and far more terrible.

It moved towards Agbeth in a lurching manner, with none of the velocity with which Corin had seen it take down the deer. As if the movement of every single limb was an effort of willpower. If it had assaulted Agbeth with the speed at which it had come upon the stag, she would have already been dead. Something was restraining it, here. And yet, despite that, it was still closing on her, just a handful of metres away from its prey.

'Agbeth, run!' Corin's shout echoed across the clearing and the lake.

She heard him but it actually had the opposite effect to what he had intended, and she paused for a moment, turning towards him. Perhaps fatally.

In contrast, the beast ignored him and lurched forwards again, swinging out its arm as it did so. Its claws missed Agbeth's face by just inches.

Corin sprinted towards them both, axe raised, and for the first time in his life he screamed. Yelled with every ounce of force within his lungs. Screaming out his bloodlust. His fear was suddenly forgotten. He would save her, here, by this lake, or he would die trying.

The creature now swung its head towards him as Corin shrieked and narrowed the distance over the ice towards it. A baleful eye locked its gaze upon him, and then once again he experienced the disorientating sensation that he was gazing out of two pairs of eyes, simultaneously. His own, as he pounded towards the beast. And its eyes, as it watched him come, claws ready.

Without conscious thought, he again found himself touching upon its mind. Feeling its animal impulses, its ravenous urge to close upon and eviscerate its prey.

And something else was there too, something which was infuriating it. A command. Embedded.

STOP!

The felrin was straining every sinew in its body to fight that instruction, but the beast knew that the command was taking root within it. And that those roots were being planted deep, burrowing into its core. An image was flashing repeatedly in its mind of being locked into place, unable to move. It was resisting that image, trying to force itself forwards. But it could not shake the order away. And it was maddening, enraging. Slowing it down. Helping the slow prey to escape.

And now the source of that command was before it. Running towards it. Small, two-legged prey. Screaming. Kill that one, and it would be free. Free to kill them both. And to feed. It wrested its body around, claws raised.

As Corin drew nearer to the creature, he concurrently both observed and experienced it swinging its body to face him. He was still screaming maniacally as he sprinted across the frozen lake towards the felrin, and he enjoyed a fleeting moment of triumph that he had distracted the beast's attention away from Agbeth. However, such victorious thoughts quickly evaporated as he realised with horror that he would close within reach of its deadly embrace in just moments.

He tried to stop his forward progress, now. However, his momentum was too great and the icy surface was too slippery. As he tried to slow down, his feet slid from underneath him, sending him out-of-balance and hurtling to the floor. He was then skidding the last few metres across the lake towards the creature, body face-forwards on the ice, axe skittering out of his hand.

He could still see through this bizarre double image. The ice before his own eyes. And, from the creature's viewpoint, he could watch himself. Sliding towards it, prostrate and prone on the ground. He could feel the beast's exultation as its enemy drew near, and as it raised its arm to strike and to kill.

Time slowed down for Corin in those final few moments, as he slid across the ice, and once again he experienced the sensation of invisible tendrils extending outwards from his thoughts. Reaching for something to grasp onto. Then finding the felrin. Locating its mind. And locking onto it.

And then, once more, Corin shrieked an order to the creature, through this connection.

STOP! STOP! STOP! STOP! STOP!

A clearer image was created this time, a mental picture which was much easier to define now that he was so close to the beast. Of it being locked in place. Arm raised, but unable to swing it. Frozen, like the lake. Unable to strike. Unable to kill.

And then his sliding momentum expired, and he banged into the creature's legs. He braced, waiting for the instant when the dagger-like claws would sink into his body, or when large paws would wrap around his neck and then rip his head off.

But the killing blow did not come.

Agbeth shrieked from some metres away, as if she herself was anticipating what Corin was also expecting. And yet, still, he remained untouched. He turned his body, feeling clumsy and slow, and looked up from his position of lying on his back on the ice.

The creature was poised above him. Poised, yet immobile, except for tiny tremors across its body. One arm was raised, claws fully extended and pointed down towards him. The other arm was by its side, the tips of razor-sharp claws just inches from his face. Its long snout was also pointing down towards him, opened to display its teeth, and drool was dripping out of its mouth. The gold-coloured eye visible to Corin was still focused upon him.

And the beast's whole body was trembling, with tremors which were almost imperceptible, but still there. It was fighting the latest command that he had planted within its mind. Struggling to free itself. Straining to move again. And failing.

He could sense this connection between them, locked securely into place, and he somehow knew with certainty that it had no means to free itself. No means to escape, despite the rage it felt at being so enslaved. He controlled it, now.

Seconds passed.

'Corin, get up, please.' Agbeth's voice, sounding terrified and uncertain.

Following the prompt from his wife, he reached out his hand to push himself up, accidentally touching the large fur covered paw on the felrin's rear legs as he did so. He could feel the tense vibrations within the creature.

He raised himself to his feet. Again, he was beset with the disorientating sensation of experiencing two minds at once. His own and the beast's. Feeling its rage, its ferocity, its frustration. And its bloodlust, the latter echoing what he had felt inside himself in those manic moments when he had charged towards the creature.

'Corin, please move away from it.'

He ignored her, staring directly at the felrin, his face on a level with its snout as it was hunched forwards. Still it could not move, but its malevolent gaze was fixed upon him. He stared into the beast's eyes.

FEAR. CONTROL. ORDER.

The words whispered seductively into his mind, and he knew with absolute conviction that the invisible connection was still locked into place, enforcing his will upon the creature.

It would be the easiest thing in the world to pick up his axe, now, and then to return to slowly chop up the beast. To incapacitate and dismember it, as it stood there helpless and unmoving. He transmitted the mental picture to the creature. Showing it. Showing it what he could do to it now, were he so to choose.

Gruesome images, perhaps drawing on the scenes of mutilation and horror that the beast itself had witnessed and inflicted during its lifetime. Images of Corin killing the felrin. Slowly and agonisingly disembowelling it. Then feeding upon it.

And for the first time, he could sense the creature experiencing an unfamiliar sensation. Fear. Fear of being prey, of meeting and being overcome by a superior predator. Fear of these things which Corin was showing that he would inflict upon it.

'Corin?' Agbeth's voice again, full of unease. And again, he ignored her.

SUBMIT! SUBMIT! SUBMIT! SUBMIT! SUBMIT!

His mind screamed the command at the creature, taking its own monstrous rage and hurling it back towards the beast, with even greater intensity. Commands contained within images and instincts which the creature understood. Images of a lesser animal bowing its neck before a greater. Presenting itself in submission, in obeisance. He could feel it resisting, struggling against him. But he enforced his will upon it.

And then he felt the felrin's willpower break. Felt it submit. Not overtly, not physically, for it was still frozen in place. But in its mind. A breaking of resistance. An acceptance, that it had met a dominant predator, and that it had no alternative here other than to submit or to die. Then its eyes dropped, no longer meeting his gaze.

And he knew that it was his, now. And so it was that he released it.

—

Minutes later, having watched the beast run away from him and Agbeth, he was standing motionless, staring towards the forest tree line.

'Corin, what just happened?'

Again, he did not respond to his wife. He was continuing to feel the association with the creature, could see through its eyes as it thundered through the woods back to its lair. Could feel and savour the tremendous power and ferocity, pulsing through its body, so different to his own weak human form.

'Corin! Answer me!' Her voice was suddenly shrill, unnerved.

'I'm sorry, what?' He was still distracted, but her tone of voice caused him to focus back on her, and he suddenly felt guilty that he had not moved to Agbeth. He did so, now, holding his arms out, and she came into his embrace.

'Corin, what just happened?' She was breathing heavily, her body trembling, and he could hear that she was close to tears.

'I'm not sure. I was inside its mind. I could control it.'

'What? I thought... I thought it was going to kill me. And then you. And then... it froze?'

'Yes. I did that.'

'What? How?'

'I... somehow, I could feel myself inside it. Seeing what it saw, feeling what it felt. And I could control it. I don't know how, Agbeth. But I can still feel it, now.'

She leaned back from the embrace, looking at him with an enigmatic expression. 'That doesn't make any sense, Corin.'

'I know. But it's true.'

He could feel her continuing to tremble. 'I thought I was going to die.'

'Thank the Gods that I got here in time, Agbeth. Thank the Gods that I saved you.' He could feel a sense of pride within himself. His actions today had been in such contrast to his cowardice in the Anath village. He had cast aside concern for his own wellbeing, and he had risked his own life to save hers. And had succeeded. He had saved her life.

'I want to leave here,' Agbeth announced, after a few moments.

He frowned. 'We don't need to, now.'

'Why not? What if it returns? How can I feel safe, with that… thing in the woods?'

'It won't hurt us, now, Agbeth. I'm sure of that.'

'But how? How can you be sure?'

'I just am.'

And he *was* sure. As he watched through the beast's eyes as it stalked into its lair, a small cave a mile to the north, he felt certain that from that moment on he would always know where it was, what it was seeing, and what its primitive instincts and cravings were. And that within this peculiar connection, he would also be able to shape and control its actions.

—

His statement that the felrin was no longer a threat to the two of them was subsequently proven to be correct. It initially stayed away from their camp, and in the week that followed he began to explore the strange association between himself and the creature.

The beast was always there, lurking in the back of his mind. It was an ever-present foreign presence, an unfamiliar entity which perceived and reacted to the world in a way which was completely alien to Corin. Its body was a mass of muscular force and energy, and in its environment everything else around it was pitiful prey. Prey to be killed and consumed.

The creature still howled out its shrieking call each night, but this was no longer a source of fear for Corin. Instead, he sometimes wanted to join in with the cry, feeling an urge to exult in the communal experience of howling out their bloodlust. He resisted doing this, lest Agbeth start to doubt his sanity.

His wife did not share in his confidence about their safety, and he could feel her shivering against him in the darkness when the beast's calls carried across the forest. Despite her obvious fear in those moments, he now found himself filled with primitive urges whenever he heard the creature's cries. Urges to hunt. To kill. To mate. But each time he also resisted these base instincts.

And on the first occasion when the felrin caught prey again, the victim being a large and slow badger, Corin also shared in the experience of the killing of the animal. Followed by the voracious sensation of feeding, of being a vicious predator devouring its captive prey. The shared experience caused his mouth to water, and his empty stomach to ache.

It then seemed like a simple progression, after a few days, to order the felrin to bring food to him. He formed an image in his mind, which he pushed across the connection between them, showing the beast dropping food at his feet. Having commanded the creature this way, Corin then observed from inside its mind as it captured and killed another animal. Then dragged it across the forest. He ordered Agbeth back inside the lean-to as he sensed the creature arriving at the edge of the lake, then he watched it emerge from the treeline. Dragging another deer.

Corin moved towards it, cautiously. The beast was standing up straight on its hind legs, presenting its full eight-foot height to him. Again, he experienced that disconcerting moment of seeing from two perspectives at the same time, of watching himself approaching through another creature's eyes.

SUBMIT! SUBMIT! SUBMIT! SUBMIT! SUBMIT!

He was transmitting the same images as he had done previously, days earlier, of a creature bowing its neck to another. And this time the beast did not fight against him, and instead bent forwards, crouching lower so it faced down to the forest floor. The back of its neck was presented to him, and its front paws were rested upon the ground.

Corin drew closer, and started to whisper words of reassurance to the creature. Its thick fur was predominantly light brown, other than on one of its front paws, which was black. *Blackpaw.* He could hear it growling as he drew closer, although not in a manner which suggested an imminent threat to him.

When he was within a pace of the creature, a rational part of him recognised what madness this was, that he was undertaking. It would be but a moment's effort for the creature to sweep out its claws, and to decapitate him. But he was sure that was not going to happen.

Instead, he slowly reached out a hand and touched the top of the felrin's head. Then stroked its fur. Its neck remained bowed in submission.

'Thank you, Blackpaw. Thank you for the food.'

—

Agbeth had ignored his instruction, and had watched the encounter from just outside of their shelter.

Later, when the creature had gone again and they were both greedily eating cooked meat from the deer, she wanted to talk about what had happened. 'Corin, how are you doing this? How did you get that... thing, to do that?'

'It's Blackpaw. I'm calling it Blackpaw. And in answer to your question, I'm not sure. I just feel like I've become connected to it. Can control it, somehow. How exactly? I don't know.'

'It's like you have some of... Mella's powers.' She said this last part shyly.

He laughed, a piece of venison between his teeth. 'I'm not sure I'm a god, Agbeth. Not quite, not yet.'

'Don't mock me, Corin. These things that you can do with the creature. Blackpaw. It isn't normal. You know that.'

'I know. I'm sorry, I didn't mean to sound like I was mocking you. But it's not just the felrin. It's other animals, too. I've been feeling this kind of... connection, with lots of animal life around us, ever since we've been in this forest. It's almost like being inside them, inside their minds.'

'But you've never had this feeling before? In Karn?'

'Never. I can only think that it's one of two things, that's causing it. Either being up here, closer to the home of the Gods, is giving me some of their powers. Or that it's somehow connected to my dream, and the Gate I keep seeing. Or both. I just don't know, for sure.'

'And what about me? Can you feel inside my mind, too?'

'No.'

'Have you tried?' She was scrutinising him as she asked the question.

'No. And I don't want to try. Ever.'

—

The next few weeks witnessed the two of them enduring and passing through the worst of the winter weather, sustained by the freshly slaughtered carcasses which were supplied by the felrin Blackpaw. With each delivery it would bow its head down low, and Corin would feel its primitive pleasure as he stroked its fur and whispered his thanks.

Corin was also able to start hunting again, and that hunting had become considerably easier. Each time he would stalk into the woods, as previously, but now he could sense and link himself to his potential prey long before he could see it, feeling it become tethered to him through an invisible connection.

And once he identified and was joined to his target, he would send the same images to immobilise it as he had first used on Blackpaw, on that day of panic. Each time, it worked, and his victim was frozen in place, helpless against his intentions. Then it was a simple task to find the doomed animal and to kill them. He tested this power extensively, without fail, and he was beginning to wonder if there was *anything* that it would not work upon.

Over time, Agbeth began to share Corin's confidence that Blackpaw was no longer a deadly threat. Despite the ongoing cold, her mood also improved again as her fear and hunger were diminished. However, the difficulties of their living conditions, and the constant icy chill under which they lived, were continuing to effect Agbeth in other ways. Only a month after she had suffered her first seizure in years, another one descended upon her.

They were both outside by the lake, in the midst of a clear and sunny day, when it happened.

'Look, Corin. At the centre of the lake. Is that a thaw?'

He was peering towards the spot which she was pointing out. 'Yes, I think it may be-'

His words were cut off as he saw her sliding to the floor next to him, falling onto her arms, and then convulsions immediately gripped her body. He ran to her, watching the seizure assailing her with the same symptoms of unfocused rolling eyes, clenched jaw, and jerking limbs.

He wrapped his arms around her, feeling horrified that this was happening to her once more. The seizure was going on for minutes. He closed his eyes, fighting back tears.

Then abruptly, the sense of the world slowing down came upon him. And invisible ethereal connections were emerging from his mind. Snaking out of his thoughts, and into Agbeth's soul. Finding her. Sharing in her experience of seizure, feeling the betrayal of her body and limbs as she was racked by the fit.

CALM. CALM. CALM. CALM. CALM.

He transmitted the message to her. Images of breathing calmly. Of a warm, safe, summer day, with the sun beating down upon her. Images of relaxation, of happiness. Images of their times together after lovemaking, cuddled sleepily in each other's arms.

CALM. CALM. CALM. CALM. CALM.

And gradually, he felt her convulsions lessening in urgency, and he knew that she was returning to him. Her breathing was restored to a normal state, and eventually she whispered, 'I'm back, Corin.'

He kissed her, and then immediately he forced himself to sever the mental connection between them. But he felt certain about something else, now. This power he owned, this strange ability, it was not just limited to the beasts of the forest around them. He was sure that he could control people now, as well.

And if he chose to, he could control Agbeth, too.

—

By the time spring arrived, his strange dream was still visiting him every other night, disturbing his sleep and leaving him with an uneasy sense of wrongness every time that he awoke from it. A wrongness at the Gate. He continued to ponder about the meaning of the dream, and what the Gate itself was, and whether it might reside in the mountains to the north. He could feel a longing building inside of himself, an urge to one day seek out the Gate, wherever it was. If, indeed, it was real.

His connection to Blackpaw continued to be strong. At a time when the ice and snow had completely thawed from the lake, he sensed the creature making its way towards their camp, but this time without prey.

He could feel a different kind of longing within the beast. A desire to go north, now that the winter had passed. Back to its summer hunting lands within the foothills of the mountains. Back to where there were others of its kind. Potential mates.

When it arrived at the lake's edge, it assumed the position of obeisance before him, which it now adopted every time it brought food to him. He moved to it, whispering words of comfort, and stroked its fur. He knew what it wanted, and after a few moments he transmitted the message to it.

GO! GO! GO! GO! GO!

Immediately the creature turned away from him, and started to sprint back into the forest, heading north. The sight of its haunches disappearing into the trees was the last that he saw of it, but shortly afterwards he heard it howl with excitement as it galloped towards the distant mountains. And he could constantly feel it there, in his head, as it travelled further and further away.

—

He and Agbeth were sitting together, that evening, arms touching, both of them feeling happy again. They were each enjoying the improving climate around them, and the re-emergence of plants and wildlife in the forest.

'What shall we do then, Agbeth? Shall we stay here, or leave?'

'Just a few weeks ago, if you'd asked me that, I would have said to leave. But now? With the weather returning? I think that I'd like to have a spring here, and another summer. It was so lovely here in the summer, last year. And then see how we feel in the autumn.'

He nodded. 'I think that, too. If you'd asked me, when you were ill, and we had no food, and were scared, I would've also said to go. But now, with the better weather, it seems so appealing to be here, again. Let's stay until the autumn.'

She smiled. 'And the beast – sorry, Blackpaw – has gone now?'

'Yes. Far into the north. But I think it'll be back, next winter.'

'And you can still feel it?'

'Yes. It's always there. In the back of my mind.'

'Could you call it back?'

'Yes, I think so.' In fact, he was certain that he could.

'Well. Don't.'

He laughed. 'OK, I won't.'

'Corin?'

'Yes?'

'I'm not pregnant. I thought I might be, by now, but I'm not. But, with what we do together… what if I get with child?'

'Then we might need to travel back. Whilst we still can.'

'But where would we go? What would we do?'

'Back to Karn, maybe.'

'To Karn? How?'

'I think I might know a way to get Borrik to let me back into the clan. A possible way.' He thought about telling her, considered mentioning that moment when he had slipped into her mind, and had controlled the ending of her seizure. But instead he decided to change the subject. 'But let's not worry about that, right now.'

He placed his arm around her shoulder, and she cuddled into him. 'I love you Corin.'

'And I love you, Agbeth. My wonderful wife.' He kissed the top of her head.

They remained like that for a long while, watching the sun disappear behind the tree line in the west. There was a vividness in the quality of the light, that evening, and the sky was painted in startlingly beautiful colours of purple and orange. The world around them was at peace.

It was an evening that Corin would long remember, afterwards, on darker nights.

18

Allana

—

Year of Our Lord,
After Ascension, 768AA

Allana continued to search for answers, as Duke Conran Sepian stared at her whilst leaning back against the desk in his antechamber.

Stop panicking, Lana! You must not lose everything that you have worked for, here. You will survive. You must survive.

Her hand slipped slowly into the pocket of her dress, seeking out and finding her knife.

'Well?' The Duke's hand casually reached down to rest upon the hilt of the dagger at his belt, unknowingly mimicking her action. 'Must I call the guard in?'

She looked at him, feeling despair. His eyes were cold but shrewd. She knew with grim certainty that he would detect any further lies.

It is time to tell the truth, Lana. It is either that, or try to lunge at him with this knife. And are you really prepared to kill again?

'My name is not Lana Marrone,' she said, eventually. 'It is Allana dei Monis, my Lord. I have no father, to my knowledge. I was

295

born out of wedlock and my mother was thrown out of our family home before I was born. I've lived my whole life until the last few months in Sen Aiduel. Not Dei Aiduel, which I've never been to.' She paused, gathering her thoughts.

Lana, should you blame the murder on Mum? Should you follow the same lie which Aiduel's Guards seem to believe? And condemn Mum's memory to be that of a murderer?

'Go on,' prompted the Duke, forcing her to decide.

'My mother is dead. She did die of the Wasting Sickness, last year. I didn't lie about that. Before her illness, she was the mistress of High Priest Ronis, the High Priest of Sen Aiduel. After her death, I was visited by the High Priest. He assaulted me. Was going to rape me. So, I...' She paused again, drawing in a deep breath. 'In self-defence, I killed him. I hadn't planned it. It just happened. But I knew I'd be burned for what I'd done, so I fled. I took the High Priest's money – that was the coin purse your men found – and bought passage on a trading ship. It was travelling to Septholme, so I arrived here by accident.'

The Duke was staring at her, impassively. 'And then what?'

'And then I set up work as a seamstress. Until I got the job here.'

'So, you're telling me you really are a seamstress?'

Given what she had already disclosed, Allana saw no point in concealing further lies. 'I'm a seamstress, now, because I've made myself become one. Before arriving here, I was a... *nothing*. A spoilt child, relying on my mum's income as a courtesan.'

'You're saying that your mother was a whore?'

For a brief second a flame of rage burned inside Allana at his use of that word, but then she controlled herself. 'Yes, my Lord. A whore.'

'So why come to this castle? Why not keep doing your seamstress work?'

'Aiduel's Guards are searching for my mother and me. They think that my mum is still alive, and was the one who murdered the High Priest. She isn't and she didn't. But the Guards are here in Septholme, as I'm sure you know, Lord, and they'd found my home. I had to leave. I thought I'd be hidden and safer here.'

'So, you're claiming that no one is paying you? That you're not an agent or a spy?'

'No one is paying me. I swear on the The Lord Aiduel, no one is paying me! That money is what I took from Ronis. I don't even know what an agent or a spy is, my Lord. I'm a seamstress, now. That's all.'

He stared at her again. 'You know what, girl? I think I may even believe you.' He laughed, although there was no mirth in the sound. 'I thought I had a spy in my home. And instead I have a thief and a murderer!'

'It was self-defence, my Lord.'

What now, Lana? What is he going to do next? And what will you do?

'And yet still murder. I was in Sen Aiduel, recently. I'd heard that that sanctimonious bastard Ronis had died – which adds credence to your story – but not *how*. How did it happen? How did you kill him?'

'He was above me, on a bed, my Lord,' she said. As she spoke these words she wondered if, for the first time since arriving in this room, there was a glint of some other untapped emotion in his eyes? 'Ready to… force himself on me. I had a small knife. I didn't think. I stabbed it into his neck.'

He stepped back away from her, moving across the room, placing distance between them. 'Who'd have thought that such a petite and delicate woman would be capable of such violence?'

'Just once, my Lord. Once only. Never again.' She tried to ignore the fleeting memory of standing beside Nionia, with a knife in her hand, battling against unforgivable impulses. Even now, she was aware of the weight of the knife sitting in her pocket.

She then watched the Duke pace across the room, noting how he maintained his distance from her. 'So, the question for me now becomes; what should I do with you?'

'Please show mercy on me, my Lord.'

'It's not a question of mercy, girl. It's a question of law. Of justice. You killed a man, by your own admission, then stole from him and fled from the crime scene. And from what you say, Aiduel's Guards are already searching for you, for your crimes.'

'What does that mean?'

'It means that... I owe you nothing, least of all mercy. It means that I want you out of my castle. Want you away from my people and my family. It means that I'm going to hand you over to Aiduel's Guards, as your countrymen. And they can make the decision whether to show mercy for the deeds you committed in your own country, or to dispense appropriate justice.'

He mustn't do this, Lana! Don't let him do this! If he reports you, and you're handed over, you're dead!

'Please, my Lord, no! They will kill me.'

The Duke stared at her with disapproval, apparently indifferent to her pleas, and he moved to the door of his bedroom. She knew with despairing certainty that once he opened that door, once he summoned in the guard, she was lost. Her downfall, and ultimately her death, would follow.

Desperation filled her, a desperation fused with a knowledge that she would do anything to avoid being delivered into the hands of Aiduel's Guards. And with that panicked realisation, three long-forgotten words re-emerged from the dark shadows within which they had been patiently lurking.

LUST. POWER. DOMINATION.

Then, as had already happened twice before in her life, once with Ronis and once with Obnel Rabnar, the world slowed down around her. The Duke's movement towards his chamber door appeared to her to transition from rapid to woefully sluggish, and Allana was once again filled with a detached sense of calm and control.

You will not accept defeat here, Lana. You will survive. You must survive.

'Conran, look at me.' She knew his name, but until this moment she would never have dared to use it.

Seemingly compelled by her words, his movement towards the door ceased and he turned to face her. Unseen tendrils sinuously spiralled out of her mind and sought out his. Finding it, pushing against his thoughts, probing for entry into his very being.

He was resisting. She could feel him sensing something *alien* curling and coalescing against his thoughts, something which he now feared. He was a man of strong willpower, a man accustomed to dominating others, and she knew that he was fighting back against what he instinctively knew was an attempt to force surrender of his own control. She sensed that he was trying to turn away, trying to renew his movement to the door, even trying to call out. With that knowledge, she redoubled her effort through the invisible connection. Freezing him in place. Locking his jaw shut.

Allana stood up, and moved towards him. She placed herself directly in front of him, facing him. She could see small vibrations in his body as he fought against the ceding of control to her, but in her detached state of consciousness Allana knew that it was inevitable that he would succumb. Her eyes sought out his, locking their stares together. She could see fear in his dark piercing eyes, and also a flicker of pleading. Was he asking *her* for mercy now?

But the closer she was, the stronger the tendrils seeking entry into his soul became. Soon they would break his will; they both knew it.

And then she was inside his mind. Entering it, and linking his consciousness to hers. Locking the connection into place. Coming closer to dominating him. To subjugating him. But he was still fighting against her, still wilfully resisting, at the moment when she started to speak to him through that connection.

Look at me, Conran. Look at my face. At my body. I know that you think I'm beautiful. I know that you want me.

He could not resist doing as he was told, and she rejoiced in the feeling of lust which she could sense stirring inside of him as his gaze suddenly poured across her.

How long since you have lain with a woman, Conran? And have you ever been with a woman who you wanted as much as you want me, right now?

As she whispered the words into his mind, she could feel the desire building inside of him, constantly magnifying and intensifying. His body was still shaking with tiny tremors as he tried to resist, but the longing he was feeling inside himself was overwhelming him.

And as had happened with Rabnar, Allana was experiencing that yearning mirrored inside of herself. She could feel the heat building within her body in waves and waves of delight, so welcome after months of denying herself this pleasure.

You want me, Conran. And you can have me. But only if you protect me. Only if you do what I want. What I need.

She saw his head move slightly, almost a shake of denial, as the force of her willpower surged against him again. His eyes widened as the last vestiges of his powerful free will fought against her, but she knew that he was on the edge of breaking.

You need me. Need me. But protect me, Conran. Keep me safe. Then I will give myself to you.

Carnal images were transmitted by her across the link between them. Fragments of memories of her encounters with Rabnar. Promises to the Duke of what might be. Further enflaming his overpowering desire and shredding his tattered remaining resistance.

Protect me. Keep me safe. Then you can have me.

And then, finally, she felt his willpower shatter. And she knew that he was hers.

—

She released her hold upon the Duke, and time sped up around her at the same moment that her enhanced state of consciousness lapsed. He lurched backwards, gasping, as she finally cast off the iron shackles with which she had held his mind. He appeared dazed and confused, his breathing heavy. As with Rabnar, she felt certain that the memory of the conflict, which had just taken place between their minds, was lost to him. However, she also knew that she had planted an overwhelmingly powerful urge deep inside of him.

She stepped forwards, standing closer to him, just a foot away. Looking up. Even though he was only of average height for a man, her petite frame meant that she was still several inches shorter than him.

How quickly this encounter has changed, Lana. And how quickly you seem capable of changing, too. But you'll do anything that you need to do to stay alive. Anything.

'You know my secrets, Conran,' she said. She reached out a hand and placed it onto his chest, fully aware of the hungry way in which he watched her movement. She could also feel his heart, hammering fast beneath her touch. 'What are you going to do?'

'I'm going to protect you, Lana,' he responded. 'I'm going to keep you safe. No one needs to know who you are or what you've done. I promise I'll protect you.'

Her other hand reached up, and slid onto the side of his neck. Lightly caressing it. 'And what do you want in return, Conran?'

'I want…' He hesitated, and despite all of the control which she had embedded within him, she sensed that there was some part of him which was still resisting, even now.

She moved closer to him, just an inch separating their bodies, mouths close together. 'I know what you want, Conran. I want it, too.' And she did. Her own body ached for the pleasure which she had been denying herself, ever since her experiences on the boat with Rabnar.

Duke Conran was not as handsome as the ship's captain had been, and he was much older than her. Too old, in any other, *normal* circumstances. However, there was something darkly intoxicating and arousing about using her beauty and her strange ability to dominate a man with so much authority and power. And there was a raw masculine ruggedness and strength in Conran, which Rabnar had not possessed.

She leaned in and kissed the Duke, slowly and softly, and felt him hungrily returning the kiss. Shortly afterwards, he was shouting an instruction to his guard in the corridor outside that he was not to be disturbed.

Then he took hold of Allana's hand, and drew her into his bedroom.

—

Afterwards, they lay together, in the Duke's bed. Allana's body was splayed across him, her head in the hollow of his neck. She was luxuriating in the pleasurable afterglow of what they had done together, in the release which she had been craving for months and had at last found.

He still appeared dazed by what had happened. 'That is the first time I have... been with someone. For a very long time.'

'Since your wife died?'

'Yes.' He sounded embarrassed, and guilty.

'Do you regret it?'

'No. Lord, no.'

'Me neither.' And she meant that.

There was a peaceful silence, for minutes after that. Finally, Duke Conran spoke again, and his voice sounded troubled. 'Lana, the thing you did. Ronis's death. You promise me that you're not a danger to anyone here?'

'I promise.'

'Because I could not forgive myself, if my letting you remain here led to harm to another person.' He sounded conflicted, as if the commands which she had placed within him were still struggling against his natural instincts.

'I'm not a danger to anyone, Conran. It was self-defence. It will never happen again. All I want is another chance.'

When he responded, he sounded more resolved. 'Then I want you to stay here, at the castle. I'll keep your secret. I'll tell no one. And

I promise to keep you safe. I'll protect you from Aiduel's Guards and from anyone else who would threaten you.'

'Thank you, Conran.'

He has no idea what you did to him, Lana. No idea that he's doing what you ordered him to do. He thinks the impulse is his.

'But Lana?'

'Yes?'

'I cannot bear the thought that this is the only time we will be together, like this. I never thought that I'd do this again, with anyone, after Meralynn. But now that we have. I could not bear the thought that…'

She kissed his neck. 'There will be other times, Conran. Protect me. Keep my secrets. Keep me safe. And there will be other times.'

—

In the weeks that followed, she became the Duke's mistress.

She was a little shocked herself at what she was doing, at first.

Are you any different to Mum, now, Lana? She slept with men for money, to stay alive. And you've seduced a man who's much older than you so that he protects you, so that he doesn't deliver you to those who would do you harm.

But Allana did perceive a difference. She had only initiated this because the alternatives had been to be delivered into the hands of Aiduel's Guards, or to be thrown into a castle dungeon. Or to attack the Duke with a knife. And faced with those choices, this was clearly the best option. Which ensured her own survival.

Indeed, after the months of abstinence, she was relishing their affair. As with Rabnar, the two of them were enjoying a mutual passion which was fuelled and intensified by what she had done to the Duke's mind. The Duke had remained celibate for years in memory of his late wife, and Allana could see that he in turn was shocked by how addicted he had become to their liaisons.

After their impetuous first afternoon together, however, their

303

following encounters were more discreet and cautious. They would agree the next night when they would meet, and then, after hours, she would creep from the outbuilding towards his chambers. They would spend the night together, but she would always be careful to return to her own bed in the outbuilding before sunrise. They spent one night of each week in the other's company, which was the longest period over which the Duke could suppress his urge to meet again.

However, notwithstanding this attempted discretion, word soon spread into the castle that Allana had become something more than a mere seamstress. She was also the Duke's mistress.

—

The first person to raise the subject with her was Ami Randle. Allana had already noticed that a number of days had passed without Ami being as friendly with her, when the older woman finally spoke out. 'You know, you need to be careful about these games you're playing, girl.'

'What games?' asked Allana, with false surprise.

'Don't act innocent with me. You know exactly what games. The whole castle does.'

'And if you're talking about what I think you are, how's it any of your business? And where's the harm in it?'

'It's my business because I gave you a job here. The harm in it is that a commoner like you shouldn't be with the Duke. And the whole castle thinks that you're a whore, girl. If I had my way, you'd be out of here. Right now.'

Allana felt a rage brewing inside herself at being called a whore, and her response was sharp. 'But you don't have your way any longer, do you? If you're so concerned, why don't you go speak with the Duke and tell him to get rid of me?'

Ami Randle tutted loudly. 'Listen to you, getting all high and mighty just because the Duke happens to let you into his bed. Mark my words, girl. You're just a short-term mistress. A nobody. He'll soon get bored of you. And when he does, Master Koss and Lord Gerrion will have you out of here before the sun's set. No one wants a little foreign whore sleeping with the Duke.'

The second time that the older woman used the insulting word, Allana lost control of herself. Her hand swung out and caught the Head of Household on her cheek with a hard slap, sending the older woman staggering backwards. Randle looked shocked and upset, a large red mark on her face. Despite her authority, she looked closer to crying than to reacting with similar anger.

How dare she call you that, Lana! How dare she! You're better than her. You're more than her. She deserves to be hurt, for what she said to you!

Allana's face was flushed as she shouted her response. 'Don't ever call me that again! Or raise this subject with me. If you do, I'll ask the Duke to throw *you* out. And if I ask him, believe me, he'll do it.'

Randle looked cowed, eyes watery, and she backed away from Allana rather than reacting again. Their relationship was irreparably damaged after that, and never again did the Head of Household sit next to Allana when she was working, or speak to her in anything other than a business-like manner.

And Allana's affair with Duke Conran continued after that confrontation, unmoved by Randle's words.

—

A more threatening subsequent encounter was with Lord Gerrion, two months after her affair with his father had started. Allana was summoned to Gerrion's chambers, where she found him standing with Charl Koss.

The two of them did not offer her a seat, but instead stood to either side of her as Gerrion spoke.

'Lana, both Charl and I feel that we should speak with you. This is a delicate matter, though. And before we begin, we need your word that this conversation will remain confidential. From *all* parties.'

She knew who he meant, from the last words. 'Everyone, my Lord? Including the Duke?'

'Most especially the Duke. Charl and I are his servants, no different to you. Sometimes we act openly in his direct interests, with his express instructions. Other times, given the troubling nature of this world, we must act indirectly. In his best interests, but without his direct instructions.'

Allana met his stare as he spoke to her, and again she experienced that peculiar sense that there was something absent in the manner with which he regarded her. She was aware that her strange recurring power was always triggered by attraction and lust within nearby men, but with Gerrion she felt as if there was nothing within him to draw upon.

'I will if I can, my Lord. As long as I'm not doing anything… against the Duke's best interests.'

He frowned as she said this last part. 'Very well. Let me speak frankly, then. We are aware of your… dalliance with the Duke. It was initially pleasing to see father appearing happy, again, after years of mourning mother. But, as time moves on and he's not lost interest in you, I start to grow more concerned. What are your intentions, girl?'

'I don't have any intentions, Lord.'

He appeared to disregard her answer as he continued. 'If you're thinking to get pregnant, and to find status that way, be aware that even to the Duke your child would be a bastard. An unrecognised nobody, with no claim to any land or titles or wealth. And you would bring shame on the Duke. And potential censure from the Church, at a time when he could least afford it. And I would then personally ensure that you and your baby would both be thrown out, penniless.'

Allana blushed. 'I… have not been planning that, Lord. I'm not pregnant.'

But you haven't been careful either, Lana. With either Rabnar or the Duke. And yet you're not pregnant? Why not?

'And don't think for a second that you've any chance of coercing him into marrying you for love, Lord forbid that he might feel that way. The Duke would never do it. He detests marriages of the Andar nobility to those of Elannis and Dei Magnus blood. And he would anyway never marry a dirty commoner like you. It would bring shame on him and all of the family.'

Allana clenched her teeth together, trying to ignore the insult. 'I haven't ever discussed that.'

'Then what?' Charl Koss asked, interrupting. 'What are you after, girl?'

'Nothing.' *Safety. Protection. To stay alive, without being hunted.*

Koss continued. 'How much do we need to pay you, to disappear? To get back on a boat to Dei Magnus?'

For just a moment, she considered it. Considered taking their money, and running again. But that would mean losing the security and protection which Duke Conran now offered her.

'I don't want to disappear. I don't want your money, either, Master. I'm staying here for as long as the Duke wants me here.'

With obvious frustration, Gerrion suddenly stated, 'Despite what she claims, she has aspirations of grandeur. Of seducing him into marrying her. Well, it won't happen. Just know this, girl. You're not fit to wipe the feet of my mother, the late Duchess. Never mind aspiring to take her place. She was a beautiful, kind, considerate noblewoman. You're just a grubby little common whore. You'll never be Duchess here. And if we think that's your intention, or we think that you're acting to cause harm to my father and his interests, be in no doubt what we'll do. We will act to protect him. And then you'll regret it. And by the time that we've finished with you, you'll wish that you were still a nothing seamstress.'

Allana felt herself bridling at what he had called her, but this time she had the good sense to refrain from any response, prior to being dismissed.

307

Despite the way that their relationship had started, and despite the large age-gap, Allana and the Duke were growing closer with the passing of time.

At the core of it were the deep roots of desire which she had planted into him at the inception of their relationship, and which had been reflected back into her. She knew that Duke Conran was physically infatuated with her. Further, having spent more time in his company, she also found him to be an attractive man, over and above the lust which her power had mirrored into her.

Although their backgrounds and lives to date had little in common, the simple act of being in each other's arms, after their nights of lovemaking, had built an emotional bond between them. This bond existed outside of the control which she had embedded into him.

The Duke had also started to confide in her. One night, she was lying in his arms, when he announced, 'Many people disapprove of us doing this, Lana.'

'I know.' She had not told him about any of the encounters with Ami Randle, Gerrion or Charl Koss, but his comment made her think of them.

'My son and Charl have told me that, for the first time ever, they are questioning my judgment.'

'They are?'

'Yes. They want me to send you away. Get rid of you.'

'Do you want to?'

'No. I promised to protect you. To keep you safe.' He sounded confused as he said these words, which she knew she had imprinted into his mind, and he paused before continuing. 'And I need you. Need this. So badly.'

'So do I.' As she said this, she wholeheartedly meant it.

'But. It's more than that. More than just need. I love... being with you.'

'For as long as you want me to stay, I will stay then.'

'But you must know, Lana. This can never progress. I can never marry you.'

'I know that.' Gerrion had made that point very clearly, but she suddenly had a devilish notion.

You could make him marry you, Lana. If you wanted to. Just control him again. And make him. It would be that easy.

She shuddered at the thought, something which he misinterpreted as her being cold, because he pulled the blanket around them more tightly. There was then silence for a number of seconds, before he spoke again.

'Even if I wanted to marry you, Lana, it would put you in danger.'

She had been starting to doze, but his words made her alert again. 'In danger? Why?'

'Because, right now, even as my mistress, you're anonymous to the outside world. Gerrion, Charl and Ami will have made sure that none of the staff or soldiers talk about our relationship to anyone outside of this castle. To anyone else, you're just a servant here. But as a wife? As a Duchess? You would be known immediately. And it would make it much riskier that you could be revealed for who you really are.'

'To Aiduel's Guards?'

'Yes. To them in particular. But to any of my other enemies, too. If I tell you something, will you promise to keep it a secret?'

'Yes, Conran, of course.' She was still thinking about his words, *'even if I wanted to marry you'*.

'When I was overseas, before I returned here, I was in Sen Aiduel, in Dei Magnus. I reached an agreement there. An important agreement, which averted war. Only me, Gerrion and Charl know about it, here. Plus Kari. As part of that agreement, Aiduel's Guards are going to build a fort to the east of Septholme, at some point in the next year. It will garrison over a hundred of their soldiers here. Their presence in and around our town is therefore going to increase massively. And with that increased presence, your risk of discovery will also grow much greater. It makes me fear for you.'

She felt a sense of disquiet at hearing these words. 'I understand what this is between us, Conran. I understand that you can never marry me. But if you want me here and will protect me, I will stay. If you want me to leave, I will go.'

'I want you to stay. I need you to stay. And I *will* protect you.' She shuddered again, as he said this last part. 'Please stay.'

'Then I will stay, Conran.'

He has sworn to protect you, Lana. And he's your lover, now, despite how this started between you. Compared to what might have happened to you, could this almost be happiness?

She fell asleep in his arms, and her dreams that night were of a different sort. Of a wedding, in a castle.

19

Arion

—

Year of Our Lord,
After Ascension, 768AA

Following the meeting at the Royal Palace in Andarron, the next two months at the Academy were a whirlwind of activity and learning. In recognition of their progress, the cadets had been issued with and routinely carried their own weapons. Arion was now accustomed to wearing his sword on his hip at all times. The cadets had also been allowed access to the Academy stables, and horse riding became an additional part of their weekly routine.

Arion continued to excel at physical and weapons skill training, and he was soon also demonstrating that he was one of the most skilled horsemen there. He was also achieving the required levels in the military academic disciplines, with Sendar and Lennion's help. He was amazed at how much he was learning in these subjects, and he felt excited about one day putting his new knowledge to use.

The negotiations with the Archlaw remained in the back of his mind, and he often wondered about how his father was progressing in his efforts to achieve a successful outcome. However, no further update was received in the immediate weeks following the Royal Palace meeting.

After six months had passed since the start of their training, Commander Roque addressed the entire cadet group in the main yard.

'Cadets!' the Commander announced. 'We're at the mid-point of the course. And fifty-three of you are still with us after this time, probably unrecognisable to yourselves from the callow boys who arrived here. By way of celebration, this coming Fifth-Day evening, we'll be holding a formal dinner here, with alcohol served. And afterwards, for those who want to, we'll allow you offsite to visit the local village's tavern for the first time!' His final words were met with a cheer from the group around him.

That Fifth-Day evening could not come soon enough for Arion. When they arrived for dinner, the seating placements had already been set out. Arion was on a top table with Sendar, Lennion and a number of other high-performing cadets, including Jarrett Berun. There was an instructor on every table, and Commander Roque himself was seated with Arion's group.

Despite Arion's dislike for Jarrett Berun, it was a relaxed and enjoyable evening. Arion realised how much he had missed red wine, and he drank a liberal amount throughout the course of the dinner. All of the other cadets were also indulging, but eventually Lennion patted Arion on the back and said, 'Careful, friend, we need to be fit to head to the tavern too!'

At that point, Sendar was in conversation with Commander Roque. 'Commander, can I ask you a question, please?'

'You can ask,' responded the Commander. 'Whether I answer it depends on what it is?'

'Well,' said Sendar. 'On our first day of Military Tactics training, you stated that you were a survivor of the Second Crusade. My question is this. How? I thought everyone on the Second Crusade perished?'

Commander Roque was drinking too, and he leaned back and looked at his glass, out of his single eye. He then lifted a hand and touched his eye patch. 'The answer is... *this*. Losing my eye saved my life.

'I was young at the time of the Second Crusade. I'd joined the army aged fourteen, and I showed a special aptitude for killing, and as such I was still very young when I was appointed as commander of a small specialist unit. My unit, well, we did some of the things that other ordinary soldiers might not want to do. Scouting, reconnaissance, sabotage, activities behind enemy lines.

'Two days before the battle on the plains before Aiduel's Gate, my unit was spotted and attacked by enemy cavalry. In the ensuing battle, someone managed to get the tip of his knife in my eye at the same time as I slashed his throat. After that, I don't remember much, other than that I woke up back in Arron, blind in one eye. They'd carried me back to the city by horse. And by the time I awoke, the battle had already taken place. Therefore, to my enduring shame but ultimate good fortune I missed the infamous slaughter on the plains. Missed the death which found so many of my fellow crusaders.'

There was silence for a few seconds. Like Arion, a number of the people around the table had relatives who had died in the Second Crusade.

'Would you go back, if there was a Third Crusade?' asked Lennion Rednar.

'No,' answered Roque, immediately. 'I've already seen too many of my friends die in that desert. A Third Crusade will be for others to lead. Not me.'

On hearing that, Arion felt a sudden worry for Delrin. *Keep safe, brother. Lord preserve you.*

'But did you get to see Aiduel's Gate?' queried Jarrett Berun, holding a half-empty tankard. 'Were you blessed to gaze upon the Holy City?'

'Not properly, no,' replied Roque. 'I saw its walls from the plains below during our scouting mission, but I never saw inside the city.

It sits on a plateau far above the plains, so all I saw were distant, and staggeringly massive, fortified walls. But that's still probably the closest that any living person from Andar has come to the city in over two hundred and fifty years. And as I'm sure you know, Jarrett, the gates of the Holy City have been closed to the people of Angall, for a long, long time before that.'

Arion stared at his wine glass, thinking, and for just a second the mention of Aiduel's Gate caused something to tug at his memory. Try as he might he could not grasp hold of the fleeting image which flashed into his mind, but in the moments afterwards he was left with a feeling of disquiet.

—

Later, half of the cadets headed out towards the local village tavern. They were all intoxicated and in good spirits, but they had been warned by the Commander not to cause problems with the local villagers.

Arion, Sendar and Lennion found themselves a table in the corner with Roliss Sonder, and Sendar produced a set of dice and proposed a gambling game. Arion had drunk too much alcohol by this stage, and with his senses dulled, he started to lose a series of small wagers as they played the game. Unsurprisingly, Sendar was a regular winner, and the prince seemed to be able to work out the odds of success or failure for his gambles instantly.

After half an hour of playing the game, Arion looked up to see Jarrett Berun and one of Berun's more devout companions, a lord named Millas Roth, standing by their table. Both were holding ale tankards in hand.

'We both enjoy dice games,' stated Berun, addressing Sendar. 'Would it be OK if we join in?'

Arion wanted to say, 'No, go away', but instead found himself groaning inside as Sendar warmly welcomed them. Shortly after this, the six of them were gathered around the table, raucously playing the game.

To Arion's annoyance, Jarrett Berun also started to win a disproportionate share of rounds. Arion did not mind losing to a good friend like Sendar, but seeing even small amounts of money pass across to Jarrett Berun irritated him greatly. Arion felt sure that Berun was smirking at him every time he won a round. Mocking him. The urge to speak out was building inside of Arion.

Smug bastard, he thought. *By the Lord, I'd love to punch that smug look off his face.*

Sendar Pavil broke off at one point to head to the privy, and with drunken rationale Arion saw this as his opportunity. At any other time, he would have held his tongue, but with the alcohol inside him the words came out all too easily. 'I'm surprised, given your tremendous piety, Berun, that you're even allowed to play a gambling game?'

'This is supposed to be a game for fun, Sepian,' replied the large youth. 'Gambling would be sinful if the amounts involved started to matter, which they don't here. Although I can see that it might not be that much fun if you're *losing*, like you are. But then again, it wouldn't be the first time you've lost to me.'

Arion again felt the urge to punch him. *Smug bastard*. He could not contain his next words.

'No, but it's the last time I'll lose anything significant to you, Berun. And it's not like I've lost my place in my Academy bedroom, or my family has lost its honour.'

'Arion, leave it!' warned Lennion Rednar.

'What did you say, you Sepian fuck?' responded Berun, his face going red. The dice game was forgotten, everyone else around the table suddenly ill-at-ease.

'You heard me, you fucking traitor. Why don't we get out of this village and settle this once and for all. Only let's use our fists this time.'

'I'll fucking kill you, Sepian. Let's go!'

—

315

The next few minutes passed in a drunken blur, as they headed away from the lights of the village. At some point Lennion had run off to collect Sendar, and the other four members of their table had gathered in pursuit as he and Jarrett Berun strode purposefully towards the darkened path back to the Academy.

When they got into the surrounding countryside, Sendar caught up with them and again tried to intervene. 'Both of you, stop this!'

This time, though, neither Arion nor Jarrett Berun were interested in his peacemaking.

'Tell him, Millas,' Berun stated, turning to his companion. 'Sepian started this. But I'm going to finish it.'

Arion looked at Sendar. 'You're not ordering me to back off this time, Sendar. He's a prick and a bully. I'm going to put him down.'

Sendar shook his head, looking exasperated. 'Very well. Get on with it, then. But know this. The two of you can deal with the consequences yourselves. Whatever happens, the rest of us weren't here and we didn't see anything.' Arion grunted his assent. Sendar then continued, 'And at least hand over your swords before you start.'

Arion withdrew his sword, fighting an urge to leap towards Berun with it, and handed it to Lennion. Jarrett Berun passed his own sword to Millas Roth.

The large youth then looked at Arion and sneered, clenching his fists. 'Anything goes, Sepian?'

Rage was building inside Arion, a rage unlike anything he had ever experienced before. He squared off opposite Berun, raising his own clenched fists.

Beat him, beat him, beat him!

'Anything goes,' he replied.

The two of them then launched themselves forwards, at the same time, each swinging a heavy hate-filled fist towards his opponent.

This time it was no controlled wrestling bout. Arion was full of a fury which powered each swing of his fists, and which allowed him at first to disregard the pounding sensations of Berun's hard return blows connecting against his own body. This was no contest for finesse or tactics, this was a drunken brawl between the two largest men in their cadet class, both of them full of loathing for the other, both with a point to prove.

On this occasion Berun had no great advantage of skill. Arion had regularly boxed his brothers as he was growing up, and it immediately felt that he and his opponent were evenly matched. He was also determined to use his punches to prevent his foe from grappling him, such that there could be no repeat of his wrestling humiliation.

Yet despite all of that, after several seconds of frantic exchange Berun's blows started to hurt him, one sharp jab connecting with his temple and rocking him backwards. He found himself backing away, fists raised, but Berun was on him again immediately, arms swinging, and Arion was abruptly defending much more than he was attacking.

Not again! I cannot let him humiliate me again!

He swung his fist in an attempted hook but missed, then felt another of Berun's blows land in his stomach, knocking the wind from him. Arion gasped and staggered backwards.

Berun sensed that he was gaining the upper hand. 'Going to beat you senseless, Sepian.'

Arion sucked in air, his senses dulled both by alcohol and by the strikes which his opponent had landed upon him, then he again spiritedly tried to launch himself into the attack. However, his forward momentum was quickly reversed by a series of heavy punches landed by Berun, one to his head, and then once again Arion was staggering backwards.

'Concede, Arion!' The voice was Sendar Pavil's, sounding like it came from the other end of a long tunnel.

Arion shook his head to reject this suggestion, aware of blood dripping from above his eye, as Berun launched himself into another attack. A barrage of blows came at Arion, and this time there were no counter-attacks by him. All he was doing was desperately defending, with more and more punches connecting against him. With despair, he realised that his legs felt weak, and he was close to collapse.

Then a blow bashed against the side of his head, and as he teetered there on the brink of defeat and surrender, forgotten words emerged from within the pain and began to ring gloriously in his ears.

STRENGTH. VICTORY. GLORY.

Instantly, his senses cast off the shackles of alcohol, fatigue and pain which had rendered them dull, and his perception of the world seemed to crackle with the intensity of lightning, as time decelerated around him.

He watched, like a fascinated removed observer, as Berun's next punch headed towards him. His opponent's fist seemed to move so pathetically sluggishly now that it was a trifling effort to turn his shoulders and to observe the punch sailing past his head, leaving his foe off-balance and exposed.

Accompanying this slowing of time, a surge of strength and energy enveloped his body. He felt instantly rejuvenated, the physical punishment that he had taken in the last few moments washed away. But it was more than that, more than rejuvenation. He felt *alive* and powerful, as if coils of energy had wrapped around every limb in his body.

By the Lord! What is this?

His right hand flicked upwards and effortlessly connected with Berun's chin as the large youth floundered for balance. To Arion's amazement, his opponent rocked backwards several steps, looking shaken.

The world around him moved in ever slower strokes as he stalked forward towards Jarrett Berun. He casually brushed aside another of the giant youth's attempted punches, and then delivered his own devastating blow to Berun's stomach.

Beat him. Humiliate him. Kill him.

Cries of merciless rage-filled victory resonated in his mind as he embraced the ease with which he was now defeating and unmanning his opponent. Memories of the humiliation in the wrestling contest gave fire to this rage, as punch after punch landed on Berun. Punches delivered with a power and fury which Arion had never known he was capable of possessing.

'Stop, Arion!'

That shout seemed to echo for seconds as Berun fell to his knees before him, whilst Arion continued to rain down blows upon his opponent.

Kill him, kill him, kill him, kill him. Take your victory.

Slurred words came from his adversary's mouth, as the big youth rocked backwards on his knees under the continued barrage of Arion's attack. 'Stop... please... I concede...'

'Stop, Arion, you won!' Sendar Pavil's voice?

Then two things happened at the same moment. Jarrett Berun slid bloodied to the floor, as a body smashed into Arion from the side, carrying him away from his opponent.

Time then sped up again, and the inhuman strength and speed which had possessed Arion was instantly dissipated, as he crashed to the ground.

—

Arion and Jarrett Berun were both subsequently disciplined for the fight, each of them having to undergo additional punishing physical training for a fortnight after the incident. The injuries that they had both sustained in the brawl were far too evident, particularly in Berun's case, for the matter to be kept private from the instructors.

The fight would also prove to be the last time that the two of them spoke to each other, as cadets.

Sendar had approached Arion in the aftermath of the fight. It was one of the few times that Arion had seen Sendar lose his cool, and the anger was directed entirely at him.

'What the fuck happened, Arion? You were ready to kill him. You lost all control.'

'I'm not sure,' he had replied, honestly. 'I'm sorry.'

'You were like a rabid dog, in the last moments of that fight.

319

That first instant after I tackled you, I thought… well, I thought you were going to turn on me.'

'No, Sendar, no. Never that.' Arion tried to say this with conviction, but he was full of doubt, and was feeling sullied by the rage and fury which had overcome his better instincts. He tried to make sense of his actions. 'He goaded me. Mocked me. Would have beaten me senseless if he could've.'

'That's not what Lennion says, Arion. He says *you* started it this time. Jarrett was just having fun playing dice.' Arion did not know what to say in response to this, and the prince continued. 'We're friends, Arion, and because of that I'll give you another chance. But if you *ever* act like that again, I will have to distance myself from you.'

'That's fair enough. It won't happen again.' *But how can I be certain of that?* He could not share what had actually happened with anyone, including Sendar and Lennion. They would think that he had gone mad.

'OK,' replied the prince. 'But maybe lay off the wine, OK?'

Arion had apologised again, feeling embarrassed, not knowing what else to say. Truly, he was still not sure what had happened, himself. But he could vividly remember the magnificent feelings which had radiated throughout his body in those latter moments of the fight.

Feelings of strength. Of power. Of speed. The glorious sensation of being alive, of bursting with energy and vigour, and of destroying his foe. Had it all been real?

The day after the fight and on subsequent occasions, when he was alone, he had tried to recapture that feeling. He had earnestly attempted to tap into it again, but try as he might, he could not trigger a repeat of whatever had happened to him during the drunken brawl.

—

Jarrett Berun left the Academy, five weeks after the fight.

Lennion Rednar was the first to hear the news, and to deliver it

320

back to his room-mates. Arion, Sendar and Roliss were all seated on their beds when Lennion hurried in.

'Have you heard?' Lennion asked, clearly excited about his information. 'Jarrett's gone. He's had to quit. He's returning home.'

Sendar sat upright. 'Why?'

'His father, Duke Berun, has died. Riders arrived this morning to deliver the news. He had a terrible fall riding, apparently, and then his wounds turned bad, and he's died from them. Can you believe it? Jarrett's now *Duke* Berun. He's inherited the Berun lands.'

'Wow,' replied Sendar. 'Poor Jarrett. He must be devastated. For all of his faults, he was clearly devoted to his father, and he was intent on finishing this course.'

'Yes,' responded Lennion. 'Poor Jarrett. No one would have wished that on him. Millas said that he saw Jarrett breaking down in tears when he first heard the news, and that Jarrett then prayed for an hour before he left here.'

Arion chose not to speak up. His relationship with Jarrett Berun was beyond repair, and he knew that it would be insincere for him to express sorrow now.

Good riddance, he thought, knowing it was not a worthy sentiment, but meaning it anyway.

—

One week after that, Sendar was summoned back to the royal palace. At the end of the day he returned, and approached Arion to deliver much more positive news.

He leaned in towards Arion and quietly said, 'It's done. The negotiation with the Holy Church. Your father was successful.'

Arion smiled broadly. 'That's wonderful news. Everything was agreed with the Archlaw?'

'Apparently so. And the final agreement is very closely aligned with what was discussed at our meeting, three months ago. The Holy

Church's support for the House of Canas claim over Canasar has been dropped. And there will be garrisons for Aiduel's Guards built outside Andarron, Condarr and, you'll be delighted to hear, Septholme.'

Arion grimaced. 'And will there be burning of our citizens?'

'Not such good news, I'm afraid. Your father and the Archprime had to concede that to secure agreement. As such, we're likely to see the grim spectacle of pyres occurring across our land, at some time in the near future.'

'But excommunication, and war, is averted?'

Sendar nodded. 'Excommunication, certainly. This outcome has allowed reconciliation with the Archlaw and the Holy Church in Dei Magnus, so the threat of religious division seems to have gone away, at least for now. In respect of war? Well, certainly, there would be no grounds for Dei Magnus to act against us now, given that this agreement has the support of the Archlaw and the High Council. And it appears that Elannis also no longer has any legitimate grounds to declare war, and they will have lost the support of the Church for any action. But we nonetheless need to keep vigilant against the threat the Emperor poses to us. But, all in all, it's the best outcome we could have hoped for.'

'That's wonderful,' replied Arion, feeling relief.

'Yes,' responded Sendar. 'Your father has done well. And it looks like he has once again protected the Sepian lands.'

—

The final months of the Academy course were as challenging as the earlier months.

Arion continued to excel at Military Skills Training, and his technique with weapons had further improved. The only person who could match him in weapons' drills was Sendar, whose natural quickness was sometimes capable of offsetting Arion's greater strength and stamina.

The wondrous moments of power and speed, which Arion had experienced in the fight with Jarrett Berun, were never repeated, despite his best efforts to call upon and to recapture that sensation. He was beginning to wonder whether it had all been a drunken hallucination, and that he had simply imagined himself to have had superhuman powers whilst under the heavy influence of alcohol.

During the final few months, Arion also made significant progress in Military Tactics and Military Strategy work. He would never be as quick-witted as Sendar was, to immediately see a solution to challenges, but the work he had put in throughout the year meant that he had gained a resource of knowledge available to draw on in the future. And he had become well versed in the techniques for drilling and manoeuvring troops, including cavalry manoeuvres. He was looking forward to discussing some of this with Charl Koss, when he eventually returned home.

He had also written a detailed letter back to Delrin during this period, setting out the events he had experienced in the last few months. No response was received, during the remainder of his time at the Academy.

The only dark cloud which he endured in that final four-month period, after Jarrett's departure, was his troubled sleep. He was waking up on a regular basis in the middle of the night, heart pounding, filled with a sense of dread from a half-forgotten dream.

At first, he had retained no recollection at all of what he had been dreaming about. A blackness had resided there upon wakening, taunting him with hidden memories of something essential. However, increasingly now flashes of images lingered in his mind after waking, and stayed there. A path. A mountain. A Gate. His companions. And something else? Something dark?

But try as he might, he could not place the images together into a coherent whole. He had considered discussing it with Sendar, Lennion and Roliss, but had decided against it. His restlessness at night-time had become a source of both amusement and irritation for them, and he did not want to add to their bemusement by sharing the puzzle of the dream.

In the last month of his time at the Academy, each of the cadets was tested in all of the four disciplines which they had been tutored in. Arion passed any Physical trials and Military Skills trials easily, the latter of which included a number of horsemanship tests. He then surprised himself by getting a clear pass in both of the other subjects. Each of his friends also acquitted themselves well in all of the end of year evaluations.

And then, close to twelve months after it had begun, his time at the Academy was over.

The full cadet group assembled in the central yard on the morning of the last day. Forty-four of the sixty cadets who had started the course were still there, to experience the successful completion of the year. Arion felt a strong sense of pride that he was one of the successful finishers. Looking around, he could see the marked differences in each of them since they had started. Each person was leaner, harder, stronger, and sharper. They were assembled in organised, uniform rows, so contrasting to the unruly manner in which they had gathered on that first day.

As at the start of the year, Commander Roque and his wife, and Sergeant Kallin, were standing in front of them.

The Commander spoke to the assembled group. 'Congratulations, cadets, men! You have completed the Academy, have successfully completed all of the challenges which we've set for you. We've lost sixteen cadets along the way, but you forty-four have stayed the course. Have shown endurance, resolve, grit, character. This has been a strong class and I can speak on behalf of myself and all of the instructors here when I say that we are proud and honoured to see you graduate from our ranks. Therefore, I'm delighted to announce that the course is complete, and each of you has earned, and now carries, the title of Martial of the Realm!'

There was a cheer in response to this, and Arion felt himself experiencing pride and relief in equal measure.

By the Lord! I did it!

Roque continued. 'You may now have a week of rest, either to spend on-site here at the Academy, or off-site as you choose. But all must assemble here again in seven days' time, when we will deliver your military assignments for the next ten months. Enjoy your time off, and again, congratulations.'

—

Arion had intended to spend the next week relaxing in the Academy grounds, with a few potential visits to the local village. However, he received separate invitations from both Sendar and Lennion, who were determined to coerce him to spend some time in Andarron.

Without needing much persuasion, he accepted both invitations. He spent a day with Sendar in and around the royal palace, this time being given a personal tour of the grand facility by the prince. There was no equivalent meeting of substance with the King or Queen this time, and the absence of a second encounter with Sendar's mother was a source of disappointment to Arion. Despite this, the two of them still had an enjoyable day together.

Arion's time with Lennion proved to be more interesting, however. Lennion's mother and younger sister had travelled to Andarron to see their family member before he was posted out to military service. Lennion invited Arion to join the three of them for a day.

They met inside the luxurious tavern which the Rednar family were staying at in town. Lennion was seated with his mother as Arion arrived. Lennion grinned and announced, 'Here he is, mother, one of the two reprobates who've dragged me through this course in the last year!'

Lennion and his mother were clearly related. She was also of average height, with auburn hair which was currently tied up in a bun, and their eyes and nose were very similar. She extended her hand, exclaiming, 'Oh my goodness, he really is as tall and as handsome as you said, Lennion!'

Arion blushed, greeting her, and Lennion quipped, 'I don't think I intended you to repeat that, though, mother?'

She laughed. 'No, maybe you didn't, but it's true anyway!'

Arion chuckled with her, and at that moment a fourth person joined them. She appeared to be a couple of years younger than he and Lennion, but again was definitely related to his friend. She was about a head shorter than Arion, with large emerald green eyes and a small upturned nose, and Arion immediately noted that she was pretty. Her hair was light auburn, and was long, falling over her shoulders and down her back.

'And this is my little sister, Kalyane,' Lennion announced, as Arion extended his hand to greet her. 'And Kaly, no telling him how handsome he is. Mother's already inflated his ego enough.'

Arion boldly replied, 'I think it should be me making the compliments to your sister, Lennion. Not the other way round.'

Kalyane blushed at the comment then laughed, a gentle demure laugh. And Arion knew that he was attracted to her.

—

He ended up spending two days in the company of the Rednar family, including dining with the three of them that first evening.

Lennion's mother, Duchess Rednar, was vivacious and flirtatious, taking fun in teasing Arion with comments about his apparent dashing looks. Lennion was also in his element, clearly enjoying the mixed company of his family with one of his best friends.

However, Arion found his attention drawn towards Kalyane. She was initially the most reserved of the three Rednars, but once they got an opportunity to speak one-on-one together, he found her to be engaging, intelligent and gently witty.

He had also never previously met a girl who asked him so many questions. She would make an enquiry, then would listen intently to even his more mundane answers, with eyes wide with apparent interest. He found this to be strangely compelling.

'So, Arion, what will the future hold for you, after your time in the military?' she asked him, when they were alone together for a few moments, on the second day.

'I imagine that I'll return to Septholme, to lead the military there after a few years. I would hope that father will also grant me an estate to manage and call my own, in return for my duties. After that, who knows?'

'And as a soldier, do you see yourself-' She paused, clearly gathering her words. 'Do you see yourself… having a family?' She looked down and away from him after asking the question.

'One day, yes, I guess I do,' he responded, choosing his words carefully. 'At the right time. With the right person.'

That answer seemed to satisfy her. Arion was later unsure whether or not her question was connected to the invite that he subsequently received from Lennion's mother, at the end of the day. Duchess Rednar embraced him prior to his departure from them, and then warmly invited him to come and spend a month at the Rednar estates near Rednarron, after his time in the military had ended.

He had enjoyed their company immensely, and accepted the invitation immediately, much to Lennion's delight. However, Arion could also see Kalyane smiling happily behind her brother in the moment after Arion had given his acceptance, and right then her response meant a little more to him.

—

At the end of the week, Arion returned to the Academy and received his new posting. He and two other Martials, neither of whom he was particularly close to, were to be posted to a military outpost on the north-western coast of Andar. To a fort which had been established to defend the surrounding coastal areas against increasing incursions by sea from Bergen raiders. He was to travel to the fort by land.

He said his goodbyes on the last day to Sendar and Lennion, feeling certain that in the two of them he had secured friends for life.

Here we go again, he thought to himself, on the day of leaving. *Now, what awaits me next?*

20

Leanna

—

Year of Our Lord,
After Ascension, 768AA

Leanna was seated at a table, inside one of the larger canvas tents, within the encampment of Aiduel's Guards. Sitting across from her were two men, both wearing the now familiar uniform of their military order. The first man was middle-aged and balding, and had introduced himself as Captain Rorker. The second, whom she had been more alarmed to see upon her arrival, was the High Commander, Ernis dei Bornere.

Lord Aiduel, please watch over me and help me to conquer my nerves and fears.

Rorker spoke first, his accent identifying him as of Dei Magnus origin. 'Thank you for coming to this interview, Leanna. And please, don't be worried that we've summoned you here. We'll be speaking with all of the novices and priests in due course, but we're starting with your age group first.'

Leanna was uncertain as to how to formally address them both,

'Yes… sir.' She did indeed feel nervous, but she took some confidence from the fact that, at the current time, no strong emotions were emanating from either of the two men.

'Before we commence, Leanna,' added Rorker, 'I would ask you whether you understand what the mission of Aiduel's Guards is? And comprehend its importance?'

'I do, sir. The High Commander explained it very clearly to us. To eradicate heresy and heretics.'

'Correct,' said Rorker, smiling, although the expression did not touch his eyes. 'And we can only achieve those goals with the aid of all of the faithful, such as you. It is essential to our success that the faithful become our extended eyes and ears.'

'Yes, sir.'

'It is therefore vital that you answer all of our questions openly, fully and honestly. Can you do that for us, Leanna?'

'Yes, sir.'

'Excellent,' proclaimed the captain. He then reached down under the table and produced a copy of the Holy Book, placing it on the surface before her. 'Swear that for me, then. Before The Lord, on the Holy Book.'

Leanna hesitated for just a moment, then placed her hand onto the book. 'Before The Lord, and on the Holy Book, I swear to answer your questions openly, fully and honestly.'

Ernis dei Bornere was staring at her as she said this, his mouth set into a hard line, making her feel uneasy.

'Very good, Leanna,' said Rorker, his words again accompanied by a smile which seemed to be entirely lacking in sincerity. 'Before we ask you any specific questions, can I check your background, please.'

'Yes, sir.'

'We understand that you were born here in Arlais. Correct?' She nodded. 'That you attended the School of Saint Amena for twelve years, and that you then joined this College twelve months ago. Also correct?'

'Yes, sir. To train to become a priestess, sir.'

329

'And how old are you, Leanna?'

'Nineteen years old, sir.' Leanna noticed that Rorker fleetingly glanced at the High Commander, as she gave this reply.

'And when was your birthday, your nineteenth birthday?'

'Just over a week ago, sir. The fourteenth day of Morningsong.' This time Rorker definitely did look across towards dei Bornere.

'Very well, thank you for confirming that. OK, Leanna, I'll start the formal questions now. Remember, we need you to answer openly, fully and honestly. My first question is; have you ever undertaken or been part of an act of heresy?'

'No, sir,' she answered immediately.

Lord Aiduel, I truly believe that these things – the vision, the dreams, the power – are gifts from you, and that I'm not answering falsely by denying heresy. I am no heretic.

'Have you ever witnessed another person undertaking or being part of an act of heresy?'

'No, sir.' The tent was hot, and she felt like she was sweating.

'Are you aware of any other person who you believe may have undertaken or been part of an act of heresy?'

'No, sir.'

'Do you know of any heretics?'

'No, sir.'

'Have you ever had visions of the future, or experienced anything else similar which might be deemed to be an act of *prophecy*?'

'No, sir.' The question had startled her, but she answered immediately.

'Are you aware of anyone else who you have witnessed or who has claimed to have the power of prophecy? The power to see the future?'

'Again, no, sir.' The High Commander was continuing to stare without relent at her face, and she was certain that she was sweating now.

'Have you ever had any unusual or recurring dreams, Leanna?'

Her heart thudded in her chest. She felt certain that her cheeks were turning crimson red. She suddenly had a vivid sense that she was in mortal danger, although it continued to be the case that no strong emotions were being emitted by the men across from her.

Lord Aiduel, please forgive me for this lie. I have no choice but to conceal this, Lord, for I truly believe that my life is in danger.

'No, sir.'

Had Rorker noticed her slight hesitation before answering? Even if he had, he continued on with his questions. 'Are you aware of anyone else who has had any unusual or recurring dreams?'

'No, sir.'

'Have you ever experienced the sensation of knowing another person's thoughts?'

'What exactly do you mean, sir? I don't understand the question.' She used her enquiry to cover the rush of anxiety which gripped her. His query brought to her mind the private emotions she had been sensing from other people for the past several weeks.

'By that I mean, reading their minds. Knowing what they're thinking.'

'No, sir.' *Lord Aiduel, this is the truth. I sense emotions, but I don't know what others are thinking.*

'Are you aware of anyone else who has experienced the sensation of knowing another person's thoughts?'

'No, sir.' She could feel a rivulet of sweat running down the right side of her face, onto her cheekbone.

'Have you ever experienced a holy vision or miracle?'

Lord Aiduel, I have sworn an oath to keep this secret.

'No, sir.'

'Are you aware of anyone else who has experienced a holy vision or miracle?'

'No, sir.'

'Have you ever manifested any unusual or unnatural powers, Leanna? Things an ordinary person couldn't do, either with their body or with their mind?'

Lord Aiduel, what does all of this mean? It is like they are looking for me, Lord? Why?

331

'No, sir.'

'Are you aware of anyone else who has manifested unusual or unnatural powers?'

'No, sir.'

'OK. I'd like to ask you some questions about the people in your age group now, Leanna. Specifically, the children who were in your year group, or the years to either side of that, at the School of Saint Amena. And also your fellow novices.' Leanna nodded in acknowledgement, feeling puzzled by this, and Rorker continued. 'First, have there been any unusual events involving any of those individuals, in all of the time that you have known them?'

Leanna frowned. 'I'm not sure what you mean, sir?'

'Unusual events. Anything out of the ordinary. Things that might have seemed odd. That might have made you suspicious about one of your peers?'

Leanna frowned again. 'I don't think so, sir.'

Lord Aiduel, why is he interested in people of my age?

'Nothing out of the ordinary? Nothing at all?'

'No, sir. Nothing I can think of.'

'Very well. Do you swear that all of the answers that you've given are true, Leanna?'

'Yes, sir.'

'OK. That was very helpful, Leanna. Now, if you reflect upon this conversation afterwards, and if you remember something – *anything* – which you might have forgotten, please come and see me as soon as possible.' Rorker again flashed his joyless smile. 'I would also insist that you do not talk about the contents of this discussion, Leanna, with anyone. Any such breach of confidentiality could potentially undermine our investigations elsewhere, and therefore we'd react to such an act of disobedience with appropriate... *disapproval*. Is that understood?'

'Yes, sir.' But Leanna already knew that she was not going to hold to that.

Rorker's false smile flashed again. 'Anyway, thank you for your time, Leanna. You may leave, now.'

Leanna smiled back half-heartedly, feeling relief, her hands trembling. She stood, and began to turn to exit the tent. That is when the High Commander spoke up for the first time. 'What happened on your last day at the School of Saint Amena, Leanna?'

She paused, feeling horror inside. 'I'm sorry, sir?'

Lord Aiduel, help me think, please. How can he know about that, Lord?

'I think the question was entirely clear, girl. What happened on your last day at the School of Saint Amena?'

She took her time to answer, sensing no emotions emanating from him. 'I said my farewells, sir. I received my Certificate from-'

'Specifically,' interrupted dei Bornere, impatience sounding in his voice, 'what happened in the chapel, at the altar?'

Lord Aiduel, please help me to choose the right words. Please help me, Lord. Who has told him, Lord? Only my parents and the two priests know about the vision.

'Oh, that. I collapsed, sir,' she said, trying to sound nonchalant. 'I think... in the excitement of it being my last day, everything got too much for me, and I fainted.'

The High Commander stared fixedly at her for a number of seconds, making no comment. Leanna could feel more sweat upon her forehead. Thankfully, there was still no discernible ripple of emotion coming from him.

'Anything else? Anything more which you think you should add, given that we already have testimonies from other people?'

'No, sir.'

He paused again, gazing at her with an inscrutable expression, then he finally said, 'Very well, then. You may go.'

Leanna exited the tent, feeling bruised and a little sullied by the interview, and her sense of dread was even greater than it had been before entering.

Lord Aiduel, what does he know? Does he know that I have

spoken falsely, today? And if he does, Lord, what is going to happen to me?

—

Following the interview, Leanna sought out Amyss as soon as she possibly could. She was not going to risk Amyss going into a similar interview unawares, and then either accidentally or purposely sharing the news about Leanna's dreams.

She proceeded to tell Amyss all about the discussion and the questioning, and specifically warned her about the need to swear an oath, and the particular questions about dreams.

'By the Lord, Lea!' said the smaller girl. 'That sounds awful.'

'Amyss, I'm scared. Truly. Of what they'll do to me if they ever find out about the dreams. Please tell me you won't say anything.'

Amyss's face bore a stern look. 'Lea, for the umpteenth time, I swear in the name of The Lord, and on the Holy Book, and on anything else you'd like me to swear on, that I'll *never* tell anyone about your dreams, or about any other secret of yours which I hold. And no oath I may ever be forced to take in future will ever override this one. There! Even if they make me swear another oath, it will not change that.'

Leanna leaned forwards and hugged her. 'Thank you.'

Lord Aiduel, thank you for the gift of Amyss's friendship.

After she had pulled away, Amyss said, 'It's scary, though, isn't it? Everyone seems so on edge, now. But why do they appear to be so interested in people who are our age?'

'I don't know,' replied Leanna, 'but it seems very likely that they'll call for you, soon, given that they are.'

Leanna was feeling equally concerned by Aiduel's Guards' interest in her age-group, but she was also worried about the questions which had been asked in relation to her collapse in the chapel. She was further unsettled that her recent strange experiences seemed to fit so many of the markers which Aiduel's Guards were looking for.

'I know,' responded Amyss. 'What fun. I'd better wash my hair and put on my best dress, for my big moment.'

'Be serious, Amyss. Be careful.'

'Oh, I am. And I will be.'

—

Amyss was indeed summoned for an interview, on the next day. To Leanna's great relief, the other girl came back appearing unruffled by the interrogation. Amyss also confirmed that there had been no specific questions about Leanna, which served to slightly ease Leanna's fears.

Leanna subsequently decided to leave the College complex on Seventh-Day, in the afternoon. She had moved up in rank from neophyte to acolyte after completing twelve months at the College, and she was now allowed to leave the College grounds on Holy Day.

As she departed, heading back towards the centre of town, she passed a number of people walking in the opposite direction. There was to be another burning today, she understood, of a man accused and found guilty of the heresy of fortune-telling. Once more, there was a large crowd assembling on the fields to the north, for the spectacle. Leanna shuddered to herself, thinking about it.

She was travelling towards the School of Saint Amena. She had resolved that she was going to speak to Senior Priestess Maris; she needed to find out what, if anything, Maris had disclosed about the events of Leanna's holy vision. The walk to the school was a comfortable and well-acquainted route, and it gave Leanna a warm feeling as she re-trod some of the familiar paths which she had walked along throughout her childhood.

It was easy to find Maris once Leanna had arrived at the School. The Senior Priestess lived in a small cottage attached to the school premises, and after Leanna had knocked on the front door the priestess quickly appeared.

'Leanna! Child! How wonderful! Come in, come in.' Leanna was ushered through the doorway into the small kitchen area at the front of the cottage.

Maris was truly delighted to see her, and for ten minutes afterwards Leanna patiently answered question after question from the older woman, about her life at the College.

Finally, Leanna brought up the subject of her visit. 'Mother, may I talk freely with you, please? But in confidence?'

Maris noted the sombreness in her voice, and put out a hand to pat Leanna's. 'Of course, child. As delighted as I am to see you here, I'm not so naive as to believe that this is purely a social visit. Please, tell me what's worrying you, and rest assured that anything you say to me will indeed be treated in confidence.'

'It's connected to Aiduel's Guards, Mother.' Maris nodded in response, as if she had been expecting this. 'You're aware, Mother, that they seem to be interviewing a lot of people who are my age?'

'I am, child,' the priestess responded. 'But before you ask, neither I nor any of the other priests in Arlais have been told why. We *have* asked, but Aiduel's Guards are choosing not to tell us.'

'That actually isn't what I was going to ask you, Mother. They interviewed me, earlier this week. I'm not meant to talk about it with you or anyone else, so please don't tell anyone I have.'

'Of course not, child. Go on.'

'Mother, they seem to be suggesting that people who have visions might also be heretics. And at one point they asked me questions about whether I'd had visions, and then later they specifically asked me about what had happened at the altar here. On my last day at the School. And I'm scared, Mother. I'm worried about what they know about the events of that day. Whether they know that I had a vision. And also about how they know.'

Maris looked concerned now. 'You didn't tell them about the vision, did you?'

336

'No, Mother. I'd sworn an oath to you never to tell anyone about it. And I was too scared, anyway.'

'Did they mention you having a vision, specifically, or did they ask you a question that was vague?'

'The latter, Mother.'

Maris made an audible exhaling noise. 'That's good. That tells me that they don't know anything which matters. I think you're safe, child. Neither Priest Hambel nor I have been interviewed, nor have we ever told anyone. Hambel and I made the same oath to each other, to never speak about the vision, as the one which you made to me. And I'm very glad indeed now that we chose not to report it, at the time.'

Lord Aiduel, so am I. What would have happened, Lord, if the Guards had been told then about my vision?

'Then what do you think they were referring to, Mother?'

'Well. Other children became aware later that you'd passed out, and had a fit, didn't they? Without knowing what triggered it. I suspect one of them reported that. And that your interviewer was fishing for information.'

Leanna also exhaled now, feeling relief. 'I hope so, Mother. But hearing that makes me feel better.'

Maris patted her hand again. 'Take care, child. Complete your training and then find a way to get away from here, far from Arlais, to somewhere where the Guards don't have such a glowering presence. Arlais has changed since they got here, and not for the better. So sad that Comrel has decided to move north.'

They shared the rest of their respective news after that, and finally Leanna walked to the doorway, ready to leave.

Maris also made her way to the door, but just before opening it she paused, and looked at Leanna. 'You know, Leanna, I've been racking my brains for any reason as to why Aiduel's Guards might have such apparent interest in your age group.'

'Yes, Mother?'

'And in answer to that question, only one thought occurs to

me. It might be a complete coincidence, but there nonetheless is a connection of time, to this event.'

'To what event, Mother?'

'To the Great Darkening. Of 748AA. The young people, whom Aiduel's Guards seem to be spending their time interviewing, are all those children who were born in the year after the Great Darkening. Children like you.'

—

Two days later, Leanna was in Priest Parmer's class for a history lesson. The old priest with the failing eyesight had been discussing The Lord Aiduel's period of time in Sen Aiduel, reviewing the events which had led to the tortures of The Lord Aiduel On The Tree. Again, it had been fascinating for Leanna to hear Parmer's learned reflections on those events. This had included him describing to the class some unknown facts collected from rare historical scriptures, which had not been recorded in the Holy Book.

However, Leanna had arrived here today, at Maris's beckoning, determined to ask the elderly priest about the Great Darkening. Maris had already given her some information about the event, but the older woman had also indicated that there would be no one better able than Parmer to describe what it was, because he had actually been in Sen Aiduel when the occurrence had taken place.

Leanna waited until the other acolytes had filed out of the classroom, before she approached the old man. 'Priest Parmer, please may I ask you something?'

He looked at her, squinting, a kind look on his face, and again she felt ashamed of that moment when she had invaded his private emotions. 'Yes, child, of course. What is it?'

'I'm interested in the Great Darkening, Father. I know only a little of it, but it intrigues me. Please will you tell me what it was, and what it means.'

He smiled. 'What an interesting question, child. Of course. I have a few moments now, if you would like, although there's not that much to say.'

'Anything that you could tell me would be interesting, Father.'

'Very well, child. It happened, as you probably know, in 748AA. I was a younger priest then, of course, serving as an aide to an Archprime, in Sen Aiduel. In simple terms, child, the sun went dark for about half an hour that day. In the middle of the day, the city of Sen Aiduel, and the palaces of the Archlaw, were all blanketed by darkness.

'It didn't just happen in Sen Aiduel, of course. In lots of other places in Angall the sky also became darker, and the sun was partially obscured. But nowhere else was it so very dark, or lasted for so long or as intensely, as in Sen Aiduel itself. I remember, on the day it happened, being terrified and getting down on my knees to pray to Aiduel.'

'What caused it, Father?'

'Well. Our curious friends studying in the field of astronomy would have us believe that the moon passed in front of the sun, thereby blacking out its light. However, my fellow religious brethren and professors of theology have also considered the event in much detail, since then. Some initially viewed it as a portent, an indication that the Day of Judgement was close at hand. That day when Aiduel would return and would judge us all. Others viewed it as a judgement in itself, that Aiduel was darkening the sky as a warning that we have become sinful and prideful in the days since He walked amongst us. Finally, others marked it as the ending of an age. A signal from The Lord that one age was passing, and another was beginning.'

'And what do you think, Father?'

'Me?' He laughed then, an oddly childish laugh for such an old man. 'That first day, I believed that the Day of Judgement was at hand, and I prayed and prayed and prayed. But since then, I've actually taken it upon myself to study all of the scriptures and old texts I could find, anything which I thought could have any relevance to the event.

'I was looking for any references to an occurrence like the Great Darkening, anything which suggested it was going to come or could be seen as a precursor to anything else. Any words of The Lord, or old prophecy, which foretold it happening. And my conclusion, after years of such study? There are none. None at all. So perhaps our learned friends in the field of astronomy are correct, and the event was merely two celestial bodies passing across each other.'

Leanna frowned, uncertain whether or not she should ask the question about the connection to Aiduel's Guards' interviews. 'When exactly did it happen, Father? When in 748AA?'

He squinted again, thinking. Despite his fading eyesight, she knew that Parmer had a near-perfect ability to recall detail. 'Let me see. The twelfth day of Eventide, 748AA.'

Leanna did not ask the next question. Her own birthday was on the fourteenth day of Morningsong, 749AA. Almost exactly nine months later.

Lord Aiduel, can this truly be a coincidence? Lord, what am I?

—

In the weeks that followed, Leanna was not approached or interviewed again by Aiduel's Guards. As a result of this, she gradually became more confident that she was not a subject of specific interest to them.

She was therefore able to return her focus to everyday life as a novice at the College. However, her lingering dread of the Guards remained, and on each Seventh-Day the religious army reinforced its threat by burning another heretic on the fields outside.

Leanna's recurring dream continued to assail her every other night during this time, while her ability to sense emotions seemed to be building in strength. And the person that Leanna was most attuned to, from whom the emotions were closest and deepest, was Amyss.

340

Leanna loved Amyss, with all of her heart. She had never had a closer friend. But she was becoming increasingly certain over time that the love the smaller girl felt towards her was fundamentally more profound. That it was romantic in nature.

Amyss had never betrayed this with her actions or with her words. In her actions, Amyss was a true friend and confidante, working hard beside Leanna as the two of them were striving to complete their priestly studies. In her words, she was fun-loving and outgoing, and clearly continued to take great pleasure in making Leanna laugh.

However, Amyss's secret feelings were repeatedly betrayed by Leanna's strange new power. Betrayed by the smaller girl's restlessly intense emotions, which pulsed from Amyss to Leanna whenever the two of them were alone together. Particularly when Amyss held Leanna at night, following Leanna's tormented dreaming.

LOVE. DESIRE. LOVE. NEED.

Leanna initially felt like an invasive intruder as these emotions washed across her, in beats, at night-time. But somehow, with Leanna having no apparent control over her Aiduel-given power, she could no more block out these feelings than Amyss could cease from emitting them. And so, over time, Leanna accepted the receipt of the emotions for what they were. Golden. Bright. Lovely. Beautiful. And although Leanna did not openly acknowledge the romantic feelings which she was almost certain that Amyss held towards her, there was nonetheless something comforting about being bathed in such loving sensations at night-time.

The two of them continued to sleep together, every other night, with Amyss's head resting on Leanna's chest, Amyss's arm lying across Leanna's stomach. In all that time, only once did Amyss's actions verge on becoming amorous, and even on that occasion Leanna was not sure if the other girl had done it inadvertently in her sleep.

Leanna awoke one night to the physical sensation of Amyss's hand, on her left breast. Softly touching her. Massaging her. Having awoken from a warm and delightful slumber as Amyss's loving emotions had rippled through her, the sensation of the other girl's hand touching her felt nice. Almost too nice.

LOVE. DESIRE. WANT.

But Leanna lifted her own hand up and took hold of Amyss's hand, and moved it back down to her side, away from her breast. Amyss did not return her fingers to where they had been, and the event was never subsequently repeated, either that same night or afterwards. Indeed, Leanna was not even sure that Amyss had been awake when she had been doing it, so she never brought the matter up in conversation. Neither did Amyss.

—

Four months after he had first made the announcement about leaving the College, the week of Senior Priest Comrel's departure finally arrived.

For the very last time, the priests and novices of the College gathered in the main central church, for an evening service with their venerable leader.

Throughout the service, a much younger man, also adorned as a Senior Priest, assisted Comrel with the holy rituals. Comrel had not introduced the newcomer before the service commenced, and Leanna started to closely observe the new arrival.

He was many years younger than Senior Priest Comrel. Whereas the elderly priest was in his sixties in age, this other man looked to be around thirty years old, with white-blonde hair. Leanna also noted dispassionately that the new priest was very handsome.

After the service had concluded, Comrel introduced the new arrival. 'My children. Sadly, tonight will be the last time that I conduct this service. How wonderful it has been for me to lead you all in these beautiful moments of worship, and how much I shall miss it in the future. Indeed, I shall be leaving to travel north in three days' time. However, it gives me great pleasure to introduce my successor, Senior Priest Rennell El'Patriere.'

Leanna heard Amyss making a gasping noise beside her, and she in turn took in a surprised lungful of air. In Elannis, the 'El' designation before a name indicated that the bearer was a member of the Elannis Imperial Family, either a direct descendent of the royal bloodline, or a close relation. Either way, the new Senior Priest of the College was a close relative of Emperor Jarrius, and carried royal blood in his veins.

'Thank you, Father,' the newcomer said, smiling to display perfectly white teeth. 'And welcome, children. I shall only say a few words now, because I would like to come and speak to each of you in person over the next few days, and *very much* want to get to know you all so much better.'

He smiled again, and Leanna felt a shiver of unease running through her. Was there a pulse of darkness emanating from the stage, or was it just her imagination?

—

Comrel departed from the College later that week. Just a couple of days after that, Senior Priest El'Patriere visited Leanna and Amyss to personally introduce himself.

The knock on their bedroom door came just after ninth hour, when they had returned to their room after the evening service, which on this occasion had been conducted by the new Senior Priest.

It was unusual for anyone to visit their room at such a late hour, and none of the male priests or novices had ever come to the corridor upon which Leanna's room was situated. She was therefore shocked when she opened the door to find the Senior Priest standing there.

'Father, please excuse us, we did not expect–'

'Hush, child,' he responded, calmly. 'No need to be concerned.' His eyes appeared to flash downwards from her face and across

343

her body, and Leanna was relieved that she had not yet started to undress. She could hear Amyss standing up hastily, behind her. 'Please may I enter?'

'Of course, Father.' Leanna stood aside from the doorway, feeling confused by his late-night appearance.

The Senior Priest walked into their room, looking around with interest. 'How tidy. How very quaint.' His voice was posh, and somehow unpleasantly oily. He then gazed at Amyss, whose long red hair was loose and had fallen haphazardly around her shoulders. 'Please forgive the late visit, my lovely children, but I had promised that I would personally introduce myself to everyone. And I noticed you both at the service this evening, and realised that we had not yet said hello.'

'Hello, Father,' replied Amyss, 'I'm Acolyte Amyss. And this is-'

'I'm Acolyte Leanna of Arlais, Father,' Leanna finished.

'What beautiful names, for such beautiful children,' the Senior Priest responded. His eyes flashed briefly back to Leanna, but he was directing his attention towards Amyss as he continued to speak. 'And I am Senior Priest Rennell El'Patriere. Please call me Father El'Patriere. Do you know what the 'El' means, Amyss?'

'Yes, Father El'Patriere,' Amyss responded, sounding uncomfortable. 'Does it mean that you're part of our beloved Imperial Family, Father?'

The Senior Priest smiled, flashing his perfect white teeth. 'Very good, child. Very intelligent.' His attention was still locked upon Amyss. 'I sometimes wish that people didn't know about my royal status, that I could keep it secret somehow, but in my case it means that I'm our beloved Emperor's *nephew*! Isn't that wonderful?'

He paused, appearing to wait for a response, and after a few moments Amyss answered, 'Yes, Father.'

'Father *El'Patriere*,' the priest corrected sharply, a suddenly stern look appearing on his face.

'Sorry, Father El'Patriere,' Amyss responded contritely, blushing as she did so.

344

'That's OK, Amyss. I will forgive you the mistake, just this one time. But only because that flush in your cheeks is so charming.'

Suddenly, Leanna began to feel a throb of strong emotion emitting itself from the Senior Priest. A wave of passion which was enveloped in shadowy colours.

LUST. LUST. LUST.

Leanna recoiled, shocked at the intensity and nature of the feelings. Which she was certain were being directed from the new Senior Priest, towards Amyss.

El'Patriere turned his head to smile briefly at Leanna, oblivious of what she was sensing, then fixed his stare back onto Amyss. 'Yes. Believe me, sometimes I very much wish that people didn't know that I'm a member of our illustrious royal family. And that therefore they would fully recognise that all of my achievements, like my rapid early ascent through the church hierarchy, are a result of my brilliance and are not at all connected to my superior birth status.' He laughed to himself, a feminine-sounding giggle.

'Yes, Father El'Patriere,' answered Amyss, who was appearing increasingly uncertain.

LUST. LUST. LUST.

'And can I tell you a secret, Amyss, as long as you promise not to tell Leanna, here.' As he said this, he was leaning in towards the red-headed girl with his hand cupped to his mouth, fully aware that he was speaking loudly enough for Leanna to hear him. 'You know, Amyss, at my last parish I had a young assistant, a devoted girl like you. And I took a special interest in nourishing her learning, in developing her spiritual enlightenment. We would pray together sometimes, in the evening, would join hands and pray to The Lord together. I've been thinking about again taking on such an assistant here, at this College. And now that I have met you, and witnessed close at hand the obvious beauty of your soul, I think I would like to grant you the honour of offering you that post.'

'Sorry, Father El'Patriere,' Amyss responded, sounding confused. 'What post?'

'Why, to come and pray with me, of course, in my private chambers after ninth hour.' The Senior Priest smiled in a way which again displayed all of his perfect gleaming teeth. 'It is a great honour, to be so asked. Which I'm certain you will say "yes" to, won't you Amyss?'

LUST. LUST. LUST.

Amyss's eyes flashed across to Leanna, betraying alarm. 'Yes, Father El'Patriere.'

'Well, why don't we start tonight then, Amyss? You can accompany me back, right now.'

Leanna looked across at her friend, feeling a sense of fear and trepidation which had been fuelled by the black emotions which El'Patriere was transmitting. She wanted to shout out to the smaller girl to stop, to refuse the invitation, but of course that was not something which Leanna could practically do. This stranger standing in their bedroom was the new Senior Priest of their College, and was an individual who now had it within his authority and instruction to end their novitiate. And all that he had done so far was to invite Amyss to pray with him. How could Leanna possibly object to that?

She therefore felt like a coward, as she instead remained silent, and heard Amyss answer, 'Yes, Father El'Patriere.'

21

Corin

—

Year of Our Lord,
After Ascension, 769AA

Corin was seated closely beside Agbeth, peering out across the placid lakeside area which had been their home for almost two years.

'So, this is it, Corin? Our last night here. In our home.'

He nodded, feeling an aching melancholy inside. He would miss this place. Miss its tranquillity. But most of all, he would miss the intimacy and peace of his life here with her. Whatever was to happen in the coming days and weeks, whatever fate was to befall him, the splendid isolation that they had both enjoyed and endured for two years was coming to an end. They would soon be returning to the lands of man.

'Yes. I know.'

'I'll miss it here,' she said mournfully and then, as if voicing his own thoughts, she added, 'I'll miss our life being just you and me.'

'Me too. But we both know that we have to do this, Agbeth. Now. It would be too easy to say, let's have another day here. Then another week. Then another month. And then, before we know it, winter will be upon us and we'll be trapped here again until spring. And I'm not putting you through another winter here.'

After their arduous first winter of living in the shelter by the lake, they had both rejoiced at the life-renewing arrival of spring, and had subsequently enjoyed another contented and peaceful eight months in their forest home. By the time that the second winter of their residence by the lake had come upon them, the hardships of the preceding wintertime were a distant memory.

But the forest and the freezing weather had bluntly reminded them of the difficulties of their choice to live here. In fact, their second winter had been colder and more traumatic than their first, with blizzard-like conditions for weeks on end. Blackpaw had returned to them at the start of that second winter, of its own volition, and without the creature's hunting on their behalf, Corin doubted that they would have secured enough food to stay alive.

'There's no certainty that I won't have my fits again, somewhere else, Corin.'

'No certainty, but I think that they'll be less likely. You'd gone six years without one, before we came here.'

Agbeth had suffered even worse privations during her second winter there, than in the first. She had endured two long and debilitating fevers, and had been convulsed by seizures on multiple occasions. During the second fever, Corin had become certain that she was going to die, and he had been desperately praying to Banta that she not be taken from him. At that point he had made the vow that if she was to recover, he would never again ask her to endure another winter there. And now, when they were in the middle of the summer and travel was still possible, it was time to act upon that promise.

'And you're still set on going back to Karn?' Her voice suggested the doubts that she had always expressed, whenever they had discussed this.

'Yes. Let's not talk about this again, Agbeth.'

'It's not my life that's in danger if we return, Corin. I still don't think that it's right.'

'Not again, Agbeth. I'm not going to stay here and watch the cold weather one day claim your life. I'd rather take my chances with Borrik, and know that you're safe. And like I've said, we've got Blackpaw to protect us, now.'

The two of them looked at the large beast, which was sleeping peacefully, metres away from where they were sitting together.

Agbeth patted his hand, sounding reassured. 'Yes, we do.'

How strange, Corin reflected, that the beast, which had once mortally terrified them both, should now be such a source of security and comfort.

—

They departed from their lakeside home early the next day, even more heavily laden with gear than when they had made the reverse journey, two years earlier. As previously, he planned to navigate his way through the forest by keeping close to the river, although this time it was on his right.

Blackpaw was not walking with them, but Corin could sense that the creature was tracking their broad direction of travel, some distance to the east. The strange connection between him and the beast had grown ever stronger over the last eighteen months. Even now, he was able to see the forest world through its eyes, as it stalked through the woods.

After spending all of the warmer months in the far north, the creature had returned to their camp with the onset of their second winter there. And it had kept them both alive, through its hunting. Gradually, Agbeth had begun to fear the beast less and to welcome it more, and a point had eventually come when it had casually settled itself down to sleep, next to their fire. They had both accepted this.

Despite the distance it had travelled to reach the far north, Corin had retained an awareness of Blackpaw's actions throughout its migration there. And he had witnessed its many kills. Had seen the foothills of the great mountains at the edge of the world, through its eyes. And he had been amazed to see it encounter others of its kind, on a handful of occasions.

Given the extended time period over which they had now been connected, Corin knew that he and the beast were both impacting the other. Each of them was influencing and changing the other's character and nature in both subtle and not-so-subtle ways. He was certain that his connection to the beast was gradually taming it. Making it less feral and wild, if no less deadly, and more amenable to his and Agbeth's company.

Indeed, he was sure that his love and protectiveness for Agbeth had also somehow been imbued into the creature over time, and he no longer felt any concern that it was a danger to her. Quite the opposite; he sensed that Blackpaw would now put itself, and its life, between Agbeth and any potential threat she might face.

On the flip-side of that, he could recognise changes in himself since the association with the beast had been formed. He felt naturally stronger, braver, and more powerful, than at any time in his life before. Sometimes the felrin's reflected instincts almost became too strong, and he found himself possessed with an overwhelming craving to hunt; not for food, but for the simple pleasure of killing. To feel the death and destruction of another creature. At those moments he had to forcibly take control of himself, to suppress such urges. Agbeth's calming presence also helped him to quash these cravings, but he never felt comfortable to share with her the full extent to which he was feeling and suppressing these darker desires.

Perhaps it was also the creature's influence on his behaviour that made him feel less trepidation about his intention to return to Karn, despite Agbeth's misgivings about this. He no longer felt the timidity which had been inside of himself, all of his life. That part of his personality had possibly been vanquished at the moment when he had first screamed out his bloodlust at Blackpaw, and had been prepared to sacrifice his own life to save Agbeth. Or maybe Blackpaw's connected influence had finally expunged it. But either way, whatever had caused the change, he knew that he was no longer a craven coward.

After its second winter with them, Blackpaw had not returned to the north. The association between the two of them had by then grown so strong, that it had been the beast's choice to stay at his side. By that point, Corin was no longer controlling the creature's actions rigidly, just subtly influencing it to do what he wanted. However, he had given it the freedom to return north if it so desired, and it had chosen not to.

Like it or not, Blackpaw had become part of their family.

—

As they travelled to the south, Agbeth was delighting in pointing out places she could remember passing on their journey northwards, on that other expedition which now seemed like a lifetime ago. Despite her concerns about their destination, she appeared excited to be travelling again.

Corin was content to listen as she chattered. He was marvelling to himself that the burden of equipment he was carrying seemed so much less effort this time around. Maybe he was indeed stronger now, or possibly Blackpaw's connection just made him feel that way.

After they had stopped for lunch that day, Agbeth chose to revisit the matter which they had discussed many times over the preceding months.

'So, will you tell me again what your plan is, Corin?'

He sighed. 'We return. I'll tell Borrik and Kernon that I've served two years of my banishment and that we're asking for forgiveness and pleading for mercy. That we need to return, because of your health. And I'll tell them that to prove my worth I'll join the next war party, and will bring a great new fighter to the clan.'

'Blackpaw.'

'Yes. They must surely see that having Blackpaw fighting alongside them will help them to defeat the Anath.'

'Yes, I know all that. But you never answer me when I ask you – what happens if Borrik says "no"? He swore to kill you if you return.'

'He won't. How can he reject the gift of Blackpaw, fighting alongside him? Imagine the glory it would bring to the clan? Borrik would look like Mella reborn.'

'Yes, but what if he rejects it? And says "no". What's your plan, then?'

'He won't say "no". Enough, please, Agbeth.' Corin had a plan for that contingency, a scheme which involved his new powers, but he had never shared that part with her, and was not about to now.

She sat quietly for a few moments, looking frustrated, but then she decided to lighten the tone of the conversation. 'Do you truly think that being back in the village, will help to…'

'Yes. I do. Truly. I think that you'll get your health back and that you'll become pregnant, Agbeth. That we'll have a child together. When things are easier again.'

Agbeth had never become pregnant during their time in the Great Forest, which had become a source of sadness for her, despite the many challenges it would have presented to them.

'That would be so lovely, Corin. To carry your child.'

'You will. And you'll be a wonderful mother, too.'

—

As they travelled south through the forest, over the next few days, the recurring dream of the mountain and the Gate repeated itself a number of times.

It was almost fully formed within his mind, now, and he could recall most of its details afterwards. However, the last moments remained elusive. Was there a figure in the Gate? A sense of wrongness also continued to linger, in the minutes after waking

He had told Agbeth all about the dream, many times, and she knew the pattern of it now almost as well as he did. In the periods when Blackpaw had been in the far north, and Corin had been witnessing remote landscapes seen through its eyes, he had stayed alert for anything which might look like the mountain pathway of his dream. But he had not seen anything even vaguely familiar.

He was aware that the urge was gradually building inside himself, to one day seek out the Gate. Once, during the previous summer, he had shared this thought with Agbeth, as they had lain together at night, under their covers.

'I think the dream is... maybe calling me. Calling me to the Gate.'

'But why?'

'I don't know. Maybe the Gods are calling me? Maybe they want me to find them? Because of this power I have. I think that the Gate is real.'

'But what if it's not? What if it's just a dream, Corin? And how would you ever find it, anyway?'

'I don't know. But I think that maybe I'm seeing the home of the Gods. Or the gateway to their home. What else could it be? And if that's what it is, it must be at the edge of the world. In the north.'

'Don't leave me, Corin. Promise me you won't ever leave, to go there, without me.' She had suddenly sounded very earnest, as she had said this to him.

'Of course not. I promise.'

She had pressed herself against him, then, her tone suddenly mischievous. 'And that we'll only go there, *together*, when we're grey and old.'

He had laughed. 'I solemnly promise that I won't take you there until I'm completely bald, with a long grey beard. And until you're a... toothless and drooling old hag!'

She had laughed in return, and he had felt her fingers digging into his ribs, playfully. 'Old hag! How dare you!'

As they continued to travel south, part of him wondered if his powers would start to diminish, as a result of becoming more distant from the home of the Gods. However, to his relief, his bond with Blackpaw continued to be as strong as ever, and his ability to control the animals in the forest around him was also unaffected.

Every time that he wanted to, after he had sensed prey nearby, he just had to form an image of invisible tendrils easing out of his mind. Then he would feel them wrapping around and entering into his victim, and the targeted animal would be helplessly frozen into place.

He had also used his powers on Agbeth a handful of times, without her knowledge, through the winter months. Specifically, when seizures had taken violent possession of her, and he had employed his strange abilities to slip into her mind, to try to calm her down and to protect her. Each time, he knew that he was using his power for honourable reasons, but he also suffered a lingering sense of shame afterwards that in some respect his action had been a violation of her. That was the reason he had never been able to muster the courage to tell her about what he had done to stop each seizure. And why he had never employed his abilities on her at any time outside of her convulsions.

He was thinking now about his contingency plan with Borrik, if the chief turned down his request for clemency. He *knew* that he had been able to control Agbeth's mind, for those few moments within the seizure, when they had been residing on their land by the lake. But he was unsure if he would still be able to do it now, having travelled further south. And when she was fully conscious.

He looked across at her, as they moved through the forest. Could he reach out to her, as they walked? In the same way in which he reached out to the creatures around them? And then order her to freeze in place? If he tried it, he would know for certain whether

354

his powers still worked here, on another person, when they were conscious. But then he would also be invading her mind without her permission.

Without planning to, he abruptly focused, and invisible tendrils were instantly easing out of his mind and snaking towards her. Time slowed down, as he felt the connection drawing closer to his wife, ready to enter her thoughts and her mind, and-

He stopped his actions, shaking his head, feeling angry at himself. He had no right to do that to Agbeth. It was one level of intrusion to do it to help her when she was in the midst of a seizure, another altogether to act on his powers when she was awake and conscious and for no other reason than to prove that he could.

No, the nature his powers would take as they travelled south, and specifically how effective they would be when he tried to apply them to a person, would have to remain a mystery from him. He would find out at the moment he *needed* to find out.

—

After eight days of travelling they re-emerged late one morning onto the fields south of the Great Forest. He stopped there, waiting for Blackpaw.

'Look, Corin. That's where we were camped. Remember what we did there, for the first time?' Agbeth was clearly delighted as she pointed out the spot where they had been camping, near the river, when they had first passionately kissed each other. He smiled at the memory, of an event which had happened only two years earlier, but which seemed so distant now.

'Yes, I can't believe you seduced me like that, when we weren't even married, Agbeth. Shame on you.'

She grinned. 'Why have you stopped, Corin?'

He looked back towards the forest. 'I'm waiting for Blackpaw to catch up. We're back in Karn land, now. I want him to stay closer to us, from now on.'

His eyes moved along the treeline at the edge of the Great Forest. They were finally leaving their home of the last two years, this place which had provided such isolation from the world. Would they ever return here, together?

After a few minutes Blackpaw emerged from under the canopy of trees, and loped towards them, and then the three of them set off into Karn territory.

—

They walked for the remainder of that day, still following the river, and covering what Corin estimated to be half of the remaining distance back to the village of Karn. They did not encounter anyone during that time, which he was thankful for. He wanted them to get as close as possible to the village, before meeting any other people.

The atmosphere around their campfire that night was subdued and muted. He knew that Agbeth was fretting about what would happen the next day, and he himself was dwelling upon it. It was unsettling to recognise that, after two years of just each other's company, they were going to be dealing with other people again on the next day. Neither of them slept well that night, although Blackpaw had no such qualms and could be heard snoring loudly near to their fire.

They set off early the next morning, and continued their trek back to the village, following alongside the river. By the middle of the day, they had reached the northern tip of the Great Lake which ran alongside the village of Karn. At this point, Corin gave an instruction to Blackpaw to stay hidden in the woods in this area. With a very clear command that any hunting to be undertaken was not to include human prey.

Corin and Agbeth then continued onwards to the village. The first people to see them were a group of older children playing to the north of the settlement. The youngsters slowly recognised them

356

both, because Corin could hear his and Agbeth's insult-names being shouted as the children ran back towards the village.

In just a few minutes a band of four adult males were in front of them, blocking any further forward progress. All of them were armed. Corin recognised his father, Akob, amongst this group.

As they closed together, Corin spoke in a conciliatory tone, and simply said, 'Father.'

There was no attempt from Akob to return the greeting. 'Why have you come back here? There is only death for you in Karn.'

'I would like to speak with Borrik, to ask him to end my banishment. To let us return here.'

'He won't do. He'll kill you.'

Corin moved forwards. 'I have a gift for the clan. But I must present it to Borrik, in person. Please take me to him.'

Akob looked towards Agbeth. 'Are you going to let him kill himself?'

Corin responded instead, his voice stern. 'Leave my wife alone, father. I accept the risk I'm taking on in coming back here, and it is my decision. Will you allow me to see Borrik?'

Akob stared at him for a few seconds, as if pondering about the apparent change in Corin's demeanour. 'Very well. Go on then. It's your death.'

The older man then stood aside and gestured for Corin and Agbeth to move ahead of him. Corin passed by him, and then started the final walk into the village of Karn.

He breathed deeply as he moved, trying to stay calm, aware of Agbeth at his side. These were his last moments to prepare. To make himself ready to face his former clan chief, and to potentially meet his own death.

22

Allana

—

Year of Our Lord,
After Ascension, 769AA

On her twentieth birthday, Allana was standing on the eastern battlements of Septholme Castle, looking outwards to the hills beyond.

She had been living in the castle for eighteen months. And for seventeen of those months, she had been the lover of Duke Conran Sepian. Sleeping in his bed for a single night each week, and delighting in the undiminished desire which she could see in his eyes whenever she was near to him.

She would be visiting his bedroom again this evening, and she shivered as she experienced a brief thrill of anticipation for the night ahead.

If only Aiduel's Guards weren't here, Lana. If only they would leave. Then you would truly have a chance to be happy and content.

Allana peered now towards the partially constructed fortress being built to house a garrison of Aiduel's Guards. It was on an

358

opposing lower hill, which was four hundred metres inland from Septholme Castle.

The fields in front of the fort were full of tents and people, many of whom were wearing the recognisable red cloak and sash. The party of the religious soldiers had first arrived outside Septholme eight months earlier. Their occupation of the shallow forested hill to the east of the town had been undertaken with the permission of Duke Conran, a condition of the agreement which the Duke had reached whilst in Sen Aiduel.

Allana recognised that the increased presence of Aiduel's Guards in and around Septholme made her life in the castle more dangerous. Because of them, for all of her time there she had never left the castle grounds. Even then, she was never completely safe, because contingents of the Guards were regular visitors to the castle. However, the Duke had insisted that the religious soldiers could only visit with prior invitation, and he always warned her of any expected visits. On those days, she made sure to stay inside her sewing room all day, and only came back out when the Duke notified her that it was safe to do so.

Today, no visitors were expected. She was therefore indulging herself on her birthday by escaping from her work in the sewing room, to walk upon the castle battlements. She was enjoying the warm sun on her neck, and was reflecting on the events of her life since she had arrived in Septholme.

How much things have changed in two years, Lana.

—

She had become the Duke's confidante, over the course of their affair. He had gradually shared the secret burdens of his office, particularly in the last half-year.

She therefore knew that the proximity of Aiduel's Guards was a source of deep agitation to the Duke. In recent months, he had often told her about this when they were alone together.

'Sometimes, I just want to muster the troops and drive the lot of them into the sea,' he had once said to her. 'And peace treaty be damned!'

'Why?'

'Because, come what may, they're determined to find themselves a victim from amongst the people of Septholme. Someone to burn on their hill.'

'And will they? Burn someone, that is.'

'Eventually, yes. The first four cases of heresy that they've brought before us have all been dismissed, by the court that we've established. But their Commander, Evelyn dei Laramin, is a fanatic. She's cool, calm, and clearly very clever. But she's fanatical, too. You can see it in her eyes. She won't be satisfied that she's fulfilling her mission here until she's burned a heretic, and there's only so many times that Gerrion and I can exercise our influence to frustrate their cases.'

The Duke had then paused for a moment, before continuing. 'I have to try to find a way to protect everyone, without it leading to conflict with the Guards and with the Holy Church in Dei Magnus. Dei Laramin has requested several times now that I allow her people to question all of the younger adults in the town. People your age, between the ages of nineteen and twenty-one. I've refused it, of course, because we never agreed to do that in our deal with the Archlaw, but the request keeps coming back. It's madness. Sheer madness.'

'Why does she want to do that?'

'I have no idea. And the Guards are not inclined to explain. I've told them that I won't even consider the request until I understand properly why they want to do it. But they keep asking, anyway. Again and again and again. Fanatics!'

Allana had frowned as he had said this, but her next thought had been a selfish one.

At least they're not directly chasing you, Lana.

—

The Duke's hunger for her had not diminished at all during the eighteen months, although sometimes he had unknowingly strained against the mental shackles which she had once placed upon him.

He was a man of strong willpower, and the ongoing exertion of this will had led her to realise that her control over him was gradually eroding away over time.

Therefore, on those occasions when she had suspected that the Duke was close to freeing himself from her subtle domination, she had repeated what she had done to him in his antechamber, that first time. And given that she had already made a connection with his mind previously, it was much easier to re-forge it on subsequent occasions.

A voice of conscience occasionally whispered to her, challenging what she was doing. *This is wrong, Lana. Very wrong. You shouldn't be doing this.*

But she had learned to ignore that voice, and to counter it with the words, *You're only doing this to survive, Lana. To stay alive. You must survive.*

She had therefore repeatedly subjugated the Duke's free will using her powers, whenever it had suited her to, and she continued to disregard the misgivings that this action stirred.

However, despite the way that their relationship had started, and despite this ongoing control which she exercised over his mind, she believed that Duke Conran had naturally fallen in love with her. Indeed, the desire which still burned within him had been joined by the regular expressions of love which he now made towards her, within the secrecy of his room.

And when sometimes she woke up beside him in distress, emerging from her troubling recurring dream of the mountain and the Gate, he was always tender and protective of her. Cradling her, until she returned to sleep.

Affectionate emotions towards the Duke were growing within her, too. She enjoyed being with him, in his arms and under his protection, and gradually other thoughts were becoming more prominent in her mind.

He loves you, and may one day want to marry you, Lana. Sometime soon he will ask you, without you needing to order him to do it. And if he does, you know how you will answer.

Even with all of the problems that such an answer might bring.

—

With the passing of time, Allana's affair with the Duke had become more accepted in the castle, if only slightly less scandalous. However, there had been no glimmer of improvement in her relationship with Lord Gerrion.

After the first discussion during which Gerrion and Charl Koss had tried to bully and then bribe her into breaking off the relationship, there had been two more such attempts over the following six months. She had rebuffed both of those efforts to entice her to leave, to Gerrion's obvious irritation. However, after the third attempt, he had finally appeared to accept that she was a fixture in the castle, albeit an unwelcome one. And the lack of any pregnancy, unwanted or otherwise, was clearly a relief to him, too.

Allana was certain now that the Duke's eldest son had no interest in women. She was uncertain whether he had that type of inclination towards men, but she was definitely sure that women held no attraction for him. On two separate occasions during the year, the Duke had expressed annoyance to her that he had tried to raise the subject of an arranged marriage with Gerrion, but the young lord had rejected the idea. Allana had never felt it wise to raise her opinion about his son's sexuality with the Duke.

Allana was also nervously anticipating the return of the Duke's youngest son. She understood from Conran that it would only be a matter of weeks until Arion returned from his time in the Royal Army. It was clear that the Duke was also looking forward to that day. Allana could remember Ami Randle's early descriptions about how handsome the youngest Sepian male was, and she sometimes wondered whether he would bear any resemblance to his father.

Both of the relationships with Conran's sons now mattered to her, if the Duke was going to do what she thought he might. One day soon he might ask her to marry him, despite the risks. And one day soon, she might be the Duchess of the House of Sepian.

Would you have ever thought that possible, Lana? On the night when you fled from your home in Sen Aiduel, two years ago? That one day you could become a Duchess?

—

Allana was daydreaming about this fantasy as she descended from the castle battlements, to the courtyard below. And because it was her birthday, and because she was preoccupied with thoughts of what might be, she was much less careful and alert than she usually was. This carelessness would lead her to blunder into a reunion that was to change her life.

She was strolling back to her room, across the castle courtyard, when she first heard the shout.

'Lana! Lana! Is that really you?' The voice was instantly familiar, and was recognisably that of a Dei Magnun.

Allana felt a thread of horror running through her body when she turned towards the source of the voice. The woman she saw, a few paces away, was tall and skinny, with closely cropped blonde hair. She was wearing the uniform of an Aiduel's Guard.

'Nionia? What-'

'It is you!' Allana watched Nionia dei Pallere come towards her, a smile on the lanky woman's face. Nionia was shadowed by a second Aiduel's Guard, a hard-faced man who appeared to be a few years older than Nionia herself. 'My friend! It's been so long.' Nionia placed her hand onto Allana's shoulder, and squeezed it in a friendly gesture.

'Yes,' said Allana, feeling alarm and wondering how to extricate herself. 'Very long.'

'Over eighteen months! But you didn't write, Lana! You promised to write. Shame on you.'

363

'I'm sorry. I meant to.'

As if the thought had finally just occurred to her, Nionia frowned and then asked, 'But what are you doing at this castle?'

'I… I work here, Nionia.' Allana could see the suspicious look on the face of Nionia's colleague, who was clearly wondering why a citizen of Dei Magnus was inside a castle in Andar.

Nionia started to laugh with apparent happiness, then stopped herself, before frowning again. 'But you said you were going back to Dei Aiduel? Didn't you?'

'Yes, I did. But at the last minute, I was offered the job here.'

Nionia frowned again. 'But then why… why didn't you contact me?'

Allana desperately willed herself not to become red-faced, under the scrutinising stare of Nionia's colleague. 'Just, very busy, Nionia. Very busy.' She knew how weak the answer sounded.

'Oh. Oh, OK.' The other woman looked crestfallen. 'This is Sergeant Monliere. We're not meant to be here today, really, but your Lord Gerrion insisted that we bring him some papers in relation to a pending case, that-'

'Enough about that, Nionia!' snapped the Sergeant. 'That's confidential.' He then gestured towards Allana, addressing his question to Nionia. 'You know this woman?'

'Yes, yes,' replied Nionia. 'Lana and I were friends, when we both first came here.'

The sergeant stared at Allana for a few moments. There was no trace of cordiality in his expression. 'What is a Dei Magnun doing here, in an Andar castle?'

She recounted her cover story, which she had said many times now. The sergeant continued to regard her with apparent suspicion, throughout this.

'OK, we have to go, Nionia,' said the sergeant, eventually. 'You can tell me about her. Later.'

Nionia looked hurt and confused throughout this exchange, as if she was struggling to adjust to the fact that her own eyes were seeing her friend in such an unexpected place. As she moved to leave, she turned to Allana again, and her voice was a little colder than it had ever been before. 'Bye, Lana. I hope that we can meet again. Though I can't help but feel that you've been deliberately avoiding me, for all of this time.'

The two of them then turned to leave. Allana watched both of their backs as they disappeared through the main archway to the road outside the castle. She was alarmed by the encounter.

Don't start panicking, Lana. You've just hurt her feelings. It's been almost two years since you fled from Sen Aiduel. They will have forgotten about Ronis, by now. Won't they?

—

That evening she was with the Duke, and sometime after their lovemaking had finished, she raised the subject of the uncomfortable encounter. It had been ever-present in her mind since Nionia had departed, and the more she considered it, the more she found it to be concerning.

'Aiduel's Guards know that I'm here,' she concluded to him, after having provided an explanation as to what had happened.

His face was sombre upon hearing this news. 'There's nothing that either of us can do about it, now. They will either decide that they want to question you more, or they won't.'

'And if they want to question me?'

'I don't know. What would you have me do?'

'If they ever question me, they'll uncover the truth. Like you did. You mustn't let them, Conran.'

'It's not that simple, Lana. If we prepare you, together, I think you can withstand their questions, and there will be nothing to worry about. And there's also a delicate balance to be maintained, here. If they were to want to question you, and it was a reasonable request, then it would be hard to deny. I have to work to protect as many of our people as possible. And if I routinely turn down reasonable requests, then it becomes harder to immediately reject *un*reasonable requests.'

'But you've sworn to protect me, Conran.'

'And I will.' His voice sounded confused.

'Then you mustn't let them take me for questioning.'

'But it's not that simple, Lana. I have responsibilities to others, too.'

'And to me! To me, above all of them! You've promised to keep me safe!'

There was silence between them, after that. She judged that this meant that he was angry at her comment and was secretly disagreeing with her, despite the prior instructions implanted within him.

Could your control on him be weakening again, Lana, at the time when you might need him most?

She decided that the matter was of such importance that she would have to use her powers on him again, without delay. She therefore swung her body above him, thighs to either side of his hips, and whispered, 'Conran, look at me.'

And he did. And once again, following a slowing down of time and a slithering of an invisible connection into his mind, she subdued his free will. And reinforced her previous instructions, with new ones.

Protect me, Conran. Keep me safe. Don't ever let Aiduel's Guards take me, under any circumstances. Don't hand me over to them. Don't let them question me. Protect me from them. At all costs.

He struggled more than ever before against her forced invasion that night, his body shaking and his face drenched with sweat as he fought to prevent her seizure of control of his mind. Indeed, at one point, she perceived that he even appeared to be in severe pain, so desperate was his attempted resistance, and his hands reached up to hold his own chest. But, eventually, he was overcome. And then, afterwards, he forgot what she had done to him.

As he always did.

—

Two days later, she received a warning from the Duke to stay hidden, since a delegation of Aiduel's Guards were expected at the castle.

She worked out of sight in her sewing room, spending her day wondering anxiously if she was one of the matters being discussed. She was interrupted in the early afternoon by one of the castle guards, requesting her attendance in the Great Hall.

She arrived at the hall to find the Duke, Lord Gerrion and Charl Koss sitting together at the main table. They were in the midst of what appeared to be a muted but tense conversation when she entered, and she had never before seen Duke Conran appearing to be so agitated and stressed.

He looked up, his face red. 'Lana. You're here.' His greeting sounded weary, lacking in his usual authority. He then addressed the guard who had escorted her there. 'You may leave us. Close the door and make sure we're not disturbed.'

Gerrion then spoke up. 'Father, I think I should conduct this conversation. It will be less... personal, for me.'

The Duke raised his hands in a gesture of resignation, and then shrugged. 'Very well, Gerrion. Proceed.'

Gerrion rose to his feet, facing Allana. 'We've just had a visit from Aiduel's Guards. Quite a difficult meeting, in fact, and we argued about a number of their demands. However, as one of the points they raised, they have presented us with a petition and other documentation, asking us to pass you into their custody, for questioning.'

Allana felt a surge of anxiety. 'Questioning? Why, my Lord?'

'You were recognised in the castle two days ago, apparently. And they have grounds to suspect that you may have been involved in the murder of a High Priest in Sen Aiduel. A Ronis dei Maranar.'

You fool, Lana. All of this, because you chose to walk in the castle grounds, when you should have been working. Be very careful, now.

'What? Why would they think that?' She did her best to sound incredulous.

'Because apparently you share the first name of one of the possible murderers, and you arrived here at broadly the same time

367

as the killers must have fled. And they think that you've been lying to one of their people, a Nionia dei Pallere.' He walked closer towards her. 'Was it you? Did you do this thing?'

'No, my Lord.' She doubted that Duke Conran would have disclosed anything.

'Well, then, you'll have no issue in sharing your story with them, answering their questions, and then they'll let you go.'

She hesitated, not knowing what to say. She looked at the Duke. 'Conran?'

'Address him as "My Lord", here, in my presence,' stated Gerrion. 'You will be fine to agree to this questioning, I presume?'

Despite the confidence which Conran had expressed two nights earlier, Allana considered that her story was no more likely to withstand questioning from the interrogators of Aiduel's Guards, than it had stood up to the Duke's own original scrutiny. She again addressed Duke Conran. 'My Lord?'

'I'm not handing her over to them, Gerrion,' the Duke muttered, eventually. His hand was on his chest again, as he said this. Allana thought that she could see sweat on his forehead.

Gerrion turned towards his father. 'Why not, father? If she's innocent of what they say, then she has nothing to fear. If she's guilty, then none of us would want her to stay here, anyway?'

'I'm not handing her over, Gerrion,' the Duke replied. 'We all know how Aiduel's Guards conduct their questioning.' The Duke's mouth was contorted into a grimace.

Charl Koss spoke up. 'We can address that, my Lord. We can insist on having an observer at any questioning, to ensure everything is done appropriately. If it would put your mind at ease, I would insist that it would be me. Then... because she is innocent, I'm sure... no harm could come to her.'

'Listen to me, both of you! I'm *not* handing her over!' The sudden bellow echoed around the room.

'But why not, father?' questioned Gerrion. He had flinched back from the Duke's anger, initially, but now he had composed himself again and his voice was still calm. 'I don't understand. Matters are tense enough between us and the Guards, right now, after the other things we refused to do today. This was their only reasonable request. Let her quickly prove she is not this person they're looking for. Why create extra conflict with them, for this issue?'

'Because I'm not handing her over, Gerrion!' The Duke's face was becoming increasingly red, as he shouted.

'There is no logic to that, father. Please help me to understand why you insist that she cannot be questioned?' Gerrion continued to appear cool and unflappable in the face of his father's outbursts.

'Because I must protect her, Gerrion. I must keep her safe.' This time the response was not shouted, but instead sounded weak and embarrassed. As if the Duke recognised how pathetic his argument would sound, and could not understand why he was taking such an irrational stance.

Allana recognised the phrases from the controls that she had repeatedly planted into the Duke's mind, and she could understand the conflict going on within him. A conflict between taking the proper course of action as he would normally have chosen, and the prohibition which she had placed inside him to prevent him from doing this. Could this conflict be causing the apparent physical discomfort which he was displaying?

Gerrion responded again. 'Protect her? Keep her safe? Why, because she warms your bed, father? Is that a reason to ignore the rule of law? Is that a reason to further antagonise Aiduel's Guards and the Holy Church, at such a tense time? We've been fighting to stop them interviewing all of our young people, father. Again, they've raised it today and have threatened the Archlaw's intervention. That is the battle we should choose to fight and hold our ground on, father. Not *her*. Not now.'

'If she is innocent, Lord,' added Koss, in a conciliatory voice, 'she will not be in danger. I will personally vouch for that. If she has committed this crime, though, then she is not worthy of your protection. Nor is it then safe for her to be in this castle, or close to you.'

'I'm not handing her over!' shouted the Duke again, in response. 'I must protect her! I must keep her safe!' His breathing was laboured, as he shouted this, and flecks of spittle were on his lips.

Gerrion replied again, still refraining from anger. 'Everything you have ever taught me, father, is to place justice and the rule of law above personal interests and emotions. And to rule fairly, for all of our people. But in this case, on this issue, this woman, your judgement is deeply impaired.' He then turned to face Allana, his tone as amicable towards her as it had ever been. 'Lana, please tell the Duke that you are fine to do this. Charl will ensure your safety in any questioning, so you can demonstrate your innocence. Please inform the Duke that you agree to let us take you for questioning.'

Allana looked across at Gerrion, his face emotionless as he awaited her answer. She then stared towards the Duke. By contrast, the older Sepian looked deeply unwell, and more flustered than she had ever seen him. She felt certain now that the conflict and turmoil she had created within him was having this impact on his health. His eyes were staring directly at her, with almost a look of pleading within them.

He wants you to release him, Lana. To release him from the promises you forced him to give to you.

Some instinct told her that if she informed the Duke that she was fine to be interviewed, then she would in some way be loosening the constraints of the commitment which she had embedded into his being. That this conflict and turmoil running rampant inside his mind, which was causing these symptoms of great stress in his body, would be eased.

But she could not do this. Could not agree to such questioning, no matter the discomfort that his inner conflict caused for the Duke. Because for her, to be taken by Aiduel's Guards, and to be questioned by them, would lead to the unravelling of her story. And in turn would lead to her death.

You must do what is best for you, Lana. You will survive this. You must survive this. Conran must protect you. Whatever the cost.

She finally addressed her answer to the Duke, her voice calm, her words deliberate. 'Don't let them hand me over, Conran. Protect me. At all costs. Keep me safe.'

Finally, Gerrion lost his temper. 'That surely confirms it, then! She must be guilty! She must be this woman they seek, this Allana dei Monis!'

The Duke had hunched himself forwards. He was again grimacing. 'We're not handing her over, Gerrion. We must protect Lana. At all costs. Must keep her safe.'

'How can you still want to protect her, father? She may be a murderer. In our home. Near Kari!'

The Duke's hand lifted to his chest again, and his face looked even redder. 'We must protect her, Gerrion. Must keep her safe.'

Gerrion turned back towards Allana. 'Why does he keep saying that? What have you done to him?'

Her voice was cool. 'I have done nothing. He loves me, that's all.' She then looked towards the Duke, again ignoring the pleading look in his eyes. Ignoring his unspoken request for release. 'And he wants to protect me, and to keep me safe. Whatever the cost.'

Gerrion appeared ready to make another angry response, but he was interrupted by an anguished moan followed by a loud thudding sound, as Duke Conran Sepian collapsed face forwards onto the table of the Great Hall.

—

Much later, Allana was escorted from the feast hall in the company of two armed guards, and she spent that night in a cell in the castle dungeon.

Duke Conran had died, in the minutes after he had fallen onto the table, clutching his heart. Even now, as she lay on a straw cot in the dark of the cell, Allana could not remember much about those frantic and horrifying minutes following his collapse.

By the time that she had finally shouted to him that she was fine if he allowed her to be questioned, it had been too late. He had been beyond hearing, by that point. The castle physician had later arrived to declare the Duke dead at the scene, from what appeared to be a massive heart attack.

But in her own heart, Allana knew what had caused it.

It was you, Lana. Whatever you did to him, and have carried on doing to him, it is not natural. You forced him to fight against his own choices. His own conscience. And finally, when you could have released him, could maybe have saved him, you chose not to. Your actions made his heart explode, within him. You killed him.

At some point in the evening or night, although it was difficult to judge time in the windowless room in which she was imprisoned, the new Duke visited her. He was carrying a candle in front of himself, and as he stood outside the bars of the cell, his face was illuminated by the single flickering flame.

'Enjoy your last night in the castle, whore,' Gerrion said. His voice was again calm. 'Or should I say, Allana dei Monis?'

'I am sorry,' she replied. She still felt numbed by Conran's demise. 'I'm sorry for your father's death.'

'Do I care whether or not you're sorry? As far as I'm concerned, you caused his death today. You. If you'd just gone when we asked you to, last year, none of this would have happened. You killed him.'

She buried her head into her knees, and started to cry.

'I wanted to let you know that we've sent notice to Aiduel's Guards, to come and collect you tomorrow,' Gerrion continued. There was no heat in his voice, just a steady calmness. 'They're going to question you. And I hope that they find the truth, whore, and uncover just who and what you are, and what you've done. Because they're desperate for a burning on their hill, and I'd rather not give them one of our own citizens. And know this. If and when you burn, I intend to be there, to watch. Standing in the front row. Smiling.'

He then turned his back on her, and left her alone in the darkness. Alone, crying, and with visions of flames running through her mind.

23

Arion

—

Year of Our Lord,
After Ascension, 769AA

A rion crouched with his men, on a hill overlooking the beach, waiting for the Bergen raiders to return to their vessels.

He was leading a company of eighty soldiers of Andar, all of whom were stationed with Arion at Fort Lennis, which lay ten miles to the south of these sands. They were preparing themselves now to ambush the raiding enemy, and this trap was to be the culmination for Arion of eight months of frustrating pursuit.

On too many occasions, over the course of the last year, Arion and the soldiers of the fort had been too far away when the alarm had been raised. They had arrived just a little too late. On three separate instances, Arion had reached the scene of the Bergens' crimes only to witness the raiders sailing out to sea on their vessels, escaping from the havoc they had wreaked. Havoc which had included murder, rape and pillage.

Arion had grown to hate them, a loathing fuelled by their vile deeds and their repeated elusiveness. The Bergens were heathen savages, and the only justice that they would understand would be written in blood for them. But in order to kill them, they must be trapped on land first. And this time, Arion and his men had them.

By the Lord. They'll all die for the crimes they've committed!

Sergeant Donnel approached Arion now, the tough old soldier climbing up the hillside towards him.

'It's done, sir,' he said to Arion. 'They're all holed.'

'Good job, sergeant.' Arion stared down at the three longboats which had been pushed up onto the beach. Donnel and his men had taken axes to the bottom of each of the boats. There was no longer a possibility that any of the longboats would be seaworthy.

The Bergen raiders had left six men to guard their vessels. Each of those guards had already been killed, their corpses dumped inside their own boats, hidden unless somebody looked over the ship's side. Arion estimated that each of the boats would hold approximately twenty men. As such, there was likely to be a remaining force of over fifty Bergen warriors returning to the beach shortly.

Arion had taken the painful decision to keep his company of soldiers here, where they had destroyed the Bergen warriors' means of escape and could spring an ambush. He recognised that by not pursuing the enemy inland there could have been more deaths and assaults of villagers in the surrounding areas. However, he had accepted that cost in return for the potential prize of giving his men a tactical advantage.

He reached down and touched the hilt of his sword. He was relishing the coming opportunity to use it in anger, finally. He had been stationed on this coastline for eight months, and he had still not been in a battle. Still had not fought a man in a situation where he was in mortal danger, and could properly test his skills and courage.

'Not long now, sir,' stated Donnel. 'I'm looking forward to giving these bastards a taste of Andar justice.'

'Me too, sergeant,' replied Arion. 'Me too.'

'Thank the Lord for your dream, sir,' added Donnel. 'I'm sick of arriving too late to catch these fuckers.'

Arion smiled. 'Pure coincidence, sergeant, I'm sure. But nonetheless, thank the Lord.'

The reason that they had come here today was that he had woken this morning, having had a vivid dream that he had been peering at three longboats on this recognisable beach. In the absence of any other missions or objectives for the day, he had obtained the Fort Commander's permission to bring a small force to this place. They had been delighted to find the raiders' vessels here, in the exact place that he had dreamed of.

'And remember, sergeant,' added Arion. 'We keep firing arrows at them until they're forced to charge us. Then we let them run up this hill towards us. And we only charge towards them when they're near the top. Do all the men understand that?'

'Yes, sir.'

'Good. I want all of these bastards dead, too. No prisoners today. But let's not waste our own men's lives.'

Arion looked around at his soldiers. All of his troops were attired in the uniform of the Royal Army of Andar; chainmail, helmet with nose-guard, and a blue tabard. All were also equipped with sword, shield and a bow. His men appeared ready and eager for the coming fight, albeit that there was an evident tension.

Arion peered towards his lookouts, next, individual soldiers crouched a hundred metres in either direction from his main force. As he did so, he saw one of the two lookouts raise his arm, in warning. The signal was clear. The raiders had arrived.

—

Arion watched the Bergen war-party move onto the beach, over two hundred metres distant. He then checked his troops again, making certain that all of his men were prostrate behind the crest of the hill, and therefore were not visible. Satisfied with this, he returned his eyes back to the raiders.

His earlier estimate had been correct, and he quickly assessed that they had a force of perhaps fifty warriors. As was typical of Bergen raiders, most were carrying an axe and shield, and were wearing leather armour. They also appeared to be hauling a variety of looted possessions.

Arion identified the man who he assumed was the Bergen leader, and he noted the precise moment when that individual spotted the lack of guards on the longboats. Immediately, the Bergen leader made a signal, following which his raiding party appeared to spread out with weapons drawn, dropping their plunder onto the beach sand.

Arion had expected this. Although the Bergen war-party was now alert to a potential threat, he knew that they would still not be able to see the dead bodies of their guards within the boats.

He growled out a command to the men around him. 'Everyone stay down until I say otherwise. But get ready to aim and fire arrows. Pass the word.'

The Bergen raiding party drew closer. When they were fifty metres away, the Bergen leader instructed a handful of his men to move closer to the boats. As Arion saw this, he made a hand signal to order his Andar soldiers to nock arrows. He then moved to a crouching stance, still hidden, and observed his men doing the same.

Lord preserve us, and bring us victory this day.

Arion observed as the small group of men approached the boats, and at the precise moment they drew close, he shouted, 'Stand! Fire!'

As one, the Andar soldiers raised themselves to their feet, and a hail of arrows flew towards the Bergen raiders. A handful of the enemy were dropped instantly, the arrows securing a lethal destination.

The Bergen warriors turned towards Arion's force on the hill, and following a shouted instruction, Arion could see them commencing a direct charge towards his company. Again, he shouted, 'Draw! Fire!'

A second volley of arrows hit the Bergen group as they reached the foot of the slope, felling a further handful. The remainder started to scramble up the hillside, axes and shields raised, fury on their faces, battle-cries resounding in the air. A third barrage slammed into them as they reached the halfway point up the hill.

'Draw swords!' Arion's bellow carried to his men, as he himself then unsheathed his weapon. 'Ready! Hold! Now charge!'

As the Bergen raiders reached the higher parts of the slope, Arion led his men in a charge down towards them. The Andar force now outnumbered their enemy by over two-to-one. Arion's eyes were focused upon the man who he had identified as the Bergen leader, a large rough-looking individual with a thick beard and shaggy hair.

Exhilaration tinged with traces of fear rushed through him as he charged towards the foe, his weapon held aloft. The momentum of the two opposing forces carried him to within a few paces of the Bergen leader, and then he was facing his first adversary, a youthful raider over whom he possessed a significant size advantage.

His opponent swung his axe around at Arion, a move which was easy for Arion to deflect with his shield, and he countered with a thrust to the young raider's neck, killing him. A surge of adrenaline powered through Arion's body with that first kill, but then he was immediately blocking an attack by a second opponent, a large black-haired brute who was wielding a two-handed axe.

That axe crashed into Arion's shield, causing it to splinter and forcing him backwards. As this second adversary yanked his axe out, Arion slammed the remains of the shield forward into the raider's face, stunning him. With his other hand he then hammered the hilt of his sword into the man's nose, bursting it.

Before there was any other combat between them, one of Arion's fellow soldiers stabbed his sword into the raider's groin, incapacitating him. The Bergen fell harmlessly backwards, away down the hill.

Arion cast off his broken shield, looking around for another foe to kill. All about him, the small but bloody battle was raging, the troops of Andar taking advantage of their numerical superiority. In the midst of this combat, this brutality, Arion felt supremely alive. So wonderfully, addictively, alive.

STRENGTH. VICTORY. GLORY.

'Andar!' screamed Arion in response to this feeling. Then, for the second time in his life, he experienced the world crackling around him as if he had been struck by a lightning bolt, with the same consequent deceleration of time. Invisible coils of energy coalesced around his limbs, making him feel suddenly superhuman, as the battle seemed to slow down around him.

He searched momentarily for the Bergen leader, before spotting him engaged in a furious struggle with Sergeant Donnel. Arion started to stride towards them, moving without fear through the battlefield on the hill.

Enemy warriors attempted to attack him as he passed, but their weapons appeared to Arion to now move with a velocity as if they were being swung through oozing mud. Each time, he nonchalantly moved his body aside to avoid the attacking blow. He then casually dispatched his assailants with his own sword as he passed, his blade and body spiralling effortlessly in a blur of graceful death-dealing.

Arion killed three raiders in that manner in the handful of seconds it took him to close to the Bergen leader. The shaggy-haired warrior had knocked Sergeant Donnel to the ground and was about to finish him.

'Andar!' Arion screamed again, catching the attention of this opponent, who turned towards him and swung his axe. Arion easily avoided the blow and then swept his own sword across the man's axe-wielding arm, cutting his foe's tendons. The Bergen leader's axe clattered to the ground as the severed tendons forced him to release it. The Bergen then launched himself directly at Arion, trying to grip him with his free hand.

Filled with an intoxicating sense of immense, unnatural power, Arion grabbed hold of the man's uninjured arm. And then, with as much effort as it would normally take to snap a twig, he broke the man's limb in two, leaving it dangling helplessly. The Bergen leader screamed and fell to the ground, by the side of Donnel.

The sounds of battle were dying out around them, and Arion could see that almost all of the Bergen raiders had been killed, other than a handful who had chosen to throw down their weapons and flee. Arion witnessed his troops charging in pursuit of them, cutting their enemies down as they ran, such that none would escape.

He then extended a hand to help Donnel to his feet. Finally, he looked down at the Bergen leader. The man was desperately using his feet to try to scrabble backwards, both of his arms rendered useless.

Arion moved forwards and put his knee and his whole weight onto the enemy leader's chest, pinning him in place. The man looked up at him, appearing defiant, before Arion's gauntleted fist crashed down into his face.

Kill him, kill him, kill him, kill him. Take your victory.

'Don't.' Arion punctuated the word with another crunching blow to the man's cheek, powered by this exhilarating force which he could still feel inside of himself. 'Come.' Another crushing blow, breaking open the raider's nose and face. 'Here.' A final blow, and the Bergen leader was dead. 'Again.'

Arion stood up, sensing that his strange power was now leeching away, but feeling triumphant. He could sense Donnel staring at him, a peculiar expression on the other man's face. And then his soldiers started cheering.

—

Arion's victory over the raiders was subsequently to earn him local renown and plaudits as both a warrior and as a leader. He soon heard the soldiers of Fort Lennis whispering about how he had personally killed numerous men in the fight, and of how devastatingly fast and deadly he had been. Their military company had only suffered fourteen battle casualties, eight dead and six wounded. To have eliminated a party of close to sixty raiders, with losses as low as these, was viewed as a great achievement. Arion had proudly written to his father, to share news of the victory.

As he entered his last month of military service, Arion was counting down the days to when he would be a free man again, and would finally have earned the title of Knight of the Realm. He was also thankful that the battle on the beach had provided him with at least one notable experience to mark his period in the Royal Army.

The prior nine months had been quite a monotonous time. Arion now understood that, in the absence of war, the existence of a soldier was often dull. His life since arriving at Fort Lennis had been a tedious routine of training, drills, equipment maintenance, and patrols. Until the successful battle, this monotony had only been interrupted by occasional and fruitless pursuits of raiders, following alerts which had arrived too late.

The location of Fort Lennis, in the more remote north-west area of Andar, had not helped. The fort was within the territory which had been the old ancestral lands of the Sepian family, and was an imposing military construction on an outcrop of headland by the sea. However, after having spent one winter there, with the freezing western winds blowing in from the ocean, Arion could understand why his ancestors had been so keen to relocate to Canasar.

In his last month within Fort Lennis, Arion received three letters. The first was a reply from the Duke:

> Dear Arion,
> Congratulations on the successful battle on the beaches near Fort Lennis. Our ancestors would have been proud of you, as indeed am I.
> I look forward to welcoming you back to Septholme as a Knight of the Realm, and in time to seeing you take over command of our army.
> Your father,
> Duke Conran

Arion experienced a surge of pride as he read this; it contained the most praise that he could ever remember receiving from the Duke. The second letter was even more unexpected, being a follow-up response from Delrin:

Dear Arion,

Hello, little brother. In case you have been wondering about this, given the fact that I have not written for eighteen months, I am indeed still alive! Barely!

I am approaching the end of my training now, and will soon be a Knight of The Order of Saint Amena. I trust that your time in the Royal Army progresses well, and that you will also soon be titled, as a Knight of the Realm? Let's agree never to bow to each other, though (OK, you can still bow to me).

The last eighteen months have been hard. I had an idea before getting here about how fragile Angall's hold on the Holy Land is, but the reality is even worse than that. There have been many assaults on our frontier castles in the last year, and the infidel armies are growing in strength. Many here fear that the five thousand recruits taken on in the last two years will not be enough. The enemy organise themselves under a warlord named Baladris, and he is as cunning as he is ruthless.

My sword has tasted blood for the first time (and numerous subsequent times), and I am no longer a battle 'virgin', as such. Have you experienced war yet, brother? It is less glorious, and far gorier, than I ever imagined.

You will be delighted to know that I have a woman now. Not my wife, since we are not supposed to take wives in the Order, but having a partner is accepted. Her name is Shalina. She is dark, exotic, and very beautiful. I hope that one day you will meet her. And stop chasing the local girls, brother! Surely it must be time for you to settle down and get married?

Write to me when you get the chance.
Your loving brother,
Delrin.

The third letter was from Lennion Rednar:

Dear Arion,

Greetings, friend.

I will keep this brief, since I hope we will soon see each other, to share our news in person.

Mother has written to me twice in the last month, asking me to contact you to remind you that you accepted an invite to our estates in Rednarron, once your military service has concluded.

I will assume that you still intend to come, unless you tell me otherwise. I am looking forward to seeing you again, friend, as is Mother. But I think we both know which member of the Rednar family is most eager to know whether you still intend to visit us?

Your friend,
Lennion.

Arion smiled when he read the last sentence, remembering Lennion's pretty younger sister. He fully intended to honour his promise to visit them, and there was a growing excitement inside himself at the thought of seeing Kalyane again.

—

Shortly after that, Arion's tenth month of service at Fort Lennis had ended, and he was formally released from his duty of service to the army. On his final day there, the Fort Commander awarded him a medal identifying him as a Knight of the Realm, and then Arion was again a free man.

The journey to Rednarron, by land and by sea, took him two weeks, and it gave Arion plenty of opportunity to reflect on the events of the last two years.

He was still confused about what had happened to him, both during the battle on the beach, and during the fight with Jarrett Berun. He had subsequently tried again to replicate that intoxicating sensation of becoming extremely powerful, but had repeatedly failed. He was certain that what he had felt in the battle had been real, and that he had truly been blessed with unnatural speed and strength for those few exhilarating moments. However, the powers only appeared to become available to him during times of danger and threat. He had still not talked to anyone about it, because he expected that any other person who he discussed it with would think him crazy.

He had also not given much thought, since the battle, to his seemingly prescient dream of the three longboats on the beach. At the time, he had dismissed it as coincidence, but he wondered now whether it was connected to his unusual physical powers.

Or, indeed, was it connected to his recurring dream? That dream still troubled him, every other night, taunting him with its elusive images of a winding mountain path and a Gate. And a figure, inside that Gate? Luckily, whilst at the fort he had been entitled to a single room, so no one else had needed to suffer from his restless dreaming. However, once he got back home to Septholme, he intended to raise the subject of the dream with his family, to see if any of them could shed further light upon its meaning.

He was still thinking about all of this as he travelled on the final leg of his journey to the Rednar Estates, by carriage. He then suddenly realised how serious and introspective his thoughts had become, and admonished himself.

By the Lord! Cheer up! I'm young, I'm now a Knight of the Realm, and I'm soon to lead the armies of a mighty House. And I'm on my way to see a pretty girl who appears to be keen on me. Lord preserve me! Lighten up!

—

The month that he was to spend in the Rednar estates, with Lennion and his family, proved to be like a paradise for Arion.

The contrast with the prior two years could not have been any greater. Whereas during his time in the Royal Academy of Knights each consecutive day had been full of trials and challenges, for each day in this month he had nothing which he *needed* to do. And whereas during his time in Fort Lennis he had lived an austere military lifestyle, here he was surrounded by luxury and opulence.

Unlike House Sepian, whose residence was a military castle, the Rednar family lived in country estates which were separate from their castle and keep in Rednarron itself. With summer arriving, the grounds of those estates were a wonderful environment within which to hunt, ride or to simply walk and relax.

Kalyane was there, alongside him, for the entire duration of his stay. She had been waiting outside the front of the Rednar country residence with her mother and Lennion when Arion had first arrived. Thereafter, she appeared politely determined to attach herself to all of his and Lennion's activities during his visit.

On Arion's first full day there, the three of them went riding together. At one point, Lennion had ridden ahead, and Arion found himself alone with his friend's younger sister.

'Was your time as a soldier everything you expected it to be, Arion?'

Arion looked up as she asked him this question. She was even prettier than he remembered, as her large green eyes focused upon him. She was wearing a summer dress which displayed her petite slim figure, and her auburn hair was again loose.

'Not always,' he replied, then laughed. 'Actually, it was quite boring, sometimes. Doing the same thing over and over.'

'Really?' She laughed, in return. 'Actually, although you may not believe it, it gets boring here sometimes, too. Doing the same things with the same people. It's nice to have a visitor.'

Arion smiled. 'It's nice to *be* a visitor.'

'But I heard from Lennion that you had a great victory at Fort Lennis?'

Arion noticed that she was again asking him lots of questions, and noted that he had never met anyone who appeared to show so much interest in him.

'A victory, yes. But a "great" victory? I think he's being kind.'

'And I think you're being modest. Please tell me about it.'

And he did tell her, although he softened his account of the violence he had delivered, and he did not share any details about his powers. Strangely though, as he recounted the story he *wanted* to tell her about the powers. She had a way of listening, with a look of fascinated interest, which made it seem natural for him to want to open up to her.

'That sounds so scary! But so exciting, too,' she exclaimed, when he had finished. 'If I was a Bergen raider, I should not want to meet *you*.'

He laughed. 'Well, I'm glad you're not a Bergen raider then.'

She laughed in response, a soft chuckling sound, then brushed her long hair away from her face, with both hands. Arion watched the movement of her graceful limbs, trying not to stare. He was very attracted to her.

—

Arion and Kalyane spent a lot of time together during the next two weeks, often in Lennion's company, but frequently without him. During his stay, Arion got to meet all of the members of the Rednar family, including the portly and stern Duke Rednar, and Lennion's older brother, Ronian.

However, there appeared to be a tacit understanding amongst all of the Rednars that the most important relationship to be nurtured, during Arion's stay, was that between him and Kalyane.

Therefore, they were given frequent and ample opportunity to be alone together. Indeed, on more than one occasion when the two of them and Lennion went out as a threesome, Lennion would then be called back to the residence for reasons which did not always seem entirely credible.

After having been asked what seemed like hundreds of questions by Kalyane, Arion was determined to find out more about her.

The two of them were sitting closely together under a tree, their arms touching. The sun was shining through the leaves above them, dappling patches of light onto her freckled face as they talked.

'Kalyane,' he said. 'You once asked me what the future will hold for me, after my time in the military. What will the future hold for you?'

'For me?' She smiled. 'I'm not very deep or complicated, Arion. I just want to be happy. To have a husband who I love and who loves me. And children who are happy and healthy and full of love. And a home full of warmth and laughter. All very boring, I know!'

'Not boring,' he said, being serious. 'It all sounds… nice.'

'Nice?' She laughed. 'Now that does sound boring!'

'No, nice! But, you being the only daughter of a leading House. Have your parents ever talked to you about an arranged marriage? A political marriage?'

'Yes. They have. I know that's a possibility. I'm eighteen years old now, and I know that the life I have here in Rednarron can't go on for ever. But Mother has always said to me, if I ever meet someone of the right… *status*, who I have feelings for, then she'll do everything she can to prevent me from having an arranged marriage.'

'And would I be of the right status?' He knew that there was a risk to asking a question like this, but in such a peaceful and intimate moment, it felt like the right thing to do.

There was no hesitation before her answer. 'I believe so, yes.'

'And could you have feelings for me, Kaly?'

'Possibly, yes. It depends.' She smiled, coyly.

'Depends on what?'

'On whether you have feelings for me, too.'

He smiled in return. 'And if I do? Because I think I do.'

'Then maybe I have feelings for you, too.' She said this flirtatiously.

'Maybe?' He grinned, sensing that she was being playful. 'Are you teasing me? OK. How do I turn a maybe into a definitely?'

She stared at him directly, her lovely emerald-coloured eyes wide open. 'Well, you could kiss me. For a start.'

And then they were kissing, softly and chastely, with just their arms and mouths touching.

—

They talked many more times, in the week after that, and kissed again on several occasions, although never in a manner which was anything other than innocent. Arion wanted more, but deliberately restrained himself. Eventually, Kalyane returned to the question of their futures.

She initiated the conversation whilst they were walking together, when there was just a handful of days of Arion's visit remaining. This time, she was more awkward than flirtatious.

'Arion. I've loved being with you, these last weeks. Loved it so much. But I need to ask you, now. What happens next?'

'Next?' He had been expecting this discussion, but he was still not quite ready for it.

'Next. After you leave here. What will become of… *us*?'

He was certain now about what *she* wanted, but the thought of where this conversation might lead was genuinely confusing to him. He liked her a lot, he enjoyed being with her, and he found her to be attractive. However, he was not entirely sure whether he had fallen in love with her, if such a thing even existed? And he was also uncertain as to whether he was ready for the kind of permanent attachment which he was sure she was looking for.

'I want us to stay in contact, Kaly. To continue to get to know each other better, and to see where this leads. Do you?'

She adopted a serious expression following his answer, and folded her arms. 'Last week, you asked me whether I have feelings for you, Arion. I do. Strong feelings. And you said that you have feelings for me, too?'

'I do, Kaly. I like you, too,' he responded. 'Like you a lot, and I love spending time with you.'

Lords! I need to choose my words carefully, now! Will I ever meet a lovelier and more suitable girl than Kalyane?

She took a deep breath. 'Let me be direct, Arion. Because our days together here are running out. I'm in love with you. I think I may have been in love with you ever since that first day when we met, in Andarron. Certainly, I've thought about you, and talked about you, a lot in this last year. And Mother has also seen how I've been feeling, and has supported me ever since then. But if you leave after this stay, with no... *commitment*, between us, other than to "stay in contact", then I think that my father will take the matter out of my hands. I think he will then go ahead and initiate an arranged marriage.'

'What commitment do you mean?' He deliberately avoided responding that he was in love with her, too. Something was holding him back from saying that, and he wondered if his apparent evasiveness was causing her hurt.

'Don't act dumb, Arion. A proposal, of course. Of marriage.'

He was conflicted and confused. On the one hand, he was not sure that he was ready to make a commitment to marriage, even for someone he liked and was as attracted to as much as Kalyane. On the other hand, if he understood her correctly, he might not have the luxury of time to consider his choices.

'This arranged marriage, which you mention. Have your parents spoken with you about this? Who might it be to?'

'Yes, they have. Father has agreed that he will also support me, if you share my feelings. But if you don't, then they have two main candidates to marry me to. The first is your brother, Gerrion, which

388

was father's preferred match, but that would be more difficult now that you and I have kissed. The second is... Duke Jarrett Berun.'

Arion's heart lurched as she spoke both of the names, and with her utterance of his rival's name he could immediately feel the old animosity boiling within himself.

Lord preserve us! How could I live with the thought of that bastard Berun marrying her, in my place? Kissing her. Touching her...

The idea made him sick.

He was still not convinced that he was ready. Still not completely sure that he was in love with Kalyane, although he was attracted to her and enjoyed being with her. But he could not bear the possibility that if he did not act now, he could lose her to his enemy. He wondered if she had any idea, from Lennion, as to just how much he and Berun despised each other. He looked directly at her, feeling suddenly suspicious about this, but her wide-eyed expression appeared innocent and nervous.

The silence stretched on for several seconds, until he eventually spoke.

'Kalyane?'

'Yes, Arion?'

'Will you be my wife?'

—

Two nights before he was due to depart, Arion and Kalyane requested an audience with Duchess Rednar. Arion suspected that the Duchess had full knowledge of what he intended to talk about, even before he had uttered the first word.

'Lady Duchess,' he started, feeling stiff and ill-at-ease. Kalyane was seated to his right, and the Duchess was sitting across from him. He and Kalyane had discussed and agreed what he was going to say. 'Thank you to you and the Duke for the month that you have allowed me to stay at your estates. And, even more, for the time that you have allowed me to spend with Kalyane.'

'Allowed?' The Duchess smiled. 'I don't think Kalyane gave us any choice in the matter.'

Arion continued, unabashed. 'As you well know, I'm a son of a Duke in a leading house, and Kalyane is a daughter of a leading house. Neither of us should therefore marry without the permission of our parents. I haven't spoken with my father the Duke yet, but before I do so we would both like to ask whether Kalyane would have permission from you and her father, to marry me?'

'Yes,' answered the Duchess, then she laughed and added, 'Yes, yes, yes, yes!'

Kalyane laughed with her, then said, 'Thank you, Mum. And in case you're wondering, he's already proposed to me, and of course I said yes!'

Arion smiled, feeling happy and excited, but also a little confused and queasy inside about the commitment which he had now made.

—

Two nights later, Arion was packing his possessions in readiness to depart, when there was a knock on his bedroom door. He opened the door to find Lennion there, looking pale. His friend was clutching a letter in his hand. Arion knew immediately that something was wrong.

'What is it?' he asked.

'Arion. Read it. Just arrived by messenger pigeon. I'm so sorry.'

Arion took hold of the letter, and a feeling of numbness struck him as he read the brief message.

> Dear Arion,
> Our Father has passed away. May The Lord preserve his soul. It was a heart attack. Please return home as soon as possible.
> Your brother,
> Duke Gerrion

Arion stared at the letter for seconds afterwards, lost for words, until his friend finally pulled him forwards into an embrace.

24

Leanna

—

Year of Our Lord,
After Ascension, 768AA to 769AA

The first night after Amyss went to pray with Senior Priest El'Patriere, Leanna lay awake in her bed, restless and fretting until her friend returned.

Amyss came back into the darkened room at some point after tenth hour, carrying a small candle which illuminated her solemn face.

Leanna spoke first. 'Hey, are you OK?'

'Yes, I think so.'

'What happened?'

There was a pause for a few seconds. 'Well… prayers, mainly. He asked lots of questions about me, and my family. Then we knelt together before his private altar, within his chambers. He took hold of my hand. And we prayed together.' The candle was extinguished, and in the darkness Leanna could hear the sounds of Amyss getting into her own bed.

'Nothing else?'

'No, but it was a bit... awkward. At the end, he told me how "spiritually fulfilling" he'd found it to be, and that we were going to do it again, soon.'

'I didn't like how he was looking at you, Amyss.'

'What do you mean?' There was a defensive quality in Amyss's voice.

'Well. Did you not feel it, too? The way he looked at you. It felt a little... sexual.'

There was again a silence for a few moments, before Amyss finally responded, 'He's the Senior Priest, Lea. Anyway, what would you know about that? Go to sleep.'

Amyss did not speak again, after that. Afterwards, Leanna remained awake, staring at the ceiling, worried about her friend and feeling a little wounded by Amyss's last comment.

—

In the weeks that followed, Senior Priest El'Patriere continued to summon Amyss to pray with him, typically once per week. After the third such private meeting, Amyss became increasingly close-mouthed with Leanna about what had transpired during their prayer sessions.

Leanna soon found out that Amyss was not the only person towards whom El'Patriere extended such personal invitations. Leanna established that a male novice, plus a mixture of male and female priests, were also invited at varying times for separate personal prayer sessions alongside the Senior Priest.

Therefore, had it not been for her peculiar ability to sense strong emotions within other people, Leanna might not have been suspicious. But she could not forget the way that darkly lustful feelings had been thrumming out of El'Patriere, as he had stared at Amyss.

On a number of occasions, particularly when Amyss had returned from the Senior Priest's chambers late at night, Leanna attempted to get her friend to provide more details about what had happened in the privacy of El'Patriere's room. But Amyss's answers had become increasingly blunt and non-committal, and the brief conversations would typically end with an instruction for Leanna to go to sleep. Amyss would then turn onto her side, facing away from her room-mate.

As the weeks went by, Leanna felt a persistent sense of worry and sadness. Worry for what might be happening to Amyss, in the secrecy of the Senior Priest's rooms. Sadness that the weekly event appeared to be changing her friend, and was creating a divide between them.

One night, three weeks after the prayer sessions had commenced, Leanna awoke from her recurring dream to find that she was sleeping on her own. She looked across and saw that Amyss was still lying in her own bed, facing away from her. Leanna's heart was pounding in the aftermath of the dream, and she felt a sense of loss resulting from the unaccustomed absence of her friend's physical presence. Leanna struggled to get back to sleep that night.

And in the following weeks, with Amyss never again coming to Leanna's bed, it took Leanna ever longer to return to sleep after waking from the recurring dream. In those hours of sleepless darkness, she had more time to ponder the meaning of the dream itself. Its images were almost fully solidified in her waking memory now. Almost. She could remember the mountains. The winding path. Her companions. And there were vaguer memories of an ethereal Gate. But she could not retain the last parts of the dream. Something in the Gate. Something she had to do. These final memories continued to prove frustratingly elusive.

—

After El'Patriere had been in his post for six weeks, Amyss was becoming increasingly withdrawn and subdued. For the first time since they had become room-mates, Leanna and her friend would reach their bedroom after ninth hour, and then there would be silence between them. Awkward silence.

Eventually, Leanna decided that she needed to confront her friend. She faced Amyss across their beds, taking the other girl's hands into her own.

'What's going on, Amyss? What's happened to change things between us?'

'Nothing's happened.'

'Yes, it has. Ever since El'Patriere arrived. It's like we're becoming... strangers.'

'Is it?'

'Yes. What's happening, Amyss? What's happening with El'Patriere? In his chambers?'

'Nothing.'

'Amyss. You're my best friend. I love you. You can tell me anything, you know that, don't you?'

'Yes.' Amyss was looking down at her knees, now, avoiding eye contact.

'So, what's happening?'

'Nothing's happening.'

'Amyss... I'm struggling to believe you. Something's happened to you, this last month. We don't laugh together any more. You don't... come to me when I have bad dreams. I miss you, Amyss. I miss my friend.'

'Whether you believe it or not, nothing's happening.' The girl looked up at Leanna, redness in her eyes, and pulled her hands away. 'It's better that I don't come to your bed any more. Better that we don't... touch each other, again. You need to learn how to cope on your own, Leanna, for after when you leave here.'

'OK. Although that thought makes me a little sad. But I still miss you.'

'You only miss me when it suits you, Lea.' There was a hardness in Amyss's voice, a tone which Leanna had rarely heard before. 'And you've only ever wanted my love at a time and in a way that suits you. We both know that, we've just been too scared and polite to say it to each other. But anyway, it doesn't matter, now.'

'That's not true and not fair, Amyss. And you know it. But why doesn't it matter now?'

'Because it doesn't. Now, leave me alone. Please.' Amyss turned away from Leanna and slid down onto her side on her own bed, facing the wall. Strange dark emotions leeched from the girl, making Leanna feel guilty about her ability to absorb and understand them.

SORROW. PAIN. SHAME.

'I love you, Amyss. That will always matter to me. And if you ever want to talk to me, about anything, I'll be ready to listen.'

There was no response from Amyss. Just waves of sorrow, beating steadily towards Leanna.

Lord Aiduel, please tell me how to protect and help my friend.

—

During this period of time, Leanna was also devoting many of her remaining free hours to her role as an assistant at the hospital.

After having spent almost a year as a regular helper for Sister Colissa, Leanna had acquired a strong foundation of knowledge about illnesses, injuries and their respective cures. Sister Colissa had already started to encourage Leanna to join the Order of Saint Helena, after her time as a novice was concluded. Colissa had indicated that she considered Leanna to have the potential to become a skilled healer, and Leanna was continuing to give serious thought to the option.

On the day after Leanna's difficult conversation with Amyss, the hospital admitted a patient who was dying from the Wasting Sickness. Although Leanna already knew much about the often fatal disease, this was her first direct experience with the illness during her time as an assistant.

The disease was feared throughout the continent. It had swept through Angall in two main waves of mortality. The first had been a significant pandemic eleven years earlier. The second lesser wave had happened two years ago, which Leanna understood had ravaged Angloss and Dei Magnus, but which had not progressed significantly into Elannis. For reasons which no one understood, the disease appeared to be less prevalent and infectious now. Indeed, Sister Colissa herself had not seen a new patient, prior to this one, for eighteen months.

The middle-aged man who arrived at the hospital was shrivelled and shrunken, a pale shadow of a comparable healthy male. He was suffering through the last ravages of the disease, with just weeks remaining of his life. His family had requested that the Order of Saint Helena tend to him during his final weeks, and had made a donation to the Order to facilitate that request.

Leanna was soon regularly undertaking nursing duties for the diseased man, during her afternoons at the hospital. His name was Kennet, and in his few lucid moments he had told her that he was a blacksmith, and a father of five children. It was clear to Leanna that the patient was a simple and good man, and it pained her to see his deteriorating condition.

On Kennet's bad days, his lucidity disappeared and he was clearly in debilitating pain. Through her strange power, Leanna also began to indirectly experience the man's suffering, but with a diminished level of intensity. She could feel his distress reaching her mind in dull, repetitive throbs, with beats which pulsed slowly out of his body in a terrible countdown to his eventual demise.

PAIN. PAIN. PAIN.

It was initially no more than a distracting level of discomfort for Leanna, but it grew worse whenever she looked directly at the man, at which point his pulsating agony took on the sinister colour of night.

One afternoon, she was alone in the hospital ward, and was again tending to the dying patient. Kennet was delirious, ranting and raving words which had no clear meaning. Leanna was steadfastly trying to ignore the steady beat of the darkness which pulsed from inside of him.

Then abruptly, and without any warning, the noise of the throbbing, pounding blackness was drowned out by a beautiful and ethereal sound. A sound which echoed outwards like a remnant from her dreams; the crystal-clear and golden voices of angels singing words into her soul.

DEVOTION. SACRIFICE. SALVATION.

Then, as had happened on another occasion in the hospital many months earlier, suddenly the world shifted, time slowed down, and the patient's vile illness came undisguisedly into view.

In the midst of this enhanced state of consciousness, Leanna could clearly see the swirls of voracious blackness circulating within Kennet's body. Pulsing darkness sinuously marking the inner corruption of this rapacious disease. This illness which was slowly suffocating his life. Poisoning him. Killing him.

Without conscious thought, she raised her arm towards the patient. Absent of any understanding on Leanna's part as to why, the gesture automatically linked their minds together. Then she felt ripples along and throughout her body, as if invisible ethereal fingers were emerging from her mind and were connecting her soul to his. Connecting to him, and to the pulsing corruption of his illness.

These ghostly fingers writhed around the blackness within the man; grasping it, pulling it, shredding it, ripping it out of him. Leanna had no true idea of precisely what she was doing, but in this miraculously alert state of consciousness, she knew exactly what the effect was going to be.

She was going to cure him. Inside of her, amongst the mysterious gifts which Aiduel had bequeathed to her following the vision, was the power to cure this illness. To save this man.

Lord Aiduel, thank you for the miracle of this gift.

And then the illness was outside of his body, dragged out into a floating ball of malign blackness, which the unseen ethereal fingers held in check. It was then a simple thing to draw those fingers tighter... tighter... and then the darkness was gone. Crushed. Obliterated.

Leanna promptly snapped out of the trance into which she had fallen, and staggered backwards

She looked around, anxiously aware of the perils of having been observed. However, no one one was nearby to witness what had happened. No one had seen her reaching out towards the patient. Indeed, he still lay in his hospital bed. Still emaciated, still looking like death would be a ready visitor in the near future.

But Leanna knew differently, now. He was cured.

—

In the two weeks afterwards, the man was restored to full health. His appetite had returned to him on the same day that Leanna had cured him, and within minutes of her miracle his delirium had also dissipated.

It took Sister Colissa a handful of days to pronounce with confidence that the illness was gone. The Sister was clearly baffled. She had seen a handful of instances of people surviving the Wasting Sickness previously, but never when the illness had been as far progressed as Kennet's.

The patient himself talked after the event about his fragmented, fever-induced memories of the visitation of an angel. How he could remember that she had been bathed in a golden halo of light as she had stood over him, healing him. However, to Leanna's great relief, given the intimidating presence of Aiduel's Guards next to the College, Sister Colissa had quickly silenced him when he had spoken about this. She had then firmly dissuaded him from making any more reference to visions and angels.

Colissa also took Leanna and a number of the other hospital attendees to one side, and warned them against referring to what had happened as a miracle. 'Whatever any of us believe happened to this man, we absolutely must not draw attention to this,' she said, to Leanna and to two other assistants. 'Even though I have heard the word "miracle" mentioned, and perhaps not unreasonably. But I do not want to draw the eyes of Aiduel's Guards onto this hospital. Not now. Not with all of these burnings.'

Leanna had nodded, being the only one amongst them who knew with certainty what had happened.

Lord Aiduel, thank you again for this miracle, and for granting me this power to do good on your behalf. Secret good.

—

Outside of the hospital, however, Leanna had stopped enjoying her life at the College. She was counting down the weeks and months until she would become ordained, and could leave.

Her first year in the College now seemed like a cherished but fading memory of happiness lost. Memories of how she had lived amongst contented and peaceful people, before the arrival of Aiduel's Guards had filled everyone there with fear and uncertainty. Of feeling safe and secure under the warm leadership of Senior Priest Comrel, now undermined by the actions of El'Patriere. Of enjoying Amyss's love and friendship, now replaced by long periods of coldness and silence.

The more interactions that Leanna had with Senior Priest El'Patriere, the less she respected him and the more she feared him. Outside of what may have been happening in his private prayer sessions with Amyss, his day-to-day manner made Leanna privately contemptuous towards him. She could not remember feeling that way about anyone, at any time, in her prior life.

The Senior Priest was a bully and a braggart, lacking any of the warmth or charity which had so clearly defined his predecessor. Any conversation on any topic in which he was involved seemed to end up being channelled towards a discussion about El'Patriere himself, and his self-professed merits. As did his evening services; any topic he chose to talk about always seemed to be a lead in for El'Patriere to discuss himself.

Leanna could have overlooked and forgiven such boasting, if that had been the worst of the Senior Priest's characteristics. However, the particular aspect of his personality which she found even more contemptible was his need to bully and humiliate others.

One day, the Senior Priest had appeared in Priest Parmer's lesson, indicating that he wished to observe for a while.

El'Patriere had been standing at the side of the classroom, smiling arrogantly with arms folded. Priest Parmer was discussing the latter period of The Lord Aiduel's life, the last years before He had returned to the Holy Land. As always, the elderly priest had a commanding knowledge of his subject. However, there had been more occasions recently when he had suffered a lapse of memory. Today was one of those days.

'And so, as it was written in the Book of... oh, Book of...' The Priest turned around, looking confused, and walked back towards his shelf of books at the end of the classroom. 'Now. Book of... now, where is it?'

'Oh, come on, you doddering old idiot!' shouted El'Patriere suddenly. 'No one cares what Book it was. They're bored enough as it is! Get on with it.'

Parmer stepped backwards, clearly taken aback by the heat in El'Patriere's comments. 'I'm sorry, Father. It is quite important that they-'

'How many times, it's Father El'Patriere, you old fool!' shouted the Senior Priest. 'Father El'Patriere! That's my name. Not just Father. Use my royal name! Remember it, before I have you thrown out onto the streets!' Leanna could feel his emotions hammering outwards in waves of dark rage.

'Sorry, Father El'Patriere,' mumbled Parmer, looking humiliated and aghast.

'You should be, you old fool!' With that, El'Patriere had turned and had stormed out of the classroom, looking like he had been grievously insulted and wronged, leaving Parmer close to tears.

In time, Leanna could perceive that all of the priests of the College were receiving similar chastisements and intimidation from El'Patriere. He was the most loathsome individual that she had ever met, and Leanna was certain that the Senior Priest's rapid rate of promotion could only have resulted from his royal status.

Lord Aiduel, how is it possible that such a man could become a Senior Priest within your Holy Church, just as a result of his royal position?

—

Parmer's public humiliation made Leanna even more fearful about what could be happening to Amyss during the private prayer sessions with El'Patriere. With less than five months remaining until their time at the College would end, Leanna was feeling a panicked certainty that she had to act to save her friend.

She had tried a number of times to get Amyss to talk, but her efforts had again been frustrated by blunt answers or silence. Leanna had decided that there was one final manner of approach which might encourage Amyss to open up, and one night after ninth hour she resolved to attempt it.

Amyss was again lying on her mattress on her side, facing away from Leanna. Leanna moved across to the other girl's bed, and sat on the edge, placing her hand on Amyss's shoulder.

'Amyss, can we talk for a while?'

'I just want to lay here.' The red-headed girl continued to look towards the wall.

'Well, in that case can I talk for a while?'

There was silence for a few seconds. 'If you want to.'

'I think something is happening with El'Patriere, Amyss. Something which is hurting you a lot. I want to help you. But I can only help you if you'll tell me what's happening.' No response from Amyss. 'I've said it before and I'll say it again, now. I love you, Amyss. You're my best friend. And I've been trying to work out how I can show you that I love you and trust you completely, so that you might be able to trust me again, too.

'I once refused to share a secret with you, Amyss, and you then asked me if I didn't trust you. And nothing could be further from the truth. Nothing. I trust you completely. You've kept my secrets from Aiduel's Guards, when it could have put you at risk, and you've cared for me and protected me from my dreams for over a year.

'So, I'm going to try to show you just how much I trust you. I'm going to break my holy oath and I'll tell you everything, Amyss. *Everything*. All of the strange things that have happened to me since my eighteenth birthday. Things that would probably have Aiduel's Guards accuse me of heresy and burn me. I'll hold no secret back from you, because I love you and I trust you.

'And afterwards, if you choose to tell me any of your secrets, I'll listen and I will try to care for you and protect you. But if you choose to tell me nothing, that's fine too. I'll still love you and I'll do everything I can to care for you and to protect you.'

Amyss did not answer, but Leanna reached out to find her friend's hand, and held it. Thankfully, the smaller girl did not flinch away from the touch.

Leanna then proceeded to tell every detail and event to Amyss. About the vision, her dreams, her ability to sense emotions, and the miracle of the man with the Wasting Sickness. Even about the emotions she had sensed from El'Patriere, and from Amyss herself. She spoke at length, getting no reaction from Amyss throughout, but at all times the smaller girl kept hold of Leanna's hand.

After Leanna had finished, Amyss still said nothing. However, Leanna could feel strong emotions pulsing outwards from her room-mate.

SORROW. SHAME. SORROW.

A pulsating, sobbing blackness existed in Amyss's mind, which Leanna could readily perceive, and could almost reach out for. But Leanna continued to sit there, holding her friend's hand, and waited. And waited. She was not going to release her hold, was not going to move away from the bed, until she was forced to.

Then, finally, Amyss began to cry. Just a series of choked dry sobs at first, then later unrelenting floods of tears. Leanna kept their hands clenched together throughout, as the dark emotions which had been bottled up inside her room-mate were unleashed as a torrent.

Eventually, after a long time, the tears ended. Leanna then said again, 'Please tell me, Amyss.'

There was another extended period of silence, until Amyss whispered, 'He's threatened me, Lea. Threatened to destroy me, destroy you, and destroy my family, if I tell anyone.'

But after that, finally, Amyss told her. Told her everything.

—

The next afternoon, Leanna was seated inside the administrative buildings next to the Cathedral of Arlais. She should have been working in the hospital at that moment, but she had feigned illness as a means to excuse herself, and then had furtively left the College grounds.

With Amyss's permission, Leanna had come to see High Priest Comenis of Arlais, the person whom she understood had authority over Senior Priest El'Patriere.

She had already been waiting for three hours. Upon arrival, she had introduced herself to an aide of the High Priest. That aide had initially tried to discourage Leanna from waiting to meet with her master, indicating that he was a busy man with no time for trivial appointments. However, Leanna had insisted that she was going to stay there for as long as it took to gain an audience with Comenis, and the aide could clearly see that she meant it.

By the time that she was finally allowed in to see the High Priest, fourth hour prayers at the College would have already happened, and she was growing nervous. However, to her great relief the door to his office was opened by the aide, and she was summoned in.

Comenis was an ageing man, in his early sixties, with a bushy grey beard and matching thick eyebrows. He looked irritated to see her. 'So, child, you're the novice from the College who refuses to leave my building until I meet with you. What do you want?'

Leanna took a deep breath, and then started to speak. 'I have a very serious matter to report, Your Eminence. A matter which, given the person involved, I felt I had to report to you directly.'

Comenis frowned, his eyes hard. 'What sort of matter?'

'A matter of abuse, Your Eminence. Bullying. And physical and sexual abuse. By Senior Priest El'Patriere, against a female novice of the College.'

Comenis sat forwards, his elbows on his desk, now more attentive. 'Go on.'

Leanna proceeded to tell him everything that she knew.

—

That night, after lights out at tenth hour, Amyss came to Leanna's bed. It was a wonderful feeling for Leanna to again have the warm reassuring presence of her friend cuddled against her, for the first time in weeks. Their friendship was renewed.

'Tell me again what the High Priest said, Lea,' said Amyss, as she lay by Leanna's side.

'He said that he'll be coming to the College tomorrow, and that he'll be dealing with El'Patriere then,' answered Leanna. 'You will never have to go to another of his prayer sessions, Amyss.'

'Thank you, Lea.' Amyss's head was on Leanna's chest. 'Thank you. I truly didn't know what to do. He… he said that if I said anything… he would throw me out of the College in shame, and would arrange to have my family ruined.'

'The High Priest will give him what he deserves. You did so well by speaking up, Amyss. You've been so brave.'

Leanna could feel emotions welling up inside of Amyss, slowly and rhythmically beating from her body into Leanna's, glimmers of gold mixed in with deeper shades of darkness.

SORROW. LOVE. SORROW. SHAME.

'I'm so sorry for some of the things I said to you, Lea. For how I treated you.'

'You don't have to apologise to me for anything, Amyss. If I'd been a better friend, I would have acted sooner.'

'I don't deserve a friend like you, Lea.'

'Yes, you do.'

Amyss squeezed her then, dark emotions still pulsing from her body.

SORROW. SHAME. SORROW.

'Lea?'

'Yes?'

'Can you cure me, like you cured that man?'

'Cure you?'

'Yes. Take this feeling out of me. This pain. This shame.'

'I don't know.'

'Will you try?'

'Yes.'

And Leanna did try, as her friend rested in her arms, Amyss's eyes closed in anticipation. And it was surprisingly easy to achieve what Amyss had asked her to do. This time, as Leanna concentrated, she fell quickly into a state of trance. Immediately, the colours pulsing from Amyss became defined and illuminated, more brilliantly intense. The blackness residing in Amyss's mind and soul, a blackness which had accumulated from El'Patriere's actions, was easy to detect.

And then, just like last time, the invisible connections from Leanna's mind were reaching out, and burrowing into Amyss. Ensnaring the darkness. Trapping it. Ripping it out. And finally killing it.

Leanna's mind continued to float within a trance as she undertook these actions. She could sense Amyss there throughout, a willing recipient of this intimate process.

Leanna lost track of time, and she became unsure whether she had been doing this for seconds or for minutes. However, she was drawn back out of her trance when, eventually, Amyss gasped, 'Wow!'

'How does it feel?'

'Like a miracle! Like you've saved me, Lea. I still have… all the memories, of what he did. But the shame. The loathing. The pain. It's like you've washed it away. Cleansed it from me. It's amazing! How did you do that?'

Leanna said nothing in response, and instead hugged her friend.

Lord Aiduel, thank you again for this blessed gift, this wonderful power which you have granted to me. Thank you for helping me to save my friend.

Amyss then spoke again, her voice now sounding sleepy. 'You're... a miracle, Lea. I think Aiduel has truly blessed you. To me, you're a living saint. An angel. Aiduel's angel. I think you're meant for greater things. Much greater things than this. I'm so proud to know you, and I love you.'

'I love you too, Amyss.'

Lord Aiduel. Truly, for what purpose have you granted me these powers? And, again, what am I?

———

The next day, Leanna was surprised when her lesson with Sister Corenna was interrupted, and she and Amyss were both summoned to Senior Priest El'Patriere's offices.

Amyss wore a frightened look as they walked there, and Leanna was also feeling anxiety as they approached the external door to the offices.

As they entered, Leanna felt a combination of relief at seeing High Priest Comenis sitting behind the desk in the middle of the office, mixed with shock as she observed El'Patriere standing to the side of him.

Comenis was maintaining an impassive expression, his mood unreadable. There was no such disguise on El'Patriere's face. His features were distorted by barely contained rage, his eyes flicking between Leanna and Amyss as if he could not decide which one of the two of them he despised more.

High Priest Comenis spoke first. 'Acolyte Amyss. Acolyte Leanna. Thank you for joining us. I'm afraid to say that there's been a terrible misunderstanding, here.'

Amyss was silent. Leanna replied, feeling the thudding beat of

El'Patriere's suddenly malevolent hatred for her hammering across his emotions. 'A misunderstanding, Your Eminence?'

'Yes. A misunderstanding. I'm afraid that certain – perhaps inappropriate, but never intentionally malicious – touching by the Senior Priest, of Acolyte Amyss, may have been misconstrued. As sexual, when that was never intended to be the case.' The High Priest said this in a completely detached manner, as if he was reading from an old religious text.

Leanna could sense Amyss's fear, as the smaller girl stood beside her, and Leanna therefore responded, 'From what Acolyte Amyss has told me, Your Eminence, it seems to me that there is no doubt at all that what happened was of a deliberately sexual nature.'

'That's not true!' snapped El'Patriere, then his voice became whiny as he added, 'I was just being affectionate, wasn't I, Amyss? Affectionate, as we devoutly prayed.'

Leanna felt Amyss recoil, but she kept her eyes locked onto the Senior Priest, witnessing his emotions pulsing from him in thrumming waves which bore the colour of night.

Comenis intervened, then. 'Be silent, Father El'Patriere! I instructed you not to speak. Please do not interrupt again, lest I lose my temper and feel that another course of action is suitable.' The High Priest then focused upon Leanna. 'From what I understand about the facts, Acolyte Amyss here – via you, Acolyte Leanna – has made certain unsubstantiated accusations. Senior Priest El'Patriere has denied those accusations. Most vehemently. There are no other witnesses. Therefore, as a neutral and objective person approaching this matter, I have no way of knowing who is telling the truth, and who is lying.'

Leanna felt herself growing angry. 'Your Eminence, why would Amyss make-'

'Quiet, Acolyte! You forget yourself. I'm the High Priest here, I am speaking, and you will listen. This is not your decision, anyway. This matter can now be resolved in one of two ways. The first way is that one or both of you try to escalate this *accusation*. And if you choose to do that, choose to seek to bring shame upon the Church and the Father's family name, be in no doubt that the life of both of you within the Holy Church will be over. Whatever then happens, I'll make sure that neither of you will ever be ordained, and you will both be thrown out of this College in disgrace. And if you *do* choose to escalate this accusation, I and other powerful people will do everything we can to defend Father El'Patriere, and his family's noble name, and to persecute the two of you and your families.'

Leanna was horrified by this response.

Lord Aiduel, how can a senior figure in the Holy Church react to an act of evil, with a response like this? With the threat of further evil?

Comenis continued. 'The second way is that Father El'Patriere apologises, here and now, to Acolyte Amyss for any way in which his actions have been misconstrued, and for any hurt caused by those misunderstood actions. Father El'Patriere will further undertake to me that he will cease these *private* prayer sessions immediately. That he will specifically stay well away from the two of you and from any other female novices, and that he will not do anything to interfere with or impede the successful completion of your training. Acolyte Amyss would then accept the Father's apology subject to those matters, and you will both agree to drop any further discussion of this accusation. And I can then forget that this distasteful matter has ever been raised before me.

'Now, for me, Acolyte Amyss, one of those routes is eminently more attractive for all parties than the other route. Don't you agree?'

Leanna looked across at Amyss. Leanna could never remember feeling as angry as this, in her life. Anger at the unfairness of it, the wrongness of it, at the casting aside by the Holy Church's representative of the right course of action. But in one respect the High Priest was correct. This was Amyss's choice to make, not hers. Whatever decision Amyss made, she would support it.

After a few seconds, Amyss replied, 'I would like to become a priestess in the Holy Church, Your Eminence. In a parish near to my home, if you're able to arrange that. And I want to put this matter behind me. Please can we choose the second way.'

The High Priest smiled in response, a self-satisfied smirk like that of a merchant who has just concluded an advantageous negotiation. 'Very wise, Acolyte Amyss. Very wise. Thank you. And I'm sure I can facilitate finding a lovely parish for you, very near to your home village. Now, onto the business of apologies.'

Leanna felt sick inside.

Lord Aiduel, is this what the Holy Church has become? An institution which persecutes and burns heretics, and conceals vile abuse? Lord, how can you tolerate such deeds?

El'Patriere started to make his insincere apologies to Amyss. He was framing his words carefully, and expressing regret only for any hurt caused by Amyss's misunderstanding about his actions. And all throughout his speech, although he did not look directly at Leanna, she could feel the overflowing cauldron of his dark emotions, directed towards herself.

HATE. HATE. HATE.

—

True to the undertakings which were given that day, El'Patriere actually did leave Leanna and Amyss alone for most of the remaining few months at the College. Leanna had to rein in her own anger and frustration every time she listened to his hypocrisies in his evening services, but otherwise, neither she nor Amyss had to interact with him.

Leanna and Amyss were closer than ever, after the dark events of the preceding months. Amyss was still focused on becoming a priestess after her two years at the College were complete. Indeed, High Priest Comenis had secured a parish for her to lead, which was close to her home village.

Leanna herself had lost great faith, after that day in El'Patriere's office. Not in The Lord Aiduel, who in Leanna's mind had given her the gifts to save Amyss, but with the institution of the Holy Church

410

She began to ponder about how much other corruption existed throughout the hierarchy of the Church, if a man like El'Patriere could be protected like that?

She had therefore spoken with Sister Colissa about spending a trial period of time with the Order of Saint Helena, following the completion of her two years at the College. Leanna had requested to move to someplace far away from Arlais, and Colissa was in the process of arranging this for her.

On Leanna's very last week at the College, however, El'Patriere found her when she was alone.

She had just left the hospital at the end of one of her afternoon shifts, and he was standing outside the building, staring at her malevolently. Leanna gasped when she first saw him, but then recovered and moved to walk past him.

He put out a hand, and blocked her path. 'You tried to ruin me, girl.'

HATE. HATE. HATE.

'We both know that you deserve to be ruined, for what you did.'

He laughed then, a soft and nasty giggle. 'Yes, perhaps I do! But even so, I wasn't, was I? I escaped without punishment here, girl, just like I've suffered no punishment in the past. Because if your name starts with "El", the Church fears you and protects you. And always will. But, anyway, enough of that. I came to tell you something, girl. Want to know what?'

'No.'

'Well, I'll tell you, anyway. With my family behind me, I'm going to rise high in our Holy Church, girl. Very high. And at some point, I'm going to destroy you for what you tried to do to me. Not now, not when Comenis is still looking. But sometime. Sometime soon. I have connections, with many powerful people. Maybe I'll even use those connections to take Comenis's job, for the way he belittled me. But one day, girl, I'll make sure that you'll suffer for your decision to try to ruin me.'

Leanna stared at the Senior Priest, feeling fear but determined

411

not to show any weakness to him. Finally, she replied, 'Lord Aiduel, make my thoughts and actions true, and deliver me from evil. May The Lord forgive you for your sins, Father, and may He protect me from those who would do evil against me.'

'You'll need more than The Lord to be saved from me, you sanctimonious little bitch!'

Then he turned his back on her, and walked away.

—

She had to face the Senior Priest one last time, in her Service of Ordainment, in the week following the end of her two years at the College. This was a public event, and the charming facade which El'Patriere presented publicly for the ordination bore no resemblance to the vile abuser which she knew that he really was.

A number of other people attended the ceremony this time, in happier contrast to the Vows of Submission which she had taken two years earlier. Amyss watched the ceremony, as did Leanna's parents, and Sister Colissa had also taken time out to attend. There was therefore no opportunity for El'Patriere to make any further threats against Leanna, for which she was grateful.

At the end of the ceremony, she had to kneel before the Senior Priest as he placed his hand onto her head and made the Recitals of Ordination. Being in his proximity like this made her feel queasy, until El'Patriere finally announced, 'I therefore pronounce you Priestess Leanna of Arlais, and The Lord Aiduel welcomes you into the ranks of his Holy Ordained.'

After that, she was at last an ordained priestess.

It was shortly following the conclusion of the ceremony that Sister Colissa approached her, and drew her to one side for a private conversation.

'Yes, Sister?'

'Leanna, a role has come up, at short notice. To work with me, within the Order of Saint Helena.'

Leanna frowned. 'Where, Sister? Here?'

Colissa shook her head. 'No. Not here. Now, what I'm about to say is highly confidential. It is not to be repeated. Understand?'

'Yes, Sister.'

Colissa leaned in close to her, whispering. 'I was asked earlier today to lead an army medical facility. A field hospital which will travel with an army of Elannis. I've accepted the role, and I'm gathering a team to travel with me. I would like you to be part of that team.'

'An army, Sister? Where?'

'They are assembling the army fifteen miles to the north of here, as I understand, on one of the nobility's country estates. I've been told that they'll be departing in less than a weeks' time. And that my team must be ready to travel with them then.'

Leanna was confused. 'Fifteen miles to the north of here, Sister? But what for? Where are they going?'

'I've not been told, officially, Leanna. But there is only one possible reason I can see why an army would be mustering in secret in the Arlais region. One possible target.'

'And what is that, Sister?'

Colissa leaned in even closer, and cupped her hand around her mouth as she spoke into Leanna's ear. 'I believe that they are planning to cross the Canas River. I believe that our army intends to invade Andar.'

Interlude Two

—

Year of Our Lord,
Before Ascension, 72BA

—

Interlude 2

A boy

—

Year of Our Lord,
Before Ascension, 72BA

The slavers had found the route to the top of the cliff, and now the boy and his four companions were trapped.

The boy had experienced a deep sense of frustration and anger, when he had first realised this. All of his prior instincts about the clifftop had otherwise been correct. This was indeed a place where they could have survived and been free. But now they were going to be enslaved again. Captured, and then dragged back in shackles to those mines which would eventually kill each of them.

Or even worse, the slavers might just choose to surround them and butcher them all in one brutal assault, as a violent lesson for any other slaves who in future might have the temerity to contemplate running for freedom.

But the boy already knew that he was not prepared to surrender himself back into slavery, even if that option was to become available to him. He would find a way out of this trap. Or he would die, trying.

The clifftop had been a revelation to the five of them, in the first few hours. It was the front edge of a massive plateau, which was a fertile oasis of plant life and water.

From the arid desert floor below there had been no visible markers of the lush greenery here. From that perspective, this plateau had looked like an innocuous clifftop far above the dry plains, with little to suggest that an arduous climb to the top would be worthwhile.

Hence, the leaders of the Angall scouting group had disregarded the place entirely. Only the boy had looked at it. Had peered towards it and had felt a yearning to escape, and an instinctive need to ascend to the top.

The cliff-edge which was visible from the desert below was a few hundred metres in width, but on moving further inwards the children had discovered that the plateau widened to a couple of miles across. It was an enormous flat and verdant paradise, enshrined within the soaring mountains which encircled and loomed above.

And as they had moved even further from the cliff edge, they had soon established that the plateau extended backwards for five miles, until finally reaching the end of the ring of encircling mountains. At that far end was a vast circular lake, which was enclosed on three sides by sheer rock walls.

But on all sides along the length and breadth of the plateau, the mountains appeared to climb into the sky in an unbroken line of vertical rock. And they had spotted no visible paths through any of them. The fertile plateau therefore also seemed to be an enormous dead-end. A trap.

—

When they had earlier reached the lake, the boy had ordered the others to rest and to drink. He had then refilled his own canteen, and had informed them that he was going to double-back to check whether the slavers had found the path up the side of the cliff. Tonnus had wanted to come with him, but the boy had instructed his larger friend to instead take care of the others, and for each of them to start exploring for places to escape or to hide, if necessary.

The boy had then run back towards the cliff edge, moving much faster now that he was on his own, whilst his eyes had been scanning ahead for any sign of the slavers. As he had neared the edge of the clifftop again, he had slowed down to a crawl, and had moved forwards with extreme caution.

Then he had spotted them in the distance, as he had crouched behind a low boulder. There were eight slavers in total. All men, all armed. They had made camp near to the clifftop edge, which confirmed that they had found the route which had taken the children up the side of the cliff. Then the boy had realised why. The slavers had two dogs with them, hunting dogs which no doubt had been following their scent the whole way to here, and which would carry on relentlessly following their trail across the plateau.

—

The boy was sprinting back to his friends, now, full of despair and frustration. For them to have overcome so many obstacles to get this far, but now to be trapped, felt so unjust.

He was gasping for breath by the time he had covered the four miles back to the others, running the whole way. When he arrived back at the lakeside, just Kellon was waiting for him.

'The slavers are here,' he told the small boy. 'They're on the clifftop. They'll be coming for us, soon.'

Kellon's expression changed from uncertainty to fear. 'How long do we have?'

'They were at the cliff edge when I left. If they decide to move, we have a couple of hours, at most. Where are the others?'

'They've split up to go round either side of the lake, towards the waterfall. They're looking for any paths or climbs out of here. They left me here to wait for you.'

'Let's go after them, then.' The boy looked across the lake. The waterfall was visible on the far side of the great pool of water, approximately a mile away, cascading outwards from a high point of one of the mountains. In other circumstances, in the afternoon light, the boy could have stood there for hours, breathlessly appreciating the magnificent view. The mountains to either side of him and on the other side of the lake towered hundreds of metres into the sky, their beautiful grandeur reflected in the lake's still waters.

However, they had no such luxury of time, now that their pursuers were so close. The boy made a quick assessment about which way around the lake would be faster, then he set off to the left.

With the exception of the shore of the lake which opened up onto the wider plateau, the lake's other edges were all very close to the surrounding mountains. From the water's edge there were perhaps ten metres of steep slope covered in rocks and scree which could be traversed with difficulty, before reaching the sheer mountain walls which extended vertiginously into the sky.

Kellon was soon panting for breath and slowing them both down as they scrambled across the loose scree, but the boy was in no mood to be patient with his weaker friend. 'Keep moving! We can't afford to let them see us.'

It took them an hour to make the journey around to the other side of the lake, and the effort was drawing each of them closer to the point of exhaustion. The boy somehow found himself with his arm around Kellon, and the two of them were helping each other move forwards.

Throughout the walk, the boy was scanning the mountainside around and above him, looking for any paths or routes which could be climbed, but the mountain walls appeared unbroken and unassailable.

In the absence of finding any such escape routes, their objective was the waterfall, which flowed out of the side of the mountain from a hundred metres above the lake, and streamed down into the pristine waters. As they finally rounded the far side of the lake, they could soon identify the figures of their three companions, who were gathered near to the bottom of the cascade of water.

By the time that they had reached their three friends, Kellon was close to collapse, and the boy himself had to resist every urge within his body to lay down and sleep for a while. All three of their companions were soaked through, as if they had been submerged in the water.

The boy repeated the words which he had first spoken to Kellon. 'The slavers are here. They're on the clifftop. With dogs. They'll be coming for us, soon.'

There was fear on each of their faces but also, he was proud to see, defiance.

'We need to escape then, or hide,' replied Menira.

'I didn't see any paths, as we were following you,' the boy replied. 'Was there anything on the other side of the lake?'

'Nothing,' replied Tennus. 'I went that way, while Menira and Pellina had gone round the same way you and Kellon have just been. There's nothing in either direction, but-'

'Then we're done for,' the boy interrupted. 'We're trapped. We each need to choose to surrender, or to figh-'

'No, we don't,' Menira said. 'Let Tennus finish.'

The boy paused, staring at Tennus as the larger youth continued. 'There was nothing in either direction, but when we got here to the waterfall, Pellina decided to go into it. To look behind it. And come with us, look what she found.'

Tennus beckoned, and then the five of them were moving through and under the waterfall, and the boy briefly enjoyed the feeling of the cool water soaking his body. On the other side, between the cascade of water and the rock wall behind, there was an available space of approximately three metres. They gathered in this small drier space, clustered together.

Menira pointed upwards. 'Look, there. Ten metres above us.'

And the boy could see it. There, in the rock face, a small alcove.

'What is it?' he asked them. 'And can we reach it?'

Menira replied. 'We can reach it, yes. Pellina was so brave, and she volunteered to climb up to it. And Pellina, why don't you tell him what you found, when you got up there?'

He turned to look at the small dark-haired girl, as she responded proudly to the request. 'It's difficult to climb, but I think we'll all be able to do it. But when you get there, there's a small ledge. About as long as me. And then there's a hole and a passageway at the end of the ledge, very low and thin, about twice as wide as me, with light at the other end.'

The boy frowned, feeling hope again. 'A passageway? Did you go through it? What's on the other side?'

Pellina smiled, again looking proud of herself. 'Yes, I had to lay down and scramble, and it took me a long time, but I did go through it. And on the other side, there's a way to escape!'

The boy put out his hand and touched her shoulder, squeezing it softly to congratulate her. 'Well done, Pellina! What's there?'

She grinned happily as she replied, 'It's a path. A winding path, on the side of the mountain.'

Part Three

—

Conflict and Betrayal

—

Year of Our Lord,
After Ascension, 769AA

25

Corin

—

Year of Our Lord,
After Ascension, 769AA

The first thing that caught Corin's attention, as he walked back into the village of Karn, was the stench. After a long period of living in the outdoors in the wilderness, the smell of a large group of people and animals dwelling in such close proximity was overpowering.

The second thing was the noise. He and Agbeth had become accustomed to just each other for company, and they had both become comfortable with extended periods of silence. Here, there was an immediate bustle of sound, which only intensified as an increasing number of the villagers recognised the two of them.

'Look! It's Runt!'

'The Cripple's back!'

The calls from the crowd, which was assembling around them, were no kinder upon their return than they had been on their departure, two years earlier. Corin glanced at Agbeth by his side, and he could see that her face displayed a look of grim resolve, not showing any weakness. He felt proud of her. She did not want to be here, and had never wanted to return to Karn, yet despite that she was showing more dignity than many of the unkind villagers would ever know.

As they walked, they were surrounded by Akob and the three warriors who had accosted them at the edge of the village, who were keeping the other villagers away. As he listened to the accompanying bile from the crowd, Corin had a moment of doubt that this was a mistake. He had come back here for the sake of Agbeth's health, but he wondered now whether either of them could ever again be content to live amongst such nastiness.

He could feel Blackpaw at the back of his mind as he walked, could see images of the creature exploring the unfamiliar woods near the Great Lake. For a fleeting moment Corin considered summoning the beast immediately, such that he and Agbeth might flee, but he resisted this urge.

Then he realised where his father was leading him to, and Corin spoke up. 'You're taking me to the cage, not to the Clan Hall?'

'That's right,' responded Akob. 'You'll meet with Borrik when he's ready to meet with you. Until then, you can wait in the cage.'

'But not Agbeth, surely? No one expects her to be caged?'

'No. The Cripple has committed no crime. *She* has always been free to return. Or to leave again.' Corin grimaced upon hearing his father use Agbeth's insult-name.

They arrived at the cage, which was located in the large open circular area in the centre of the village. Akob opened the cage door, and Corin moved inside without protest, placing his equipment down onto the floor inside the wooden bars.

After Akob had closed and latched the cage again, instructing two of the other men to guard it, Corin called out to him. 'Father!'

Akob turned around. 'What is it?'

'When you speak to Borrik, please make sure to mention that I have a gift for the clan. A very important gift. But I have to present it to him, in person.'

426

'Very well.' Corin's father started to move away, but then he paused and turned around again, a look of reflection on his face. 'You've changed, you know, Runt. You're bigger, certainly, than when you left. Not by much, but it's noticeable. And you look stronger. But it's not that, either. It's... at some point, since you left here, you've stopped behaving like you're a weakling.'

Akob then moved off in the direction of the Clan Hall.

—

As she had done previously, on a sunny day two years earlier, Agbeth was sitting against the bars of the cage, on the outside. Corin was leaning against the other side of those bars, and their hands were clasped together.

'We shouldn't have come back here, Corin.'

There was still a large crowd gathered around them, a few metres away, and the jeers and catcalls were continuing as they waited there. 'It'll be OK, Agbeth. Trust me.'

'Trust you? Don't tell me to trust you, Corin, when I'm having to see you in a cage! Surely you didn't expect to be caged like this?'

'Nothing bad has happened, yet. Please stay calm.' Corin knew that he could not bear it if she was to suffer from a seizure now, in these circumstances. 'It'll be alright.'

'But they've put you in a cage, Corin! What else might they do to you?'

'Please be calm.' He then lowered his voice. 'Blackpaw's near. If we need him, he'll come.'

She shook her head, a grim expression on her face. 'This is all my fault. Me and my stupid fits. We shouldn't have come back here.'

But despite her frustration, she continued to hold Corin's hand, as the afternoon sunshine beat down upon them.

As Corin waited, his other family members appeared in the crowd. His mother, Orga, was there, as was Kernon and two of his other brothers.

427

Kernon walked forwards from the assembled mass of people, and after a word with the guards was allowed to approach the side of the cage. He knelt down by the bars on the opposite side of the wooden frame to Agbeth, with a sneering look on his face. 'Ah! So the Runt has returned to the litter, even though he knows it means death. Couldn't you survive in the world, brother?'

'Hello to you, too, Kernon. It was time to return.'

'Well, it'll be a quick return. Thought I'd better come speak to you now, before Borrik comes to kill you.'

Kernon looked slightly different, and Corin realised that his brother's nose was more flattened than he remembered, a clear after-effect of the fight in the Anath village.

'Kernon, I never said it at the time. But I'm sorry for what I did, in the raid. I should not have run. If I ever have the opportunity again, I won't run. I will fight. I promise that.'

'Ah! An easy thing to say, when you're cowering in a cage, Runt, and there's no chance you'll ever get to prove it.' Kernon then looked towards Agbeth, and a malicious smile appeared on his face. 'Is she your woman now, Runt?'

'Agbeth is my wife, Kernon.'

'Is she, now? So, you've fucked the Cripple at last?'

'Please don't call her that name, Kernon. Her name is Agbeth.'

'No. It's Cripple. I'll call her something different when she learns to walk properly.'

Corin did not lose his temper, this time. But he was no longer going to accept casual insults being cast at his wife. Nor did he feel fear as he calmly spoke his next words. 'After my business with Borrik is finished, if you ever call her that again, Kernon, I swear on all the Gods that I'll kill you.'

The older brother sneered. 'Will you, now? Again, an easy threat to make, right now. Because after you've finished "your business" with Borrik, you'll be dead. And let me make a promise in return, now, Runt. After you're dead, I'm going to find your wife, and I'm going to fuck her. Fuck her until she screams my name. Not because

428

I'd want to, but because it's what I want you to be thinking about, in your last seconds of life.'

'As if I ever would!' Agbeth hissed the words.

'Oh, I won't need to ask for your permission, woman. Not after you're the widow of a dead outcast.' Kernon then stood up and walked away.

Corin knew that it would be easy to embrace anger and fear in response to Kernon's words, but he forced himself to control these emotions. Made himself push them away. More than ever at this moment, he needed to remain calm. Focused. Ready. Borrik would accept their gift. He would not casually kill Corin. He would allow them both back into the clan. He must.

—

Corin had been confined for thirty minutes, before Borrik Greataxe, Clan Chief of the Karn, appeared in the clearing outside of the wooden cage.

The crowd parted to allow Borrik, Akob and two other senior warriors through. Corin watched their arrival, and noted immediately that Borrik was carrying his two-handed war axe in his right hand. The clan chief towered above the men around him, the large muscles on his arm visibly corded as he held the weapon.

'Stand back, clear some space!' Borrik's commanding shout carried across the central area of the village. Everyone assembled there moved back a few paces, forming a large circle around the cage. Corin judged that most of the village must now be present. 'Bring him out!'

The cage door opened, and Corin exited the structure, leaving his possessions on the floor behind him. He looked towards Agbeth, and with a gesture instructed her to stay where she was, by the side of the cage. He then moved a couple of paces away from the wooden bars, distancing himself from her, all the while making sure that he remained out of reach from Borrik's axe. The assembled crowd had gone quiet around them.

429

'So, Runt, you've returned.' Borrik's words were announced rather than spoken, intended to carry to all of the surrounding gathering. The purple scar beneath his eye added a sinister distortion to his expression.

'Yes, I have Borrik. I've come-'

He was interrupted before he could finish. 'You've come back, despite my clear vow that you would be killed if you returned here?'

Corin paused. He was trying to achieve his focus, to find the necessary level of concentration. But it was difficult amidst the apparent hostile tension of the crowd, and under the threat of Borrik's stare. 'I've returned, aware of your promise, yes. But I'm seeking your pardon now, and a way to make amends to the clan for what I've done.'

'Why should I overturn your banishment?'

Corin closed his eyes for a moment, and again he could see through Blackpaw's eyes, as the felrin lurked in the woods to the north-west. He transmitted an instruction to the creature.

COME. COME. COME. COME. COME.

He opened his eyes, holding Borrik's gaze, and answered loudly enough for the whole crowd to hear. 'Three reasons, Clan Chief. I was a coward, and you were right to banish me for that. But I'm no longer a coward. I've been away for two years, and in that time I've changed. I want to prove that to the clan. I seek forgiveness, to allow me to prove that.'

'My decision was final, and was sworn before the Gods. It cannot be changed, just because you want it to be changed.' Borrik rotated his great-axe as he said this, such that the long shaft was now held in both hands, in front of him. He then moved forwards slightly, towards Corin.

Corin stepped back, staying out of reach of the deadly weapon. 'Second. Agbeth is my wife. Her health has been bad, recently. She needs to come back to live in the village.'

Borrik shook his head. 'She can stay. But my decision was final. Sworn before the Gods. Stay away from here, or return and be killed.' He stepped forwards again,

This time Corin held his ground, on the edge of the axe's reach, forcing himself to concentrate. For the briefest moment he experienced the sensation of invisible tendrils swirling out of his mind, moving towards Borrik. But then there was a shout from the crowd of, 'Kill him!'

And Corin's focus was shattered, the tendrils dispersing instantly. He gulped. This was not how it was meant to be happening.

'Third,' he continued, trying to overcome his fluster. 'I have a gift for the clan. A great gift. For the clan, and for *you*, Borrik. One that will bring glory to the Karn, and most of all to its chief.'

'What gift?'

Corin closed his eyes again. He could see the image through Blackpaw's eyes, of the beast pounding along the path at the side of the Great Lake, getting closer to the village. There was little chance of it encountering a person, given the masses gathered here in the centre of Karn. Corin passed another instruction to the creature. He knew exactly where he wanted it to appear, and he told it that now.

Corin needed to secure a few more moments of time. 'A great gift, Borrik. A gift to lift the Karn to victory over the Anath and the Borl. To make you the greatest chief.'

Borrik's voice was lower, impatient. 'What gift?'

Again, Corin tried to focus on the clan chief, and tried to send the unseen tendrils spiralling out towards him. For a brief moment he achieved this, and they circled around Borrik's mind, probing against it. However, the giant warrior shook his head angrily, and again Corin felt the connection shatter.

'The gift of a great new warrior,' Corin finally responded. He was becoming more worried by the failure of his strange ability, and he still needed to stall for time. 'A warrior who will bring victory to the Karn.'

Borrik stepped forward two paces, angry this time, and started to raise his axe. His next words were a snarl. 'What gift?'

Finally, Corin sensed Blackpaw arriving in place, and he issued a further instruction to the beast.

'That gift!' he shouted, pointing at the roof of the Clan Hall, across the village. Borrik and the assembled crowd turned as one, to stare towards the indicated location.

And there, at the highest point on the conical roof above the village's largest building, stood Blackpaw. The felrin was fully upright, extended to its full eight feet in height. One of its paws was wrapped around the central beam which emerged through the building's roof. Blackpaw's muscles rippled, its jaw was open, and with the sun in the sky behind it, a terrifying and magnificent silhouette was formed.

The beast then tilted its head back and howled, a cry as ghastly as any which Corin had ever heard it make before. The cry lasted for seconds, before finally dying away.

'That gift,' Corin repeated, more quietly this time.

—

In the seconds afterwards, there were frightened shrieks from a number of the villagers surrounding them, and calls from some of the warriors to take up arms.

Borrik was calmer, although he appeared to grip his great-axe more tightly. He looked at Corin. 'By the Gods. That is a felrin?'

'Yes.'

'How is it here?'

'It follows me, and Agbeth. It fights for us. It will fight for the Karn.' As Corin said her name, he glanced towards his wife. She was still standing by the side of the cage, looking worried. He gestured for her to move further away from him, but she shook her head and remained in place.

'How? How does it follow you?'

Corin knew that he could not share the truth of his connection to the beast. At least, not yet. 'We found it. We tamed it.'

Borrik shouted an order. 'Akob! Assemble ten warriors! Aim your arrows at that thing. If it moves towards us, kill it!'

'That's not necessary,' said Corin 'It won't attack.'

432

'Unless you tell it to?'

Corin hesitated, before replying. 'Yes.'

'So, is this a gift, or a threat?'

'A gift.' Corin paused again, before adding, 'Unless I'm killed, in which case I'm not sure what it would do.'

Borrik spat, followed by a mirthless bark of a laugh. 'Akob, make that twenty men!'

Corin closed his eyes for a second, concentrating.

GO. GO. GO. GO. GO.

In response, in a flash of movement Blackpaw descended from the Clan Hall roof down the far side, disappearing out of view behind that building. The gathered villagers now shifted their positions such that the warriors were on the outside of the circle, facing outwards with weapons raised. The women, children and elders were standing to the inside of them, also with eyes trained on the surrounding buildings.

Borrik then shouted again. 'People of Karn! The Runt returns here, and he threatens us!'

'No, that's not true, I-'

'Stand firm, now,' interrupted Borrik. 'If the beast comes closer, we'll kill it. *I* will kill it. Know now that the Runt seeks to make me change my vow, which I swore before the Gods. That for the rest of his life, he is banished, and will suffer death if he returns here. And instead he brings a monster here, amongst us, a deadly beast which he believes brings the threat of death to us. And he seeks to use this to scare me into breaking my oath.'

'That isn't true!'

'But if my word is not law,' continued Borrik, 'and my vows to the Gods are untrue, what use then is a clan chief? I'd rather cut off my own balls than break my oath. And so, the Runt must be punished. I sentence him to death. And I'll deliver that death. Here and now.' He raised his axe and turned towards Corin.

Corin was shocked by the swift rejection of his offered gift. This had not been meant to happen. He stepped urgently away from the clan chief, also creating further distance from where Agbeth was standing. No one moved to stop him, because the majority of the villagers were now facing outwards.

He needed to divert Borrik from the clan chief's chosen course of action. Corin therefore strove to find concentration, to use his power to take control of the other man's mind. Again, invisible connections spiralled outwards from Corin towards the giant warrior. They located their target, then started probing and burrowing with all of the force of willpower which Corin could muster.

However, there was a powerful resistance, as Borrik's mind struggled against this unknown assault. Corin realised that doing this with a strong-willed person was much more challenging than anything that he had ever encountered before. With animals, and even with the felrin, he had been able to dominate their will easily. In the case of Agbeth, he had only slipped into her mind in moments of seizure, and she had never been aware of his actions in order to be able to resist him. But with Borrik, there was a clear effort to repel his attempts to take control.

Corin's mental assaults had at least resulted in Borrik pausing in place with a look of uncertainty on his face, with no forward movement to carry out the death sentence which he had declared moments earlier. Corin retreated, sensing that if he could just hold Borrik for a few seconds longer, he could still secure a peaceful outcome. Could he somehow encourage the clan chief to change his mind, and to see sense and accept the gift, before it was too late?

But Corin then stumbled backwards over a leg and a boot which had been extended behind him, and he was suddenly tumbling onto his back, banging his head into the ground. Instantly, he could see his brother's sneering face above him, and he realised that Kernon had tripped him. In the same moment, he knew that his focus and attempted control over Borrik was gone.

The clan chief roared with rage as the tendrils assailing him dispersed harmlessly. Corin was flat against the ground, and would have no time to stand again before Borrik was upon him. And Corin's concentration was shattered.

Borrik drew nearer, raising his axe. His weapon was poised above Corin. Ready to strike.

At that instant Corin felt a weight landing on top of him, blocking his view, a small form covering his face and his body. A person and a smell which was as familiar to him as his own hands.

'Don't kill him!' Agbeth screamed the words. 'Don't kill him!' She had thrown herself directly on top of Corin, between him and the axe that would have delivered his death. Her arms wrapped around Corin's neck.

Corin shifted his position so that he could see beyond her, could see Borrik with the axe raised, and he was thankful that the clan chief was delaying the killing blow.

'Get her off him,' ordered the giant warrior, grimly, directing his instruction to Kernon.

Kernon appeared to take great delight in roughly prising Agbeth's arms off Corin, which Corin also gently assisted with. He wanted his wife out of harm's way. The last outcome he could possibly desire would be one which could cause any physical hurt to her.

As soon as she was clear of him, however, the axe would fall, and then he would be lost. He needed to think of something. Anything. To delay the moment of his death, to allow him the time to get his focus back.

Then the answer emerged, at the instant as Kernon finally pulled Agbeth away from Corin's body.

'I challenge you!' Corin's shout carried across all of the villagers.

Borrik paused again, with the axe still raised above him.

Corin shouted once more, as he rose to his knees. 'I challenge you, Borrik, for the clan chiefdom!'

Borrik snorted, but still the killing blow was held back. 'You're banished. For life. Challenging me doesn't change that.'

'You're wrong! You banished me for as long as you're clan chief. Not for my life. But for yours! I challenge you! I challenge you! Your death would end my banishment.'

Borrik stepped back, his face a mixture of amusement and derision. 'Maybe that's true. But right now, you're banished. No longer part of the clan. I don't have to accept your challenge, pathetic as it is.'

Corin had no alternative now. He needed to secure time for himself, to get his concentration and poise back. If he was sentenced to death for breaking his banishment, as Borrik had already declared, then the whole village would be entitled to attack and kill him. But in a challenge with Borrik, he at least had the slim chance of a one-on-one fight. He therefore doubled-down on his words, saying things which at one time he would never have imagined possible to come from his own mouth. 'Borrik is scared! Of a challenge by the Runt!'

Borrik snorted again and twisted his neck as if to control his rage. 'Is this a trap? This is a challenge to fight just you, yes? Not the beast?'

Corin raised himself to his feet. 'Me. Not the felrin. Me.'

He then glanced at Agbeth. Kernon was gripping her upper arms to hold her in place, and Corin's brother was grinning with malevolent interest. In contrast, there was a look of confusion and fear on Agbeth's face, with evident uncertainty as to what Corin was now doing.

'Corin, please stop this madness,' she said.

Corin shook his head, knowing that he must ignore her, that he had to proceed. However, the proximity of his wife to Kernon, accompanied by the remembrance of his brother's earlier threats, added to Corin's sense of alarm.

He took a deep breath, steadying himself, before again shouting, 'I challenge Borrik Greataxe to a fight to the death! If he dies, my banishment will end! Does he accept?'

Borrik laughed derisively and shouted in return, 'And I accept his pathetic challenge! Here and now!'

436

It had been many years since the village had last seen a challenge against the clan chief. Eight years since a foolish young warrior had dared to attempt to take Borrik's position, and over fifteen years prior to that since Borrik himself had taken his role by beheading his predecessor. Despite that, the villagers knew the protocol of the event, and the circle around the two combatants closed again, forming a fighting arena. There was mocking laughter from some individuals, but largely the atmosphere was now subdued and nervous, with eyes still cast to the buildings around them for signs of the felrin.

Borrik stepped away from Corin, to the far side of the enclosed circle. He casually swung his axe around his head, before saying, 'Pick your weapon, Runt.'

'Axe and shield,' said Corin.

'Very well,' said Borrik. 'Give him his axe, and get him a shield. Which I'll try not to damage, as I kill him. Otherwise, no armour, for either of us.'

Corin waited, whilst his weapons were brought to him. He was trying desperately to focus. To concentrate. To shut out all of the distractions around him, and to ignore the tightening dread which was now in his chest.

He took hold of the axe and shield. He was stronger than the last time that he had held this combination of weapons, during the attack on the Anath village. And this time, at least, he was conquering his fear and his hand was not trembling. However, compared to Borrik, he was still a weakling. In a fair fight, he would not last for more than a few seconds.

There was only one way that he could win this combat, and that was by using his powers.

'Ready, Runt?' The clan chief looked to be supremely confident about his coming victory. 'I need to make this quick so that we'll still have time to hunt and kill your beast today.'

437

Kernon had pulled Agbeth to the side of the circle. She again looked at Corin, then called, 'Corin, please don't do this! Call Blackpaw!'

Once more, he shook his head, then mouthed the words, 'Goodbye, my love.'

Agbeth closed her eyes then turned her head away, blinking back tears.

Corin knew that concentration was needed. Focus. Needed immediately. But he still could not achieve what he required. There was silence in the circle around them, as he gathered his thoughts. At least Agbeth's defence of him and his challenge for the clan leadership had bought him this much; the chance to stand up and to face his attacker. And some slim opportunity for his powers to save him, if he could access them.

Eventually, he replied, 'Ready.'

From outside the village, Blackpaw howled again, ferocious and wild. As if that sound was a signal, Borrik moved forwards, ready to kill.

26

Allana

—

Year of Our Lord,
After Ascension, 769AA

Allana spent her first day in the fort of Aiduel's Guards on the floor of a cold and austere cell.

She had not yet had sight of the inside of her new prison. When a contingent of Aiduel's Guards had arrived to collect her from the dungeons of Septholme Castle, her hands had been bound and a cloth bag had been placed and tied over her head. She had then been marched from one captivity to another, in a blinded state throughout.

Whilst being moved, she had tried on a number of occasions to ask questions of her new captors. However, each attempt had been met with silence, or with ungentle shoves to her shoulder.

When the lack of further forward movement had signalled that they had arrived at their destination, she had been stripped naked, other than for the cloth covering on her head. She had experienced a crippling sense of humiliation as unseen hands had pulled the clothes from her body, leaving her completely exposed to whomever might be looking. Another single piece of clothing had then been pulled over her, which felt like a coarse sackcloth shift. Then they had left her there, still tied and unable to see. Feeling utterly disorientated.

In the minutes thereafter, she had wandered sightlessly around the small room in which she had been placed. Cautiously reaching her bound hands out to test its boundaries, which she established were barely eight feet across. Confirming that there were no comfortable furnishings of any sort, only hard stone walls and a cold floor. And a foul-smelling and soiled bucket, which had been placed in the corner.

Eventually, she had dropped to a sitting position, leaning back against one of the walls. The presence of the cloth bag around her face was making it harder to breathe, and was inducing a stifling sense of claustrophobia.

Alone, in that surrounding blackness, she was trying to find courage, and was fighting against the tears which again threatened to come.

Don't despair, Lana. Try to be strong. Remember to stick to your story. You can survive this.

———

In the many hours which followed, during which the passing from day to night was marked only by the increasing darkness inside the cloth bag, her captors started to torment her.

She was given no food or drink throughout the first day, and her mouth quickly became parched. No one responded to any questions, whenever she called out.

The only form of communication which she received from her jailers was the repeated clashing of metal objects against the cell door, several times each hour. Although she was trying to steel her nerves in readiness for this, the clanging sound still shocked her every time it came. It was clearly intended to unsettle her, and was causing her ears to ring painfully.

In the daytime, this was an annoyance. However, as night arrived, it was a severe hindrance to sleep. She finally slumped into a sideways position on the floor, bound hands before her, feeling desperately thirsty and tired. But each time that the escape of sleep would start to embrace her, the clanging would start again, jolting her out of her nearing slumber.

She therefore could not find rest for any longer than short bursts, and through the passage of the night her mind was becoming increasingly muddled.

Sometimes, she thought about Duke Conran, such thoughts mixed between grief at the dawning realisation that he was gone forever, and guilt for her own role in his death. These considerations served to add to her sense of torment and inability to sleep.

And she spent the entire first night like that.

—

The following day and night also passed within the sightless isolation of the cell. The cycle was broken only twice, when the cloth covering was partially raised above her mouth, and a cup of water was pressed to her lips. On both occasions, it was taken away again before she had been able to swallow any more than a mouthful.

As her captivity continued, she was feeling increasingly thirsty and hungry. And also tired and scared. She longed to remove the confining bag from her head, and to suck in a clean lungful of air along with a delicious gulp of water.

Finally, after what Allana guessed must have been two days in captivity, she was pulled to her feet, and manhandled into a forward walk out of the cell. She could feel herself being manoeuvred through a series of corridors and doorways, before firm hands on her shoulders pushed her down into a chair. After this, the cloth bag on her head was untied and was at last removed from her face.

Allana shook her head, striving to clear the befuddlement from her mind, and she squinted her eyes in response to the sudden exposure to the glaring light of day.

Seated across from Allana, on the other side of a table within a small room, was an elegantly tall woman with jet black hair. The woman appeared to be in her late-thirties in age, and she was wearing the uniform of Aiduel's Guards. In other circumstances she could have been described as beautiful, with high cheekbones and exotic, slanting dark eyes. However, there was a coldness to her expression which overrode any other immediate physical impression. Her eyes were locked directly onto Allana's.

'Hello, Allana,' said the woman, softly. Her accent identified her as of Dei Magnus origin, and she sounded highborn.

Wake up, Lana! Wake up! Be careful. Watch every word!

'It's Lana,' Allana replied, still blinking as her eyes adjusted to the light. 'Lana Marrone. Not Allana.'

The woman smiled, then reached down to pick up a cup on the table. She took a long drink, then sighed with exaggerated satisfaction as she placed the cup down again. 'Ah, yes. Lana. Lana Marrone. Of course it is.'

Allana did not respond to this. Her mouth and throat were dry, and she gazed at the cup with envy. She could sense that there was at least one other person present in the room, who was standing behind her, but she could see no one in her peripheral vision.

The woman opposite her spoke again, her stare fixed on Allana, the corners of her mouth upturned. 'Don't worry, though, Lana, about me getting things wrong. We'll have the truth of what you are and what you've done before you leave this fortress. All of it, with no mistakes. Because we've plenty of time to spend together, you and I, and I'm not in any rush. And nor is our young Duke Gerrion displaying any eagerness to have you back. You must have been a *very* naughty girl, Lana, given how keen he was to hand you over to us. Or perhaps his grief has overwhelmed him? Such a tragic loss.' She smiled again. 'But how dreadfully rude of me, I haven't introduced myself. I am High Commander Evelyn dei Laramin.

442

You know, that Laramin from the province which borders Monis, to the north? Or perhaps you don't? Anyway, now that we know each other's names, maybe we can become friends, Lana? And confidantes. And in time, I feel certain that you'll be able to tell me anything and everything.'

Allana dropped her eyes down, not wanting to hold the woman's gaze. There was a fierce intensity in dei Laramin's stare, which gave the impression that she was peering directly into Allana's soul and could discern the truth. Allana could remember the Duke's frustrated descriptions of dei Laramin, as a fanatic.

She's trying to scare you, Lana. She wants to intimidate you into blurting everything out. Don't let her! Wake up. Be brave. Think clearly!

As much as she tried to do this, however, Allana felt as if her mind was caught within a dense fog, clearly undermined by the lack of sleep.

Dei Laramin leaned forwards. 'Have you gone shy, Allana? Well, let me set some ground rules. I'm going to ask you some questions, and if you answer me truthfully, you and I will become friends. Special friends. And I may even let you have a drink of this lovely water. But if you don't answer me, Allana, or if I think that you're answering falsely, then that will upset me. And when I get upset, I have other ways – other more *painful and distressing* ways – of getting to the truth. And you wouldn't want me to be forced to hurt you, in my quest for the truth, would you?'

'No. But it's Lana.'

'Of course it is. Very well. I think that we're really starting to understand each other now, *Allana*. So, Allana, let me start with this question. Tell me who you are, and how did you get here?'

—

The initial series of questions went on for what felt to Allana like a period of hours. During this interrogation, despite her lack of sleep, she acquitted herself more capably than she had done in the equivalent long-ago encounter with Duke Conran. Her answers to

443

dei Laramin were complete and cogent, and the holes in her story which had existed previously were artfully addressed.

Keep going, Lana! You're doing so well. Might this convince her to release you?

However, just when Allana was beginning to hope that her cover story was being believed, the High Commander abruptly ordered her to stop speaking.

Dei Laramin's face bore an impassive expression as she looked up to address someone who was behind Allana. 'Enough of this! She's not ready to shed this veil of lies yet. Truthseeker, take her and purify her tainted soul with water.'

Before Allana had any inclination or time to protest, the cloth bag was pulled down over her head, and she was being dragged away from the table.

'Please,' she said, as she was marched out of the room. 'What did I do wrong? I told the truth. Please.' Her words were met with silence.

After just a few moments she was lifted and then manhandled into an awkward position, lying on her back on what felt like a sloping wooden table. Her face and eyes were covered by the cloth bag, and she could not see the nature of the apparatus onto which she had been placed. Her head was several inches lower down than her feet, and the crown of her head was pressed against what she assumed was a wooden block. She could hear people moving around her, and she felt her breathing growing quicker with anxiety for what was about to happen.

Then her unseen captors started to strap her to this strange tilted table. She could feel leather straps being tightened painfully across her ankles, her thighs, her waist, and then her chest and arms. Finally, a looser strap was bound across her neck. She had no idea as to how much of her body was still being covered by the sackcloth shift in which she was dressed, but again she felt exposed and vulnerable.

All the while, no one else spoke and Allana had no idea as to how many people were in the room with her. The situation was causing panic to rise within her; she had heard vague stories about the acts which Aiduel's Guards undertook when questioning a heretic, but she had never focused upon the possibility that she could fall victim to such deeds. All of her fears in fleeing from the Guards had been concentrated onto the final horror which they might inflict upon her; that of being burned alive. But, until this moment of being helpless on this table, she had never properly contemplated that there were many more vile acts and tortures which they might commit against her before that final release of death.

Into the vacuum of the silence in the room, she started to plead. 'Please. I haven't done anything. Please. Let me go. Please.'

Be brave, Lana. Be brave. They might just be doing this to scare you. Be brave.

But then the water began to pour, onto the cloth on her face, and with horror she knew that this was no mere scare tactic. The wet cloth pressed down onto her nose and mouth, blocking her air passages, and in response to this her body began to arch in terrified objection, struggling against the various restraints now holding her in place.

And in the midst of this horrific sensation of drowning, any determination to remain brave was immediately and utterly destroyed.

—

By the end, Allana had lost track of for how long she was subjected to the water torture. They repeated the act of pouring water onto the cloth on her face, many times. On each occasion, she felt her chest heaving to find breath, and by the time the water ceased to flow her lungs were bursting with pain.

Between the bouts of torture, there was a pause, sometimes of minutes. Always with silence around her. At first, Allana dispelled that quiet with pleas for mercy, but eventually she recognised that this would solicit no response or reprieve. Instead, she tried to steel herself for the next traumatic assault. But she could never make herself ready for the terrible sensation of drowning under the wet cloth, once the torment started again.

Finally, after the worst minutes or hours of her life, she was unstrapped from the table and forced to stand. The wet cloth bag was still on her head, but she gave thanks to Aiduel as it fell away from her nose and mouth. She gasped and sucked in air, feeling tears in her eyes. Then she was again steered away, by ungentle hands. Her sackcloth dress was soaked in water, and she was starting to shiver.

When the cloth covering was finally removed from her head, she was once more seated across from Evelyn dei Laramin.

'Hello, Allana,' said the High Commander, the corners of her mouth again upturned. 'I do hope that we're still friends, and that you're grateful for the purification of your eternal soul as delivered by the water?'

Allana did not speak. Dei Laramin seemed oblivious to the lack of response and smiled, and Allana suddenly understood that the other woman was enjoying this. Was enjoying the torture and humiliation which she was inflicting, and the power which she held over Allana's life and wellbeing. Allana felt an abrupt surge of hatred towards the other woman. Dei Laramin was a fanatic, and Allana recognised that her captor would be able to justify all manner of evil deeds in the service of her religion.

'Now, Allana. I would like you to start again and tell me the truth, as friends should. The *truth*, Allana. Otherwise, I will ask the Truthseeker to immediately take you for another session with the water. I do sincerely hope that we understand each other better now? Certainly, better than before?'

Allana nodded, slowly. Her eyes were still red from where she had been crying, and her lungs were sore. She was not brave enough to face a recurrence of the trauma which had just been inflicted upon her. And she did not dare to repeat the story that she had already told and been punished for.

What can you do, Lana? What can you do? Think!

'Yes.' She paused after uttering this word, and swallowed against the pain in her throat. She had to give them something, something closer to the truth, and hope that it would be sufficient for them to stop hurting her. 'I am sorry for lying to you, High Commander. So sorry. My name is Allana dei Monis, and my mother murdered High Priest Ronis dei Maranar.'

—

The questioning by the High Commander continued for a long time afterwards. Dei Laramin asked astute and probing questions, but during that session of further interrogation she did not expose the critical lie about Seilana dei Monis's role in the killing.

The harrowing water torture had at least roused Allana's mind from the befuddled state caused by her lack of sleep. This allowed her the dexterity of thought to plausibly retell her own true story, but with the added central deception of Seilana's involvement.

The events were relayed largely as they had happened, but for that deceit. The truth of who Allana was and where she had come from. The murder of Ronis dei Maranar, following his attempt to rape Allana. The escape through Sen Aiduel. The journey by boat on *The Flower of Andar*. The arrival of Allana in Septholme. And what she had subsequently done whilst living in this town.

Where the story was altered was that Seilana was blamed for the murder. Allana then described how her mother had stayed on the ship and travelled on to Andarron, to distance Allana from her crime. Of course, Allana claimed to have no idea as to where her mother was now. And she made no mention of her own affair with Duke Conran.

Allana felt a modicum of guilt about blaming her mother for the murder. Part of her also wondered whether she might be condemning Captain Obnel Rabnar to death, for his part in her escape. Her story would stand up to scrutiny only for as long as it

447

took someone to find the captain, when they would establish that Allana had travelled alone. However, anything she could say right now which could halt the torture, and which could delay or prevent her own punishment, had to be acceptable to reveal. She did not have the luxury of being selfless and virtuous. Her own survival mattered more than her mother's memory, or Rabnar's safety. And Nionia had once told her that Aiduel's Guards thought that Seilana was the killer, so Allana was merely confirming their preconceptions.

Survive, Lana. Survive this! That's the only thing that matters.

She did not say anything about her recurring dream, or about her strange power, and nor did the High Commander question her about any of this.

As Allana finished answering the final question posed to her, dei Laramin was staring at her, a shrewd look in the woman's eyes. 'Very good, Allana. Much better than the first story you told me. I can now understand why you lied to Nionia. And do you know what? I believe you. Well, most of what you've said, anyway. Such that we're almost friends again. Almost. And tonight, I'll reward you for being my friend with some food and drink. Would you like that?'

'Yes,' answered Allana, immediately. She wanted to ask what would happen next, and what her fate was likely to be based on what she had already disclosed. However, she restrained herself. Any question would just be likely to encourage dei Laramin to bait her further, and she would not receive a meaningful response.

'OK. But I still don't think we have the *full* truth, Allana. Not yet. Not quite. So next time we speak – maybe tomorrow, maybe the day after – we'll start again. And next time, I'll have some other questions, too. Something we want to ask all of the young men and women, who are your age. Won't that be nice? Won't that be something special to look forward to?' Dei Laramin smiled, this time with no effort to conceal her malice, and again Allana felt a rush of hatred towards the other woman. 'And next time, if you upset me, my Truthseeker might not want to cleanse you with water. Perhaps,

448

if I'm not convinced by the purity of your soul and the complete truth of your words, I'll let him use fire.'

—

The third and fourth nights in the cell within the fort of Aiduel's Guards passed as miserably as the first two. The banging of metal against the other side of her cell door continued throughout both nights, at frequent intervals. The unseen Guards could be heard laughing as they did this, taunting her lack of sleep, as she lay wretchedly on the cold floor of the cell.

Allana's stomach was now aching from lack of food, to add to her various other discomforts. Her hunger brought back memories of the last weeks with her mother, of that time when she had been close to starving, living on the meagre scraps bought from the sale of their remaining possessions.

Her jailers had given her a small hunk of bread to eat, at the end of the third and fourth days. They had not removed the cloth covering for this. They had merely raised the bottom of the cloth past her mouth, and had fed the bread to her as she leaned forward on her knees, like one might feed a dog beneath a table. It was yet another degrading act, to add to her accumulating sense of shame and humiliation.

The cloth bag had been on her head for days now, and it smelled stale inside. As she was fed at the end of the fourth day, with the lower edge of the cloth held against her nose, she begged the person who was feeding her to take it off.

'Please,' she said. 'I just want to breathe clean air. For just a few moments. Please take it off me.'

The person standing in front of her paused, giving Allana a brief flicker of hope that they were considering her request. She was able to look down to see the feet standing before her, the stance suggesting that the individual who was feeding her was male.

Then a hand touched her chin, and stroked up along her

449

cheek. 'You want me to remove this hood?' It was a man's voice, gruff and common-sounding. And was there a trace of desire in those words?

Be ready, Lana. If he takes this off, be ready to look at him. Use your power. Do whatever you need to do, to survive.

'Please, yes. For just a few moments.'

Two hands took hold of the lower edge of the cloth bag. Allana readied herself.

But then there was a nasty chuckle, before the cloth was pushed down and tied again, and with despair she heard the man's footsteps moving away from her, and out of the cell.

—

On her fifth day of captivity, she was again brought before the High Commander. If Allana had thought herself confused when they had met two days earlier, that disorientation paled in comparison to what she felt this time, as the cloth covering was removed. Four consecutive nights of broken sleep were proving severely detrimental to her ability to focus and to concentrate.

And after such a long period within the dark of the hood, the sudden exposure of light onto her eyes was extremely painful. She felt like shutting them and putting her head down into her arms, on the table.

Dei Laramin showed no sympathy, as she addressed Allana. 'We're tracking down your Captain Rabnar as we speak, Allana. So, we'll soon find out if you've been telling me the *whole* truth. But I have some other questions for you today. Something we're asking all of the young people of your age. Now, do you promise to speak truly to me, Allana?'

'Yes,' said Allana, immediately.

'Very well. But I sincerely advise that you answer the rest of these questions openly, fully and honestly, Allana. If I believe that you've failed to do so, I'll hand you over to the Truthseeker for the afternoon, with an instruction to do whatever is necessary to correct your ways. Is that understood?'

'Yes.' Allana was trying to sound meek and compliant. The threat of further torture by the Truthseeker truly terrified her.

'To start, how old are you Allana?'

'Twenty years old.'

Dei Laramin's eyebrows arched, as Allana said this. 'And when was your birthday, your twentieth birthday?'

'It was on the eleventh of Morningsong. The day that Nionia saw me.'

'Really? That's interesting, Allana. Next. Have you ever undertaken or been part of an act of heresy?'

Allana looked at her, feeling confused by the question. It was such an odd thing to be asking her, in the wake of the other serious matters to which she had already confessed. 'No, I truly believe in The Lord Aiduel and the Holy Church. I always go to church on Seventh-Days.'

Dei Laramin stared at her again, and then the questioning continued.

—

Afterwards, the water torture was inflicted upon Allana for a second time. She did not believe that on this occasion dei Laramin ordered it because the High Commander suspected that she was being lied to. The highborn woman simply instructed for Allana to be tortured again, because she chose to.

As Allana was once more strapped to the tilted table, with knowledge of what was to come, she was begging for mercy from the outset. But these desperate pleas were quickly curtailed by the water again closing over the cloth on her mouth and nose.

Her only reliefs were that afterwards she was returned to her squalid cell, and not back to dei Laramin for more questioning. And that they had not used fire upon her, as threatened.

She sobbed for a long time as she lay upon the cell floor, feeling cold and hungry and thirsty. And miserable and humiliated. But gradually, as she forced herself to calm down, the unusual questioning of the day returned to her. Dei Laramin had selected such strange matters to query.

Did Allana see the future? Of course, she had honestly answered 'no' to this question.

Did she have any unusual or recurring dreams? The real answer was 'yes', but Allana had managed to conceal this truth during the questioning. The excited glint in dei Laramin's eyes had told Allana all that she needed to know; that saying 'yes' could worsen her already desperate plight. She was partially thankful now that her captors were tormenting her at night, such that she had never had the opportunity to dream restlessly in front of them.

Don't mention the dreams, Lana. Don't mention the mountains or the Gate.

Did she have any unusual powers? As she had been asked this, and had meekly denied it, Allana had glanced up at dei Laramin, and had hidden her own hostile thoughts behind bloodshot eyes.

If only she was a man, Lana. If only she desired you. Then she would find out what unusual powers you have.

Dei Laramin was still the only person who Allana had actually seen since her arrival. There was no attraction or lust in the cold, mocking eyes of the High Commander, no opportunity for Allana to use her powers on the woman. Allana needed to see a man there, to attempt to improve her situation using her strange ability. But there would be no possibility of that while the cloth bag was on her head.

Allana was slowly realising that the likelihood that she would ever leave this harrowing imprisonment was diminishing with each passing day. Would this be her life now, until she was led to a pyre to burn?

—

During Allana's fifth night in the fort, she felt the external presence for the first time.

She was in the small cell, within the enclosing darkness of her cloth covering.

At first, she assumed that she was either dreaming or hallucinating. But after blinking her eyes several times, she knew that she was awake. And that there was something *there*. A golden shimmer in her mind, calling to her from some distance away. Shining. The presence pulsed from a consistent distance and direction, although with her lack of sight she had no certainty as to where that might be. But it was certainly not in the room with her, or in the fort. Further away than that, but still close. In Septholme?

But a definite presence which she could feel. Something. Or someone? Somehow connected to her dream?

The presence stayed in her mind all of that night and was still there during the next morning. Pulsing. Glowing. Golden. In some peculiar manner, it soothed her to sense it there, to feel less alone, and it made her feel stronger and more refreshed in the midst of her misery and torment. Clearing away some of the fog from her thoughts.

What is it, Lana? What can you feel? And can it sense you, too?

—

She was again brought before dei Laramin, on the following day. Once more the cloth covering was removed as she was pushed into a seat, and this time her hands were also untied.

There was a piece of parchment laid out on the table before her, next to an inkpot and quill.

Dei Laramin smiled at her. 'You'll be pleased to know that we have a date set for your trial next week, Allana. None of us, certainly not me, want to see your suffering being prolonged like this. So, better that we bring things to a conclusion, eh?'

Allana nodded, taking the opportunity without the hindrance of

453

the cloth bag to breathe in fresh air. The call of the golden presence still resounded in her mind. It felt like it was a few hundred metres to her left, the direction easier to discern now that she was sitting here with the covering removed. And it was having the effect that she did not feel as dazed and confused as on her previous meetings with the High Commander. Despite the hopelessness of her situation, it gave her renewed courage.

Dei Laramin continued. 'All I need you to do, now, Allana, is to sign this document for me. And then we can return you to your cell, and there'll be no need for you to spend any more time with the Truthseeker.'

'What is it?'

'Just a simple record of what you've said to us, Allana. All you have to do is to sign it.'

Allana looked down at the document. Her eyes scanned through the words, and she could immediately see that it was a written confession which appeared to condemn her:

I assisted my mother, Seilana dei Monis, as she murdered High Priest Ronis dei Maranar. I made no effort to prevent the murder or to save the life of the High Priest. I then aided my mother to steal from the High Priest and to conceal his body. I did nothing to report the murder. I made no effort to see justice brought to the High Priest's killer. I assisted Seilana dei Monis to escape from Sen Aiduel and from Dei Magnus. I created a false identity to avoid justice. I lied repeatedly to Aiduel's Guards to cover up my own and my mother's crimes against The Lord Aiduel and The Holy Church. I remain unrepentant for my crimes.

'You want me to sign this?'

'Yes. Just sign it, Allana. Then soon your suffering will be ended.'

Signing that seals your death sentence, Lana. She wants this for the trial. Does she need it? Better that you fight to survive than to surrender meekly to this.

454

'No.' Allana muttered the word. Without the external presence somehow fortifying her, she doubted that she would have found the inner bravery to reject the High Commander's instruction.

'No? Truly? Are you absolutely certain that you want to give me that answer, Allana?' There was a look of cold outrage on dei Laramin's face.

'That doesn't record what I said. I'm not signing it.'

'Very well. You disappoint me so much, Allana, for doing this to me, just when I thought that we understood each other, and were becoming such special friends. I could waste my time, right now, seeing if I can persuade you to change your mind. But I won't. We'll see whether you have a different view when we meet again, tomorrow.' Dei Laramin looked up, staring towards the hidden person standing behind Allana's shoulder. 'Today, Truthseeker, introduce her to the fire.' She raised her long-fingered hand, thumb and forefinger pressed close together. 'Just a little, though. I don't want her to be marked or crippled for her trial.'

—

In the hour after that, they burned Allana. Burned her as she screamed and begged. Not with flames, but with the tips of heated pieces of thin metal, placed against her legs.

Allana had never known such pain, coming close to passing out each time a small red-hot tip pressed against her skin. Throughout, the distant golden presence remained in her mind, and it bolstered her, helping her to endure the agony and the sickening smell of her own charred flesh.

Frustrated rage welled up inside her as this torture was done to her. She was again hooded, and was unable to anticipate when the agonising heat would touch her. But, for just a few moments, she thought that she could feel the presence of the Truthseeker near to her. Could sense someone's twisted satisfaction and enjoyment as the work was carried out. And Allana wanted the pain within herself

455

to explode. To burst out, and to sweep over the Truthseeker and over every other sadistic person in this cursed place. To wash all of her tormentors away in a flood of her agony.

But no such thing happened, and eventually, after a handful of such pinpricks of red-hot metal, she was dragged back to her cell. But this time she was not weeping.

All the while, the golden presence was with her. Sustaining her. Making her feel stronger, and somehow giving her the courage not to surrender to despair.

You will survive this, Lana. You will survive. And they'll pay for what they've done to you. They will pay.

—

Later that day, her grim routine of cloth-covered darkness in the cell was at last broken.

Allana was lying on the cold floor when she heard the cell door open and then close again. Her legs throbbed painfully in the places where she had been burned, but the hurt was endurable. She had earlier touched the spots where the damage had been done to her, each of them feeling like small blisters of pain.

She raised herself to her knees, wondering if it was time to be fed again. Readying herself for an opportunity to get the cloth bag removed, and to gaze upon her captors.

Instead, she heard a familiar female voice. 'Lana? Oh my. What have they done to you?'

'Nionia, is that you?' Allana experienced a faint glimmer of hope when she heard the other woman's voice.

Soft hands were then reaching for Allana's covering, and pulling it up and off of her head. As Allana's eyes adjusted to the dim light, taking in the surroundings of her cell for the first time, she could see the blonde-haired young Guard kneeling in front of her. Nionia looked horrified. 'Oh, Lana. What have I done?'

'Please help me, Nionia.' Allana's throat was dry, and her voice

456

cracked with emotion from at last being with someone who did not appear to hate her.

Nionia was reaching down and untying Allana's bound hands. 'I can't, Lana. Quiet. We shouldn't speak. Someone's coming. I have to get you ready.'

Allana could see the dress that she had been wearing when she arrived, held in the crook of Nionia's arm. 'They're hurting me, Nionia. Going to kill me. Please help.'

'Shhhh, Lana. I can't. I'm sorry.' Nionia reached around Allana and pulled the stained sackcloth dress over Allana's head. Allana had been humiliated so many times in the last week, that she no longer cared that she was suddenly naked in front of the other woman. 'I didn't mean for this to happen, Lana. Please believe that. I was just so upset that you'd lied to me.'

'They're killing me, Nionia.'

Nionia had a wet cloth and a pail of water, and she started to wipe Allana's face and arms, and then the rest of her body. When the damp cloth came near to the blistered skin on Allana's legs, the blonde-haired woman paused and looked as if she was going to cry. 'Quiet, please, Lana. The other guards might be listening. I've got to get you ready for your visitor.'

'What visitor?' At the moment that she said this, Allana realised that the golden presence which had been inside her mind for the last day was closer. Much closer. Possibly within the fort? And that with its proximity she was feeling revitalised, suddenly full of energy, despite all of the adversity which she had suffered over the last few days.

Nionia started to pull the clean dress down over Allana's head. She leaned in close as she did so, such that her mouth was near to Allana's ear. 'I'm not meant to say, Lana. But he's a lord from the castle. Lord Sepian. Lord Arion Sepian.'

27

Arion

—

Year of Our Lord,
After Ascension, 769AA

Arion knelt by the side of his father's fresh grave, within the family burial area behind the chapel of Septholme Castle. The plot was marked by a simple engraved headstone. This would eventually be replaced by a more ornate headstone alongside his mother's resting place, but for now a humble block of granite was the only marker of the passing of the great Duke Conran.

Goodbye, father. By the Lord! Even now, being here, it doesn't seem real.

Arion knew that he should maintain this respectful pose, for a sustained period. The castle retainers might be observing him, and expecting such behaviour. He was also aware that he should be praying to Aiduel for the delivery of his father's eternal soul into heaven. But despite being here, and in mourning, he was deeply distracted.

By the *presence*. An external pulsing presence was resonating through his mind and body, as it had been ever since the ship carrying him had made anchor in Septholme harbour, during the previous night. It was something alive. Seductively alive. Each time that he felt the surging throb of the presence, a flood of energy washed across his body. Renewing him. Making him feel stronger. It was a similar sensation to that which had flowed across him on the two strange occasions when he had been in conflict, and had suddenly felt supremely fast and strong.

Whatever this thing was, or whomever it was, it was located somewhere to the east. He could feel it there, and he was certain that it could sense him, too. The intrusive awareness of it was making it difficult for him to concentrate on anything else. Or to linger beside this grave, achieving nothing.

He finally stood up and walked back towards a stairway to ascend to the eastern battlement. A few long strides and he was up high on the castle wall, looking outwards to the east. He had first come to this place in an agitated state at dawn, but now he felt compelled to stand here again in the light of morning.

The partially built fortress of Aiduel's Guards stood before him, a few hundred metres away. It was an ugly building, a scar on the shallow forested hill on which it was being constructed. In Arion's mind, its existence was also a stain on the sovereignty of Andar and of House Sepian. He had been a witness to the discussions in Andarron with the King, which had led to this foreign army's fort being built here. However, the idea of it had not felt as awful as the reality of now seeing the red-cloaked troops in the middle distance, enemy soldiers teeming in the midst of their half-built fortification.

The presence pulsed again. Confirming what he was now close to certain about. It was coming from the fortress. Whatever it was that was touching his mind, and energising his body, he felt sure that it resided within those walls.

As he stood there, considering this, a further question occurred to him. Was this presence, which repeatedly pulsed into his mind, somehow responsible for or connected to the new dream which had beset him, on the previous night? Had it triggered the dream? He did not know.

The memory of this new dream was still vivid in his mind, even now. After he had arrived back at the castle, in the middle of the night, he had been escorted to his room. And then the dream had taken him, this time not being the usual recurring vision of a mountain or of a Gate...

—

He was watching the young woman as she walked through the enormous and raucous crowd. She stepped slowly between two lines of red-cloaked soldiers, who appeared to be holding the jeering mob at bay.

The young woman was wearing a pristine white dress and a long white hooded cloak, the latter with its hood raised. Despite the ignominy of her situation, she walked with a dignified and almost regal gait, and without seeing her face he knew that if she were to lower that hood she would be beautiful.

Then he looked towards what she was approaching. It was an unlit pyre of wood, with a large raised beam in the centre. And he understood with horrified certainty what was going to happen here. The young woman was going to die, within an inferno of flame.

NO! STOP! NO!

He screamed the words to the people around him. This was wrong. A sickening mistake. Something which, once done, could never be undone. But his words were lost amongst the cacophony of the crowd.

He was continually trying to push forwards through the mass of bodies, attempting to get closer to her. But he was too far away, too far back in the throng of people gathered there, to prevent the terrible thing that they were about to do.

He watched as the young woman was tied to the pole in the centre of the wood. Throughout, she maintained her quiet poise, her face hidden, as a member of Aiduel's Guards announced the charges against her.

And then he saw the flaming torches, being brought closer. Being placed against the wood. Still, the young woman maintained her dignity. But as the pyre lit, she jolted her head back, and her hood fell...

—

After jerking awake that previous night, his sheets wet with perspiration, he had immediately recognised that it had been no ordinary dream. It had displayed a vividly real quality throughout, like the recurring dreams of the Gate, and was even more akin to the dream of the Bergen raiders' boats on the beach. But, if indeed it was possible, it had felt even more substantial and tangible than either of those.

He had chosen to dismiss the true nature of the Bergen raider dream, and at the time he had discounted his prediction of the boats on the beach as mere coincidence. It had been easier to believe that than to face the truth that he had somehow seen the future. But he was no longer fooling himself as to what his dream from the night before had been.

It was prophecy. He had been a witness to something awful, which was going to come to pass. The girl in the dream was going to burn on the pyre.

—

After a period of troubled reflection whilst standing on the castle battlements, Arion headed back into the castle to speak with Gerrion. The two of them had shared only brief greetings after his arrival during the night before, and Arion knew that there would be much for them to discuss.

Gerrion was in his new larger personal chambers which, until days earlier, had belonged to their father. The older brother was seated at a desk in the antechamber when Arion arrived, and he looked relieved to see that his visitor was his younger sibling.

461

Gerrion spoke first. 'Hello, Arion. Have you seen the grave now, brother?'

'Yes. It's hard to believe that father's buried there,' replied Arion. 'Still harder to get my head around the fact that he's gone. That you're Duke now, Gerrion.'

'I know. And to be honest, I didn't expect it for another twenty years. Maybe longer. You know that I've always had a lot of responsibility here. Father insisted on it. But the Duke – sorry, Father – was always there to make or to support the final decision. Now it's all on me.' The older Sepian brother had bags under his eyes, and he looked less stoical than Arion could ever remember.

'Not all on you, brother. Charl is still here to advise you. And with my knighthood and training, let me take the burden of military matters away from you, as soon as possible.' He put a hand onto Gerrion's shoulder.

'Thank you, Arion. It's truly good to have you back here, at this time. Thank you.' Gerrion gestured towards the spare chair by his desk. 'Take a seat, brother. There's much for us to talk about.'

'You look troubled, Gerr?'

The older brother shrugged. 'It's been a hard and lonely few days. All of this sudden and unexpected responsibility. Grief for father. Guilt.'

'Guilt?'

'Yes, guilt. I've blamed it all on the whore, but I was as much to blame. When father died. I chose to make an argument of it, when I could have just backed down. But I was so angry, with the way that she was manipulating him. The trouble that she was going to cause us. And it all led to Father's heart attack.'

Arion frowned. 'You'll have to slow down for me, Gerr. What are you talking about?'

'Of course. Forgive me, brother, I'm not thinking clearly. You don't know anything about it, do you? Father took himself a mistress, from within the servant staff of the castle. A seamstress, young, same age as you probably. From Dei Magnur.'

'A mistress? Father? Really?' Arion suspected that his voice expressed as much incredulity as he was feeling.

'Yes. The whole castle knew about it, though I think that we managed to keep the secret within these walls. I tried to make her leave, you know, a few times, but she wasn't having any of it. And do you know what was worse? Father was clearly in love with her. A foreign commoner. With Father.'

'Someone *my* age? Really?' Arion felt bewildered. He had never seen Duke Conran express any interest in other women, since their mother had died. Let alone having an affair with someone less than half his age, who was not of the nobility.

'Well, your reaction's the same as how I felt about it, at first. Shocked and disgusted, if I'm honest. But I grew to accept it, even if I worried that one day he was going to ask her to marry him. But then we got the accusation from Aiduel's Guards – who are a fucking pain in the backside, by the way – that she was living in Septholme under a false identity, and may be a murderer. And all I wanted to do was to hand her over. To let them interview her. If she was innocent, then fine, but if she was guilty then good riddance. I was worried about Father, and about Kari. So I asked this woman, this Lana Marrone, to agree to be interviewed. But she refused. And once she'd refused, Father wasn't having any of it, either. He defended her. We argued. He went red in the face. And then he had his heart attack and died. It's my fault.'

Arion could see tears in his brother's eyes, and he sensed that this was the first time that Gerrion had been able to share any of these feelings. 'Surely that's not your fault, then, Gerrion? From what you've said, all you were trying to do was the right thing?'

'I was. Honestly, I was.' Gerrion was staring down at his desk, his hands trembling, his usual calm now definitely broken.

'And Father wouldn't let you?'

'No.'

'Then none of what happened was your fault. Stop blaming yourself, brother. If it was a heart attack, it might have happened at any time, under any circumstances. But even if it could be anyone's fault, it would be this woman, this mistress, surely?'

Gerrion paused before responding. He took a deep breath, clearly composing himself, then nodded. 'Yes. That's right. Of course. Thank you, brother. It means more to me than you can know, to hear you say that.'

Arion again placed his hand onto his older brother's shoulder, to comfort him. 'What's happened to the woman then, this Lana?'

'Her? Well, it's now been established that she was indeed a fugitive on the run, and that her real name is Allana dei Monis. And she's already confessed to her role in the murder of a High Priest.'

'Then surely, even more, you did the right thing, brother? For Kari and for Father.'

'Yes. Yes, you're right. Thank you. You wouldn't believe how cold-blooded she was, though, Arion, in the moments before Father died. Almost like she'd cast some sort of spell on him. Used some kind of witchcraft. It made me so furious, I found myself wanting to hurt her, in the hours afterwards.'

'Witchcraft, really?' *Is prophecy witchcraft? And could witchcraft be responsible for this presence that I can feel?* 'And where is she now, brother?'

Gerrion looked up again, and the emotion had gone from his voice. 'I've handed her over to Aiduel's Guards, Arion. She's in their fort. She's confessed, and we're going to try her next week under a special Holy court. After that? Well, I'm sure that after the trial they're going to burn her.'

—

Arion discussed various other matters with his brother during that first meeting. They shared a number of happier memories about their father and mother. They also talked at length about Arion's engagement with Kalyane, and finally they spoke about ending Delrin's banishment from the family.

464

Arion was relieved to hear Gerrion expressing delight about his provisional engagement with Kalyane. Gerrion talked enthusiastically about how a wedding would be good for the morale of their people after the old Duke's death, and of how it would be good for Kari to have a woman in the family. He gave his immediate approval for the marriage, and stated his intention to write to Duke Rednar in confirmation, and to make arrangements for the wedding as soon as possible.

Lord preserve us, Arion had thought as his brother had said all of this, *this is moving very quickly!*

They were also both in agreement that Delrin's banishment was going to end. Gerrion resolved that he was going to write to their brother in the Holy Land. He planned to notify Delrin about their father's death, and to inform him that he was welcome to return home, if The Order of Saint Amena permitted it.

However, despite the importance of these discussions, Arion's mind had been distracted from the moment that Gerrion had stated that Aiduel's Guards were going to burn the woman. This *Allana dei Monis*. Arion could not stop thinking about the images in his dream from the night before, and of how he had been sure that a terrible mistake was going to be made. He felt certain that the parallel between the scene in his dream, and Gerrion's expectations for this woman's fate, could not be a coincidence.

Nor could it be pure chance that the strange presence he was feeling, which was now indelibly associated with this new dream, was emanating from the direction of the Guards' fortress. Where this young woman was being held. Could it be coming from her?

By the Lord! What's happening to me, here? Why should this woman matter to me? What's going on?

As the conversation with Gerrion proceeded, Arion became increasingly resolved that there was something which he needed to do. And that his mind would not be at ease until he had done it.

He was on the verge of speaking up about this when he suddenly felt a change in the surging external presence, as it throbbed outwards from the distant fort. Pain. Extreme pain. Agony. Something awful being done. He winced, leaning forwards with hands on his knees, and a stinging hurt on his thigh. ·

Gerrion noted his state of consternation. 'What is it, Arion? What's up?'

The pain disappeared, quickly, but the remembrance of its bite lingered. 'Nothing, brother. I'm OK. But... I need your permission, to do something. Something which doesn't make any sense, but which I need you to let me do, anyway.'

Gerrion frowned, quizzically. 'My permission? For what?'

'I want to meet this woman. This Allana dei Monis. I think that I *need* to meet her.'

—

Three hours later, Arion was inside the fortress of Aiduel's Guards. Gerrion had initially been reluctant to agree to Arion's request, and Arion had struggled to articulate why it was important for him to meet with the woman. However, after Arion had made a simple plea for Gerrion to trust him, the elder brother had eventually agreed.

Gerrion had then sent a messenger to communicate with the High Commander of the garrison, and after some initial resistance he had secured her consent for the meeting.

Arion was waiting in a small room with a single door, a table in the centre, and two chairs on opposite sides. He was sitting facing the door, trying to adopt a casual pose. The pulsing external presence was now much closer, and he was more nervous than he could remember being for a long time.

Why I am so ill-at-ease? She's just a young woman, barely more than a girl. I'm a Knight and a Lord. She should be the nervous one.

The pain which had echoed outwards from the presence had occurred four more times, after the initial discomfort which he had suffered. If the external presence was indeed somehow connected to this woman, then he was grimly certain that she had been tortured during this day. That thought made him furious; torture was not permitted as part of the agreement to let the Guards into Andar, and he regarded its use as vile. He intended to ask her. If there had been such abuse, he would have to do something about it.

He could feel the presence getting ever closer, as he waited. It was clear that the Guards had not wanted him to come here, and had definitely not wanted a stranger walking through their partially completed fortress. They had been wise to be concerned about that, because he had taken the opportunity to note the composition of their defences, as he had been led to this room. It was worthwhile being alert now, in case he ever needed to use the information at a later time.

The external presence was now looming outside of the room, pulsating with energy, and then the door opened. But the first person to enter the doorway disappointed him. It was a plain-looking gangly woman in the uniform of an Aiduel's Guard, her blonde hair closely cropped. She addressed Arion with a drawling Dei Magnus accent, sounding nervous. 'Lord Sepian?'

'Yes.'

'I am Nionia, of the Guards. The prisoner Allana dei Monis is with me. Are you ready to see her?'

'Of course.' *That's not her. Thank The Lord.*

'I've been asked to stay with you while you meet with her. Is that OK?'

If she had made the request forcefully, he may possibly have agreed to it. However, after sensing her apparent lack of authority and confidence, he simply replied, 'No. Get out. I'm a member of the Sepian noble household, and you're in our territory. Leave her with me. I don't intend to be insulted by having an observer forced on me.'

The woman's face paled, but he had correctly judged the weakness of her character, as she nodded and said, 'Oh. OK. Sorry, my Lord.' She moved back through the doorway, then stated, 'Allana, you may come in now.'

The second – and much smaller – woman to appear was not even looking at Arion when she walked into view. She was staring backwards, at someone or something, as she edged past the lanky female Guard. She then paused for a moment in the doorway, half-turned facing away from Arion, with a look of intense concentration on her face. Still not taking note of him.

But he knew immediately that she was the source of the external presence which he had been feeling for the last day. It resonated from her, bombarding and assailing his senses.

Then she turned to regard him.

—

Instantly, he wanted Allana dei Monis.

Her eyes met his, locking onto his stare. They were a mesmerising deep hazel colour, set within a beautiful heart-shaped face, which was framed by long black hair. That face was slightly gaunt right now and her hair was matted, perhaps hinting at her sufferings in the last few days. However, those imperfections only acted to emphasise the raw, magnetic allure of the girl.

She was the most physically desirable woman that he had ever encountered. Without any exception. The only person whom he had met who could compare to her natural beauty was Queen Mariess. However, whereas the Queen's features had a delicate exquisiteness which compelled admiration from afar, this girl elicited an intensely more primal response within him. He knew that he needed to possess her. Wanted her more desperately than he had ever wanted any woman before, and far more than he desired his merely pretty new fiancé.

She entered the room, her limbs moving gracefully as she walked, and seated herself at the table opposite him. He was noting the way that her dress clung to her body, emphasising the slim but voluptuous figure contained underneath. He had to wilfully resist from reaching out to touch her hand, as she placed it onto the table in front of him.

And he could feel an aura around this woman. That vibrant external presence, which he had been aware of for the last day, was surging and swirling about her. It was undoubtedly emanating from her. Making him more aware of Allana dei Monis and her immediacy than anyone else that he had ever met before.

As an afterthought, he made a gesture to order the blonde-haired Guardswoman to get out, without taking his eyes away from the young woman seated across from him. He had come here with a reasonable idea of what he was going to say. How he would first address her. How he would frame his questions. But instead, he found himself gawping at her. Her expression was mysteriously enigmatic, hinting at a mix of emotions which he could not properly interpret, but that wide-eyed stare continued to hold his own.

After the door had closed behind the blonde Guardswoman, Allana eventually broke the silence, with an unexpected question. 'What... what *are* you?'

Her voice was low, husky, drawling. Clearly Dei Magnun. And as seductively enticing as her perfect physical features. But hearing the words at least brought him back into self-awareness.

I'm like you. The same as you. What are you?

That thought flashed into his mind, before he filtered his spoken answer. 'I don't know. But I can *feel* you. For the whole of the last day, I've felt you here, and been aware of you, somehow. Is that what you mean?'

'Yes. At least, I think so.' She paused, blushing. 'And I can... feel you, too. For the last day. And right now. In my mind. In my body. And I feel... alive. Awake.'

As she said this, he became more aware of the physical effect that her proximity was having on him. As had happened when he had fought with Jarrett Berun and the Bergen raiders, it seemed as if coils of energy were coalescing around his limbs. He realised that he felt wonderfully alive and strong. Part of him wondered whether he could even punch a hole in the stone walls of this room, were he to attempt it?

He had intended to ask her questions about his father. About their affair. About the Duke's death. Instead, an enquiry which he had never planned to ask came into his mind. 'Do you have any powers, Allana? Strange powers?'

She glanced nervously towards the door, before turning back to him. Then she nodded, looking excited, and leaned in towards him conspiratorially. 'Shhhh. Be careful of what you talk about, here. And talk quietly, so they can't hear us. But yes, I have a power. A very unusual ability. Do you?'

'Yes, I do,' he replied, aware of how close her face was to his. He had to restrain himself from leaning forwards to kiss her. He was consumed with an urgent need to touch her and to feel her touch, a need so passionate and persistent that he was struggling to maintain his control.

Lord preserve me! What's happening to me? What is she?

His voice was cracked, as he asked the next unplanned question. 'And do you dream about the Gate, Allana?'

Her cheeks were flushed as she responded. 'Yes. So many times. The mountain. The winding path. The Gate. The others. You have the dream then, too?'

'Yes. Almost every other night. All of it. How is this possible, that we share the same dream?'

'I don't know. But it's amazing. It must mean… something. Something important. But these Guards are looking for people who dream, and who have powers. Like us. You must be careful as to who you tell. Or don't tell anyone.' After mentioning her captors the excitement vanished from her face, and again her expression became more mysterious, and more cautious. 'You seem so… familiar. But we've never met? Who are you, really? And why have you come to see me?'

Why am I here? By the Lord, can I really tell her that it's because I've had a vision about her being led to a pyre to die? And that I had to see the girl in that prophecy?

He tried to gather his thoughts. 'I am Arion Sepian. Youngest son of Duke Conran.' As he said this, an image flashed into his

470

mind of this Allana dei Monis with his father, and he was abruptly consumed with an irrational jealousy. 'As to *why* I'm here? I don't properly know.' He could not bring himself to tell her that he had foreseen her death. 'But I could feel you, sense you, here. I had to come. I know who you are and what you did. With my father, and before. But even knowing that, I had to come.'

Her face adopted a stern expression, and she folded her arms in front of her breasts, elbows on the table. 'And what did I do, Arion?'

'You were my father's mistress? And before you came here, I understand that you were involved in the murder of a High Priest?'

'Don't judge me! High Priest Ronis dei Maranar was an evil man who was going to rape me! He was killed in self-defence! And I've been hunted for it, for years!' She hissed her reply, sounding upset by the perceived criticism in his words. 'And then I seduced Duke Conran, who was going to hand me over to be killed, to save myself! Does that make me such a horrible person? Does it? Do I deserve this awful treatment?'

'I'm sorry! I don't know anything about it. About you. Please don't be upset.'

'I'm not upset,' she answered, but the tears welling in her eyes gave the lie to that statement. 'So, you're here, Arion. What now?'

'I don't know.' And he truly did not.

'They're torturing me, Arion! Drowning me and burning me. And they're going to condemn me and burn me to death. So, what now?'

'I don't know!'

I know what she says is true. I've seen it. If I do nothing, she's going to die on that pyre.

Allana dei Monis took a deep breath, and appeared to compose herself. She then reached out and placed her fingers onto his hand, as her eyes again locked with his. 'Look at me, Arion.' He was overwhelmingly conscious of her touch as he met her stare. She had lowered her soft drawling voice, into an even more compelling and seductive tone. 'We're alike, you and I, Arion. We've just met, and neither of us know how or why we know it. But we're alike. We're the same. You know it. I know it. Maybe we've always been meant to meet. Always been meant to be… together.'

The way that she said the last word had multiple meanings, a deliberately sensual connotation, and again he wanted her desperately. Wanted what she was suggesting, and what she was appearing to offer. As she spoke, it seemed to him that there were echoes of her words in his mind. Echoing whispers, making promises. Tantalising and delightful promises. The room felt like it was spinning around him, causing him to feel dizzy.

'Together?' The word came out from his mouth with a half-choked sound. Was it possible that he had fallen asleep, for just a few moments?

'Yes. Together. In *every* way possible.' Her eyes were still locked to his. She stroked the back of his hand with delicate fingers as she said this last part, and leaned in even closer to him. The whispers in his mind intensified, and he was overcome with desire for her. 'Every way. But only if I survive, Arion. I have to survive. I have to escape from this place.'

I want her. I need her. Need to protect her. To keep her safe.

'But what would you have me do, Allana? I can't just break you out of here. I can't attack a fortress full of Aiduel's Guards.'

'I think I may have a way to get outside of this fort, Arion. But if I do, I need you to help me to escape. To get me away from here. Far away from here, to somewhere safe. To take me away from the Guards, and to stop them from recapturing and killing me. I need you to protect me. To keep me safe. Will you do that for me, Arion?'

At that moment, within the entrancing enchantment of her presence, he felt as if he would do anything for her. Would cast off any prior commitments, whether to his family or to his land or to Kalyane. And he would devote himself to this young woman, to Allana, above all other things. He wanted her, needed her, and that primal desire overrode all other rational thoughts or loyalties.

'Yes, Allana. I will.'

His thoughts were still consumed with her as he lay in his bed that night, in the moments before sleep. Her presence pulsed, from the distance of the fort, and he was therefore vividly aware of her, as she no doubt was of him.

We are something different. To everyone else. But she and I are the same.

Removed from her immediate proximity, the encounter had already taken on something akin to a dreamlike quality. As if he had been drawn under a spell, whilst in her presence. He had wanted her, had shared secrets with her which he had never divulged to anyone else, and he had listened to her plan. And had agreed to his part in it.

His heart was beating fast as he remembered the lust which she had stirred within him, and as he reflected on the promise in her words of the rapture that could await him if he enabled her escape. But was he truly ready to abandon his home, his family, all of his past loyalties, and his future with Kalyane, for a fugitive girl – albeit one who was breathtakingly desirable – who he had spent less than thirty minutes with? And to go where, and to do what?

Now, with the physical separation between them, his rational mind was more capable of raising objections about the madness of what he had agreed to do. And to sow doubts. But, as he closed his eyes and evoked the sensual memory of her image, he was still resolved upon his chosen course of action.

I want her. I need her. Need to protect her. To keep her safe.

She had leaned in to kiss his cheek at the end of their encounter, her soft lips pressing for just a moment against his skin. He reached up to touch that spot, now. That final act had seemed to seal the pact between them.

He was still thinking about the mysterious girl, Allana dei Monis, as he drifted into sleep. And that night, another prophetic vision slid into his dreams.

—

The military force was crossing the ford in the river, in the early morning light. Thousands of men, their allegiance identifiable by the yellow tabards that they were wearing. This was an army of Elannis.

The fording point was narrow, barely enough for eight men to walk abreast, and the crossing was slow. In the middle of the river at that very moment, in the midst of the army, was a group of mounted knights adorned with gleaming, resplendent armour. Royal knights.

He was watching them from an elevated position, some distance away, and after a few moments he recognised the location. He had been here, long ago, as a teenager. They were in Western Canasar. And that recognition caused a mixture of fear and anger. This was a large enemy force, and it was brazenly crossing an Andar river, a tributary of the Canas. On a route which led to Septholme.

The Elannis soldiers were forming into orderly ranks as they reached his side of the river, apparently preparing for battle.

Then he spotted the small second army moving towards the soldiers of Elannis, from the south-east. This new force had the rising dawn sun at their backs, and they were wearing blue tabards. Soldiers of Andar. They were also massed in the thousands, but were significantly outnumbered by the enemy. He looked for the banner of a noble of the House of Sepian, but it was not there. Men of Western Canasar were marching into battle, and neither he nor any other member of his family was leading them.

He felt horrified, as he realised that this small army of Andar appeared to be marching to its doom. This would be a one-sided slaughter.

What was this? When was this to come? And why wasn't he there?

—

The next morning, immediately after they had taken breakfast, he requested a meeting with Gerrion and Charl Koss.

He could see the scepticism in their eyes, as he finished relaying his story.

'I know it sounds mad,' he said to them both, as he was finishing. 'It sounds mad to me, even as I'm saying it. But I had a dream like this before the battle at Fort Lennis. And I acted on it. And we won. I tell you, the place I dreamed about was Moss Ford on the Sept River, and their army was crossing there. We have to get there before them, and in force.'

'But we cannot muster our army, based on a dream, Arion, surely?' Gerrion at least paid Arion the respect of taking his words seriously, but the doubt was clearly evident in the older brother's voice.

'I don't know,' replied Arion. 'At the very least, we could start some preparations? Send orders to some of our banner-men to start mustering troops locally. And send messages to all of the forts and watchtowers on the Canas River, to warn them to be on high alert?'

'That could create a lot of uncertainty and fear in our people, particularly given that they're still recovering from the shock of Father's death.' Gerrion shook his head. 'And if it was to be proven false, my first major act as the new Duke would make me look like a fool.'

Arion knew that his brother was talking sense in the circumstances, but he also believed in the truth of his own dream. 'Yes, I understand your concerns about the impact of Father's death. But could that also be why they're invading? To take advantage of any uncertainty here following the death of the Duke? When we're most vulnerable.'

Gerrion frowned. 'Charl, what do you think?'

Charl Koss addressed both of them as he replied, looking aged by the grief that he had suffered after Duke Conran's death. 'At the very least, we do as Arion has suggested in relation to sending messages. I'll arrange for carrier pigeon messages to be sent immediately to all Canas River forts and watchtowers, telling them to be on high alert.

And asking them to confirm that all is well. There's nothing to lose by doing that, to be cautious.'

'And the mustering of the troops?' asked Gerrion.

Koss responded. 'Well, we could start the process of local musters while we investigate what Arion is saying. If there's no apparent threat after a day, we can cancel it and claim it was a drill. There'd be no loss of face in doing that.'

Gerrion looked from Charl Koss to Arion, clearly deliberating.

Arion spoke up. 'Gerrion. Please, brother. Trust me on this.'

Gerrion appeared to consider this for a few seconds more, before nodding. 'Very well. Charl, please put this into place. Messages to the river forts first. If they all confirm all is well, we may end the muster sooner. And then instructions to the banner-men. Local musters only. Let's not announce an invasion which hasn't happened.'

—

Arion spent that day with Captain Menion Thatcher and the troops of the Household Guard. He was familiarising himself with their officer group, and was focused on getting the troops of Septholme ready to march on short notice. This helped to distract him from his thoughts of Allana dei Monis, and the promise that he had made the day before. But he was aware of her enduring presence, throughout the day.

In the early afternoon, he was summoned alongside Charl Koss and Captain Thatcher, to meet with Gerrion.

When they arrived in the Great Hall, Gerrion was clutching a piece of paper. The new Duke spoke first, his voice trembling. 'Arion, you were right.'

'How so?'

'All of you, read this. It's a message we received a few moments ago, by pigeon. From the Eighth Fort.'

Arion took the message, holding it such that he, Charl Koss and Thatcher could read it at the same time.

> *My Lord,*
>
> *An army of Elannis has attacked and captured the Ninth Fort, and is using the Ninth Bridge to cross into Western Canasar. Massive forces, estimated at fifteen thousand. We have closed the eastern and western gates to the Eighth Fort and are preparing for attack. We have also sent messages to all forts south of us on the river. Western Canasar is being invaded. We will defend to the last man, but otherwise await your instructions, Lord.*
>
> *Yours,*
>
> *Commander Buller, Eighth Fort*

Arion could see that his brother's hand was shaking, as he passed the parchment back to the new Duke.

Gerrion then spoke the words that they were all thinking. 'We are being invaded by Elannis.'

Arion thought for a moment about a beautiful girl imprisoned in an Aiduel's Guards' fortress, and a promise that he had made to her, just a day earlier. During the time when he had been in her enchanting company, in her physical presence, when all other loyalties and aspirations had been washed away. Had been rendered trivial. All he had been able to focus on was her, and the intense lustful desire which she had evoked within him. Saving her. Escaping with her. Ultimately being with her and making love to her. Nothing else had seemed to matter, when compared to that promise of sensual bliss.

But this was the moment that he had worked towards, for his entire life. He was a Knight of the Realm, trained to lead men to war, and his land was suddenly under attack. How could he be expected to keep his promise to Allana, in these circumstances? How, at a time like this, could he choose a girl who he barely knew, and abandon his people and the army of Western Canasar?

Because if I don't save her, she's going to die. But if I abandon House Sepian, we're going to lose this coming war.

477

He was certain that both statements were true. Both outcomes appalling.

But he had to decide what he was going to do, and quickly. And right now, she was not physically present to remind him of why he might be willing to forsake everything else for her.

Without pausing for further reflection, he dropped to his knee in front of Gerrion, and bowed his head before his brother. 'Please appoint me as leader of our armies, brother. I hope that you now believe in me, and in the truth of my vision. I know that I can lead our armies to victory. I know where the enemy is going to be. And I believe that I know how to defeat them. Before The Lord, I swear all of this to be true.'

28

Leanna

—

Year of Our Lord,
After Ascension, 769AA

Within a few hours of having been approached by Sister Colissa, at the Service of Ordainment, Leanna had accepted the offered position of healer in an army field hospital.

The day after that, she had already packed up all of her clothes and equipment, and was saying her tearful goodbyes to her parents and to Amyss. She had been unable to provide them with a clear explanation as to where she was going, or for how long she would be gone, and it had pained her to see the worry in their eyes as she was ready to depart.

Amyss had pulled her into a vice-like hug at the last moment, pressing her forehead into Leanna's neck as emotions of love had emanated from the smaller girl. 'Take care, Lea. I'll miss you so much. Our room at the College already doesn't feel right, now that you're not there. And don't you forget me.'

'I could never forget you, Amyss. And I'll miss you, too, more than you can know. But the next time that we meet, you'll be a priestess, too.'

After finally departing from the three of them, Leanna had felt fortified to know that there were three people in the world who loved her so deeply, and who would be praying for her in the weeks to come.

She travelled to the army encampment in the company of Sister Colissa, along with four of the other ordained healers from the College of Aiduel, and one of the lay assistants. They were travelling on an open-top horse-drawn wagon, in a small column with two other such carts which were laden with medical provisions. After years of confinement in and around the College of Aiduel in Arlais, Leanna was excited to be heading out into the countryside and into the wider world. She felt particularly happy to be escaping the oppressive presence of Aiduel's Guards and Senior Priest El'Patriere. Indeed, the whole group was in good spirits, on the way to their destination.

Within a few hours of their departure, they arrived at the military encampment to the north. The army, which Leanna was soon to learn was titled the Army of Western Elannis, was being assembled in the centre of a sprawling royal estate in the northern Arlais region. Maintaining the secrecy of the muster was clearly regarded as important, and guards were posted at all of the entrances to the royal lands. After Leanna's party had been authorised to pass through the southern entrance, they continued on to the location where the army was camped, which was two miles to the interior. Well away from prying eyes.

Upon her arrival, Leanna was amazed by the spectacle of an assembling army. Tents were pitched in perfect lines into the distance, with thousands of men gathered on the land around her. She could see massed ranks of infantry troops drilling in the fields beside the tents, marching in perfect unison as they practised their manoeuvres. Cavalry ranks were also assembled, with hundreds of horses contained within an enclosure to the west of the main camp. Siege equipment was also visible, in various shapes and forms, on the far side of the site.

She had never seen so many people gathered in one place, and under such apparent discipline and organisation. All of the soldiers were wearing tabards coloured in the yellow of the Imperial Sun of Elannis. After the uncertainties of the recent months, just being witness to such an immense feat of organisation gave her a renewed sense of pride to be a citizen of the Empire. Her faith in the purity and dignity of the Holy Church had been damaged by Comenis and El'Patriere, but in front of a gathering such as this there was no doubting the magnificence of her nation.

In that moment, she also peered around the site, looking for any glimpses of red cloaks and red sashes. But to her great relief, there were none.

Lord Aiduel, thank you for bringing me into such a great undertaking. And thank you even more, for not calling the Guards to join us.

—

Leanna was to spend three days waiting at the muster site. There was a steady stream of new arrivals across those days, which continually bolstered the number of soldiers amassing there.

A second group of healers arrived a day after the Arlais party. They had travelled to the encampment from the city of Boralais, which was further to the south. They were led by a Brother Perrien, who was a very tall and skinny grey-haired priest in his late fifties in age. He and Sister Colissa clearly knew and respected each other, although Leanna noted that their exchanges were largely formal and professional, rather than warm or friendly.

At night-time during those first few days, Leanna was sharing a tent with three other female healers. She quickly realised that someone other than Amyss would now be witness to her often-troubled dreaming. The first morning after she had suffered from the recurring dream and had woken the others, it was indeed remarked upon. But the comment was only delivered in a wry manner by an elderly priestess from Boralais, and with no acrimony, which Leanna was thankful for.

Leanna had plenty of opportunity during the waiting days to wander around the site, and to more closely observe the soldiers and their preparations. She was particularly interested to walk closer to a large and impressive marquee tent, which was in the centre of the encampment.

This tent's canvas was coloured yellow and gold, and it was emblazoned with the symbol of a hawk. Waving from a pole raised through the centre of that tent was a flag which she understood carried the colours of the Emperor's son and heir, Prince Markon El'Augustus. His banner bore the image of a blazing Imperial Sun, with the same silhouette of a hawk across it. Leanna understood from Sister Colissa that 'The Hawk' was the moniker which had been ascribed to the Prince by his adoring soldiers, after his victories in the conquests of the countries of Sennam and Patran. And now he was here, to lead the Army of Western Elannis to similar glory.

Leanna saw the Prince from a close distance only once during the three days at the muster site. She spotted him on that occasion as he was inspecting the cavalry, while she was walking by. He was easily discernible by the gleaming armour worn both by him, and by his surrounding retinue of bodyguards. The prince was a tall man who appeared to be in his early thirties, with hair as blonde as his cousin El'Patriere. But there the similiarities ended. Even a brief observation highlighted to Leanna that the Prince demonstrated a sense of camaraderie with the men around him, and moved with an air of nobility, which the Senior Priest would be incapable of replicating.

Lord Aiduel, please bless Prince Markon, and keep him safe.

—

On the morning after Leanna's third night of camping at the site, Sister Colissa gathered all of the healers for an announcement. She informed them that they were to pack away their tents and equipment, and that they would be setting out to travel to their next destination after sunset.

One of the lay assistants asked a question in response to that, voicing what they were all thinking. 'Does that mean that the army is going to war, Sister?'

Colissa nodded, and said, 'I think so. Everyone, get some rest during the day today. We'll be travelling tonight. And tomorrow... well, I suspect that tomorrow we will have some work to do.'

Later that day, in the final hours of the afternoon, Colissa called all of the healers together again for a final briefing. She talked in detail then about how they were to organise and conduct themselves once the army went to war, and once casualties started to be suffered.

After that briefing, they gathered for a last meal before their pending departure. Colissa was again asked to share any information which she had gleaned about the army's intentions. Leanna and the other healers were sitting in a semi-circle around her, fully attentive, as the senior healer replied.

'This is as much as I know,' said Colissa. 'But I've been told it by someone who was told it by someone else, so who can be sure if it's correct? But anyway, I understand that our beloved Emperor, may Aiduel bless him, wants to add Western Canasar to the Empire. I've been told that the army's plan is to invade and conquer the western side of the Canas peninsular, and then to hold it until Andar surrenders it.'

Brother Perrien was seated beside her, and spoke up in response. 'I've heard the same thing, Colissa, so there must be truth in it. We shall all be blessed to be part of a glorious moment of history, as the Empire expands into the west!'

Colissa shook her head, smiling ruefully. 'You'll have us all singing the imperial anthem next, Perrien! But you and I know better than any of us here that this war will be an ugly business, and that thoughts of glory don't survive for long after the first cartload of bodies has arrived. But I must admit to sharing your optimism. I understand that we now have over thirteen thousand infantry and archers gathered here, and a further two thousand cavalry. And that more will be following behind, to join the army at a later time. So I confess to sharing your sentiments, Brother. I think that we're all going to be part of a difficult, but glorious, endeavour.'

Leanna had nodded, listening to their exchange with rapt attention, and experiencing a mixture of excitement and apprehension. She could also feel that sense of nervous anticipation and uncertainty being echoed in the emotions emanating from all of the other healers.

Lord Aiduel, please help me to serve my country and to save lives, and please bless the brave soldiers of the Empire.

—

They set off on their wagons at dusk that day. Leanna's open-top wagon was towards the back of the snaking procession of people, horses and carts which were organised to depart with meticulous efficiency.

The column of soldiers and camp-followers initially travelled southwards to leave the grounds of the royal estate. They then joined with the main road between Arlais and Andar, and turned westwards. The sun was disappearing below the western horizon in front of Leanna, as her wagon finally made its turn onto that road and towards the west.

'This confirms my expectations,' said Colissa, from the front of the wagon, as she gestured towards the setting sun and their direction of travel. 'We're heading west. Towards the Ninth Bridge. I'm guessing that will be the place where our armies attack.'

Leanna knew enough about geography from her time at school, to be aware that the wide Canas River marked the boundary between the Empire of Elannis, and the country of Andar. And that there were twelve separate bridges across the hundreds of miles of the great river, each of which was sandwiched between opposing military forts. At the western end of each bridge spanning the mighty water was a fortress owned and manned by troops of Andar. At the eastern end, an Elannis fort,

'Why the Ninth Bridge, Sister?'

'That's the northernmost of the bridges leading into Western Canasar,' replied Colissa. 'The Tenth, Eleventh and Twelfth bridges lead into the lands of Berun, which I don't believe are our target. All of the land south of the Ninth Bridge is Western Canasar. I believe that our armies intend to capture the enemy fortress, and then turn south. But again, I'm just speculating.'

Their wagon continued to travel through the night, covering the twenty-five mile distance to the border. They moved at a reduced pace, that was consistent with the marching soldiers which the cart journeyed behind. When darkness had come fully upon them, Colissa led all of the healers in quiet prayers. Leanna joined in with these prayers fervently, as she clutched a small statue of The Lord Aiduel On The Tree.

Lord Aiduel, please bring us victory tomorrow, and protect your faithful.

Colissa then encouraged all of the healers on the wagon to lie down and to try to sleep. Leanna did this, sandwiched between Colissa on one side and a male healer on the other side. Sleep was initially hard to attain, with the wagon jolting regularly and with constant exposure to the chilly night air, but eventually she dozed off into a restful slumber.

—

Leanna's first experience of the grim nature of war came on the following morning. The Army of Western Elannis, at the Ninth Bridge of the Canas River, was to storm the enemy fortress at dawn.

Leanna was awoken on the now stationary wagon in the pre-dawn half-light, prior to the attack. She sleepily raised herself up and looked to the west as she stretched. Immediately, she spotted a mighty castle sitting on the banks of what had to be the Canas River, half a mile away. The castle appeared to be eighty metres across, with grey stone walls which were ten metres high. However, it was dwarfed in scale by the grandeur of the river, which she estimated was hundreds of metres in width. Leanna could not see a bridge.

She turned to a Brother healer from Arlais, while still blinking the sleep from her bleary eyes. 'Where are we?'

'We're to the east of the Ninth Bridge.'

'I don't see a bridge? And what castle is that?'

'That's our Ninth Fort, Leanna,' he replied. 'If you squint, you can just about see the Imperial Sun flag waving from that right hand tower. But we can't see the Ninth Bridge from here, or the enemy's fortress, because they're both hidden behind our castle. Come on, Colissa needs us to start setting up the field hospital.'

All of the healers worked together to rapidly erect and prepare the hospital. Their hospital tent was at the front of an enclosure of army followers, at the side of the main road which led towards the river. There were few remaining infantry soldiers with them now, but the Elannis cavalry troops were assembled in massed ranks to the east.

At dawn, with the hospital pavilion fully established, Leanna and the others took their breakfast. There was a palpable sense of nervousness across the group of healers, which Leanna could have picked up on even without her ability, and there was no chatter in these final moments. But for just a few minutes the area around their tent was quiet and serene, with the white canvas walls disturbed only by the gentle breeze rippling across them.

Then the noises of distant battle started to carry across to Leanna. Men shouting and screaming. Weapons clashing. More screams. The sounds were muted by distance, and were sometimes confusing to define. But they were deeply unsettling, nonetheless.

Lord Aiduel, please take care of our soldiers. Please protect them.

Leanna and her fellow healers started to bustle around each other as they finished their preparations. Were the surgical instruments clean? Were the painkilling brews available in sufficient quantities? And were the unoccupied beds made tidily enough to satisfy Sister Colissa's inspection?

Then, within half an hour of the battle starting, the first cart of wounded and maimed soldiers was rolling along the road from the west, and arriving at the tent entrance. Suddenly, Leanna's world was transformed into a maelstrom of blood-soaked bandages and agonised screams. Addressing the anguished suffering of men who had been cut, impaled, crushed and burned.

Lord Aiduel, she thought to herself in those first chaotic moments, *please give me the strength to endure this, and to do my best for these poor soldiers.*

In the following three hours, she was exposed to more death and gore than she had witnessed in eighteen months of assisting in the hospital at the College of Aiduel. But without the limited experience which she had already gained from those duties, she doubted that she would have been able to cope. One moment she was dressing or stitching a wound, and the next she found herself summoned to hold down an injured soldier as a limb was gruesomely removed.

Sister Colissa was directing matters, alongside Brother Perrien. These two senior healers were also the lead surgeons within the field hospital. However, there were moments during those first hours when Leanna considered that butchery would have been a more accurate description of the work which the surgeons were required to carry out.

The carts carrying the injured continued to arrive for over two hours after the first one had trundled into view. By the time of the final cart, over fifty grievously wounded and an even greater number of less seriously injured soldiers had entered into or passed through the field hospital. A number of the critically injured casualties entered the canvas tent with only a frail hold on life, and left it having lost their personal battle to stay alive.

For the duration of those hours, Leanna was assailed from every angle by the emotions of these suffering men.

PAIN. FEAR. PANIC. PAIN. SORROW. TERROR. PAIN!

The intensity of this anguish varied from man to man. She was thankful to Aiduel that her experience in the College hospital with

Kennet had prepared her for such external agonies, otherwise she would have been unable to bear it.

Lord Aiduel, please help me to ease their suffering. And give us all the strength to endure this, Lord.

As she moved from patient to patient, and from corner to corner of the field hospital, there was little time to pause or to reflect amidst the bustle of activity. There was never an opportunity for her to fall into a trance-like state, or to attempt to use her Aiduel-given power of healing to save more lives. Nor would she have been comfortable to attempt it, with so many witnesses.

Instead, she tended to the wounded using conventional means, her robes soon becoming covered with blood and gore. By the time that the tide of new casualties had finally ceased she was breathless, her arms aching, and her ears ringing with the cries of the maimed and the dying.

—

After the flow of the wounded had ended, word soon came through to all of the camp followers that the enemy fortress had fallen, and that Elannis had secured victory.

Within minutes, the cavalry was passing by their hospital to travel westwards towards the Ninth Bridge. Shortly afterwards, various other camp followers, including the supply and mess wagons, started to follow the route towards the river.

Leanna and the other healers remained at the field hospital, tending to those of the wounded who were too seriously injured to move themselves. At various times during the following hours, Leanna could see rising spirals of thick smoke in the west. This reminded her of the grim spectacle of the pyres lit to the north of Arlais, on Seventh-Day.

Colissa saw her staring at one point, and the older woman's voice was emotionless as she stated, 'They're burning the bodies of the enemy, Leanna.'

Leanna could not think of anything meaningful to say in response to that. Instead, she made a small prayer to The Lord to ask him to ensure the safe passage of the souls of the dead into heaven.

Later that afternoon, they were instructed that the army intended to move off again, on the following day. The remaining injured were to be transferred into the Ninth Fort of Elannis before then, to be tended to by the physician at the fortress. Colissa organised the loading and transportation of the wounded, and then Leanna accompanied one of the wagons of injured men towards the fort and the river, sitting on the front seat next to the driver.

The Canas River looked magnificent in the afternoon sun as she approached it, as sunlight glimmered across the surface of the sparkling water. Again, it seemed to render the Elannis fortress rising from its banks insignificant. As Leanna drew closer to the fort, she could more clearly see that a rectangular tunnel ran through its centre. The tunnel was maybe six metres high by eight metres across, appearing large enough for carts and wagons to pass through in opposite directions. She observed that the tunnel ran for approximately forty metres through the fort, and that there were four separate and massive portcullises along its length, each of them currently raised. Right now, the tunnel was a bustle of activity, with soldiers clad in the colours of the Imperial Sun moving hurriedly in all directions.

Her wagon passed into the mouth of the tunnel, and from this position she could at last gain sight of the Ninth Bridge. This grand structure appeared to run for over three hundred metres, and was raised ten metres above the powerful waterway beneath. It ended at a fortress on the far banks which mirrored the one which she had just passed into. Soldiers of Elannis were still crossing over the bridge to that fort on the western side, and she immediately noticed that the flag of the Imperial Sun was raised high above that far castle.

She wondered about how many men of Elannis had died today to capture that fortress? And how many of the enemy had lost their lives in an attempt to thwart that victory? The thought made her shiver, but she knew that today's deaths would not be the last casualties of this invasion.

Lord Aiduel, please give me the courage to help the men of Elannis, and to save lives.

—

Shortly after sunrise on the following morning, the Army of Western Elannis had departed from the Ninth Bridge. The army was moving swiftly southwards into the land of Western Canasar, marching deeper into foreign and enemy territory.

The horse-drawn wagons of the healers were again towards the rear of the column of troops and army followers. For this first day of travel within Andar lands, the massive procession of people and animals remained on a wide carriageway which was called the River Road. The River Canas remained on their immediate left for the entirety of the day, iridescently glorious under the beating sun.

On a handful of occasions, the army passed through or near to small Andar settlements, which were adjacent to the River Road. At those times, Leanna observed the efficient and ruthless way in which stores were raided and goods were requisitioned. This work of looting typically took place just before Leanna's section of the Elannis column arrived. However, on several occasions she could still hear the shouted objections of the locals as her wagon passed by. She was also often witness to raging fires which had been started by the passing army.

Their travel that day ended in the late-afternoon, when they reached another massive bridge across the river, which was again flanked by a pair of fortresses. Leanna deduced that they were at the Eighth Bridge. The fortress at the western end of the bridge still flew the flag of Andar from its highest tower. From a distance, Leanna could see that its portcullises were lowered, and that enemy soldiers lined its battlements.

The camp of the Elannis army was promptly established on open ground a few hundred metres away from the Andar fort, and once again the hospital tent was erected. Leanna spent the remainder of the daylight hours staring towards the enemy fortress, and wondering if and when her country's army was going to launch their assault. She later watched with interest as a number of Elannis soldiers dug what Brother Perrien explained were earthworks, one hundred metres from the fort, blocking all of its approaches.

However, at no point was an attack ordered, and Leanna went to her bed that night grateful that there were no freshly wounded soldiers to tend to.

—

The next day, Leanna was surprised to observe that the vast majority of the army was decamping to move south again, without an assault on the Eighth Fort of Andar having been ordered. As her wagon passed along the closest spot to the western fortress, still on the River Road, she could see that a detachment of Elannis troops had been left behind. These soldiers were manning the earthworks, facing towards the fort.

The third day of the invasion followed a similar pattern to the one which had preceded it. The army covered a significant distance along the River Road, and passed through a number of swiftly ransacked settlements. One of the other healers, who Leanna understood had grown up near to the Canas River, pointed out that there was no visible traffic on the water. They told Leanna that this was unheard of in their lifetime.

The army ended its day at what Leanna knew must be the Seventh Bridge. Once more, a contingent of soldiers were tasked with the construction of earthworks, facing the western Seventh Fort. Andar soldiers again stood defiant behind their battlements, making insulting gestures towards the Elannis forces.

Leanna was gradually becoming more accustomed to this new life as a follower of the army, but she and the other healers were all agitated as to when there would be another significant battle. Each night, she would kneel before her bedroll and pray to Aiduel for the safety of the soldiers of Elannis. She wondered whether the news of the invasion of Western Canasar had reached the city of Arlais, and if so whether her parents and Amyss now realised what Leanna had become involved in.

Lord Aiduel, please look after my parents and Amyss, and give them the reassurance that you will keep me safe.

—

On the fourth day of the invasion of Western Canasar, the Elannis army continued to travel southwards along the River Road. Colissa noted that they would reach a major Andar town called Canasholme, if they remained on the road all day. Canasholme was built on the land to the west of the Sixth Bridge.

At midday, Leanna was leaning back against the side of her moving wagon, daydreaming whilst rubbing her leg to ease a cramp. A crash of noise from up ahead jolted her out of her reverie. She looked up, and felt an instant rush of fear when she spotted enemy cavalry, wearing the blue tabards of Andar. They were attacking the Elannis supply wagons, and assaulting the occupants of those wagons. This was happening just over a hundred metres ahead of Leanna's own position.

There was then a frenzy of activity around Leanna, as she watched the events of the attack. She could see at least fifty of the mounted enemy, who were ruthlessly attacking the Elannis folk who were now rushing in panic from the wagons up ahead. Screams carried to her, and Leanna and the other healers huddled down on the inside of their wagon. Elannis infantry soldiers hurried past and around their vehicles, some remaining to stand guard beside them while others rushed directly towards the melee. Then a larger contingent of Elannis cavalry appeared from the south, smashing into the enemy ranks, and within seconds the Andar force had turned and fled.

Leanna's heart was beating hard throughout, and she could feel the fear pulsing towards her from all of the other occupants of her wagon.

The whole of the fray had taken no more than a handful of minutes, but that was sufficient time for there to have been a significant number of wounded amongst the Elannis column. For the first time, Leanna properly understood that this invasion posed a genuine risk of death or injury to herself and her colleagues, even in the company of such a mighty army. Prior to that, she had been holding onto a misplaced sense of security. But if the attack had been launched just a minute later, her own transport would have been in the middle of the assault. She could easily have been one of those casualties.

Leanna's wagon was soon rolling forward again, and then passing alongside the place which had been at the heart of the sudden skirmish. Two supply wagons were ablaze, and a number of bodies – predominantly those of Elannis camp supporters – were scattered around the wagons. The majority of the victims appeared to be dead, but a handful were calling out pitifully for help. Leanna spotted a young boy amongst the wounded. She guessed that he was thirteen years old at most. He had a deep gash running down the entire left hand side of his body, from his shoulder to his stomach.

Colissa shouted for their wagons to be brought to a halt to allow them to assist the wounded, but an Elannis cavalry officer immediately rode towards her. The man banged on the side of the wagon and barked his order at the senior healer and the driver. 'Keep moving! We've been ambushed. You're not stopping here.'

Leanna peered around at the moaning injured forms, realising that they were about to abandon their wounded. She pointed towards the teenage boy, his hand raised towards her wagon. 'Him! At least carry him onto here.'

A couple of infantrymen responded to her request. They hurriedly lifted the boy, and rolled him over the side of the wagon.

Leanna and her colleagues moved the youth into position in the centre of their floor area, as the vehicle started to move again.

Now that she was near to him, Leanna noted that the injured boy was even younger than she had first estimated. He had mousy hair and a thin, freckled face. He was breathing too quickly, too erratically, and his expression portrayed a mixture of pain and panic. His clothing was shredded along the line of the red bloody gash. Emotions burst outwards from the boy.

PANIC. TERROR. PAIN. TERROR.

Leanna leaned over him. 'Try to stay calm. We're with you now. What's your name?'

'It's Hann, Sister,' replied the boy, his voice high-pitched and weak. 'Where's my Dad, the Cook, Sister? Where's Dad?' His face was pale, and his breathing was becoming more frantic.

'Shhhh, try to stay calm,' replied Leanna. She then turned to the others. 'Where's our equipment? We must try to save him—'

Leanna felt a hand on her shoulder, and looked around to see Colissa crouched beside her. The older woman shook her head, sadly, then whispered, 'It's too late, Lea. Ease his passing.'

Leanna turned back to the boy, and as she properly regarded his wounds, she knew that Colissa was correct. The long gash ran through the boy's stomach, and was deep, and it was clearly a mortal wound. She placed her hand to cradle the back of his head, and whispered, 'You just rest, Hann. We'll find your dad. We'll bring him to you.'

The boy did not answer, his face becoming paler and his chest heaving ever more urgently, as if he was struggling to find his breath. His body was shaking.

And for just a fragment of a moment, Leanna thought about her power. Of the gift of healing, which had been granted to her by The Lord Aiduel. In that instant, even in the midst of the bustle of the wagon, she slipped into the trance-like state which she had transitioned into three times before in her life. The boy's injury exploded into view. Black agony running along the length of the wound, writhing and pulsing. Dark, throbbing, fatal agony. With a wound like this, what would happen if she tried to repeat what she had done with Kennet? Could her gift do anything to restore an injury that was so severe?

Lord Aiduel, can I save him? Can I use the powers that you've given me to save him, Lord?

But, even in the tranquillity of the trance, she was too aware of the people around her. Much too aware of the number of observers who would witness any action which she might take, whether or not it succeeded. Including some of the healers from Boralais, who she did not know well. Any of them might be potential accusers who could declare her a witch or a heretic, if she acted now. Or who might report her to Aiduel's Guards.

Therefore, influenced by this awareness, it was her own conscious decision to pull herself out of the alertness of the trance. She was again just an ordinary healer, holding a dying boy.

He died within minutes, his life bleeding away on the wooden floor of the wagon, and afterwards she felt ashamed by her inaction.

Lord Aiduel, please forgive me for my weakness and for my fears, and please grant this boy's soul a safe journey to heaven.

—

Later, in the early evening, the Army of Western Elannis established camp to the north of the Andar town of Canasholme. The sturdy town walls and battlements were visible half a mile to the south. Even further away than that, Leanna could see the imposing structures of the Sixth Bridge and the Sixth Fort, enclosed within the walls of the town.

After sunset, Sister Colissa again gathered all of the healers together. 'I've just had instructions about what's going to happen at first light tomorrow,' she announced. 'The army is going to split. As I understand it, three thousand infantry and five hundred cavalry are going to remain here to capture the town of Canasholme, and

495

to take control of the whole of the River Road and the bridges. I've decided to leave three healers here to remain with that army; Sister Dotsi, who'll be in charge, Brother Reuben and Sister Willow. The remainder of you will stay with Brother Perrien and me, with the main army under Prince Markon. That army is to move off at first light tomorrow.'

Leanna was pleased that she would continue to stay under Colissa's charge.

Perrien asked the only question. 'Do you know where we're heading for, Colissa?'

'I think so,' replied the Sister. 'From what I've been told, the main army will be leaving the River Road now, and heading inland, to avoid being delayed by the battle against and capture of Canasholme. I understand that Markon's army will then at some point plan to cross the Sept River. I can only assume therefore that our target must be the capital, Septholme.'

After the attack on the moving column earlier that day, Leanna was more aware now of the danger of the undertaking of which she was part. That awareness made her more appreciative that such danger must only increase, the further that they moved into enemy land. If they travelled to Septholme, they would be deep within Andar territory. Would they at some point encounter its main army?

She shuddered at the thought of the bloodshed and carnage which could result from such a confrontation.

29

Corin

—

Year of Our Lord,
After Ascension, 769AA

Corin watched as Borrik stalked towards him across the circular fighting area formed in the centre of the village of Karn. The clan chief moved with a quick confidence, his axe held in two hands in front of him.

The fearsome warrior was not charging recklessly, but nor did he look like he had any fear about the threat which his opponent posed. Corin knew that if he came within reach of that axe, he was as good as dead. Perhaps one swing of the mighty weapon to break his shield and his arm, and then a second to end him.

Corin focused, and once again invisible tendrils emerged from his mind, this time erupting outwards with greater velocity. They arrowed in towards Borrik as the large clan chief approached. Then, as the giant warrior arrived within striking range of Corin, once again raising his great-axe, the tendrils surged against his mind. Fighting for control.

The mental assault caused the clan chief to pause, for just a moment. His axe did not swing downwards, and Corin took that opportunity to skip past and away from his opponent, moving himself out of reach of the weapon. He heard Borrik roar with frustration, and once again Corin could feel the unseen connections being expelled from his opponent's mind.

Borrik spun around, his face angry. 'What is this? What shaman's tricks are these?'

This time, he charged directly towards Corin, axe drawn back. Corin instinctively renewed the assault on his opponent's mind. At the same time as Borrik closed into range, Corin's mental attacks struck home, decisively, and he screamed his order to Borrik.

STOP! STOP! STOP! STOP! STOP!

Borrik's assault changed from decisive to stilted and hesitant, the great-axe again failing to swing. In that moment, Corin swept past him and sliced his own axe-head against his opponent's left arm. His attack struck home, scything across the triceps of the arm, cutting flesh and muscle.

Corin dodged away as quickly as he could, as Borrik roared again, although this time in reaction to pain. The connection of metal on flesh, and the hurt it triggered, appeared to give Borrik a surge of extra willpower to repel the mental assault. Once more, Corin felt himself cast out from his opponent's mind.

Corin could hear the shocked excitement of the crowd around him while he backed away from his opponent, as realisation grew amongst them that this could actually be a contest. Borrik's arm had a deep gash on it, and blood was pouring from the wound. The clan chief's face had adopted a maniacal look, and he screamed in fury before charging again.

Corin watched his opponent's feet pounding towards him, and he redoubled his efforts to take control of Borrik's mind. On this occasion, as he was doing so, time seemed to slow down around him. Making Borrik's movements seem more sluggish, and causing the cries of the crowd to echo morbidly in Corin's ears. The unseen connections swirled around Borrik's thoughts, seeking entry, and then with an effort of willpower Corin emphatically overcame his opponent's resistance. This time, the instruction which was carried across the link between them was resounding.

FALL! FALL! FALL! FALL! FALL!

It worked. The clan chief appeared to lose balance as he closed the distance between them, and then he was toppling over, falling onto his front, directly before Corin. Immediately, Corin chopped his axe downwards, and the blade bit deep into the back of his opponent's leg. Cutting into the upper thigh, slicing through to the bone. Borrik screamed in agony, then rolled his prone body over as Corin once again dodged away from him.

Corin knew that he had control of this fight, now. Knew that the contest was his. He watched as Borrik tried to raise himself to his feet, at the same time as he could feel the clan chief trying and failing to push this invading presence out of his mind. Corin stepped several paces away, again keeping out of reach of the axe.

Borrik called out, and Corin thought that he could detect fear in the giant warrior's voice. 'What witchcraft is this?' The clan chief addressed his words to the gathering of villagers. 'He uses spells. Witchcraft! He's cursed.'

There was a grumble from the crowd in response to this. Corin did not look around, keeping his eyes on his opponent, but he was alarmed by the cries that he could hear.

'Witchcraft!'

'Demon!'

Borrik had by now managed to raise himself to a standing position again.

Then Corin heard another shout, this time from Agbeth. 'He's not a witch. He's blessed. By the Gods! They visited him, in the far north! And gave him powers. How else can he control a felrin?'

There was more murmuring in response to this, some positive, as Borrik tried to stagger forwards, dragging his badly injured leg.

This time Corin did not step away, secure in the knowledge that he still controlled Borrik's mind.

STOP! STOP! STOP! STOP! STOP!

The clan chief ground to a halt. The large warrior was losing a lot of blood, from both his arm and his leg, but he resolutely maintained this upright position.

Corin raised his axe and shield. He was feeling out of breath, but otherwise was in much better condition than his opponent. 'It doesn't have to be like this, Borrik. I never wanted this. Just let me back into the clan. Please. Accept my gift, end my banishment. I don't want to be clan chief. I don't want to do this. Just end my banishment.'

Borrik roared again and shouted, 'Fuck you, shaman!'

Corin could feel his opponent pushing back against his domination. Pushing back with a fury which caused Corin sudden concern that the clan chief might yet break free of his control.

Borrik then lurched forwards, in a manner reminiscent of how Blackpaw had pursued Agbeth on the frozen lake. Corin sensed the clan chief's fury lashing against the controls which had been placed over his mind. This might not be over.

STOP! STOP! STOP! STOP! STOP!

But Borrik was wilfully resisting, and Corin was not yet ready to kill the other man. He had never killed another person, and he did not want to start like this. 'Please surrender, Borrik. End this. I don't want to do this.'

Borrik lurched forwards again, still fighting Corin's control. Coming closer, axe raised. 'Fucking kill me, or get ready to die, shaman!'

Corin retreated several steps, experiencing an unpleasant echo of the paralysis which had once come upon him in the Anath village. He had failed to strike a killing blow on that occasion, an act which had indirectly led to all of this, and even now he did not want to kill the other man. Borrik did not deserve to die. But what choice was there?

The giant warrior pushed forwards again, albeit sluggishly, and this time he was only two metres from Corin. Straining to make the killing attack. Still, Corin hesitated.

Then Agbeth's voice carried over the combat, once more. 'Kill him, Corin! You must kill him! For me!'

A recollection of Kernon's earlier threat to Agbeth came into Corin's mind. An image of what might happen to his wife, were he to lose. At that moment, he acted.

Corin's axe chopped down, slicing deeply into the join between the neck and shoulder of the clan chief, and killing him instantly.

Borrik crashed lifelessly to the floor. Corin stepped away, breathing heavily.

Around him there was sudden silence. Silence, broken only when Blackpaw howled, announcing his master's victory across all of the lands of the Karn.

—

As Blackpaw's howl faded away, in the immediate aftermath of Corin's defeat of Borrik, a stunned silence pervaded the crowd gathered in the village of Karn.

Corin raised his bloodied axe, arm extended above his head, and made a slow, weary rotation to face each of the surrounding villagers in turn. There was uncertainty and anxiety on each face; Borrik had ruled their village for over twenty years, and none of them could have anticipated this outcome. Worse than that, hostility was expressed on a number of faces, particularly amongst those who were part of Borrik's inner circle of family and friends.

Corin transmitted a message to Blackpaw. It was time for the felrin to come to his side, in case things got any nastier.

It was Agbeth who finally broke the silence, once again crying out in her loudest voice, 'All hail the new clan chief! Corin! Chosen by the Gods!'

Corin stared at his wife, feeling bewildered. She was no longer being restrained by Kernon, and she was regarding Corin with pride. However, there was no response to her proclamation for a number of seconds. Corin's arm remained raised, holding the killing axe aloft. He could sense Blackpaw getting closer.

The next voice to speak surprised him. It was that of Akob, who in turn had now raised his weapon. 'All hail the new clan chief. Corin. Chosen by the Gods!'

Corin looked at his father, feeling surprise that his true name had been used. There was an unfamiliar expression in Akob's face, something almost akin to respect.

The call was then repeated, by Orga, Corin's mother. Then others took up the shout. Within seconds, the vast majority of the surrounding villagers were repeating the cry. Only Kernon, and a number of those closest to Borrik, were not adding their voices to the chorus.

Corin was sombrely bemused. Of all of the outcomes which he had planned and imagined for today, this one had not featured. Borrik's body lay face-down on the floor, close by, reminding him of the life that he had just taken. And although he could hear the words of the crowd, the dawning reality that he was suddenly clan chief of the Karn left him feeling dazed.

He was aware that Blackpaw was in the village, and was hidden out of sight behind a building. He also knew that he had to speak to the gathered crowd, and the nearby presence of the creature gave him greater courage to do this.

'I did not come here today, seeking this,' he announced, turning slowly on the spot as he spoke. 'Nor did I want Borrik's death. Or seek the chiefdom. But if this responsibility has become mine, then I will take it. I will lead the Karn as best as I can. I will try to protect our people and our lands. And I will be just and fair.'

There was not much reaction as he was speaking. However, he could see a sullen expression on Kernon's face. How appalled must his elder brother be, at this moment, to see the Runt of the family in such a position?

Corin continued. 'I brought a gift for the clan, today. A felrin, to fight for us. Borrik would not accept it, but it remains my gift. I will call it to us, now, and I ask that no one attacks or threatens it. It will not harm anyone in this village, unless I tell it to, or it is attacked. Understood?' There were muted nods, around him. 'Very well. Don't panic, when it appears. Remain calm. Blackpaw, come.'

At the same instant as saying that, he transmitted the instruction to the creature, and within moments it appeared, silently striding towards the edge of the circle of people. Its claws were extended and its jaws were open, revealing its deadly fangs. There were more gasps and cries from a number of the villagers, and Corin repeated his advice to them to stay calm.

The people on the side of the circle closest to the felrin backed away from it, and it stalked through the gap which appeared, stopping by Corin's side. It bent its head down, and he stroked the creature's neck.

Corin gestured for Agbeth to come forward, and she limped into the centre of the clearing. 'I will treat everyone here right, and with respect. And I ask the same of all of you. My name is Corin. Not Runt. My wife's name is Agbeth. Not Cripple. I will not accept that name any longer.' He looked towards Kernon in particular as he said this. 'And the felrin's name is Blackpaw. It will protect anyone here, unless you attack it, me or Agbeth.

'And now, I ask everyone to go from here. Borrik's family must move his body, and tonight we must follow the rites to honour his death. He was a great leader of this clan, for a long time. Tonight, we will mourn Borrik. Tomorrow, I will talk about the future.'

—

That night, some hours after the funeral pyre for the giant warrior had faded to embers and ashes, Corin and Agbeth were cuddled together. They were inside the building which served as the home of the clan chief, lying in what had been Borrik's bed.

503

Borrik's wife had been moved out of the home, and henceforth was to live with one of his adult daughters. Although both Corin and Agbeth had felt guilty about this eviction, Akob and the other elder warriors had insisted that they take immediate possession of the residence.

By the standards of Karn, it was a large home, and far more impressive than the small lean-to which they had lived in for the last two years. Blackpaw was resting outside the front entrance, a fearsome deterrent to anyone who might seek to endanger them.

'Don't ever do that to me again, Corin,' Agbeth said, as she rested with her head on his chest, hugging him tightly. 'I thought that I was going to lose you, today.'

'That makes two of us. I promise that I had no idea, though, Agbeth, that it would all happen like that.'

'Are you feeling OK? About killing Borrik?'

'I'm not sure. I feel a little... sick inside, about it. I didn't want to do it. But, in the end, I think I did everything that I could to prevent it. That at least makes me feel better.'

'You're the clan chief, though, Corin. Can you believe it yet?'

'No. It doesn't seem real. Clan Chief of the Karn. Me. No one would have believed it possible. Least of all me.'

'You did it, though, Corin. I'm so proud of you.'

'And I'm so thankful for you. I couldn't have done it today, Agbeth, wouldn't have survived, without your bravery. You saved me.'

'I was more scared than brave. Scared of losing you. I don't think I've ever moved so fast though as when I jumped on you. And my ribs are still hurting.'

He hugged her, then laughed. 'And those things that you said. Blessed by the Gods? Chosen by the Gods? Where did all of that come from?'

She chuckled. 'They could see you controlling a felrin, Corin. And somehow controlling Borrik. Better for them to think that the Gods have chosen you, than that you're a witch or an evil spirit. And what's more, I think almost all of them believe it now, too.'

'And you're going to make me keep pretending that's the case, aren't you?'

'You have to. The more they believe that the Gods have given you powers, the more they'll follow you. And I must admit, there's something a little exciting about being married to the clan chief. And to the Chosen One.'

'Oh, really? Wife of the Chosen One, eh? I'm not sure *all* of them believe it, though. But really, Agbeth, can *you* believe it? I've become the clan chief. From now on, they're meant to follow what I say. I make the decisions, and I judge the law. But compared to some of them, I'm just a boy, and they must already be thinking that. I've only been on one raid, and that was a disaster. How can I lead them? How can they trust me?'

'There's more to leading them than war and raids, Corin. You maybe don't see it yet, but I know you and I see it clearly. Even if you haven't been on lots of raids, you're clever and *wise*. Certainly, wiser than most of them, and wiser than Borrik ever was. And you are kind, and fair, and good. My good husband. Most of them only know how to be nasty and vicious. But you and I know better. You know better. There's a different way to rule them. To teach them. To be better people. And I believe in you to find that way.'

'You have so much faith in me, Agbeth. What shall I say to the elder warriors tomorrow, then?'

'You need to think about it. Think about what you would like Karn to be. What you would like it to become. I trust you to find the right way.'

He kissed her head, and she turned her body onto her side and snuggled back against him. She fell asleep before he did, and he lay there, reflecting on the events of the day, and thinking about the responsibility which he had taken on. And pondering about what he would say, on the next day.

The next morning, prior to the village council, Corin was approached by Kernon. Corin had decided that the safest place for Blackpaw to be for the next few days was directly at his side, and the felrin was walking alongside him at this moment, hunched forward on its front paws. Corin observed that his brother's eyes were glancing nervously towards the creature, as he drew closer.

'Corin? May I speak?'

Corin noted that his proper name had been used, which he took as a positive sign. 'Yes, Kernon.'

'I wanted to talk about what I said yesterday. About Agbeth. It was just a joke. You know I didn't mean it, yes?'

Corin sent an instruction to Blackpaw, and the creature stood up and stretched out to its full standing height, by his side. Corin could see the intimidating effect that it had on his brother, which pleased him, but he also recognised that Kernon had just used Agbeth's real name.

'Just a joke, that you were going to rape my wife, in the moments after I was killed?'

'Yes.'

'Hardly a funny joke, Kernon? But let's move on from it. It's history now.'

'That's good. Oh, and congratulations, Corin. Chief.'

'Thank you.' Kernon started to move away, but before he did so Corin spoke again, his voice calm. 'Kernon. One last thing. I meant what I said, you know, about Agbeth's insult-name. If you ever call her that again, ever, I'll have you banished or killed. And if you ever threaten or act to cause harm to her, or to me, or to any member of my family, ever again, I'll set Blackpaw on you. I promise you that. Is that understood?'

Kernon's face twisted, like he wanted to make an angry response, wanted to challenge Corin. But then he glanced again at the felrin, before his features softened and he said, 'Yes, Corin.'

'Good. And now we understand each other, brother.'

—

Later that morning, Corin gathered with the elder warriors of the village, in the Clan Hall.

In total, twelve warriors had joined him in the Hall, including Akob and Kernon. Corin had also insisted that Agbeth be present at the meeting. He valued his wife's opinion, but he specifically wanted her to be there to observe how the leading warriors reacted to his words. Blackpaw was also inside the Hall, resting near to the entrance of the building.

Corin had spent several hours deliberating about what he was going to say at this meeting. At some point in the night or early morning, the answer had finally come to him. A decision to do something which he knew was going to shock them all, and appal some of them. When they had all gathered around him, Corin started to talk.

'Welcome, to all of you, to the leading warriors of the Karn. Thank you for meeting with me. None of us, including me, could have expected me to be sitting here before you today, as clan chief. But that is what I now am. The leader of the Karn. Under our law, until my death. But I will only stay leader with all of your support. If I do the right thing for the Karn.' There was nodding around him. 'I can see that some of you are looking at Agbeth. Wondering why she's here. Know that I trust my wife above all others, and when she gives me advice, I listen. Agbeth will now attend all of these meetings.' He looked towards Kernon. 'If any man objects, let me know, and he can leave this gathering.' No one raised an objection.

'As my first decision, I want to appoint Akob and Marrix as my military advisers.' The two named individuals were the most senior warriors there, Marrix being the head of a large family with a lot of influence in the village. 'As you all know, I don't have experience in the ways of war. I will therefore be trusting Akob and Marrix to teach me what I need to know, and to give me advice if battle ever approaches.' He then considered that it was time to address a matter which many of them might have been contemplating. 'I know that two years ago, I left this village in shame, for an act of cowardice. Even now, having defeated Borrik using my powers, I am no great warrior. However, be certain, in the last two years I have found my courage. I will lead you all bravely.'

'Tell us about those powers, then,' said Marrix, folding his arms. He was tall and lithe with greying hair and a long, wild beard. 'And tell us about the Gods. How can you control the felrin? How did you do what you did to Borrik?'

Corin paused to consider his response, and instead Agbeth answered the question. 'The Gods visited him, when we were in the far north. In his sleep. His sleep is still often restless, when they are speaking to him. But he was given the power to control beasts, and to control men. Only Mella before us could control the felrin. He has been chosen by the Gods.'

Corin did not contradict her, despite his discomfort at the words. 'It is true, I have that power. The felrin does what I tell it to.'

Marrix asked, 'Then we have a mighty weapon?'

'If we need a weapon, yes, we have it,' answered Corin. 'But that is connected to what I want to talk about, today. For all of my life, and no doubt for all of Akob's and Marrix's lives, we have been at war. With the Anath. With the Borl. We kill their men, their livestock, burn their buildings. They do the same to us. We both bleed the lives from each other's young men.'

'It is the way,' stated Akob. 'They are not Karn. They are animals.'

'Is that really true?' Corin looked around the group. 'Really? I stood in the Anath village. Their homes are like ours. They settle into families like ours. We speak the same language, worship the same Gods. They fight like us. And yet we are sworn to kill them. And they swear the same of us.'

'It is the way,' repeated Akob.

'It has been the way,' said Corin. 'The way for too long. Borrik was a great warrior, and he knew war. Rejoiced in it. But how can we Karn grow and prosper, how can our children and wives be safe, when we stay in this endless fight?' He could see the dubious expressions on the faces of those gathered around him. 'In Blackpaw, we have a deadly weapon, yes. I would dread to think what the beast could do if unleashed upon a village of our enemies. But there has been too much blood. I do not want to use that weapon for *killing*.'

Marrix asked the next question, scepticism in his voice. 'What *do* you want to use it for, then?'

'For peace,' replied Corin. 'It is time for the Karn to end their wars. Time for us to make peace with both the Anath and the Borl. To bring peace from a position of strength.'

The stony-faced silence within the room told him everything that he needed to know about how popular his announcement was.

30

Allana

Year of Our Lord,
After Ascension, 769AA

In the aftermath of the encounter with Arion Sepian, Allana's hope was reborn. After she had been returned to her cell, and even after she had been stripped and hooded again by Nionia, she could feel the embers of excitement stirring into life within herself.

She could clearly remember her last words to him, after having explained her plan. 'Do you promise, Arion? Do you promise to do the things that I've asked of you, and to save me?'

He had looked at her, and had solemnly whispered, 'Yes. I promise.'

In response to this, she had leaned forwards to kiss him, on the cheek. Softly and tenderly. Sealing the compact between them.

The mere thought of him now, and the memory of her lips against his flesh, stoked a fire inside of her. He was the most beautiful man that she had ever seen. From the moment that she had walked into that room, and had stared at him for the first time, she had wanted him. Had desired him, despite the gravity of her situation.

And he had wanted her, too. The look of lust in his eyes had been unmistakeable, even before she had used her powers to compel him. And had there ever been a more amenable victim of her compulsion?

And he was like you, too, Lana. You can somehow feel him, even now, somewhere out there. He shares the dream of the Gate. He said he has powers. The two of you are alike, and this was meant to be. You were meant to meet him. To be with him.

She shivered at the thought of it. Imagining his touch upon her. He was nothing like his father. Taller, broader, far more handsome. And lighter-haired where Duke Conran had been dark. If she had not been told that he was the Duke's son, she would never have guessed it. Her former lover was but a pale shadow of his offspring.

The encounter with Arion had been strangely dreamlike, throughout. As if there had been an aura surrounding him, which had beguiled and confused her. It had felt like the air around him was crackling with energy, with life, and being close to him had made her feel rejuvenated and revitalised. When she had kissed him, a flow of energy had rushed into her body. She was sure that she was not deluding herself that the wounds to her legs hurt less afterwards, and that the fatigue had been cast out of her body. And it had left her tingling.

'What are you?' she had asked, moments after meeting him, and even now she was not sure of the answer. Other than that he was different. As she was different. And that they were forever linked by their distinctness.

They were also now connected by the instructions which she had implanted within him. Which he had readily succumbed to. Although even that had been different to the other occasions when she had used her powers to compel someone, whether that had been with Obnel Rabnar or the Duke. During those earlier instances, she had felt invisible tendrils forcing themselves into the person's mind, fighting through a barrier of resistance, and gripping the target's

511

thoughts. With Arion, those unseen connections had just dispersed into the invisible energies wrapping around his body, her own power coalescing and mingling with his. Filling her with even more energy.

And yet, the end effect had seemed to be the same. He had appeared to be transfixed. Mesmerised, and full of lust for her. And he had agreed to everything which she had asked of him. Had made his promise to her.

And they were joined. In some way, forever connected. Right now, she could feel his presence, somewhere in Septholme Castle. She shivered once more, feeling a glimmer of arousal even within the squalor of her enclosed, dark conditions.

He will save you, Lana. And then you will be together.

—

The next day, she was again brought to meet with Evelyn dei Laramin. However, the High Commander had no idea of how much things had changed inside Allana's mind, since their last encounter.

Once again, the confession document was set out on the table before Allana.

'So, Allana, here we are again,' said dei Laramin. Her lustrous dark hair was loose around her shoulders, today. 'I was so disappointed by you yesterday, Allana, do you know that? So very disappointed. I thought that we had become friends, and had grown to trust each other. But then you took that trust and you spat it in my face. I was very hurt and upset.'

'I'm sorry,' said Allana, meekly.

'Well, I hope so. The last thing that I wanted was to see you hurt by the Truthseeker, yesterday. Or to see you hurt again, today. And again. And again. It truly troubles me. But you must understand that The Lord Aiduel needs me to find the truth, Allana, and to see justice done. And I must unflinchingly do what The Lord requires of me. You do understand that, don't you, Allana?'

'Yes, I understand.'

Dei Laramin pushed the document forward again. 'Very good, Allana. Very good. I do much prefer it when we properly understand each other. So, Allana. Your confession. Read it. Sign it. And then we can be friends.'

Allana glanced down and could see that it was the same document as had been presented to her the day before. If she signed it, it condemned her to death. But only if she was still here. Only if she was still captive. And Arion had restored her hope of freedom. She picked up the quill, dipped it in the ink, and then signed her name.

You won't give them the chance to use this against you, Lana.

The High Commander smiled, and drew the document back towards herself. 'Excellent, Allana. What a good girl.' She looked up then, at an unseen person behind Allana's shoulder. 'Although I can tell that my colleague appears to be a little disappointed. The Truthseeker has found your sessions together to be so... professionally satisfying. But, hold on! I've had an idea. A splendid idea! Shall we let you and the Truthseeker spend another afternoon in each other's company, anyway? To really explore your threshold for pain and suffering?'

Allana experienced a moment of horror, her face going pale.

Dei Laramin suddenly laughed. 'Oh, Allana dear. Your expression, it's a delight! Truly! You're so gullible. So very gullible, it's almost sweet. As if I would do that to you when you've already confessed. What do you take me for? A monster?' She laughed again.

'No, High Commander. I'm sorry.' Allana mumbled the response, feeling immense relief.

'Don't be sorry, Allana. I'm very pleased with you today. Very pleased. With this, I can confirm that your trial is going ahead. And very soon, all of this uncomfortable business will be over for you.'

'Thank you.'

'No, thank you, Allana. You've given me what I need. What *this garrison* needs.' Dei Laramin leaned back in her chair and put both of her hands behind her head, clearly enjoying the moment.

'High Commander, please can I ask something?'

'What is it, Allana?'

Allana had already taken the first steps on her escape plan, so she was not entirely reliant upon the granting of the request which she was about to make. However, it would certainly make matters easier for her. 'Now that I've confessed, please will you allow me to have the cloth bag taken off my head, when I'm in my cell? I'm finding it very difficult to breathe.'

'Why, yes, Allana. Consider it gone.' The High Commander lifted her eyes to again address someone who was standing behind Allana. 'Did you hear that? Get rid of it. And even more, but only because I'm in such a good mood today, I'll also tell them to stop all of those horrid banging noises outside of your cell door, too. How kind am I to you, Allana?'

Dei Laramin grinned again, acting for all intents like a generous benefactor distributing gifts. Allana stared at her and then, for the first time since she had arrived in captivity at the fortress, she smiled in response.

—

After the meeting with the High Commander, Allana was returned to her prison cell, this time unhooded. On the way back to the cell she was subtly turning her head to observe her surroundings, and was trying to memorise the placements of guards. Every detail that she noted might matter now. Could mean the difference between escape and failure.

She observed that there were a large number of Aiduel's Guards in the fortress, and that the fortifications on the western side facing Septholme were almost fully constructed. However, she was pleased to note that the eastern walls of the fort were not even close to finished. There were large gaps in the external structure there, with some elements of the walls not even started. The forest to the east of the fortress was clearly visible through these gaps in the walls.

If you are to escape from this place, Lana, it will be that way.

When she arrived back at the prison cell area, she passed by two guards, both of them males. They were standing in a cramped rectangular space which was surrounded by a number of cells, including her own. One of the guards was staring at her as she passed, with undisguised hunger in his eyes. He was a brutish and ugly middle-aged man, short but very heavily built, with thinning hair and a grizzled chin. He appeared to be seeking some sort of acknowledgement from her, an indication that she noticed him and recognised his interest. She returned his stare boldly, keen to nourish his desire.

It was not the first time that she had looked at him in this manner. Yesterday, when she had been led to the meeting with Arion Sepian, this man had been her second accompanying guard. Nionia had been in front of Allana, leading the way. This gruff male had followed behind, with a meaty hand gripping Allana's arm. As she had walked ahead of him she had intuitively sensed that he was relishing touching her, and that his eyes were roaming across her body.

She had looked back, then, glancing at him briefly, and she had become certain that he wanted her. She had guessed at that moment that he had been the guard who had stroked her chin and cheek, after feeding her. Could he have been watching her, all week? Enjoying the power which he held over her? Imagining what he would do to her if they were alone, with no other guards present?

She had made the immediate decision then that she was going to use her ability to try to control him, as soon as she had a chance to. And that opportunity had quickly arisen, in the moments when Nionia had first walked into the meeting room to speak with Arion Sepian. Leaving Allana alone with the brutish guard, in the corridor outside.

In the time which had been available during Nionia and Arion's brief exchange, Allana had turned to stare at the brutish-looking Aiduel's Guard, and she had mesmerised and dominated him. It

515

had been easier and quicker than on any prior occasion. Indeed, his will had crumbled before her assault in just moments. Possibly he was weak-willed, or maybe the lust burning inside of him had made him a willing victim? Or perhaps it had been the proximity of Arion Sepian, enhancing her powers, making the domination of the Guard that much easier? Or maybe she was just becoming more powerful?

But however it had come about, she had been able to subdue his will easily, and in just moments he had become hers. Ready to do anything for her. She had walked into the meeting with Arion Sepian holding that knowledge, and it had shaped what she had subsequently said to her visitor. By the time that her meeting with Arion had concluded, she had known that she possessed two men, both of whom were willing to risk their lives to help her to escape from this place.

As she was pushed back into her squalid cell, now, she was thankful that for the first time her hands were left unbound, and no covering was placed over her head. She turned to face the door as it was closed and locked behind her. The ugly brutish guard had moved to stand on the other side of the cell door, and he was looking through the small head height hatch, staring at her. Again, she returned his stare.

—

Later that evening, she watched as the brutish guard entered the cell. He was carrying a hunk of bread and a small jug of water. Her stomach was aching, and it rumbled as she saw the food.

She moved towards him, to take the bread. Again, she could sense the lust boiling within him. He was a truly repugnant man, with thin squinting eyes and oversized ears and nose, and there was no apparent kindness in his demeanour. He clearly enjoyed the power which his Aiduel's Guard uniform afforded him.

As she reached for the bread, he pulled his hand back, and shook his head. Then he gestured downwards, with an ugly smile on his face.

She knew what he desired, and she felt repulsed. He wanted her on her knees before him, and to feed her as he had done before. In other circumstances, she would have revolted, and pulled away. But she knew that she needed him. To escape. To survive. And if she acquiesced to this, and magnified his craving for her, it would make her control on him that much stronger.

She dropped down to her knees, looked up at him, and opened her mouth. And as he placed the hunk of bread to her lips, she began to speak to him, through the connection between them.

Imagine having me. Whenever you want. But only if you free me. Only if you help me to escape. Then I'll be yours. To do whatever you like, whenever you like. But only if you free me.

He spoke, only once. 'I'm Donnus.' It was the same gruff and common-sounding voice which she had heard once before.

She took a bite from the bread, and began to chew, slowly, savouring the food. Her eyes were still fixed to his cruel stare. Then she began to whisper spoken words to him. Soft, seductive words. She watched him listen, rapt with attention and seemingly transfixed upon her, as she told him everything that she would need him to do.

—

The next night and day were a time for waiting. Despite the removal of the cloth hood and the freeing of her hands, Allana was still cold, hungry and thirsty. The cell was still squalid and austere. And with each passing day, the moment of her death by fire drew closer.

However, hope burned inside her now. During the third night following Arion Sepian's visit to her, she was going to escape from this grim fortress. Arion would be waiting for her, in the place that they had agreed, and then they would escape together. Flee to somewhere far away. And begin a new life, finally free from this hunted persecution. Together.

You will survive this, Lana. You must survive this.

517

She could feel Arion there, with her, throughout the period of waiting. He was a constant reassuring presence, from somewhere in the direction of Septholme. In the moments before sleep took her, she wondered about what he was doing and what he was thinking. Was he imagining her, as she was conjuring visions of him? Or was he reflecting upon the promise that he had made to her, which he was to carry out on the following night? Or thinking about kissing her and making love to her, as she was having such thoughts about him? Imagining his arms sensually wrapped around her, as her head was on his chest?

She had never felt like this, before.

Are you in love, Lana? Is this what love feels like? Does it embrace and entrap you so quickly and so deeply?

The night after she had whispered her instructions to the brutish guard Donnus, she slept soundly, under the dim flickering light of torches hung outside of the cell. True to Evelyn dei Laramin's word, they had ceased from tormenting her with the banging noises against her door. And the bread had eased her hunger pangs, slightly. Therefore, despite the squalor and chill of the cell, Allana rested her head on her arm and fell into a deep and unbroken sleep.

The next day, she was left alone in her cell. Not interviewed, or tortured, or in any other way harassed. Just waiting. Tense, agitated, and nervously excited. Steeling herself for the night ahead. And anticipating her reunion with Arion.

—

The enactment of her planned escape began with an innocuous sound, close to the midnight hour. A strangled half-cry, cut-off quickly.

Then her cell door opened. Donnus entered, dragging a body behind him. In the half-light cast by the torches outside of the cell, Allana could see the smear of blood on the floor as Donnus's fellow prison guard was dragged in.

She looked up at Donnus, enquiry in her eyes.

518

'Cut his throat,' announced the brutish guard, as if it was a trivial matter. He dumped the corpse into the corner of the cell least visible from the door. The dead man's eyes were open, staring sightlessly upwards with an expression which suggested bewilderment about what had just happened to him.

A wave of nausea rose within Allana, which she wilfully stifled. An image of High Priest Ronis's bloodied throat flashed into her mind, taunting her. 'Did you really need to do that? Couldn't you have just... knocked him out?'

'You told me to get rid of any other guards. Easier, this way. Didn't want him shouting for others.' He stopped, and then spat towards the dead body. 'Never liked him, anyhow. Arrogant twat.'

Allana shuddered, feeling repulsed by the man's casual callousness. She was trying to keep her eyes away from the corpse, as blood continued to seep out of the grim neck wound.

You did this, Lana. Another man is dead, because of you. Another death. How many more?

She shook the thought away, annoyed with herself for thinking it. Donnus's fellow guard had died because he had chosen to join Aiduel's Guards, and to be part of its evil. And because they had unfairly imprisoned her. None of that was her fault. All she was trying to do was survive. If they had not brought her here, his death would never have happened. It was *not* her fault.

'Do you have the clothes for me?'

'Yes,' he replied. 'One moment.' He headed back outside of the cell, then returned with a sack, which he threw to her. 'Yours.'

She looked inside, and her clothes and shoes were there. She pulled the clothing out of the sack, ready to change into it. Her hands lifted the hem of the sackcloth prison dress which she was wearing, but then she hesitated. Donnus was staring at her, clearly anticipating the moment when she would strip off her clothing.

She would have preferred to tell him to turn away, but she knew that would risk both the wasting of time and the potential lessening

519

of her control over him. Instead, she swiftly pulled the sackcloth shift over her head. As quickly as she could she then put on her own clothing, smoothing down the dress over her thighs. Donnus's eyes were boring into her throughout this process, clearly savouring the sight of her bare flesh, and his desire was palpable.

'Ready?' Donnus grunted the question, after she had pulled on her shoes.

'Yes. To the eastern wall?'

'Yes.'

'How difficult will it be to get there?'

'A little difficult. Not too much. Most of the garrison is asleep in the barracks or the tent camp. Maybe twenty awake and about, at most. Handful patrolling the fort, maybe ten on guard duty. Only one guard we definitely have to pass, though.'

'How will we get past him?'

'Not him, tonight. *Her*, I think. How to get past?' He raised his hand to his throat, and made a slicing gesture. Allana shuddered again. She started to move to exit the cell, but Donnus put his hand out to stop her. 'When you're free, you're mine, yes?'

'Yes. Yours. Always.'

'Later, woman. When we're away from here, and can stop. I'm having you. Tonight.'

'Yes. Tonight.' She had to strain to keep the look of revulsion off her face, as she gave the answer.

'I've always wanted a woman like you. Had no idea I'd do all of this to get one, though. But it'll be worth it. For you. OK, let's go.'

Let him have his crude fantasy, Lana. If you're being honest with yourself, you know that he may not survive this night.

She recognised this for the cold thought that it was, but she knew that there was no possibility that she could stay with this man, once they were out of here. Nor could she let him touch her, in the way that he wanted to. She had not worked out how or when she would detach herself from him, but one way or another she would be free of Donnus before the dawn.

They then moved out of the cell, and he locked the door behind him, before pocketing the key. Her escape had begun.

—

Allana was not precisely certain about how she had envisaged that the next few minutes would proceed. But she had definitely not expected to find the fort as quiet and deserted as it was.

They did not encounter anyone along the forty metres of corridor which they needed to pass through, before reaching an external door. When they arrived at that exit, Donnus growled, 'Wait here.' He then headed through the doorway, shutting the wooden door behind himself. Allana pressed herself back into the shadows, glancing around nervously, until her brutish companion finally returned. 'I was checking for patrols. There's none here. We move. Now.'

He grabbed her wrist and pulled her through the door. His hand was wrapped tightly around her slender limb, and he was half-dragging her behind him. She emerged into a murky area which was inside the fort walls, on the north side of the complex. The walls were complete on this edge of the fortress, and occasional torches in sconces provided a dim gloom of illumination. However, the shadows here were deep and it would be difficult for anyone else to see them unless they came very close. Donnus steered Allana quickly to the east, staying tight to the wall, sneaking towards that part of the perimeter where the fort walls were incomplete.

She was peering into her surrounds throughout this, looking for any signs of movement which might indicate the presence of patrols. Her heart was pounding and her mouth was dry. If they were detected and captured now, she would be unlikely to ever have another chance to escape. And dei Laramin would undoubtedly make her pay in a currency of screams for the failed attempt.

She could sense the comforting external presence of Arion, throughout. He was there, to the north, in the place which they had agreed. Waiting for her. That knowledge aided her to keep control of her nerves. She longed to be out of this place, and to once again be in his company.

Donnus stopped suddenly in front of her, and with hand gestures signalled for Allana to stay where she was. He put a finger to his lips, and then pointed. She stared in the indicated direction, and spotted a sole Aiduel's Guard. The figure was standing in the centre of a small gap in the eastern wall, illuminated by a nearby flaming torch. The individual appeared to be female, with long hair tied in a ponytail, and she was facing outwards.

Allana had a queasy feeling in the pit of her stomach as she stared at the solitary female figure. Was she about to witness a murder? Did this person have just seconds to live? Her mind fleetingly questioned whether they could approach this differently, whether they could spare the woman's life. Knock her out, or tie her up? Or something like that? Allana knew that it was in her power to encourage Donnus to use a less deadly approach.

Don't be a child, Lana. This isn't a game. You have to escape. You have to survive.

She stayed silent, trying to convince herself that she was still deliberating about whether to speak up. But in her heart she knew that any approach, other than a quick strike, would make it more likely that the woman could call for help. And that their escape would be detected.

The opportunity to suggest any alternative approach to Donnus was then lost, as the man had released her wrist and was moving again. He strolled forwards with a casual saunter, making no effort now to disguise his presence, coming closer to and then hailing the solitary Guard. The female Guard returned the welcome. Allana knew that if she called out, even now, there was still a possibility to save this unknown woman's life. But she remained silent.

There was a flash of a knife in the darkness. Allana watched the form of the female Aiduel's Guard go limp, saw her legs buckle, and then witnessed the body collapsing to the floor. Allana was suddenly fighting to hold back a rush of vomit which was rising in her throat.

How many more people must die for your survival, Lana? How many more? You could have found another way. You could have spared her!

Again, she shook away the thought with anger, fighting against her nausea as she ran over to where Donnus was standing.

It's not your fault, Lana. It's their fault. All of them! They've forced you to do this.

'Get her feet,' Donnus said, sounding unperturbed about having just killed another colleague. 'We'll carry her to the treeline.'

Allana looked down at the dead female. She was plain-looking, with long red hair. And now she was dead. Did she have a family? A husband? Parents? Had she been dreaming happy thoughts, in the moments before the knife had slashed across her throat? Allana felt another rise of nausea.

'Come on,' urged Donnus, sliding his arms under the woman's armpits. 'If we get her out of sight, we'll have the most time possible to get ahead of any pursuit.'

Allana took hold of the Guard's legs, and then they were carrying the dead body. They stumbled with their burden across the open ground between the eastern perimeter of the fort, and the woods fifty metres away. The woman was heavy, a dead weight, and Allana struggled to move with any speed. She again felt anxious that someone might see them here in the open, even in the murkier light away from the fortress.

But no shout of challenge or of alert came. They entered under the treeline, just for a few metres, and Donnus indicated for them to drop the body behind a large tree trunk, hidden from view of the fort. 'That's far enough,' he said. 'We're out. We may have hours now until they see something's wrong and come after us, or only minutes. We have to move. You said we'd have horses. Where?'

'At the fork in the road to the north of these woods. Someone's meeting us there.' She could still feel Arion's presence, from that direction, and once again she felt a glow of satisfaction and excitement that he had been true to his word.

'Let's go, then.' Donnus started moving immediately, trudging through the edge of the wood, not waiting to check if she followed.

Allana took one final lingering look at the dead woman. Then she reached down and pulled a short dagger from the woman's belt, and gripped it in her right hand. Immediately, having the weapon in her possession gave her an extra layer of reassurance. She took a deep breath, savouring being out in the open again after a week within the claustrophobic conditions of the prison.

You've escaped, Lana. You did it. You can survive this. You must survive this.

Then she started to follow after Donnus, and towards her rendezvous with Arion. She was no longer a prisoner. But, once again, she was a fugitive, and she was on the run.

—

They followed the edge of the woods northward, heading towards the location where she was to meet with Arion. Their agreed meeting place was a fork in the road, which had been clearly visible to her from the eastern battlements of Septholme Castle. It was to the east of the town of Septholme, and a quarter of a mile to the north of the fortress of Aiduel's Guards. At that point, the highway which ran south-to-north split, with one branch continuing northwards, and the other curling towards the east.

As she trekked through the edges of the dark woodland, she could remember the moments of her encounter with Arion when she had explained her plan to him.

'On the third night from now,' she had explained, 'sometime around midnight. Wait for me at the fork in the road to the north of here. You know where I mean?'

'Yes, of course. I'll wait out of sight, but near the signpost.'

'And you must work out where we're going to go and how we're going to get there. I don't know this land, at all.'

'I will.'

'Good. And bring whatever we'll need, for when we escape together. Horses. Money. Possessions. Clothes. Food. Weapons. Whatever you think we'll need. Because once we leave, we can never come back here. Do you understand?'

'I understand,' he had answered, immediately.

'Do you really, Arion? Do you really comprehend what I'm asking you to do? To give up? Truly?'

'Yes.'

'And you'll do all of this for me, Arion? Even though we've only just met? You'll give up everything else for *me*?'

'I will,' he had answered, steadfast in his certainty, and her heart had leapt with exhilaration. Even despite knowing the impact that her compulsion over him might be having on his responses. It had been at that point that she had asked her final question, and had sought her final reassurance. And following that answer, she had leaned forwards, and had kissed his cheek. Had sealed their commitment to each other.

Despite the gravity of her current situation as she followed Donnus, Allana smiled at the memory. She had never been as stirred by a single encounter with any other person as she had been in that meeting. Never as stimulated with anyone else, to compare to the way that she had felt as his eyes had devoured her form. And never had she relished the sight of someone else as much, the ability to gaze upon and admire their physical perfection. He had been so flawlessly masculine and handsome.

He is so beautiful, Lana. And he will be yours, after you have escaped together.

She could still sense Arion, getting closer to her as she walked northwards. However, mixed in with the thrill of encountering him again was a sense of trepidation, about what would happen when Arion and Donnus faced each other. Allana wanted to rid herself

525

of the brutish ugly Guard as soon as possible, but she had not yet worked out how to do it.

She had needed Donnus to get this far, and indeed had used him to get this far, but now he was an unwanted danger. A threat to herself, but also to Arion. She had witnessed Donnus's casual and skilled violence twice already this night, and she was concerned now that he might do the same thing to her young lord. She had no idea how ably Arion would acquit himself against a thug like Donnus, and when she had explained her plan to Arion she had not told him to expect her to be accompanied when she arrived. She would be reliant on his reactions and quick wits.

The place where the road forked came into view, blanketed in darkness at this midnight hour. Allana stared at the back of Donnus, as he moved towards the signpost at the point where the road split. Allana's hand was still clutching the knife which she had picked up.

Donnus hissed the words at her. 'Where are the horses?'

She was about to reply when she heard a whinny from a grove of trees which were a short distance to the north-east of the fork, and then she saw a rider appear. She recognised the figure as Arion, and she could feel his presence that much more intensely now that they beheld each other again. He was riding a horse, and appeared to be leading a second mount which was tethered to his.

'Allana?' Arion's voice was clear in the darkness, although pitched at a low level so as not to carry beyond her.

'Arion, it's me!'

'Who the fuck is this?' asked Donnus, addressing the question to Allana. He then turned back towards the shape of Arion. 'You! Leave us the horses and then fuck off!'

There was no answer from Arion for a few moments, before Allana heard a swishing noise. A sound which she had often heard when the Septholme Castle guards were practising their skills; a sword being drawn from a scabbard. Arion spoke up again, his voice surprisingly calm. 'Allana, who is this man? Do you want him here?'

Allana heard Donnus uttering a curse, and witnessed the brutish

Guard moving towards Arion. She had no time within which to consider her answer, and she instinctively shouted, 'No! He's going to try to kill you, Arion! Kill him!'

Whatever happened next, it occurred too quickly for Allana to properly register it in the dim light. There was a closing of the distance between Arion and Donnus, a lightning quick sound of metal clashing, and then a stifled scream. In the midst of that contest, for just a moment, she thought that she could feel a surge of energy emanating from Arion. Then Donnus had collapsed to the ground.

She watched as Arion leaped down from his horse. He effortlessly lifted the limp form of Donnus, dragging it into the nearby grove of trees. Arion then ran back to his mount.

'Quick!' His voice was sharp. 'Get on the spare horse!'

'Is he d-'

'He's dead. We must get away from here. Get on!'

'I can't ride! I've never ridden a horse!'

There was a pause, suggesting that this was an obstacle which he had not anticipated, before he spoke again. 'Come here, then. Ride in front of me.'

—

Then they were riding away from the fork in the road. Following the road east, and putting distance between themselves and the fortress. Leaving behind the three people who had died that night, including Donnus's body in the grove of trees.

You're not to blame, Lana. None of this was your fault. Donnus was a murderer. He killed the others. And Arion had to protect himself from Donnus. You just did what you had to do.

Arion had one hand on the horse's reins, with his other arm wrapped tightly around her stomach as she sat in front of him. She could feel her back pressing against him, with his breath hot against her ear. And she felt renewed and alive in his presence. Intoxicated by his proximity, and by the sensation of an aura of vitality around him, which she could feel enveloping her. Her heart was beating fast within her chest.

She had never ridden on a horse before, and she felt some nervousness even at the steady canter at which the animal was moving. However, she felt sure that the muscular arm across her stomach would not allow her to fall. Arion would protect her. He would keep her safe.

He had initially enquired as to whether she was being pursued and then, once she had responded, for an extended period they did not speak. They continued to follow the road eastwards in silence through the night hours, covering a distance of ground at a fast pace. The second horse cantered along beside them, loaded with saddlebags which appeared to carry whatever possessions he had brought with him. She had earlier tucked her knife into one of those bags.

Eventually, she broke the silence between them. 'Arion, thank you.' He did not answer, and after a few seconds she added the words, 'Thank you for coming for me. For saving me.' She turned her head slightly, and from the corner of her eye she could see his chin, close to her. So close, and so tempting to turn and to kiss it.

His answer surprised her by being curt. 'I made a promise.'

She felt a little wounded by the brevity of the response. 'Even so,' she replied. 'Thank you.'

He did not respond, and his continuing silence elicited a first flicker of doubt within her. One which she tried to suppress.

He is here, Lana. He came for you, as he promised. And he's right to concentrate on your escape. There will be much time for talk. Later, when you're safe. Time for talk, and also for other things.

—

They covered miles of ground as the hours of night passed by. He drove the horses hard, and at one point he stopped to allow them both to switch to the second mount. At that time, he also lit a lantern

528

attached to each of the saddlebags, and led the horses from the main road onto a much smaller side trail. This smaller path was on the left of the main track, and appeared to wind northwards.

'Where are we going?' Her thighs and calves were aching as she swung down from the first horse, his hands on her waist to assist her. There had still been little conversation between them, and she chose this moment to attempt to renew their connection, trying to look into his eyes as she spoke.

He was peering back along the road behind them, rather than at her, as he answered. 'This trail is not well known. Certainly, Aiduel's Guards wouldn't know it. It runs parallel with the River Road, to the east.'

'And where does it lead?'

'It runs north. I need to get you as far away from Septholme as I can, tonight. You will need to go north.'

He said you, *Lana. Not* we.

She tried to shake that thought away as they mounted the second horse. But the doubts were becoming more prevalent within her as they rode along the thin trail, travelling for a further extended period.

The lantern provided the only illumination of the verdant countryside in the lands around them. There was still no glow of dawn in the sky, at the point when Arion finally stopped their mount. Allana estimated that they had been in the saddle for over three hours. Again, Arion assisted her down from the horse.

This time, after she had dismounted, she came and stood before him. 'Arion,' she said. 'What's the matter? Arion, please look at me.'

It was not her intention to use her powers against him. She merely wanted to peer into his eyes, even in the murky light, and to better try to divine his thoughts.

For a moment, he looked away. Then he turned towards her, still not meeting her eyes, his expression stern. 'I'm sorry, Allana, I can't come with you. I must leave you. Here.'

'What? But your promise-'

'My land has been invaded, Allana. We're at war. I must go to lead our armies. Tomorrow – sorry, today now – we march north. I can't abandon everything, and everyone, that I love. For you. However much that I may want to.'

His tone of voice was different to that which he had used, back in the fortress. Lower, more reserved, more stoic. But with a noticeable tinge of shame. And still he was not meeting her stare.

'But what would you have me do, Arion? You would abandon *me*, instead? Here? In the dark, in the middle of nowhere?'

'I have to go back, Allana. I have to. But you can still escape. In these bags, I've brought clothing for you, and money which you can use to travel north.'

'But how?' She tried to keep the despair and pleading out of her voice. 'I don't know where I am. My accent will betray me, anywhere I go. You promised to help me escape, Arion.'

'I've helped you escape! I'm doing this, right now, Allana, when I have no time. I should be resting or planning for war!'

'That isn't what you meant! You know it isn't! You promised!' This time the plaintive upset was clearly evident in her voice, and she was aware that she must be sounding childishly petulant. Still he avoided meeting her eyes, clearly embarrassed by his actions.

'We're over thirty miles from the fort, now,' he said, after a pause of a few seconds. 'No one will pursue you, Allana, other than Aiduel's Guards. The concerns of my brother and House Sepian are far greater than you, now. And even if Aiduel's Guards have dogs, you have a big lead over them.'

'But Arion–'

'I don't have much time, Allana! I have to get back to Septholme before dawn! I need you to listen! Will you listen to me, Allana? Now?'

She was stung by his sharp words and rebuke, but she nodded and whispered, 'Yes.'

'Listen to all of this, carefully. Remember it, all of it, and you *will* escape. Keep moving. Always keep moving. Go east across these fields.' He pointed to signal the direction. 'Keep going straight. In less than two miles you'll come to the River Road. Follow that north, always with the Canas River on your right. Within another two miles you'll come to the town of Eastholme, by the Third Bridge. The bridges will all be closed now, but there are regular horse-drawn carriages that you can get on from there which run the whole length of the River Road. One will be ready to leave, going north, shortly after first light. Get there before dawn! Be on that carriage, and stay on it, but for no further than Canasholme, the Sixth Bridge. Sleep on the carriage. Get some rest. After that, get off the main roads, always keep moving, and stop and rest as little as possible. And steer clear of any armies. Well clear. This land is at war now. But go north, keep going north, and get out of Western Canasar. Get to Rednarron, there'll only be a handful of Aiduel's Guards there. Get there, find a safe place, and wait. Then write to me, at Septholme Castle. I'll come to you as soon as I can, when the war is over. Please believe me.'

'Believe you?' There was a hint of derision in her response, but despite her upset about his intentions, she was trying to retain everything that he was saying. 'What about the money? And clothes?'

'In these two bags.' He lifted the bags off the saddle, and placed them in front of her. 'In here are clean dresses, which were yours at the castle. I suggest that you change into one, in case Aiduel's Guards are looking for the colours of your current dress. There's also money in a purse in the bag. More money than you could need. And food.' He then reached into the pocket of his tunic, and passed a sealed letter to her. 'And this is a letter carrying the seal of House Sepian.'

'Saying what?' She pocketed the letter as she asked the question.

'Saying that the bearer of the letter is carrying out business for House Sepian, and that she should be given any assistance she requires, to get to Rednarron. Only show it if you absolutely have to, but if the need arises, use it.'

He has planned all of this so carefully, Lana. Has given so much thought as to how he is going to leave you. But he must not leave you.

'Thank you, for what you have done. But you're set on leaving me?'

'Yes.' Again, his response was curt and cold.

She had to do something to change this. Had to attempt to restore and reignite whatever emotions had been enflamed within him, when they had met in the fort. She stepped closer to him, and placed her hand on his cheek, forcing him to look towards her. 'Arion. Please look at me.'

His eyes focused upon hers, the first time tonight that their gazes had locked together, and at last she could detect the barely contained emotion which he was holding within. There was still desire there. He still wanted her. She was suddenly certain that his icy demeanour was an act, an effort to keep her at bay. To maintain his stated resolve when what he really wanted to do was to flee with her. To become her lover. All was not lost.

She could also sense the powerful aura around him, as she had sensed it when in the fort. Alive. Vital. Full of energy. Pulsing.

And then time slowed down around her, and invisible tendrils started to sinuously emerge from her thoughts, snaking towards him. And she began to speak to him.

You want me, Arion. You want me. And you can ha-

But then the tendrils touched the aura around him, and dispersed. Harmlessly, and ineffectively. As if they had never been. He continued to stare at her, his face a tormented mixture of desire, shame and duty. But he was untouched by her power. And she realised then that she had never truly enchanted him during their first meeting, in the fort. At least, not in the way which she had imagined.

No, on that occasion he had *allowed* himself to be seduced and to fall under her power. But she had never really dominated or controlled him, not in the way that she had done with others. His will was too strong.

She knew now that he had simply chosen to fall under her seductive spell, inside the fortress, and to make his promise to her. And now he was choosing to break it.

She tried one last time, her voice as soft and appealing as she could make it, given the circumstances. 'Please don't leave me here, Arion. Please come with me. I *know* we were meant to meet. Meant to be together. To be lovers. Soulmates. You know it, too.' She inched closer towards him.

But he abruptly moved backwards, taking her hand from his cheek, and then his face hardened. 'I have to go, Allana. Now. I'm nearly out of time.' He then turned away from her, and jumped back onto the saddle of his horse, creating distance between them.

She watched his action, then lowered her head to hide the tears that were forming in her eyes.

'So, that's it? You're really leaving me here? Knowing that I'm going to be hunted, and that you're sending me into a war?'

'Yes, I'm sorry. I've done everything that I can for you. But I have to go now. I'll follow a different return route which circles back to Septholme along the western coast road, and I'll hopefully lead off any pursuit. But keep moving, do the things that I said. Stay safe. Get to Rednarron. Then write to me at the castle. Please.'

'OK. Go then.'

'Goodbye, Allana. May The Lord protect you.'

She did not answer, turning her back on him, and shortly afterwards he and the two horses had departed. The lantern which he had left for her cast a small radius of light, and the shape of him was quickly swallowed by the darkness outside. Leaving her alone, in an unknown countryside in the middle of the night. She reached into the bag before her, pulled out a dress, and started to change.

She took a deep breath, forcibly trying to maintain her calm, despite the unknown threat suggested by the surrounding blackness. He had abandoned her, despite his promise. And her upset at his decision was quickly hardening into anger, tinged with a trace of fear.

But she had been in worse situations than this, and she had survived. She had saved herself from Ronis. Had escaped from Sen Aiduel. Had made it to Andar. Had survived torture. And only tonight, by her own efforts she had escaped from certain death from within the fortress of Aiduel's Guards. She had survived it all. And she would survive again. With or without him.

You will escape from here, Lana. You'll use his plan, and his money, and his letter, and you'll get to Rednarron. You will escape, and you will survive.

And after that? After, you'll remember the choice that he made here, on this night. You will always remember it.

31

Arion

—

Year of Our Lord,
After Ascension, 769AA

In the hour before dawn, four days after he had departed from Allana, Arion was standing outside in the open air. He was cold, but he was completely alert.

He had much time to contemplate matters, within the blanketing darkness. However, his thoughts were drawn towards the radiant external presence located somewhere to the north-east. Pulsing towards him, from the direction of the Elannis army encampment.

He had been feeling this presence for all of the night, and even now it continued to stimulate his senses. And every time that it radiated outwards again, it energised and revitalised him, and was helping him to remain fully awake despite the unsociable hour.

It was the same sensation as when he had first become aware of Allana dei Monis. This presence therefore had to be the Dei Magnun girl who had so entranced him, and that realisation made his stomach knot with anxiety. Despite everything that he had done, despite all of his efforts, could she somehow be there right now, a captive in the midst of the enemy camp?

Four days and nights had passed since he had parted company with Allana, and had abandoned her by the side of a little-used trail. He could clearly recall the look of anguish and fear on her face after she had realised that he was determined to leave her. And he could picture the way that her distress had gradually hardened into something else until, at the end, her expression had appeared closer to bitterness.

He knew that he had done everything that he could for her, in the circumstances. Without his intervention, she would undoubtedly have been captured within a couple of miles of Septholme. He had given her a significant head-start over her pursuers, had gifted her the money and provisions which she would need, and he had provided her with a plan of escape.

And yet, in those last minutes together, she had looked at him as if he was a betrayer and a breaker of promises. She had ignored all of the things that he had done and was doing for her, and she had focused purely on what he was not doing. Not escaping with her. Not fleeing together.

Lord preserve me. I had only just met her. I saved her. I killed a man for her! How could she have expected more?

But he knew the answer to that question. In the meeting at the fortress, he had promised more. And he had wanted more. Even now, just thinking about her in these darkness hours, made him imagine the tantalising possibilities if he had decided to go with her. If they were together, right now, sharing a bed. Making love under thick warm covers, and feeling cocooned in each other's embrace.

Rather than standing outside in the cold of the night, and counting down the hours until he would be in mortal danger.

Being in her presence on that night of escape had again flooded him with energy and vitality. He could clearly remember the way that her body had felt as she had pressed herself back against him, on his horse. It had made him want her even more, even amidst the danger of their escape, although he had battled within himself to suppress those feelings. He had reached such a level of inner crisis, during that flight from the fort, that he had been unable to look at her lest his willpower break. He had been relieved when he was no longer holding her, and had even tried to avoid speaking with her.

But he could vividly recall some of her last words to him. 'I *know* we were meant to meet. Meant to be together. To be lovers. Soulmates. You know it, too.'

Part of him had known that she spoke the truth, and he had almost succumbed in the moments after she had uttered those words. Had almost allowed her to move in, and to kiss him. And if she had done that, he doubted that he would be here, now. A brush of her lips against his would probably have been enough for a lifetime of accumulated loyalty to his family and country to be undone. He would instead be somewhere away from here, fleeing northwards with Allana.

But he had pulled away from her, and the frailties and doubts of his inner turmoil had been lost on her. She had felt abandoned and betrayed. He had then sent her off into the expanse of Western Canasar, alone and possibly in great danger. Under threat from her pursuers, and from warring forces, in a land which she did not know.

After leaving her that night he had wondered; would he ever see her again? And after her abandonment, would she ever *want* to see him again?

But he was surely sensing her again, now. Feeling her vibrant pulsing presence, to the north-east. Sensing her as she must be sensing him. And her location had to be within the encampment of the massive Army of Western Elannis.

The army which Arion was determined to destroy, in the hours ahead.

—

The prior week had been extremely busy and challenging for Arion, and for the entire Sepian household. All of their collective efforts had been focused towards a single defining battle, which would come to pass on this day.

The muster of the armies of Western Canasar had taken place rapidly and efficiently, as House Sepian had scrambled to assemble its troops in response to the unexpected invasion. The work and planning put into place by Duke Conran and Charl Koss in the preceding years had come to fruition, and had allowed Arion to quickly gather a critical mass of force.

Arion had set out from Septholme on the morning after his parting from Allana, leading a contingent of fourteen hundred infantry and six hundred cavalry. Charl Koss and Menion Thatcher had joined this assembled army, but they had all agreed that Gerrion should remain in Septholme. The new Duke was to lead the defence of the town if necessary, but his principal reason for remaining was to co-ordinate actions with the royal Pavil family, and with the other major Houses of Andar.

Arion had been regularly updated on the various diplomatic developments, ever since the invasion had begun. The news of the attack on the Ninth Fort had been followed a few hours later by an approach to King Inneos, in Andarron, by the Ambassador of Elannis. The Empire's diplomat had communicated that his country had no desire to go to war with the whole of Andar, and merely wanted to reassert the rule of the House of Canas over Canasar. The Elannis attack had therefore been restricted to the Canasar region, and any conflict would end once Andar ceded the territory.

Arion was aware that the King had rebuffed this approach, and that Andar had now declared war on the Empire. The King's diplomats had also attempted to contact the Archlaw, demanding that the Emperor of Elannis be threatened with excommunication, unless the illegal invasion was ceased. However, as far as Arion was aware, there had been no response from the head of the Holy Church.

Gerrion had also written to request immediate aid from both of the noble families which held lands bordering Western Canasar; namely, the Houses of Rednar and Berun. The response from Duke Rednar had been swift, promising that he was mustering a relief force. This army would be marching into Western Canasar within the next two weeks, under the leadership of Lennion Rednar.

The response from Duke Berun had been very different:

> Dear Duke Sepian,
>
> Thank you for your warning about the invasion of Western Canasar, by Elannis. The armies of Berun are mustering immediately in response. However, our intentions are to bolster our river forces at the Tenth, Eleventh and Twelfth bridges, and to defend the southern borders of the lands of Berun. We will not be marching our forces south into Western Canasar unless we are responding to an attack against our own land. I will seek to protect my own borders and people, as you must do with yours.
>
> Yours sincerely,
> Duke Jarrett Berun

Arion had cursed when he had first been told of this response. However, he knew that it was predictable given the animosity between himself and Jarrett Berun, and the prior dislike between the two Houses. The armies of Berun would anyway not have arrived in time to influence the decisive coming battle.

Arion was resigned to the fact that Western Canasar had to hold out without external assistance for as long as possible, and certainly until relief forces arrived. That meant protecting the capital, Septholme, which in turn required them to intercept and defeat the main enemy force.

And that would happen here, today, at Moss Ford.

Arion's initial force had moved northwards from Septholme, and then had started to gather additional numbers at a muster point three miles to the south of Moss Ford. Over the two days subsequent to the assembly camp being established, many local lords and commanders had arrived with their troops, bringing a further three thousand infantry and twelve hundred cavalry. Over six thousand soldiers in total, forming Arion's main army of defence. But still not enough against the massed ranks of over ten thousand of the enemy, which he had witnessed crossing the river in his dream.

Arion was aware that he had taken a significant risk by ordering the defence to be set up here, to the south of Moss Ford. Other than at Moss Ford, where rocks widened the river and lowered the water level, the Sept River was a fast-flowing and deep body of water, thirty metres across, and it was unpassable on foot or by horse. However, if the enemy army had chosen to travel directly towards Septholme from Canasholme, following the main roads, then a bridge twenty miles to the east of Moss Ford would have been the most natural route for them to pass over. And today, they would have found that bridge to be defended by only a token force.

But Arion had trusted in his dream. The prophecy in the dream had told him that the enemy intended to cross at Moss Ford, and he had gambled to concentrate all of his forces here.

An even riskier decision several days ago had been to send messages to the towns of Canasholme and Eastholme, and to order them to immediately transfer almost all of their cavalry to this place. To leave the defence of those towns to their infantry and their walls, such that he could gather as many mounted troops as possible in one location. And it had worked. His order at first had been questioned, but Gerrion had supported him to insist that it was done as soon as possible. The massed cavalry from those two towns had arrived just the afternoon before. Barely in time. But giving him enough troops to now have a belief in the possibility of victory.

The pieces of his military plan had therefore arrived in the right place, at the right time, and in sufficient numbers. Then, late yesterday evening as the sun was setting, from a hidden vantage point he and Charl had watched the Army of Western Elannis arriving on the opposite banks of the Sept River, on the northern side of Moss Ford. He had watched that army set up its camp there, on the far side of the waterway, as darkness fell.

And at that moment, Arion had at last felt certain that his dream was a true prophecy of what was to come.

—

He turned around, now, looking for the soldiers who were near to him. The first hints of dawn had appeared in the sky, with the sun soon to emerge on the eastern horizon. It was time to act.

'Lord Arion? Is it time?' The question was asked by Captain Menion Thatcher. The captain was waiting twenty metres away, with a number of other soldiers and their horses.

'It is. Issue the orders. Every man to his horse. They must be ready to ride within fifteen minutes, and I want them assembled in this valley within fifteen minutes of that. In silence. And for the avoidance of blunder, repeat this instruction down the chain of command again. No man or horse is to climb that hill or to be visible over that crest until we're ready to charge. I'll hang any man who breaks that order. It's that important.'

As Arion spoke, he pointed to the crest of a shallow hill to the north, a gentle elevation which lay between their position and the Sept River. The hill acted to block the view from here of the water, of Moss Ford, and of the Elannis encampment. It therefore also kept Arion and his accompanying soldiers out of the enemy's line of sight.

Thatcher reissued the orders to the men around him, and a number of those soldiers quickly mounted their horses and rode away. Back towards the place where half of Arion's total cavalry strength was waiting, further out of sight a few hundred metres to the south.

Arion was left in the company of Thatcher and four other

541

soldiers. Arion ordered the remaining soldiers to hold their horses, and then he gestured for Thatcher to follow him up the shallow hill.

As they neared the top, Arion first crouched, then dropped to a crawl, and then finally he lay flat out on the ground at the crest of the hill. The tip of the sun had still not appeared over the horizon, but there was sufficient light now to fully reveal the Elannis army camp which sprawled before them.

The enemy army was camped on the northern side of the river, on the land next to Moss Ford, less than a quarter of a mile from Arion's current position. Arion's vantage point at the crest of the hill was twenty metres elevated above the river and the camp. There were approximately two hundred metres of open grassy fields between his position and the waterway. Arion could see hundreds of tents set out in straight lines within the encampment, suggesting thousands of enemy soldiers.

Lord preserve us, there must be over ten thousand there.

Even now, in the half-light before dawn, the enemy camp was coming to life, with fires appearing in various places. The Elannis forces had arrived too late the night before to attempt to ford the river before nightfall, but Arion had no doubt that such a crossing was going to take place early today. And that it would be expedited when the enemy witnessed an army of Andar marching towards them.

'There's a lot of them,' said Thatcher, echoing Arion's thoughts from a moment earlier. 'Awful lot of men.'

Arion turned to him, forcing himself to appear more confident than he felt. 'That's to the good. They've gathered themselves in one place for us. Made it easy. We break this army, we break the invasion.'

Arion had already spotted and recognised the insignia on the flag flying from the main central tent of the encampment. Prince Markon El'Augustus was here, leading the army. Arion's opponent was the Emperor's firstborn son, and a man whose many monikers spoke of his substantial military accomplishments and infamy; The Hawk, The Golden Heir, The Conqueror of Sennam, The Victor

542

of Patran. A man who had known war for the last fifteen years, and whose campaigns Arion had once studied in a lesson at the Academy. This man had come to conquer Western Canasar and to destroy House Sepian, and this would be the foe who Arion must pit his wits against to secure victory.

Arion could still feel the radiant external presence as he lay watching the enemy camp, and his eyes scanned around the site now. Where was Allana? Which tent was she inside? And what was she doing there? There was no way to discern her precise location from this distance, but he was certain that she was close. And that she would be able to sense him, too. With every pulse of her presence he continued to feel refreshed and renewed. And strong.

Arion was also glancing towards the south-east, tracing the route of the Sept River as it meandered away. Somewhere along that river, in that direction, were the other two parts of the Western Canasar army. Arion had taken the bold decision, which Charl had at first argued against, to split his forces. Arion had acknowledged to Charl that it was not conventional military tactics to separate an army, but to achieve his objective today required him to do just that. But somewhere in that direction, Charl would have his force ready to move. Waiting.

Arion continued to watch the sky to the east. Finally, the tip of the sun appeared above the horizon. That was the signal for Charl to move. The plan was underway.

—

Arion was then a spectator for a period of time, his eyes moving between the Elannis camp and the place to the south-east where he knew that Charl's force would first appear.

Eventually, after twenty minutes of agitated waiting, the anticipated ranks of Andar troops appeared in the distance. They were marching from the south-east, on Arion's side of the river, towards the Elannis camp. Arion exhaled, then glanced back

543

towards the valley at his rear. His own ranks of cavalry were forming up there.

The Elannis encampment had already demonstrated lots of activity before anyone had caught sight of the approaching Andar army. Soldiers in the camp were eating, and some tents were being dismantled. However, once the Elannis sentries spotted Charl's force, there was a whirlwind of activity throughout the site. Arion could not help but be impressed by the speed at which men were assembled into organised ranks. Then he smiled as he saw the first of those ranks moving to cross the ford.

This was the key moment; Markon could have decided to maintain his position and to defend the ford on the northern side, in which case his army would have been unassailable. However, he had instead chosen to cross his men at speed, clearly confident that he would be able to form up sufficient ranks in time to keep the ford open. And to allow the rest of his army to subsequently cross and to secure victory.

Charl's advancing force was on the same southern side of the river as Arion, to the south-east. Arion had determined the troop numbers which had been allocated to Charl's command; four thousand eight hundred infantry, and four hundred cavalry. Upon spotting such numbers, Prince Markon and his advisers might have believed that they were facing the whole strength of the main army of Western Canasar. And they might also have perceived an opportunity to destroy that outnumbered enemy, by swiftly crossing the ford.

Arion continued to watch the two opposing armies moving across the vista in front of him. The mighty Elannis army was splashing across the narrow river ford, and the smaller Andar army was advancing along the path of the river. As the Elannis troops cleared the ford on the southern side, they were immediately forming into orderly ranks. Facing in a south-easterly direction, towards Charl's advancing force, and away from Arion's position.

Then Arion observed Prince Markon and his retinue of

bodyguards starting to cross the ford. They were in the midst of hundreds of men who were also making the crossing. The Prince and his bodyguards were all mounted knights, each of them wearing gleaming, resplendent armour. The Prince rode beside his Hawk banner.

As Arion regarded all of this, there was a moment when he recognised exactly what he was witnessing. He was seeing the *exact* images which had been in his prophetic dream, from the precise same vantage point. He felt an abrupt moment of unsteadiness, and then he knew that his vision had been correct. He had foreseen this moment in his prophecy, he had made all of his tactical plans and had staked their lives on the back of it, and now it was proven to be true.

But the significant difference was that in the dream he had not known what he was seeing. In the haze of the dream, he had thought that the Andar force marching northwards was alone and heavily outnumbered.

Now, he knew the truth. He turned around, looking at the land to the south of his position. Fifteen hundred Andar cavalry were now assembled there.

—

In the handful of minutes following that, Arion watched Charl Koss forming his army up into six companies; three infantry companies in the front rank, a block of archers and a separate infantry company in reserve, and a small cavalry force protecting their left flank. Arion was also able to observe the Elannis army manoeuvring into formation opposite them, while a hail of arrows flew across the neutral ground between the two armies.

At the moment when the opposing forces on the southern riverbank seemed ready to launch into each other, Arion estimated that half of the army of Elannis had already forded the river. There were several hundred more in the midst of making the crossing, and the remainder were clustered on the northern bank, waiting for their turn to wade across. Prince Markon's banner was to the rear of his army and still close to the southern mouth of the ford, within a cluster of several hundred of his cavalry.

Arion stayed in his hidden position, lying down, two hundred metres from these events. He waited until the precise moment when he could see Charl's infantry starting to charge forwards.

He then immediately turned away, descending the hill as rapidly as possible as he ran towards his own cavalry, with Thatcher following him. Their horses were brought to them, and Arion mounted quickly, before donning his helmet. He was armoured with the standard cavalry equipment of helmet, breastplate and chainmail, the latter covered with the blue tabard of Andar. His sword and shield were passed up to him, and once they were in his gauntleted grip, he wheeled his horse around and rode in front of the assembled lines of mounted soldiers, his weapon raised high.

There would be no time for rousing speeches now, not when he could already hear the clash of weapons and screams from the southern bank of the river. Not when Charl's men were already engaged in battle.

Instead, he simply shouted, 'For Andar! For House Sepian! For Canasar! And for glory!'

Then he turned his horse, pointed his sword towards the crest of the hill, and he started to ride back up the slope and towards the enemy.

Within moments, the earth-shaking trampling of thousands of hooves told him that his cavalry was undoubtedly following him.

—

In the moment when his horse crested the hill, riding alongside hundreds of other charging Andar cavalry, Arion was alive with energy and excitement.

He was invigorated by the natural thrill of being part of such a mass cavalry charge. And he was also still vibrantly aware of Allana's nearby presence. It continued to radiate from somewhere inside the enemy's camp, and in this exhilarating moment it was further fuelling and strengthening him.

'For Andar!'

Once his mounted force appeared over the crest of the hill, the time for subterfuge was over. Arion was one of the many hundreds of voices yelling out those words as they galloped towards the enemy, who were just two hundred metres away. Combined with the thundering sound of galloping hooves hammering against the ground, their massed charge was deafening.

The enemy infantry were initially all facing away from Arion's cavalry, many of them already engaged with Charl's forces. Arion knew that fear would be flooding through their ranks as they first noticed the formidable cavalry charge, which was heading towards their exposed flanks and rear.

This was Arion's plan. He intended to strike the Elannis army when it was divided by the Moss Ford crossing. He would drive his cavalry into the vulnerable sides of the troops who had managed to cross, and then he would see them crushed against the banks of the river.

As he closed the distance towards the enemy at full gallop, Arion again experienced the miraculous sensation which had erupted within him twice before; once with Jarrett Berun, and again in the battle with the Bergen raiders. Time abruptly decelerated around him, and he could feel coils of energy rippling around and through his limbs. This time, the feeling was even more intense, perhaps given strength by his exhilaration or through the nearby presence of Allana? And now that he recognised the sensation, he rejoiced in it. He felt alive, and brimming with vitality. He instinctively knew that he would be more powerful and strong and quick than any man there.

The world had slowed to a crawl around him, and therefore despite closing the ground to the enemy in less than thirty seconds,

Arion was able to witness and digest all of the Elannis reactions to the Andar cavalry charge. He could see Markon's immediate response, as the Prince's body of cavalry wheeled to protect the Moss Ford crossing point. And he was able to observe as the Elannis infantry reserves started to manoeuvre to face towards the new threat.

But their efforts would be too little, and too late. Too many of Markon's men were still trapped on the ford or on the other side of the river, and too many of his infantry on this side of the river had their flanks fatally exposed.

STRENGTH. VICTORY. GLORY.

The power within Arion was building with every passing moment. In the exhilarating final seconds as they closed upon the enemy, his body felt like it would burst with simmering energy. And then it felt instinctive to be releasing some of that energy. Letting it discharge outwards, cascading over the Andar cavalry who were about and around him. Letting his own troops share in the feelings of invigoration, speed and strength which now coursed through his own body.

Then they smashed into the enemy. Many of Arion's line slammed directly into Markon's company of cavalry which was charging in response, near to the ford crossing point. Others crashed into Markon's body of infantry reserves, which was massed behind his main force. And many more ripped into the exposed flanks of the Elannis main infantry line, which was already engaged with Charl's infantry.

Arion himself was engaged directly with the Elannis infantry reserves. And it was carnage. The enemy infantry had gained no opportunity to advance pike-men to their front ranks, and as such Arion's cavalry simply ploughed through and over them, trampling and crushing hundreds of men within seconds. Arion found himself at least ten ranks deep within the enemy before his momentum was slowed, and then his sword was whirling about him in a blur of death and bloodshed.

As had happened with the Bergen raiders, time was moving so slowly around him that it was an easy matter to avoid or block each incoming blow, and it was effortless to slaughter his opponents. Within minutes, he had personally killed over ten men, and each personal victory acted to fuel his vigour and strength even more.

He again screamed the words, 'For Andar!'

Without conscious effort, his power was streaming out across all of the Andar soldiers around him. He was not aware of how he was achieving it, and could not know for sure whether they were experiencing it with the same intensity which he was, but his men were fighting with a speed and ferocity which was astonishing. This further served to add to the advantage which they already possessed, while fighting from horseback.

The men of Elannis were putting up sturdy and brave resistance, given the sudden adversity of their situation and their early casualties. Arion was certain that he was fighting tested veterans. But he also knew that it would not be enough for them, under such vicious assault. The enemy was retreating backwards steadily under the ferocious pressure, but they were already trapped against the river, and the logjam of the ford was their only outlet of escape.

—

After several minutes of battle had passed, Arion gained a small respite from the fighting. He used this as an opportunity to move his horse backward up the shallow slope away from the river, from where he sought to gain a better perspective of the developments around him.

To his right, he could see that the cavalry charge against the Elannis infantry had caused the enemy line to collapse on its right flank. The mass of the Elannis infantry was now trapped between Charl's force to the south-east, the river to their north-east, and the masses of their own men and Arion's cavalry to the west. The fighting between that main infantry force and Charl's men was bloody, but

Arion could quickly see that Charl's army had now gained a clear numerical advantage.

Directly in front of Arion, the infantry reserves of Elannis were a broken force. They had been pushed back to the river, and were surrounded by Arion's cavalry. Even now, Arion could hear splashes and screams as men were forced over the river banks and into the water, under the press of bodies. It would only be a matter of time before that body of men was obliterated. Already, some of the Andar cavalry who had been engaging them were free to turn against the rear of the remaining encircled Elannis infantry.

But to Arion's left, in the area in front of the mouth of the ford, the strongest Elannis resistance remained. Prince Markon's banner still stood tall in front of the ford entrance, and Arion could see that the troops of Elannis in that vicinity were now making a slow and orderly retreat back across the river.

Markon's body of cavalry appeared to have beaten off the Andar cavalry charge against them. Arion now spotted the Prince himself. The Elannis leader was exhorting his mounted troops to hold their ground, clearly attempting to facilitate an escape back to the northern bank for as many of his soldiers as possible. Arion knew that the enemy must realise that the day was now lost for them; Prince Markon's objective would be to retreat to and hold the northern bank, with as large a fighting force remaining as possible.

There were still several thousand of the Elannis army either on Moss Ford, or on the northern banks, so Markon might be able to regroup with a fighting force which remained dangerous if he achieved that objective. Indeed, several hundred Elannis soldiers on the northern bank had now formed up on the river edge, and were firing volleys of arrows across the water into Charl Koss's ranks of infantry. Arion's eyes scanned to the east with frustration, searching for other activity on the north side of the river.

Where are you, Berker? Lord preserve us, where are you?

Then he spotted the final element of his plan, coming into sight in the distance. Over a thousand more Andar cavalry, the contingents from Canasholme and Eastholme, led by Commander Berker of Canasholme. Yesterday, Arion had ordered these men to cross the distant eastern bridge, to the northern side of the river. They had been given precise instructions as to when and where they were to attack. Now, this second mounted force was charging towards the Elannis troops on the northern banks. Towards the Elannis encampment.

This was the moment when Arion knew that he must act to finally shatter the will of the Elannis army. Even now, under such adversity and losses, they were holding together and maintaining discipline for their Prince. But if Arion could capture the Prince's banner and destroy the cavalry ranks guarding the mouth of the ford, he felt certain that that the enemy would be ready to rout.

'Andar cavalry! To me! To me!' Arion shouted the words as loudly as he could, whirling his sword above his head. The cry was lost to many of those around him within the cacophony of battle sounds, but at least twenty of his cavalry noted his shouts and gathered around Arion and his horse. Arion pointed towards the ford. 'Prince Markon! We want Markon!'

Arion started to charge towards the enemy Prince's position. At the same moment, the Andar cavalry on the northern banks swept into and over the enemy archers, who had been firing across the water. The mounted troops under Berker's command then smashed into the enemy companies clustered around the northern entry to the Moss Ford crossing, and heavy fighting also immediately ensued there.

More of Arion's mounted troops were joining him as he closed the distance towards Markon's retinue of bodyguards and accompanying cavalry. 'Markon! Markon!' The cry was repeated many times, and each of the Andar horsemen in this new charge now knew who their target was.

The world was still slowed down as Arion watched the last metres close towards Markon's cavalry, and he was feeling no fatigue from the battle as energy rippled and coursed through his limbs.

Then he was again bashing into the midst of the enemy, this time fighting knights and experienced veterans on horseback.

In the minutes that followed he was lost in a frenzy of battle and bloodletting. His opponents still moved in a snail-like fashion in comparison to his hyper-alert senses, and his blows relentlessly cleaved and sliced the foes around him. Each personal victory gave him more strength and vitality, and he knew that this energy was constantly flowing outwards and over his own men.

Kill them! Kill them! Kill them! Kill them!

The enemy cavalry was now being pushed steadily backwards, towards the mouth of the ford. More and more of Markon's elite knights were falling under the sustained and frenzied attack of Arion's cavalry. At the same time, Elannis's remaining infantry on the southern banks of the river had been fully surrounded, and were trapped and squeezed against the riverbank. In their tens, then in their hundreds, enemy soldiers in armour were being pushed into the fast flowing water. On the northern bank, the attack by Berker's cavalry had closed the ford escape route there under the weight of battling forces. Many Elannis troops were now trapped on the ford.

'Save the Prince! Save the Prince!' Arion heard the cry from Markon's personal bodyguards as he drew closer to Markon's banner. With the trap having been closed by the Andar cavalry charge on the northern bank, Arion knew that the Elannis Prince must now be in no doubt as to the mortal peril he was in.

Arion cut down another opponent, then another, but men were throwing themselves into his path, and he could see the Prince's banner moving slowly away from him. Could see the Prince and his remaining bodyguards entering the ford, and literally riding over their own infantrymen to attempt to cross it. The remaining Elannis cavalry on the southern bank were desperately trying to hold their ground, trying to sell their lives dearly enough to secure time for their Prince's escape.

'Markon! Markon!' Arion repeated the cry, and renewed his assault on the foes before him. Cutting down one. Then another.

Then another. He was covered in blood by now, roaring with anger, and he knew that he must be a terrifying and dreadful prospect for the men opposing him. 'Markon! Markon!'

Kill them! Kill them! Kill them! Kill them!

Arion's cavalry force surged forwards again in support, finally shattering the last line of defence against the entry to the ford. Arion and his men charged towards the crossing. Markon and his bodyguards were now halfway across, having forced many of their own men off the ford and into the deeper water around it, in their attempt to flee.

This was the point when the discipline of the Western Army of Elannis finally collapsed. Men who had attempted to hold their ground during a battle that was going disastrously, and who had remained in formation, eventually lost their nerve and started to panic. On both the southern and northern banks of the river, Elannis soldiers started to either throw down their weapons in surrender, or began to flee. And that attempted flight quickly turned into a rout.

Arion and his cavalry charged across the shallower water of Moss Ford five abreast, and Arion was unforgiving of any enemy soldiers who remained on the ford in his path. Markon and his bodyguards had almost reached the mass of men on the northern bank of the river, when Arion finally caught up to them. Elannis soldiers there were routing, fleeing to the west along the banks of the river, trying to escape the pursuit of Berker's cavalry.

Arion could finally see the enemy prince up close. Markon was a large man, whose armour was now looking significantly less resplendent, and a lot more battered, than it had at the start of the battle. The prince and his remaining bodyguard of over ten knights appeared to be the only Elannis soldiers on the battlefield who were not fleeing mindlessly. Markon wheeled his horse to face Arion's group, and then shouted, as if in recognition that the day was utterly lost, 'To the death!'

The fighting which ensued was fast, bloody and brutal. These were Markon's best troops, his elite bodyguard, and the narrow width of the ford meant that only five Andar cavalry could face five of the enemy at any one time. But Arion's speed, strength and reactions were the difference. He battered his way through his first two opponents, and then he was in amongst the enemy, slicing and cutting his sword through armour and flesh. In moments, Markon's banner-man and his banner had fallen.

Then Arion was facing Prince Markon, after the prince's retinue had been slaughtered. The enemy leader came at Arion with anger and skill, his sword delivering a flurry of quick attacks. But with Arion's enhanced powers it was a simple matter for him to deflect these, and then to find an opening. In a split second, Arion instinctively thrust his sword forwards, putting all of his might into the blow. The blade pierced the armour of the Elannis heir, entering deeply into his stomach. The Prince gasped and dropped his sword as the blow struck home, and then he slid sideways off his horse, crashing to the ground below.

Arion watched the enemy prince fall, and was barely cognisant of the rout and the massacre which was now taking place all around him. They had won.

—

Within minutes, the battle had ended. The surviving Elannis soldiers on the southern bank of the river had now all thrown down their arms and surrendered. Those to the north of the river were in heedless flight, being pursued and cut down by the cavalry under Berker's command. The Army of Western Elannis had been humiliated and destroyed.

By the Lord, we did it. We won!

After he had defeated Markon, Arion's battle frenzy seemed to ebb away in moments. He suddenly felt a whisper of fatigue, despite still being aware of Allana's external presence, which was now much closer and more palpable given that he had crossed the ford. He leaned forward to hold the pommel of his saddle, trying to collect his thoughts. He could see the many thick splatters of blood and gore covering his breastplate and chainmail, and he wondered grimly as to how many lives he had personally ended on this day. Thirty? Forty? Fifty? He was not sure, but he had been an unstoppable bringer of death to his foes.

Arion noticed then that the last of his victims, the enemy prince, was actually still alive. Markon was writhing in the shallow water of the ford, moaning and clutching his stomach.

Arion resolved that he needed to quickly find Allana, amidst the chaos which was now enveloping the enemy camp. And now that he was calming down, he realised that he had been reckless to strike the final blow against Prince Markon. There could be great leverage to be gained by holding the Emperor's son. He needed to try to keep the prince alive, despite the apparent severity of the wound.

He shouted an order to the Andar cavalrymen around him. 'Get Markon on a horse! Follow me! We must find a healer!'

They were riding into the enemy encampment in moments, with Markon's body hoisted over a horse following behind Arion. There was panic all around the camp, as non-combatant followers of the Elannis army were taking flight and were being cut down by pursuing Andar soldiers. Arion was aware that he could try to stop this, and could call a halt to the revenge attacks taking place around him, but right now he had other priorities. And anyway, all of the people being struck down had knowingly and willingly joined this invasion. They had been party to the aggressive actions of their army, and they did not deserve his mercy.

He peered around, trying to gain sight of anything which might be an enemy field hospital. Finally, he spotted a larger white tent, standing slightly separate, on the far side of the site. He could also feel the presence of Allana, coming from that same direction.

He rode towards it, feeling her radiant aura ever more strongly as he came closer. Drawing nearer to her rejuvenated him, and coils of energy surged around his limbs again, causing the fatigue which had briefly assailed him to be cast away. Despite the horror of the morning, he felt a thrill of anticipation and nervous excitement that he was going to reunite with her.

He swung down from his horse, shouting for four of his soldiers to bring Markon's now unconscious body. He pushed open the entrance flap on the tent.

'Allana! All-'

He stopped speaking when he properly took note of the scene in front of him. He had indeed located an Elannis field hospital. This was evident from the beds, tables and equipment which were set out within the pristinely clean interior space.

His eyes were drawn to the nine priests and priestesses, all of whom he assumed were healers, who were gathered in a circle in the centre of the tent. Each person was down on their knees, praying, but they looked up as he entered. He could see the fear and shock in their eyes as he regarded them, and then even more horror as the Andar soldiers dragged in the badly wounded prince.

A priestess in her late-forties in age, with long black hair, stood up to face him. She looked scared, but was clearly trying to control her fear in front of the others. 'Yes, sir knight, can I help you?'

Arion lifted his hand, palm forwards, instructing her to be silent. His eyes scanned across the assembled healers, but he could not see the person who he wanted to see. Allana was not here. And yet he could feel her here, within the tent. Her presence was crying out to him.

'Where's Allana?' His voice sounded hoarse, and more aggressive than he had intended.

'I'm sorry, sir knight, we don't-'

Again, he raised his hand, instructing the black-haired priestess to cease talking.

His eyes had fallen upon another figure in the circle of kneeling healers. While the others had since lowered their heads, appearing to cower from him, this one had raised her chin towards him. And she was staring at him with a wide-eyed expression on her face, which seemed to convey a mixture of terror and wonderment.

He stared back at her, his eyes locking onto hers. She was not Allana, and indeed was nothing at all like Allana. This young woman's eyes were a dazzlingly clear blue, and her hair was long and straight and golden blonde.

But he could feel her, inside himself. Pulsing. Alive. Radiant. Pure. This girl, this priestess, was the source of the external presence which he had been sensing for the several hours before. Which had energised and sustained him, throughout the battle.

And he knew that she could feel him, too.

32

Leanna

—

Year of Our Lord,
After Ascension, 769AA

Leanna was not certain as to when she had first become aware that the battle was turning into a disaster.

Perhaps the doubts had started when the enemy cavalry on the south side of the river had charged thunderously into the men of Elannis? However, she suspected that she had still been harbouring naive delusions of victory, even then.

But that delusion had been shattered when the second cavalry charge had smashed into the troops on her own side of the river. In that latter instant, she had known without any doubt that she was witnessing a devastating defeat for her countrymen.

And she had understood then that she and all of the other healers were in grave danger.

—

Earlier that day, Leanna had been awake for several hours before the battle had commenced, and she had been deep in prayer.

She had awoken in the middle of the night from her recurring dream, having experienced it as vividly as she could ever remember. Had there been a figure in the Gate, raising a single finger?

Thankfully, her restlessness had not woken the other healers who were sharing her tent. However, she had felt a pang of longing for Amyss to be there in the darkness, holding her. As she had held Leanna on so many other occasions across the last two years, in the aftermath of Leanna's troubled dreaming.

But then Leanna's musings had been cut short by her awareness of the external presence. She had felt Him there, with her, in the night. A vibrant presence, suffusing her with energy and courage, as she lay on the cot in her tent. Coursing around and through her. Filling her with vitality.

She had known immediately that it must be The Lord Aiduel. He was watching over them. Watching their camp. From somewhere close. Blessing the Army of Western Elannis with His presence.

The knowledge that she was near to Him again had made her feel replete with glory and wonder. He had once come to her at the altar in her school, and He had called her to His service. And now He had come to her again in these dark hours, when she and the army needed His protection and love. She had fallen to her knees at the bottom of her cot as she had realised this, joyfully clutching her small statue of The Lord Aiduel On The Tree. She had then started to pray.

Lord Aiduel, thank you, thank you, for coming to us in this time of fear and danger. Please bless this army, Lord.

And she had known that He was listening, because her body had continued to be bombarded with life-giving energy. Making her feel wonderful and loved, and keeping her awake for the remainder of the night.

—

His presence had still been with her as the sun had first shown its face to the day. Her eyes had been drawn to a specific point at that moment, to a shallow hill to the south of the river. It had felt like He was there, watching her from the crest of that hill. His presence was repeatedly announced with regular throbbing pulses, like the beating of a loving heart.

She had been standing outside of the hospital tent, staring towards that hill, when an alert had been raised that an approaching enemy army had been spotted, on the opposite side of the river. She had watched with admiration as the encampment had come quickly to life, and the army of Elannis had started to cross the river in orderly ranks to face the enemy.

Colissa had been standing at her shoulder in those moments, also watching, and at one point the older woman had leaned closer to Leanna and had said, 'This will be the decisive battle.'

Leanna had understood then why The Lord Aiduel had come to them, in this place. He was there to fortify them and to protect them. To be their sword and their shield, on this momentous day.

Lord Aiduel, please watch over us, and bring victory to our men today.

Then the two mighty armies had clashed, on the other side of the water, and the spectacle had been both awesome and terrible.

'There will be much work for us, today.' This statement had been made by one of Leanna's colleagues, as the sounds of battle had carried across to them. Leanna had only nodded, her eyes still drawn to the small hill on the southern side of the river.

Many soldiers of Elannis had still been queuing to cross the ford and to join the battle, at the instant when she had first spotted the hundreds of horsemen appearing over the crest of that hill. Leanna had been amongst the first to notice them, since her eyes had already been drawn that way. Despite the fear that she had experienced at seeing hundreds of Andar cavalry suddenly emerge, there had also been a frisson of awe at such an imposing sight.

She had shouted and pointed, and there had been gasps of horror around her as they had all watched that mass of cavalry thundering towards their own troops. Had all heard and seen the way that the enemy smashed into and through the Elannis infantry men. Had all observed as Prince Markon's cavalry had suddenly become encircled by teeming masses of Andar horsemen.

And yet, even then, as it had seemed as if a wave of life-giving energy was suddenly washing over her from the south, Leanna had still not properly recognised the jeopardy facing the Elannis army. Thousands of Elannis men still queued up on her side of the river, ready to join the battle and to deliver victory.

Lord Aiduel, please give our men the strength and courage to endure this.

And it had felt like He had come closer to her, in response to her prayers. Like He had moved to support the faltering army, in the midst of the battlefield.

However, sometime afterwards, the second Andar cavalry charge had crashed into the Elannis encampment on Leanna's side of the river. Enemy horsemen had scythed through the troops waiting beside the ford, cutting into them and scattering them.

And then the panic had started.

—

Leanna was frozen with shock as she watched this latter attack unfold. It was happening within two hundred metres of her position, to the south of the encampment, and there was an air of unreality about it.

The field hospital tent where Leanna was standing had been placed on the northern edge of their encampment. If it had been located on the southern side, she now realised, they would be in the midst of that bloody conflict.

Leanna was still standing motionless, her mouth open in horror, as she watched the killing spread out across the most southerly of the tents in the camp. People were fleeing from in and around those tents, and they were being cut down as they ran. It was developing into carnage.

But it felt as if The Lord was coming ever closer to her.

Lord Aiduel, why is this happening? How can you allow this to happen, Lord?

Leanna was finally shaken out of her stunned paralysis by Colissa shouting, 'Quick, everyone inside the tent! Now!' Leanna looked around, dazedly, and saw Colissa, Perrien and the other priests and lay assistants moving back into the hospital tent. Colissa noted that Leanna was slow to move, and again shouted, 'Leanna! Get inside!'

Leanna turned and rushed into the tent, and Colissa immediately closed the entrance flap behind her, enclosing them within the white canvas walls. Colissa then said to them all, 'We're in great danger. We must hope now that they recognise us as healers and priests of the Holy Church, and show us mercy. But do nothing to upset or anger the men of Andar. Now, everyone, gather around me. Let us kneel and pray.'

Colissa dropped to her knees in the centre of the tent, and Leanna, Brother Perrien, four other healers and two lay assistants gathered with her. They formed a circle facing in towards each other, and Colissa started to lead them in quiet prayer.

Leanna was able to sense the anxiety emanating from her companions. She herself was full of fear; she could hear the screams and cries coming from the encampment outside, such noises gradually drawing closer. People were dying all around them, while the nine of them were as yet untouched. She closed her eyes and prayed, fervently.

Lord Aiduel, please do not abandon us. Lord, please protect your faithful on this awful day.

Despite all of her fears, it seemed like The Lord was closer to her than ever, and He was continuing to fill her with energy and vitality. But how could He be here, watching this battlefield, and yet be allowing this terrible outcome to happen to His faithful? Then an awful thought occurred to her; perhaps The Lord had deemed the cause of Elannis to be unjust, and was instead supporting the soldiers of Andar? Perhaps they should not have invaded this place? Could that be the only true explanation for the collapse of the Army of Western Elannis?

Lord Aiduel, please do not abandon us. Please protect Sister Colissa and the others from harm.

She hoped that The Lord had heard and was responding to her prayers, because His holy presence seemed to be coming closer and closer.

Everyone in the circle around her was murmuring in prayer, and the noises of horror in the encampment were drawing ever nearer. Then Leanna heard the sound of horses' hooves, from outside of the tent, followed by shouts. She opened her eyes to stare at the entrance flap of the tent, and her heart pounded with fear.

A voice was still shouting as an arm pushed the tent flap open. A male voice, deep and hoarse-sounding. 'Allana! All-'

The figure who entered the tent was the very personification of death and horror. He was extremely tall and broad, a towering presence within the enclosed space. A helm with a long nose-guard covered his head and much of his face, leaving just his eyes and the grim set of his mouth visible. His chin was red, clearly covered in blood. He was also wearing a breastplate and chainmail, with a blue Andar tabard, but all of these items were also coated in blood and gore, in streaks and spatters and globs. This *killer* had been deep in the midst of death today.

And yet, he pulsed towards her. And was vibrantly alive. Magnificently alive.

The iridescent emotions which emanated from him were like nothing that she had ever encountered before. Erratic. Unreadable. Incapable of interpretation. Yet so many and such varied emotions were being emitted from him, rapidly pulsing outwards with every heartbeat. In rainbow waves of golden white, black, and every colour in between. It stunned her.

563

The man's eyes roamed around the room, flashing quickly across Leanna. He was clearly searching for something. Then the tent flap shifted again, and four other Andar soldiers moved inside, half-carrying and half-dragging a limp figure between them. Leanna felt a rush of anxiety when she recognised the bloodied and motionless man who was placed on the floor inside the tent; Prince Markon lay before them, an apparent victim of this horrific killer. The prince's stomach was a fearsome wash of red. There were no ripples of agony coming from the prince, however; he was unconscious and seemed almost too far gone to be aware of any pain which he might be feeling.

Leanna's eyes returned to the large man standing inside their tent, and she was astonished by the energy which she could feel inside of him. Calling to her. Filling her with vibrant, pulsating life. Could this have been the person – the *thing* – which she had been mistaking for the presence of The Lord Aiduel? Just what was he? Despite the grim nature of his appearance, she could not take her eyes off him. She did not realise that she had lifted her head, mouth agape, and was staring at him whilst others around her looked away.

Lord Aiduel, please tell me what I'm seeing. Have you blessed him with powers too, Lord?

Leanna was vaguely aware of Sister Colissa rising to her feet, and walking towards the man. She was admiring of Colissa's bravery as the older woman asked, in a steady voice, 'Yes, sir knight, can I help you?'

Rudely, the man raised his hand to Colissa's face, to silence her. His voice was low and guttural as he spoke, sounding impatient and threatening, sending a chill through Leanna. 'Where's Allana?'

Colissa answered, 'I'm sorry, sir knight, we don't-'

Again, the man's hand was swiftly raised to silence Colissa, but on this occasion Leanna felt a rush of fear as for the first time his eyes found her, and locked upon her. Cold blue eyes, intensely scrutinising her. Leanna knew with certainty at that moment that he *was* the source of the external presence which she had been feeling, for the hours before and throughout the battle. And that in his direct presence and under his regard that feeling was magnified tenfold. Like being in the proximity of a blazing and life-giving sun.

And she knew with certainty then that he could feel her, too.

—

They continued to stare at each other for a few seconds. Who and what was this man? Could he possibly be what she had thought he might be? She spoke the word, still maintaining eye contact with him, but it came out as a half-choked whisper. 'Lord…'

Lord, is it you?

But then he took his gaze away from her, and addressed Colissa again, no more cordiality in his voice than before. 'Are you in charge here?'

'Yes, sir.'

'I'm Lord Arion Sepian, leader of the Army of Andar. Save this man. Keep him alive.' He gestured to Prince Markon, who lay unconscious on the floor.

'Of course, Lord,' replied Colissa. 'Please, carry him onto our operating table. Perrien, please help me.'

The four Andar soldiers lifted the prince again, and then carried him across to the table indicated by Colissa. They deposited him there, and then Leanna saw Colissa leaning in close to the stricken prince, checking his pulse. Perrien had joined his colleague beside the table, and Leanna herself rose to her feet, waiting to see if Colissa required further help.

As this was happening, Leanna sensed that the stranger, this Arion Sepian, was looking at her again. This time she did not return his stare, and she was trying to focus on the events taking place around the operating table. But she could feel him there, a palpable aura of energy whirling and cascading around him. Sometimes surging outwards, and enveloping her.

After a few moments, Colissa announced, 'He lives. Barely. Quick, Perrien, we must get this armour off him and inspect the wound.'

The two surgeon healers acted quickly to slice through the straps which held Prince Markon's plate armour in place. As the breastplate was peeled away, the wound to the prince's stomach came more clearly into view. Markon's shirt was awash with blood, and as Colissa cut the cloth apart, the full deep hole in the prince's stomach was revealed. Leanna observed Colissa staring at the wound for a few seconds, then saw the older priestess glance up at Perrien and shake her head. Perrien acknowledged the conclusion, with a grim expression on his face.

'Well?' Arion Sepian spoke up again. 'Can you save him?'

Colissa was quiet for a few moments, then finally replied, 'No, Lord Sepian. The prince's wound is mortal. We must pray for him and ease his passing, Lord.'

Sepian appeared to consider this, then shook his head, and bellowed, 'That's not good enough! If you value your lives, you'll save him!'

Leanna observed Colissa and Perrien recoiling backwards under the ferocity of the man's shout. However, these interactions were already starting to lose importance. She was becoming detached from the events around her, as she stared at Markon's fatal wound. She could feel herself slipping unerringly and willingly into that trance-like state, which had claimed her on a number of prior occasions.

Within a moment, she was observing Markon's injury with a vision which was unique just to her. The wound ran through his body, a condensed hole of blackness along the line where a blade had been thrust into and through him. That blackness was seeping out with fingers of death into the rest of his body; swirling towards and gripping his mind and his heart. Whispering to the prince. Calling him to surrender to his inevitable death.

In a seemingly faraway place, Leanna heard Colissa responding fearfully that there was nothing more which they could do. That it was a stomach wound and it was fatal. But the older woman's conversation seemed to be happening in another, distant, setting. A world from which Leanna was now distinct and separate.

In Leanna's world, where time had slowed so much that it now moved forwards in mere fractions, there was just her, the prince, and the wound. And one other being, this nearby vibrant, pulsating presence in the form of Arion Sepian, whose proximity was continually bombarding Leanna with energy and power. A bombardment which made her feel as if The Lord Aiduel was inside her, and renewing her. Making her His vessel for the action which He now wanted her to undertake.

She focused again on the prince's injury, not aware that she was walking forwards to the operating table, her arm outstretched before her. The wound in Prince Markon writhed and throbbed in its whorl of darkness, and she knew that it was gradually smothering its victim within its deathly embrace. And was close to finishing its work.

A remote voice – *Colissa's?* – was asking her what she was doing, but then the way to the table was cleared before her, and she was standing over the prince, her arm pointing directly towards him. Leanna could distantly hear Colissa objecting, and then the stranger – Arion Sepian – brusquely ordering Colissa and the others not to interrupt Leanna's actions.

Leanna had once saved Kennet, using her Aiduel-given power. But just days before this one, she had foregone the attempt to save a young boy from dying, on the back of a cart. Had decided not to even try to save him, because of the fear that others were watching. And even if she had found the courage to try, on that occasion, she had doubted whether she possessed sufficient power to close the wound and to save the boy.

But right now, she was overflowing with power. Was full to the brim with it, from whatever Arion Sepian either was or was doing, and her energy felt ready to burst outwards. And she was suffused with an overwhelming feeling of purpose and holy bliss, which rendered any other considerations of fear or secrecy moot. This power was a gift from The Lord Aiduel, and it was a gift which He intended her to use, not to hide.

Lord Aiduel, please help me to save Prince Markon.

Her arm was pointed towards the wound, and she felt unseen ethereal fingers spiral out of herself, closing onto that blackness which resided on and within the prince's flesh. Connecting to the prince, to his mind, and to the injury which would otherwise kill him.

Once again, these invisible ghostly fingers wrapped around and enveloped the blackness of the wound. Before, with Kennet, in a body which had been beset with disease, she had simply torn that illness out, and had thus restored him. This time, it would be different. This time she must join flesh which had been severed, must repair that which had been rent apart.

And there, before them all, in a room full of five men of Andar including this Arion Sepian, and containing Sister Colissa's group of healers, Leanna unveiled her power to the world. The unseen fingers started to knit together the torn flesh, to repair the punctured wound, and to drag the remaining blackness out of the prince's body.

Lord Aiduel, thank you for this gift. I do this in your name, Lord.

Power poured through her, and in her detached state of consciousness a part of her noted that she was ablaze within a golden halo of light, as energy flooded along the connection between her and the prince. This stranger, this Arion Sepian, was feeding her with power, and she was unsure whether she would have been capable of achieving this feat without his proximity.

But in this stranger's vibrant presence, her power was saving Markon's life, and was restoring him. The blackness which she had dragged outside of the prince's body was swiftly crushed into oblivion, and after it had disappeared the place where the wound had been was visible once more.

Where just minutes before there had been a gaping hole, there was now a tiny pink scar over sealed flesh, with scant evidence that it had once constituted a fatal injury. The prince's chest was rising and falling steadily, with little suggestion that he was still close to death.

In that moment, a wave of fatigue swept over Leanna. She had saved Prince Markon, and had worked an apparent miracle in front of a room full of people, but now she was exhausted.

She felt herself slipping out of her trance-like state, suddenly feeling unsteady and faint. She placed her hand down onto the side of the operating table, to try to balance herself. Looking around, she could see the faces about her, most of them containing expressions of wonder and awe. Colissa's mouth was wide open, and the older healer was staring at Leanna with what appeared to be a childlike expression of delight.

Then, feeling ever more light-headed, Leanna turned towards the stranger. She stared at Arion Sepian, who she knew had helped her to achieve this. His expression was inscrutable, but his eyes bored into her. What was he seeing? Recognition? And for just a fleeting moment she thought that she knew him, too. That she remembered him.

But then that thought was gone, and she collapsed to the floor, unconscious.

—

Leanna awoke later, within a small tent. She opened her eyes slowly, taking note of her surroundings and recognising where she was. She was lying on her back, on her cot. She looked to her left, and was surprised to see Prince Markon on the cot next to her. He was in a deep sleep.

'You saved Kennet, too, didn't you?' The soft question was asked by Sister Colissa. Leanna raised her head, and could see the older woman sitting near to the entrance of the tent. The emotions emanating from the healer were confusing.

'Yes.' Given what Colissa and others had already seen, Leanna saw little point in trying to deceive her.

'How?'

'I don't know. I think… The Lord Aiduel has granted me this power, to do His work.'

'That's so wonderful. That… thing you did earlier, was a miracle, Leanna. I've never seen anything like it, but miracle is the only word for it. You… healed Prince Markon. Brought him back from death. And at the end, you were covered in a golden light, as you were doing it. I had goosebumps all the way up and down my back, watching it. Knowing I was watching a miracle. Aiduel was in you, Leanna, and we could all see Him working through you.'

Leanna blushed. 'I've had to keep it secret, Sister. In the eyes of others, I'm a dangerous heretic, now.'

'Not in my eyes, Leanna. Not at all. No, to me, you're the most important person that I've ever met. To think that I've grown to know one so blessed by Aiduel. And that I've tutored you. I feel so honoured.'

Leanna was embarrassed, unsure of how to respond to such gushing praise from a woman who was so much more senior and experienced than herself. 'Where are the others, Colissa?'

'Perrien and all of the others are still in the field hospital. Under orders to tend to Andar's wounded. I was ordered to come here and to watch over the two of you.'

'Where is…?' Leanna could not give voice to the man's name.

'Lord Arion Sepian? A fearsome man, that one. You wouldn't believe the way that he was looking at you, Leanna. And he was asking me lots of questions. About you. He told me that he'd come back for you, later today. That he needed to speak with you. You must be very careful, with him.'

'What has happened, Colissa? To our army?' There were no more sounds of conflict from outside of the tent, although Leanna could hear regular cries of anguish from the wounded survivors of the battle.

'We've lost, Leanna. Lost badly. The Army of Western Elannis has been destroyed. It's been a tragic, awful day for our country and for our prince.' Colissa looked like she might have been crying

'They've killed thousands of us, and appear to have captured the rest. And those of us who survived are all prisoners now.'

'Have you looked outside, to see what's going on?'

'No. I'm not allowed outside. There are eight guards around this tent. I've looked out of the entrance flap, but I can't see much from there. And we're to stay in here until they tell us otherwise. And watch the prince.'

Leanna looked towards Prince Markon again. 'Is he OK?'

'Yes. Exhausted, like you were. And not woken up, yet. But alive, Leanna. Alive! As is Kennet. Both because of you, and your miraculous power. And you're alive too, Leanna. That last point alone will sustain me through this dark day. We have lost an army, Leanna, but the Holy Church has gained a living saint. Aiduel bless you, child.'

—

Andar soldiers came to collect Leanna from the tent that evening, by which time Markon had still not awoken. The near-death experience had clearly drained the prince, but Colissa was otherwise happy with his condition.

As she left her tent, Leanna could taste the lingering smokiness in the air. Pyres had been burning all day, disposing of the vanquished of Elannis. There would be no death rites for these unfortunate men, and instead Leanna stared towards one of those still flaming pyres and gave a mournful and silent prayer to Aiduel.

Leanna was led towards her own prince's hawk-emblazoned tent. As she drew closer, she spotted a number of Andar officers leaving the structure. On reaching the entrance, she saw Lord Arion Sepian sitting alone inside, at the end of a large table. Two plates of hot food were set out at that end of the table, and Leanna's empty stomach rumbled in response.

'Priestess Leanna Cooper. Please sit down, and join me to eat.'

His voice was not as rough and hoarse as it had been during

their first encounter. He had removed all of his armour, including his helm, and had clearly washed before donning clean clothes. Now that she could see his face properly, it was immediately noticeable that he was very handsome, with blue eyes and a strong jaw. Such a contrast to the monstrous appearance that he had presented, when he had first burst into the hospital tent.

'Thank you, Lord Sepian.' She said that warily, then seated herself. Again, in his presence she could sense an aura of vitality and energy flowing about him, which invigorated her as it rushed into her body and mind. She could also sense strong emotions in him, but they were still unreadable, the aura around him somehow acting to muddle her senses. However, the intensity of his energies and emotions was greatly reduced from how they had been earlier, in the immediate aftermath of the battle. Had he calmed himself down, in the intervening period?

Lord Aiduel, please keep me safe, while in the company of this man.

'Please, call me Arion. And may I call you Leanna? Sister or Mother would sound so formal.' His voice could even have been described as gentle, now, and his manner was apparently friendly.

'Yes, Arion. Please, call me Leanna.' She was being reserved and polite, and careful. She could not forget how he had acted earlier, or that this man was the enemy leader who had been responsible for the deaths of thousands of her countrymen. This was a dangerous person, no matter how he chose to portray himself now.

'I'm sorry for my rudeness and threats, earlier today. Being in the middle of all that… killing, being forced to do that by this invasion, it makes a man lose touch with his senses. His decency. I'm not a monster, Leanna, whatever your first impression of me may have been.' She did not respond, and he continued. 'I asked you to come here and have dinner with me because I saw what you did. Everyone saw what you did. It was miraculous!'

He paused, appearing to wait for a reaction from her. Eventually, she said, 'If you say so.'

He frowned. 'By the Lord, I do say so. I do. Now answer me this honestly, Leanna. Could you sense me nearby, before you saw me?'

She hesitated, then answered, 'Yes.'

'And I could sense you, too, Leanna. I could feel you nearby, hours before we met. There's something between the two of us which I don't understand. Something which connects us… and one other. Do you have the dream?'

'What dream?'

She of course knew to what he was likely referring, but she wanted to be certain before saying any more. She had been asked a similar question to this in a tent with two officers of Aiduel's Guards, under the threat of a charge of heresy. But the way that he asked it was completely different. Eager. Excited, even, the boy he might once have been becoming visible in his eyes. Making him more attractive, and making it easier for her to overlook the potential threat which he posed.

'*The* dream. If you'd ever had it, you'd know. The mountain. The winding path. The-'

'Gate.' She finished his sentence, feeling shocked but also thrilled. 'Yes. I do. A lot.'

Lord Aiduel, what does this mean, that others have shared the dream?

'That's amazing! So do I! All the time! And so does Allana! And we both have powers, too, Leanna. Mine are very different to yours, but still powers. How is that possible, that three people with strange powers could all dream the same dream, over and over?'

'I don't know.' A multitude of questions were running through her mind. 'My power is… a gift from The Lord Aiduel.'

His eagerness was replaced by a quizzical frown. 'From The Lord? Do you really think so?'

Lord Aiduel, please excuse those who are lacking in faith.

'Yes, I do,' she responded politely. The sceptical tone of his response suggested that he thought her comment to be nonsense, but she refused to allow that to upset her. 'Who is Allana?'

At that question, his expression shifted again. 'Another. Like us. Right now, I'm not sure where she is. But I promise I *will* find her again.' He said this last part with such passionate intensity that Leanna immediately wondered whether he was in love with this Allana woman.

There was a myriad of questions which she wanted to ask him about now; about the dream, his powers, and this other woman, Allana. But the first thing which Leanna wanted to establish, despite his apparent friendly demeanour, was his intention for her.

'I know that you won the battle, Arion. And I recognise that we seem to share certain… unusual attributes. And I thank you for treating me with courtesy, when I am part of an enemy army. But what is going to become of me, and Colissa and the others?'

'There'll be plenty of time to talk about that, Leanna. You'll all be prisoners of war, of course, until this war has ended. Most of your survivors will be taken to a prison camp. The other healers will be put to work in our own field hospital, until I choose to release them. But I'll not be sending *you* to a camp. Or Markon. No, I'll be keeping the two of you close to me, from now on.'

'So, I'm to become your prisoner?'

'In some ways, yes. But you'll not be chained or tied or locked up. And you'll be treated well, as long as you abide by my rules.'

'And what do you want of me, Lord Arion?' It felt suddenly appropriate to remind him of his title, and of the wide current imbalance of power between them.

'Arion, please, Leanna. For one thing, I need *you* to make sure that Markon stays alive, so that I can try to end this war. But I could employ your Sister Colissa, if it was just that. More importantly, I want someone I can talk to, about this dream and my powers. Someone to help me to understand them better. To share our knowledge.'

'And you would hold me prisoner, to force me to do that?'

He frowned again. 'I'm not going to force you to do anything with me, Leanna. Although this is a war, and you're an enemy prisoner, whether you welcome my company or not. But anyway I would've thought that you'd be as interested in this as I am?'

She did indeed share that interest, but her response was again neutral. 'OK.'

He paused, clearly reflecting on his next words, and then asked, 'Can I make you a deal, Leanna?'

She hesitated, feeling guarded against the question. 'What deal?'

'I'm going to promise to trust you, Leanna. That may be reckless, but something about you makes me feel that, if you give me your word that you'll keep my secrets, then there's never been a safer person for me to trust. And then I'll tell you everything that I know about the dream and my powers. All of it. And I ask for one simple thing from you, in return.'

'What's that?' But she had already guessed what his demand would be.

'That you do the same thing for me. Tell me everything you know. And if you do, I give you my word now Leanna that anything you'd tell me would stay secret between us. Which, of course, is only worth something if you think that you can trust me.' He paused for a second, staring at her, and again his expression took on a hint of the roguish boy hidden within the Lord and soldier. A smile was playing at the corner of his mouth. 'Do you think that you can trust me, Leanna?'

She stared back at him.

Lord Aiduel, let your wisdom guide my actions.

Finally, she was ready to respond. And, despite who he was, and despite the bloody circumstances of their first meeting, she was certain about her answer.

'Yes, Arion. I think that I can.'

33

Allana

—

Year of Our Lord,
After Ascension, 769AA

Allana reached the outskirts of the town of Eastholme as the sun was starting to rise. She had walked for close to four miles since her abandonment by Arion. Four miles in the darkness of an unfamiliar country, with only the light cast by her lantern to illuminate the blackness around her. The last two miles had been trekked with the noisy accompaniment of the Canas River on her right hand side, as she followed the River Road northwards.

She was starting to feel tired and sleepy. During her time in Arion's company, she had felt refreshed and without any need for rest, but now her eyelids were heavy. Arion had told her to get onto the carriage and sleep, and she knew that she needed to do exactly that, before she succumbed to fatigue.

During the four mile walk, which had taken her almost two hours, her nerves had been constantly on edge. She had been listening for any sounds of horses' hooves in pursuit of her, or for

576

dogs barking in the distance. She was certain that her escape from the fortress must have been detected by now, including the discovery of at least one of the dead bodies which she had left in her wake. They would then have started the pursuit of her, to obtain revenge for the deaths of their colleagues.

Allana could see the silhouetted shape of Eastholme as she drew closer to it. The settlement was situated directly alongside the Canas River. It was a small town, certainly smaller than Septholme, although it still had the protection of sturdy town walls. The most prominent structure in the settlement was the castle fortress, located on the edge of the town nearest to the river. Peering towards that castle, Allana could also see the impressive shape of the bridge which emerged from Eastholme, and straddled the mighty waterway. Arion had described it as the Third Bridge.

She had repeated the instructions that he had given to her over and over since their parting, trying to engrave them onto her memory.

Get to Eastholme, Lana. Get the carriage north to the Sixth Bridge. To Canasholme. Then get off. Go north.

Arion had done much to help her. He had taken her far from Septholme, had given her provisions, and had clearly thought about how to facilitate her escape. But he had not stayed with her, despite his promise.

Now is not the time to think about him, Lana! Concentrate on getting through Eastholme, then you can spend time thinking about Arion Sepian later.

As she approached the town's southern gate, the sun was close to clearing the horizon. The gate was open, but four Andar soldiers were stationed across the road below the entrance arch. They stared at her as she drew closer, assessing whether or not she was a threat, but none of them challenged her.

However, as she walked past one of them commented, 'Dangerous time to be walking alone on the roads, girl. We're at war now, you know.'

She did not answer, but merely nodded and hurried on by. The less people that she spoke to, and revealed her accent to, the better. Particularly to gate guards, who would be the first parties that any pursuers would be likely to question.

She continued through the gate, heading towards the centre of the town. She was becoming more conscious of time now, given that Arion had mentioned that the northbound carriage left shortly after first light. The town was coming to life around her, and she stopped a passing middle-aged woman.

'Excuse me,' said Allana. 'Where would I go to catch a carriage, please?' As she spoke, she was trying to mimic an Andar accent as best as she could, such that her origins were less evident.

The woman looked at her with a hint of suspicion. 'Town square, that way. Not sure they'll be running though, what with this war.'

Allana hurried on again, moving at a half-jog, beginning to feel a slight alarm that either she would miss the carriage, or that it would be cancelled. She realised that she had not actually asked Arion about the war, or who Andar was fighting against. She guessed that it must be Elannis, given that he had said that all of the bridges had been closed.

Upon reaching the town square, she was relieved to see two large wooden carriages there. Both had a team of four horses hitched to the front. There was a bustle of people clustered around the driver beside one of the carriages, but the other vehicle had just a driver seated upon it, with no passengers. She moved towards the latter carriage, to speak to the solitary driver.

'Hello, is this the northbound carriage?'

The driver was in his early thirties, with mousy thinning hair and a gaunt face. 'Yes ma'am, although I'm currently deciding whether to change route.' He gestured with resignation towards the other carriage. 'That's the carriage to and from Septholme. Lot of people wanting to get inside Septholme's walls, right now.'

'I need to get to Canasholme, please. How much?' Again, she was trying to mask her accent, but she doubted that she was succeeding.

578

'Canasholme? You're a brave one, ma'am. We're at war, you know. Talk is, there's an Elannis army descending on Canasholme from the north. Even if I *was* going north today, which I've not decided on, I wouldn't take you that far.'

'How far would you take me?'

'No further than the Fifth Bridge, certainly. But *look*.' He gestured again to the other carriage. There were arguments breaking out around it, as it was already stuffed full of passengers, and a number of people appeared to have had their entry refused. 'No one else is wanting to go north. Not worth me braving that journey, for a single passenger. I can get at least eight passengers from the looks of it, if I head to Septholme.'

Allana sensed that the man was not trying to negotiate with her, and that he was merely being honest and open about his thought process. 'What would the normal fare to the Fifth Bridge be, for a single person?'

'Five crowns, ma'am. It's a sixty mile journey, so not cheap.'

'Make it fifty crowns to take me to the Fifth Bridge, then. But only if I have the carriage to myself, and if we leave in the next five minutes. I *need* to get north. As soon as possible. Please.' Arion had left her with hundreds of crowns in the purse in the bag. Even more money than she had once brought to Septholme. She had exclaimed aloud when she had first checked it.

The driver's eyes widened. 'I'd only consider it if you've got the money to pay in advance. But why do you want to go north, anyway?' There was now a trace of uncertainty and suspicion in his voice.

Allana saw little point in not exploiting the letter which Arion had given to her, which she had tucked into her pocket. She extracted the document now, and flashed the seal at the driver. 'Can you read?'

He shook his head. 'No. Not much. Sorry, ma'am.'

'No problem. See this seal?' He nodded in response. 'This is the seal of House Sepian. Your lords and rulers. This letter says that I'm carrying out business for House Sepian. And that I must be given every assistance possible to get north. Urgently. This is very important to them, and to me. Do you understand that?'

Given the length of the conversation, she had no doubt now that he would know her to be a foreigner, which might make him more suspicious. But she needed him to believe her. She needed to get away from here, and to put more distance between herself and any Aiduel's Guards pursuers. She waited for his response, knowing that, if it was negative, she would use her powers to coerce him. Even out here in the open.

After a few seconds, he nodded. 'Very well, ma'am. Give me the money, and we'll set off immediately.'

—

Allana was alone inside the horse-drawn carriage, as it headed north along the River Road. The driver had stated that it was a sixty-mile journey to the Fifth Bridge, and that they would be travelling all day.

The carriage was rolling along quickly, for which she was thankful. Even if she was being tracked by dogs, the animals would not be capable of matching the pace at which she was now moving.

The Canas River was to their right as they proceeded. In the initial part of the journey, she extracted some of the food and drink provisions from her pack, and ate greedily. Her stomach was relishing the richer food, after days of the stark and meagre provisions in the fort of Aiduel's Guards.

After that, she lay down on her side on the carriage seat, and was fast asleep within seconds.

She was awoken by the driver opening the side door of the carriage. Looking outside, the sun was high in the sky, and she must have been sleeping for hours. The carriage had come to a halt beside another large fortress on the river.

'Ma'am, sorry for disturbing you. Just wanted to let you know, we're at the Fourth Fort. I've checked, and they've confirmed that there's no reports yet of any Elannis soldiers between here and the Sixth Bridge. We're OK to proceed.'

'Thank you.'

She felt greatly refreshed by the deep sleep that she had enjoyed, and after that she sat and stared out of the side window as the carriage rumbled along the road.

She was on her own in the carriage, under no immediate threat or duress, and she sighed as she recognised it as a moment of peace. It was the first time since the day of Duke Conran's death, and since Gerrion Sepian had handed her over to Aiduel's Guards, in which she could properly reflect upon some of the things that had happened to her.

The events in the fortress of Aiduel's Guards had been horrific. She shuddered suddenly as she remembered the things which had been done to her, under Evelyn dei Laramin's orders. Foul, horrible, torture. The excruciating experience of drowning as they had poured water onto the cloth on her face. The agony of her legs being burned. That memory of how they had burned her was still vivid and sickening, even though the pain from the physical wounds had diminished by now to just a dull throb.

She shivered again as her thoughts lingered on the torments which they had inflicted upon her. She knew that she would never be able to forget the trauma of those sufferings, for as long as she lived. The experience was too intense and tangible, even now. It was repugnant, to think that some unseen and sick individual had relished making her endure such dreadful hurt and terror. She knew that if she were to surrender to the emotions which these memories evoked, then she would end up putting her head in her hands and would weep, uncontrollably. But she resisted this; she had to stay strong, until she was safe.

You survived it, Lana. They didn't break you. They didn't destroy you. You endured. You escaped. And you survived. As you will keep on surviving.

But she knew with certainty that if they managed to track her and capture her, then her sufferings next time would eclipse what had gone before. The High Commander would take this escape as a personal insult and betrayal. She would make Allana suffer unbearable agonies before finally ending her life on the pyre. Allana could not let them catch her.

Allana's thoughts also turned to Arion Sepian, as her journey continued. If only he had not abandoned her. If only he were still with her, right now. Protecting her. Keeping her safe. How could he have chosen to leave her? He had shared her dream. They both had powers. And every moment with him had convinced her that they were meant to be together. As lovers. Soulmates. She shivered once more at that thought, this time the tremor driven by a different kind of emotion. The way that she had been able to sense him, and his vibrant vitality, had promised a blissful level of carnal intimacy. *If* they were ever to consummate their relationship.

But, despite all of that, he *had* abandoned her. Had left her alone, with an escape plan which now extended only as far as the Fifth Bridge. After that, she was completely on her own, needing to traverse an unknown country at war to reach Rednarron. And he was dependent on her making contact with him, if they were ever going to see each other again. Would she ever choose to do so?

Just survive, Lana. Escape. Get away from Aiduel's Guards. Get to Rednarron. Then you can decide what to do about Arion Sepian, after that.

—

Allana dozed for a little while longer, that afternoon. The sun was starting to set when she finally spotted the Fifth Fort and the Fifth Bridge coming into view. There were a number of Andar soldiers stationed on the River Road outside of the fortress, and Allana heard the driver conversing with them after the carriage had come to a halt.

After a few moments, the driver again opened the carriage door. 'We're at the Fifth Fort, ma'am. I daren't go any further than this. I've checked with the soldiers, though, and they've confirmed that the road is still open to Canasholme, although the enemy are expected to close on the town tomorrow. The soldiers say to either get inside the walls of the town, or to steer well clear of it, ma'am. Either way, I wish you a safe journey.'

Allana thanked him for his help, and then set out on the road northwards, on foot. She was carrying the two bags with her possessions, although she had extracted the knife first and had placed it into the pocket of her dress. She was determined to continue walking until after nightfall, and then to sleep that night for only a handful of hours. She was conscious that for every minute that she was on foot, her pursuers might be travelling more quickly. Therefore, she walked at a brisk pace, and stayed on the faster main road given that the soldiers had vouched that it was still safe.

Keep moving, Lana. Always keep moving.

Now that she was outside of the security of the carriage, she was more paranoid that any stray noise was that of dogs barking, signifying that her pursuit was drawing close. However, every time that she succumbed to the nagging urge to turn around, there was nothing there.

Once in a while, Andar soldiers on horseback passed her on the road, travelling quickly. There was also an occasional cart travelling southbound, laden with a family and its possessions, but otherwise there was little road traffic.

The sun disappeared and the land slipped into darkness as she walked, and by the time that she finally decided to stop for the night, she estimated that she had covered half of the remaining distance to Canasholme. Her night-time camp was more comfortable than she had been expecting, after she spotted an abandoned farm, to the west of the road. Possibly the owners had passed her, heading southwards, at some time earlier that day.

She found a comfortable spot on a bed in the farmhouse to lie down, and then determined that she was going to set-off again well before sunrise. Sleep came easily, but as she settled down, she wondered again if her pursuers were on her trail, and if they too were sleeping.

Allana did indeed rouse herself before dawn, and was on her way soon after waking. Her plan for the day was to continue to follow the River Road northwards, until the town of Canasholme came into sight. After that, she intended to cut inland away from the river and hopefully well away from any armies, until she found a route to turn north again.

The morning passed uneventfully, although she trekked through a number of small settlements on the River Road which appeared to have been abandoned. It was a strange environment to be walking through, a place where all of the people seemed to have been spirited away. She suspected, with news of the enemy army so close, that everyone living on the River Road had decided to either head for Canasholme, or to travel south.

The large settlement of Canasholme came into sight in the distance, at midday. The town's high walls and castle were visible from far away, as was the Sixth Bridge. Upon spotting those markers, Allana decided to leave the main road and started to head away to the north-west, in order to circle the town.

The countryside that she moved into was less deserted than the settlements which lay along the River Road. On a couple of occasions, she passed close by to farms, and witnessed the occupants coming out to confirm that she was promptly departing from their lands. There was clear suspicion on the inhabitants' faces towards any strangers, which she could well understand given the fraught circumstances. A number of farm dogs also barked at her which, given her anxiety over her pursuit, further set her nerves on edge.

Gradually, Canasholme's relative position moved from northerly to easterly. She was passing across meadows and between copses of trees as she walked, following any trails which she could find, and occasionally cutting through planted fields. However, her pace of progress was much reduced compared to when she had been walking on the road. On more than one occasion, she found herself frustrated to have to backtrack or detour, when she was blocked by impassable hedges or brambles.

It took Allana a couple of hours before she re-emerged from her cross-country route onto the south side of another major road, this one running east to west. Canasholme was visible to the east now, over a mile in the distance. To the north of the road the land was more forested than farmed, with a dense wood of trees stretching out in front of her.

She spent a couple of minutes considering her options. She would be able to travel more quickly on the road, but she would be following it to the west rather than heading in a northerly direction. She also had no idea as to what sort of fellow travellers she would meet on this highway, and she had been warned that the Elannis army could be near. It therefore seemed to be too much of a risk to walk on such an exposed route.

She therefore took the decision to cross the road, and to head into the forest to the north. Once there, she set off in what she assumed was a north-westerly direction, heading broadly away from the highway, from Canasholme and from the river.

Keep going, Lana. A few days ago, you could never have dreamed of being free and being here. Keep going.

She walked through the woodland until after dusk, putting several miles of distance between herself and the main road. By this time it was too dark to see clearly, and she risked breaking an ankle if she tried to proceed further.

She had never been in a forest before, but now she was deep in these woods, on her own and after dark. However, after the torments in her cell at the fort, the threats posed by the forest seemed tame by comparison. After she had stopped, she ate some of her remaining provisions, and then leaned back against a tree. There were many sounds of rustling in the forest around her, and a number of animal or bird calls, but she fell quickly asleep.

The recurring dream came to her that night. A figure was there. Waiting. In the Gate. Raising a single finger.

—

For the next two days, she trekked northwards. Arion's words kept repeating in her mind. Keep moving. Always keep moving. She was pushing herself relentlessly to comply with this; rising to start travelling at dawn, and continuing for as long as possible in the fading light. She reached the forest's edge after a few hours of daylight on the first of those days. After that, she was travelling over a combination of rough trails, fields and woodland. She was trying to judge the sun's position throughout the day, to ensure that she maintained a northerly direction of travel.

Occasionally, she approached farms which she was passing. The locals here were less suspicious, and for some of them she was the first provider of the news that their land had been invaded. There was certainly no evidence of the Elannis army in these parts. Through a combination of friendliness and being willing to pay, she was able to procure new provisions of food and water, and she also obtained confirmation that she was heading in broadly the right direction.

On the second day, she met with a kindly husband and wife, who owned a large number of cattle. After she had shown her letter to them and had offered to pay, the husband agreed to take her northwards on his horse-drawn cart. This gave her a four hour respite, during which she was travelling along a country road at a much greater pace than she would have managed on foot. She used this opportunity to sleep soundly, in the back of the cart.

She was beginning to dare to hope that she had escaped from any pursuit by Aiduel's Guards. There had certainly been no sign of them since her departure from the fort. Was it possible that they had never tracked her with dogs, or that they had never picked up on her scent? Or could she even hope that in the midst of this war, they had other considerations which were far more important than her? She cast these thoughts aside, however; if she began to believe them she might start to slow her escape, and she could not afford to ease up until she was in Rednarron, at the very earliest.

When the farmer finally dropped her off, after taking her as far as he was prepared to travel, she asked, 'Am I nearly out of Western Canasar, yet? How far to the border?'

The man nodded. 'Yes, about thirty miles until you get to the northern border. May The Lord bless your journey, young lady.'

She covered a number of miles further that day before finding herself a suitable barn, as the sun was setting, within which to secure another short night of sleep.

—

On the fifth day after her escape from the fort, she emerged from fields onto a wider and dusty road, which appeared to be heading broadly northbound.

She again gave consideration as to whether she should stay off the road, and head back into trekking through fields and woodland. However, she concluded that she was sufficiently remote from the Canas River here, such that she could stay on the main highway, to make better time. There was no visible traffic on the road, in either direction, at the point when she joined it.

The sky was overcast, and threatening rain, as she started to trek northwards. She was on the lookout for any carts or carriages passing her from the south, from which she could seek to purchase passage. However, no suitable candidates overtook her throughout the morning, during which time she guessed that she had covered over half of the remaining distance to the northern Canasar border.

She had gradually become less jittery about the sounds of dogs, during the several days of her escape. There had been too many farms that she had passed over the last few days, which had contained mongrels yapping in their yard, for her to feel as nervous about the noise of barking as she had at first.

But at lunchtime on this fifth day, when she had stopped for a few moments to eat, the sound of dogs carried to her.

Not one dog. But several. To the south, still far away.

She stood and quickly packed her food into her bag, staring into the distance and listening. She could not see anything, but the sound was still there.

She promptly started off again, walking to the north, just as it started to rain. She was trying to remain calm, but she soon found herself increasing her pace from a brisk walk to a jog. Within minutes, her clothes were wet and her lungs were hurting. She needed a carriage or a horseman to appear now, someone who could transport her rapidly away from here. But no one appeared.

The road was sloping up from a shallow valley, and around her now was all fields, leaving her position on the highway exposed for anybody nearby to see. And the sound of the dogs barking was getting louder. She briefly considered getting off the main road, but she knew that if they had tracked her this far, she would not find sanctuary by hiding in a wood or in a ditch.

Her jog had turned into a run, and her lungs were bursting for air. Her dress was soaked through and heavy, and was plastered to her body, and the rain was getting heavier. Thunder rumbled across the sky, somewhere in the distance.

Run, Lana, run! Don't let them catch you!

But the barking continued to become louder and more frantic. Her arms and legs were aching, and her lungs were struggling to catch the next breath, when she finally reached the crest of the hill out of the valley. She turned around when she got there, and looked back.

There was a party of riders, on the other side of the valley, coming towards her. Three dogs, and eight horsemen, each of the latter wearing a familiar red cloak. The horses were galloping, now that the riders had spotted their prey, directly in sight of them.

Aiduel's Guards were here. Despite all of her efforts, they had found her.

34

Corin

—

Year of Our Lord,
After Ascension, 769AA

Two weeks after he had become the new clan chief of the Karn, Corin was sitting directly across from his counterpart from within the Anath. They were meeting on open land, several miles to the east of the Great Lake.

The request for the two leaders of the clans to meet had been delivered by an unarmed elder female of the Karn, just days after Corin had first announced his decision at the village meeting. The old woman had walked to the Anath village, making the Gods' sign of peace as she arrived. After delivering the requested message, she had been allowed to leave. Unharmed.

And so here they were, blood-sworn tribal enemies facing each other in a peaceable manner, under the midday sun. The place at which they had chosen to meet was equidistant from their two villages. It was in an area which both clans still claimed as part of their territory, but which neither held true dominion over. They were sitting on a small hillock which rose perhaps ten metres above the surrounding open fields, and which offered a clear view for several hundred metres in every direction. The spot had been chosen to prevent either side from having an inclination to spring an ambush.

Corin was accompanied by Akob and Marrix, and by two of the Karn's other strongest fighters. The Anath Chief, named Rekmar, was also escorted by four warriors, all of them hard-looking individuals. Every man in attendance was armed and armoured. Corin had decided against bringing Blackpaw with him, despite encouragement from Akob to do so. Corin had not wanted to engage in a conversation about peace while in the shadow of a beast which threatened so much potential for violence. He was already regretting that decision.

'So, tell me again,' said Rekmar, interrupting Corin's thoughts. They had been here for over thirty minutes, and so far had achieved little of worth. 'It was really *you* who killed Borrik Greataxe? You?'

The Anath leader was a vicious-looking individual, dark-haired and in his mid-thirties. He was of average height, but was heavily muscled, with a fluid movement to his limbs which suggested potentially deadly speed. The wild look in his eyes also indicated that he would have little hesitation to employ that speed for violent purpose.

'Yes. I challenged Borrik to mortal combat, and I defeated him. I am clan chief now.' There was a time when Corin would have cowered before one such as Rekmar. But today, although he still felt disquiet as he faced such a fearsome looking adversary, he was determined to control his nerves.

Rekmar laughed, scornfully. 'Borrik Greataxe, killed by a boy of your size! By the Gods, who'd have believed it? But how? Tell me again how you beat him?'

Corin remembered the words which Agbeth had been repeating to everyone in the village, for the last two weeks. 'I travelled to the far north, Rekmar, as I said. And while I was there, I was visited by the Gods. They gave me the power to control beasts, and to control men.'

Rekmar laughed again, making little effort to conceal the

590

derision in his voice. A couple of the Anath warriors, seated behind him, echoed that laughter. 'Ah, yes, the Gods! Of course, they visited you. In the far north. And you also control a felrin. But which you decided not to bring today. So, this beast, this felrin, it was that which killed Borrik?'

Corin sighed, feeling like the discussion was going round in circles. 'No, Chief. *I* killed Borrik, as the warriors here can confirm.' He gestured to Akob and Marrix, who both nodded. 'And I didn't bring the beast today, because it wouldn't be fitting to start a talk of peace, with a threat of death.'

'You and your beast don't scare me!' snarled Rekmar, and in response the warriors seated behind him shifted in their places, displaying either real or feigned agitation. 'And any man who threatens Rekmar and the Anath will soon learn to regret it!'

Corin remained calm and unflinching, as he replied. 'I do not wish to threaten you, Rekmar. But I see that you doubt that the felrin exists. And why would you simply take my word on this, given that we've only just met? But if you'd like to meet again, I can bring my felrin, to prove that I speak the truth.'

The chief of the Anath appeared to take control of himself, and Corin sensed that this was all part of a game by the other man, testing whether he could intimidate his younger counterpart. 'Let's say I believe you, for now,' said Rekmar. 'What is it that you want?'

'I want peace between us, Rekmar. I want us to stop killing each other's people. To fairly agree our borders, and to stop attacking each other. There's been too much blood shed between our clans. And there was too much hate between you and Borrik, for peace to ever be possible during Borrik's reign. However, I'm a new chief. There'll be no better time for peace, than now. A new clan chief of the Karn, and a fresh start between our people.'

'So, you're scared of the Anath, now, eh?' The other man grinned maliciously as he said this. 'Without Borrik to protect you? Perhaps you Karn are scared you're not strong enough any more. Coming to us begging for peace, when you now fear conquest?'

Corin heard Marrix tutting angrily behind him, the older warrior clearly feeling unhappy with how the conversation was proceeding. Marrix and Akob had continued to protest against Corin's decision to seek peace, arguing that the Anath would regard the offer of truce as a sign of weakness. Rekmar's last words seemed to accord completely with that viewpoint.

Corin chose his words carefully. 'No, not scared, Rekmar. We *do* have a felrin to fight for us, whether you believe it or not. We're not scared. But we're tired. Weary. Of the Anath killing the Karn, and the Karn killing the Anath. So much death, so much blood, and for what gain? We're not coming to you from a position of weakness, but of strength. What better time to extend the hand of friendship and peace to our neighbours?'

Rekmar's top lip curled into a sneer as he appeared to contemplate this. Corin watched his counterpart, wondering what the man was thinking. Corin felt that there must be some aspect of the Anath chief which also craved peace, or why else would he have responded positively to Corin's request for this meeting?

'All clever words, Chief Corin of the Karn. But with so much blood between us, how do I, Rekmar, Chief of the Anath, know that I can trust you? How does Rekmar know that this is not a trap?'

'Neither of us knows that, Rekmar, for certain. But trust can only be built over time, by our actions. Both of us have come here today, and we've followed the rules of truce which we agreed for this meeting. That is the first act of trust between us. Maybe there could be more?'

'Maybe there could,' replied Rekmar, nodding, the sneer gone from his face. 'There is much to think on, here. Much past blood spilled. Much hatred. But also maybe much hope. For a better future. Tell me now, Clan Chief, are you also speaking with the Borl, this way?'

'Not yet,' said Corin, 'but we will be, shortly. Peace between the three clans will make us all stronger.'

Rekmar stared at him. 'You're a small man in size, Corin of

the Karn. That is the truth. But maybe you're also a mighty man in wisdom. I cannot give you an answer on this, today. But I give you my word that Rekmar will think on it. And I'll discuss it with my elders. And then you will have my answer.'

Corin nodded in response, feeling some relief that perhaps this had not been a complete waste of time, after all.

—

Later that day, Corin and his companions were arriving back at their village. Even from the outskirts of the settlement, the physical changes which had been made to Karn in the last two weeks were immediately visible.

A raised embankment had been built up around the village. Many thick wooden stakes had already been cut and implanted into that embankment, creating an eight feet high external palisade wall. This wall currently covered a third of the village boundary. A deep trough had also been dug, on the external side of the embankment.

Corin peered at this ditch and wall, with satisfaction, as they drew closer. It had been his idea and his instruction for this to be built. A number of villagers were working on extending the barrier, even now, as he watched. This was just the first of his ideas about how to improve the village. He was already formulating plans as to what should be done next.

Marrix was still protesting about their actions with the Anath as their group came alongside the defensive barrier. 'Rekmar is a hound, Corin. A low wolf. He doesn't understand peace. Only death and killing. He'll betray you, and he'll bring war.'

'I understand what you're saying, Marrix. And maybe he will. But if there's to be a chance for peace, it has to be taken now, when I'm new.'

'Rekmar thinks you're weak,' stated Akob. 'We both saw the fight with Borrik, and we both know the truth, now. But he didn't. He thinks you're weak. It was in his eyes. There will be no peace.'

'You don't know that yet. You can't know that,' replied Corin. 'He said he would think on it. And I'll give him the time to have those thoughts, and to speak with his people. But I'm not blind to his threat or deaf to your advice. That's why we're building this wall. We should have done it a long time ago. Two gated entrances in and out of the village, and the rest of our boundary protected by the wall and the ditch. Much safer, when raids happen. We must aim for peace, but prepare for war.'

Akob nodded, looking at Corin with a measure of respect, and again Corin marvelled at the change in his father's attitude towards him since the fight with Borrik. Having been treated for his whole life as the son whom his father was ashamed of, Akob's sudden support and apparent pride made Corin feel awkward.

Marrix spoke again. 'So, you still intend to have the meeting with the Borl, tomorrow?'

'Yes,' answered Corin. 'But with one change.'

'What's that?'

'Next time, I'll bring Blackpaw. Even if I tell him to stalk in the distance, I want the felrin to be somewhere that the Borl can see it. Then they might believe me when I tell them that I control it.'

—

That night, Corin and Agbeth made love, as they had done regularly since their return to Karn. Afterwards, they were snuggled together, both feeling content. His arm was wrapped across her stomach.

'Being here is starting to feel more normal again,' she said. 'At first, I never thought I'd ever get used to the smells and the noise. And all of the people. But now, it's starting to feel like our life again.'

'I know what you mean. Although I feel like I spend all my day talking, now, rather than hunting and fishing. And being the chief still takes some getting used to.'

'You're doing a good job, Corin. Just keep doing what you think is right.'

594

'Thank you, Agbeth. And are the women treating you with... respect?'

'Yes, they are. No one's called me Cripple, at least not to my face. And they're listening to my ideas.'

'Well. You're always full of good ideas. They should listen to you.'

'Thank you.' She was then quiet for a few moments. 'You know, Corin, after the number of times that we've tried, I hope this will be the month that I finally get pregnant. So I can give you the son that a clan chief deserves.'

'I hope so, too. Or the daughter a clan chief's wife deserves.' He kissed the back of her head.

'I love you, Corin.'

'And I love you, Agbeth.'

—

The meeting with the Borl on the following day had a more successful outcome than the equivalent discussions with the Anath. Clan Chief Munnik of the Borl appeared more receptive to the idea of peace than the Anath had. Indeed, the Borl chief even went so far as to say it was a thought which he had held for many years, but had seen no merit in pursuing for as long as Borrik was chief.

Corin believed that the presence of Blackpaw had also helped. He had brought the felrin to the meeting, which had been held on neutral open territory an hour's walk to the north-east of Karn. Corin had kept the creature in sight in the distance throughout. He had observed Munnik and the other members of the Borl party glancing nervously towards the beast on several occasions, during the meeting. Corin could recognise the extra respect he had gained from his counterpart, as a result of the creature's presence.

At the end of the meeting, he and Munnik had stood and clasped hands. They had both resolved to talk to their people about how peace could work, with agreement to meet again two weeks later.

Corin was feeling satisfied with his day's work as he headed back towards Karn. Indeed, both Akob and Marrix also seemed more content with the outcome of the meeting, and were less suspicious about the motivations of the Borl chief. The two elder men walked to either side of Corin as they covered the one hour journey back to Karn, none of them travelling with any urgency.

Blackpaw loped along at the side of them; Corin would allow the creature its freedom to hunt later, but for now it accompanied them on the trip back to the village. As Corin watched the felrin's long bounding strides, he was feeling a sense of hope that his actions could end war in this region.

'Look!' Akob's shout interrupted Corin's reverie.

Akob was pointing in the direction of Karn. Corin looked up, and it took him a few moments to register what Akob was highlighting. Then he saw it. There, in the distance, a thick plume of smoke billowed up into an otherwise clear blue sky.

Akob had already drawn a conclusion as to what he could see. 'The village is burning! We're under attack! Anath betrayal!'

The other members of the party reacted immediately, setting off at a sprint towards the village. Corin was slower to react, and he was already several paces behind by the time that he started to chase after them.

As he ran, a sudden fear gripped him. Not fear for himself, but for his wife. She was there, in the village, without him. He immediately sent an instruction to Blackpaw, across their bond.

AGBETH! AGBETH! AGBETH! AGBETH! AGBETH!

Find her. Guard her. Protect her. The image of Agbeth sent through their connection told the beast all that it needed to know.

The felrin launched itself towards the village, bounding forwards on four paws. It overhauled the progress of Corin's party of running warriors in moments, and then disappeared into the distance in long, loping strides. It was making its eerie shrieking howl as it ran, which Corin hoped would put fear into the enemy and would cause them to flee prematurely from their attack.

He was worried for Agbeth. That moment from long ago, when he had raced towards the frozen lake to save her, flashed into his mind. He had arrived in time, then. Barely. But he was too far away here to make any difference.

The village had been at least half a mile away when Akob had spotted the smoke, and whatever attack was being inflicted upon Karn might well be concluded before the five of them reached it. But Blackpaw at least might be able to influence the outcome and protect Agbeth. Corin could feel the felrin's muscles pounding across the ground as it entered the village, and fleeting images of violence witnessed through the creature's eyes reached Corin's mind.

Corin was struggling to keep up with the rest of the group, as they ran ahead. Despite the influence of Blackpaw over the last two years, he knew that he would never be physically strong. His breathing was becoming more and more laboured as he covered the distance back to Karn. Finally, however, the village came into view, hundreds of metres away. And the damage inflicted by the attackers was now more visible. At least three building were aflame, including the Clan Hall, each raising its own terrible plume of smoke into the clear sky.

Corin hoped that Agbeth was hidden away. Out of sight, and out of danger.

He could now hear a series of repeated howls and shrieks released by Blackpaw, from the direction of the village, eclipsing all other noises from the battle. It sounded like the creature was in a ferocious fight. Corin had hoped that the sight of the felrin in full fury would put the attackers to flight, but Blackpaw was clearly in the midst of a deadly struggle. Images and sounds flashed into Corin's mind, from the creature. Images from the space where it fought outside Corin's home; claws slashing, blood spattering, weapons swinging, agonised screams. Anath warriors, fighting Blackpaw. Corin could feel a feral bloodlust pouring into him, through his bond with the creature.

KILL! KILL! KILL! KILL! KILL!

Blackpaw was fighting for its life, as Corin neared the village boundary, and it needed no further encouragement to strike against its attackers, but Corin repeated the deadly instruction anyway.

And was some other emotion being received by Corin through the connection with the beast? Grief? Followed by a momentary vision of an explosion of violence inside his own home? Corin shook his head as he ran, not daring to explore that thought.

As Corin finally entered the village from the east side, he could see the attackers running away to the west, towards the Great Lake. They were apparently fleeing, with Akob and Marrix in pursuit. Corin gripped his axe in his right hand and sprinted towards the village centre.

'Agbeth!' He yelled the word as he ran, wanting her to come to him, but there was no response.

He could hear screams and anguished cries all around him, a chilling reversal of the attack he had once participated in against the village of the Anath clan. Bodies were scattered about, some clearly dead, others moaning with pain.

But right now, Corin had no interest in any of them. He pounded through the village towards his own home. He ran through the central area, where there were more bodies visible, worryingly more of them Karn than the enemy. If he had been attacked at this moment he would have been an easy and unwary victim, because he could think of only one thing. One person.

'Agbeth!' Still, no answer.

Then he came to his own home. Blackpaw was standing outside it, at full height, and upon seeing him the creature raised its head and wailed. A cry which was unlike any sound which Corin had ever heard the beast make before. Doleful. Mournful, even.

There was blood on the creature's arm and a gash on its chest, and it was panting heavily, but it otherwise looked unhurt. Around it were the strewn remains of what appeared to be five Anath warriors. They had clearly tried to attack the felrin, and had been ripped apart in the ensuing melee. Arms and legs were detached from bodies, and were scattered on the floor around the

598

building. One of the dead had been disembowelled, and even more gruesomely a decapitated head was settled in the dust near to the entrance to Corin's house.

Corin's heart was gripped with dread as he noted that the door to his home was open.

He moved towards the entrance. The first thing that he observed inside was the dead Anath warrior, who was spread-eagled on the floor in front of Corin and Agbeth's bed. The dead man was decapitated, but was still holding a blood-stained and crude misshapen club, in the spot where he had fallen. The floor around this corpse was covered in a pool of blood.

The second was Agbeth. She was on her back on the bed, unmoving. Her eyes were closed, her arms and legs splayed as if she had fallen bonelessly backwards onto the bedding.

He moved closer, and then he saw the large red wound on the side of her head, surrounded by ugly swelling.

'Agbeth?'

There was no response.

'Agbeth?' He could hear his voice quaking, as he spoke to her.

She did not awaken. His hand moved to hold hers.

'Agbeth? My love?'

There was a weak, shallow breath, her chest moving slightly. Corin exhaled, desperately relieved and anxious all in one instant. His wife still lived. But the wound on the side of her head looked grievous.

And she did not wake.

—

Several hours later, after the sun had set, almost all of the surviving villagers were gathered within the open central area of the village.

Twenty-two of the Karn had been killed in the attack. This was estimated by the clan elders as one-in-twelve of the village's population, and the dead included fourteen warriors. A similar total had received injuries. They had also lost livestock, had suffered

599

burnings to four buildings including the Clan Hall, and had incurred damage to two of their longboats.

Twelve Anath corpses had been left behind in the village, after their fellow attackers had retreated by longboat. Half of these Anath dead had been killed by Blackpaw alone.

In the history of the Karn, it was one of the darkest days. Only Blackpaw's arrival had averted catastrophe. Corin could feel both the eyes of the villagers, and their blame, directed towards their new chief and his seemingly naive overtures for peace.

'We brought this upon ourselves,' said Marrix, angrily addressing the clan. 'We bared our open throat to the wolf, with this talk of peace. And what did the wolf do? He pretended to be tame, to get close to us, and then he leaped. The Anath have shamed us, today.' He looked towards Corin, as he said this last part.

Corin was aware that he was being criticised, but he did not respond. He was struggling to give his attention to the discussion going on around him, even though he knew that it should be his responsibility to lead and direct it.

His concentration was fractured, his thoughts split in sharply contrasting directions. The first was towards Agbeth. She had still not woken. Two of the elder village women, with more knowledge of healing, had been left to care for his wife's comatose form. Before coming to this meeting, Corin had tenderly lain Agbeth out straight, on top of the covers of their bed. In the moments before leaving her, he had watched her shallow breathing and unmoving face, and he had kissed her softly.

And now, every time that he thought about the wound on the side of her head, he felt sick inside. When would she wake? Would she ever wake? Or could she be slowly dying? Could it be possible that he would he have to face the rest of his life, without her? That last question was too devastating to contemplate, and he was trying not to allow his anguished mind to descend and linger there.

The second focus of his thoughts was towards trying to contain his rage. Anger, blossoming out of fear, had been building within him from the moment that he had found his wife. Anger unlike anything that he had ever known, and which even now was making his hands shake.

Anger at the Anath, that they would betray their talk of peace like this. That they would attack the village. That they would hurt Agbeth! That they would try to kill her!

And hatred. Pure hatred, for Clan Chief Rekmar. Violent, destructive, hatred.

These wrathful thoughts were alien to him. He had once been incapable of even touching upon such rage as he felt inside himself, right now. But the seeds of these raw dark emotions had been planted inside him at some point during his long-term connection with Blackpaw. And now, in the midst of his anxiety for his wife, he could feel them taking root.

His feelings had been shared with the felrin for several hours now, which in turn was making the beast more agitated, and fuelling its own fury. Blackpaw was sending that feral rage back towards him through their bond. They were feeding on each other's wrath.

Corin had allowed the beast out to hunt tonight. And he had felt it make three kills, in the forest to the north. The first had been for food. But the last two, he was sure, had been for the pure pleasure of inflicting pain and death. Corin had shared that emotion, and it was so tempting at this moment to submit to the most primitive instincts of the felrin; to kill, to rend, to sever and to savage. To commit ghastly violence. But how could he allow himself to surrender to that?

He was a good person, wasn't he? Certainly, he had always considered himself to be a good person. A kind, and peaceful, person. He had always rejected the casual nastiness and violence which had marked the day-to-day life of so many of the Karn. He had tried to treat others well.

That was how he saw himself, and it was how he felt that Agbeth regarded him, too. Why she loved him. Because he was a good, kind and peaceful man. The rational part of him, the person

601

he had always striven to be, did not want violence. He had always wanted peace, and the chance to live his life happily, with Agbeth. Even his murderous action against Borrik had been a last resort, to protect himself and Agbeth, when there had been no other choice. And his first decision as clan chief had been to seek peace.

But if all of that were true, then why did he feel right now like he wanted to commit bloody violence? Awful, unspeakable, violence, against somebody. *Anybody*. Rekmar. The Anath. Why did he feel as if he wanted to kill every single last member of the Anath clan?

He looked down at his hands, which were still trembling as a result of the tension which he was holding inside himself. His power to control others felt like it wanted to explode out of his mind, and this constrained tension was making his head pound. Part of him felt that, if he so desired, he had the ability, at this instant, to take control of every single member of the village.

'We cannot let this go unanswered.' Akob said then, addressing the clan. 'If we don't respond, they'll know we are weak, and they will come again.'

Kernon followed up on his father's statement. 'Yes, we must raid them. As soon as the boats are fixed, we must raid. We must answer blood with blood.'

Corin looked away from his hands, attempting to concentrate on the discussion around him, trying to subdue the dark emotions that threatened to take control of him.

'I agree,' said Marrix. 'And it must happen within days.'

The elder warrior then paused, and all eyes turned towards Corin, waiting for him to speak. No raid could take place without the authorisation of the clan chief.

Corin stood up. His ability to control had never felt so powerful. So alive. It was time to decide, and to act. But as he started to speak, he still did not know what action he was going to conclude upon.

'There will be no raid,' he stated. There were a number of calls of disapproval in response to this, before he continued. 'There will be no raid, because it achieves nothing. They kill us. We kill them.

602

Then they kill us again. But I must protect this clan. We must act, and act now, to stop them from attacking us again. We must end this, end this fighting, for all of time.'

'End this, how?' asked Akob.

Corin's hands were still trembling. What would Agbeth say, if she were beside him right now? What advice and counsel would she give him?

FEAR. CONTROL. ORDER.

The words whispered into his thoughts, suggesting a different answer, and then his decision, and his plan, became clear in his mind. He paused for a few moments, before he replied. 'There could have been two ways to end this. One was peace. Which I wanted, and which we offered. But the Anath have rejected this. And have hurt and have killed our loved ones.' There was a tremor in his voice, as he said this last part. 'So, we must choose another way.'

Marrix responded, 'What other way?'

Corin looked around at the whole clan, assembled before him. 'We will not raid the Anath. The time for raids has ended. Tomorrow, I will have vengeance, for what has been done here today. And either the Anath will accept peace, and order, and will kneel to me, or I will destroy them. Get ready. Prepare your weapons. At first light, the warriors of the Karn will march on the Anath village. And the Anath will find out what happens when you choose to go to war with a felrin, and when you face a clan chief who has been chosen by the Gods!'

Corin stood up, feeling satisfied with his words, and in turn he could hear an approving murmur from the gathered villagers. He knew that he was still full of anxiety and fury, and that he would find no calm or rest during the coming night. But at least he was now resolved upon a course of action.

By the end of the following day, the Anath clan would know its fate. As would the clan of the Karn. And perhaps, Corin in turn might also know his. And Agbeth's, too.

35

Arion

—

Year of Our Lord,
After Ascension, 769AA

'So, tell me again, why are you so sure that our powers come from The Lord Aiduel?' After Arion had asked the question, he suppressed a smile as he noticed the wrinkling on the upper part of Leanna's nose, as she in turn appeared to suppress a frown.

'Because they are powers which are more than are natural,' she replied, calmly and with apparent sincerity. 'Our lives, and the whole of the natural world, are a gift from The Lord, and were delivered by His sacrifice. Why then should we view our powers any differently? Only The Lord could grant such abilities. My power to heal. Your power to have great strength and speed, and from what you've said, to also see the future. The Lord must have given us these powers for a purpose. To use for His purpose.'

This was the fifth straight night that they had taken an evening meal together, since the Battle at Moss Ford. At first, the meals had been an opportunity for both of them to share what they knew about the recurring dream and their powers. He had perceived that she had been guarded with him for the first two of those meetings, which had been understandable given the bloody circumstances in which they had met. However, from the third meal onwards she had become more relaxed and expressive in his company, and he was now relishing their encounters.

'But how do you know that we didn't just catch our powers? At random. Like a disease?' He strove to maintain a straight face as he made the query.

'Catch them? Like a disease? But, that's ridiculous! The Lord-' She stopped herself as she appeared to spot the slight upturn at the corner of his mouth, which he had been unable to conceal. 'Oh. I see that you're teasing me again, Arion. Please excuse me for being so gullible. And so apparently devout and naive.'

He smiled more broadly. 'I'm sorry for teasing, Leanna. And I don't for a second think that you're naive. A little gullible? Possibly. Devout? Yes, definitely. But naive? No. But you get so serious when you start talking about The Lord, I can't help myself.'

Her nose wrinkled again for a second, before he saw her mouth widening into a grin. 'I am a priestess, remember, Arion? But, yes, I suppose I do get a little serious. And you're not the first person to have teased me about that.'

Her smile was guileless and joyful, and in Arion's eyes it transformed her, from pretty to radiantly beautiful. He felt strangely pleased with himself, to have elicited that reaction. 'I enjoy hearing your views, Leanna, I really do. But on the subject of the source of our powers, I think that we should probably agree to disagree?'

She lifted her hand to brush her golden-blonde hair back behind her ear, her blue eyes shining. 'Yes, I think that perhaps we should. And if we do, I'll plan to find time to pray for your immortal soul, given your apparent impiety. But in all seriousness, my powers only came after I was called to and committed myself to the Holy Church. And that's why I genuinely believe them to be a gift from

The Lord. He gave them to me, and I will use them in His name and in His service.'

Arion nodded, attempting to appear respectful of her response. He was truly enjoying being in Leanna's company, despite the differences in their backgrounds and their outlooks. Even in these peculiar circumstances, in the middle of a large army camp where he was the leader and she was his prisoner.

As had been the case when he had been near to Allana, it was invigorating for him to be in Leanna's presence, and to be continually experiencing the glowing energy which flowed through and around her. He felt vibrantly alive and alert, whenever he was close to her.

But over and above these feelings of vitality, and the dreams and powers which they had in common, he genuinely found her to be likeable. There was an unmistakeable quality of *goodness* about her. She clearly had a lively intelligence, and a strong will, but there was no detectable trace of arrogance or artifice within her. He had known almost immediately that he could trust her.

After each of their previous meetings, Arion had noticed that he was feeling happier, and more contented and relaxed. The contrast with when he had met Allana, and had emerged from each encounter excited and agitated by a turmoil of surging emotions, could not have been any greater.

True to the pact which Arion and Leanna had made during their first meeting, they had shared a lot of information with each other over the course of the last few days. As far as they could establish, the recurring dream which they both experienced was identical. Their shared dream included all of the same features, although they were each equally frustrated that the memory of the figure in the Gate remained elusive. Both of them knew that there was *a* figure there, but neither could remember what form it took, or what it wanted of them.

She had told him everything about her powers. Had revealed that she had an ability to sense emotions, and had described her power of healing. He had told her about his strange strength and speed, and of how he had been able to share something of this with his men during the Battle of Moss Ford. He had also disclosed the details of the two prophecies which had come to pass, that of the Bergen raiders and Moss Ford. However, he had held back from telling her about the dream of Allana on the pyre. That had seemed to be far too personal.

He had felt a mixture of alarm and excitement when she had first told him about the story of the Great Darkening, and the apparent link to her birthday. They had compared birth dates, and had been shocked to realise that they had been born only eight days apart. It had made him wish that he had asked Allana about her date of birth, although he now suspected it was likely to be close to his and Leanna's.

He had been concerned when Leanna had described her interrogation by Aiduel's Guards, and that the religious order appeared to be seeking out people like the two of them. And regularly burning ordinary citizens as heretics on Seventh-Day, in the city of Arlais and in other cities across Elannis. He had anyway not liked the Guards, but to know now that they might be hunting for him gave him greater cause to dislike them. It also made him more fearful on Allana's behalf, that they might catch her and discover what she was. Where could she be, right now? Was she safe?

'Is everything OK, Arion?' Leanna's voice disturbed his thoughts. 'Are you thinking about Allana again?'

'Yes. Yes, I was.'

'I… can't read your emotions, usually. Not in the same way that I can do with others. But… when you think about her, it's like they come screaming out of you. You've not confessed to it yet, but I believe that you're in love with her.'

By the Lord. Am I? Is it that obvious?

He knew that this was a problematic subject, given his betrothal to Kalyane. 'No. I'm not.' Leanna did not respond, but her raised eyebrow suggested that she thought that he was not being honest with himself. He sought to explain. 'I… am to be married. Have

607

I told you that?' He knew that he had not. 'To Lady Kalyane, of Rednar. So, of course I'm not in love with anyone else.'

'Oh. I understand. And do you love her?'

'Who?'

'Lady Kalyane.'

'Yes. Of course.' He saw Leanna nodding, in careful acknowledgement of his response. 'I just want to find Allana. And save her. She may be in great danger.'

'OK. I hope that you do, then. She seems to be of... great importance to you.'

There was an awkward silence for a few seconds, until he said, 'I think that this might be the last time that we can meet like this, at least for a few days.'

'Really? Why is that?' Did he detect a trace of disappointment, in her voice?

'My brother, Duke Gerrion, is due to arrive at our camp tomorrow morning. And tomorrow afternoon, we'll both meet with Lord Bornhaus, commander of what's left of the Army of Western Elannis. We hope to turn this current armistice into a permanent surrender. So, I'll most likely be with Gerrion tomorrow evening. After that, well, if our meeting with Bornhaus is successful, then after that you may not be my prisoner for much longer.'

'Oh. OK.' Again, did he hear a hint of regret? 'It's not been so terrible, being your prisoner, Arion. I thank you for allowing me to return to tending to the wounded, following Prince Markon's recovery. And you've treated me and my colleagues well, and with kindness. Certainly better than I thought that I might be treated, when a blood-soaked monster burst into our tent!'

He laughed. 'Blood-soaked monster? That's a new one. I think I prefer to be called The Hero of Moss Ford!'

She smiled again in response, and then laughed, her eyes sparkling and her whole face illuminated by the action. She was truly beautiful, when she smiled. There was no doubt about that. And also familiar. Which was the oddest thing. It made him feel like he knew her, or had known her. But they had never met before, so how could that be possible?

However, he felt a surge of happiness in response to her laughter, and a sudden unexpected desire came upon him. He wanted to hold her in his arms, and to kiss her.

Lord preserve us! Must I develop a childish crush on every attractive woman that I meet? Even if she is like me, she's a priestess! And what about Kalyane? And Allana!

He did not try to kiss Leanna, much as he might have wanted to. And he suspected that she would have strongly rebuffed him, were he to have tried.

—

That night, as he lay in his cot under the canvas of his tent, the dream of the burning came to him for a second time…

—

…*He watched as the young woman was tied to the pole in the centre of the wood. Throughout, she maintained her quiet poise, her face hidden, as a member of Aiduel's Guards announced the charges against her.*

And then he saw the flaming torches, being brought closer. Being placed against the wood. Still, the young woman maintained her dignity. But as the pyre lit, she jolted her head back, and her hood fell…

—

Arion woke up from the dream, sweating. The prophetic vision of Allana had come again, as if it had been triggered by the earlier discussion about her. He lay awake in the darkness, contemplating what he had witnessed.

Allana had to be in trouble. He had hoped that he would never experience this dream again, and that his prior actions to help her escape had somehow changed her future. But this had been identical to the dream from his first night back at Septholme Castle. And in its lucid nature it was clearly the same as the visions of Moss Ford and the beach near Fort Lennis. Both of those dreams had proven to be a true portrayal of real future events in his waking life.

Which meant that his efforts to help Allana escape had either failed or were going to fail. She must still be alive, but she seemed destined to be captured, and she was still going to be led to a pyre to die.

He closed his eyes again, trying to recall the details of the dream. There was some small element of the scene that was nagging at his mind, and unsettling him. Something wrong, or out of place. But try as he might, he could not determine what it was.

But there were a number of matters of which he *was* certain. He was running out of time to find her, and to prevent this. And to have a chance to do that, he had to bring the war to a close, and quickly. Or she would die.

Only he could save her.

—

The next morning, Arion was on horseback, waiting for Gerrion to arrive at their military camp. He was wearing his full battle armour, which had been cleaned and burnished on his behalf. Alongside him were Charl Koss, Menion Thatcher and Commander Berker.

Shouts carried across to him, from Andar soldiers who had spotted him waiting there, in the centre of the encampment. 'Hero! Lord Arion!'

'I think that they're waiting for their Hero to give them a wave,' said Charl Koss, dryly. Charl had been effusive with his praise after the battle, but he had also been making sure that Arion did not let his success go to his head.

Arion raised a hand to the troops, in embarrassed acknowledgment, and heard a cheer arise in reaction.

Five days had passed since the Battle of Moss Ford. Five days in which he had realised that his place in the world, and the way that people perceived him, was changed forever.

His men had already taken to calling him 'The Hero of Moss Ford'. A pride had taken hold within the army about their achievements at the battle, and he was already being acclaimed as the architect of that victory. His feats as a warrior on the battlefield that day were also gaining great renown. Stories were circulating of how he had led the charge into the enemy, and had personally killed countless soldiers of Elannis. Tales of how the men of Andar had felt more inspired under his leadership than at any time in their lives. How they could recall being filled with energy and power, when near to him on the battlefield. And how he had personally pursued and struck down the enemy prince.

Arion had also been able to observe a change in the demeanour of his more senior commanders, in the last few days. Prior to Moss Ford, he had seen some doubt and lack of faith in their eyes as he had explained his plans. Yes, he had been their lord, and a knight, and the appointed leader of their army. But he had also been a relatively unproven soldier. Now, they were following him unwaveringly.

But for the ordinary soldiers, he had already taken on a heroic status. His appearance amongst their ranks now repeatedly elicited cheers and cries. Part of him felt slightly uncomfortable with this new level of attention. But another part, if he was being honest with himself, was enjoying his newfound emergence from obscurity. He had always believed that he was destined to achieve great military deeds, and now at last he had also proven his worth to the world. Now the world knew who Arion Sepian was.

He was the Hero of Moss Ford.

As Arion was contemplating this, his brother Gerrion emerged in the distance, in the midst of a body of cavalry over fifty strong. When the elder Sepian arrived, the two brothers dismounted, and then embraced with genuine warmth.

Gerrion spoke into Arion's ear, his voice animated, as they hugged. 'You did it, brother. You did it! You beat them! It worked out, exactly as you said.'

'Thank you for trusting in me, Gerr.'

'That trust has been repaid a thousand-fold, Arion. Come, let's sit with Charl, and we'll finalise the terms for the Elannis surrender.'

—

Three hours later, Arion, Gerrion and Charl were meeting the remaining senior officers from the Army of Western Elannis, on the outskirts of the Andar army camp. They were meeting under the luxurious canopies of Prince Markon's tent. Charl had suggested that this could be utilised as a reminder to the Elannis delegates of the scale of their humiliation.

Arion's army was camped to the west of the town of Canasholme. The remainder of the Army of Western Elannis was situated to their east, alongside the Canas River and to the north of the town. A temporary truce had been reached between the two opposing armies only the day before, to avoid a further battle which could cost thousands of lives and which threatened obliteration for the residual Elannis forces.

Today's meeting had been arranged to discuss the terms on which the surviving Elannis army would surrender, and the war would be ended. Arion was aware that Gerrion had corresponded with the royal household prior to coming, and had been granted the King's permission to negotiate any settlement. Gerrion had also informed him that the conflict between the countries had not currently spread beyond the bounds of Western Canasar.

Canasholme itself remained under the control of Andar, as did all of the western river forts to the south of the town. Indeed, the only fortress on this side of the river which Elannis controlled was the Ninth Fort, which their army would be unable to reach with Arion's cavalry force in such close proximity

612

Gerrion was reinforcing this point to the enemy Commander, at this moment. 'You say that our terms are unreasonable, Lord Bornhaus. And yet, you invaded us. You're now cut-off, in a foreign land, with no means to cross back over the river. We outnumber you over two-to-one, having already smashed an army three times your size. And, in case you've forgotten, we have custody of your prince. The Emperor's son.'

The leading enemy commander was named Lord Bornhaus. The lack of an 'El' in his name indicated to Arion that he was not part of the Imperial Family. However, he nonetheless appeared to carry the authority for the Elannis army, in the absence of Prince Markon. Bornhaus spoke now. 'You don't want this battle any more than we do, Duke Gerrion. You'll lose too many men. Your proposed conditions go too far.'

Gerrion replied, calmly. 'It could easily be argued that they don't go far enough, Lord Bornhaus. You started this war. Not us. And the Archlaw has now *finally* come out to signal the Holy Church's disapproval of the invasion, now that he and everyone else knows that your position is militarily useless. So not only is your tactical position impossible, but the Holy Church has turned against you, as well.'

Bornhaus frowned. 'The Emperor will not accept this. He will insist that Prince Markon is returned to our custody, immediately.'

Arion stared at the man, feeling anger building.

By the Lord! Doesn't he realise that they were the aggressors, and that they've lost?

'Then he'll be waiting for a long time,' replied Gerrion. 'We'll return the Prince only after all war damage reparations have been paid, and after twenty four months minimum has passed. We'll otherwise return all other non-combatant prisoners once your army has surrendered, and we'll repatriate all other military prisoners over time, in line with the payment of those reparations.'

Bornhaus was silent for an extended period, staring at them, with his arms folded. Arion met the man's gaze, becoming more and more annoyed. He was feeling a building urge to strike the Elannis commander down.

Gerrion finally broke the silence. 'In case you're confused about the terms, Lord Bornhaus, I'll repeat them again. The Ninth Fort is to be surrendered to us, immediately. You and all remaining Elannis troops in Western Canasar will lay down your arms and armour and surrender to us. We will requisition your arms, your horses, all of your provisions and your siege equipment. At that point, we will allow your non-combatants to be repatriated. The Emperor will then write to King Inneos, to myself and to the Archlaw to apologise for his illegal aggression, and to renounce any future claim to Western Canasar. Then Elannis will start to repay the war reparations we outlined earlier, following which we will progressively allow your surviving soldiers to be repatriated. Then, after two years and payment in full, and only then, Prince Markon will be returned. I trust that all of this is clear?'

Bornhaus said nothing for a few seconds, before repeating, 'The Emperor will not accept this.'

Arion had reached his boiling point. He answered, before Gerrion could respond. 'The Emperor is not here, Bornhaus! But you are, as are the three thousand men in your camp, who are your responsibility. Make your decision, and make it in the next two hours!' He had started to shout, but he did not care; he and Gerrion had agreed in advance that if Bornhaus was proving stubborn, Arion was instructed to lose his temper and bare his teeth. 'Because if you choose not to surrender on these terms, I promise you that we'll crush you, as we crushed your Prince. Your situation is hopeless. You have a river on one side, Canasholme on the other, and us to the west. If you try to flee north, we'll catch you and cut you down. And if you force me to do battle, I promise you this. Next time, we won't take prisoners. I'll kill you, I'll kill your officers, and I'll kill every last one of your men! None of you will ever see Elannis again! And if you choose to fight today, we'll try your prince as the war criminal he is, for burning our settlements, and he'll go back to the

614

Emperor in pieces. With a letter indicating that you were the man who made the decision to let him be killed. Do you understand all of that, Bornhaus?'

Arion knew that Gerrion and the King would never permit such a murder of the Elannis prince. However, right now all that mattered was that Bornhaus believed it, otherwise thousands more would have to die before the invasion was over.

Bornhaus regarded him, a cold look on the man's face, but his hand was shaking. 'So speaks the Butcher of Moss Ford.'

Arion was for a moment taken aback by the moniker, but then he decided to embrace it. 'Yes. The Butcher of Moss Ford. And if you force me into another battle here, they'll be calling me the Butcher of Canasholme as well. But, do you know what? I've changed my mind. If we do battle here, I'll keep you alive, Bornhaus. Just you. And we'll ship you back with the Prince's body parts. Do you want to be known forever as the man who sentenced the Emperor's son to death?'

Bornhaus's face had turned red, with barely suppressed anger and shock. He looked at Gerrion, now. 'You would allow him to kill our Prince?'

Gerrion did not hesitate. 'Yes. If the Prince has committed war crimes against our people, which I understand that we can establish.'

Bornhaus continued to stare at the young Duke, trying to gauge any weakness there. 'And we have two hours to make a decision, yes?'

Gerrion nodded. 'Yes. Two hours, that's correct.'

'Very well.'

Two hours later, Bornhaus accepted their terms of the surrender.

—

Before dusk on that same day, the physical process of the surrender of the Army of Western Elannis was completed. Arion was there for the formal process of surrender, as the Elannis troops marched past in single file, depositing all banners, weapons and armour in an agreed position.

By the Lord! We did it! We won this war!

He felt an immense sense of achievement, as he realised that the conflict was finally over. It had been a matter of mere weeks since the enemy had first captured the Ninth Fort, but for that entire period there had been a threat of destruction looming over his family and his land. Now, that threat was ended, at least for the foreseeable future.

The end of the war also had implications for his relationship with Allana. Would he now be able to free himself from his duties to allow enough time to find the Dei Magnun girl? And how he would be able to explain any such intended absence to Gerrion? The older brother had no idea of the extent of Arion's interactions with or feelings for Allana dei Monis.

But the repeat of the dream of seeing her on the pyre had renewed Arion's sense of urgency that he had to act to find Allana. Before it was too late.

—

That evening, Arion and Gerrion had the captive Prince Markon brought to meet with them. Again, they decided to hold the meeting in Markon's own tent.

Whilst the war had been continuing, Arion had conducted only a very brief discussion with the Elannis heir, who had refused to answer any military questions. Given the status of the prisoner, Arion had thereafter left the prince alone, and closely guarded, until now.

Gerrion gestured to a chair as Markon arrived, under armed guard. The Elannis prince was tall, with blonde hair and a strong chiselled face. He walked now without any apparent pain or impediment. Arion was amazed by this, given the condition the prince had been in after he had been struck down.

By the Lord! Leanna's deed that day was a true miracle. It deserves more renown than anything that I achieved at Moss Ford.

After introductions, Gerrion described the surrender of the remaining Elannis soldiers, and finally stated, 'The war is over, Prince Markon. You're to be held for twenty-four months now, at a secret location somewhere in Andar, as surety of your father's compliance with the surrender conditions. Please be assured that you'll be held in good conditions under house arrest, as is befitting of your royal rank.'

The prince twisted his neck, appearing relaxed. 'Twenty-four months? That's not so bad, although it's a shrewd choice of period on your part. Any shorter and you're probably letting me go before you'd like to. Any longer, and father will probably pass me over for the throne and move on without me.' His voice was calm and refined, and there was no trace of rancour in his tone.

Gerrion took hold of a jug of red wine, and set out three glasses on the table before them. 'May I ask a question?'

Markon shrugged. 'Go ahead. That tent you're keeping me in has become very dull. I'm in the mood for talk, if you'll pour me a glass of that wine.'

Gerrion did as requested, passing a full glass to the prince. 'Why did you choose to invade, *now?*'

Markon shrugged again. 'My decision. We all knew that an invasion of Western Canasar was going to come, at some point. After Sennam and Patran, where else can the Empire possibly expand to next? It was inevitable. And my forces had already been assembling and planning an invasion, for weeks before. But after the news of Duke Conran's death, I made the decision to act, as soon as possible, thinking that you'd be in turmoil. Too quickly, as it turns out, such that we marched before a full third of my army had been assembled. That was my first mistake.'

'And your second mistake?'

'I grew overconfident. I underestimated your defences. And I underestimated *him*.' He pointed at Arion as he said this. 'Your brother is the most dangerous man that I've ever encountered. But I know that now, and I won't be underestimating him, ever again. So, there it is. We lost a battle.'

Arion noted the word that Markon had used, and quietly said, 'You lost the war.'

Markon looked at Arion, his face calm and his demeanour polite and even close to friendly. 'Oh, no. We lost a battle, as we sometimes lost battles in Sennam and Patran. But we didn't come close to losing a *war*. If there's to be a war between Elannis and Andar, this wasn't it. This was mainly about testing the willpower of the Pavil family, to see how far they'd be prepared to go to retain Western Canasar. And do you know what? They surprised me.' He then smiled. 'But trust me, you will all know about it, if and when Elannis ultimately does decide to go to war.'

—

Later, after Markon had left them, Gerrion turned to Arion and said, 'I haven't forgotten the discussion that we had on the day that you returned to Septholme, brother.'

'Discussion?'

'About your marriage to Kalyane Rednar.'

'Of course. Yes, I remember.'

'I want to make it a special event for you, Arion. The people need it, to raise their spirits. They'd needed it anyway, after father had died. But now, after such a traumatic event as an invasion, even more they need something to celebrate. Something to give them joy. What better than a marriage between the daughter of one of our closest allies, and the Hero of Moss Ford!' He clapped Arion on the back as he said this last part. 'We shall make it an occasion for all of Septholme and Western Canasar to celebrate, and we must do it as soon as possible!'

'Yes, brother. Of course. Are you sure?'

'I've never felt more certain about anything, Arion. A great reward for you, and also a celebration of our victory. I will start the arrangements as soon as we've returned to Septholme. And given your newfound fame, we should ask for a member of the royal family to attend. Of course, we can invite your friend, Prince Sendar! I assure you brother, it will be a great day!'

Arion smiled in response, outward enthusiasm on his face. But inside, his stomach was churning.

—

As Arion lay on his camp bed at the end of that day, his brother's comments came back to him. And made him reflect once more upon his earlier considerations, as to how he would be able to escape, to rescue Allana.

So much had happened since he had spent time with Kalyane in Rednar. He closed his eyes now and tried to picture her, and to recall her voice. Auburn-haired, green-eyed and pretty. Softly spoken and gentle. But it was difficult to properly evoke and form the memories, since two other images pushed their way into his mind. One was of a tall and serene priestess, with golden-blonde hair and a dazzling smile. The other image, even more compelling, was of an incomparably desirable petite young woman, with dark hair and hazel eyes.

Both of whom were somehow connected to him, somehow like him, in a way which Kalyane would never be. Both of whom shared the same recurring dream, and had strange powers. Both of whom radiated energy and vibrancy when near to him, and made him feel capable of achieving the most wondrous feats imaginable.

And Allana alone made him feel like he would cast off all other loyalties and commitments, just to satisfy the temptation and need that she created within him. Even though he barely knew her. How could it be possible that she enflamed such intense feeling in him, even now? Had he fallen so madly in love with her, in such brief encounters?

If he had met either of these two women before meeting his fiancé, would he ever have proposed to Kalyane Rednar? He did not know, but he did know that in the eyes of Gerrion and the rest of the Sepian and Rednar households, he and Kalyane were now committed to each other. Irrevocably and forever. Withdrawing his proposal of marriage would most likely sever all friendship between their respective noble Houses.

And once Gerrion had announced the wedding occasion to the world, Arion would be unable to back out, without shaming his older brother. Again, Arion felt torn apart, inside. But he could not share any of these doubts with Gerrion.

What should he now do? When he had known that war was threatening his country, he had decided not to abandon his family and his land for Allana. He had instead abandoned her, on a trail in the middle of nowhere, in the midst of a war. Had left her there, with nothing more than a flimsy plan of escape and a bundle of possessions. And now the prophetic dream told him that her escape had been unsuccessful, and that unless he found a way to alter her future, the pyre awaited her.

But at this moment, even following the end of the war, he had to face the reality that his commitments to his family, to his land and to his betrothed had not gone away. If anything, they had increased. He had been transformed, in the space of a few weeks, from a largely anonymous third son to a victorious general. His betrothal to Kalyane would soon become known to the world.

Was he to accept that Kalyane was his future, that she would be a good and loving wife, and therefore proceed with his marriage to her? Or should he choose to desert her and his position, and set off in pursuit of Allana, to again try to save the beautiful Dei Magnun girl?

He truly did not know, but he would have to decide. And soon.

36

Leanna

—

After the evening of her fifth dinner with Lord Arion Sepian, Leanna was lying on her cot in the middle of the night. Thinking about him.

She was starting to greatly enjoy their meals together, and they had become something akin to a guilty pleasure for her.

She had initially surprised herself, by expressing trust in him during their first conversation. She had agreed that she would trust him, despite him being one of the enemy, and despite the traumatic nature of their initial encounter in the hospital tent.

But as the days had passed since then, she felt certain that she had been correct to express that trust. He was open, engaging, and interesting, and there was an undercurrent of excitement between them about the dreams and the powers which they shared. He was very different to her, in both his background and in his view of the world, but she considered him to be a good and honest person. And so strangely familiar.

He was very handsome, too. There had been one fleeting moment this evening, during their meal, when she had thought that he was going to attempt to kiss her. He had been watching her laugh, at which point his expression had altered, and he had leaned closer towards her. Then he had pulled himself back, looking suddenly awkward.

Better that he had. Of course, if he had tried such a thing, she would have pushed him away. Would have reprimanded him most severely for such an inappropriate action towards an ordained priestess. Of course, she would have. Or would she? She shuddered.

Lord Aiduel, please forgive me for my sinful thoughts. He is a handsome man, but I have chosen to give myself only to you, Lord.

She did trust Arion now, though. In less than a week, she had shared a number of important secrets about herself with him. More than she had ever disclosed to anyone else, other than to Amyss. The only aspect of her powers which she had concealed from him was the vision in the School of Saint Amena, because she did not want to break her vow to Senior Priestess Maris for a second time. But other than that, he knew all about her powers, and she knew about his. That mutual disclosure had to some extent entrusted each of their lives to the other's hands, given the threat of Aiduel's Guards. But Leanna accepted that.

Arion's birth date, being so close to her own, had added to the mystery of the Great Darkening. He had also thought that the Allana girl was the same age as them both. How could it be possible that three people, each sharing the same recurring dream and displaying unusual powers, could all have been born at the same time?

Lord Aiduel, if you have a purpose for each of the three of us, please show me what it is. Why have you given us these powers, Lord?

Leanna also recalled the matter which she and Arion had discussed, the night before.

'How many of us are there, do you think, that are like this?' She had asked the question. 'We both know now that there are at least three of us, who share the dream and who have powers. But are there more? Many more?'

'There are five in the dream, including myself,' he had replied. 'So, it's possible that there could be five of us, in total? Or could that mean nothing, and instead there may be hundreds or thousands of us, all in hiding from Aiduel's Guards? Who knows?'

She had shrugged, in response. But lying here now, in the dark, she believed in her heart that there were five. Her. Arion. This Allana girl, who Arion appeared to be in love with, despite his denials. And two others. But if that was true, what did it mean? And how would it ever be possible to find the others?

Lord Aiduel, please protect those to whom you have given these gifts. And allow us to use them for good, Lord.

—

Towards the end of the following afternoon, Leanna was working in the field hospital, in the company of her fellow Elannis healers. She had just finished cleaning and re-bandaging a patient's wound, when the news arrived that the remaining forces of the Army of Western Elannis had surrendered.

'So, that's it,' announced Brother Perrien, near to her, his voice sounding bitter. 'The war's over.'

Leanna did not say anything, in response. Ever since she had been allowed to return to the other healers, three days earlier, it had been awkward to be in their company. A number of her colleagues appeared to be displaying a state of reverential awe towards her. They had seen her carry out a miracle, had witnessed the powers of The Lord flowing through her, and now they seemed unable to converse with her in a normal manner. No one was making small-talk with her, as if they considered that inappropriate, and she was often finding herself alone with her own thoughts.

Their hospital was now only dealing with Andar's wounded, treating soldiers who had suffered more serious injuries and who needed longer to convalesce. As a result, there had been no more frantic periods of tending to the freshly injured. She had not needed to use her power of healing again. Following the surrender, there would be no new casualties, for which she was very thankful.

As if he had heard her thoughts, Perrien looked at her, and added, 'No chances for you to work any more of your *miracles*, Leanna. You must be very disappointed.'

Of all of the healers, Perrien had been acting the most peculiarly towards her since she had returned. He had made several sharp and sarcastic remarks, and was far less friendly than he had been before the Battle of Moss Ford. The emotions which she could feel emanating from him towards her were consistently dark and negative.

Sister Colissa was present to witness Perrien's comment. Minutes later, she took Leanna to one side, and whispered, 'Please excuse him, Leanna. We're all feeling upset, but the losses at the Battle of Moss Ford have affected him the most.'

Colissa was looking uncomfortable as she said this, and Leanna asked, 'But that's not all, is it?'

'No. Your... miracle, which we saw in the tent, has also impacted all of them, including Perrien. In different ways. But in Perrien's case, it's something else that's upsetting him. He doesn't like the fact that he believes that you've been... how do I say this? Consorting with the enemy. With their leader.'

Leanna was taken aback by the comment. How could such an accusation be fair? She had been given no choice but to meet with Arion Sepian, each day. She was a prisoner, too, and her captor had demanded it. And if she was enjoying their meetings now, then so what? She had done nothing wrong, surely? Or had she?

'Please excuse me, Sister Colissa, but I think that's unfair. Lord Sepian has insisted upon the meetings.'

'But what does he want to talk about, Leanna?'

'The miracle he saw. Of course.' But Leanna knew that even the miracle would not explain five consecutive evening meals, together. 'Beyond that, I cannot say.'

Colissa regarded her in silence, with scepticism in her eyes, and Leanna blushed.

624

After that, Leanna resolved to steer clear of Brother Perrien.

—

The day after the formal surrender of the Army of Western Elannis, Leanna witnessed Prince Markon being escorted away from the Andar army camp.

The heir to the Elannis throne was visible mounting a horse in the centre of the encampment, where he was surrounded by a significant number of Andar cavalry. After a few moments he rode off, in the centre of this armed contingent, in a westerly direction.

It *was* a miracle that the prince was alive, and it was something that she was proud of having achieved on behalf of The Lord. Without her intervention, and without The Lord acting through her, the prince would have been just one more dreadful casualty of the horrors of Moss Ford. Instead, the worst of his suffering had been to sleep for two whole days after she had healed him, his body clearly exhausted by whatever she had done to him. But he was otherwise completely healed, without any apparent adverse effects.

As Leanna watched Prince Markon disappear into the distance, she recalled the single conversation she had held with him. This had taken place shortly after he had awoken, and had asked for her.

He had been sitting on the edge of his camp bed, his face solemn, when she had arrived at his heavily guarded tent. He had glanced up at her, and unexpectedly he had smiled. 'Ah. I'm assuming that you must be Priestess Leanna of Arlais, the lady responsible for the miracle of my deliverance from death.'

She had bowed her head, unsure of how to act in the presence of royalty. 'I am Priestess Leanna, Your Majesty. Although The Lord delivered you from death, not me. I was merely… His vessel for the act.'

He had smiled. 'Ha! Religious semantics. But either way, I'm greatly in your debt, Priestess. Perhaps some will say that it would have been better if I'd died at Moss Ford, given what a disaster it was. And certainly, some of my troops would have wished death on me, that day. But not me! Oh no. I would much rather live to fight another day, and you – or The Lord! – have given me that opportunity. So, I thank you.' He had bowed towards her.

'Thank you, Your Majesty. I'm honoured to hear that.' It had seemed remarkable to her, just how different he was to his cousin, El'Patriere. The Senior Priest had never displayed any humility or manners, in all the time that she had known him.

'No, the honour is mine. I understand that it was a true miracle, and there have been few enough of those, since the days of Aiduel. As I say, Priestess Leanna, I'm greatly in your debt. And that debt should extend to anyone who cares to see me on the Imperial Throne one day. But I'm not sure when I'll be able to repay my obligation to you. I suspect that I'm to be taken away, and imprisoned for some length of time, until they've ransomed me. But when I'm free again, I promise that I'll find you, and that you'll be honoured and rewarded for what you've done for me.'

She had thanked him once more, and after that had left him alone in the tent. Alive and well, thanks to her and to The Lord Aiduel.

—

Three nights after the surrender, Leanna was again summoned to dinner with Arion Sepian.

After she had taken a seat opposite him, he said, 'I'm afraid that this will be our last evening together, Leanna. The war has ended. And the non-combatant prisoners, including you, are to be escorted through Canasholme and across the Sixth Bridge, tomorrow. By the end of the day tomorrow, you'll be in Elannis again. And free.'

'Really?' She had been half-expecting such an announcement, but even so she was surprised by how it made her feel. Happy, but a little melancholy at the same time.

'Yes. Really. The war's over. We're going to hold the captured soldiers until war reparations have been paid, but there's no longer a reason to hold the Elannis camp followers. So, much as I can sense that you're delighted to spend time with me, I shall have to let you go.'

The dinner that followed was the most relaxed and light-hearted of any of their encounters together. For the first time, their conversation did not touch at all on the recurring dream or their powers. They simply chatted, as two young adults who both felt relieved to be coming towards the end of a challenging period of their lives. Again, Leanna found herself to be greatly enjoying his company. For the first time, she guiltily accepted the wine which he was offering her, and which he was indulging in liberally himself.

Towards the end of the dinner, he asked her, 'So, where will you go next, Leanna? What does the future hold for Priestess Leanna of Arlais?'

'I'll return to Arlais, first,' she answered. 'After being ordained, I'd been planning to spend some time with my parents, before getting a posting to a hospital somewhere else in Elannis. Arlais is… not the place it once was, though, so I'll be glad to leave it. After that, I want to continue to work as a healer. Using my power, secretly when I can, to make people better.'

'All very worthwhile,' he said, his voice serious. 'But I shall miss our conversations, Leanna. I would very much like to stay in contact with you.'

'As would I.'

After she had said this, his eyes locked with hers, and he started to speak more rapidly, and with less confidence than usual. 'Could there be any way in which you could be persuaded to stay in Andar, Leanna? In Western Canasar? Not as my prisoner, of course, but as a free person? As a Priestess in the Holy Church, here? It's just… now that we both know more about what we are, and the… things we share, I'm feeling a strong sense of regret. That you'll be leaving tomorrow. That we may not see each other again. Is there any way I could persuade you to stay? Or at least, to stay for a little while longer?'

She paused, contemplating his apparently heartfelt words, and

627

she noticed that her own heart was beating a little faster than usual at the unexpected request. Could she stay? Did she want to? It was an idea that had not occurred to her, until this moment.

However, after a few seconds of reflection, she answered, 'I'm very flattered that you would want me to stay in Andar, Arion. Very flattered. But Elannis is my country. My family is there. My best friend. My Church. I can't imagine leaving it. And anyway, I think that you'll soon have... someone else to spend your evenings with.'

He nodded, looking disappointed and embarrassed. 'I knew that you'd say that, and yet I decided to embarrass us both by asking, anyway! Forgive me, that's the wine talking! OK then, Leanna, at least promise that you'll write to me. The Third and Sixth Bridges at Eastholme and Canasholme will no doubt open again soon, and trade will resume between our countries, as will the postal services. Will you write to me, at Septholme Castle, once you get to wherever you're going?'

She did not hesitate in her response. 'I would like that, Arion. Very much. And will you write to me?'

'Yes, of course. It will be good to know that my letters will remind you to keep praying for my immortal soul.'

She smiled. 'I will. Fervently. And what will *you* do next, Arion? Now that this war is over?'

He furrowed his brow, in contemplation of his answer. Eventually, he shrugged, then laughed and said, 'Do you want to know something? I have no idea!'

'You have no idea?' She was uncertain whether to laugh with him, or to take his comment seriously. 'You said that you're to be married?'

'Yes, that's right.' He looked uncomfortable, and was staring down at his glass, swirling the red liquid within it. He then downed it in one long gulp, before continuing. 'I'm to be married. Soon. Possibly, very soon. To Kalyane. It will be a great occasion.'

'And what about finding Allana?'

His emotions pulsed out of him, as she said the name. 'Finding

Allana! I know. Somehow I have to find her, when I've no idea where she is. Before it's too late. *And* continue leading the armies of Western Canasar. *And* get married, to someone who isn't Allana! All at the same time.' He paused, then laughed, infectiously, as he poured himself another large glass of wine. 'It's a real dilemma, isn't it?'

She smiled. 'Yes. It appears so. But I wish you luck in resolving it, and may Aiduel help you to make the right decision.'

—

The next day was dull and overcast. Leanna and the other healers were in the middle of a column of over two hundred Elannis non-combatants. They were being marched through the town of Canasholme, towards the Sixth Bridge. Andar soldiers accompanied their party, and lined much of the route to keep the townsfolk at bay, but the atmosphere amongst the crowd was hostile.

These were Andarrons who had seen their land invaded, their people killed, and their town besieged. They were in no mood to be magnanimous victors, and the hatred emanating from the crowd was palpable. Leanna stayed towards the centre of the road through the town as much as possible. Nonetheless, she experienced numerous taunts, and some people spat towards her as she walked past. She was carrying a small bag of her clothes and possessions, which she clutched tightly to her side; all of the medical equipment and carts had been requisitioned by Andar, and therefore the journey home was to be on foot.

The uncomfortable march through the streets of the town lasted for less than half an hour. The column then reached the mighty castle fortress in the centre of Canasholme, which sat astride the western entrance to the Sixth Bridge.

Leanna and her companions were directed through the fortress and over the bridge, heading eastwards. As she crossed over the Canas River, she was feeling a confusion of conflicting emotions. The mighty waterway flowed majestically beneath her, oblivious to the events which had taken place on its shores, over the preceding weeks. And oblivious to Leanna's newfound knowledge, that there were others like her in the world, and that she was leaving one of them behind.

The reception from the occupants of the eastern fortress, under the control of Elannis, was cold and unwelcoming. Leanna's party was returning with the ignominy of failure and defeat attached to them, rather than as conquering heroes. But anyway, as she crossed under the eastern fortress portcullises, Leanna reached down to clutch her small statue of The Lord Aiduel On The Tree, and she gave thanks.

Lord Aiduel, thank you for guiding me safely home.

—

The party of healers split up, once they had departed from the eastern fortress. The majority of the Boralais healers turned eastwards to head for their home, while the Arlais contingent took the northbound road towards their own city. The only exception to this was Brother Perrien, who indicated that he wanted to accompany them to Arlais, without offering proper explanation as to why.

This made Leanna uncomfortable, given the ongoing coldness of the elder healer, but she largely stayed away from him on the walk back. Indeed, she found herself walking alone for most of each day, not joining in with any of the chatter around her. And she was faintly surprised to realise that she was missing the daily encounter with Arion.

They took shelter at a number of churches on the main road as they headed back to Arlais. The walk took them five days and four nights, and all of the remaining healers were sleeping in close proximity during that period. The recurring dream visited her twice during the journey, waking her from her slumber in the midst of thrashing and shouts, and disturbing the sleep of all of the people around her. At Arion's insistence, she had been sleeping in a tent on her own after the Battle of Moss Ford, and it was mortifying to see

630

so many of her colleagues witnessing her in that state. Had she been shouting about the Gate?

After the second occasion that it had happened, as she was about to close her eyes to try for sleep again, she noticed that Brother Perrien was staring at her. There was a quizzical expression on his face. She quickly shut her eyes again, but afterwards it left her wondering as to what he had been thinking.

The day before Leanna's party was due to arrive back in Arlais was Seventh-Day. That day, the group did not recommence their journey until lunchtime, having stayed for the morning to participate in the local Holy Service.

On the evening of that same night, as Leanna was sheltering with the others in a Priest's cottage next to a small church, she realised just how much she was looking forward to being back in Arlais. To reuniting with her parents, to sleeping in her own soft bed in their house, and to having some home comforts again.

Lord Aiduel, please keep my parents well, and bring happiness to us all tomorrow.

She arrived at the outskirts of Arlais on the next day. She had already decided that she wanted to head straight to her parents' house, rather than travelling first to the College of Aiduel and risking an encounter with El'Patriere. She therefore said her farewells to the priests and priestesses around her, hugging many of them as they said their goodbyes.

The tightest hug which she received was from Sister Colissa. The older healer whispered in her ear, as they embraced. 'Remember, child, you are a gift. A gift to the world. Aiduel bless you, Leanna.'

Then Leanna was on her own, holding her small bundle of possessions under one arm as she walked through the streets of Arlais. How much had changed within her, in the two years since she had given herself to the Church? And how much more had she

631

been changed, in just the last few weeks, as she had been exposed to the horrors of war?

She had become something more than she had once been, during these last two years. She was no longer ordinary, no matter how humble and selfless she might in future strive to be. In the moments when she had healed Prince Markon, she had revealed herself to her colleagues and to others. What she was, what she could do, was no longer a secret. She was changed by that act, and was unveiled, and it could never be undone.

She felt a little numb as she reached the street where her parents lived. It was a place full of familiar cobbles, and even more familiar stone houses. And her own home. Where she had lived, for the first eighteen years of her life.

She knocked on the door. Twice, softly. It no longer felt right to just walk in, no matter how long she had once resided there for.

After a matter of seconds, the door opened, and Elisa was there. And this time, the hug which enveloped Leanna made Colissa's parting effort seem tame by comparison.

—

The afternoon of that day was spent talking with her mother, and being pampered and fed by her.

Later, when her father Jonas arrived home from work, he broke down in tears when he saw Leanna sitting in their kitchen. That acted as a release for Leanna and her mother, and soon the three of them were huddled together in the centre of the room, sobbing and embracing.

That evening, Jonas led them in prayer, and gave repeated thanks to Aiduel for the safe deliverance of his daughter.

And that night, as she snuggled down under the blankets on her own bed, Leanna slept soundly and peacefully. The dream of the mountain and the Gate did not disturb her, and for the first time in weeks, she was truly happy and content.

And deeply thankful to the The Lord, for bringing her home.

37

Allana

—

Year of Our Lord,
After Ascension, 769AA

After she had spotted her pursuers coming towards her, Allana knew that the time for running was over.

She stepped off the road, crossing over a low ditch and into a neighbouring field. There was a copse of trees in the middle of that field, and she decided that she would make her final stand, in that place.

She walked towards the trees, knowing that the riders would be drawing closer to her with each passing second. The barking of the dogs was growing ever louder, clearly audible over the constant patter of the rain. But she did not hurry. If they were going to catch her, she wanted to be able to face them with courage, with breath in her lungs. Better that than to be ridden down from behind, out of breath and hysterical.

As she walked, she dropped her two bags, and pulled the knife out of her pocket. She stared at the blade of the weapon, as she reached the edge of the trees in the centre of the field. Then she looked at her wrist.

You can't go back there, Lana. You can't face the tortures that they'll put you through, if you surrender to them.

An eerie sense of calmness had come upon her. She had spent two years running, and hiding, then running again. And for what? To be hunted down in a field in an unknown land, alone and friendless. To be at the mercy of Evelyn dei Laramin again. She had spent her entire adulthood living in fear, and now those fears were going to be realised. *If* she surrendered.

She placed the blade of the knife to her wrist, touching it against the wet skin, and she closed her eyes. A simple slice of the knife, and it would soon be over. She would cheat dei Laramin of her revenge and her burning.

You can survive this, Lana. You must survive this.

But, for once, the words held insufficient power for her. After all her efforts to escape, she felt defeated. She had no one, and nothing. She had watched both of the people in the world who might truly have loved her lose their lives; her mother to the Wasting Sickness, and Duke Conran to her own selfishness. And just when she had thought that there might be another who cared for her, Arion Sepian had abandoned her. Left her alone, as she was alone now.

A simple slice of the knife…

And yet. She could not do it. Her right arm shook, so tightly was she clenching the weapon, trying to force herself, but she could not bring herself to deliver the killing motion. Something within her resisted, even now.

You will survive this, Lana. You must survive this.

Her eyes opened, and she stared towards the road. She could not end her own life. No matter the fate which might await her were she to be captured, it was not within her to take that action. In that moment she knew that she must fight, and would have to resist her pursuers until they were forced to strike a killing blow. She moved the knife away from her wrist, and held it to her side.

The copse of trees was at her back as she waited, and the sky was dark grey above her, with the downpour of rain continuing unabated. Her hair was damp, pressed against her head and neck, and her dress clung wetly against her body, exposing the curves underneath.

The party of Aiduel's Guards appeared, seconds later, turning their horses onto the field. Three hunting dogs with long leashes were tethered to the lead rider, yapping excitedly, and then behind them a further seven riders followed.

The riders slowed when they caught sight of Allana, and then trotted towards her, fanning out into a semi-circle around her as they came closer. Allana's eyes swept across the group. Two figures were immediately recognisable. One of those was the High Commander, Evelyn dei Laramin, who took a position in the centre of the group as the riders spread out. The second was Nionia, the lanky Guardswoman looking downcast as she steered her horse to Allana's extreme right. The other six Aiduel's Guards were comprised of five men and one woman.

The dogs continued to bark frantically, restrained a handful of metres away from Allana by their male handler. None of the riders had drawn a weapon, but Allana could see that they all were equipped with swords. Each of their weapons looked much deadlier than the knife which she held in her own hand.

Dei Laramin spoke first, the High Commander's usually lustrous hair hanging wet and lank against her neck. 'So, Allana. Here we are. You've been a very naughty girl, do you know that?'

Allana did not answer her, but instead raised her knife. She positioned it in front of herself, pointing it towards the High Commander.

'Oh, come now, Allana. Enough of this nonsense. You've already wasted enough of my time, with this daring escape. Don't make me get off this horse and take that knife off you.'

Allana chose to speak, then. 'I'm not going back.'

Dei Laramin smiled, and then laughed. 'I'm *not* going back!

How delightful! Well, if I'd known that I wouldn't have bothered chasing all this way after you. Come on, everyone. She's not going back. So I guess it's time for us all to go home now, and to let her get on her way.'

There was no laughter from the High Commander's colleagues in response to this, as Allana moved her eyes around them. From Nionia, no eye contact was made in return, and the lanky guardswoman looked appalled to be there. On the faces of the other woman and from most of the men present, there were grim expressions. Had they known the three victims from the night of Allana's escape, and were they looking forward to gaining their revenge?

But from one of the men, positioned to Allana's left, there was something else. His eyes were focused on Allana, but they were directed at her body. Staring at her dress, and at the way it was plastered against her flesh. The look on his face suggested an emotion which Allana recognised well. And could always now sense. Lust.

Dei Laramin moved her horse forward a step, causing Allana to move backwards and to raise her knife again. 'Oh, I'm sorry to mock you, Allana. You know, I'm actually rather impressed with you, despite how much trouble you've caused me and how angry you've made me, these last few days. How very resourceful of you, to somehow induce one of my Guards to help you to escape. And to get this far! Extremely impressive. It almost makes me wish that it wasn't going to end so very badly for you. Almost.'

'I'm not going back.' Allana's eyes had now switched to the male Guard who she could sense desired her. He was watching her, intently. And she realised now what she would have to do. She moved the blade of her knife such that it was at the top of her chest, above her breasts, close to her throat. Directing their eyes. Directing his eyes. 'I'm not going back.'

'Really? You're threatening to kill yourself? Go on, then, Allana,' said the High Commander. 'Stop posturing. If you're going to do it, do it. Then we can at least put your worthless corpse on the back of

636

a horse, and go and find ourselves somewhere to shelter from this rain.'

You will not accept defeat here, Lana. You will survive. You must survive.

Allana brought the knife closer to her throat. Her left hand reached up and grasped the neck of her dress, holding it tight. Then, in one steady, firm motion, she sliced the blade down through the front of the garment. Slowly cutting through fabric all the way down across her chest to her abdomen, but leaving the skin below untouched. The front of her dress parted, revealing the naked flesh beneath, and displaying the perfect form of her body to the party before her.

LUST. POWER. DOMINATION.

The world slowed to a crawl around her, and her eyes locked onto the Guard who had already shown lust for her. On this occasion, there was no time for subtlety or finesse as he returned her gaze; she thrust the force of her willpower against him, attempting to overpower him. Launching invisible tendrils of dominance into his mind. Gripping and assailing his free will, and striving to make him her slave.

You want me. And you can have me. But only if you protect me. Only if you do what I want. What I need.

He resisted, for mere instants, looking dazed and mesmerised. But within moments his will was shattered. He was dominated. Hers to control.

Kill them. Kill them all.

But one would not be enough. Even as she saw her first victim reaching sluggishly for his sword, her eyes were sweeping across the semi-circle of riders. Seeking out another target.

She locked onto the male rider who was controlling the three dogs. And there she found a new spark of sexual attraction in his eyes. Her act of cutting the dress had drawn his attention to her bare flesh, to her breasts, and a burgeoning flame of desire existed within him. That was more than enough for what she needed to do, in this moment, as her willpower started to attack him.

As she strove to subdue this dog handler, her first victim was already drawing his sword from its scabbard, and was starting to swing it at the man to his right. As that blade struck home, cleaving into the head of its target, Allana could feel the will of the dog handler breaking in turn.

You want me. And you can have me. But only if you protect me. Only if you do what I want. What I need.

Then he, too, succumbed to her.

Set the dogs on them. Kill them. Kill them all.

After that, chaos broke out amongst the line of Aiduel's Guards, as two of their own number turned against them, and their own hunting dogs were set upon them. Allana witnessed all of this in a continuing detached state, where everything about her seemed to occur at a snail-like pace.

The first Guard whom Allana had enslaved had already killed two of his colleagues, before dei Laramin had even had time to draw her sword and engage him. On the other side of the group, the male dog handler released his hounds against the line to Allana's right, before drawing his own sword.

Allana backed away as the fighting started. The rain was torrential now, rivulets of water running down her bare chest as she watched. Despite the violence playing out in front of her, she felt strangely unmoved. She had already witnessed so much bloodshed and death in her life, such that it was beginning to lose its power to disturb her. And anyway, none of this killing was her fault. It was theirs.

Allana watched the three dogs leaping at the female Guard positioned alongside Nionia. The hounds quickly dragged the woman down from her horse, before she drew a knife and started to frantically stab at the three animals. In the same moments, the dog handler attacked the final unengaged Guard next to him. Allana could see Nionia watching all of this with panicked horror, before the lanky Guardswoman's horse reared in response to the actions of the dogs. The blonde-haired woman was thrown backwards to the ground.

The conflict lasted for only a few seconds more after that,

although in Allana's decelerated world it seemed to go on for much longer. Evelyn dei Laramin skilfully dispatched Allana's first dominated victim, at the same time that the dog handler killed his unprepared opponent. The Guardswoman on the floor was screaming as one of the dogs had its jaws clamped on her throat. Two of the three hounds lay limp and bloodied near to her, and she was plunging her knife into the side of this third attacker, but its bite was not releasing.

Nionia had survived the fall from her horse, and the lanky woman was scrambling backwards away from the chaotic melee before her, panic in her eyes. Allana watched dei Laramin approach the dog handler, both of the combatants still on horseback, both holding drawn swords aloft. There was a ferocious exchange of blows between them, before the High Commander turned her opponent's blade and thrust the tip of her sword into his neck.

Then the world sped up again.

The Guardswoman on the floor had by now fallen limp, a bloodied and dead animal laying across her. All of the male Aiduel's Guards were also now dead, including the pair who had succumbed to Allana's power, both of whom had fallen to the High Commander's sword. Nionia was still scrambling away from the carnage, on her back, looking hysterical.

Which left only Allana and dei Laramin, facing each other, as the rainfall suddenly ceased.

The High Commander was panting for breath, and for once her cool and unruffled demeanour had been shattered. Her teeth were bared in a rictus of fury. 'What did you do?' She hissed the words, as she swung herself down from her horse.

Allana's reply was resolute. 'I'm not going back.' She lifted the knife.

Dei Laramin's reaction was frighteningly quick. Rather than speaking again, she dropped her sword and launched herself forwards. Allana did not have time to react before the High Commander had closed the distance between them. In a moment, dei Laramin's hand was on Allana's wrist, twisting it painfully and then pushing the arm holding the knife up behind Allana's back.

Allana felt as if her arm was going to snap as dei Laramin continued to force it upwards. The High Commander was much stronger than her.

'Give me the fucking knife or I'll break your arm!'

The pain was agonising, and Allana had no choice but to comply. Her hand opened, and the knife was grabbed by dei Laramin. As soon as Allana had released the weapon the High Commander spun her around, and then punched her in the stomach. Hard. Allana doubled over, and then the back of dei Laramin's hand struck the side of her head, sending her stumbling backwards to the floor.

Dei Laramin stood over her. 'Fuck, you're one of them, aren't you? One of the ones we've been looking for. Fuck, how could I not see it! You lying little whore! What are you? What did you do?'

Allana looked up, feeling hatred towards the other woman, her ears ringing from the force of the blow. Once again, she was being forced to listen to dei Laramin's questioning, although this time in very different circumstances. 'I don't need to answer your questions. I'm not your prisoner. I'm not going back.'

The High Commander lunged forwards again, and her boot swung into the side of Allana's leg. Dei Laramin's icy calm demeanour was completely shattered now, and she looked close to rage. 'We'll see about that. You think you're free, because you've killed the others? So what? I'll truss you up on my horse. I'll take you back. I'll torture you. And then I'll burn you. And the Archlaw will reward me for destroying you, you lying little whore.'

'I'm not going back.' Allana tried to stand, and found that the strength had gone from her legs. But despite that, she felt defiant. Dei Laramin's repeated use of the 'whore' word was starting to infuriate her, and was fuelling that defiance. 'And I'm not a whore.'

'You will, whore. And next time, when the "Truthseeker" tortures you, I'll take your hood off. So that you can see that it's me, doing it to you.'

'What?'

'What? Didn't you know? There was no Truthseeker, Allana. It was me. And it was so… satisfying, to see you in pain like that. Sobbing and begging. And sobbing some more. So very satisfying. But when I get you back, it will be so much worse. Much, much worse. Everything that you've already suffered was just an introduction. An introduction to the horrors that I'll inflict upon you, before I end your life.'

Allana stared at her, noting the malice in the woman's eyes, and she knew that the High Commander was telling the truth. The woman had not merely ordered the torture which had been inflicted upon Allana. She had carried it out. And she had enjoyed it.

Allana could feel a cold fury building ever more intensely inside of herself. She moved to try to raise herself to her feet again, but once more dei Laramin's boot swung out. It crashed into Allana's hip, and she fell back to the floor, winded and in pain.

Allana closed her eyes, gasping. It felt like she hurt everywhere. In her head, her stomach, her hip, her arm and her leg. Rainwater still trickled down her face and into her mouth, evoking those moments of torture when she had thought that she was going to drown. And the burns on her legs throbbed anew, reminding her of the agony which she had experienced at dei Laramin's hand.

Fear. Agony. Terror. Trauma. Submission. She had suffered from all of the worst of emotions. All at the hands of this woman.

She did all of that to you, Lana.

Allana had reached the point when she could no longer endure and accept this. She had crossed that point. For two years now she had lived in fear. Hunted. Hiding. Tormented. Humiliated. But no more. She could no longer live like this. The rage at the unfairness of it all gripped her and threatened to overwhelm her.

Then, for the first time, she felt that she could sense these emotions inside herself. As a physical, tangible, thing. As a cluster of darkness, lurking in her heart and in her mind.

The icy rage that she was feeling gave her added clarity, and

641

unveiled a new possibility. She had the power to confront each of these dark emotions. To confront them, and to pour them all out of her body, along with the fury which now roared through her. They were something palpable which could be seized, gathered, and used.

'Well?' Dei Laramin was speaking again. The calm and superior tone had returned to her voice, now that she had regained control of the situation. 'Are you going to surrender to me, whore, or do I have to kick you again?'

Allana opened her eyes, and she smiled. At that moment, she was certain that the blackness lurking inside herself was hers to control. To release. To unleash.

'Surrender to you?' Allana spoke the words calmly, as she sat up. 'Yes, High Commander. I will surrender to you. I'll surrender *everything*.'

And then she released the darkness. She let it pour forth from her, and into dei Laramin. All of the fear, and hatred, and pain, and sorrow, and anguish. Torrents of dark emotion, in an unbroken stream of horror and agony. Sharing her worst ordeals with the High Commander, and magnifying them as they were unleashed.

Within seconds, dei Laramin had hunched forwards, and her hands had scrunched up into claws, causing the knife to drop to the floor. Allana rose calmly to her feet, knowing that the darkness continued to wash through her and into the other woman. Enveloping the High Commander in a cocoon of suffering. Allana's own physical pain was forgotten.

Dei Laramin's eyes had rolled up in their sockets, as the woman fell down to her knees. Her face had taken on a rictus of terror, and then she started to scream. Allana watched this dispassionately as she moved towards the woman, and she picked up the knife.

The High Commander had raised her hands to the side of her head, as if she was trying to shut out whatever foulness was now running through her mind. She was completely oblivious to the new threat, as Allana came to stand beside her.

'High Commander. Let my voice be the last thing that you ever hear. I *do* have dreams. And I have powers. And I *will* survive. Whatever the cost.'

Then Allana swept the knife across dei Laramin's neck.

—

Sometime afterwards, Allana came back into her senses. The bloody knife was in her hand, her dress was still torn and her body exposed, and dei Laramin lay dead before her.

Bodies were strewn about the area around her, a ghastly tableau of mingled corpses of humans and animals. A number of agitated and now rider-less horses were milling about nearby, while others had galloped away from the place of the killing.

In contrast to the grim scene of death, the clouds had now broken in the sky above, and sunshine was re-emerging into the world around Allana.

Are you free of them, Lana? Free, at last?

Only then did she detect the sound of breathless sobbing, and she turned towards it.

Nionia was twenty metres away. The lanky Guardswoman was the sole survivor of the party of Aiduel's Guards which had pursued Allana. The woman was sitting on the wet grass, her knees tucked into her chest, with her arms wrapped around the knees. Her sword must have been thrown aside at some point, and she was unarmed.

Allana walked towards her, still carrying the knife. She was unsure as to what she intended to do with it.

Nionia looked up, as Allana approached. The woman's voice was high-pitched and breaking as she said, 'I didn't want to come, Lana. I didn't want to come. Please don't kill me.'

Allana looked at her, and back at the knife. Nionia was a witness to what had happened here. She had seen Allana use her power of compulsion, and had been present as an even worse new power had been unleashed on dei Laramin. Could she be allowed to live?

Allana replied, after a few moments. 'I'm so tired, Nionia. Tired of being scared. Tired of being hunted. *You* were the reason that I had to leave my house in Septholme. And you were the reason why I was handed over to Aiduel's Guards. And tortured. All of this, it's because of you, and your stupid mouth.' She stepped closer, resolved that if Nionia was to try to move now, she would strike her down.

'I'm so sorry, Lana. So sorry. You were my friend, Lana. My best friend, here. I didn't mean any of this. I didn't. Please don't kill me. Please.'

Allana stared at her, and then moved forwards again. She stepped behind Nionia, and placed the knife at the Guardswoman's throat. 'I've had enough, Nionia. Enough. I don't want to be chased for my whole life.' The blade was pressing against Nionia's skin.

The woman released a loud sob. Her eyes were streaming with tears. 'Please, Lana. Please. What can I do?'

What can she do for you, Lana? What use can she possibly be now, other than to die?

If the blade slashed across, Nionia would become just one more victim. One more unfortunate individual who had died as a result of Allana's actions. And with so many already dead, what would one more matter?

But the one solace that Allana could hold onto, as she thought about the trail of death which she was leaving in her wake, was that everyone else had died because they had to. By contrast, she was not sure that it was still necessary that Nionia should be killed. And it was the truth, that the woman had once been a friend.

Then a firm reason for sparing Nionia's life came to Allana. She kept the knife at the lanky woman's throat, as she began to articulate this. 'If I kill you, Nionia, I might be able to escape and disappear. Flee somewhere, and hope that I'm never found. But someone in Aiduel's Guards could still be looking for me. And wondering what happened to you and dei Laramin and all of the others.'

644

Nionia's teeth were chattering with fear, and her only response was a whimper.

'But if I spare you, and you go back and tell them that I'm dead, then no one will come. If you tell them that... Elannis raiders killed the other Guards and me, after you'd captured me. That Allana dei Monis is dead.'

'Yes, yes, Lana. I would say that. I promise.'

'And if we burn all of the bodies, they'll never know any different. But... only if you tell the story.'

'I would, Lana. I promise. We captured you. Raiders came. They killed the others and you. I would. I promise.'

Can you spare her, Lana? Can you trust her?

Allana leaned in closer to Nionia, so that her mouth was next to the other woman's ear, and she whispered the next words. 'Know this, Nionia. And believe it. If I let you go, and you either don't tell this story, or if you tell anyone what really happened here, I will come for you. I'll find you, and I'll do to you what I did to dei Laramin. But worse, much worse. Understand that?'

'Yes. I'll tell the story. Exactly as you said. I promise. I promise! Please don't kill me, Lana. Please.'

Finally, Allana removed the knife from the other woman's neck. Nionia immediately rocked forwards, and started to sob again. Allana was satisfied that the woman would do as she had been told. Nionia was clearly terrified of her, and was completely cowed.

Allana recognised the unbridgeable divide between the two of them, which had allowed her to so thoroughly intimidate the other woman. Nionia was soft, weak, and incapable of killing. But she, Allana, was forever a killer.

—

Later that day, the two of them burned the bodies of the Guards and their dogs. The sun had quickly evaporated the moisture from the ground, and they built a large pyre within a dry area inside the copse of trees.

Allana had also thrown her torn dress onto the gathered pile of wood, and had put on her sole replacement dress from the bags. The earlier rain felt like it had washed the grime from her body and her hair, and she felt cleaner than she had at any time since leaving Septholme Castle.

As the flames from the fire rose into the sky, the irony was not lost on Allana that she was the one responsible for Evelyn dei Laramin being burnt on a pyre. As she stared at those flames, the memory of what she had done to the woman came back to her. Of the darkness, which she had unleashed. And of dei Laramin's torment, in her final moments. Allana shuddered, but then pushed the image away.

She had another means to protect herself, now. Her power of compulsion had always been available to her, whenever she had needed it. And she had a belief that she would also be able to draw on this new, and deadlier, power, if future circumstances ever demanded it.

And she knew without any doubt that she would be prepared to use it again. If necessary.

—

She parted company with Nionia that afternoon, making a last warning to the woman that no one was to know that Allana had survived this day. There was no warmth on their parting; Nionia was too frightened of her now, and seemed eager to separate.

After that, Allana returned to the road and walked northwards. Her body ached from the beating given by the High Commander, and her hip and leg were bruised, but these were trivial ailments in comparison to the prize of having avoided capture.

Her thoughts returned briefly to Arion Sepian, as she walked. Nionia's story would act to sever her link with Septholme and with

646

Aiduel's Guards, but any contact with Arion would risk re-forging that connection again. She had still not decided whether she wanted to see him again, after his abandonment. But this was just one more factor to complicate her decision.

Despite that, there was a lightness in her footsteps as she covered the ground. A tremendous weight had been lifted from her shoulders. She was no longer being pursued. No longer being hunted. As far as the world was concerned, the girl who had once been involved in the murder of a High Priest in Sen Aiduel, was dead. That part of her life, which had haunted her since her eighteenth birthday, was at last over.

She was free.

After two hours of walking, she wondered whether she had yet crossed out of Western Canasar and into the land of Rednar. She was still thinking about this, when she first noticed the riders in the distance, to the north. There was a band of possibly forty or fifty such horsemen, heading in an easterly direction. She groaned inside when she noted that they had also spotted her, and saw the column of horses wheeling in her direction.

Please let them leave you alone, Lana. Haven't you already endured enough, today?

The riders quickly closed the distance towards her, and as they arrived they fanned out around her. The manoeuvre was disconcertingly similar to that undertaken by her Aiduel's Guards pursuers, earlier that day. The horsemen were wearing tabards which appeared to be of Andar design, although with a slightly different shade of blue to that with which she was familiar. But they were heavily armed, and it was clearly a military company.

Once the mass of riders had arrived, the group appeared to part in the centre, and a giant black stallion passed through the gap created.

Allana could quickly perceive why the horse needed to be so substantial; its rider was the largest man that she had ever seen. He was wearing shining black armour beneath the blue tabard, and she noted the delicate intricacy of the golden engravings across that armour. This was a man of wealth. He was also wearing a gleaming black helm, which completely covered his face.

The man on the horse alongside the black stallion called out, 'You are in the presence of the Duke. Show proper respect!'

Allana started to curtsey, confused, but she saw the enormous man make a gesture to quiet his colleague. Nonetheless, Allana finished her curtsey, and said, 'Forgive me, Lord.'

The giant lifted his hand, and raised the visor on his helm. A broad face with a neatly trimmed black beard, and piercing dark eyes, was revealed. 'How peculiar. The only traffic that we've seen on this road for two days is a beautiful woman travelling on her own, and an exotic foreigner at that.'

'I'm fleeing the war, Lord.'

'Ah. Then you're safe. The war has not breached our borders, and you'll be glad to know that you have left the land of Western Canasar.' He moved his horse closer to her, and she could see an interest in his eyes which she immediately recognised. She returned his stare, trying to display more confidence than she felt.

'Am I in Rednar, Lord?'

He smiled, and there were a number of laughs from the men surrounding them. 'Rednar? No. But why would anyone want to go to Rednar, when they can come to Berun?'

You're in Berun, Lana! You've travelled too far to the east. Then who are you speaking to?

The giant man gracefully dismounted from his horse, and walked closer to her. On foot, his enormity was even more apparent. He towered a foot and a half above her. 'What is your name, my lady, if I may be so bold as to ask?'

'Lana, Lord.' She said the name before she had time to stop herself. It was too engrained in her.

'And are you devout, Lana? Do you adhere to the one true faith, and to the Holy Church, and do you follow the word of Aiduel?' His eyes were focused on her, dark and alert, and she knew that he was attracted to her.

'Yes, Lord. Of course, I'm a devoted follower.' She noted that he was wearing a small statue of The Lord Aiduel On The Tree, on a chain around his neck.

'Then you are welcome in my land, Lana. I am Duke Jarrett Berun, lord of these lands.' He swept his arm out and then bowed his head towards her, an oddly charming act of courtesy given his status.

'Thank you, Lord.' She curtsied again, surprising herself.

'And as you are in my land, Lana, I become your liege lord. So, I would ask this question of you, if you would humour me. What favour will you ask of your liege lord, if you decide to stay in my land?'

There was an awkwardly flirtatious tone to his voice. She was aware that his men were watching the two of them. She also knew that he was trying to play to that audience, making a show of flirting with the beautiful woman whom they had just met on the road. But she could also sense the immediate desire within him, for her. There was a deeper intent to his apparent attempt at charm, than a mere display of showmanship for his men.

She contemplated her answer for a few seconds, before she responded. Her voice was soft and low as she spoke, making her words audible just to him, and her eyes were locked onto his. 'I will ask nothing of you, Duke Berun, other than what any true and devout member of the faith would ask of their liege lord.'

'And what is that, Lana?'

'To protect me, Lord. And to keep me safe.'

38

Corin

—

Year of Our Lord,
After Ascension, 769AA

The conflict raging within Corin had still not abated, as he led the warriors of the Karn into the lands of the Anath.

A day had passed since the attack by the Anath on the village of Karn. A single day since that moment when an Anath warrior had swung a club into the side of Agbeth's head, felling and grievously wounding her. Throughout that time, Agbeth had not woken, had not opened her eyes, had not responded to the people around her. Corin's beloved wife remained unconscious, and his unbroken anguish and fury burned ever more fiercely within him.

Corin had found little rest, the previous night. He had lain beside Agbeth, watching her shallow breathing, sometimes holding a water-soaked cloth to her mouth. And he had remembered. Frozen images of their time together. Memories of those many actions and interactions which, over the passing of the years, had led to the roots of their lives becoming so deeply intertwined.

He had finally conjured into his mind his favourite recollection, of a long ago night at the side of their tranquil lake. They had been sitting together, both of them imbued with a sensation of peace, as the sky had been ablaze with colour. That memory had in turn drawn his first tears.

When he had eventually found sleep, the recurring dream had in turn sought and captured him, as if it was taunting him in the midst of his distress. It was almost fully shaped within his mind now; the walk along the winding path on the side of the mountain, his shining companions, the Gate, and a terrible figure in the Gate. All of it clear, apart from the confused final moments, after a single finger had been raised. What happened next?

He could never remember that element of the dream, but it had always caused him to waken with an unsettling and pervading sense of wrongness. Something terrible had happened, or would happen, in those final moments. Something perhaps so awful that his mind would not allow him to remember it?

Last night, when the events in the dream had forced him gasping out of slumber, the sense of unease which had lingered afterwards had seemed stronger than ever. And his ability to grasp the hidden memory had teased at being closer than ever. Was it possible that his frame of mind, since Agbeth's injury, had opened a clearer pathway to the darkness which might lurk in this obscured heart of the dream?

But after waking, the reality of Agbeth's condition had still been there. And his inability to speak with his wife, to tell her his thoughts and to hear her response, felt more out of place – more unnatural, more horrific – than anything which a dream could ever torment him with.

He had left her with a gentle kiss to the forehead, that morning. Wishing that she would wake. Terrified that her condition might worsen, whilst he was gone. Not daring to think about the worst possible outcome.

And here he was, now, journeying through the lands of his enemies.

His axe was clenched tightly in his hand as he marched towards the Anath settlement. However, he knew that the successful delivery of victory today would not rely upon the blade of that weapon.

Blackpaw walked by his side, the beast moving forwards on all four legs. The connection between Corin and the creature throbbed with barely contained violence. For almost two years, the nature of Corin's interactions with the beast had been marked more by his nature than by the felrin's. He had controlled the creature and had gradually suppressed its most primitive urges. But today the beast's nature, its feral core, was striving to be the dominant impulse. It continued to whisper to Corin seductively, promising to shield him from his pain, if only he would unleash bloody violence and carnage.

The warriors of the Karn walked behind him. Their numbers had been depleted by the events of the prior day, and Akob had indicated that there were only slightly more than four boats' worth of fighters. The older man had told Corin that he expected the Anath to have that number and at least half as many again. There had been no apparent fear in Corin's father as he had made this statement, though. Just an acceptance that his clan chief had made a decision, and that if the Gods willed their victory it would come to be.

Corin had not shared his precise plan with Akob, or with Marrix, or with any of the warriors of the Karn. They would see what he intended to do, at the same moment that the Anath experienced that action. But he was certain that the men of the Karn would follow him.

As he covered the last mile towards the enemy settlement, Corin reflected upon how much had changed since that day, over two years ago, when he had first approached the Anath village. There were many simple contrasts between today, and that last assault. This time, they had not come by boat, or in stealth under the cover of darkness. This time, they walked in the daylight, and their approach would be clearly visible.

But there were more poignant differences, too. He had been a callow youth, and full of fear, the first time that he had come here.

He had been completely untried and untested. And he had been oblivious to his fate, that he would soon be banished for cowardice. But he had also known, on that long ago and scary night, that Agbeth would be waiting for him, when he returned. Waiting, with the promise of a new dawn for their relationship.

Would he take back everything that had happened since then, discard every event and memory from the last two years, to return to that day? And to know that she would be there, alive and well, upon his return? Waiting for him, with a loving smile on her face. He shook his head, trying and failing to force the thought and his frustrated self-pity away.

Eventually, at a distance of four hundred metres from the enemy village, Corin halted his war party.

He intended to line his force up outside of the enemy settlement. Corin wanted Rekmar to bring himself and his warriors outside, such that he could face them on the open fields beside the village. The visible presence of the Anath warriors, gathered all in one place, would make what Corin wanted to do that much easier.

Akob and Marrix immediately shouted instructions for the warriors of the Karn to spread out, into a line which was two-men deep.

Then it was time to wait.

—

Within twenty minutes, the Anath war-band had assembled opposite the warriors of Karn, on the fields outside of their village. Corin watched their ranks form, and he realised that Akob's estimate had probably been on the low side. The Anath force was considerably larger. The opposing armies were two hundred metres from each other.

When the full strength of the Anath was amassed, Corin walked forward from the line of Karn warriors. He indicated to Akob and Marrix that he wanted them to follow him. Corin then waved and gestured at Rekmar, signalling to the enemy chief that he wanted to speak. This was the start of Corin's plan.

'Why are you attempting to hold discussions, Chief?' asked Marrix. 'Surely the time for talk is over?'

Corin turned to the other two men, as they reached the point which was almost halfway between the opposing forces. 'Akob, Marrix. Today, do *nothing* to interrupt or contradict me, when we're with Rekmar. Whatever you think. If you start to have doubts, just remember what happened, with Borrik. And stay quiet. Say nothing. And trust me.'

Marrix frowned, but he did not say anything else. Akob simply nodded.

Corin observed Rekmar walking forwards, also accompanied by two of his warriors. As Rekmar drew closer to their position, Corin could feel the pent-up energy inside of Blackpaw, from where the felrin waited within the ranks of the Karn. The beast craved to surge forwards and to unleash itself upon the Anath chief. Corin resisted that urge, and held the creature back.

When the Anath chief was twenty metres away from him, Corin shouted, 'You betrayed my offer of peace, Rekmar! It is no longer possible that we can have peace while I'm clan chief of the Karn, and you are chief of the Anath.'

Rekmar laughed scornfully in return. 'So what? We piss on your pathetic offer of peace. Why bargain with the weak? All of you Karn will die here today, and then we'll take your village and your women. This day is long overdue.'

Corin stared at the man, staying silent for a few moments. Unseen connections were spiralling out of his mind and towards the Anath chief. Probing. Finding where the weakness was…

Corin smiled, feeling satisfied. 'Why waste our men on this fight, though, Rekmar? Whoever wins between us, the losses will be too great. Even the victor's clan will be too weak, afterwards. I know that. Surely you know it, too.'

'What? So you bring your men here, and now you're too

scared to fight us?' The Anath chief spat into the ground, after saying this.

Corin took a step towards the man. 'How would you like to be clan chief of the Karn, too, Rekmar? To be chief of the Anath *and* the Karn?' Corin heard a loud intake of breath from behind him, from either Marrix or Akob, but he ignored it.

'What, are you so scared, now that you're here, that you want to stop being clan chief? And run away?'

'No, not run away,' replied Corin. 'I want you to try to take the chiefdom off me. To fight me, and to try to kill me.'

'Fight you?' Rekmar laughed with derision, then spat again. 'I'll do that on the battlefield, anyway. Rekmar will chop the head off your fucking felrin, and then I'll chop you up, piece by piece, as you watch your men dying.'

Corin could feel that the rage within himself was surfacing again. This arrogant and vicious thug was the person responsible for Agbeth's injury. The raid against Karn must have taken place on Rekmar's command. Corin longed for the moment when he would make the Anath leader regret his actions, and would cause the man to suffer. And he *would* make him suffer. But Corin knew that he had to keep control of his fury, such that Rekmar's punishment happened at the precise right time.

'You're not understanding me, Rekmar. As clan chief, before the Gods I can adopt anyone into the clan of the Karn. *Anyone*, including you. Which I'll do, before the Gods. Once I've done that, if you were to defeat me in a challenge in single combat, you would become clan chief of the Karn. The warriors of the Karn would have to follow you.'

'And why would you do this?' Rekmar stared at him, his eyes scrutinising Corin, appearing to look for a trap.

'Because I require you to do the same for me. Adopt me into the Anath. Such that if I kill you, I'll become the Anath chief. Then we can have one single combat, and the winner will become chief over both clans. And the Anath and the Karn will not have wasted their best warriors on this field, on this day.'

Rekmar continued to stare at Corin, regarding him silently.

Corin decided that it was time to goad the other man. 'But if you are scared, Rekmar, then let's just have the battle between our armies, and suffer the losses. There's no loss of face in being scared of the man who killed Borrik Greataxe, even if there is such a great prize available for the victor.'

'Scared of you? Rekmar will piss on your rotting corpse, you little shit!'

'Then prove it. Fight me. But let me make it easier for you to decide, Rekmar. I'll fight you without weapons or armour. Unarmed. But you can select whatever equipment you like.'

Rekmar barked a laugh. 'Are you a fucking madman, Corin of the Karn? And if Rekmar chooses to accept this offer, what next?'

Corin's face remained impassive, despite how much he now wanted to hurt the other man. 'We need to bring our men closer. They need to hear us take the vows to adopt each other into the other's clan. And we need them all to swear before the Gods that they'll follow the winner of our fight.'

'And you will be unarmed? Without your felrin in the fight? But I can have weapons? Yes?'

'Yes, to all of that. The felrin won't join the fight.' The need for vengeance was burning inside Corin, and he had to restrain himself from smiling, as he gave this response.

'Very well. Rekmar agrees.'

—

Some minutes later, the massed forces of the Karn and the Anath had moved much closer to each other. There was a distance of perhaps thirty metres between their lines. Blackpaw was in the centre of the Karn line, hunched over, resting on its front paws. There was a gap of several metres between the creature and the wary Karn warriors around it.

Just Corin and Rekmar were now standing in the area between the opposing armies. The Anath chief was wearing leather armour which covered his body and shoulders, leaving his muscular arms and legs bare. He was carrying an axe in one hand, and a wicked-looking curved knife in the other.

Corin had stripped off his own leather armour, and had thrown his axe to the ground near to the ranks of the Karn. He recognised how relatively puny he must look, compared to his armoured opponent.

Corin had already made his vows to adopt Rekmar into the clan of the Karn. He was listening now, as Rekmar made the equivalent vow.

'I, Rekmar, Clan Chief of the Anath, adopt Corin of Karn into the clan of the Anath. Before the Gods, I swear this to be true.' Rekmar snarled the words as if they were a curse, and at the end of his pronouncement he spat into the floor again.

Corin could feel the darkness building inside himself, once more. The rage, which he had been experiencing ever since Agbeth's injury, was threatening to take control of him again. He was eager to soon release at least some of it, onto Rekmar. His plan here today might result in the preservation of life for the vast majority of the people there, but the Anath Chief would know no such mercy. The end which Corin had planned for him was going to be horrific, but Corin needed it to be that way, to teach a lesson to every other man gathered there.

After Rekmar had finished speaking, Corin turned towards the Karn warriors and shouted, 'Men of Karn! Recognise Rekmar into our clan, before the Gods. And recognise that he will be clan chief of the Karn, if he defeats me. Repeat my words. Before the Gods!'

The shout from the assembled Karn warriors was muted, and disgruntled, but nonetheless Corin's call was echoed by them. 'Before the Gods!'

Rekmar repeated similar words to the Anath men gathered there. Corin was satisfied to hear the Anath warriors also give their affirmation, although again with little enthusiasm.

Corin stepped forwards, such that he was a few paces away from his opponent, and asked, 'Ready, Rekmar?'

'Ready.'

Even before Rekmar had responded, Corin was taking control of the man. Corin's ability to control others felt more accessible, and more powerful, than it had ever done before. Perhaps he had learned vital lessons from the fight with Borrik, or more likely his rage was fuelling his ability? But it seemed so effortless on this occasion for the invisible tendrils to whip out of Corin's mind towards the Anath leader, and to bludgeon their way through to their target.

STOP! STOP! STOP! STOP! STOP!

Borrik had resisted, for minutes. Rekmar's will was broken in an instant.

Corin observed the Anath Chief attempting to move forwards, and then stopping. Rekmar's limbs were locked in place, and he was paralysed. One of the man's arms was holding the axe aloft, and the other with the curved blade was down at his side. Corin noted the trembling in Rekmar's arms, as the man tried to break free of the unseen bonds which were wrapped around all of his limbs.

Corin moved towards the Anath Chief, hearing the confused mutterings of the assembled Anath warriors, as Rekmar made no move to cut Corin down. Corin stood before them, in striking distance of Rekmar's weapons, as he addressed his foes.

'Warriors of the Anath. I stand before Rekmar, Chief of the Anath, as an adopted son of your clan. I have challenged Rekmar to single combat. And he knows that if I win, I will become chief. But he does not choose to strike me down, even though I'm unarmed. Why not? Because the Gods have willed my victory! I went to the north, and I saw the Gods, and I returned. And I have been given powers, powers above any other man. Powers to control beasts. To control felrin. And to control men. And the Gods will protect me, from the likes of Rekmar.

'I told this to Rekmar, when I spoke with him. I told him this, and I offered to make peace between us. But what did he do? He spat on that offer, and you attacked my village. Attacked and hurt my wife. So things cannot be as they were. I cannot leave the Anath village as it was, ruled by Rekmar.'

Out of the corner of Corin's eye, he could see the Anath chief straining to release himself from the paralysis which had been implanted inside him. The man's eyes were wide, and were bulging with the effort. But this time, Corin had learned the lessons from the fight with Borrik, and his anger and his hate had made him much more powerful than he had ever been before. There would be no release, until Corin was ready. There was no threat from Rekmar.

In the same moments, further invisible tendrils were spiralling out from Corin, sliding around and through all of the assembled Anath. In seconds, Corin knew that he could control each and every last one of the Anath warriors. If he needed to.

'I could have chosen to come here today, and to make war against you. And if I had chosen that, I could have done to every one of you what I'm about to do to Rekmar. Could have killed every single man, woman and child of the Anath. On my own. Think on that, if any man here is considering attacking me. Because if you do, you'll share Rekmar's coming fate. But instead, I've chosen that only one man needs to die here, today. Rekmar.

'After I've finished with Rekmar, and have become your chief, I'm going to offer you a choice. Join me, and follow me. Become a single clan, of Karn and Anath. Accept me as your clan chief, as chosen by the Gods, and know peace between our villages. Peace for your families, and for your children. Do that, and I'll spare your lives, and there'll be no more vengeance or bloodshed between us after today, from anyone, whether they be Karn or Anath. Reject my offer, and you will die, today, on this field. In a few minutes I'll ask you to make that choice. But before doing that, I must hand out punishment. To Rekmar, who thought me weak and who pissed on my offer of peace.'

Corin walked towards the Anath clan chief. There was hatred and defiance in the man's eyes, but this was overlaid by fear, and mounting desperation. Perhaps Rekmar wanted to speak, but Corin had no interest in hearing his words, and had already ordered him into silence.

Corin knew what he was going to do next. What he had decided, the night before, at the Karn gathering. And he recognised the darkness of it. Would this be an act of violent evil? Or, by avoiding mass bloodshed, would he be doing a good deed today? Either way, the part of him which sought vengeance for Agbeth, was relishing what was about to happen.

'Rekmar, drop your weapons.'

Corin transmitted the instruction to the Anath clan chief, at the same moment that he said the words. The axe and the knife both clattered to the floor.

'Rekmar, get down on your hands and knees, like a dog.'

There was some futile further attempt at resistance, but then the Anath leader collapsed downwards onto all fours. This resulted in shocked gasps and mutterings from the assembled Anath warriors.

'Rekmar, crawl towards the felrin. Offer yourself to it.'

As Corin said this, and as Rekmar found himself moving forwards against his own free will, appearing to drag his reluctant body across the ground, Corin could at last see the unconcealed terror in the man's eyes. Rekmar had realised what was going to happen to him.

Corin transmitted an instruction to Blackpaw, and the creature sat up, eyes focusing upon the Anath chief. Its jaws opened, displaying sharp glistening teeth within its long maw. Corin turned in a circle, and addressed every man there. 'There *will* be peace between us! This is the fate of any who would break that peace!'

Rekmar's body was still dragging him forwards, against his volition. Corin could feel the man fighting with every sinew of his strength, to try to stop the forward movement. But it would do him no good. In seconds, the Anath chief came within range of the felrin. Came inside the embrace of the creature's thick arms.

The beast could have decapitated and killed the man in a second. But that would not have served Corin's purpose, on this day. Instead, the felrin gently put one paw onto Rekmar's back, and slid a thick arm under his legs. It pulled the Anath chief in towards itself, holding him in place, close to its own body. Appearing to cradle him, as a mother would cradle a child. Its snout dropped, it sniffed Rekmar's bare upper arm, and drool slid out of its open mouth onto that limb. Corin could hear whimpering from the Anath chief.

Corin then released the control which had been prohibiting Rekmar from speaking. He wanted every man there to hear what the Anath chief was about to endure. He issued a final instruction to Blackpaw, and he accompanied it this time with spoken words. 'Blackpaw. Feed. Slowly.'

Corin watched everything that took place, thereafter. And experienced much of it, through Blackpaw's eyes. It was his responsibility to see every moment, even as other hardened warriors blanched and turned away. This was *his* vengeance, his release of violence. One grim, ghastly death, to pacify his rage over what they had done to Agbeth, and to avoid the darker temptation to otherwise unleash his fury on every last one of the Anath.

One death, to avoid the bloodshed of a massed battle between the clans, here today. And to avoid the slaughter of the Anath.

As awful as the deed was, he had concluded that something as terrible as this was necessary, if he was to stop the conflict between the clans. After becoming clan chief, he had naively sought peace through friendship. And disaster had resulted. But perhaps peace could only be more permanently secured, if each and every person was terrified of the alternative. Terrified of *him*.

And that day, as their old clan chief screamed and begged for the many agonising minutes before his death, minutes during which his limbs were slowly crunched, chewed and severed by a creature arising out of legend, the surviving Anath learned the lesson of fear.

A lesson which was also not lost on the warriors of the Karn.

After today, Corin knew with certainty that each and every one of them would fear him. And if they all feared him, he would control the Karn, and he would control the Anath.

And there *would* be peace between them.

Corin stood in silence for several seconds after Rekmar's screams

661

had faded away to ghastly memory. Then he turned back to face the surviving Anath. 'Choose, now. Accept me as your leader, choose to follow me, and join a greater combined clan of the Karn and the Anath. And you will know peace. Or choose to challenge me. Now. And choose death.'

They all chose to follow him.

—

After that, Corin's thoughts returned to Agbeth. He allowed the Anath warriors to return to their village, after they had pledged their loyalty to him. He left them with a promise that he would be returning soon.

Corin then walked back to his own village, with Blackpaw and the other warriors of the Karn. There would be time aplenty later to work out how best to unify the clans. How best to ensure that there was no further return to violence between the longstanding enemies. And time also to proceed in securing peace with the Borl. But all of that could wait. He had to be with his wife again.

When his party arrived back at Karn, they were bombarded with questions about what had happened, from villagers who were relieved to see all of their loved ones returning unscathed. Corin left it to Akob and Marrix to provide them with answers. He returned directly to his home.

The two elderly healers were still by Agbeth's side, and a quick shake of the head by one of them told Corin simply that his wife still lived, but that there had been no change in her condition. He dismissed them, and walked closer to the bed. The swelling on the side of Agbeth's head looked even worse, and was now showing a bruised yellow colour. Her breathing sounded hoarse, and shallower than previously.

He lay down alongside her, feeling numb. He reached out for her hand, then gently held it in his own. He wished that she would turn to him and smile, then roll onto her side and invite him to snuggle behind her. He wished that she would ask him how his morning had gone, and allow him to relieve some of the horror of what he had done by sharing it with her. But she was not going to do any of these things.

Corin lay on the bed beside his wife, and he wept.

In two years, he had gone from being a nothing, and an exile, to clan chief of two tribes. And yet he felt no sense of triumph, or of achievement. Instead, he felt lost, and dirty. Soiled. He had discovered and released something from within himself in this last day, had unleashed something awful upon his own soul, and could there ever be an undoing of that? Could he ever forget the darkness of the deed which he had done to Rekmar?

The Anath chief had suffered an excruciating and ghastly end. Yes, that suffering had been inflicted to teach a lesson to the warriors there. And to secure peace. But Corin knew, in his heart, that his actions had really been undertaken for the purpose of vengeance. For the satisfaction of watching the other man scream and beg, and of knowing that some small revenge had been taken for what had been done to Agbeth.

Corin sensed that his actions on this day could have scarred and altered him, irrevocably. What had become of the gentle man, who had once lain beside Agbeth under the canopy of the Great Forest, and had asked her to be his wife? Was that person now gone forever? And how would Agbeth regard him, how would she judge him, if she knew of what he had done?

But his wife did not wake.

He moved closer to her, placing his forehead onto her shoulder, while still weeping. Slowly, he settled into a more relaxed state, something closer to sleep, and his sobbing gradually ended.

With him being there, so close to her, it seemed entirely natural for unseen tendrils to slide out of his mind, and to gently ease their way into hers. And what he found there was unlike anything which he had ever experienced previously when doing this, with her or with others. There was an absence. A nothingness.

When he had done this in the midst of her seizures, he had felt her presence there. Each time, he had felt himself residing in her soul, pained though it was by the seizure. But now, it felt as if he was floating in a great emptiness.

And yet, he pleaded.

COME BACK, AGBETH! WAKE UP! PLEASE COME BACK!

His entreaties disappeared into the void of her mind.

He concentrated again, trying to focus all of his force and willpower.

COME BACK! WAKE UP! WAKE UP!

Still the words disappeared into the nothingness, trailing out of sight and memory.

For the last time, he tried, his thoughts begging.

PLEASE, AGBETH! I NEED YOU. SO MUCH. PLEASE. WHAT SHOULD I DO?

And then, silence. She was not there.

Corin pressed his head against her shoulder, feeling distraught. He missed her. Missed her so much. Missed all of the intelligence and wit and warmth and love that was Agbeth.

Had the injury rendered her like this, forever? And if that was the case, what was the point of Corin himself carrying on? Everything that they had survived together, everything which they had achieved together, everything that they had loved together, might be undone by the cruel act which had led to her injury. How could Corin possibly endure this?

Better to cast himself into the nothingness, and to join her.

But then a soft voice carried to him, in ethereal whispers, from somewhere in the distant void. Agbeth's voice? Reverberating in his mind, although he was uncertain whether it was her words, or simply her gentle voice applied to some other thoughts.

Gather them. Open the Gate. And claim the power.

There was someone there. Someone who could be reached. Someone who was responding to him.

'Agbeth?'

He gathered his strength, and when he communicated again, he screamed the thoughts, driving all of his remaining rage and willpower into the message.

YOU MUST COME BACK TO ME! YOU MUST WAKE UP!

And then there was a stirring, beside him on the bed. A jerking of her arm. Excited, he immediately sat up, staring at her face. There was movement there, a barely discernible twitching of the mouth. He observed more closely, watching her eyelids flutter, daring not to hope that he had healed her.

His hand moved to cradle her cheek, on the side of her head which was not injured. Waiting. Watching, as her eyelids flickered.

And finally, her eyes opened.

39

Arion

—

Year of Our Lord,
After Ascension, 769AA

'And now, before The Lord Aiduel, I pronounce you husband and wife.' As the priest announced these words, there was a smattering of applause from the audience within the chapel of Septholme Castle.

Arion looked at his new bride upon hearing the pronouncement. He noted that she had a beaming smile, and he leaned forwards to kiss her. There was a cheer from the gathering in the chapel as he did this, followed by another round of applause.

After the kiss had ended, Kalyane moved in closer to slide her arms around his back, and to lean her head onto his chest. She was squeezing him tightly, as he turned his head to peer around at the assembled audience. Happy faces returned his stare, and he grinned back in response, displaying an outward joy which he did not feel inside.

The bells of the castle had started to ring, jubilantly announcing to the citizens of Septholme that Lord Arion, the Hero of Moss

Ford, was now married to Lady Kalyane Rednar. Those sounds would mark the start of a day of Fifth-Day festivities, in celebration of the victory in the war, and of the wedding.

He closed his eyes momentarily, and *her* image appeared in his mind. He knew that it was not right to picture *her* at this moment, as his new wife was hugging him. That it was an act of betrayal to think about *her* in these circumstances and these surroundings. But she had been constantly there, tormenting his thoughts, ever since he had heard the news.

Allana was dead. And now he was married. To someone else.

—

He had heard the news of her death, the day after he had returned to Septholme, just over a week earlier.

Upon his return, he had still been undecided as to what he was going to do. He had been agonising over whether he should stay in the town, or head off to try to find Allana. In the midst of that indecision, he had realised that he could try to obtain more information before concluding upon his course of action. Specifically, that he could speak to Aiduel's Guards again first, to gather any clues as to where she was or whether they had recaptured her.

He had therefore visited the Guards' fortress on the hill outside of Septholme, and from the moment of his very first enquiries he had sensed that something was wrong. The officer on duty at the front entrance had looked sheepish, and then had asked him to wait.

Eventually, Arion had been led towards a meeting room, the same one in which he had first met Allana. After a few minutes of waiting there, two people had entered the room. The first was a swarthy male officer, whose insignia suggested that he was a captain. The second was the lanky Guardswoman, who Arion had remembered from his first visit there. The woman's eyes had been cast downwards as she had entered the room, apparently uncomfortable about the conversation that she was about to have.

'Lord Sepian? I am Captain Pellyron. I understand that you've been asking about the prisoner, Allana dei Monis?'

'Yes, I have.'

'May I ask why?'

'She was a retainer at the castle, for a long time. I have an interest in her status, because of that.'

'Very well. But I regret to inform you that she's dead.'

At the time, Arion had felt as if he had been punched in the heart. Hard. He had felt momentarily winded, but had tried to keep the shock and sudden grief from his face as he had replied, 'Dead? How?'

'You may not have heard, but she escaped from here. Fled northwards. Guardswoman Nionia here was part of a pursuing party that captured her far to the north. They were bringing her back when they were attacked by rogue Elannis cavalry. Other than Nionia, who escaped, they were all killed. Including our courageous leader, may Aiduel guard her soul, High Commander dei Laramin.'

By the Lord! It cannot be true!

Arion had switched his attention to the blonde-haired woman, who had been quiet so far. Her eyes had still been staring downwards, focused on the table between them. 'You saw her die?'

She had lifted her eyes, at that question. Had met his gaze. 'I didn't see her die, no. I was fleeing. But later, when I came back, I saw her body. I saw all the bodies.' She had shuddered.

'How did she die?'

'Cut down. They were all cut down.'

Not on a pyre? She must be mistaken!

'Where did she die? Where are the bodies?'

'I burned them all. After I came back. I dragged them to a pyre, and I cremated them. Tried to give them funeral rites.'

'But. That cannot be right. She was definitely amongst the dead?'

'Yes. I knew her, before she was a prisoner here. As I knew all of the people who died that day. I was the only one to survive. If you knew her, then I'm sorry. Very sorry. But she's dead.'

—

Later, during his walk back to Septholme, Arion had realised that his prophetic dream had been proven false. After the accuracy of the visions of the raiders on the beach, and of the army at Moss Ford, he had been certain that the dream of Allana on the pyre was somehow going to come to pass. Unless he prevented it.

And yet it would not. He had abandoned her, and her fate had been to be caught by Aiduel's Guards, then subsequently to be cut down by an Elannis war-party. After that, she had indeed been burned on a pyre, but not in the manner which he had foreseen in his dream.

He had crouched down at the side of the road then and had vomited, tears in his eyes, feeling stricken by the outcome. Her perfect physical form had been cut and bloodied, and then burned. Life and vibrant energy had left her body. She no longer lived or breathed. She no longer existed. He had abandoned her, and she had died.

Perhaps his actions on the night of the escape had somehow managed to twist her destiny, but ultimately had not done enough to avert her death? He had no means to know whether that was true or not, and he would never know.

Guilt, regret and doubt would now be his secret companions, for a long time to come. But at least, with the knowledge of Allana's death, his torment of indecision had finally ended. His sole solace within the grim news was that he no longer needed to abandon his home and his family, in pursuit of her.

Later that day, when Gerrion had approached him again about the wedding plans, he had therefore meekly acquiesced. He had agreed to a very quick wedding, if that was also acceptable to Kalyane and the Rednar family.

Within two days of that, after a flurry of communication between Gerrion and Duchess Rednar, the wedding had been confirmed. For Fifth-Day, the following week.

And now he was here, in the Great Hall of Septholme Castle, in the midst of a splendid feast which was celebrating his and Kalyane's nuptials.

It was a lavish event, with a high table which was seating a number of members of the nobility. Arion and Kalyane took centre stage, in the places of honour at the head of the table. Even with his thoughts distracted, Arion recognised how lovely his bride looked. Her long auburn hair lay glossy and full down her back, and she appeared to be radiantly happy.

To their right, Gerrion was seated between Duke Rednar, and Prince Sendar Pavil. The three men were engaged in a serious-looking conversation, although the prince had a typically wry-looking expression on his face. As soon as he had heard the news of the wedding, Sendar had made it clear that he would attend, and Arion had been delighted when the ship carrying his friend had arrived that morning.

To Arion's left, Duchess Rednar was seated alongside Charl Koss, the Duchess laughing frequently at a tale being told by the aged adviser. Further along from them, Lennion Rednar was sitting beside Karienne. The youngest of the Sepians was now sixteen years old, and Arion could see that his younger sister and his friend were getting along very well, with their heads close together as they were chatting. Arion had gained little opportunity since his return to spend time with Karienne, and he knew that he would have to remedy that. But for now, it appeared that the last thing that she wanted was to be interrupted from her conversation. It was good to see her smiling again, after their father's death.

That thought gave Arion a pang of sadness. His father was not there today, and only a few weeks had gone by since the Duke had passed away. It was another source of regret to Arion that he had never got to see his father again, after his military training had ended.

When he had departed from Septholme over two years earlier, his farewell to Duke Conran had been muted and lukewarm. It had been tempered by Delrin's treatment, and by his own arguments with the old Duke. But the last letter from his father had expressed pride about the battle near Fort Lennis. And how would Duke Conran have reacted to Arion's accomplishments at the Battle of Moss Ford, and during the war with Elannis more generally? Undoubtedly with pride, if he had been there to witness any of it.

'What's up, my husband? You look a little sad, again.' Kalyane's voice was gentle, as she asked the question.

'Just thinking about my father. Wishing that he was still here. That he could be here, now.'

She reached out and placed her hand over his. 'I'm sure that he'd be proud, to see you now. To know what you've achieved. As am I.'

He smiled at her. 'And I'm proud, and honoured, to have married you.'

She beamed happily in response to his words, making him feel again like he was a fraud and a liar. She would never know what had been in his thoughts, for these last few weeks since their betrothal, and he would never tell her. Kalyane was his wife now, and she deserved better than the way that he had almost disregarded her, in recent weeks. He must make her happy. And she would never know about Allana dei Monis.

As he would never know, for certain, whether he ever would have married Kalyane, had Allana still lived.

—

Later, he was gathered with Sendar and Lennion. All three of them had been drinking for an extended period, and they were in good spirits. A group of musicians had arrived in the Great Hall and were now playing a variety of famous songs, and there was soon to be dancing.

'So, here we are again,' said Sendar, smiling. 'The elite Academy class of 768AA, reunited again. Although, while Lennion and

671

I continue to be mere mortals, one of us has moved on to greater things.'

'I think all three of us always knew that was going to be the case,' said Arion, neutrally, trying but failing to maintain a straight face. 'When greatness is surrounded by mediocrity, it always finds a way to rise to the surface.'

Lennion snorted. 'I can think of something else which rises to the surface, and there was plenty of it in that statement!'

The three of them laughed. Sendar then added, 'Anyway, I can't believe that our fourth room-mate, a certain Duke Berun, didn't get an invite, too?'

'Jarrett?' Arion grimaced. 'Ignoring the fact that I hate his guts, which of course I do. But I like him even less now, given that he made no effort to help us during the invasion. So, no invite from me for the big, annoying, pious bastard!'

Lennion laughed, then looked at Sendar. 'Is the King going to do anything about Jarrett's actions during the invasion?'

Sendar shook his head. 'I doubt it. Jarrett didn't break any direct orders, as such. He mustered his soldiers, and he protected his borders. Just didn't want to march them into Western Canasar. I doubt that my father will want to pick a fight with Duke Berun, right now, given the other things that are going on with the Archlaw.'

'The Archlaw?' Lennion repeated the words. 'What's going on with the Archlaw?'

'Not good news, I'm afraid,' answered the prince. 'My father is furious, and unfortunately this time he doesn't have Duke Conran, may his soul rest in peace, to calm him down. We only barely managed to persuade the King to accept the armistice with Elannis; he was all set on pursuing an all-out war against them. But now we see that the Archlaw is refusing to take any action against anyone from the Empire, to punish them for the invasion. And father is yet again accusing the Holy Church of hypocrisy and double-standards.'

'Can we expect any different?' asked Arion. 'We all know that if Andar invaded Eastern Canasar, then condemnation and the threat of excommunication would come to King Inneos, and anyone else involved, within days. But when Elannis invades us? Nothing!'

Sendar shook his head. 'We should be able to expect fairer treatment. Particularly after all the concessions that we agreed to, following the Grand Council. But we can't. Too many members of the Elannis hierarchy are now on the High Council of the Holy Church. Too much Elannis money gets donated to the Archlaw. There's too much corruption. I fear that father is returning to where he was in his thinking, two years ago.'

'What do you mean?' Arion could clearly remember the King's anger and petulance, from the meeting in the palace almost two years earlier.

'What I'm about to say is confidential, between the three of us,' replied Sendar. 'Although I have also told the two Dukes, today, to gauge their reaction. The King is again considering breaking off from the Holy Church in Sen Aiduel. Starting with the expulsion from the country of all of those vermin from Aiduel's Guards. He's not yet decided, but I fear that if father sees no meaningful punishment taken against the Emperor or Prince Markon, then he might take the action.'

Lennion frowned. 'Whew! That would be quite a step.'

'I know,' replied Sendar. 'We all know. But one way or another, at some point, things will come to a head. I think that your deeds have bought us peace, Arion, but only for a time.'

'Do you really think so?'

'Yes, I do. One way or another, it feels inevitable that war will be coming again. And next time, it may also be a religious war, and one which encompasses the whole country. We must use the time which you've won for us, now, to prepare for it.'

—

Later in the evening, Arion was approached by Gerrion. Arion was watching Kalyane on the dancefloor at the time, his bride laughing

673

happily as she twirled in a circle with her mother, brother and Karienne.

'I am proud of you, Arion,' the young Duke said, as he drew close.

'Thank you, Gerr.'

'We'll be OK, I think, without father. At first, if I'm being honest, I was scared by it. A little overwhelmed. But no longer. With me to run our lands and economy, and you to lead our armies, we'll be just fine. We'll be a great team. They will talk about the achievements of the Sepian brothers, for years to come.'

Arion raised his glass. 'I'll drink to that.'

There was then a moment of hesitation by Gerrion, before the older sibling leaned in closer and said, 'I hope that your marriage to Kalyane will be blessed with children, brother.'

'So do I, brother.' As he said this, Arion realised that he meant it.

'And perhaps, if you have a son… one day, that son could be named my heir.' Arion looked towards his brother, a puzzled expression on his face. Gerrion put a hand onto his arm. 'Keep this between us, Arion. And it's a conversation for another time. But it's a conversation I'd like to have with you one day. Soon.'

—

At the end of the evening, Arion and Kalyane retired to Arion's chambers. They were ushered from the Great Hall amidst clapping and cheering, and Arion was eagerly anticipating the physical act which he knew was coming. They were kissing as they entered his chambers, alone together now, and they were locked in each other's arms.

His new wife was attractive, and it had been a long time since he had been with a woman. And he was undoubtedly full of desire for her, as she undressed before him. He was fully aware that he was a lucky man, and that thousands of other men would have envied his position at that moment.

674

And therefore, it seemed churlish, as he led Kalyane by her hand to their bed, to have a momentary pang of regret that she was not Allana.

—

Afterwards, she lay in his arms, drowsy and content in the aftermath of their lovemaking.

'I love you, my husband.'

'And I love you, my wife.' Was it the first time that he had ever said this to her? Did he truly mean it, or were they just words?

'Forever.'

'Forever.'

She fell asleep, with her head on his chest, and was soon snoring softly. He, however, remained awake, staring up at the darkened ceiling of their room. Deep in contemplation, and ill-at-ease.

He should be overjoyed.

Just over two years ago, he had been facing a life in the priesthood. A life of servitude to the Holy Church, of inaction, and of chastity. But since then, his life had been transformed. He was a Knight of the Realm, the leader of the armies of Western Canasar, and the Hero of Moss Ford. He was a man who was blessed with an extraordinary power. And someone who had already achieved fame and renown, at the age of just twenty. And he was married to a lovely and pretty young woman, who had a kind and gentle nature, and who seemed devoted to him.

He was blessed, and he should be overjoyed. And yet.

And yet, he was in mourning. Not, if he was being honest with himself, for his father, although that grief was still raw. No, he was in mourning for a girl who he had met on only two brief occasions, and who he did not truly know.

A girl who had needed him. Who he had made a promise to. And who, in the final reckoning, he had failed. He had failed her, and now she was forever lost to him. He blinked his eyes rapidly, trying to shed the tears which had formed there.

He was still thinking about the tragic young woman with the dark hair and beautiful hazel eyes as he drifted into sleep, and as his new wife snored softly with her head on his chest.

And then, in the midst of slumber, the prophetic dream of the girl on the pyre came to him for the last time…

—

…He watched as the young woman was tied to the pole in the centre of the wood. Throughout, she maintained her quiet poise, her face hidden, as a member of Aiduel's Guards announced the charges against her.

And then he saw the flaming torches, being brought closer. Being placed against the wood. Still, the young woman maintained her dignity. But as the pyre lit, she jolted her head back, and her hood fell…

—

He jerked up out of sleep, feeling disorientated and confused. His heart was pounding. Kalyane had moved away from him since he had fallen asleep, and she now lay on her side at the edge of the bed.

It had been the same dream, of the girl being led to the pyre. The same dream of Allana. But how could that be possible, if she was already dead? If she had died at the hands of Elannis raiders, as the Guardswoman had stated, then why was he still witnessing a prophecy of her?

For a brief moment, he dared to hope that she was alive. Perhaps the Guardswoman had made a mistake? Perhaps Arion had been lied to? Perhaps he could still save her from this fate, if he acted quickly enough?

He sat up in bed, considering this, full of agitation and excitement. But, as had been the case on the last occasion when he had experienced this vision, something from within the dream was nagging at him. Some detail, something important.

He closed his eyes, trying to retain the last images from the vision. Trying to discern what element from within the dream was giving him this sense of discomfort.

And then he identified an incongruity. There was a flag, which had been fluttering in the distant background behind the crowd. How could he not have noticed that, previously? But it was not the flag of Andar, or of House Sepian, or of Septholme. He concentrated, trying to picture the image more vividly. Striving to recall what the symbol on the flag represented. And finally, the answer came to him. Arlais. The city of Arlais.

Next, he focused on the very last instant of the dream, in the moment before he had awoken. Allana jolted her head back, and her hood fell… and then he saw it, for the first time. A few stray strands of hair, falling loose out of the hood of the white dress as that hood started to fall.

Hair that was golden-blonde.

Not dark. Not Allana.

And he realised that he had made a terrible mistake.

40

Leanna

—

Year of Our Lord,
After Ascension, 769AA

Leanna spent less than twenty-four hours at home, before they came for her.

She was at breakfast with her parents, on Second-Day, the day after her return to Arlais, when the pounding on the front door started.

'What the-'

There was irritation in her father's voice as he heard the noise, which was so out of place in their quiet neighbourhood. But there was also fear. Leanna and her mother looked at each other, with worry, as Jonas moved towards the door.

Jonas opened the door, but before he had an opportunity to speak, a loud voice questioned, 'Is Priestess Leanna here?'

'Yes,' replied Jonas. 'What is it?' But even as her father was speaking, Leanna saw a hand reach in and push him forcefully out of the way, causing him to clatter against the far wall.

Two large men walked into the room, both of them wearing a red cloak and a red sash, and both with their right hand on the hilt of their swords.

Leanna's heart sank as she took note of the three men who entered the house behind the two bulky Aiduel's Guards. The first was High Commander Ernis dei Bornere, adorned in the same uniform as his men. The next was Brother Perrien, looking sullen and angry. And the last, mouth open in anticipation and displaying his perfect white teeth, was El'Patriere. The Senior Priest's eyes sought out Leanna, and he smiled.

Dei Bornere had also spotted and recognised her, and he was the first to speak. 'Priestess Leanna of Arlais. You will come with us, immediately. You are accused of heresy, and of witchcraft. We have multiple witnesses, of both your heretical deeds and your vile dreams. You are to be questioned, you will confess, and then you will be judged.'

At dei Bornere's words, the two Guards moved towards Leanna, standing to either side of her.

Leanna rose to her feet, knowing that there was little point in protesting, given the individuals present. She also knew that, if Perrien was involved, there could be no denial of their accusations. They knew who she was, now, and they would be fully aware of what she had done.

She smiled wanly at her parents, trying to reassure them, but in her heart she already knew that she should have stayed in Andar.

She would be questioned. She would be judged. And on the next Seventh-Day, she knew what the outcome would be.

—

After having been marched across Arlais, within a few minutes of arriving at the fortress of Aiduel's Guards she was taken to a meeting room. In that room, she again encountered High Commander Ernis dei Bornere, and Captain Rorker.

The High Commander stared at her dispassionately, as he commenced their discussion. 'Let me make one thing clear, Priestess Leanna. I don't like torture. I'll use it, if I have to, on you or your loved ones. But unlike some of my colleagues, I don't derive any satisfaction from it. And I'd rather not use it on you or anyone else, unless I have to.'

She returned his stare, unsure of what to say. 'OK, sir.'

As had been the case on her previous meeting with dei Bornere and Rorker, no dark emotions were being emitted from the two men. However, there was an undercurrent of excitement emanating outwards from dei Bornere, as he addressed her.

'Therefore, I want you to help me to help you, Priestess Leanna. Please be aware that we already have enough evidence to secure your condemnation. You were witnessed by a room full of people, working dark magic to heal a fatal wound. And you are assailed by traumatic recurring dreams, again testified to by multiple witnesses. Those facts alone are enough for me to declare you a heretic. But adding these to your date of birth, I'm close to certain that you're one of the ones that we've been tasked to find. Therefore, if this goes to a trial, I'm certain that you'll be found guilty. So, I don't want or need your help for that, Priestess Leanna.'

'What do you want, sir?'

'First, I want the certainty of a confession. Sign a confession for me, confirming who you are and what you've done, and then we can bypass a formal trial. Second, I want to know all of the details of your recurring dream. All of them, so I can confirm what you are and can report back to the Archlaw. Third, I want to know all about your powers. Again, so I can report back.' Leanna stared at him in silence for a few seconds. 'Do all of that for me, Priestess Leanna, and there will be no need for us to torture you. Or your parents. Or your old room-mate, Amyss. As I said, help me to help you.'

'And if I do all of that, sir, what will happen to me?' She was already certain of the answer, but she wanted to hear him say it.

'Well, you'll be purified on the fire, on this coming Seventh-Day, Priestess Leanna.' His tone was entirely business-like, as he spoke. 'Purified so that your heretical soul can return to Aiduel's Holy path. But of course, you already knew that, and that's going to happen whether you assist me or not. The conversation we're having right now is solely about whether or not I have to treat you like filth, and to torture you and everybody else that you love, between now and then.'

—

Therefore, later that Second-Day, Leanna confessed to being a heretic, and she told dei Bornere and Rorker about the dream and her powers. She had decided that such a confession was her only option, in order to try to keep her loved ones safe.

She was open and transparent about the elements of the recurring dream which she could remember. And she gave them a full description of her abilities to feel emotions, and to heal people. Throughout this discussion, she watched as Rorker eagerly wrote down everything she said, knowing that he would be drafting the written confession for her to sign.

At one point, she stated to them, 'I've always believed that my power of healing is a gift from The Lord. The Lord Aiduel Himself healed the sick, many times, as you'll both know. And if I've only ever used my gift for good, and only intend to use it for good, as The Lord did, then how can it be heretical and evil?'

Dei Bornere replied to that statement, his voice becoming more passionate as he did so. 'Because The Lord deems it so! The Archlaw was visited by The Lord, Priestess Leanna, and The Lord told him that the deeds of you and your kind are evil. Therefore, whether you yourself consider your actions and intent to be "good" is irrelevant. The Archlaw has spoken, on behalf of The Lord. The Lord has stated that your heresy, if allowed to go unchecked, will undermine the Holy Church and the faith. Therefore, you and your kind must be eliminated in order to eradicate that heresy, no matter what you think your intent is.'

'Me and my kind?'

'The Illborn. Unholy spawn. You're the second that we've found, and you'll be the second to die. But, in time, we'll find you all. And as you burn on Seventh-Day, Priestess Leanna, you should give thanks to The Lord Aiduel and to the Holy Church. Your purification is being undertaken at The Lord's behest, and by sacrificing yourself to the flames, you'll strengthen and preserve the Holy Church, for all of time.'

Given the circumstances, and her need to protect her loved ones, there were only three matters of substance that Leanna concealed from her captors.

The first of these was the vision on the altar, at the School of Saint Amena. Leanna had no desire to get Senior Priestess Maris in trouble by disclosing the events which had taken place on that long-ago day. Therefore, she did not mention this.

The second was Amyss's awareness of what Leanna was. Leanna tried to protect her friend by stating that the dreams had only become outwardly noticeable in recent weeks, and that she had never shared any other information with her room-mate. She believed that she was successful in her efforts, since neither of her interrogators showed any significant interest in the small red-headed girl.

The third was the existence of Arion and Allana. Even if she herself was fated to have been caught and to be burned, that was no reason for her to betray her knowledge of the others. And thankfully, dei Bornere seemed so delighted, to have identified and captured Leanna, that he did not press her about whether she knew of any others.

But she had a name, now, for what the three of them were. A name apparently given to them by either The Lord, or by the Archlaw.

They were Illborn.

—

682

In the days that followed, she was imprisoned in a small cell, which was just a few metres across. It had a cot bed on one side, and was austere but clean. During her time in the cell, she either prayed or read from the Holy Book. But sleep did not come easy to her.

She was treated relatively well, for the duration of her captivity. With her confession signed, High Commander dei Bornere appeared satisfied that he had obtained what he needed from her, and he seemed content not to torment her further.

On Fourth-Day, dei Bornere visited her, briefly. He notified her that a panel of Aiduel's Guards had reviewed her confession and the testimonies against her, and that she had been found guilty of heresy. He then reconfirmed what she already knew; that she was to be purified by flame, on the Seventh-Day. On Holy Day.

Throughout the days that she was waiting in the cell, Leanna was frightened, but she was also resolved to accept her fate with as much dignity as she could. Despite her fear as to what awaited her, she took comfort from knowing that this must be the destiny which The Lord had determined for her. And if He had decided that it was fitting that her life should end in this way, then who was she to wail and to protest and to cling on to that life?

She prayed many times over the course of her imprisonment, whilst clutching her small statue of The Lord Aiduel On The Tree. Prayer, and memory of The Lord's own sacrifice, were her main sources of solace.

The Lord Himself had submitted His Body for suffering on The Tree. He had meekly accepted as the heathens had bound His arms and legs to the wood. And He had endured the pain as they had fired the two arrows into His body, piercing under both of His shoulders and pinning Him against The Tree. He had suffered all of those agonies with dignity, knowing that His salvation awaited Him in heaven. He had suffered, and without complaint He had endured, until the moment when He had been set free.

Leanna knew that she would have to strive to follow His example.

683

Lord Aiduel, please help me to remain strong when the pain begins. Please help me to endure the suffering, as you did, Lord.

But despite her faith, and her acceptance of death, it was the horror of what her last moments would be like, as the flames devoured her still-living body, which was keeping her awake at night. The fear of being undone by the unbearable agony, and dying whilst her mind was consumed by faithless hysteria.

—

On the afternoon of Sixth-Day, she was allowed a visit by Amyss.

The small red-headed girl rushed forwards to pull Leanna into a fierce embrace when she saw her, and then she started sobbing. Leanna wrapped her own arms around Amyss in turn, and hugged her back. For the first time, tears came to Leanna's eyes, in response to the emotions cascading out of Amyss.

LOVE. PROTECT. FEAR. LOVE. PROTECT. FEAR.

'They can't do this to you, Lea. They can't.'

For a long time, Leanna just hugged her, but eventually she replied, 'If The Lord wills it, Amyss, it will happen, and it was meant to be. And if He doesn't, He will stop them. They can do this thing to me, but they'll never change who I am. They will never take my faith from me.'

Amyss continued to hold her, and was still crying. She appeared unwilling to let Leanna go. 'But how can you be so calm, Lea? What you can do is a miracle, a wonderful miracle. And for them to do this to you, it's so wrong. Everyone thinks so, everyone except Aiduel's Guards and El'Patriere. How can you be so calm?'

'How else can I be, Amyss?' Leanna lifted her hand to wipe her eyes. 'What choice do I have? I'm so scared, but I need to keep my faith.'

They were silent for a couple of minutes after that, still holding each other, the silence broken only by Amyss's choked sobs.

Eventually, Amyss pulled back from the hug, and looked up at

Leanna. 'I love you, Lea. I always have, and I always will.' She then lifted herself onto her tiptoes, and softly kissed Leanna's lips. Love radiated outwards from the smaller girl, as she did this.

Leanna savoured the gentle kiss, which lasted for just a few moments, and when Amyss pulled away, Leanna whispered, 'And I love you, Amyss. I always will.'

—

The next morning, in the early hours of Seventh-Day, she was finally allowed a visit by her parents. As with Amyss, their greeting started with an embrace between the three of them, which lasted for several minutes.

When they finally separated, Leanna noted that her mother was carrying a dress and a cloak under her arm. Both were pristinely clean, and white. Leanna immediately recognised the dress.

'Is that what I think it is?'

'Yes,' replied Elisa. 'It was to have been your wedding dress. I wasn't sure if you'd recognise it.'

'You kept it, for all of this time?'

'Yes. And the cloak, for afterwards. And I thought... that you could wear them, today. I never saw anyone as beautiful, as when you tried this dress on. I know it sounds stupid, but I want them to see you in this, Leanna. To see you so pure, and beautiful, and good. So angelic. And to realise what they're doing. How wrong and evil what they're doing is.'

'Then I'll wear them, Mum. Thank you.'

'There's so much anger, Leanna,' stated Jonas, and indeed there was bitterness in his own voice. 'We've all grown used to their burnings. Numb to it. But the ones they've picked before have all been loners, freaks, outsiders. Nobodies. But to do this to one of our own, and to a priestess, everyone's so angry about it. I've been telling everyone that I know. The guilds, the tradesmen, our neighbours. Everyone's so angry. If they can do this to you, where will it end?'

'We've all heard, Leanna,' said Elisa, more gently. 'About Prince Markon, and what you did. Sister Colissa is telling everyone, since they arrested you. You saved the Prince! Colissa says it was a miracle. She even stood on the stage in the town square and had a large crowd listening to her, as she was telling it. A miracle! And this is how they repay you. As your father says, no one understands it, and there's so much anger.'

After that, Leanna turned their talk to more trivial matters, and they reminisced about certain events of her childhood, sharing stories. Subsequently, all three of them knelt at the side of Leanna's bed, and for a while they prayed to The Lord. Each of them was holding a statue of The Lord Aiduel On The Tree, as they did so.

—

Her last visitor was far less welcome. In the early afternoon that day, the cell door opened, and Senior Priest El'Patriere entered the room.

She had already changed into the pristine white dress by then, and she noticed his eyes lecherously running up and down her slim body, as he shut the door behind himself.

He grinned, flashing his teeth, and said, 'You're soon to be purified by fire for the heretic you are, Priestess Leanna. But as a member of my flock, albeit a vile and sinful one, I wanted to offer you the opportunity to pray with your Senior Priest, before the end.'

Dark emotions pulsed from the man, indicating clearly that there was only ill intent behind his visit. Leanna refused to allow herself to be goaded by him, and she politely replied, 'I thank you, Father, but I will respectfully decline. I would like to be alone with The Lord in this last hour.'

The grin disappeared. 'Father El'Patriere.' Leanna felt a degree of pity for the Senior Priest, that such a trifling matter of address should continue to hold such importance for him. 'Anyway, enough pretence. The real reason that I'm here is to remind you about what I

686

once told you. That you'd suffer for what you tried to do to me. And here you are, now.'

Leanna stopped looking at him, and instead took hold of her statue of The Lord. She started to silently pray, ignoring El'Patriere.

The Senior Priest continued, clearly intending to finish what he had really come to say. 'Just so you know, when the flames are burning you. It was me who arranged for Brother Perrien to keep a watch on you. Me who offered Perrien an incentive to report back about you; he's the new Senior Healer in Arlais, now. And me who ordered Perrien to notify dei Bornere. So, the reason all of this is happening to you, is because of me.'

Dark emotions continued to emanate from him. He was clearly trying to elicit a reaction from her. Whether he wanted anger, or sorrow, or begging for mercy, she was not sure. But she did not intend to give him any satisfaction.

Instead, she looked at the statue, and said, 'Lord Aiduel, make my thoughts and actions true, and deliver me from evil. Lord, please forgive Father El'Patriere for his sins, and please protect me from those who would do evil against me.'

She then continued to repeat these words, over and over, not listening to anything else that the Senior Priest had to say. Eventually, she did hear El'Patriere uttering a foul curse, and then the cell door slammed behind him as he left the room.

—

The Guards came to collect her, a couple of hours after midday. They started to escort her through the fortress, and towards the field outside.

Prior to leaving the cell, she had put on the white cloak over the back of the white dress, and she now lifted the cloak's cloth hood. The raised hood covered the back and sides of her head, immediately shutting out her view of the world to either side of herself. This allowed her to ignore the people in the fort who were gawping at her, as she passed by.

There was a dark irony that she was wearing what had once been intended to be her wedding outfit. Everything had started with her rejection of the event at which she would have worn this dress. She had turned her back on Lohan, over two years earlier, and had accepted a calling into the Holy Church. She had therefore never worn the garment for its intended purpose. But her decision back then, to reject her marriage, had led her unerringly to this moment and to this place. Where she would wear the dress as she walked to her death, rather than into a new life as a married woman.

Would it have been better if she had taken her mother's advice, all that time ago, and was now happily married and leading a quiet and anonymous life? A life in which she had never encountered El'Patriere, or gone to war?

But she knew that she could not think that way. She had been called by The Lord Aiduel on that day in the School of Saint Amena, and she had answered that calling. And in return, The Lord had given her a wondrous, miraculous power. The ability to work miracles of healing, in His name. How could she now choose to reject and scorn such a gift, to wish it had never been, simply because it had led her to this moment?

No, she should be thankful for what He had given to her. For the purity and holiness of the moments when she had healed Markon, Kennet, and Amyss. Everything that had happened subsequently, and everything that she would soon endure, would be at the will of Aiduel. And if she followed His will, and if she maintained her faith throughout, He would call her unto Him in heaven, when it was all over.

And therefore, no. It would not have been better. She would wear this dress now. She would try to walk with dignity. And she would meet her fate, as bravely as she could.

Lord Aiduel, please give me the courage to endure. And please accept me, Lord, at the end.

—

The moment when she emerged from the fortress, to the fields outside, was shocking. She knew where the pyre would be, where it had always been, and she immediately looked in that direction. But between her and that place, there were thousands of people. A massive and raucous crowd was sprawled across the whole area, suggesting that a high proportion of the population of Arlais had come to view this spectacle.

In response, it seemed as if the entire garrison of Aiduel's Guards was also present there. Perhaps over two hundred heavily armed red-cloaked soldiers. The majority of the Guards formed a narrow corridor of steel through the crowd, a pathway to the waiting pyre, around which yet more of their number were clustered.

Leanna took a deep breath, and started to walk forwards, flanked by the two Guards who had led her from the fortress. She felt abruptly nervous, and was concentrating on completing each single next footstep.

Lord Aiduel, please don't let me fall. Please don't let me fall.

She was thankful for the hood around her head, to block out her peripheral vision. She was worried that if she began to start to recognise people in the crowd, if she noticed friendly faces, then her steady footsteps might falter. Her courage might begin to fail. Instead, she just wanted to look forwards, out through the opening of the cowl, towards the pyre. She would focus solely on that, taking one step at a time, and she would strive to maintain her composure.

Each footstep took her closer to her death. As she walked forwards, she could see that the red-cloaked soldiers were pushing back against the crowd to either side of the corridor. She realised then that the mass gathering was hostile. There was much shouting, and cursing, and she was uncertain whether it was directed at her or at others.

Emotions surged out at her from all directions, from thousands of souls within the throng of people, assailing her and confusing her senses.

ANGER. ANGER. ANGER.

She tried to shut it out, lest it wreck her composure and destroy her courage and dignity. Instead, she strove to continue to walk tall, her back straight, refusing to allow herself to cower or to stumble.

She thought about The Lord Aiduel as she walked closer to the place where she would die, and as fear was building within her. The pyre of wood was stacked several feet high, in the middle of which was a raised platform, with a large vertical pole running through the centre. She shivered. Was this how The Lord had felt, when he had been led to The Tree? When He had known that they were going to torture Him, and kill Him, and yet he had allowed Himself to be taken?

The Lord had faced His own suffering, to prove His courage and His faith, and His willingness to sacrifice Himself for His people. And whilst Leanna was uncertain whether her own courage would hold, she was determined that she would prove her faith, here today.

She had arrived at the centre of the field, had reached the stacked pile of wood, and now they led her to the centre of that waiting pyre. She was lifted onto the raised platform, and her Guards proceeded to tie her wrists together behind her back, her arms around the sturdy pole. They then tied a rope around her waist and legs, locking her in place against the wooden beam. She could feel her breath quickening, and becoming more erratic, as the ropes were tightened.

Lord Aiduel, please help me to endure this. Please help me to endure this. Please.

The platform had elevated her to four feet above the ground, and she could see across the whole crowd now, through the opening of her hood. She was therefore able to properly appreciate the enormity of the audience which had gathered for the event. And she continued to feel the dark and hostile emotions being emitted by that throng of people, which were continually bombarding her senses and shocking her.

Her eyes settled on the three figures at the very front of the crowd, close to her platform. Her mother, her father, and Amyss.

690

Each of them looking desolate. But she could not hold their regard for long, lest it undo her own resolve, and she moved her eyes away from them. Even nearer to her, dei Bornere, El'Patriere and High Priest Comenis were in an open patch of ground beside the pyre, standing within a central area surrounded by armed Guards. She spent even less time, looking towards those three individuals.

Then the High Commander moved onto the platform beside her, and began to speak. 'People of Arlais, we are gathered here today to see the burning and purification of a heretic…'

His words proceeded on after that, but Leanna was suddenly distracted, and she did not continue to follow dei Bornere's speech. She could feel something peculiar; a foreign sensation, a core of energy sprouting inside of herself, spreading across her mind and her body. It was a feeling which she had not experienced since the Battle of Moss Ford, and since her encounters with Arion Sepian.

What was this? How was this possible?

She was distractedly aware that the High Commander had finished his declaration. She observed the two Guards moving towards her, each of them carrying flaming torches, which were emitting heat and light. But a completely different form of energy was still burgeoning within her. Pouring into her from an external source, which felt like it was getting ever closer.

Then the torches were placed against the edge of the piled wood, and even though just the corners of the pyre caught aflame, Leanna felt an immediate wash of heat. As that happened, she jolted her head backwards in shock, and the hood of the white cloak fell away. It drifted downwards, revealing her long and flowing golden-blonde hair to the gathered audience.

The fire was spreading quickly across the pile of timber, and the heat was building on the pyre beneath her platform. At the same time, the external energy was now surging through every limb of her body, infusing and embracing her in vitality and power. She turned her head towards the left, towards what she thought was the source of that energy. But in front of her was a massed crowd, thousands of people,

691

and it was impossible to identify any individual in such a throng.

But the heat continued to build on the pyre below, mounting beneath the soles of her feet. Soon, the flames would reach her platform, and she would start to burn. Soon, she would begin to feel unbearable pain.

She closed her eyes, praying, beseeching The Lord.

Lord Aiduel, please help me to endure this. Please give me the strength and faith to endure this.

She thought again about His sacrifice, on The Tree. The Lord Aiduel had been willing to surrender Himself, to renew the world. He had submitted, He had been pierced by the Arrows, and in the midst of such suffering He had looked up blissfully to heaven and to salvation. And He had endured.

As she must endure.

She thought also about the pain that He had suffered, as she awaited her own pain, that first sensation of blistering on the soles of her feet that would herald the excruciating agonies to follow. Arrows had pierced The Lord's flesh, and He had bled. Blood had poured from his deep, agonising wounds. And yet He had not cried out, had not flinched, had not begged.

She must show that same faith, that same strength.

And at that moment, as ever-stronger energies continued to flow and swirl across and around her body, familiar words returned to her.

DEVOTION. SACRIFICE. SALVATION.

The words called to her, with the clarity of beatific angels singing. And the combination of the power of these words, and the vast energies which were rushing through her body, acted to lift her into a seemingly transcendent state.

And she knew with absolute certainty then that The Lord had come to her, as He had come to her once before, in the School of Saint Amena. That He was with her, now. That He had always been with her. Watching her. Guiding her. Protecting her.

With that knowledge, she was filled with ecstatic holy bliss.

692

With rapture. The Lord was with her. With closed eyes, she could see Him, bleeding, suffering, on The Tree. As she was prepared to suffer, for Him.

And then she too started to bleed.

She was almost oblivious to the gasps and shouts from the crowd, as the two spots of blood started to sprout and blossom through the fabric of her white dress. Two pinpricks of red initially, then spreading outwards on the white cloth, in perfect circles in the place beneath her shoulders. Blood, where The Lord had once bled.

All she could think about in the midst of her holy ecstasy was that He had endured, as she had been ready to endure. And He had survived.

As *she* was going to survive.

She opened her eyes, now. Vast quantities of energy coursed through and around her body, cocooning her within a golden halo of light, as the flames rose around her platform. More energy than she could have ever thought possible. The inferno enveloped her. But there was no pain, and her fear was forgotten.

In the midst of her Aiduel-given power, the flames were mere decoration. She did not burn, and she was untouched. Her clothes were untouched.

The Lord was shielding her from the flames. The Lord was protecting her. And she was bleeding, as He had once bled.

Cries were mounting from the crowd. 'She bleeds! She bleeds!'

Fingers were pointing at the blossoming circles of blood on the white dress, and witnesses were noting that they were in the very spots where the Arrows had once pierced The Lord's flesh. Emotions of awe and wonder were washing over her from the gathered throng, from all directions.

Lord Aiduel, thank you. Thank you. Thank you.

Leanna raised her chin, and looked up to the sky, to heaven. She was unconsciously mirroring a pose which all of the followers of the faith had seen thousands of times before, when beholding The Lord

Aiduel On The Tree. Golden light radiated from every pore of her body.

'She bleeds like The Lord! She bleeds!'

'Release her! Release her!'

The cries were mounting throughout the crowd, growing in volume and fervour. Leanna was unaware of the struggles now taking place between the ordinary citizens of Arlais, and the soldiers of Aiduel's Guards who stood between them and her.

Flames raged high on the pyre now, enveloping her whole form, but failing to penetrate the blanket of shining golden energy which was coating her body. It was The Lord's energy, defending her from harm, and it continued to leave her unscathed by the inferno which was engulfing her.

But that energy and the feeling of holy bliss was still mounting to a crescendo, within her. Multiplying in power, and becoming more than she could contain. It was ready to burst forth. Ready to erupt.

Lord Aiduel, make my thoughts and actions true, and deliver me from evil.

And then the energy exploded out from her, an explosion marked by a thunderous booming noise which carried across the whole field. It erupted outwards, and it tore the pyre and the flames away from her. Sent the wood and the heat flying into the air, and launched it into those around her.

But only into red-cloaked soldiers, and into El'Patriere.

The energy released was immense. A wave of force followed behind the explosion of timber and flame. This energy wave washed across the field before crashing against the walls of the fortress of Aiduel's Guards, and it knocked the entire crowd from their feet as it surged through them.

Leanna remained upright, in the centre of the field, still bound to the pole on her raised platform. Alone, and undamaged but for the blood seeping from beneath her shoulders. Her white dress was still pristine, but for this mark of the stigmata.

It seemed as if every other person there had been knocked flat onto their backs.

But then she twisted her neck to the left, to look towards a place where she could still feel a vibrant, but diminished, pulse of energy. And in the midst of a sprawl of collapsed bodies, one single figure was standing.

Arion.

He was upright, alone, and was staring at her with awe. He looked haggard and wearied, but was untouched by the force of the explosion. And she knew that The Lord had called for him, in her darkest hour.

And he had come, to deliver her salvation. And he had saved her.

And the destiny of the world was forever changed.

Some months later

A travelling merchant

—

Year of Our Lord,
After Ascension, 769AA

'...nd they're calling her the Angel of Arlais, now. I swear before
The Lord, everything that I've said is true, or may He strike
me down. There are many who are now saying that they were there,
that day, you know. Many of whom are liars. But I genuinely was, I
swear. It was a miracle, I tell you. A miracle.'

As he finished his story, the merchant looked across at his
drinking companion, enjoying the look of rapt attention which he
could see in the stranger's bloodshot eyes.

'I don't doubt you for a second, friend,' said the other man,
eventually, his speech slurred. 'A tale like that, told the way you tell
it, it has to be true. The Angel of Arlais, eh? A worthy and interesting
tale, about an apparently remarkable and miraculous young woman.
Here, let me buy you another drink.'

The merchant grinned. He was in a tavern on a road far to the east of the city of Elannis, and he was enjoying the free drinks which his story was securing him. Which was only fair. He actually *had* been at the pyre, that day.

But the drunken stranger had shown more interest and enthusiasm for the tale than anyone else before him. And, despite an initially melancholy demeanour, more generosity in buying drinks. The merchant stared at the other man, now. His companion was large, very tall and wide with grey hair, a thick grizzly beard, and a ruddy complexion. But friendly, too.

As the stranger started to order drinks, he leaned forwards, and for the first time the merchant spotted the weapon on the floor beside them. It was an object comprised of three feet of solid oak shaft and a formidable steel head. A mace.

'Do you always bring your weapon into the tavern with you?'

The merchant asked the question flippantly, but the stranger looked up, suddenly appearing more alert and sober, and seeming to take the query seriously. The man then patted the mace reassuringly.

'Please, pay the weapon no mind, friend. It's my travelling companion, and keeps me safe on the road, sometimes. No need for a good fellow like you to be concerned by it.'

And then he smiled.

Epilogue

—

Year of Our Lord,
Before Ascension, 72BA

—

Epilogue

Something which was once a boy

—

Year of Our Lord,
Before Ascension, 72BA

How does the opportunity ever arise for one person to alter the destiny of a world?

The boy did not consider this question as he sat beside the waterfall, on the shores of the remote mountain lake. Instead, he cried and cried and cried.

He was still wet, from where he had scrubbed his arms and his face, and his sandy-coloured hair, in the icy waters before him. His elbows were both cut, markers of his frantic return scramble through the passageway behind the waterfall.

Don't think about it! Don't think about it! Don't think about it!

As he sat there, he was dimly aware of the newcomers – the slavers – approaching to either side of him, circling around both sides of the lake.

That was just one piece of new knowledge, amidst many others which were now spinning within his head, contorting and twisting

701

like tendrils. Each of them enflaming his senses, and torturing his thoughts.

The slavers did not worry him, now. Their cautious encirclement would do them no good, at the moment that he chose to act. Their fate was already sealed.

He squeezed his eyes shut, trying to destroy the images, the memories. But they were written in stone, in blood, and he knew that nothing other than his own death could now cause him to forget.

After what seemed like an eternity within this state of heightened awareness, although he was still crying as they arrived, the slavers were surrounding him. A dog was barking close by, and he could hear the metal whisper of a sword being drawn from a scabbard.

He could also feel them. Feel each of them. And determine their life, or their death.

'What's your name, boy?' The voice was vicious. 'And where are the others?'

He chose not to answer the question, at first. He did not want to answer the question. But he stopped crying.

Don't think about it! Don't think about it! Don't think about it!

There was a vague sense of the man with the drawn sword moving closer to him, and raising it in a threatening gesture.

The questions were repeated. 'What's your name, boy? And where are the others?'

He looked up, staring at them, his face impassive. He could afford to tell them the truth, he knew that. Tell them the truth and then end them.

And therefore, eventually, he answered.

'My name is Aiduel. And my friends are dead. They're all dead.'

THE ILLBORN SAGA
WILL CONTINUE IN BOOK TWO
OF THE SERIES...

 Matador